continued . . .

"Fast-paced ... Berg creates a troubled world full of politics, anarchy, and dark magic. ... The magic is fascinating."
—SFRevu

"Carol Berg has done a masterful job of creating characters, places, religions, and political trials that grab and hold your attention. ... Don't miss one of 2007's best fantasy books!"
—Romance Reviews Today

"[Berg] excels at creating worlds. ... I'm eagerly awaiting the duology's concluding volume, *Breath and Bone*. ... An engrossing and lively tale, with enough action to keep you hungry for more."
— *The Davis Enterprise*

The Bridge of D'Arnath Series

"A very promising start to a new series."   —*The Denver Post*

"Berg has mastered the balance between mystery and storytelling [and] pacing; she weaves past and present together, setting a solid foundation. ... It's obvious [she] has put incredible thought into who and what makes her characters tick."
—*The Davis Enterprise*

"Berg exhibits her skill with language, world building, and the intelligent development of the magic that affects and is affected by the characters. ... A promising new multivolume work that should provide much intelligent entertainment."
—*Booklist*

"Imagination harnessed to talent produces a fantasy masterpiece, a work so original and believable that it will be very hard to wait for the next book in this series to be published."
—*Midwest Book Review*

"[Seri] is an excellent main heroine; her voice, from the first person, is real and practical. ... I'm truly looking forward to seeing what happens next."   —SF Site

"Gut-wrenching, serious fantasy fiction."
—Science Fiction Romance

"Excellent dark fantasy with a liberal dash of court intrigue. ... Read this if you're tired of fantasy so sweet it makes your teeth squeak. Highly recommended."   —Broad Universe

Song of the Beast
Winner of the Colorado Book Award
for Science Fiction/Fantasy

"The plot keeps twisting right until the end ... entertaining characters." —*Locus*

"Berg's fascinating fantasy is a puzzle story, with a Celtic-flavored setting and a plot as intricate and absorbing as fine Celtic lacework.... The characters are memorable, and Berg's intelligence and narrative skill make this stand-alone fantasy most commendable." —*Booklist*

"It would be easy to categorize it as another dragon fantasy book. Instead, it is a well-crafted mystery ... definitely recommended for libraries looking for high-quality fantasy and mystery additions." —*KLIATT*

Transformation, Revelation, and *Restoration,*
the Acclaimed *Rai-Kirah* Series

"Vivid characters and intricate magic combined with a fascinating world and the sure touch of a Real Writer—luscious work!" —Melanie Rawn

"Grabs the reader by the throat on page one and doesn't let go ... wonderful." —*Starburst*

"Berg greatly expands her world with surprising insights." —*The Denver Post*

"Superbly entertaining." —*Interzone*

"Vivid characters, a tangible atmosphere of doom, and some gallows humor." —*SFX Magazine*

"An exotic, dangerous, and beautifully crafted world." —Lynn Flewelling, author of *Traitor's Moon*

"Berg's characters are completely believable, her world interesting and complex, and her story riveting." —*KLIATT*

"Epic fantasy on a gigantic scale ... Carol Berg lights up the sky with a wondrous world." —*Midwest Book Review*

Breath and Bone

CAROL BERG

A ROC BOOK

ROC
Published by New American Library, a division of
Penguin Group (USA) Inc., 375 Hudson Street,
New York, New York 10014, USA
Penguin Group (Canada), 90 Eglinton Avenue East, Suite 700, Toronto,
Ontario M4P 2Y3, Canada (a division of Pearson Penguin Canada Inc.)
Penguin Books Ltd., 80 Strand, London WC2R 0RL, England
Penguin Ireland, 25 St. Stephen's Green, Dublin 2,
Ireland (a division of Penguin Books Ltd.)
Penguin Group (Australia), 250 Camberwell Road, Camberwell, Victoria 3124,
Australia (a division of Pearson Australia Group Pty. Ltd.)
Penguin Books India Pvt. Ltd., 11 Community Centre, Panchsheel Park,
New Delhi - 110 017, India
Penguin Group (NZ), 67 Apollo Drive, Rosedale, North Shore 0632,
New Zealand (a division of Pearson New Zealand Ltd.)
Penguin Books (South Africa) (Pty.) Ltd., 24 Sturdee Avenue,
Rosebank, Johannesburg 2196, South Africa

Penguin Books Ltd., Registered Offices:
80 Strand, London WC2R 0RL, England

Published by Roc, an imprint of New American Library, a division of Penguin
Group (USA) Inc. Previously published in a Roc trade paperback edition.

First Roc Mass Market Printing, January 2009
10 9 8 7 6 5 4 3 2 1

For all who dance

Acknowledgments

Again, incalculable thanks to Susan, Laurey, Glenn, Brian, Catherine, and Curt for two years of hard-nosed reading; to Linda for listening; to Markus, the Fighter Guy, for combat review; and to the doc-on-the-net, Doug Lyle, for more gory consultations. No words can express gratitude for my family's support, especially this past year. And last, but certainly not least, to those ever in the hunt for inspiration, my thanks to National Public Radio for a small feature called "The Last Lighthouse" that launched me into these wild and wondrous realms.

PART ONE

Tarnished Gold

Chapter 1

"I don't understand why I must remain locked in this god-cursed chamber all morning, dressed like a ducessa's lapdog," I said, scraping the frost off the window mullion. The distorted view through the thick little pane revealed naught but the snow-crusted ruins of the abbey brewhouse, a sight to make a stout heart weep. "You seem to forget that I'm yet a vowed novice of Saint Ophir's Rule. I should be helping the brothers rebuild their infirmary or salvage their stores if there's aught to be found under the rubble."

Storm, pestilence, civil war ... the world was falling apart all around us. Abbot Luviar's hope to protect the knowledge of humankind against this growing darkness dangled by the thinnest of threads. A monk I had believed holy ... and my friend ... had abducted a child I'd vowed to protect. And I was stuck here in Gillarine Abbey with a guard who never slept, awaiting who knew what. I needed to be doing something useful.

I wrenched the iron casement open and let the snow-riddled wind howl through for long enough to remind me of the dangers abroad. Setting off alone on a mad chase through the worst winter in Navronne's history was a ludicrous idea for anyone, much less a man who was like to lose his mind at any hour.

My unlikely nursemaid, a warrior whose presence turned men's bowels to water even before they glimpsed his mutilated face, blocked the doorway of the abbey guesthouse bedchamber. A pile of velvet and satin garments draped over his arm, and a pair of low-cut doeskin court boots— large enough they might possibly fit my outsized feet— dangled from his thick fingers. He waited until I slammed the casement shut before vouchsafing a comment.

"His Grace wishes you to dress as befits his pureblood adviser. You must be ready whenever he summons you, so you should do it now." Voushanti twisted the unscarred half of his mouth in his unsettling expression of amusement. "And you're as suited to be a Karish monk as I am to be a pureblood's valet."

Though my dealings with Voushanti were anything but amusing, I could not but laugh at the bald truth stated so clearly. My novice vows had bought me a haven here two months previous, when I'd been a wounded deserter with no prospects of a roof, a meal, or a kind word anywhere. That my attachment to Gillarine Abbey had grown into something more was a virtue of the people here and no reversal of my own contrary nature. Circumstances—the law, my loathsome family, and the contract with which they had bound my life's service to the Bastard Prince of Evanore— had halted my brief clerical career . . . and every other path of my own choosing.

I peered into the wooden mug on the hearth table, discovered yet again that it was empty, and threw it across the chilly room. "Let me dig graves, if naught else, Voushanti. The brothers have not had time to bury their dead since the Harrower assault. Prince Osriel has not yet *arrived* at Gillarine, so he couldn't possibly need me before afternoon. I'll not run away. I gave him my word. Besides, I'm still half frostbit and wholly knob-swattled from the past seven days, so I'm hardly likely to wander off into this damnable weather again."

Were I the same man who had claimed sanctuary at Gillarine two months past, I'd have broken my submission to Osriel the Bastard, bashed Voushanti in the head with a brick, and gone chasing after the villain monk and his captive, be damned my word, the weather, and the consequences. But for once in my seven-and-twenty years, I had tried to think things through. Brother Gildas wanted Jullian for a hostage, a tool to manipulate me; thus he would keep the boy alive. I had already sent word to the lighthouse cabal, people who were far more likely to be able to aid my young friend. And in my own peculiar interpretation of divine workings, I believed that breaking my oath of submission, given to save Jullian's life on another day, would somehow permit the gods to forsake the boy. Two months past, Jullian had saved my life. Perhaps the best service I could do for him was to behave myself for once. *Dear Goddess Mother, please let me be right.*

Voushanti tossed the fine clothes on the bed. "Dress yourself, pureblood. Remain here until you are summoned. You don't want to know how sorely Prince Osriel mislikes disobedient servants."

I pulled off the coarse shirt the monks had lent me and threw it to the floor. Propping my backside on a stool, I began to untie the laces that held up the thick common hose so I could replace them with the fine-woven chausses Prince Osriel expected to see on his bought sorcerer. Deunor's fire, how I detested playing courtier to a royal ghoul who wouldn't even show me his face. Though, in truth, if Osriel's visage was more dreadful than Voushanti's purple scars and puckered flesh, it would likely paralyze any who saw it. His Grace of Evanore had the nasty habit of mutilating the dead, and was reputed to consort regularly with the lord of the underworld.

Argumentative murmurings on the winding stair slowed my fingers and stiffened Voushanti's spine as if someone had shoved a poker up his backside. The prior of Gillarine, a black-robed monk with a neck the same width as his shaven head, swept into the room, laden with drinking vessels and a copper pitcher. A ginger-bearded warrior burst through the doorway on Prior Nemesio's heels.

"I'm sorry, sir," said the frowning warrior, a robust Evanori by the name of Philo. "The monk insists on seeing the pureblood. I know you said to keep everyone away, but to lay hands on a clergyman—"

A second warrior, also wearing my master's silver wolf on his hauberk, joined his fellow. Their drawn swords appeared a bit foolish with none present but one stocky, hairless monk, one gangle-limbed sorcerer wearing naught but an ill-fitting undertunic and one leg of his hose, and their own commander.

"For mercy's sake, Philo, Melkire, sheath your weapons," I said, stuffing arms and head back into the shirt I had just shed. "Father Prior! Iero's grace." Hose drawn back up and laces retied, I jumped to my feet and touched my fingertips to my forehead. "I was shocked to find such devastation here, holy father. If I can do aught to help . . ."

Though protocol ranked any pureblood, even an illiterate, incompetent one like me, above nobles, clerics, or any other ordinary, I prayed my respectful address might prevent Voushanti and his men from hustling Nemesio away. The prior was my only link to my friends of the lighthouse cabal. I hoped for news of Jullian.

Nemesio's nostrils flared as if an ill odor permeated the room. Difficult to imagine this unimaginative and slightly pompous man conspiring with the passionate, aristocratic Abbot Luviar to create the magical cache of books and tools they called the *lighthouse*.

The prior set his copper pitcher on the table and arranged the five cups beside it in a neat row. "Indeed, I have come to request your aid, Brother Valen."

Voushanti rumbled disapproval.

I acted quickly, lest protocol violations end the visit. "You must not address me directly, Father Prior, but only Mardane Voushanti, as he represents my contracted master, Prince Osriel. But I'm sure the prince would hear your petition favorably in appreciation for your hospitality."

I held no such assurance, of course. Though I had served him less than a fortnight and met him only twice, Prince Osriel seemed even less likely than most of his ilk to express gratitude of any sort. But perhaps he liked to *pretend* he was reasonable.

Prior Nemesio's thick shoulders shifted beneath his habit. He clutched the silver solicale that hung about his neck as if the sunburst symbol of his god could protect him from these minions of the Adversary. The dark blots in his wide, pale face spoke of a sleepless night. "Mardane, a few weeks ago, one of our young aspirants disappeared. We have searched, questioned, and expended every resource to find him without success. We fear greatly for his life. Perhaps you remember Gerard, Brother Valen? A good, devout boy, just fourteen."

I nodded, a chill more bitter than Navronne's foul winter shadowing my spirit. Of course, I remembered. This recital was for Voushanti's benefit. Only the previous night had I shared with the prior my new-formed belief that Brother Gildas, scholar and traitor, had not only stolen young Jullian away, but murdered his friend Gerard.

Nemesio straightened his back and spoke boldly. "We of Saint Ophir's brotherhood are Gerard's family. If he lives, then we must locate him and ensure his safety. If he is dead, he must be returned here where we can afford him proper rites. We understand that Brother Valen's pureblood bent involves tracking and route finding, thus request his aid in our search for the boy."

Fool of a monk! I wanted to strangle Nemesio. Gerard's body must be retrieved, and I was more than willing to lend my paltry skills to the task, but Voushanti was Prince Osriel's man and could not be permitted to know of the place I believed the boy lay—or its significance. The Well was secret. Holy. And Voushanti and our master were not. "Father Prior, I couldn't possibly—"

"Cartamandua is not brought here to serve you, monk," Voushanti snapped. "Prince Osriel has chosen this monkhouse as a neutral meeting ground suitable for his royal business. The pureblood is required to attend his master. Nothing else."

Nemesio's hairless skull and wide neck glowed crimson. "Well, then. It was but a thought. We would never wish to distract a man from his duty. Here, I've brought refreshment for you all." He filled the five plain vessels from his pitcher, handing them around first to Voushanti and the two warriors, then to me. "In all the excitement of your arrival yestereve . . . the various comings and goings of so many . . . we lapsed in our sacred rituals of hospitality."

Nemesio raised his cup to each of us. His hands were shaking. "May the waters of Saint Gillare's holy font bring good health and serenity to our guests."

Voushanti shrugged at Philo and Melkire and the three of them raised their cups and drank. I raised my cup in my two hands, but only touched my lips to its rim. Since the day I turned seven, the day my mother the diviner first pronounced that I would meet my doom in water, blood, and ice, only desperation could drive me to water drinking. And were I naught but a withered husk, I could not have touched *this* water. The holy spring that fed the abbey font had its source in the hills east of Gillarine—in the very pool where I believed Gerard's body lay.

A glance across my cup revealed Nemesio glaring at me as if I were defiling a virgin. I had no idea what I'd done, but his shoulders sagged a bit as I lowered my cup. He snatched away the vessel and gathered the emptied cups from the others.

"I'd best leave you gentlemen to your preparations," he said. "The guesthouse is yours for as long as you need, of course. Though we can provide but meager fare since the Harrower burning, we shall send what refreshment we can for His Grace when he arrives. Our coal garth is intact . . ." Nemesio's nervous babbling slowed as Melkire sagged against the doorframe, rubbing his eyes.

I glanced from the prior to the soldiers. Something untoward was going on.

"Mardane Voushant . . . s'wrong . . ." Philo's voice slurred as he dropped to his knees and slumped to the floor. Melkire tumbled on top of him with a soft thud.

"Gracious Iero!" said the prior softly. But he made no move to succor the men.

"What treachery is this?" Voushanti's hand flew to his sword hilt, and the core of his eyes gleamed scarlet. But before he could draw, he blinked, sat heavily on the low bed, and toppled backward.

"Father Prior, what have you done?" I said, my stomach lodged so far in my throat, my voice croaked as if I were a boy of twelve.

Nemesio dropped his vessels on the table. "They'll sleep for a few hours and wake confused, so Brother Anselm told me. We'd best go right away."

I could almost not speak my astonishment. "Nemesio, are you absolutely mad? These men serve Osriel the Bastard, the same prince who conjured horses and warriors the size of your church from a cloud of midnight, the same who, not two months ago, cut out the eyes of a hundred dead soldiers who lay in your fields. We know neither his capabilities nor his intentions in this war. Great Iero's heart, for all we know *he* may have dispatched the Harrowers to burn you out!"

"I'm well aware. If the Bastard Prince wishes our destruction, then he'll do it. I cannot control that. But *you* have made a grievous charge against Brother Gildas—the lighthouse Scholar—and we cannot know how to proceed until you prove it. As we've only these few hours until Prince Osriel takes you away, and as only you can find this place in the hills, I see no alternative."

"Did you send my message to Stearc and Gram?" Thane Stearc was likely the leader of the cabal now that Abbot Luviar lay dead and Brother Victor lay comatose somewhere in Prince Osriel's captivity. Stearc despised me and would no more believe my charges than Nemesio did, but Gram—Stearc's quiet, pragmatic secretary—was a man of reason. He'd see that a search was mounted for Jullian and Brother Traitor.

"Indeed I sent news of your safe return. I also informed them of your foul accusation and my determination to seek the truth. You claim that you are one of us—sworn to Abbot Luviar's memory to aid us in our mission—and *this* is the service we require of you." Without waiting for my hundred arguments against this lackwit plan, he stepped over the two warriors and vanished down the stair.

Gods preserve me from holy men. It was Abbot Luviar's persuasive passion that had got me caught up in his mad scheme to preserve the entirety of human knowledge in his magical library. Now his splayed and gutted corpse hung from a gallows back in Palinur. Crossing Prince Osriel . . . laying out his men with potions . . . the prior would have us end up the same or worse.

Yet as I pulled on a heavy cloak, I could not deny the virtue of retrieving poor Gerard. Unlike Jullian, a wily, experienced conspirator at age twelve, simple, good-hearted Gerard had been but an unlucky bystander. He should not lie forgotten.

For the fiftieth time since we'd left the abbey, I glanced over my shoulder and saw no one. A frost wind gusted off the mountains to the south, whipping the snow into coils and broomtails that merged with the gray-white clouds, hiding Gillarine's broken towers. Ahead of me the prior, his black cowl billowing, strode eastward across the wind-scoured fields toward the valley's bounding ridge, leading Dob, the abbey's donkey.

Though the calendar marked the season scarce a month past Reaper's Moon, the once-fertile valley of the Kay lay blanketed in snow. The Karish said Navronne's past ten years of increasingly cold summers and bitter winters were caused by the One God Iero's wrath at mankind's sinfulness. The Sinduri Council claimed the elder gods' bickering among themselves had shifted the bowl of the sky. Those of the lighthouse cabal feared the cause lay with the earth's guardians—the mysterious, elusive Danae, who had withdrawn from all contact with humankind. Though I had no sensible arguments to make, my instincts told me that matters were worse than they imagined. Whatever the cause, famine and pestilence had taken on bony reality and crawled into our beds with us.

"We should be hunting the living, not the dead," I said, puffing out great gouts of steam in the cold air. "Don't you understand, Nemesio? Not only does Gildas have Jullian, he has my grandfather's book of maps. And the god's own fool that I am, I *unlocked* the book to him. Given rumor of a Danae holy place . . . given even a guess as to where one might lie . . . he can follow the maps and take the Harrowers there to destroy it. Once Prince Osriel takes me away from here, I'll not be able to help you anymore. And without me or the book, you've no hope to find the Danae and ask for help."

"Brother Gildas has been a member of Saint Ophir's order for nine years." Nemesio's voice quivered with suppressed fury. "With unmatched scholarship, holiness, and devotion, he has devoted himself to work and study that he may carry the world's hope into the future. You, sir, are a liar, a charlatan who has mocked our faith and suborned the weak-minded with your unending prattle, a hedonist and libertine, an illiterate wastrel who has spurned Iero's greatest gift—the magic in your blood—and accomplished nothing of value in your life. Why would anyone accept your word as truth?"

Knowing that his every charge had merit did nothing for

my bitter temper. "Have you no fear of walking out alone with such a rogue?"

"Two of our brothers hold missives to be forwarded to Thane Stearc should I fail to return."

"Spirits of night . . ."

Nemesio halted where the land kicked up sharply into the ridge, motioning for me to take the lead. "Abbot Luviar, the most admirable and perceptive of men, insisted that you were more than we could see. Yet he also named Brother Gildas as the Scholar. In which man was he deceived?"

And so was I silenced. I could not argue Gildas's guilt without confessing my own—that my slug-witted reaction to an excess of nivat seeds had prevented me rescuing Luviar from his hideous death. The fact that Gildas himself had abetted my perverse craving could never exonerate me.

Our path twisted upward through gullies and rockfalls, every crevice and shadowed nook treacherous with ice and crusted snow.

"Not far now," I said, as I led Nemesio and the flagging donkey up the last steep climb and onto a shelf of rock that abutted a shallow cliff.

Shivering, uneasy, I gazed back out over the valley of the Kay and the slopes we had traversed, shrouded in snow fog that teased the eye. Drifting clouds mantled the cliff tops above us. I could not shake the certainty that we were being watched. How could I have been so stupid as to come here? Only one day ago I had narrowly escaped a trap set by the trickster Danae down in the bogs of the River Kay. And now we were to intrude on their holy place, an unassuming little hollow that touched on the most profound mysteries of the world.

Chapter 2

Sila Diaglou, priestess of the ragtag Harrowers, wished to send Navronne back to the days before cities and roads and tilled soil, to a time when women hid in caves and men cowered in terror of night and storm. She named all gods false: Iero, the benevolent deity of the Karish, as well as Mother Samele and Kemen Sky Lord and the rest of the elder gods, worshiped in Navronne since time remembered. Harrowers ridiculed belief in Iero's angels, called the impish aingerou naught but fools' wishing dreams, and denied the existence of the Danae, whose dancing defined the Canon—the pattern of the world.

I could not name which gods were real and which but story. Nor could I argue the truth of angels or aingerou, though I spat on my finger and patted the naked rumps of those cherubic messengers carved into drainpipes and archways in hopes my prayers might be carried on to greater deities. But Danae ... As boy and man I had scoffed at my grandfather's claims to have traveled their realms. But Danae existed. Since I'd come to Gillarine, I had glimpsed at least two of them for myself.

The prior and I trod slowly along the snowy shelf path. Repeated melting and freezing had left small glaciers along the way.

"Are you having second thoughts, pureblood?" asked Nemesio, blowing on his rag-wrapped fingers to warm them. "Why would Brother Gildas choose this particular spot to hide a body when any of these gullies would do? Perhaps you'll tell me this is the wrong location after all."

There was no mistake. "He chose this place because killing Gerard was not his object. He wanted to kill the Danae guardian."

Despite their claims, at least *some* of the Harrowers believed in the Danae. It could be no accident that their savage rites murdered Danae guardians one by one.

Legend said Danae lived both on the earth and in it. Everywhere and nowhere, my mad grandfather said. Most times they took human form to walk their lands—our lands, for the human and Danae realms were both the same and not the same. But for one season of every year a Dané became one with a sianou—the grove, lake, stream, or meadow he or she had chosen to guard. The protection of a Dané infused the sianou and the surrounding land with life and health.

Our destination was such a sianou, a pool I had located at the bidding of Abbot Luviar, before I even understood what kind of place it was. I had brought my friend Brother Gildas there, and in the weeks since that night, Gerard had gone missing, blight had infected Gillarine's orchards and fields, and disease had come to its sheepfolds. When I touched my hands to the earth in the abbey's cloisters, I could no longer feel its living pulse. Harrower raiders had left the abbey buildings in ruins, but I believed the cause of its underlying sickness lay here and that Gildas was responsible.

Snow and ice packed a jutting slab beneath its slight overhang. Dob balked and brayed in protest at the tight corner. As the prior slapped the donkey's rump and hauled on the lead, a horse whinnied anxiously just ahead of us.

Startled, beset with imaginings of lurking Harrowers, I hissed at Nemesio to keep silent.

Footsteps and jostling spoke of one man and one beast. "Easy, girl, it's friendly company on the way. We'll be about our business and be off again to hay and blanket."

The quietly persuasive voice brought a smile to my lips. Gram could convince a cat to play in the ocean.

"How in great Iero's mercy do *you* happen to be here?" I said, abandoning the prior to the donkey while I hurried around the rock and along the shelf toward the slender, dark-haired man stroking a gray mare. "Did you get Nemesio's message about Jullian and Gildas? Well, of course, you must have done. That's why you've come. Gram, you must believe me. Gildas has taken Jullian and the book. He's murdered Gerard . . ."

I wanted to pass on everything I knew: what I had sensed in the abbey's cloisters, the truth about my damnable perversion and how Gildas had thought to use it to bend me to his will. My determination to rescue Jullian—perhaps the only true innocent left in this blasted world—had become a fever in me. Ever-sensible Gram would understand the importance of prompt action. The man spent his days as the calm center of the lighthouse cabal, juggling his testy employer, Thane Stearc, and Stearc's ebullient daughter, Elene. But I'd scarcely begun my tale when Gram raised his gloved hand.

"Hold, friend Valen," he said. "We are already moving. Thane Stearc and his men have spent the night scouring the countryside between here and Elanus for the two of them. Mistress Elene leads another search party between here and Fortress Groult. We told Thanea Zurina that a wayward monk had kidnapped a young friend of yours and asked her to keep an eye out along the roads west as she makes her way home."

The flushed Nemesio joined us, hauling Dob behind him. "What are you doing here, Gram?"

Gram bowed politely. "Good Father Prior, your god's grace be with you this morning. As I was just telling Valen, Thane Stearc has dispatched several parties to search for Jullian and Brother Gildas. As he wished to move swiftly, my lord left me behind at Fortress Groult. So I rode up here, hoping to make myself useful."

The secretary's pale skin took on a hint of scarlet. Though no older than I, Gram was sorely afflicted with ill health.

Prior Nemesio shook his head. "Brother Valen's story is nonsensical. How could a scholarly man such as Gildas give hearing to Harrowers? Even if he be apostate to divine Karus and the One God, which I cannot credit, who but mindless lunatics could imagine that a world without tools or books is what any god intends?"

Sila Diaglou claimed her dark age would be a time of appeasement, a time of cleansing, required because we had forgotten our proper fear of the Gehoum, the elemental Powers who controlled the land and seasons. The bitter wind whined through the crags, as if to answer my skepticism with a reminder of our wildly skewed seasons, and the disease and starvation that howled at Navronne's door like starved wolves.

Gram stroked the mare's neck and fondled her ears. "Men are driven in such varied ways, Father Prior. Brother Gildas relished his task as Last Scholar, destined to be the holder of humankind's accumulated wisdom. Perhaps—and who can say what is in a man's heart?—he does not relish the task of First Teacher."

Nemesio tightened his full lips. "We have only Brother Valen's surmise. I'll not believe ill of Brother Gildas without some proof. So where is this pool, Brother? We must get you back before the demon prince's heathenish servants awaken."

I'd been to the Well only once, in conditions of light and weather so different I didn't trust my memory to recognize the cleft in the wall. So I crouched down, recalled the passage, the grotto, and the pool, and allowed magic to flow through my fingers into the stone beneath my feet. Cold, harsh, its cracks filled with frost crystals, the stone gave up its secrets far more reluctantly than earth. But I stretched my mind forward, swept the path and the cliff, and after a moment, a guiding thread claimed my senses—a surety something like that birds must feel when the days grow short and they streak southward beyond the mountains toward warmer climes. Such was the gift of the Cartamandua bent, the legacy of my father and grandfather's bloodline—a gift I had spurned because of its cost to my freedom. "This way," I said, moving northward along the shelf path.

"You said Prince Osriel himself comes to Gillarine tonight?" said Gram to the prior, as they trudged behind me, leading the beasts and sharing a flask Gram had brought.

"Aye," said the prior. " 'Twas only out of respect for good

King Eodward's memory that I could stomach hosting such a visitation. How could a noble king breed such a son?"

Gram downed a long pull from his flask. "Abbot Luviar himself could not explain the ways of the gods sufficient to that question."

Dikes of dense black stone seamed the pale layers of the limestone cliff with vertical bands. Some twenty paces along the cliff, a wide crack split one of these dark bands. "Here," I said. "We'll find him here."

The gray morning dimmed to twilight in the narrow passage. We stepped carefully. A dark glaze of ice sheathed the straight walls and slicked the stone beneath our feet. Ahead of us, beyond a rectangle of gray light, lay the little corrie, centered by a pool worn into the stone.

Clyste's Well, the pool was called, named for the Dané who had last claimed guardianship there. On one of his journeys into the Danae realms, my grandfather had involved Clyste in a mysterious theft that had driven humans and Danae apart. For his part in the crime, the Danae had tormented his mind to madness. For hers, they had locked her away in her sianou, forbidding her to take human form again. She had lived on all the years since, enriching the lands watered by her spring, including Gillarine Abbey. But no more. My every sense insisted she was dead. Murdered.

Heart drumming against my ribs, I bade Nemesio leave the ass where he stood. A few steps more and we reached the entry, the point where the passage walls expanded to encircle the grotto like cupped hands. *Ah, Holy Mother . . .* I clamped my arms about my aching middle. I would have given my two legs to be wrong.

Translucent, blue-white cascades of ice ridged the vertical walls and sheeted the smooth ground. The pool itself lay unfrozen, dark and still, no matter the wind that whipped the heights, showering us with spicules of ice. Gerard floated on the glassy water, naked, bloodless. Rain must have washed his shredded flesh clean of blood and what scraps of his abbey garments the knives had spared. The thorough savagery could have left no blood inside him. Iron spikes had been driven through his outstretched hands, tethering him to the rocky bank like a boat to its mooring. But one hand had torn through as he struggled to escape his fate, and now dangled loose in the water. Harrowers left their ritual victims to suffer and bleed, for it was both their blood and their torment that poisoned the sleeping Danae and the lands they guarded. So my grandfather had told me.

Nemesio choked, and I shoved him ruthlessly back into the passage to empty himself, though it was likely foolish to worry about further desecrating a place so vilely profaned. Gram pressed his back to the cliff wall at the entry, his pale cheeks as stark and drawn as the frozen cascades. "I cannot go here," he whispered. "I'm sorry. I can't help you with this."

"No matter. Rest as you need." I retrieved a worn blanket from the donkey's back and entered the grotto. Kneeling at the brink of the pool, I touched Gerard's tethered hand. *Cold. Great, holy gods . . . so cold.* Darkness enfolded me, threaded my veins and sinews, tightened about my heart and lungs until I felt as if I shared the terrifying, lonely end of this child's short life, and with it, the cold suffocation of the dead guardian. I needed desperately to empty my stomach, too, to cry out my sickness, to run, to be anywhere but this dreadful place. But I could not leave the boy. *Forgive. Please gods and holy earth, forgive us all.*

Stretching out from the brink, I drew him close, then worked awkwardly to wrap the blanket around him. By the time I had pulled his weakened flesh from the remaining spike, an iron-faced Nemesio had rejoined me. Together we used the blanket to lift the boy from the pool, then wrapped him in an outer blanket and carried him into the passage.

As the three of us tied the gray bundle to Dob's back, a movement caught the corner of my eye back in the corrie. A glint of sapphire brilliance quickly vanished in the gray light.

"Go on out," I whispered, still fighting to contain my own sickness. Gram looked ill, and the prior's teeth clattered like a bone rattle. Nemesio and I were both soaked. "I'll be along before you start down the steeps."

Nemesio clucked softly to the donkey. I slipped back down the passage toward the rectangle of light, flattened myself to the icy wall, and peered into the grotto.

A tall, naked man, every quat of his lean flesh ridged with muscle, knelt on one knee beside the pool. Back bent, head bowed, he extended his long arms over the water in a graceful curve as if to embrace the very essence of the pond. Red hair twined with yellow flowers curled over one shoulder. Patterns of blue light scribed his skin—a sapphire heron on his back, vines and flowers the color of mountain sky on his powerful limbs, a spray of reeds drawn in azure and lapis along one thigh and hip.

The Dané lifted his head, and a single anguished cry tore through him—echoing from the ice-clad walls, resonating in my bones. And then, stretching his arms to the heavens, he rose on his bare toes and whipped one leg around so that he spun in place. A quick step and then he spun again . . . and then again, moving around the pool in a blur of flesh and color and woven light, one arm curved before his chest, one above his head. The very rocks wept with his sorrow. I thought my heart might stop with the beauty of it.

When he reached his starting point, I stepped farther into the grotto. He halted in midspin and dropped his hands to his sides. He was not at all surprised to see me. And I recognized him. Three times I had glimpsed this same one of them . . . but never so close. Never in the fullness of his glory.

His eyes glowed the fiery gold of aspen leaves in autumn. On his left cheek the fine-drawn pattern of light scribed a dragon, whose wings spread across brow, shoulder, and chest, and whose long tail wrapped about his left arm. Below the graceful reeds that curved from his hip across his belly, a hatchling dragon coiled about his groin and privy parts. He appeared no more than thirty, but Danae lived for centuries and did not age as humans do.

"I didn't know this would happen," I said. "The man I brought here pretended to be what he was not. The child he slaughtered was an innocent . . . chosen because he was my friend. Never . . . never . . . did I mean to bring this on the one who slept here—this Clyste. My grandfather—" I caught myself before saying more. The Dané wouldn't care to hear that a human wept for her.

"As wolfsbane art thou, Cartamandua-son," he said, speaking fury and grief in the timbre of tuned bronze. "Beauty and poison. Taking life. Giving it back. Speaking the language of land and water, but with words graceless and ignorant. Intruding where thou shouldst not, violating—" He broke off, trembling, and swept his hand to encompass the grotto. "Thou dost lead me here, cleanse the Well so I do not sicken, return it to my memory so I cannot escape knowing what is lost—though I must lose it all over again as I walk away. Is this thy pleasure to taunt those thou dost not know? Dost thou think my love for Clyste can shield thee from the judgment of the long-lived?"

As flint to steel, his indignation sparked my anger, erasing all caution. "I know naught of you, Dané, save that you once offered me a haven in my need, then stood back and observed my captivity as if I were a performing bear chained for your amusement. I know that Danae vengeance has left my grandsire a madman. And I know that you or one of your fellows tricked me and my companions and our enemies into the bogs as if *all* humans were naught but beasts worthy of a slaughterhouse." Naught would ever erase the memory of luring my enemies into the freezing mud to save my companions' lives, of hearing . . . feeling . . . them drown. "I once believed your kind to be the blessed finger of the Creator in this world. But you are no better than we are."

"Pah!" With a snarl of disgust he turned away. Kneeling once again by the pool, he scooped water in his hands and poured it over his head. "*Askon geraitz, Clyste,*" he said, his voice breaking. "Live on in my heart, *asengai.* Let me not forget thee."

"Kol, don't leave. You must— Please hear us!" I had forgotten Gram. The wan secretary stood framed in the dark band of the passage entry, astonished . . . stammering. "Many of us . . . most . . . despise these murderers. The Everlasting is in upheaval, to the ruin of our land, our beasts, and all humankind. Whatever the cause, we desperately need the help of the long-lived to understand it . . . to make it right again. The gard of the dragon names thee Kol, friend and foster brother of Eodward King, brother to shining Clyste, who danced as none before her. In Eodward's name we beg hearing. Please, take us to Stian Archon or to any who might heed our message . . . our need . . ."

The Dané shifted his gold eyes to Gram. Cocking his head, he flared his nostrils and inhaled deeply. His lip

curled. "Human speech is briar and nightshade. Human
loyalty is that of wild dogs and weasels. Stripped is Stian of
his archon's wreath." His finger pointed to the dark pool.
"These evils are the gifting of Eodward to those who sheltered him. Begone! Thou dost bear the stink of betrayal
and shalt not pass one step into our lands until his debt is
paid." He strode toward the ice-clad wall, but before he
reached it, he vanished in a ripple of air and light.

Never had I stood in a place so unforgiving, so empty.
Gram might have been frozen into the wall. I gave him a
nudge, and we abandoned the grotto.

Halfway down the dark passage, a spasm of coughing
caused Gram to stumble and skid on the ice. I grabbed his
arm and steadied him. "You should come back to the abbey
with us, Gram. You look like walking death."

"I might as well be dead. I should have listened better
at Caedmon's Bridge, but I didn't want to hear their judgment. I should have believed what you told us about the
Harrower rites poisoning sianous."

"My grandfather said it is the Danae's greatest secret.
But when I walked into Gillarine yesterday and found it ruined . . . when I touched the earth in the cloisters . . . Gram,
I felt the world broken. I know it sounds presumptuous.
I've meager skills and a history of lies, but you must believe
that every breath, every bone, every drop of my blood tells
me that this breaking is cause of the world's upheaval . . .
the weather . . . the sickness . . . I'll swear it on whatever
you like."

Someday, perhaps, someone might believe what I said
without the backing of god-sworn oaths. My myriad swear-
ings had my life tangled upside over and backside front.

"We did not doubt your sincerity, Valen. We just believed
that no human action could compromise the Canon itself.
We assumed your grandfather's tale was but guilt speaking
through madness. And now I've wasted this opportunity. I
should have been better prepared. Ah, cursed be this weakness . . . inept . . ." The racking cough forced him to stop and
lean on the wall. He slapped his hands against the stone in
frustration, his reserve shattered for the first time since I'd
known him.

"If all this is true," he said, when he caught his breath at last, "if the Danae forget a place when it is corrupted and lost to the Canon, then how could Kol be here?"

"He follows me," I said, able to answer that one question, at least. "I saw him the first time on the night I tried to escape from Gillarine. He waited in an aspen grove and offered his hand—tried to rescue me. Then he watched me every day of my punishment exhibition in the streets of Palinur. I even glimpsed him in a courtyard of my family's house. I saw a Dané in Mellune Forest, too, but I'm not sure it was he. I didn't know the one with the dragon on his face was Kol. Spirits of night, Clyste's brother . . . he likely *was* the one who tried to drown us in the bog. My grandfather warned me that I was in danger from the Danae."

Gram stared at me for a moment in the dim light, then rested his back against the passage wall and averted his eyes. I'd never met a more private man. "That makes no sense," he said, collecting his scattered emotions. "Your grandfather is being punished for his crime and will continue to be until whatever he stole is returned. Thus his debt is being paid. The Danae would never take vengeance on others, even his family, unless they believed those others complicit in Janus's crime. Their law—the Law of the Everlasting—forbids it."

He ran his long fingers through his hair as if to drag ideas from his skull. "Danae justice is quite clear and quite specific. Everything is balance. Bargains. Exchanges. Think of what Kol said and how he said it. Death and life. Violation and restored memory. He clearly did *not* blame you for Clyste's death. He would blame the one who did the murder. Perhaps he was already following you about when it happened. Yet he implied that you've raised the ire of other Danae . . . *the judgment of the long-lived* . . . and with your grandfather's warning . . ." He looked up at me again. "Valen, do you have what Janus stole?"

"No!" I said. "I didn't even know of my grandfather's crime until a fortnight ago. And he refused to tell me what he took. If their 'justice' is so balanced, then why does Eodward's betrayal bar us all from their realms?"

"I don't think he meant all humans." Shivering, Gram bundled his cloak tighter. "I've got to consider all this . . .

inform Thane Stearc and see what he makes of it. Our plans may have to change. Come, we'd best get back."

"Brother Valen!" As if in echo of Gram's conclusion, Nemesio's call bounced urgently through the passage. "Get out here now!"

"So you go back to Osriel?" said Gram as we hurried toward the light.

"I would rather do anything else. But I must honor my word or else— Well, I don't know what would happen, but my word is the only thing I've ever held to. I promise you, I'll be no good to him."

He stopped me as we approached the mouth of the passage. "You said something similar back at Mellune. What do you mean?"

No need for him to know what my nivat-starved perversion was like to make of me. I pulled my arm from his hand. "Be well, Gram. Give the thane and his daughter my regards."

"*Teneamus*, Valen," he said.

We preserve—the Aurellian code word of the lighthouse cabal. Gram's invocation of it expressed the sincerity of his concern for me. I had no answer for his kindness. "We'd best go before Nemesio bursts."

It was as well I chose not to further compromise my vow of submission. When Gram and I stepped from the cleft into the open air, Nemesio and the donkey waited with Gram's gray mare. Beside them stood Voushanti.

Chapter 3

No argument of mine could persuade Voushanti that I'd no intent to run. "His Grace will decide your punishment," he said as he bound my hands to the donkey's harness. "And you *will* be there to heed it."

Though pale and quivering, Nemesio bore Voushanti's impossible arrival with a straight spine and unbowed head. I should have warned the prior about Prince Osriel's favored commander. I had seen Voushanti recover from terrible wounds in a matter of hours. I had witnessed his resiliency as we tramped day and night through the winter nightmare of Mellune Forest. More than once I had looked into the red core of his eyes and suspected he did not sleep. What common sleeping draft would affect such a man, if man he was?

At least the mardane showed no interest in exploring the cleft. Whether or not Prince Osriel was Sila Diaglou's rival in the pursuit of chaos, the last thing I wanted to do was teach him a way to interfere with the Danae.

When we reached the flats, Voushanti dismissed Gram with a promise to report his interference both to Thane Stearc and Stearc's liege lord Prince Osriel. The last I saw of the secretary, he was vanishing at a gallop into the frozen haze that had settled in the valley. Voushanti, the prior, the ass, and I slogged toward the abbey afoot.

With no silken cords binding my hands to stay the flow of magic, I could have unlocked the chain that linked my wrists to the donkey even with my limited skills. But in truth I could not summon the wits to work a spell. A storm of blue light filled my head—the image of the Dané as he danced out his grief. I had never imagined such expressive power in mere movement, as if his body formed words and music I could not hear. My own feet dragged like brutish anvils through the snow. My arms felt stiff as posts. Compared to his, my body was no more living than a wall of brick.

Remnants of our exchange swirled in my thoughts like water through a sluice. He'd said that I had cleansed the Well, as if it were some marvel. Yet I'd done naught but remove the dead boy, hardly difficult for a man of his strength.

Kol, the son of the Danae archon who had sheltered King Caedmon's infant son more than a century ago . . . My mind balked at the imagining. My grandfather, a cartographer with a sorcerer's bent, had discovered Caedmon's heir living in the realm of the Danae—the realm of angels, legend called it. Life spent differently in Danae lands, for a century and a half after his royal father's death, Eodward had just been passing from youth to manhood. A Karish hierarch and a high priest of the elder gods had persuaded the young man to return to Navronne and revive the wreckage of his father's kingdom. Though Eodward had promised the Danae to return to them after only a few years, he never had. Navronne had needed her strong and honorable warrior king, who had freed her from the disintegrating Aurellian empire and a succession of invasions from the barbarian Hansker.

Three years ago, good King Eodward had died, abandoning Navronne to his three sons—a blustering brute, an effete coward, and my master, rival to the lord of the netherworld. Between my grandfather's unexplained theft, Eodward's betrayal of his word, and the depredations of the Harrowers, it was no wonder the Danae brooked no dealings with humankind.

Nemesio unlatched the wooden gate in the low eastern wall of the abbey. The prior had been silent on our return journey. Praying, I thought. Mourning. *Deunor's fire, Gerard . . .* an unscholarly boy with a quick smile and an innocent heart. What punishment would be dreadful enough to requite this crime? Gildas . . . the Harrowers . . . Sila Dia-glou . . . I *would* see them brought to account for it.

As soon as we left the field path for the abbey walks, the monks began to gather, like blackbirds to a rooftop. De-spite their anonymous robes and hoods, I recognized them by their shapes—short, tight Brother Sebastian; willowy Brother Bolene; squat, stooped Brother Adolfus—and by their hands, roughened by cold and hard work or stained indelibly by buckets of ink. These men, who had so kindly welcomed me as a vagabond into their brotherhood, of-fered no signs of blessing, greeting, or welcome. Why would I expect it? Most of them had last seen me a month past, when my sister had led me from the abbey with shackled feet and silk-bound hands—a disgraced *recondeur*, named trai-tor to god and king, a liar and thief who had mocked their vows by pretending he could be worthy of their company, even for a season. And now . . . chained to the ass that car-ried Gerard's body . . . as if I were responsible . . . My skin heated with shame.

"Set me loose," I said to Voushanti through my teeth. "I'll not run. Please. They'll think I did this."

But he wouldn't until we reached the bedraggled garden maze in front of the church. As the brothers lifted the boy gently and carried him toward the lavatorium where they would clean and wrap him properly, Voushanti detached my chain from the ass and led me toward the guesthouse like a troublesome dog.

Philo and Melkire awaited us in the guesthouse bed-chamber, dark rings about their eyes and glaring resent-ment pouring off them like steam from a lathered horse. Voushanti unlocked my manacles and jerked his ugly head to the fine clothes, still strewn on the bed, and a cop-per washbasin sitting beside the hearth. "Clean and dress yourself."

Days of fear and frustration boiled over despite my best intents. "What, no whips? No dungeon? The abbey has a prison cell, you know. If I'm to be treated as a brainless dog, why not kennel me?"

Voushanti grabbed the laps of my cloak and dragged my head down to his, where I could not ignore the scarlet pits of his eyes. "I would gladly whip sense and respect into you, purebold. Be sure of it. Your flesh is weak and your mind undisciplined. But our master has charged me to preserve your skin and your mind for *his* pleasure, and his will is our law. Now prepare yourself for his arrival." He shoved me away.

I clamped my hands under my folded arms, fighting to control my anger. Deep in my gut an ember flared in warning. Before very long—a day or two at most—its fire would grow to encompass my whole body, triggering the hunger for blood-spelled nivat seed. Ravaged with guilt on the day Luviar had died, I'd sworn off the doulon—the enchantment that transformed fragrant nivat into an odorless black paste that warped the body's experience of pain and pleasure. I'd thrown away my implements and the last of my nivat supply, so when the hunger came on me next, I had naught to feed it. That's when I would go mad.

"Have we word of His Grace?" Voushanti blocked the narrow doorway.

"Santiso rode in not an hour since," said Melkire. "He says the prince should arrive at any time. The other parties to the parley are expected tonight as well."

As the three of them discussed horses, guard posts, and the best places to billet Osriel's retinue, I stripped off my sodden garments. The water in the copper basin was tepid. A clean linen towel, many times mended, lay beside it. They'd left me no comb, but my hair had not grown much since it was trimmed to match my regrowing tonsure. I dunked my head in the basin and thought fleetingly of not pulling it out again.

I had to put the morning's events aside for now. I needed to use the next hours to the cabal's advantage. Perhaps I could acquire some notion of Osriel's plans in this damnable war or learn the nature of his power. His mother had been purebold and clearly he had developed his magic far beyond the weak capabilities of other mixed-blood Navrons. But I didn't even know what parley was to happen here.

For three years, Osriel had sat on his gold mines in his mountainous principality of Evanore, weaving devilish enchantments while his half-brothers' war ravaged their own provinces of Ardra and Morian. Theories abounded on why he raided his brothers' battlefields and mutilated the dead—none of them pleasant. I had believed the stories of Osriel's depravities exaggerated until the night when Prince Bayard of Morian had flushed his brother Perryn to Gillarine's gates, slaughtering a hundred of Perryn's Ardran soldiers along the way. Hellish, dreadful visions had descended on the abbey that night, and by morning every corpse lay under Osriel's ensign and stared toward heaven eyeless. The monks had called it Black Night.

As I laced my chausses, Philo raced up the stair, snapped a salute, and reported Prince Osriel's arrival. "The prior has given him his own quarters and offered any building save the church for his use. His Grace sent me to fetch you, Mardane."

Voushanti eyed my half-dressed state. "Inform His Grace that I am unable to yield my charge until he summons his pureblood. I will deliver the sorcerer and my report at the same time."

Philo pressed a clenched fist to his breast and bowed briskly.

I refused to rush my dressing. The clothes were of the sort expected of purebloods: a high-necked shirt of black and green patterned silk, ruched at neck and wrists, a spruce-green satin pourpoint, delicately embroidered in black and seeded with black pearls, and a gold link belt. The doeskin boots felt like gloves. Ludicrous apparel for wartime in a burnt-out abbey. But if my master wished me decked out like a merchants' fair, so be it.

Voushanti's impatience came near scorching my back, but eventually my hundred buttons were fastened and fifty laces tied. I lifted the claret cape and mask and raised my brows. He jerked his head in assent. So other ordinaries were to be present, not just my master and his household.

The lightweight cape of embroidered silk fastened at my right shoulder with a gold-and-ivory brooch, shaped like a wolf's head. The mask, a bit of silk light as ash, slipped onto the left side of my face like another layer of skin and held its place without ties or bands of any kind. Someone had given my exact description to the one who had created and ensorcelled it. Of all pureblood disciplines, I most hated that of the mask.

Then we waited.

Though the great bronze bells had fallen from the church tower, the monks rang handbells to keep to their schedule of devotions and work. I would have preferred to get on with whatever vileness Osriel planned for me. It would save me fretting over the worthwhile tasks I ought to be attempting while I yet had a mind: rescuing Jullian, retrieving the book of maps, discovering where Sila Diaglou hid her supplies and trained her Harrower legions. I wasn't even sure whether or not the lighthouse yet existed after the ruinous assault on Gillarine.

I had believed the magical domed chambers and their astonishing cache existed underground below the abbey library and scriptorium, but I'd seen no evidence of the downward stair in the rubble. Why hadn't I asked Gram what had become of it? If Osriel chose to lock me away in one of his mountain fortresses, I might never learn. My contract with the prince, negotiated by my father and approved by the Registry, lacked the customary protections afforded more tractable pureblood progeny, thus allowing my master to do whatever he wished with me.

I slammed my fists against the window frame, rattling the glass in the iron casement. Voushanti snorted, but said naught.

By the time Philo brought the prince's summons, Vespers had rung through the early dusk. The ginger-bearded soldier led Voushanti and me past the charred hollows of the west-reach undercrofts, where the fires had been so fierce that the entire upper structure of the lay brothers' dorter had collapsed, and around behind the squat stone kitchen building to the refectory stair.

"His Grace will speak to the mardane first," said Philo. "The pureblood is to wait inside the door, where he can be seen." The ginger-haired warrior pulled on his helm, took up a lance propped against the wall, and joined Melkire in a proper alert stance flanking the wide oak door.

We entered the refectory halfway along one side of the long chamber. The barreled vault of the roof stood intact, but the tall windowpanes were broken and the pale yellow walls stained with smoke. The long tables and backless stools had been shoved together at the lower end of the cavernous hall.

The refectory had been my favorite place in the abbey. But no robust ale or steaming bowls of mutton broth sat ready to warm the belly on this eve. No beams of light streamed from the soaring lancet windows to warm the spirit. No grinning boys or teasing monks awaited to warm the heart. I splayed my five fingers and pressed my palm to my breast, praying Iero to welcome Gerard and to comfort Jullian, boys who had honored their god with such cheerful service.

Two braziers provided the only light or heat. They flanked a single plain wood chair set before the delicate stone window tracery that gaped empty at one end. There, robed and hooded as severely as any monk, our master awaited us.

"Stay here until you're called," muttered Voushanti.

An enigma, Voushanti. His touch left me queasy, and his glance induced me to spread my fingers in ward against evil. Yet for all his single-minded ferocity and spine-curling presence, the mardane had never harmed me. Together we had survived the ordeal in Mellune Forest.

He hurried across the worn wood floor and prostrated himself at Osriel's feet—an elaboration more suited to an Aurellian emperor than a Navron prince. The prince motioned Voushanti up, but only as far as his knees. I could not hear what was said, but felt the Bastard's anger stirring the shadows like the first breath of a storm wind.

If Voushanti's presence disturbed my stomach, Prince Osriel's disturbed my soul. My imagination conjured a thousand horrors beneath his hooded robe. Some said the prince was crippled; some said his body had been corrupted by his dealings with the Adversary.

The wind whistled and moaned through the broken windows, swirling the detritus of dust and glass that littered the floor. I twitched and fidgeted, fussed with my cloak, with my belt, with the iron latches of the lower windows. I strained to hear the monks' Vesper singing down in the ruined church, and tried to recall the words of the psalm and the comfort they promised. Deunor's fire . . . what was taking so long? Voushanti must be reciting every detail of the eight days since we had left Prince Osriel in Palinur. I tried not to imagine what punishments Osriel could devise for my morning's misbehavior. My every sense, every nerve, felt stretched to breaking.

The light wavered. For a moment I thought the flames in the braziers had gone out. But rather the shadows were creeping in from the corners and vaults to envelop the prince and his kneeling servant, roiling and thickening until I could scarcely see the two men. Sweat beaded the base of my spine beneath my fine layers, even while the night air pouring through the empty window frames froze my cheeks.

A quick strike of red light fractured the gathered darkness. Voushanti's shoulders jerked, and he could not fully muffle a groan. Twice more, each eliciting a similar cry, and then the mardane bent down as if to kiss Osriel's feet.

The prince, shapeless in his enveloping robes, leaned back in his chair. Voushanti climbed slowly to his feet. Stepping back a few paces, the mardane motioned me to approach.

Wishing myself five thousand quellae from this place, I took a deep breath and crossed the expanse of floor through the swirling dust and snow. Heat radiated from Voushanti's body as if he had swallowed the sun. As he bowed and withdrew, blood trickled from the unscarred corner of his mouth. *Mighty gods . . .*

Remembering Osriel's instruction from our last meeting, I whisked off my mask and looped it over my belt. My knees felt like porridge, my skin like cold fish.

"My lord prince," I said, touching my fingers to my forehead and bending one knee—the proper pureblood obeisance to his contracted master.

The flames in the two braziers shot into the air in spouts of blue and white flame, pushing back the rippling shadows. Not enough to reveal the prince's face. Only his hands were exposed. Long, slender, pale fingers, one adorned with a heavy gold ring. Their smooth firmness reminded me that Osriel was no older than I. He twitched the ringed finger, and I rose to my feet.

"Magnus Valentia." The harsh whisper came from behind and beside and before me, raising the hair on my arms. "The reports of your behavior puzzle me."

In our previous interview, the prince had expressed a

preference for honesty over feigned deference, for boldness over cowering. Swallowing hard, I shoved fear aside, clasped my hands at my back, and hoped he'd meant it.

"How puzzled, my lord? Since leaving your side in Palinur, I have followed Mardane Voushanti's direction, and I've not strayed from his sight save when his sight was clouded with sleep. We traveled companionably. Indeed, we worked together to preserve the lives of your Evanori subjects on our journey from Palinur. Never once, even when Mardane Voushanti and his men were ... debilitated ... by the severities of that journey and we were separated by necessity, did I break my submission to you. Nor did I have any intention of doing so this morning when I aided the good prior to retrieve one of his abbey's lost children. Mardane Voushanti had no basis to assume I would run away." The weight of Osriel's attention slowed my words.

"Yet this morning's excursion occurred over his objections, and only after a monkish potion laid him low—he has reaped his proper harvest for *that* slip of attention. I instructed you to obey him as if his word were my own. So tell me, shall I punish *you* for disobedience, or shall I punish this Karish prior for poisoning my servants and abducting my pureblood for his own purposes?"

The questions and accusations nipped at my skin like the claws of demon gatzi. I kneaded my hands at my back, expecting to feel bloody pricks and scratches. *Hold on to your mind, Valen,* I thought. *No supernatural power exists in this room. You have felt the stirrings of true mystery in the Gillarine cloisters, and you have witnessed a living Dané dance his grief.* Whatever Osriel of Evanore might be—and I had no doubts he possessed power unknown to any of my acquaintance—he was neither god nor demon.

"Prior Nemesio believes that my novice vows, made but a few weeks ago, give him a claim on my loyalty. Though my oath to you is more recent, I saw no compromise of your interests in helping him retrieve a dead child."

I stepped closer to the chair and did not squirm. "As for potions and poisons, the unfortunate effect of the abbey's blessed water on Mardane Voushanti and his men is perhaps a reproof from their gods at some failure in their devotions. For surely, my cup was filled from the same pitcher, yet I did not fall asleep. Then, too, Mardane Voushanti arrived at the sad scene of this boy's death not half an hour after I did, thus he could not have been much affected. Were the prior's water poisoned, would not the mardane have suffered its effects longer? Or is there some reason his constitution does not succumb to the effects of potions or poisons?" I braced, expecting red lightning to strike.

But instead, the prince leaned his elbow on the arm of the chair and propped his chin on his hand. "Ah, Magnus, your tongue is as soft and quick as a spring zephyr in the Month of Storms . . . and just as deceitful. Unfortunately I've not the time to test your stamina at this game tonight. But I believe I shall reap great pleasure from our sparring in the deeps of this coming winter. Snug in my house, I shall strip you of your pureblood finery and raise the stakes for untruth."

I bowed, hiding my satisfaction, as well as my face, which his throaty humor had surely left void of color.

"And now we must discuss a few things before my guests arrive."

"Of course, my lord." I straightened my back and forced myself to breathe.

The prince angled his head upward, then waggled his hand toward the floor. "Sit," he said impatiently. "I've no wish to break my neck gaping upward. Is your father or brother so tall as you? Your grandfather, perhaps? Purebloods are of wholly modest stature."

"I am an aberration of pureblood lineage in countless ways, my lord. My own father would gleefully deny my birth had he not scribed it in the Register himself and seen the entry countersigned by two unimpeachable witnesses."

Off balance from his abrupt shift from chilling threat to peckish complaint, I settled on the wood floor and wrapped my arms about my knees. The hairs on the back of my neck prickled. The shadows that reeled and twirled on the refectory walls had no correspondence to the flames in the braziers. Nor did their shapes—heads, limbs, writhing torsos—correspond to those of the prince or my own body.

"An aberration? Yes, I suppose you could be," the prince mumbled.

I did not flinch or turn my head when his next comment seemed to come from behind my left ear. "So tell me who would be considered unimpeachable witnesses to a child's birth? Truth and lies are of infinite interest to me. I might like to interview such a person."

At least this answer was easy, though I could not fathom the intent of the question. "For good or ill, lord, the witnesses to my birth are beyond your inquiries. Indeed, they are more a part of your own history than mine. Two of my grandfather's oldest friends happened to be visiting our house on the day I was born—Sinduré Tobrecan of Evanore and Angnecy, the seventh Hierarch of Ardra, the very two clergymen who brought your father to Navronne from the realm of . . . angels."

"A most interesting coincidence."

Though forced to parrot the facts and validation of my lineage since I could speak, I'd never considered them at all interesting.

The prince settled back in his chair and did not move. Thinking, surely. Watching, too. The velvet hood might mask his own face, but I did not believe it obscured anything he wished to look on. Rather than squirm under his scrutiny, I stared back at him. From this angle I could glimpse his jaw—fine boned, square, clean shaven—and mouth—generously wide, lips pale but even. Unsettling. *Well, of course,* I thought, after a moment, *he is Eodward's son.* Though I had met the king only once, every coin in the realm bore the imprint of those fine bones. What was so dreadful about Osriel's face that he kept it hidden, when his man Voushanti walked freely with his own ruined flesh bared for all to see?

"Tell me, Magnus, what magics can you work? You've said that you paid no mind to your tutors and that your inability to read prevented your study of pureblood arcana, but Voushanti's report indicates you are not incapable of spellworking. What have I received for my hundredweight of gold?"

No wisdom lay in *under*reporting my paltry skills in some hope that Osriel would set me free of my contract. He might decide my best use was that he made of corpses. *Over*reporting might yield me a better position in his house. My grandfather constantly babbled that I had talent beyond the usual for purebloods. Of course, even before he went mad, my grandfather had an overblown opinion of our family's talents, and I'd never seen evidence of anything extraordinary in myself.

"Honestly, my lord—you see, I remember you are very strict about honesty, even if the honest statement fails to please you—my catalogue of spells is thin. Beyond my family bent of route finding, tracking, identifying footsteps, and the like, I've meager skills in spellworking. Opening locks is perhaps my strongest, and I can accomplish voiding spells—making holes in things." I closed my eyes and wished I had more to report so that I might hold back some small secret advantage for the future. "I can work inflation spells—that is, I can create an illusion by exaggerating an existing object. For example, I once conjured a tree stump from a weed with spreading roots. Creating an illusion from nothing is beyond me . . ." Truly it was a pitiful collection when one considered the vast possibilities of magic.

I was straining to come up with something more to boost my worth, when the refectory door burst open and Voushanti hurried toward us. "My lord prince, your guest has arrived. As you commanded, I informed him that only the two principals and his pureblood would be allowed in your presence. He was not pleased, but neither did he leave."

"Well done, Mardane. You've taken the measure of his desperation, it would seem. Let him cool his heels for a moment, while I instruct my sorcerer."

The visitor had a pureblood in attendance. He was nobility, then, or clergy, or a civic official wealthy enough to purchase a pureblood contract, someone who thought to profit from traveling to this remote site to wait on the Bastard Prince, even as Osriel's eldest brother was ready to declare victory in Navronne. All parties to this war were realigning themselves since Prince Bayard's alliance with Sila Diaglou and the Harrowers had broken three years of stalemate.

Voushanti left as he had come. Once the door had closed behind him, Prince Osriel returned his attention to me. "I require your complete obedience tonight, sorcerer. Without reservation or any of your clever deceptions. You will stand to my right and slightly in front of me, angled where you can see my hands and I can see your face without moving my head. I wish you to listen carefully to all that's spoken and observe all that remains unspoken. You will say *nothing* without my permission. Do you understand? Nothing, even if you are addressed directly. But if I require you to respond or offer an opinion, you will speak in perfect honesty, without subterfuge or withholding. Is this clear or must we argue it? I promise you, I *will* prevail."

Though such threats could not but raise my hackles, innate perversity no longer drove me to pointless rebellion. For the sake of my friends in the cabal, I needed to learn what I could of Evanore's prince and those who came seeking his favor. So I rose and bowed, touching my forehead. "As you command, Your Grace."

If my master thought my presence would lend him some kind of prestige in a lordly negotiation, he had an unhappy lesson coming. By now every pureblood in the kingdom would know of Osriel's contract with the infamous Cartamandua renegade.

Moments after I slipped on my mask, straightened my cloak, and took my position at Prince Osriel's right hand, the great door burst open, and I gaped as if I'd seen a fish walk out of the ocean. Prince Bayard of Morian walked in, followed by his half-brother, Perryn of Ardra, and Bayard's attendant pureblood sorcerer—my own brother, Max.

Chapter 4

――✺――――――✻――

Bayard and Max, layered in mail, leather, and fur-lined traveling cloaks, each made a quick survey of the room. The two of them were similar in build, though Max's tight bulk came in a smaller package than the Duc of Morian, called the Smith for his brutal manners. The last I'd seen of Max, he had been chortling at the news of my father contracting his rebellious younger brother to the most feared man in Navronne.

Perryn, Duc of Ardra, remained near the door, shivering in grimed silk and torn lace, his once golden hair greasy and unkempt, his head bent, and his arms wrapped about his middle. His furtive glance took in Osriel and the dancing shadows. Then, as if he had seen enough, he hugged himself tighter and closed his eyes.

Max bowed respectfully to Osriel, touching his forehead with his fingertips. His eyes reflected humorous irony as he pivoted to face me, touching one middle finger to the center of his brow—the proper greeting of one pureblood to another while in the presence of ordinaries.

I made sure to close my mouth, which still hung open in astonishment. Unsure whether my master would consider a returned greeting as speech, I remained motionless, my hands at my back, grateful for the mask that might hide the extent of my surprise. What possible circumstance could bring Bayard supplicant to his despised youngest brother in the very hour of his triumph? Every notion of politics claimed the Smith should be seated on Caedmon's throne at this moment, planting his brutish foot on the necks of groveling Ardran nobles.

"So is this the kind of foolery the terrifying Osriel spends his time on? Playing with shades and gargoyles in a Karish ruin?" Bayard's posture, feet apart, hands resting lightly at his waist, spoke everything of self-assurance. But deep creases in his brow and stretched smudges about his eyes hinted that victory did not rest firmly within his grasp . . . as if his presence at this assignation so far from Palinur was not indication enough.

"Is one fool's occupation to be preferred to another's? My shades leave no one bleeding." Prince Osriel's cool jibe heated his elder brother's cheeks. "You requested this parley, brother. And you said I should choose a neutral venue."

Osriel snapped his fingers. The flames in the twin braziers surged to the height of a man, causing the shadows to lengthen and dance wildly. Two armless wooden chairs took shape out of nothing, positioned to face him. Bayard paled and shifted uneasily.

My master gestured toward the chairs. "Come, brothers, sit. I would not have you stand like servants or courtiers. I've missed our long dinners with Father, talking of history and geography, building and art. Should I send for food and wine? Perhaps we could begin again in his memory." The words pelted the faces of his brothers like hailstones, evoking a cascade of expressions, even as they whetted my own curiosity.

"No need for games, Bastard. You know why I'm here." Bayard snatched one of the chairs, realizing only after he'd sat how awkwardly it suited. It was much too small for his blacksmith's frame. Max moved to Perryn's side, touched his arm, and gestured to the second chair. The blond prince shook his head and huddled deeper into his own embrace. One might have thought him cowed, save for the occasional glance of purest hate that speared Bayard's back.

"I am guessing you've at last seen Father's writ of succession," said Osriel. "And that you are preparing to proclaim to the people of Navronne that it names you heir, just as you've insisted all these years that it would. But we know the truth of that, don't we? As does our frighted brother. Have you found a better forger than his?"

The truth laid out so quietly exploded in my head. My gaze snapped from one to the other. Osriel—Eodward's named successor? I recalled the grand depiction of the *ordo mundi* painted on the walls of the Gillarine guesthouse and imagined it flipped end over end, the denizens of heaven and hell dislodged and poured out to mingle with the tangled creatures of earth's sphere. Horror, wonder, denial, and awe mastered me in rapid succession.

One would think Bayard chewed iron. "You will never wear my father's crown, Bastard. I'll gift it to a Hansker chieftain first."

"So what do you propose to do about this little disappointment?" Osriel's throaty whisper exuded subtle menace. "Do you think to snatch those few who know the truth and feed them to Sila Diaglou? I hear her executions are most efficient, if a bit gruesome. I quite resent your allowing the bloodthirsty priestess to destroy *my* city and slaughter *my* subjects—even holy monks, I've heard."

All confused bulk and outrage, Bayard spluttered. "Navrons will never accept a crippled, half-mad sorcerer as king. You've no warrior legion and no strength to lead one. That's why you've never pressed a claim. Fires of Magrog, you sneak onto our battlefields and mutilate the dead. You squat on your treasure, waiting for the two of us to kill each other off—"

"You and Perryn chose your own course of fraternal mayhem," snapped Osriel. "I warned you at the beginning I would not play. As for the rest, I have my own purposes. Now, what do you want of me? I will never kneel to you. Put that right out of your thoughts."

Osriel . . . king. Every belief must shift and skew at the imagining.

Bayard burst from his chair, swung around behind it, and gripped the squared oak back, as if wrestling a hurricane into submission. Both face and posture declared he would prefer to open his belly with a dagger than speak what he had come to say. "The woman Sila Diaglou is a demon gatzé. But using her legion of madmen was the only way I could get this sniveling imbecile to heel before he burnt my ships and yards—our only hope to hold off the spring raids from Hansk. I agreed to cede her territory—some wild lands, a few villages, a town or two. She said that with sovereign territory 'properly cleansed,' she could prove to the rest of us the power of her Gehoum. But this lunacy she's wrought in Palinur ..." He spat his words through the bitter edge of humiliation. "I gave her no mandate for executions. I ordered her to stand down and withdraw her filthy lunatics from the city, but her partisans goad everyone to their own madness. Now the witch has presented me with a list of demands, threatening to raze Palinur and set her madmen on Avenus and other cities if I don't comply. I've squeezed Morian's treasury dry to get this far, believing I'd have Navronne's wealth—mine by right—to control her at the end. But what have I found?"

He strode to Perryn, huddled against the wall, dragged him to Osriel's feet by the neck of his silk tunic, and shoved him sprawling. Perryn threw his arms over his head and lay quivering, and I cursed myself once again for ever believing he was man enough to lead Navronne.

"This parasite," snarled Bayard, "this weak-livered vermin, did not merely exhaust Ardra's patrimony, but Navronne's, as well. Our father's treasure house sits empty, its gold squandered on oranges from Estigure, on brocades and perfumed oils from Syanar, on follies, jugglers, and lace, on miniature ponies for his whores, on puling spies and legions of mercenaries from Aurellia and Pyrrha who have never set foot in Navronne, if they exist at all. If I am to crush this devil woman, I must have Evanore's gold."

Osriel perched on the edge of his chair, coiled tight as a chokesnake. Bayard bulled ahead without a breath. "You will not have to kneel. You will have autonomy in your own land until the day of your death, and I will recognize you publicly as my sovereign equal in Evanore. Together, we can prevail. Together ..." Bayard's speech trailed away in the face of his brother's frigid stillness.

"What does she want?" said Osriel, quiet and harsh.

Bayard's beard quivered with pent rage. "It doesn't *matter* what she wants. She's a madwoman. We yield on these demands and she'll come back for more. I see that now."

Osriel leaned forward slightly, and I knew Bayard felt the pressure of his brother's will as I had earlier. "Tell me what she asked for."

Heaving a sigh of suffering patience, Bayard whipped his hand toward Max. "Tell him."

My brother stepped forward and bowed slightly to his master. "First, she demands the province of Evanore, whole and entire. Second, she desires that one of my lord's brothers, either one, be turned over to her as mortal forfeit for the offenses the line of Caedmon has wrought against the Gehoum." My brother cataloged the unthinkable as if the items sat on a shelf like tin pots.

Osriel tented his pale hands, his fingertips just touching his chin. He did not speak.

Max bowed again and flicked a glance at me. "Third, she desires a piece of information—the location of a secret library that she claims is anathema to the Gehoum. It does not appear to exist where she was told. And lastly, she wishes to own the contract of a particular pureblood sorcerer."

"A pureblood?" Prince Osriel dropped his hands abruptly into his lap. "Who? For what reason?"

The public half of Max's face remained perfectly neutral as his position required. But an eye accustomed to looking past a pureblood's mask could not miss the wicked humor behind the sheath of dull blue silk. "She insists on controlling one Magnus Valentia de Cartamandua-Celestine, lately returned to the discipline of the Pureblood Registry. She did not explain why."

Magrog's teeth! My suddenly sweating hands came near slipping out of each other behind my back.

Bayard shoved his chair away so viciously it tipped over and clattered to the floor. "The cheek!" he fumed, striding to the windowed wall only to reverse course and return to kick the toppled chair. "As if I would go scrambling about the city like her pet hound, hunting libraries and purebloods. My own sorcerer's brother, as if that would make her my equal." He paused and glared at me as if Sila Diaglou stood behind me with her hand on my shoulder. "What does she want with you, pureblood, eh? I hear you are a renegade, a liar, and a thief."

Mind reeling, I pinned my gaze on Osriel's hands. They were still, so I kept silent and asked myself the same question. Why would the Harrower priestess want me? Not merely for the Cartamandua blood. Max ... Phoebia ... my father had no contract, for the gods' sake. They all displayed the bent of my grandfather's line. Unlike me, they were trained and skilled and intelligent enough to read books and make sense of the world.

"You'd best keep an eye on him, little brother," said Bayard with a sneer. "By the Mother's tits, I'd give her Perryn and offer to gut him myself, save for the damnable impertinence of her insisting on a kill of my own blood. But Evanore ..."

Perryn had crept to the foot of Osriel's chair and hunched there in a shriveled knot. "You wouldn't let him give me over, brother," he said. "I was ever kind to you. It was Bayard played the bully. He swears he'll do this bargain, and throw you in as well if he can persuade the witch to forgo Evanore's gold."

"Does anyone outside this room know that you two have come to me?" Osriel spoke over Perryn's head as if the fair prince were some whining hound.

Bayard spluttered. "My aides know, of course. My field commanders. I'm not a fool—"

"Tell me the truth, Bayard, or I'll send you back with an ox head instead of your own. Does *anyone* but these two know you've come to Gillarine to meet *me*?"

"No one else knows," said Perryn, emboldened like a lapdog that finds its courage only at its master's feet. "He says we must be secret, else she'll find out he's plotting against her. He near pisses his trews at the thought. She sees everything."

"Good." Osriel pointed to a spot in front of his chair. "Now stand here, the both of you, and listen. Yes, you, too, Perryn. Your 'kindness' fell short back when your pleasure was to lock me into emptied meat casks. Stand like a man and listen to me."

Perryn slouched to his feet, while Bayard stood his ground ten paces back, bristling like an offended boar. My master waited silently. Only when Bayard expelled an exasperated oath and moved to Perryn's side did Osriel speak again.

"You came here seeking my help, brothers. Did you think I would shovel gold into your pockets and allow you to continue sending my people to the slaughter as you've done these three years? You've countenanced crimes that make my activities look tame, and I should rightly take your heads for it."

Reason. Assurance. Command. Of a sudden this mad parley felt grounded in something more than terror.

"I am the rightful High King of Navronne, whether anyone beyond this room ever understands that or not, and you will stand or fall by my will."

"You are a crippled whelp who knows nothing of warfare." Bayard spat the brave words, but held his position in the place his half-brother had indicated. He must be at the end of all recourse.

Osriel raised a hand in warning. "I am allowing myself to believe that the two of you have been stupid and blind these three years, rather than vile and malicious, and that your excesses have been as misreported as my own deeds. Either we work together to salvage this mess you've made, or you can walk out of here this moment. As for the fool who attempts to touch my gold without my consent, I will take his eyes living from his head and hold his soul captive in everlasting torment. Choose, brothers. For Navronne. For our father, who foolishly believed in all of us."

A seething Bayard, his complexion the hue of bloomed poppies, whirled and strode away. I was certain he would broach the door, but instead he circled the refectory. Perryn lifted his chin, sneering as if ready to defy both brothers, but glanced at the ceiling, peopled by writhing shades, shuddered, and dropped his head again. Osriel waited. I held my breath.

Halfway between his brothers and the door, Bayard slowed, growling with resentful fury. "What do you propose? I concede nothing until I've heard your plan."

Osriel flicked his ringed hand toward me. "Magnus, tell me: Is your brother trustworthy? I will send him out if you say."

Max stiffened as if one of Silos's firebolts had fused his spine. Not the least hint of a smirk appeared on either half of his face. For a pureblood adviser to be dismissed in a negotiation accounted him as useless to his master. If report spread of such a thing, it could ruin Max.

Past grievance, childish pride, and my every base instinct gloated in such opportunity. Yet, for some reason surpassing all speculation, my brother and I stood at a nexus of Navronne's history. My master, who astonished and mystified me more by the moment, required me to offer a fair measure of a man I scarcely knew. And I'd begun to think I'd best heed the Bastard's wishes. Petty vengeance had no place here.

"My brother is not and has never been my friend, Lord Prince," I said. "Neither has he been my enemy save in the petty strife of family and as a danger to my freedom in my years away from my family. I have encountered him only briefly as a man, thus I can say nothing of his honor or his moral strength. But he has ever supported and embraced the strictures of pureblood life. Thus I believe he would do nothing to the detriment of his bound master. In any matter of contractual obligation, I would trust him completely."

"Good enough. He stays." Osriel's brisk assent near sucked the words from my mouth before I could speak them. He nodded to Bayard. "Here is what I propose, brother: Send your pureblood back to Sila Diaglou. Tell her you accept her terms."

"What?" Bayard bellowed.

The green shoots of hope that had sprung up so unexpectedly in the past hour were sheared off in an instant. The Harrower priestess had plunged a stake through Boreas's gut, reciting her blasphemous incantations: *sanguiera, orongia, vazte, kevrana*—bleed, suffer, die, purify. And then she had licked my old comrade's blood from her fingers. I struggled to hold my position without trembling.

"Great Kemen preserve!" said Perryn, looking as if he would be sick. The blond prince backed toward the door. "You can't do that, you twisted, depraved—"

"Have your man say that your brother Perryn is already forfeit because of his treasonous looting of Navronne's treasury and his forgery of our father's will." Osriel pressed forward, his words harsh, decisive, shivering the air. "Have him report that your bastard brother is mad and can be persuaded to yield his land, his pureblood, and the secret of the library. Set a meeting with the woman and use it to haggle with her over the gold and apportioning of Evanore—she will never believe you would concede it all. Let her think she is going to win, while you control the damage as you can. At the last, settle for the best deal you can make, with the stipulation that her legions enter Evanore at Caedmon's Bridge and attack my hold at Renna on the winter solstice. Tell her that I submit myself to Magrog at Dashon Ra each year at midnight on the winter solstice; thus my magic will be at an ebb."

"And then?" Bayard growled in contempt and snatched Perryn's sleeve, before the cowering prince could run away.

"Either the joined might of Eodward's sons defeats her, or the world we know will end."

The simplicity of this declaration left Bayard speechless. My head spun; my stomach lurched at the speed of events. Even Max's mouth hung open.

"Osriel, you *are* mad," said Bayard, recovering his wits sooner than my brother or I. "And I must be mad to listen to you. Yet Father's writ claims— Tell me this, Bastard. What do you do with dead men's eyes?"

The challenge echoed from the vaults as if the hideous beings dancing there had joined in the question. I wanted to cry out in chorus, "Yes, yes, tell us."

"Ask first of Sila Diaglou how long she plans to let you rule," said Osriel with such quiet menace as to raise the hair on my arms. "Bring me her truthful answer, and I'll give mine."

Osriel uncurled one slender hand to reveal a white ball of light, pursed his lips, and blew on it. A shivering lance of power split the air between Max and Bayard, causing Perryn to yelp and crouch into a ball at Bayard's feet. "This will keep our brother quiet for the nonce. Lock him up safely, where no one can harm him. I'll send a messenger to your headquarters in Palinur on the anniversary of Father's coronation. At that time, you can inform me of the outcome of your negotiations, and I'll notify you of any change in plan."

Perryn pawed at his mouth and tongue in a wordless, animal frenzy I recognized. Poor, stupid wretch. How many words did his tongue-block forbid?

Bayard folded his arms and stared boldly at the man

in the green hood, reclaiming something of the pride he had brought into the hall, but little of the arrogance. "You wear Father's ring. I assumed this sniveling twit had stolen it from his dead finger, then feared to wear it publicly."

Osriel's slim fingers caressed the gold band. "Father gave it to me the night he died. Believe that or not as you choose. Perhaps I stole it. Perhaps my devilish magic twisted his mind."

Testing. All of this was testing. Would Bayard believe? Would he accept what was offered or balk in arrogance, in self-deception, in fear? Would I? For I could not shake the notion that all of this was my test as well. Osriel had no need of me in this confrontation. I brought no power, no prestige, no insight that such a perceptive mind could not have come up with on its own. Yet a man of such well-considered purposes would not have me here without specific intent. Perhaps it was only to witness a kind of power I had known but twice in my life: in an abbey garden when an abbot had peered into my soul and found it worthy of his trust, and long ago beside a battlefield cook fire, when these princes' father had shared his love of Navronne with a youthful pikeman.

After a moment, Bayard shook his head. "Father's writ purports to explain why he chose you over me. Reading it, I heard his voice as clear as if he spoke to me aloud. 'Twas the Ardran hierarch showed me the thing, and I destroyed his chamber after. Had the Karish peacock shitting his robes, I did, naming him a cheat and a forger, as mad as you to believe our father wrote such lies about a crippled weakling."

"Father valued you, Bayard. If you read the entire writ, then you know he named you Defender of Navronne and your sons after you, believing that your strong arm and stubborn temper should hold the righteous sword that mine cannot." It was the nearest thing to an apology I ever thought to hear from royalty. A gift offered without coercion, without demand for reciprocation, with humbling generosity.

I thought Bayard would pounce on Osriel and grind him in his jaws. "Why didn't he *tell* us? He knew what I believed. What everyone in this kingdom believed. Every day of my

life I trained to be king, and he never told me elsewise."
Pain, not anger, drove his fury—a familiar anguish, rooted
in family, in a child's expectation and betrayal.

"You trained to be a warrior, Bayard, not a king. Father
made his decision only after I turned one-and-twenty and
showed some prospect of living for more than a moon's
turning. He told me first. Then Perryn. But you were off
pursuing Hansker again, and he would not have you hear
such news from any lips but his. Nor would he shame you
by telling another soul before you. But you spent more
time on your ships than in Navronne those last few years.
How many times did he summon you home? He risked everything to save your pride and lost the gamble." A gentle
reproof, taking its power from unbending strength.

"I could not abandon my men halfway between Hansk
and Morian just so I could play courtier. Let up the pressure,
and barbarians lose all respect. I saved Navronne. I—"

Bayard cut off his own protest. Even he could hear how
foolish it sounded now after three years of war and thirty
thousand Navrons dead. He spat on the floor. "You'll never
rule; you know that. A bastard. The evil stories told of you.
Clerics of either stripe won't accept it. The people won't. Not
when there's a strong, legitimate elder son. The hierarch's
paper is ensorcelled so it cannot be destroyed, sad to say, but
without a valid second copy no one will believe it."

Osriel did not accept the gauntlet Bayard threw, but
rather slipped it back on his brother's hand. Only time
would tell whether he had left a spider in its folds. "We
will preserve this kingdom first, brother, and then turn our
minds to its ruling. I'd recommend you not go setting any
crowns on your head before the solstice."

Bayard jerked his head in assent. "I'll see you on the
solstice, then. Betweentimes . . . I'd recommend you look to
your back, little Bastard. I think you're the only thing in
this world the mad priestess fears."

Bayard grabbed Perryn's collar and shoved the moaning princeling toward the door. Max hurried ahead and
held open the door, casting me a long, curious gaze before
following his master from the room.

As soon as the door had closed behind Max, the flames
in the braziers faded. The shadows flowed together, pooling

in corners, settling over the monks' tables and stools. The man in green slumped backward in his chair and leaned his head tiredly on his fist.

My mind, numbed with wonder and shock at what had just unfolded, slowly began to function again. Should I kneel to my king or should I topple his chair through the gaping windows and protect Navronne from a madman, a honey-tongued servant of Magrog who had convinced me that even the evils he acknowledged would admit to rational explanation?

Before I could choose any course, he swiveled his head my way, still resting his temple on his pale fingers. His eyes remained shielded behind his green velvet hood, but I felt their scrutiny. "So advise me on my plan, Magnus Valentia. Perhaps I should allow this bargain with the priestess to stand. The land is mine. The pureblood is mine. I know the whereabouts of the lighthouse. My brother Perryn has fallen to ruin in defeat and is useless to anyone. Bayard has too many dead Navrons on his conscience to be trustworthy. I could throw him into the bargain and allow Sila Diaglou to take care of all my problems."

Slowly, deliberately, I removed my mask and tucked it into my belt. A hundred responses darted through my head. I could not be easy, not with my fate bandied about as a bargaining chip of less worth than a slip of gold from Evanore's mines. Yet neither fear nor resentment shaped my answer. "You wish me to be honest, my lord. So I must confess, I am very confused."

Confused was too simple a word. I could not shake a growing admiration for this man—the same villain who had bound Jullian in terror to manipulate me, who claimed pleasure in bending minds to his will and refused to deny he stole the eyes of the dead. In the space of an hour I had both learned the unthinkable truth that the Bastard of Evanore was the rightful king of Navronne, and heard enough to suspect that choice not so unthinkable. Even as he quipped of betrayal and surrender, the echo of his charge to Bayard fed a mad and greening hope. Beyond shadows and sparring, nothing this man did was a lie—which frightened me to the marrow. Yet . . .

He laughed, deep and convincing. And familiar. Was I

again recalling his father who had smiled as he watched me dance away the horrors of battle so long ago?

"I, too, sit confused," he said, "for I know why Sila Diaglou wants the lighthouse. She wishes to destroy it so there will be no healing or recovery from the ravaging she plans. And I know—"

"Iero's everlasting grace!" The shattering explosion of truth set my mind reeling. *Healing . . . recovery . . .* spoken like good Eodward's chosen heir . . . a prince who hid wisdom and reason behind a gargoyle's mask . . . who had sent his newly acquired pureblood out to rescue two holy men that a villain had no reason to aid. No discretion, no forethought, no tactic could keep my discovery from my lips. "You're Luviar's man!"

Chapter 5

"My princely pride prefers to think Luviar was *my* man. You understand, pureblood, that your tongue will blacken and rot before I allow you to speak those words outside this room." A red glow suffused two fingers of Prince Osriel's left hand as he made a slight circular gesture.

I clamped the back of my hand to my mouth, battling a sudden nausea as my tongue grew hot and swelled to half again its normal size. The taste of decay ... of rotten meat ... flooded my mouth. *Spirits of night!*

At the very moment I believed I must choke on my own vomit, the sensations vanished. I took a shuddering breath. "Not a word to anyone, lord. Not a word."

"Only five living persons—and now you as a sixth—know that Luviar de Savilia was my first tutor. He remained so until I was ten, when my father built Gillarine and installed him as its abbot. He would have schooled me here, but ... circumstances prevented it."

My mind raced. Who else would be privy to such a secret? Brother Victor, of course; if Luviar had been one face of a coin, Victor was its obverse. And Stearc, who was himself a student of Gillarine, and the first to bear the title of lighthouse Scholar, would surely know. But Elene had been horrified ... disgusted ... when I asked her about Osriel, so perhaps Gram, not Stearc's daughter, was a third. Yet Gram was wary of this prince.

I must be wary, too. Perhaps this was but a ploy to pry

names from me. "Lord, these other five . . . they must be Luviar's people as well."

"Some are. Some are not. If you are attempting to discover whether I know that Thane Stearc and his daughter and his secretary have plotted with Brother Victor, Prior Nemesio, your sister the Sinduria, and even young Jullian to salvage what they can of learning before Sila Diaglou remakes the world, the answer is yes. If you are asking me to tell you which of those conspirators might know of my involvement with the lighthouse cabal, I will not, for you are not to speak of it with *anyone*."

I licked my dry lips. No need to remind me of that. "But *Brother Gildas* did not know?"

"Ah. Indeed that is perhaps the one favorable circumstance of this betrayal."

"So you know that Brother Gildas . . ."

". . . has taken the boy and the book of maps. Yes. And we must assume he is taking them to Sila Diaglou. Which means we must wonder if her demands of my brother will change once she knows what she has." He held up four fingers and ticked off one and then a second. "It is obvious why the priestess wants the lighthouse. Its treasures thwart her aims of an ignorant, helpless populace. As for why she desires one of Caedmon's line to go under her knife: My family is consecrated to Navronne—I will be displeased if you laugh too openly at that consideration after such close viewing of us three together—and she has long held that our blood will be all the more potent for these purification rites she works, releasing a great deal of power at the same time."

He wagged his third finger, offering me no opening to respond. "As for Evanore . . . she hungers for it. Not solely for its gold, for which she has little use, but because my land is the true heart of Navronne, which is the Heart of the World. You have not seen such magic as can be worked in Evanore."

The prince wriggled his remaining finger. "But you, Magnus Valentia de Cartamandua-Celestine . . . why did she ask for *you* instead of your grandfather's book? You have already unlocked the maps to her man Gildas. To seek out Danae holy places so that she can work her abominations, all she needs is the book and time enough to use it. You've no more insight than the monk as to *which* places in the book are significant—perhaps less—and a book is far easier to manage than an obstreperous pureblood. Certainly purebloods have skills in magic—most of them superior to yours, it seems—but Sila considers your kind a disease akin to royalty and practors, an affront to the Gehoum, and she vows to dispossess purebloods of their favored place in the world. Did you not know that? So lay your mind to the question. Why does she want you?"

The wind moaned through the jagged glass. A quick review of everything I had learned and experienced over the past weeks, most especially my grandfather's fractured testimony, brought me only one conclusion. "I suppose because I can take her past the boundaries of the maps. Gildas can lead her to any location on the maps, but to travel deeper into the realms of the Danae, they'd need my grandfather or me. My grandfather told me that my bent could take me anywhere . . . even to places he had not mapped . . . even to the boundaries of heaven or hell. Silly to think . . . No one would believe such a thing."

The prince settled back in his chair. "The boundaries of hell . . . I doubt you'd care for that."

My skin crept. He spoke as if he'd visited there.

Dread encircled and choked me like smoke from the braziers. "I've told the others, and so, I suppose you know that these murderous rites the Harrowers perform destroy the Danae guardians and corrupt the Canon. If Sila Diaglou were to lead her Harrower legions into their land . . . My lord, what better way to accomplish her ambitions than to destroy them all?"

He fell into a deadly stillness. Then he rose from his chair and grasped the back of it for a moment, as if to steady himself. "Well then, we certainly can't allow you to fall into her hands."

He turned away and moved in measured steps, not toward the outer door, but toward the kitchen stair. His shapeless green robes hinted at a slender man slightly more than average height.

This could not be the end of the subject. Luviar's passion . . . the certainty of the darkness to come . . . only in

these past few days had the urgency penetrated my understanding: the end of the Danae . . . the death of Navronne . . .
the long night, the end of the world we knew become a reality as palpable as the wood beneath my feet.

"My lord, protecting *me* is not enough," I said to his
back. "What if they've other ways to make the attempt?
What if they abduct my grandfather? The danger—"

"Your sister has secured your grandfather and hidden him somewhere not even I can find." He paused at
the edge of the pool of light cast by the braziers. "You've
tested well, Magnus. Better than the first reports led me
to expect. That morning in Palinur . . . Voushanti doubted
your mind's clarity."

"My lord, what use do *you* think to make of me?" Even
as the essential question took shape in my head, I was not
sure I could bear the answer. Such a deep-buried longing
gripped my heart, far deeper and more profound than the
doulon hunger, I thought my chest must burst.

"I think you have just answered that question," said Osriel, as if plucking thoughts from my head. "The Danae dance
on the solstice; did you know that? Whatever magic exists in
the world is renewed on that night. The music of the universe reaches its crescendo, so they say, and without magic
we will not prevail. That's why I chose that day for our confrontation with Sila Diaglou. The assistance we need from
the Danae must be arranged before they dance. And someone must warn them of the priestess and her plot."

The treacherous, trickster Danae. Blue fire spun in my
head . . . dragons and herons and long muscled limbs. Glim-
mers of light and shadow shifted and leaped on the bur-
nished wood floor. I stared unblinking, as if these things
might form some pattern I could comprehend.

"Good night, friend Valen."

Startled, I glanced up to see his pale lips graced with
quiet amusement. And for the first time that evening, he
spoke without whisper or throaty harshness. So familiar.

Words rushed out of me. "Your Grace, this night has left
my curiosity pricked beyond all reason. Excuse my impertinence, but you are not at all the person I expected. And I
have a fancy . . . foolish, I know . . . that we are not strang-

ers. I would look upon your face, lord, that I might know my rightful king."

"You're not afraid? Even my eldest brother, who regularly dropped me down the sewage sluice at our father's house in Avenus, fears me. And rightly so." His gold ring gleamed in the dying light, defining his hand against his shapeless robes.

"I do fear you, lord. Reason demands it. Instinct insists upon it. Yet I do not find myself afraid."

"I've planned to force your service blind," he said. "How can I trust you—a proven, skillful liar? I've been given reason to believe you involved in the matter of this murdered boy. And you could easily have betrayed Luviar and Victor, hoping to buy yourself a more comfortable future."

"No, my lord! I never—" Guilt aborted my protest. For certain he must feel the heat of my shame about Luviar's death. Yet some circumstance had gained me his favor. "The mission to rescue Abbot Luviar and Brother Victor . . . you were testing me."

"Luviar, may his Creator cherish his great soul, trusted you. That—and desperation—bought you that morning's chance. I *do* regret I had to use Jullian in such vile fashion, but I had no time to argue or explain or devise a better trial." He raised a hand and the flames in the braziers flared, bathing us both in yellow light. "I suspect Luviar was right. He said you were but lost and searching for your place. Perhaps that place is at my side . . . for as long as I can survive." His smile widened, and he lifted his hood.

I gawked like a crofter's child brought to a palace. Then a pleasured warmth suffused both flesh and spirit. Reclaiming sense, I sank to one knee and touched fingers to forehead, making proper obeisance to my bound master and sovereign lord . . . to the Thane of Erasku's intelligent and persuasive secretary, Gram.

"My Lord Voushanti!" The urgent voice and pelting footsteps from the bottom of the guesthouse stair halted my ascent and spun Voushanti halfway round.

The mardane was escorting me to my bedchamber. No matter that for me the sun had shifted in its course,

Voushanti's zeal to ensure my security and compliance with our master's wishes had not.

"We've trouble!" Philo, chest heaving, cheeks ruddy, beard and leathers dusted with snow, appeared at the bottom of the stair carrying a lantern. "Harrowers accosted Ervid and Skay on the road to Elanus. When the orange-heads found the prince's safe passage letter on Skay, they tore into him. Left him for dead. Ervid fought free, but instead of pushing on with his dispatches, the fool bided and brought Skay back here."

"Has he lost his mind?"

"They're lovers, lord. He could not—"

"Were they followed?" Voushanti's question punctured Philo's excuses like a bodkin.

"He believes not, sir. Skay lies in the monks' kitchen. His life ebbs quickly, lord. If the prince—" The warrior's voice quavered and halted. Fear for a friend's life? Fear of Osriel's wrath?

Of course, Philo would not be privy to Gram's secret. This facade of horror . . . the gruesome stories . . . had been spread to shield a frail man with too few warriors to hold his own in war. And he had devised this masquerade to allow him to move freely through the kingdom, for his brothers' supporters would have no qualms at removing the inconvenient bastard from the reckoning of power.

"Post Havor's men about the abbey's inner walls," snapped Voushanti. "I'll inform His Grace."

I'd wager my life that Voushanti—the loyal bodyguard, messenger, nursemaid—was one of those few who knew Osriel's secret. Yet the mardane was not a true member of the cabal. He served Osriel only.

Philo pressed a fist to his breast and vanished into the gloom below. Voushanti motioned me up the stair. "Get to your bed and sleep, pureblood. We'll likely be traveling tomorrow. And I'll advise you: Do not wander. It's a dangerous night to be abroad."

In the depths of his black eyes the warning gleamed like molten iron. This was a dangerous *season* to be abroad.

"Will your duties permit you sleep tonight, Mardane?"

Amusement lifted the unscarred corner of his mouth. "Matters do not seem promising."

As he galloped down the steps, I slogged upward again. Sleep ... after such a day. My body felt as if the clouds had opened and rained stones on me. Yet how could my mind ever still itself enough to sleep? The prince had not lingered in his hall after his revelation, but assured me that we would talk more in the morning when Stearc and his daughter would join us. If they did not have Jullian and Gildas in safekeeping, we would set out in search of them by midday. The prince ... Osriel ... Gram.

No mystery now how the cabal had come by the journal of Eodward's tutor. Or why Stearc offered his secretary such deference and care. Perhaps Elene had been near panic when I inquired about Osriel, not from distressed sensibility at her lord's depravity, but fear that somehow I had guessed a perilous secret. Eodward's chosen heir ... I had witnessed Gram's intelligence, reason, judgment, his calm strength that had naught to do with arms. Aye, but therein lay the peril. How could a man with no legions hold a fortress, much less win a kingdom?

I rounded the last spiral of the stair carefully, wishing I carried a torch. Only a faint wash of a rushlight in the upper passage touched the steps, leaving most of them dark as spilt ink. I grabbed the rushlight from its bracket and carried it with me. The coals in my bedchamber hearth were carefully banked, but I let them lie for morning. Instead I threw off my cloak and attacked my legions of buttons, hoping Gram would not require such grandiose attire too often.

Great gods ... Gram ... Every time I thought I had accepted what had just happened, a wave of excitement washed over me. I'd never felt like this before ... a part of something so important, something that felt so right. Of course, not even the most foolhardy gambler would risk his coin on our chance to put Gram on Caedmon's throne, much less to hold off the plagues and famine that augured the coming years of trial. Even if Bayard kept to this truce of necessity, the prince must confront Sila Diaglou on the winter solstice, some two months hence. A night of magic, perhaps, but even devout Karish folk believed the longest night of the year to be the apex of the Adversary's strength, when he set in place his schemes to ensnare the innocent, while the angel legions sang in holy chorus and formed up ranks to face him.

The choice of that particular night for Gram's first step was perhaps the finest irony of this whole tangled story. For I had been born at midnight on the winter solstice, so the family tale had always run—the ill-famed winter's child of bardic rhymes, the get of gatzi, conceived when Magrog's demonic servants infiltrated the bawdy rites of spring. And on this birthday would I turn my grandfather's mysterious eight-and-twenty. My ears itched with his whispering: *Thou shalt be the greatest of the Cartamandua line. Thou art of my blood, incomparably strong in magic.* I, the least gifted of men. Grinning like a fool, I shed the satin pourpoint, wondering if it was too late to learn a bit of spellworking.

And then, from out of nowhere, an invisible ax shattered my skull. Knives ... lacerating ... my flesh bathed in fire. Paralyzed with dread ... awash in pain ... drowning in blood ...

Choking, gasping, I dropped to my knees. The weak glimmer of the rushlight seared my eyes with the glare of a thousand suns. Gray, transparent faces, twisted with hate, hovered above me, striking ... cutting ... I felt my bones shatter. Blade-rent, beaten, my body reported every color of pain, and my mind every nuance of grief, of rage, of regret, of unfounded horror and hatred.

Even as I experienced the agony of such wounding and felt a frigid numbness creep upward from my toes, I knew my limbs whole and unmarked, my palms resting on cold, solid stone. No one stood beside me.

The physical pain ceased as abruptly as it had begun. The emotional tumult dwindled more slowly into a directionless anger. Then that, too, faded until I was empty of all but my own terror. I lay curled on the floor, trembling, my arms wrapped about my knees, afraid to move lest I trigger another assault.

My disease, surely. Yet this was not the familiar ground of doulon perversion. The pain ... the searing dread and anger ... never in all my years had I experienced such a ravaging, as if my sickness had itself become some live thing inhabiting my body, wreaking purposeful vengeance now I'd sworn I'd no longer service it with nivat seed.

After a time I sat up. Slowly. My blood started flowing again, and reason crept out from hiding, dragging with it a dismal conviction. I had to tell the prince. Tonight, while this pain remained fresh, reminding me of the madness to come. The hopes raised in the past few hours could not overshadow that inevitable result. Nor could they shake my certainty that one more use of nivat would destroy both soul and body. Life's last great joke. I had found a master I was willing to serve, but my irredeemable folly had ensured my service would be cut short. I could not allow Osriel to imagine he could rely on my help.

I pulled on the heavy cloak I'd worn in the morning and hurried down the stair. One might have thought the world had already ended. The abbey ruins lay burnt and frozen, dark and silent. One faint gleam shone from the kitchen building in the south cloister, where the prince had been summoned to succor his fallen messenger.

The night air frosted my lungs, and I clutched my cloak around me. The world felt askew, as if my body were besotted with mead.

The grimed windows of the kitchen flickered with odd light of purple-streaked scarlet. I shoved open the plank door and stepped into a dark vestibule. Wet heat slapped my face, and with it the sweet, ripe alchemy of human dying—sweat, piss, emptied bowels, and the overwhelming iron taint of blood. A young man in padded leathers stood off to one side, his one arm held tight across his breast, clenched fist at his heart, the planes of his face eroded with grief. Voushanti's wide hands gripped the young man's shoulder and pressed him against the bricks of poor Brother Jerome's beloved hearth. But it was the tableau in the center of the room that turned my blood to sand.

The kitchen worktables had been shoved aside to clear the stone floor. Fire blazed—a broad ring of tall flames, scarlet and purple and the deepest blue of midnight, of storms, of bruises and pain. No fuel fed the flames; no hearth contained them. Within the fiery ring a stocky warrior lay dead, his body hacked and battered, the top of his skull caved in. Far worse than those mortal wounds were the fresh bloody holes that gaped where his eyes had once looked upon the world.

Prince Osriel—the gaunt, dark-haired man I knew as quiet, persuasive Gram—knelt beside the body, his velvet robes stained dark. Gore adorned the prince's face, not random splatter, but precisely marked patterns of circles and lines on brow, temples, cheeks, and chin. The blood signs burned with a power of their own that thrummed in my head as music—songs of pain and bondage, of striking whips and cries of despair. The prince's cupped hands, bloody to the wrist, held a calyx of carved stone—a shallow offering vessel as Iero's worshipers used to carry fragrant oils to his altar. Wisps of gray smoke trailed from the vessel.

". . . come weal, come woe, bound to my will and word until world's end. *Perficiimus*." Osriel's chant rang clean and hard and sure.

As he lowered the bowl, I backed away, cracked open the door, and slipped unseen into the bitter night. A haze of smoke and freezing fog obscured the stars. Somewhere soldiers softly called the watch.

Pressing my back to the stone wall, I tried to erase what I had seen, to silence the truth articulated by that sonorous incantation. Holy gods, how many times had he done this? What use did he have for souls withheld from whatever peace lay beyond this life? The wall of midnight that had smothered the fields of Gillarine remained etched in my memory—behind the fire-breathing horses and monstrous cloud warriors, I had seen gray, transparent faces in the blackness, hungry . . . lost . . . angry. And now I understood what I had experienced this hour past.

Life or death. In alleyways, on battlefields, in taverns and hovels and fine houses, I had always been able to determine whether a wounded man was like to live or die, no matter if the last breath had left him. But never before without my hand touching his body. And never before had I lived the actual rending of the victim's flesh and spirit. Somehow Osriel's dread enchantment had opened a door, and my talent had taken me through it to a place I had no wish to go. Navronne's rightful king, the world's hope, my bound master . . . Holy Iero, preserve us all.

For better or worse, my stomach was long empty, thus I left little trace of my retching in the snow. Had matters been different, I might have spent the night in the open air trying to purge the odor of unclean magic that clung to my spirit. But cold and exhaustion drove me back to the guesthouse, along with a vague sense that the prince must not know I'd glimpsed what he was about. I was certainly not as ready as I'd thought to bare my own weaknesses to my master.

Every bone and sinew demanded that I bolt like Deunor's fiery chariot from what I had just seen. It was one thing to accept Osriel's admission of unsavory practices, and wholly another to feel their blight upon my own soul. Could I, who prated of free choices, serve a man who enslaved the dead?

Abbot Luviar had taught me that I could not sit out this war. And if I were to take a battle stance at Caedmon's Bridge on *this* night, I would yet choose Osriel and his lighthouse over Sila Diaglou and the world's ruin. But obedience . . . the loyalty I had been so ready to hand over not an hour since . . . that would be another matter.

Once back in the guesthouse bedchamber, I stripped and rolled up in the coarse wool blankets. But I did not sleep. Instead I traveled the boundaries of hell in the company of savaged corpses with bloodied eye sockets, of a master whose face was marked with blood signs, of a whirling Dané who spat gall. The agonies of a dying soldier wrote themselves over and over again in my soul, and a diseased knot burned in my gut, fiercer with each passing hour.

Chapter 6

The day birthed as gray and forbidding as my spirits. Voushanti did naught to improve matters. When I inquired what had become of the wounded messenger, he said only that Skay had succumbed to his injuries, and that Ervid had lapsed into a forgetfulness, so that he could not even remember how his lover had died. I wanted to be sick.

The scent of spiced cider, mingled with woodsmoke and the abbey's ever-present residue of charred wool, wafted up the stair as I followed Voushanti down to the second floor of the guesthouse to meet the new arrivals. The mardane motioned me toward an open doorway to the left of the landing, then slipped down the stair before he could be seen.

Voushanti had reminded me forcefully that the prince's disguise must be strictly maintained unless Osriel himself signaled otherwise, even with members of the cabal. Never had a man's character confused me so. I had taken to Gram's kind, morbidly cheerful ways in our first dealings, admired his intelligence, humility, and equable humor in the face of his employer's irascible nature. I had believed him my friend and the only honest member of the lighthouse cabal. The absurdity near choked me as I pulled on the silken half mask and stepped into the room.

The sound of friendly argument welcomed me to the modest retiring chamber. Prior Nemesio was conversing energetically with a big man with a narrow beard, a beaklike nose, and the scuffed leathers and jewel-hilted sword of a noble warrior—Stearc, Thane of Erasku.

The talk ceased abruptly at my appearance. Rapidly melting snow dripped from the cloaks flung over chairs drawn close to a blazing fire.

"Cartamandua," said Stearc, sounding wholly unsurprised. He finished removing his gloves and tossed them onto the drying cloaks. "So Prior Nemesio was right that Mardane Voushanti has left you here alone this morning?"

At Stearc's right hand stood his daughter, Elene. Her close-woven braids gleamed the same bronze hue as her father's hair, and her rugged garb and weaponry reflected the same martial seriousness. I hated that I could not give full attention to her blooming loveliness. But Osriel . . . Gram . . . sat bundled in blankets beside the fire.

"Prince Osriel and his main force departed in the night," said the prior before I could answer. "Voushanti rode out to Elanus before dawn in search of fresh horses. I was something surprised the vile fellow would leave Brother Valen unguarded after yesterday's unpleasantness, but he told me he did not wish the pureblood to be seen in town."

I was grateful that Nemesio's eager report prevented me having to affirm this nonsense.

"Fortunate for us," said Gram. "Valen, we could use your talents to aid us in the search for Jullian and Gildas. Neither Lord Stearc nor Mistress Elene has found any trace of them."

"You may have whatever you need of me," I said, trying not to imagine his sober, pleasant face marked with unholy blood. "I just want to find the boy."

"It is nonsensical to go chasing off into the wild until we receive the reports from the Sinduria's spies," said Elene sharply, clenching her fists as if to extract some sense from the air. "We've no idea where Sila Diaglou might be, and we're all more tired than we'll admit. Each of us would give his heart's blood to see Jullian safe, but we need *everyone* fit, so perhaps, for once, insufferable pride and infernal stubbornness won't trump reason and planning. Our purposes are ill served if one of us falls off his horse and must be scraped up and put back on again."

Gram threw his blanket aside and rose from his chair,

his lean frame straight and confident beneath his sober garb. The heat of the fire had painted his gaunt cheeks scarlet. "Mistress, you know how many days must pass until we can gather reliable reports. If Valen's talents can give us direction, we should use them. If it is *my* infirmities that concern you, let me ease your mind. I've not been floundering in weakness all morning, but rather trying to give some thought to strategy. May I speak freely, Lord Stearc?"

Stearc nodded. Elene folded her arms across her breast and shot Gram a murderous glance. The little chamber shimmered with heat. I retreated to the window niche in search of the colder air that leaked through the iron seams of the casement. Urgency pulsed in my blood like battle fever. The doulon fire was rising in my gut.

Gram shoved a renegade lock of hair from his eyes. "Firstly, our overarching goal remains the preservation of the lighthouse, and as the lady suggests, we cannot lose sight of that in our fears for Jullian. As Gildas has the book of maps as well as our young friend, we must pursue him and hope we can retrieve both at once. Meanwhile, Prior Nemesio must find us a new Scholar. Whether he is selected from the survivors here at Gillarine or from elsewhere in Navronne, that one must be brought here as quickly as possible to study and prepare."

The prior sagged onto a couch, his round face stunned, his gaze flicking uncertainly at the man he believed little more than a lord's scribe. "But I am no Luviar, Gram. I've no wisdom to bring to such a task. How can I—?"

"None of us can replace Luviar," said Gram, clasping his hands behind his back. "We must do with our own talents. He chose you to run his abbey, Father Prior, to care for his brothers whom he loved. Thus he had clear faith in your judgment. If Valen's accusations are correct, then Gildas deceived even the abbot. Perhaps a more practical man will make a better choice."

Though his manner was entirely calm and logical Gram, Prince Osriel's eyes had taken on the character of iron when fire, hammer, and coal have had their way. No wonder he kept his gaze shuttered as he played this role. No meek secretary had such eyes.

A cramp tightened my left calf. I propped the toe of my

boot on a stone facing and stretched out the muscle. *It's nothing. Nothing.*

Prior Nemesio kneaded his chin, staring at the patterned rug. "Luviar had a great respect for Jon Hinelle, a merchant's son in Pontia who once studied here," he murmured, "and for Vilno, a self-taught practor who once traveled as far as Pyrrha. Hinelle, I think—he's younger, more practical, if not quite so powerful a mind. With the abbey library in ashes, the new Scholar will need access to the lighthouse. And he'll need protection."

Over Nemesio's head, the prince lifted his eyebrows at Stearc and flicked his gaze from the bemused prior to the door. Stearc nodded brusquely.

"We shall open the lighthouse the moment the new Scholar is in place, Father Prior," said Stearc. With a firm hand, the thane dislodged Nemesio from the couch and drew him to the door. "And I'll leave a small garrison here at your disposal for the new man's retrieval and protection. Fedrol is a capable commander and will ask no awkward questions. I'd advise you heed his recommendations . . ."

As their voices faded down the stair, the prince poured himself a cup of cider from the pot on the polished table, lost in his own thoughts as he sipped. I kneaded my aching left forearm and breathed away a sharp spasm that pierced my rib cage.

Elene graced me with a rueful smile. "It is the gods' own gift to see you safe, Brother Valen." Her voice sounded as rich and potent as fine mead, warming even my cold spirit.

I mustered a smile and bowed, pulling off my mask and looping it on my belt. "Just Valen, mistress. I make no further pretense to holy orders."

"Two days ago, when we saw what the Harrowers had done to the abbey, and then Voushanti straggled in, saying you had stayed behind to face our pursuers alone, we feared your brave heart lost. So when your message came to Fortress Groult—" Her red-gold skin took on a deeper shade. "While we could not rejoice at your conclusions, we did rejoice that you were alive to make them. And now"— she jerked her head at the prince—"we've no need to hide certain facts from you. For better or worse."

"For better or worse," I said softly. So she knew Osriel's secret. "Mistress, do you know—? Last night, I—" The prince looked up from his cup, expressionless, and I dared not speak what I had seen, lest he overhear. "Lady, I am unsure of whom I serve." Perhaps I had found the source of her bitter enmity for Gram. I could not imagine a woman so devoted to justice and right, herself so rich with exuberant life, countenancing practices so abhorrent.

"We are an inharmonious collection of comrades, to be sure."

The clamor of boots on the stair signaled Stearc's return, accompanied by a blast of cold air—and Voushanti. Elene promptly moved away from me, poured a cup of cider, and plopped onto the dusty couch.

Welcoming the fresh air, I pressed even closer to the window. The stifling heat was near choking me. Another cramp wrenched my back. I blamed the overbuilt hearth fire and the previous day's climbing. *Please, gods . . .*

"We should inform the prior of your identity, Your Grace," said Stearc, squatting by the fire and rubbing his hands together briskly. "If he is to be an effective ally, he should know all."

The prince shook his head. "Too many secrets have escaped our grasp of late. Nemesio is stalwart and intelligent, but unimaginative in deceit and poor at conspiracy. That Gildas cannot expose me is one slim consolation amid Valen's ill tidings."

"I don't understand why you believe all this about Gildas. The boy's body is proof that he was murdered, not that Gildas did it. We've a far more likely candidate right here." Stearc glared at me with undisguised contempt. "Did your own guilt catch up with you, pureblood? Did you realize you'd be found out, and so turn on the very one who compromised himself to aid you? Perhaps you didn't know that Gildas confessed how he'd induced you to strike him and run. How he sent Gerard after you with supplies for your escape. The monk's testimony shook even Luviar. Now you say some magical *insight* has shown you the boy's resting place? I don't accept it. You were half crazed that night. I say you struck down the boy so he couldn't give you up to the purebloods."

Voushanti shifted his position slightly, intruding between Stearc and me. "You should listen to the pureblood, Thane. Whatever else, he's no coward. Eight days ago I was ordered to kill him did he step wrong, but I found reason enough to leave him walking. Save for his diverting the Harrowers, you, your daughter, Prince Osriel, and the rest of us would lie dead on the Palinur road."

This casual confirmation of how close I had come to dying by Voushanti's hand did naught to cool my burgeoning anger. I'd given Elene the benefit of the doubt, but this . . . Damn the woman; she had been there. She had allowed these lies to fester.

"I am certainly no innocent," I snapped. "But bring me the man or woman who says I have ever used a child ill, and I will show you a liar. As it happens, I've a witness that Gildas himself brought me supplies the night of my escape, that I forbade him send the boys, and that I had no contact with either boy before I was slammed senseless near the aspen grove. As that witness has not come forward to speak for me, perhaps the coward prefers I stand guilty of the crime."

Osriel looked surprised. "A witness?"

Stearc snorted. "I don't believe—"

"You planned to *kill* Valen?" Elene rose from the couch, her face crimson. Had Osriel spouted blood from her glare, it could not have surprised anyone. "You told me you would question him and seek the truth about that night. I never thought— Are we no better than the murderous madmen we fight?"

The prince's face hardened like mortared stone. "We did as we thought best."

"Your secrets blight your life far worse than any illness, *Gram* of Evanore. Twisted pride and a corrupt soul will be the death of you, not Sila Diaglou or your wretched royal brothers."

"Daughter!" snapped Stearc. "Mind your vixen's tongue!"

Wrenching her glare from Osriel, Elene crossed her arms, touching opposite shoulders, and bowed to me. "I beg your forgiveness, Master Valen. I had reasons for my silence that seemed compelling at the time but were clearly selfish, foolish, and inexcusable. Please believe, if I had imagined such murderous folly, I would never have left the matter in doubt."

She turned back to the others. Though her arms remained in the penitent's gesture across her breast, her fists tightened as if to contain a fury that matched my own. "Papa, Mardane Voushanti, my lord prince, I indeed followed Brother Valen out to the dolmen that night. He did not leave my sight until the purebloods gave chase through the fields. All is as he has said. Only Gildas came. Not Gerard. I heard Brother Valen adamantly refuse to involve the boys in any way. He could not possibly have seen anyone that evening without my knowledge."

"You returned at dawn, girl!" bellowed Stearc, his cheeks burning. "You said you'd been with some ailing pilgrim woman in the Alms Court all night. What were you doing with Cartamandua? And where were you after he was taken?"

"That has no bearing on Valen or Gildas, so I'll not waste our time just now, Papa," said Elene, acid on her tongue. "But I *will* tell you. What misdirected loyalties induced my silence are now moot."

I had no wits to sort out what she might be talking about, save that it surely had to do with Osriel.

"I am satisfied that Valen is innocent of these crimes, Stearc," said the prince, putting a sharp end to the matter. "After yesterday's encounter with Kol, I fear our hopes of aid are even flimsier than before. Yet before we can consider how to approach the Danae, we must attempt to retrieve the boy and the book . . . and Gildas. We ride within the hour."

Voushanti had passed around cups of cider, and now stood across the room, observing me curiously. Every time I blinked, the world seemed to waver. I gulped the cider and set the cup aside before the mardane could notice how my hand shook.

Stearc jerked his head at Elene and snatched up his cloak. "Let's be off, then."

"Not you, Thane. You are to remain here." The prince pivoted on his heel. "You and Fedrol will detail your men as you see fit for the prior's needs and for the security of the lighthouse and the brothers."

Stearc flushed and glared at me. "My lord, if this is punishment for my accusations—"

"This is not punishment," said the prince sharply. "We've no time for petty guilts and reprisals. Believe me when I say I would prefer to have your strong arm at my side. But Luviar has fallen. As the only living lighthouse ward-holder, your personal safety is paramount, and we've no time to transfer your charge to another. Thus, if you perceive the least threat to your person in these next weeks, you will entertain no foolish ideas of brave antics, but will run and hide, no matter the brothers' safety or your daughter's or mine. Do you understand me?"

"Aye, Your Grace. Of course." Stearc gritted his teeth and bowed.

The prince shifted his attention to Elene, who looked as near jumping out of her skin as I felt. "Mistress, though it grieves me to say it, you cannot go with us either."

"I thought we had no time for petty reprisals!" she snapped. "I have not faltered in my duty to this cabal, no matter our personal disagreements. I have not hesitated."

"I would not think of underestimating your determination," said the prince, as frosty as the windowpanes. "My only hesitation is for the dangers I must ask you to venture instead. Thanks to a few brave souls, Brother Victor lies safely at Renna. To move him was a risk, but not so much as leaving him in Palinur. Saverian will keep him alive if any physician in the world can manage it. Mistress Elene, I would ask you to meet Victor at Renna and take on the burden he and Luviar kept safe from Sila Diaglou. Saverian can work the necessary rite. We cannot leave your father the only ward-holder. Are you willing?"

"You wish me to be a lighthouse warder?" Astonishment wiped Elene's fine-drawn features clean of anger and outrage. "Of course . . . of course I will."

"Good." The prince turned briskly to Voushanti while Elene was yet stammering. "Dispatch Philo and Melkire to safeguard Mistress Elene on her travels, Mardane. They're our best, and if they remained with us . . . Well, I'd not wish them to confuse Thane Stearc's secretary with their prince just yet."

Voushanti nodded, as did Elene, only a rosy flush remaining of her surprise.

"I believe we have some time, if we take care," said Osriel to all of us. "Sila Diaglou has some use for Valen beyond his grandfather's book. As long as her attention is distracted with her own plans and she is left guessing as to mine, a small, fast party should be able to move unnoticed to intercept Gildas."

"Gildas knows I'll come after Jullian," I said. I wished I shared Elene's determined composure. My knees squished like mud and my bowels churned like a millrace.

"But you are Osriel the Bastard's bound servant, and Osriel's cruel games would never permit you such freedom," said the prince. "Secrets and deceptions grant us opportunities that fate denies."

No one could have missed this reproof of Elene. But I could read the prince's expression no better than any other time. His cool sobriety revealed no hostility.

"Now that Gildas holds the book," he continued, "Valen is our only hope to warn the Danae and enlist their help. As his safety is critical, and I've still some notion of ruling my father's kingdom, Voushanti must keep the both of us alive through this venture."

Voushanti bowed. "How many men?"

"Only us three."

"My lord, no!" Voushanti and Stearc erupted in unison. "Impossible . . ."

Stearc argued himself hoarse about Osriel's foolishness in taking a single bodyguard "no matter his exceptional talents." Osriel allowed him to rant, but altered the plan not a whit. As Stearc moved from sputtering at Osriel to showering Elene with warnings and advice, the prince took up pen and paper to set his plan into motion.

Osriel took Gildas's threat too lightly in my opinion. The monk might believe me the Bastard's bound servant, but he also knew how I felt about villains who abused children. Worse yet, he knew my weakness; he'd left a box of nivat seeds to taunt me. I'd destroyed the box and yet clung to the belief that I could manage a few more hours of sanity—long enough to set Osriel on the right path. I could not abandon the boy. I had sworn to protect him.

Voushanti charged off to see to horses and supplies, and conversation shifted to a brisk discussion of message drops and rendezvous and other details that needed no input from me. As the moments slipped by, the knot in my belly launched a thousand threads of fire to snarl my flesh and bones. My companions and their concerns and, indeed, the entire world outside my skin began to recede, until they seemed no more than players and a flimsy stage. My time had run out.

"My lord," I whispered from my place by the window. It was all the voice I could muster from a throat that felt scorched. "I need to tell you . . ."

No one heard me. Elene held Osriel's sealed orders for his garrison at Renna and for this Saverian, his physician and house mage. Voushanti returned and hoisted the leather pack that contained the prince's medicines. Osriel donned his heavy cloak and tossed his extra blanket to Voushanti, telling him to pack it. "A dainty flower such as I cannot afford to leave extra petals behind."

My body burned. I tried to unfasten my cloak and padded tunic, but my hands would not stop shaking.

Soon Osriel and Stearc were laughing. They embraced fiercely. Elene clasped her father's hands, biting her lip as she mouthed sentiments I could not hear.

I fumbled with the iron window latch and shoved the casement open far enough I could gulp a breath of frigid air to cool my fever.

"Magnus, it's time to go."

"Magnus Valentia!"

The calls came as from ten quellae distant. I lifted my anvil of a head, sweat dribbling down my temples. The four of them stared at me.

"What's wrong, Valen?" said the prince.

"I can't," I said, pressing one arm to my belly as a vicious cramp tied my gut in a knot. "It's too late. Gildas knew—" But I could not blame Gildas for this betrayal. He had merely taken advantage of my own sin; the excess nivat he'd given me in Palinur had but sped up what was going to happen anyway. "I'm afraid I'm no good to you after all."

"Are you ill, pureblood?" Voushanti dropped the satchel. "You should have spoken earlier."

I shook my head, as waves of insects with barbed feet swarmed my skin. "You'd best go now. Retrieve the book, or you'll have to discover another way to the Danae."

The prince appeared in front of me. Though his years numbered only six-and-twenty, fine lines crisscrossed his brow and the skin about his eyes. Concern settled in the creases as in a familiar place. "You seemed well enough yesterday. Have you some hidden injury? We can fetch Brother Anselm."

When he touched my chin, I jerked away. But trapped in the window niche, I could not evade him. I closed my eyes, though behind my eyelids lay naught but flame. "No, my lord. A disease."

"But not a new one." I felt his gaze penetrate my fever like a spear of ice.

My molten gut churned. "It comes on me from time to time."

"Have you medicines for it? How long will it hinder you? A day? A week?" Spoken with the understanding of a man who had dealt with illness every day of his life. Did his remedies skew his mind until he could think of naught else, until they became indistinguishable from the disease? Did his salves and potions leave him muddleheaded so that he killed the people he was trying to help? I doubted they tempted him to slash his flesh or scald his feet just to make the healing more pleasurable.

"You're our best hope to reach the Danae, Valen. We'll get you what you need. Just tell me."

There it was. The temptation I feared most.

The doulon hunger sat inside my head like the Adversary himself, whispering its seductions. *One spell and you can hold together for a few days . . . help them rescue Jullian . . . retrieve the book. Then they won't need you anymore, and you'll have kept your vow as best you could. Too bad you threw the enchanted mirror away—so easy to do when your gut is not on fire—but this devil prince can surely enspell another. And he'll have a supply of nivat as a gift for the Danae. Surely . . .*

The fiery agony was my disease. For all these years, no

matter its torment, no matter how I rued my folly, cursed the stars, or told myself otherwise, deep inside the darkest core that held a man's unspoken sins, I had welcomed its pain in aid of its remedy. My chest clenched with hunger. My loins ached with need no woman could satisfy. Saliva flooded my mouth. No amount of washing had removed the scent of nivat that clung to my skin, to my fingers that had opened the little box Gildas had left me. So enticing . . .

"Valen?"

Luviar had died an unspeakable death because the doulon had left me slow-witted and confused. Brother Victor lay half dead and Jullian was captive because servicing my need demanded my first and clearest stratagems, and every other matter must yield to whatever the doulon made of me. Nivat gave me an illusion of control, but I knew better. A cramp wrenched my back like an iron hook.

"You cannot help me. You *must* not." *Saints and angels, make him believe it, for you'll never be able to repeat these words.* My darkest core prayed he would not listen.

"Look at me, Valen." His icy fingers shook my chin. "Open your eyes. I am your lord and your bound master. I command you tell me what's wrong."

Best let him see the raging hunger. Best see his reaction in turn, to crush hope and understand my fate. I allowed his clear gray gaze to capture mine, then spoke so that only he could hear. "The doulon."

"Ah."

He dropped his hand but not his eyes, his expression such a strange compounding of comprehension, curiosity, and calculation, I could not read it. But at least I saw no judgment. Perhaps a man who enslaved souls saw no perversion in teaching the body to crave pain in order to release one moment's ecstasy and gain a few weeks' comfort.

"You are full of surprises, friend Valen." His voice was soft. Puzzled. Kind. Almost as if he were Gram alone and not the other. "But this one—"

He turned away abruptly, leaving me slumped against the window, where I tried to inhale enough cold air I would not erupt in flames. I was relieved to hear him dispatching the others about their duties, telling them he would set out after Gildas as planned. Good. Maudlin sympathy was no better an asset for a worthy king than self-righteous judgment. Somehow it made my shame easier to bear that he was proceeding with the kingdom's business.

Eyes closed again, stomach heaving, I slid slowly down the wall, trying to decide what to do with myself once these four were dispersed on their missions. I could not remain in the guesthouse. Stearc would not be so matter-of-fact about this betrayal as his prince was. Horrid to think of the thane filling my last hours of reason with bullheaded insults. But I also hated the thought of burdening the brothers . . .

"Come, come, you're not going to get off so easy." A firm hand caught me under the arm and halted my downward slide. "Stand up, Valen. Gather what's left of your wits and come with me. We must find our young friend and your book and this villain who thinks to use them."

"Your Grace, if I could—please believe me—I would. Do you have any idea—?" I lowered my voice so the others would not hear. "Doulon hunger destroys mind and body. I'll be of no use to you."

"I have a *very* good idea. I was born with saccheria."

Saccheria! No wonder reports named him a cripple. Joint fever, a rare and brutal rogue of a disease, could crack a man's limbs or bend them into knots. Even if the first bone-twisting onslaught of fever didn't kill you, you were never free of it. It would attack again and again, vanishing abruptly for weeks or months at a time before the next assault, manifesting itself in a hundred cruel variants—one time as grotesque skin lesions, the next as mind-destroying fever, a lung-stripping cough, or a palsy that transformed a robust warrior into a bed-ridden infant who fouled his sheets. Always lurking . . . always unexpected . . . always, always painful.

He released me as soon as I was standing again. "One cannot live as I have without learning every remedy the world provides for pain. And the first and most difficult thing you learn is that there exists no remedy without cost. I was fortunate that my father forbade me try nivat or poppy until I was old enough to understand their price. I won't give you either one." His calm assurance eased even so blunt a condemnation. "Unfortunately for you, I also know you're not going to die in the next few days."

"I'll want to," I said. And even if I shed the doulon hunger, I would have to face the disease itself.

He pulled my cloak around my shoulders and tugged it straight. "So you will. But I won't allow it, and perhaps you will have accomplished something useful before you expire."

Chapter 7

"I can't eat this," I yelled, knocking away the spoon, spilling hot soup over my clothes, my blanket, and my unfortunate companion. "Tastes like drunkard's piss." I rolled to one side and drew my knees to my chest, the sound of my own croaking voice threatening to burst my eyeballs. I was shivering so violently I could not catch hold of the blanket to draw it over me, and so lay exposed to the frigid evening.

One of my tormentors threw the blanket over me—over my head, so that every breath was tainted with the stench of horse, smoke, vomit, and my unclean body. Moaning, I clawed at the damp wool to get it off my face before I could not breathe at all.

"Just stick a knife in me," I said between gulps of the frosty air that froze the slime leaking from my nose. "It's quicker than poisoning or suffocation." Quicker than devouring oneself from the inside out.

"I give you no leave to die. You vowed without reservation that you would not run away from me. Remember?"

My chief tormentor was no more than a shadowed outline between me and the fire. I closed my eyes and clung to his voice. Calm. Cruel. Kind. The fragile thread of reason that held my body and mind together. Days . . . blessed angels, how many days since I could think, since I could move without screaming, since I could sleep? And now it was almost night again, and we lay on a bleak hillside in a forest of charred trunks, all that remained of a spruce and aspen forest. I had tracked Gildas and Jullian into this desolation somewhere west of Gillarine, but I could not have said where.

"Tell me, Valen, what is it you do when you put your hands on the earth? Do you work a spell to find the way? Or do you ask ... someone ... something ... to show you ... as with a prayer? Or is it something else altogether?" Gram ... Osriel. Of course I knew the one who held me on his leash. It was just difficult to remember the two were the same man. "Answer me, Valen."

"Don't know. I feel. I see. It hurts." I swiped at my face with my trembling hand, only to sneeze again—a great wet gobbet of a sneeze. Samele's tits, I was disgusting. I hunched tighter as the sneezing set off another barrage of cramps. Chokesnakes writhed in my belly, clamping their wirelike bodies about my stomach, liver, and gut. The two swallows of piss soup I'd got down came ravaging back up my gullet, as did everything my companions tried to shove down me.

When I was done with the latest bout of retching, a warm wet rag wiped my face. "I've seen that the seeking pains you, as does everything just now. But Voushanti says it didn't seem to distress you in Palinur or Mellune Forest. So perhaps when you are yourself again, it will be painless again."

The prince's patient baritone never changed. If I could find a blade, I might slip it between his ribs just to see if the next time he said, "Tell me, Valen," it might sound something different. But my eyes watered so profusely, the world and its contents were never in the places I expected them, and my two companions hid their weapons from me.

"Please let me sleep," I whispered, rolling tighter, clutching my blanket to my chest, trying to hold still so the cramps would ease. "Have mercy."

"I'll not give you what you want. I told you that. Sleep will come when it will. Perhaps later tonight. Now it's time to search for Jullian again. You told us this afternoon that we were close. You made me promise to force you to this again when we reached higher ground."

No ... no ... no! Impossible when rats fed on my brain, when my parched soul shriveled, when marvelous, glorious life had shrunk to this frozen, wretched, burning hell.

"Come, Valen, will you try?" Ever and always patient.

"Aye, lord. Just help me move."

The two of them unfolded me, supported me as I knelt beside a patch of cleared earth, and then gently unclenched my fists and laid my shaking palms on the cold ground.

"Find the boy, Valen. You are gifted beyond any man I know. You've kept us close these four days, though we've traveled in entirely unlikely directions. This child, your young brother, stolen by a traitor who would use him to destroy you . . ."

Somewhere in the ragged, hollow shell of my being, where the shreds of reason, talent, and sense had collapsed like the walls of Gillarine, anger smoldered. When my tormentor's voice touched that ember, I could grasp my anger, use it to steady my shattered nerves, which in turn gave life to my magic.

Where are you, Archangel? I promised to protect you. Where?

My will drew my mind into the earth, and I sought through soil and roots, frozen now, the cold penetrating deeper than these lands had known since before men walked the earth. The roots tore at my mind's fingers like metal thorns, the dirt and rocks scraped like ground glass, leaving my soul raw and my gut bleeding. But anger held me together, and I swept my inner vision across and through the landscape, seeking the footsteps of the traitor and the boy . . . and discovered they had diverged. *Where are you, boy?* Saints and angels, if I but had a drop of his blood to link a path . . .

I poured my soul into the seeking, existed as worm, as beetle, as root, listening and smelling and feeling the cold grit as I groped for some hint of human footsteps. Gildas had led us on a lunatic's path. This high, rocky wasteland had welcomed few humans, but hosted every kind of wild goat, squirrel, and rock pig for generation upon generation. Most of them dead now. A sickness festered in this desolation.

Cold . . . frigid, searing, mind-numbing cold . . . a thread of ice . . . suffocating . . . drowning . . .

I snatched my hands from the ground and clamped them under my arms, rocking my body to soothe the urge to vomit. "Water!" I gasped. "Gildas has left him in the water. A spring or a seep. Holy gods, in this cold. Hurry . . . hurry . . . no time." I flapped and floundered, struggling to rise. What if Gildas had left him bleeding as he had the hapless Brother Horach, as he had poor Gerard, attempting to poison another Danae guardian? Jullian's brilliant mind and noble heart, his determined courage that had stood up to mad sorcerers and powerful priestesses, laid waste by knives and despair . . . the imagining drove me wild.

"Wait!" Osriel crouched in front of me and clamped his hands on the sides of my head, demanding I look him in the eye. His features swam in the light of the crescent moon that shone bright and heavy in the west. "Be clear, Valen. Jullian is abandoned? Where is Gildas himself?"

I blinked and squinted in the moonlight, trying to connect the wavering landscape with the images in my head. We crouched just below the summit of a rocky bluff, a vantage where the prince and Voushanti could survey the steep-sided, narrow gorge.

"Northwest," I mumbled, shaking my head to clear it. "Over that ridge at the end of the gorge and into the earth. Moving fast as if he knows this country."

"That makes no kind of sense," said Voushanti from behind me. "This is bandit country, riddled with hiding places, true enough, but what purpose for a scholarly monk? Into the earth . . . a cave, then? Does he think to be a hermit like the wild holies in Estigure?"

The two of them had speculated endlessly on why Gildas traveled so far from the impoverished Moriangi villages and failing Ardran freeholds where Sila Diaglou enlisted most of her support, and so far from the estates of Grav Hurd and Edane Falderrene, the two nobles who trained her legions.

The prince's attention did not waver though he had to squeeze his questions between bouts of coughing. His saccheria had flared up a day out of Gillarine. "How far, Valen? Can we reach Gildas before you lose your sense of him?"

"If we stay high . . . traverse the ridge. But Jullian is down. Straight west and down. This side of the ridge." To get down these icy slopes to fetch Jullian and then back up again and over the ridge to catch Gildas would be impossible. And I would lose the monk's track long before we could travel the long way around out of the gorge and up the easier slopes to the ridge. Tears and mucus ran down my face unchecked. "The boy will die down there in the water. Die alone. We can't leave him ... not fair ... not right ... an innocent ..."

"We should go after the book," said Voushanti. "The monk believes us weak. He's planned to make us choose. The boy is likely dead already."

"Not yet," I said, holding tight to my anger so I could think. "I'd know."

"I'll not build our future on one more dead child," said the prince hoarsely. The saccheria had left thorns in his breathing. He moved carefully, as if his joints grated upon one another. "If we cannot protect our own, then how can we protect the rest of the kingdom? Valen and I will fetch the boy. You can go after—"

"No," said Voushanti flatly. "I am here to protect you and your pureblood. You have bound me with that duty, and no whim—even yours, lord—will sway me from it."

"You—are—my—*servant*." A flash of red lanced from the prince's fist to the bottomless black of Voushanti's eyes ... and held.

Muffling a groan, the mardane dropped to his knees. Even in his submission, he struggled and writhed, his body seeming to bulge and swell until he twisted his thick neck sharply, wrenching his eyes from Osriel's lock. In that same moment the red lance broke and vanished. The mardane yanked his sword from its scabbard, laid it crosswise on his upturned palms, and thrust it at our master. "Do with this as you choose, lord, as is your right and privilege," he said, curling his half-ruined mouth into a demonic leer, "but I will not leave you."

I wiped my eyes with the back of my hand and confirmed that the sword's crimson glow was not some artifact of blurred vision.

"By the mighty Everlasting!" Osriel's upraised fists shook and spat white sparks that showered down on Voushanti's dreadful face.

Surely Magrog's own presence would not taint the night with such a stench—death and brimstone and scarcely bridled violence. The earth shivered at Osriel's wrath, or so it seemed to me, who would gladly have exchanged my body for that of one of the cold worms I had touched. I laid my head on the ground and shrank as small as I could manage.

"You will pay for this, Voushanti. When your day of trial comes next, you *will* pay."

The dispute was quenched as quickly as it had flared. The night became only night once more, rather than the vestibule of hell. Before I could sort reality from nivat-starved illusion, the two of them had tied me to the back of a horse and we were descending the slope into the darkening gorge. I could not fathom why Voushanti yet lived. In what kind of bondage did *he* serve?

The nervous animal's hooves slipped more than once. Voushanti cajoled the beast to stay afoot and me to balance my weight back to help keep it so. But every jogging movement set off my cramps, and before we'd descended halfway to the bottom of the vale, I had stopped worrying about Osriel's scarce-contained furies and was begging Voushanti to throw me from a cliff.

"Tell me which way to the boy, Valen," said the prince, laying his hand on my knee as he walked beside me. Fifty times he had said it, between his hacking coughs. Even through my layered chausses I felt the heat of his fever.

"Water," I said, my chin bouncing on my chest, lips numb, drool freezing to my chin. "Find the water. Down."

The beast beneath me jolted forward. I muzzled my screams in the crook of my arm. Gildas must not hear us.

The night's black seemed washed with silver. Details of the land crept out of the dark—scrubby trees, snow, crooked slabs of ice-slicked rock. Could it be morning already? *Please, holy Iero, no.* After a night in freezing water, the boy would be dead.

No, this light was something else. Not moon. Moon and stars were lost in cloud. Yet I could see . . . there, the guide thread itself laid out on the landscape, a gray pattern that sparked and shimmered of its own light, scribed atop the landscape, like the sigils of the Danae that shone from within and yet apart from their bare flesh. I dared not ask if my companions could see it, too.

"Bear left," I croaked. Red sand hardened into stone and twisted by wind and water had formed a narrow rift. Thistles and scrub sprouted between its thin layers. "It's narrow. Choked with boulders." Beyond the boulder field a wall rose like the facade of a temple, an oddly flat face in this rugged wilderness.

We halted, and before I comprehended he had gone, Voushanti returned from a scout. "It's as he says, my lord. Great slabs fallen everywhere. Dead trees. No sign of anyone, boy or man. But the place has an odd feel. We'd best leave the horses and the pureblood out here. Neither will manage the boulders."

They untied my hands and feet and helped me to the ground. Propped my back against a rock. Bundled blankets around me and gave me a sip of ale.

"Are we in Evanore, lord?" I mumbled, my speech vibrating through my skull.

"No, Valen. Why would you think that?" Gram's endless patience at my shoulder. Profound weariness. Perhaps the netherworld I had witnessed in his eyes had been but my own madness.

"Brains boiling."

Soft laughter fell about my head and shoulders like autumn leaves. "Should we ever travel to my wondrous land, I'll shield your poor brains, Valen. Now tell me: Is the boy close? We can't take the horses any farther."

I clutched my belly and rolled to the side, onto my knees, pressing forehead and hands to the churned snow and dirt. All I could sense was the blistering heat of my skin. "I can't feel, lord."

"Do we need to warm your hands? We daren't make a fire."

"Can't raise my magic." I could not even remember why I searched.

"Heed me, pureblood." The presence swelled and darkened just behind me, close to my ear, sending thrills of terror up my spine. "Your father and grandfather used you to fuel their war with each other. Do you think I do not understand why a child's pain touches your soul so deeply? Stop playing at this and find the boy, or I will break you."

The boy . . . The ember yet burned. I grasped it and dived into earth. And from the deep crevices between the rocks came the faint trickle of water and a rhythmic tapping.

"Holy Mother, he's trapped in the boulders," I mumbled, hands clawed into the frozen mud, pebbles digging into my forehead. "In the crevices between. Look down. Seek the water."

"Hold on just a little longer, Valen. Not a sound as we fetch him."

"Careful on the ice." Voushanti's parting whisper carried through the night air as clearly as Gillarine's bell.

My every sense stretched to fevered refinement. The crunch of their boots sounded like the tread of a retreating army. The horses snorted and tore at the dead grasses that poked through the snow, their mundane noises the cacophony of the world's end. The hot stink of their droppings choked me.

I shivered and a spasm raked me from belly to lungs like a lightning bolt, near rending the bones from my flesh. "Archangel," I mumbled into my knees. "Jullian! Where are you, boy?"

My agitated mind would not stay still, and I reached farther into the boulder-filled rift ... into the earthen banks beyond the boulders, past the stone wall ... where something breathed ... men, unmoving, waiting, ready in a great hollow. Gildas was *there*, gone *through* the rocks, not over them. And a woman beside him ... pale-haired, cold, deadly ... roused with unholy lust to serve her fearsome Gehoum. Great gods ... a whole citadel buried behind these steep banks. Sentries ... watchers ... ahead and to either side of us. Trap.

I clawed at the boulder behind me, willing my useless body upward. Stumbling into the rift, I dodged fallen slabs until the piled ice, stone, and rubble wholly filled the narrow gorge. I scrabbled up the boulder pile, at every touch reaching for their footsteps ... Voushanti the devil, Gram my friend ... Navronne's king ... *Must be silent.* Though I could hear my skin ripping on the sharp rocks. Though I could feel the blood leaking out of me.

There ... ahead of me ... Voushanti's dark bulk, and ahead of him a muffled cough that sounded like a wild dog's bark. "Who's there?"

They heard me. Saw me. Caught me as my foot slipped on an icy slab.

"Trap," I sobbed, pain lancing every sinew like hot pokers. "Ambush. At least twenty of them ahead. Sentries on the cliff tops to either side. And beyond them—gods have mercy—a fortress. Hundreds of them. We can't—"

"Do they know we've come? Answer me, Valen. Do they know someone's here?"

They held me tight, and I reached out with my tormented senses and felt the night ... the watchers ... listening ... a shifting alertness ... stiffening ... ready. "Aye. They know."

Gram held my jaw in his hot hands. His face was distorted ... swollen to ugliness with the scaly red signature of saccheria ... a gatzé's face with dark, burning pits for eyes. "We're going to control this. Voushanti is going to get you out of these rocks and then you're going to scream a warning to *Gram* and his companion *Hoyl* that this is a trap. You must be silent until Voushanti tells you. When you shout, you will think of me only as Gram, and Voushanti only as Hoyl. Do you understand? You *must* do this, no matter how it pains you."

"Aye," I said, though whips of fire curled about my limbs. Though I had no idea why he wished me to do it.

Big hands grabbed me and hefted me across a broad shoulder. Jostling, bumping, slipping, every jolt an agony. I bit my arm to muffle my cries, until at last he threw me across a saddle and bound me tight. I took shallow breaths. Somewhere in the braided silence a hunting bird screeched, and the man with red eyes whispered a count from one to two hundred. Then he snapped, "*Now*, pureblood. Warn Gram and Hoyl of the trap."

Somehow I understood how important it was to do this right. The listeners mustn't know I'd learned about the fortress. They mustn't know I'd brought Osriel and Voushanti here. So I lifted my head and bellowed like a bull elk until I was sure my skull must shatter. "Gram! Hoyl! It's a trap! Come back! Four ... five of them waiting! Run!"

My shouts set off a riot of noise—shouts from right and left, clanking weapons, drawn bows. But before one arrow could loose, a thunder of moving earth raised screams beyond my own. Voushanti cursed and mumbled until pelting footsteps joined us. "Ride!"

We rode as if Magrog's hellhounds licked our beasts' flesh with their acid-laced tongues. I wept and babbled of Sila Diaglou and the fortress I'd discovered hidden behind the stone, and I swore I had not caused the earth to move and kill the sentries, though I feared I had done so. I cried out the anguish of my flesh until we stopped and Gram tied rags across my mouth. "We'll find the boy again, Valen. On my father's soul and honor, I promise you, we'll save him."

That was the last thing I heard before my brains leaked out my ears.

"Magrog devour me before ever I touch nivat seeds!" Words took shape as if they sat in the bottom of a well. "Are you sure he should travel, my lord? The brothers would gladly keep him here at the abbey. It's astonishing; they still consider him one of themselves—even Nemesio."

The cold air that brushed my face stank of manure and mold and mud. Mind and body were raw, gaping wounds.

"Ah, Stearc, I don't think traveling could make things worse. He'll be safer at Renna while he endures this siege. If he has a mind left by the end, Saverian will find it. Right, Valen?" The muffled voice of my tormentor moved closer to my ear. "My physician's skills are exceptional, complemented and honed with a mage's talents. You will marvel."

I could not answer. My mind was long dissolved, my tongue thick and slow. They had tied rags over my eyes and plugged my ears with wool as I screamed. Light, sound, touch tortured my senses like lashes of hot wire.

"As you're the only one can draw sense out of him, Lord Prince, it's good he'll be with you. And if it makes *you* ride in the cart and keeps you out of the wind until this cough is eased, that's a double blessing."

"I'll survive. Brother Anselm has refilled all my bottles and salve jars. It's still more than a month until the solstice. Valen is the concern for now. I need him well. It was *I* that Kol forbade from entering Danae territory, not Valen. Unless I can think of some gift to placate them, it will be left to Valen to warn the Danae of Sila Diaglou's plot to exterminate them."

"But if the pureblood's vision was true, and we've actually found Sila Diaglou's hiding place . . . that's more promising than any of this Danae foolishness. Fedrol has already set up a discreet watchpost on the hill."

"Carefully, Stearc. I'm still debating whether I was mad to set off the landslide, minute though it was. The priestess must not suspect that Valen recognized the place as more than a convenient site for an ambush. Was Gildas a fool to lead us there or are we the fools to believe we've gained a slight advantage?"

"We are certainly fools. Godspeed, Your Grace. Tell my daughter I will see her at the warmoot."

"I doubt she'll hear any greetings out of *my* mouth, but I'll do my best."

When the world jolted into movement, I screamed. They had bundled me in blankets and cushions and moldy wool, but to little avail. My bones felt like to shatter.

For hour upon hour, aeon upon aeon, I existed in darkness, in company with Boreas as he sobbed out his torment, with Luviar as he cried out mortal agony, and with Gerard, alone and freezing, as he fought so desperately to live that he tore his hand from an iron spike. I felt my own hand rip and my own belly tear, spilling my bowels into the cold to be set afire. I screamed until I could scream no more. Tears leaked from beneath my aching eyelids. Life shrank until I felt trapped like a chick in an egg.

Only the one voice could penetrate my mad dreams, and I clung to it as a barnacle to a ship's sturdy keel. I tried to croak in answer, just to prove to myself I yet lived.

"We *must* travel to the Danae, Valen," he said one mad hour. "Luviar believed that the world's sickness derives from their weakness. Everything I know confirms that. Our estrangement from them surely exacerbates it. But, tell me, should we walk or ride as we approach them? My father said the Danae ride wild horses when they please, but most prefer to walk, to feel the earth beneath their feet. Perhaps it would show our goodwill to walk into their lands."

"I hate horses," I croaked, "and they hate me."

He laughed at that and I hated him. Gram was Osriel; Osriel was a gatzé, Magrog's rival.

We traveled onward . . . and the voice touched me again

and again. I cherished it like sanity itself and loathed it like the cruelest Registry overseer.

"Tell me about your grandfather, Valen," he said. "What did he steal from the Danae? They wear clothes only when they wish to hide among us or when the whim takes them. They carry nothing from place to place save perhaps a harp or pipe and would as soon leave it and make another as carry it. What do you steal from such folk? Tell me, Valen."

Everything hurt—my hair, my eyebrows, my fingernails. He could stop it, but he wouldn't, and anger enabled me to muster moisture enough to spit in the direction of his voice. "Their eyes, perhaps. Their souls."

In the ensuing silence, pain came ravaging, and I wept and pleaded. "I'm sorry. So sorry. Please speak to me, my lord. The silence hurts."

His breath scraped my face like hot knives. "Do not speak of matters you do not understand, Magnus Valentia. I am your master and your lord. My purposes are not yours to judge."

As the flood of misery swept me along, my tormentor spoke less and less, and I sank deeper into chaotic dreams. I drowned in fear and pain, suffocated in madness, too weak to claw my way out. Though I feared him above all men, only my master could grant me breath.

"Here, taste this. It's very sweet—makes Voushanti heave. But your sister told me you had a special love for mead."

"Bless you, lord," I whispered as the wagon jolted onward. "Bless you." I licked what he dabbed on my lips and mourned because it tasted like pitch instead of mead. But I did not tell him so, because I was afraid he would abandon me to the dark and the visions. "Please speak to me, lord."

"I'm sorry for my reticence, Valen. I've naught of cheer to report. So if you'd have me speak, then you must excuse my mentioning serious matters when you are so sick. Every hour brings us closer to the solstice, and I am in desperate need of a plan. How do I find the Danae? How do I persuade them to trust me? If you don't get well—of course, you will—but if you don't, I'll be in a pretty mess."

"Likely I'll be sicker on the solstice," I mumbled into the moldy wool. "Even if I survive this."

"And why would you be sick on the solstice? I expect you to have your head clear of this cursed craving long before then. From what your sister told me, you're never really sick."

"Solstice is my birthday." The effort of conversation made my head spin. "Always sick."

"Indeed? You must have been a horrid child. Did you make yourself sick on your birthday? Too many sweets? Too much wine?"

This birthday ... what was it? I had thought of something ... before sickness and mania took me. Something nagged, like dirt left in a wound. Mustering every scrap of control I had left, I dug through the detritus of memory. *Seven.* The mystery of seven. My grandfather had confirmed it.

"On some birthdays, my disease got worse. On my seventh birthday, I set fire to my bed and ran away. On my fourteenth, I hurt so wicked, I took nivat the first time. Twenty-first, thought my prick would fall off. Almost killed a whore ..." The wagon lurched and bumped. I clutched the blankets, shivering, and fought to keep talking. The dark waters of madness lapped at my mind. If I sank below the waves, I would never rise. "Gods, I am a lunatic. Always have been. But Janus says I'll be *free* on this birthday— twenty-eighth. Dead, more like. Every seven years, I go mad."

He was so quiet for so long, I panicked, flailing my arms in the darkness. "Please, don't leave me, lord. Please!"

"I'm here, Valen." He caught my arms and laid them gently at my side. I welcomed the searing torment as he laid a firm hand on my head. "That's an extraordinary tale ... seven, fourteen, twenty-one ... and now twenty-eight. It reminds me of something in Picus's journal. Picus was my father's tutor, himself a monk as well as a sturdy warrior, sent to protect Father as he grew up in Danae fostering, and to ensure he learned of his own people. Picus wrote endlessly of numbers and their significance, especially seven and four. He it was who calculated the sevenfold difference in the spending of life in Aeginea. The Danae them-

selves pay no heed to numbers past four—the completion
of the seasons that they call the *gyre* and their four *remasti*,
or bodily changes: separation, exploration, regeneration,
maturity . . ."

Moments seeped past in the dark. The horses whinnied.
The cart jostled. The hand on my head quivered. My master's voice shook when he took up again, though he had
dropped it near a whisper. "You have always been rebellious . . . out of place . . . never sick, save for this peculiar
disease festering in your bones. Your grandfather favored
you above all his progeny . . . the same man who stole a
treasure from the Danae . . . to which he claimed a right.
Janus de Cartamandua, by coincidence the very same man
who provided unimpeachable witnesses to your pureblood
birth—his own two boyhood friends."

Of a sudden, hands gripped my shoulder like jaws of
iron.

"How blind I have been," he said, "I, who have read
Picus's journals since I was a child. Think, Valen. Of *course*
you can't read. Of *course* confinement and suffocation mad-
den you . . . make you feel as if you're dying. Confinement
within the works of man kills them. But *you* don't die from
it. Remember on the day your sister was to take you from
Gillarine, Gildas gave you water—I'd swear on my father's
heart it was from the Well, already tainted with Gerard's
murder—and it poisoned you. But, again, you did not die,
only got wretchedly sick, because you are *both* and *neither*.
By all that lives in heaven or hell, Valen . . ."

And the truth lay before my crumbling mind, as gleaming and perfect as the golden key of paradise, as solid and
irrefutable as the standing stones of my long questioning
now shifted into a pattern that explained my father's loathing and my mother's drunken aversion and every mystery
of my broken childhood. My father's damning curse hung
above it all like a new-birthed star in the firmament: *You
are no child of mine.*

Indeed, my blood was no purer than Osriel the Bastard's, at most only half Aurellian—and that half given me
by *Janus* de Cartamandua, not Claudio. But unlike that of
my rightful king, the taint that sullied my pure Aurellian
heritage was not the royal blood of Navronne, but that of a

pale-skinned race whose members were exceptionally tall, had curling hair, and could not read. *Thou, who art without words, yet complete.*

"...you are Danae."

The cart bucked once more, and I lost my feeble hold on reason. The tides of pain, fire, and madness engulfed me, and I heard myself wailing as from a vast and lonely distance.

PART TWO

The Waning Season

Chapter 8

⇒——⇐

The angel sponged my chest with warm water and chamomile. I scarcely dared breathe lest she realize I was awake—or as much awake as I ever seemed to get amid my cascading visits to hell and heaven. The sponge moved lower. A pleasurable languor settled in my belly and spread to my knees and elbows. This moment was surely wrought in heaven. But who would ever have expected heaven to smell like chamomile?

She lifted the sponge, sloshed it in a metal basin, and squeezed it, the sound of dribbling water setting my mouth watering as well. Her washing was always quite thorough, the water deliciously warm, her fingers ... ah, Holy Mother ... her fingers strong and sure. Her hands were not the tender silk of a courtesan's, nor were they rough and calloused like those of a dairymaid or seamstress, but firm and capable. Tough, but unscarred. Her voice named her female, but when she leaned across me to reach my sprawled arm, her body smelled of clean linen hung out in the sun to dry. An angel, then, not a woman. But her hands ...

"I think you are beginning to enjoy this too much, Magnus Valentia." The angel's breath scalded my ear. "Either you are feigning sleep or your dreams have broached the bounds of propriety. Know this, sirrah: I would as soon tongue a goat as indulge a man's pleasure—no matter the marvels of his birth."

The warm sponge touched my groin ... I groaned as gatzi drove me back into hell.

*   *   *

Magnus Valentia. The name attached itself to me in some vague fashion throughout my ensuing visit to the nether-world. As familiar spiders crept through my bowels with barbed feet, breeding their myriad children, who then flooded out of my nose and mouth and other bodily orifices, and as gatzi strung me up on a cliff of ice and lashed me with whips of fire, I examined the appellation carefully. Shoving aside pain and madness—what use to heed the twin keystones of my universe?—I turned it over and over in my ragged mind: *Magnus Valentia.* It wasn't quite right. Not a lie, but not truth either. The few bits of truth I experienced—the angel's sure hands, clean smell, and astringent tongue, the clean cold air that blasted my overheated face from time to time, an occasional taste of pungent wine, the plucked notes of a harp—had a certain rarefied quality about them, a hard-edged luminescence that distinguished them from mania.

The uncertainty of name and birth dogged me until I next came to my senses—or at least what portion of them I could claim. A flurry of hands rolled me over in the soft bed and restrained my wrists and ankles with ties of silk. I could not fathom why my caretakers bothered with such. The only movement I seemed able to command was licking my parched lips.

A hand on my forehead brought the world beyond my eyelids into sharper focus. I smelled . . . everything . . . dust and stone, the faint residue of burning pennyroyal, rosemary, oil of wintergreen, medicines and possets, old boots and dried manure, cinnamon and ale, evergreen branches, chamomile, and soap. But unlike the usual case of late, the varied scents did not corrode my flesh. Hell's minions had been using my senses as instruments of torture.

"The spell seems to be taking hold," said the woman—the angel. Her voice crackled like glass crushed under a boot. "His last seizure spanned only an hour, and each seems milder than the one before. He no longer tries to injure himself. His body now responds to pleasure as well as pain. As Your Grace has rejoined us, perhaps he'll open his eyes. He reacts to your presence as to none other. And not entirely with terror. Does that annoy you, lord?"

Someone drew up a sheet of soft linen to cover my naked shoulders and the touch of its fine-woven threads did not make me scream. I almost forgot to listen as I contemplated this odd experience.

"Will he have a mind left after all this? I need him capable. This very hour would be none too soon." The man's voice slid into my thoughts like a sharpened stake into soft earth, rousing a frantic need for sense and strength. Despite his intriguing language of sanity and reason, instinct screamed that to lie here bound and muddleheaded in his presence was dangerous.

Filled with eager dread, I fought to open my eyes, but succeeded only in stirring up remnants of madness. Just punishment. I had broken vows ... indulged perversion ... done murder ... soiled my bed ... and now I had to pay. Dancing shadows swirled in the landscape of my head, parting to reveal scarlet light glaring from the empty eye sockets of sprawled corpses, a brawny man pinned to the earth with wooden stakes, skeletal fingers drawing me into the snow-blanketed bog, pulling me down and down into the icy mud. Drowning ... suffocating ... freezing ... yet never, ever dead. Seven times seven times seven years was I condemned to live and die, buried in the ice. A wail rose from my hollow chest.

The angel's hand on my back silenced my cry before it reached my throat. Her sere voice swept away the nightmares as if they were no more than ash, drifting like black snow about my bed. "I cannot even venture a guess as to his state."

She moved away. A clank of iron, various rustlings and thumps, and a mumbled "*flagro*" produced a rush of sound and a moment's blistering heat behind me, surging to attack the legions of winter.

"Yet indeed the fellow's constitution is extraordinary," she continued. "A *fortunate* man—that is, one who did not die gnawing his own appendages—would experience the most acute nivat sickness for six weeks after quitting the doulon. Certain effects—nausea, high-strung nerves, tremors, and sweats—would then linger for nigh on a year, and susceptibility to the craving for the rest of his life. This man, or whatever you think he is, is emerging from the acute illness after only a fortnight. Perhaps your theory as to his birth explains why. Whatever the source of his resistance to nivat's worst effects, each succeeding hour convinces me that this sensory disorder that remains is, indeed, fundamental to his body's humors. Yet I see no more evidence of immortality or inhuman strength in him than I see of wings or halos or blue sigils glowing from his skin. Look at the scars on his thigh and shoulder. He's been wounded a number of times, and he's been enslaved to the most virulent of all enchantments for near half his life. No physician could tell you more of his nature than that. Consult priests or talespinners, if you insist on more."

"I've not yet confirmed the details of his birth," said the man. "And we've no idea the implications of dual bloodlines—such bloodlines. Of course, he would be neither immortal nor invulnerable. You've not mentioned this to anyone else?"

"Certainly not. I'd sooner spread plague than dose idiots with more superstitions. It's wretched enough to see their response when I confess that my employer is Magrog the Tormentor's rival, while I am forbidden to reveal that he's naught but a disease-ridden celibate with a diabolical bent for magic and an overgrown opinion of himself."

"Someday, mistress, you truly will overstep." Frost edged the man's words, so bitter that my tattered soul curled into a ball and hid, certain I was fallen to hell again.

But my astringent angel laughed, her fearless merriment a silver sword banishing the demon gatzi that tried to take shape behind my eyelids. Pillows lay soft beneath my cheek; tendrils of warmth wafted from her hearth. Even the silken ties that bound my wrists and wrapped each finger made me feel safe and protected in her presence.

Receding footsteps crossed my muted chamber, then clicked on tile as they passed into a place of echoes. Behind my eyelids I envisioned a long, wide passage of clean white stone, bordered by arches hung with brightly woven curtains. The lamps that hung from the high ceiling shone, not with burning oil or lit fingers of wax and braided wick, but with the pure blue fire of daylight, held captive within their glass panes. The image held the same hard-edged truth as the angel's hands and stray moonbeams.

Whence came such certainty? I could not have *seen*. I'd been a raving lunatic since well before they brought me here, my eyes covered, my ears and nose stopped to tame the agony of my senses.

"Someone's coming to sit with him? I don't begrudge you rest after this long siege, but I'd not have him left alone." The man's voice echoed faintly down the passage.

"The fellow must have some charm about him," she said, sere as the uplands of Ardra. "Everyone seems eager to take a turn to help—even your little heart's bane. I've made a schedule . . ."

Gatzi surged out of the corners of my mind, pricked at my skin, and drew me downward into the frozen bog. Mud and water filled my lungs, so I could only choke and gurgle, not scream.

"There, can you feel it, Brother? A marvel as we've not seen since we left Palinur. Awkward as this might be for us were you sensible, Saverian said that to expose your skin might do more good than harm, so . . ."

Hands drew stale linens away, tugging gently where they snarled my tucked limbs, carefully settling the scant weight about my hips. The touch of air on skin set off a defensive tremor deep within me where some primitive function kept my heart beating and lungs pumping. Yet it was merely sharp-edged heat that bathed my flesh.

Every nerve burst awake in that moment, not in the overstretched agonies of madness, but in a fevered baptism of delight. My lungs filled with light. My ears rang with its brazen song. I tasted its tart and searing flavor. And as heat filled my veins, I groaned and uncurled, stretching to gather more of it before hell's minions snatched it away.

"Dear Brother, I'm sorry if this hurts you!"

My eyes flew open to dazzling brilliance, and a sweetly curved form shimmering red against the haloed light—my angel. The memory of her strong hands tending my naked flesh sent the liquid sunlight in my veins surging toward my groin and possessed me of such aching desire, I dared reach for her wrist, even as I breathed fire. "O blessed one . . ."

"Brother Valen, the Mother be praised! What are you—?"

I drew her close and kissed her—gently, for angels are but cloud and music and divine light, thus bruise easily. Her lips were as sweet and rich as heaven's cream. Her silken gown flowed as water on my skin. And underneath that fabric ... As my left hand fingered her bronze corona of soft hair, my right released her wrist and smoothed the gauzy robe from her shoulder. *Great gods of earth and sky, what gift of mortal substance have you granted your holy messenger?* My mouth followed my hand's guidance, as it unmasked the tender hollow below her shoulder and the firm swell of her breast ... skin so like silk ...

"Brother, what magic do you wield? Ah, Holy Mother ... your hands are unbound. I've never felt such. We ought not ..."

I kissed her lips to quiet her. Suffused in exquisite radiance, she yielded to my embrace, only a sighing breath as my hands slipped away her layered raiment, until she lay entwined with me, her skin cool against my fever, no sexless divinity, but full and ripe and enduringly female.

Hands cupping her firm backside, I drew her sweet center against my swollen need and buried a groan in her neck. Gods, I had been ready for an eternity. I tumbled her over, released her to the pillows, and straddled her. She lay beneath me in the brilliance of winter sunlight, arms flung over her head. Her eyes were closed, long lashes delicate on her cheek, lips full and slightly parted, golden skin flushed. Ready, too. I inhaled deeply.

As if a finger had snatched a blindfold from my eyes, her scent snapped me awake. *Fennel soap. Thyme and leeks. Woman. Elene.*

I hesitated, quivering with the difficulty of restraint, trying not to let thought or fear intrude where they had no place. Naught had changed but my perceptions. I touched two fingers to her lips and drew them down the fine line of her jaw and her neck, across her breast, and down to her belly. She shivered deliciously.

I smoothed my palm across her belly ... and a certainty intruded on my overcharged senses, one of those spine-rippling moments of prescience I'd experienced throughout my life. I must not lie with her. Some heated core within her insisted I had no right.

Shaking with pent desire, I snatched my hand away.

"Lady . . ." I drew a wavering breath and shifted to the side, making sure not to touch her again. Then I spread the fallen red silk over her, gathered the tangled bedclothes into my lap, and turned my face away as if I had not looked on her abandon. Assuredly this was not her first time to lie with a man. Was it my own past sin that burned my conscience and stayed my hand? Fire-god Deunor, what had I done?

"Forgive me, lady." My voice sounded coarse and strange, scarcely audible. "My madness has drawn you in. Or some magic of the sunlight. Unable to control— By the Goddess Mother, I would not take you unconsenting. By magic. Even mad, I can't believe I would."

She stiffened and drew away, the catch in her throat no longer healthy lust, but shock. *My* body's demands were not so speedily dismissed. *Great gods* . . . I clawed the bright-woven blanket and clamped it in my lap. Perhaps I'd best keep babbling.

"Your kindness seems to have brought me back to life," I said, as hurried fumbling took her clear of the bed. "My head so muddled . . . a lunatic . . . I thought you an—"

Tell her I'd believed her an angel, and she'd be sure I was mad and have me bound again. I could scarce argue with such a judgment. I had no idea of year or season, of where we were or what had brought us here. Only now were life and memory settling into some explanation of this eternity of pain and nightmare. Nivat. The doulon. Disease.

"You've cared for me all these wretched days . . . Iero's hand of mercy . . . and I so disgusting in my perversions. I'd no idea that I had . . . I don't know what to say."

She didn't run away. Scarce controlling my urge to wrestle her back into my arms, I could not but shove the wadded bedclothes tighter into my treacherous parts and shut my foolish mouth. A warrior woman of Evanore. She likely had a knife to hand—though where hidden in that gown I dared not imagine. What business had she in red silk instead of her habergeon? Yet truly, mail as sturdy as her father's might not have resisted my urgency this day. Her father . . . Now there was a remembrance made my shaft begin to shrink.

The silence stretched long enough, I ventured a glimpse to make certain she was no stray illusion after all. She stood at the wide window, where the unexpected brilliance of sunlight split by mullioned panes had set off my befuddled misbehavior. Red gown in disarray, bronze hair tousled, she folded her arms and pressed one hand against her lips as her shoulders shook.

Just as I, shamed and regretful, returned my attention to the rumpled sheets, muzzled laughter burst that fine barrier and brightened the room even as the sunlight. "Dear Brother Valen," she said, when her first spasms had eased, "when you wake, you *wake*. Though I must appreciate, and approve, your gracious conscience, I don't know if I will ever, *ever*, forgive you for stepping back. I've imagined this occasion since I first took you walking out of Gillarine. Were I living in my grandmother's day, I might have carted you off to my fastness that very night! Somehow you cause a woman to lose her mind and forgo all other . . . yearnings. Indeed your fingers carry magic."

Unable to keep my gaze from her, I gaped, uncomprehending.

She shook her head in mimed rue. "What's more, honesty requires me to confess that this is the first time I have visited you this tenday of your stay at Renna. Other tasks have occupied my time. It is Renna's physician, Saverian, you must thank for your care. Though I'll warn you: Play your finger tricks on her, and she'll have you a eunuch before you can sneeze."

The astringent angel. How could I ever have believed that sexless messenger of the heavenly sphere to be Elene, who was abundant earth itself? I felt ridiculous . . . and marvelous . . . and then, of a sudden, weak as a plucked chicken, as the sunlight faded into flat gray.

Elene produced a comb from her pocket and began to tame her hair. Chilled and chastened under my rumpled sheets and blankets, I curled up around my regrets and considered the mysterious certainty that had halted so fine a pursuit. I was no diviner. The only thing I'd ever predicted with accuracy was whether a sick or wounded man was like to live or die.

Life or death . . . I closed my eyes and recalled that core

of heat beneath Elene's silken skin ... that core of life ...
My eyes popped open again. "Oh, good lady!"

My face as hot as the color of her garments, I motioned
her near. What I had discerned might be more dangerous
than any magical indiscretion. She approached my bedside,
brows raised in amused speculation, her face at a level with
mine. Not even the spider on the windowsill could have
heard my whisper. "Mistress Elene, do you know you are
with child?"

Clearly not. For a second time the sun vanished behind
burgeoning clouds, and I existed once more entirely within
the bounds of disastrous winter.

"You're wrong! No god would be so cruel ... so foul ...
the Mother would not permit it!" She spun in place, her
arms flailing in helpless frenzy, until her bloodless fists
gripped a warming iron and she smashed it onto the bed
not a tenquat from my head. "Damnable, accursed madman! How could you know?"

I didn't take the warming iron so much for a personal
assault, as for a measure of shocked desperation. Her earlier confessions affirmed the child was not mine, begotten in some lunatic frenzy I could not remember. I kept
a wary eye out for a second strike. "I've always had this
instinct—"

I began to say it was a scrap of talent inherited from my
mother, the diviner. But returning memory swept through
me as a spring wind through an open door, swirling away
dead beliefs like dried leaves. My hands trembled, no longer
from frustrated lust, but from evidence revisited and truth
laid bare. Josefina de Cartamandua-Celestine, drunken diviner, wife of Claudio, was not my mother.

"Valen, are you ill? Did I strike you? Holy Mother,
I'm sorry. You've been so— I didn't mean— Let me find
Saverian."

The warming iron clanked onto the floor, the noise making me wince. Elene streaked out of the room in a blaze of
scarlet, while I flung off the bedclothes and examined my
naked flesh. What did I expect to see? Blue dragons tearing
through my skin? Surely the doulon sickness had unstrung
my reason.

But my mad grandfather's words popped into my head

as clearly as I'd heard them that last night at my family's home. *Everything is secrets and contracts... I stole from them. A treasure they did not value. I had the right, but they could not forgive the loss of it ...* Only, Janus de Cartamandua-Magistoria was not my grandfather. He was my father.

I stumbled to my feet and strode the length of the chamber, an expansive room of whitewashed stone walls, of clean curves and arches and broad paned windows. Swelling anger gave strength to limbs too long cramped and idle. My skin buzzed as if I'd been buried in a barrel of flies.

Thou canst not know! He'll think I told thee ... Claudio exacted such a price ... keeping me from thee. His babbling made sense now. I could reconstruct the history: Janus de Cartamandua, whose pureblood wife was long dead, had brought home an infant, a child of his own body, and struck a bargain with his son, Claudio. *Raise this child as your own,* Janus would have said, *and I'll not announce to the world that the Cartamandua bloodline is corrupted. I will even supply unimpeachable birth witnesses for the Registry.*

Claudio, furious, filled with hate for the man who put him in such a position, would have agreed in a heart's pulse ... on condition that Janus stay away ... never tell the child the truth ... never interfere. For seven-and-twenty years Claudio had pretended to the world that the loathsome child, whose very existence promised ruin to the family, was his own pureblood offspring. And all the anger he dared not show for his own father, he had expended on the child he despised—the son of Janus de Cartamandua and a Dané named Clyste.

"Spirits of night ..." Truth pierced my heart like a sword of fire, as painful as any remnant of my madness: I had heard my true mother's voice. Beyond a barrier of mystery in Gillarine's cloister garth, I had felt the pulse of her lingering life ... experienced her grief and wordless tenderness, heard her music that had touched places within me that I didn't know existed. But I'd not known it was she, imprisoned for Janus's crime ... trapped, condemned to slow fading. So he had described her fate. Now she was dead, and I could never know her. And I ...

I propped my hands on a long bare table of scraped pine, my whole body shaking.

"Return to your bed, and I can keep the others away from you for a while longer."

In an arched doorway stood a tall whip of a woman, dressed in riding leathers. Though her height spoke contrariwise, her nose, as long and straight as my own, her skin, the hue of hazelnuts, and her hair, straight, black, and heavy, tightly bound in a thick braid, testified unmistakably to Aurellian descent. Pureblood or very near. Tangled as I was in the unraveling of long deception and a loneliness that threatened to unman me, I had no capacity to guess who she might be.

"On the other hand, if you roam the halls of Renna, I'll take no responsibility for the consequences, especially if you insist on wearing naught but your skin. The housemaids rarely see such sights. Evanori are a modest people."

The prospect of visitors and questioning nauseated me. "I thank you for the offer, lady, but I doubt Kemen Sky Lord himself could keep Prince Osriel away once he hears a report of my state." Once he knew his captive half Dané could speak.

"What state would that be?" Decisive footsteps brought her up behind me, and her leather gloves skittered onto the table. "As a physician, I propose *dead* as your most likely condition and that what I see before me must perforce be an apparition. Surely no human body could withstand what you have gone through this tenday and stand here speaking as if he'd a modicum of sense."

"Physician?" I whipped my head around. She stood three or four paces away, her brows raised. "You're Saverian . . ." The astringent angel.

"Please don't bother me with 'What an odd name for a woman,' or 'How could such a *young* woman possibly know enough to be a physician?' or 'You must mean hedge-witch, do you not?' or 'How could a *modest* woman bear to mess about with such nastiness as physicians must?' So, Magnus Valentia, are you human or apparition or . . . something else?"

I averted my face, propped my backside on the table, and rubbed my aching head. Someone had trimmed my hair short again, disguising its telltale curl—so unnatural for a pureblood. "I don't know what I am."

To my discomfiture, the woman briskly installed herself in front of me and held out one open palm as if to demonstrate it held no weapon. Then she touched me with it—raised my chin, felt my forehead, and lifted my eyelids, peering inside me as if I were a vat of odd-smelling stew.

"For one, you are a doulon slave," she said, as she retrieved my hand from my groin where it was attempting to maintain a bit of dignity before a stranger. She attended the beat in my wrist veins as dispassionately as ever Brother Robierre the infirmarian had done at Gillarine. "No matter how remarkably fast you have sloughed them off this time, nivat's chains will ever bind you. I would be remiss if I did not say that here at the beginning. A fool should know what his stupidity has cost him."

I examined her face, all unrelieved planes and angles. A small mouth and ungenerous lips. The pureblood nose narrow and sharp. Small creases between her dark brows, and crinkled lines clustered at the outer corners of her eyes, as if she spent a goodly time at her books, though the smoothness of her dusky skin testified that she could not yet have seen thirty summers. Naught of warmth or passion in that face. Naught of disgust either, which spoke decently of her philosophy as a physician.

Using both hands now and spitting a few unintelligible epithets under her breath, she explored my neck, strong fingers poking and prodding in search of who knew what. Yet the annoying agitation of my skin dulled, even as she produced a silver lancet and glass vial from out of nowhere and nicked and milked the vein in my left arm.

"What does that mean?" I said, watching her stopper the vial containing my blood and slip it into her pocket. "About the doulon. I'd not dared hope—"

"It means you'd best put nivat seeds right out of your head. To touch or even to smell them risks waking your craving again. And it means that you must find some other way to deal with this." She blew on her fingers and touched my ears.

The world exploded in sound. Bleating, crunching, crackling, drumming . . . the noise trapped inside my skull felt as if it were bulging my eyes from the inside out.

Birds scrabbled on the roof. Pots rattled in a distant kitchen. Two women argued. A sick man moaned and mumbled in drugged sleep. A rhythmic crashing could only be someone raking hay. Horses chomped ... mice scuttered ... this very structure—a house of wood, not stone—creaked as the wind pushed on it. My heart rumbled like an avalanche beside the woman's steady drumbeat.

I cringed and clapped my hands over my ears. "Blessed Deunor!"

Saverian's warm hands covered mine and, at her muttered word, mercifully damped the clamor. Strong, capable hands. I would never mistake them.

"Thank you," I whispered as the din in my head subsided. To my relief, my voice remained a whisper and not the onslaught of a whirlwind. "For *all* your kindness these days."

"Kindness had nothing to do with it," she said, dry as the desert winds of Estigure. "Prince Osriel insists that he needs your functioning mind as soon as may be. Yet each one of your senses seems to suffer this same incontinence. This muting enchantment is a somewhat brutish remedy, but the only way I see to solve a problem I've been given no leisure to investigate. It is far from a permanent solution to your excess sensitivity, as it fades quite rapidly. Perhaps if you could tell me more about the progress of the disease. Do these symptoms vary?"

"When I was seven, attacks came every month or two, and lasted a few days at a time. Over time, they became more frequent, more severe, and lasted longer, but still coming and going. By fourteen ... well, I started the doulon at fourteen, and after that ..."

"... everything was a muddle. Yes. I would imagine." She gestured insistently toward the rumpled bed and offered me her arm. "Elene indicated that the sunlight roused your member. Is that true? Is there some connection?"

Since I'd first discovered the merry art, I'd never understood why so many shrouded it with shame. But her brazen questioning made it sound as if one could set down a recipe for desire as Brother Jerome had seasoned stewing parsnips. Disconcerted, I refused her assistance and set out for the bed on my own. "I don't— Perhaps. The light fed whatever— I've never noticed a connection."

By the time I'd gone half the length of the chamber, I decided I should have kept her beside me instead of leaving her behind to observe my naked rump. Of a sudden I could not get myself back under the bedclothes soon enough. I certainly had no mind to tell her that it was the memory of her hands had done the rousing.

I sank to the low bed—a boxlike wooden platform, built right into the floor—dragged a blanket from the tangle, and bundled it around my shoulders. I was shaking again, this time from the cold. The sun had lost itself in the gray and white world beyond the window glass.

Saverian knelt by the hearth, threw three logs onto a heap of glowing ash, and snapped her fingers. The ash glowed brighter, but the logs remained inert. "*Flagro*, you misbegotten twigs!" she shouted with a certain cheerful virulence. Bright blue flames as high as my knee burst from the logs with a throaty roar before settling into a tidy, robust blaze.

"You'll find clothes in the chest and cider by your bed. I'll have food brought. Though you may yet experience nausea or poor appetite, you should eat and drink. Someone will sit with you until we're sure my conjuring can sustain you, but by heaven and earth, keep your appendages to yourself! If someone had found you with Thane Stearc's only child . . . You'd not like thinking on what meager bits of you would be left for me to study." The woman retrieved her gloves from the table and moved briskly to the doorway. She paused, thoughtful. "You don't fancy *men*, do you? Should I warn them as well?"

An abortive laugh burst through my heavy spirit. "Not in that way. At least, not recently." Then again, one heard so many different tales of Danae. Who knew what was true? Some tales said Danae mated with the wind or the sea or with animals or kin. My stomach lurched unpleasantly.

"Osriel has told me your history, and of his theory as to your birth. I must tell you that I'm skeptical. Even if there exist beings who live for centuries and can conjoin themselves with trees or mud, I doubt you're one of them. These past days . . . if you could have escaped the consequences of this unforgivable injury you've worked on an otherwise healthy body, you'd have done it."

"Perhaps I just don't know how."

"Pssh." She leaked skepticism.

As her departing footsteps echoed in the passage, I tried to imagine what it might be like to yield my soul and body to a tree and be confined by its immovable bark and leaf or to find myself locked into the barren stone and blue-white ice of Clyste's Well. I lurched from the bed to the night jar, threw off the copper lid, and heaved up bile from my empty belly.

Chapter 9

I held the spell fragments—the essence of the turned wood cup, the image of the large wooden bowl I desired, the linkages of power, the rearrangement of perception, the connecting threads of what *was* to what would be—and then, carefully, slowly, I unleashed the flow of magic. Nothing happened. I closed my eyes, focused on my fingers and on the warm center somewhere amid lungs and heart and spine whence I drew magic, and tried again, this time with less caution. Failed again.

A stupid test. But my question had been answered. Either the doulon sickness had drained me of magic or Osriel had somehow precluded my use of it. And without working magic, I could not begin to understand what the nonhuman part of me might bring to it.

I tossed the cup on the bed and ran my fingers about the window frame, searching in vain for the faint prickles that would indicate a barrier to sorcery. My fears that the *power of Evanore* might explode my small illusion or bloat my cup into a house now seemed absurd. Evanore . . . the haunted realm.

The view beyond my window was stunning—a sprawl of blue-white mountain peaks and plunging chasms, shrouded in wind-whipped cloud. Nearer, dominating a tortuous slope, a small, solid fortress backed up to a low bluff, the two appearing to have sprouted together from the stone core of the mountains. Scattered about the lower slopes, colorful tents billowed like the sails of a Moriangi fleet.

Riders streamed from the encampment and the lower valley toward the fortress gates, banners fluttering, squires, servants, and soldiers trudging alongside.

More than the barren, windswept slope separated this house—where I was kept—from the fortress. These clean open arches, the finely carved ceilings, polished woods, and expansive windows were altogether unlikely for an Evanori war lair.

Of course, Osriel himself made no more sense than this house. It would have been easy to dismiss him as a cynical and unprincipled sorcerer, the most skilled manipulator of men I had ever encountered, able to convince abbots and nobles that he held the interests of Navronne preeminent, while using cruelty and torment to ingratiate himself with the lord of hell. Yet I knew the answer to his mystery was not so simple. He had risked his own life on our last venture, not just to retake Gildas and the book, but for Jullian, whom wise men would name the least of our cabal. And some quality in the prince had reached me through pain and madness and kept me from losing my mind. No matter how much I wished to distance myself from his red lightning and blood-marked rituals, I owed him a debt.

I snatched up the green sash and knotted it about my waist. I'd found it along with a knee-length tunic and wool leggings in the carved clothes chest at the foot of the bed. True to her promise, Saverian had sent a serving man with a wooden dish heaped with bread, cheese, and dried apples. I had made it through one rubbery slice of apple before my rebellious stomach halted further attempts. She had come herself an hour later. Inspected my tongue and eyes, taken more blood, sat at the table to write extensive notes in a worn book. She had refused to say when I could travel or whether anyone was out searching for a captive child.

Gods . . . Jullian. The thought of him held by Harrowers tore at my heart. Unfortunately this past hour had left me no nearer choosing a course of action. I had sworn not to run. Yet, did a man's oath bind when the one who'd sworn it discovered he was something altogether different than he believed? Not entirely human. I kept staring out the window half hoping, half terrified to see a Dané with a dragon on his face. My uncle. Holy Mother . . .

"Hsst! Valen! Over here." The whisper came from the corner beyond the empty table and a yellow painted washing stand stacked with towels.

My heart's stuttering calmed when Elene poked her head through a heavy curtain woven in colorful stripes. Against the rich greens and blues, her complexion took on the color of whitewash. She beckoned me to join her. Not at all a difficult summons to obey. Truly the woman was more addictive than nivat, especially as I now had a true memory of her unclothed, instead of mere imaginings. The truth outshone the image as an angel outshines a frog.

"Great gods be thanked," she said softly, inspecting me from head to toe, her very presence lifting my spirits. "Saverian told me I'd not harmed you, but I kept imagining a great charred dent in your skull."

I spread my arms and twirled about, then ducked my head so she might view its integrity. "Your weapon never touched me. Rather, it's I who must apol—"

"Valen, you *must* not tell anyone what you told me. Please, promise me. I beg you."

I could not help but smile at this ferocious reversal of her earlier indignation. Glancing about to ensure no weapon was at hand, I spoke softly. "So it's true, then?"

"By the Mother, promise me! On your word—the same oath you gave Osriel!"

Though I could foresee no circumstance that would make me betray such a confidence, the prospect of one more binding oath filled me with misgiving. I was already hamstrung by my submission to Osriel. Yet I did need a friend in this house, and I could well understand her desperation. An unexpected pregnancy was no happy news for an unwed girl of any parentage. So I raised my hand.

"I could never be such a madman as to betray the confidence of a daughter of Evanore. But if it eases one worry, mistress, then by the Mother I swear you my silence without reservation. And perhaps in return you'll be kind enough not to mention my ... indiscretion ... of this morning to any who might take offense." I didn't need irate warlords drawing practice targets on my hide.

She rolled her eyes. "I'm hardly likely to speak of it. Remember *you* are the lunatic, not I. Well ... clearly I am, as well . . . but you can be sure my tongue is mute. I told Saverian you'd made an advance. In the confusion of your illness, of course. I had to report your . . . condition. For your sake. You can be sure the frost witch will bait us with it, but she'll not tell anyone else. Though she's wholly Osriel's creature, it suits her to keep her patients' counsel. She'd not have them withhold information she needs to succeed in her work."

This barren bluntness belied any assumption of a womanly confederacy.

"So, what of you, lady? Will the man be upright about all this? What will you do?" Though I was ferociously curious, I chose not to risk Elene's wrath by asking who had begotten the child. She lived in a world of men. One glance from her and she could have her pick. Her fury had not implied an unconsenting liaison, which precluded any temptation for noble reprisal on my part. But jealousy could easily lock my fingers around the damnable oaf's neck. Better not to know.

"I should have some time before anyone will guess— except perhaps Saverian. And I'll just stay out of her way. Whatever must be done, be sure no *man* will decide for me."

She beckoned me to duck my head again and startled me with a ferocious kiss planted square atop my head. "You've a good heart, Valen. The Mother shield you from your master's vile works."

Brisk footsteps echoed from the main passage. Elene paled. Stung by her warning, I caught her shoulder before she could duck beyond the striped drapery. "The prince . . . Voushanti . . . all these warnings . . . I feel as if I'm running blind down the road to hell. Someone needs to explain what I should fear, and you're the only person I trust to be honest with me."

Her brown eyes flamed amber. Resolution stamped her face. "You're right. But later tonight . . . during the warmoot. This last night is mostly ceremony. The main gates of the fortress face westerly. When the lords start singing, get you to the rock gate behind the east end of the hall, and I'll show you what to fear. Now, please . . ."

I released her, and she vanished. Snatching up a towel

from the painted stand, as if I'd been washing, I spun in place and greeted my master as he hurried into the chamber. Garbed in an ash-gray tunic and black leggings no finer than my own, his hair tied back by a purple ribbon, he appeared more servant than prince. His pleasure as his first glance assessed me reflected that part of him I would ever name Gram.

I sank to one knee and touched fingers to forehead. "My lord."

"Will you never cease to astonish me, friend Valen?" he said, cocking his head to one side as he gazed down at me. A smile played over his fine countenance—noble Eodward's handsome features writ on a darker, frailer, sterner canvas. "I expected to find you weak and woolly on your waking day."

I dared not meet his eyes. Had our king known what his favored son played at? "I am both of those things, lord."

He touched my shoulder. "Come, get up. I won't keep you long. I've a hundred warlords in my hall, drinking my ale and spoiling for battle. Do you feel up to a walk?"

I held out my incapable fingers. "As long as you don't expect me to seek out our route."

He laughed quite genuinely and motioned me toward the passage. "That's Saverian's doing. She found silkbinding your hands tiresome and dodging your nightmares dangerous. You'll learn, as have we all, to avoid annoying Saverian. Thus you must tell me promptly if we need to get you back to bed. I doubt I could carry you, even underfed as you are."

Despite his claim of warlords waiting, we strolled down the passage—the very one I had envisioned so clearly in my madness, even to the patterns and colors of the woven hangings. Above every arch hung a shield of beaten gold, each shaped as an animal—a fox, a lion, a boar, even fanciful beasts such as a dragon, phoenix, or centaur. One was a gryphon, its feathered wings spread from its lion's body, as on the Cartamandua family crest.

Bearing left around a corner, we arrived at a long gallery where weavings no longer blocked the arches. On one side of the gallery, the openings held paned windows that overlooked the descending slope, the grim fortress, and the grand mountain landscape; on the other, the openings stood unblocked, accessing a courtyard garden almost as large as Gillarine's cloister garth. Trees, shrubbery, and flowers grew in healthy profusion in air that held the warmth of late spring rather than winter's bite.

The notion struck me that I'd mistaken Elene's reference to my stay at Renna as a mere tenday. But when I looked to the sky to verify the season, I gasped in wonder. A dome of faceted glass separated us from the gray sky. Snowflakes flurried and danced, melting when they touched the intricately patterned glass.

"It's very like the domes in the lighthouse," I said, recalling the twin mosaic vaults of colored brilliance that had imbued the storehouse of books and tools with magic and majesty.

"This was an early experiment," said the prince. "It told me that what I wanted to do was possible. Luviar and Victor had created the underground chambers early on—did you know that Victor is a pureblood stonemason?—but his design was very ... monkish. We had no time to cache works of art, but I felt our lighthouse ought to include something of no worth beyond its beauty. We'd not want humankind to forget something of such importance."

Once I would have marked this unsentimental declaration as the wisdom of ever-sensible Gram, and reveled at the new knowledge he'd let slip. Now I worried at his purpose, sure his every utterance hid meanings within meanings. And, too, a knife of guilt twisted in my heart at the reminder of my forgetfulness.

"Brother Victor ... how fares he?" I'd heard a sick man struggling to breathe and wondered if it was the little monk. "I'd like to visit him. And Jullian ... have we word of his fate? Plans for his rescue?"

His expression grave, Osriel clasped his hands behind his back. "We've had no further word of Jullian, and no word on the negotiations between my brother and Sila Diaglou. Be assured I remain committed to getting the boy back safely. As for Brother Victor ... he improves daily, but his injuries were dreadful. Saverian has kept him asleep as she works to repair them. We hope he'll wake again when they've healed enough to cause him less pain. Best leave him in peace for now."

I was hardly surprised at his putting off my visit to the chancellor. "Later, then. As soon as he's able. I would never have guessed Victor pureblood."

"A humble man is a rarity among purebloods."

"True," I said, glancing at the magnificence above us. "For certain, I am no judge of men."

I longed to pour out my myriad questions to my friend Gram, but I dared not expose my ignorance to Osriel. Which was a wholly foolish sentiment. After weeks of raving mania, what part of me could be left private?

We ambled down one of the paved walkways that interlaced the garden, pausing when we came upon a fountain tucked into a grove of elders. Water bubbled from the feet of a statue depicting a tall, nude woman with an eagle taking flight from her upraised hand. Beside her, a sculpted man bent one knee and stretched the other leg behind him in a straight line with his muscled back. His fingers touched the center of his forehead in a gesture of respect, as his stony eyes gazed on a small tree bursting from the earth just beyond his bent knee. My skin slithered over my bones when I noted the fine whorls and images carved into the figures' marble flesh.

The prince stood at my shoulder. "My obstinate physician declines to reveal what the two of you discussed this morning. So I must ask if you remember our last conversation?"

I stared at the statues and forced my voice steady, as if on every day I spoke the unthinkable. "Janus de Cartamandua-Magistoria sired me. The Dané named Clyste was my mother."

"It explains a great deal, don't you think?" he said. "So you believe it's true?"

"Yes." Though questions piled upon questions, like a flock of sheep at a narrow gate, each pushing to get through. "I wonder . . . did they lock her away in the earth for lying with a human or for allowing a human to steal me away?"

I stole a treasure they did not value, but could not forgive the loss of, so Janus had said. I could not yet think of the old man as my father.

"Almost certainly the latter," said the prince. "My father and the monk Picus left Aeginea well before you were born. But I have Picus's journals, where he recorded all he learned of the Danae. He wrote that once past the third change—the passage of regeneration—a Dané is capable of mating and can choose his or her partners at will. As long as a joining is consensual, none may gainsay it. Certainly for Clyste to conceive a child could have been no accident. Danae females are fertile on the four days of season's change and no other. No matter that her family, the archon, and every other Dané would disapprove her choice, we must assume she chose Janus, and she chose to make a child with him."

They'll never have thee. I saw to it. The mad old man's words hung in my memory like stars in the firmament, sharpening the familiar aching void in my chest. Of a sudden, no caution could restrain my questions. Half my life had been denied me, the other half twisted out of all recognition, and this prince held some answers at least. "Then why would she let him take me? Everything he said leads me to believe she consented."

"Danae dislike halfbreeds"—he squatted beside the fountain and ran his fingers over the marble branches of the new-birthed tree—"but they believe no one else has any business raising one of their blood. Unlike Aurellian purebloods." He flashed a grin up at me. "Once *our* blood is proved tainted, the Registry cares naught what becomes of us. Perhaps you'd like to send the Registry a notice of your changed status?"

I had already considered that. "They'd only believe it another of my lies."

"Mmm . . . likely so." He removed a stone cup from a niche beside the fountain, scooped water from the font, and drank it down. I declined his offer of the cup, and he replaced it in its niche.

"So Clyste's child vanished," he continued. "The Danae believed the child belonged with them and punished her. But as to Clyste's purpose . . . A Danae mother is responsible for her child's education, including preparation for the remasti. She selects the child's vayar—the dance master. This preparation is the most serious and sacred duty among the long-lived. Perhaps she meant for Janus to bring you back at some time."

I hadn't even known the right questions to ask that night in Palinur, and my grandfather's ragged mind had skipped from one thing to another. But there had been something . . . "He said she bade him destroy his maps to keep other humans away from the Danae lands, because he could 'keep his promises' without them. And he said he'd failed her. But that could mean a thousand things." It was all very well to explore past intents, but the future concerned me more. "Why did he say I would be *free* when I turned eight-and-twenty? What happens then?"

"Four times in their lives—at the ages we would name seven, fourteen, one-and-twenty, eight-and-twenty—Danae undergo these bodily changes they call remasti or holy passages. We know little about the passages, save that each results in new gards—their skin markings. They consider the whole thing very private. Most of what Picus learned of them came from the confidences of one disaffected Dané female—a halfbreed girl named Ronila who left Aeginea before making her fourth change. He knew only the results of the fourth: The newly matured Danae are bound to a sianou and allowed to dance in the Canon itself for the first time, and from that day they are free to walk the world as they choose, subject to no person, law, or duty save the Law of the Everlasting as interpreted by their archon."

"But Janus had no intention of me living as a Dané. He wanted me to stay clear of them until I passed my birthday." *'Tis no life for thee,* he had told me. "Perhaps that was it. He had promised Clyste that he would send me back and then changed his mind."

Osriel nodded as he picked dead blooms from the violets massed about the fountain. "Therein, too, lies freedom of a sort. Picus wrote that those Danae who choose not to undergo the fourth remasti, or are forbidden to do so, or are incapable of it, lose the power to become one with a sianou. They revert to an ordinary life span—longer than humans live, but far short of the centuries a mature Dané would expect. It sounds as if you will become wholly human on your birthday. That must be what Janus wished."

"There must be something more," I said. "He told me I would be the greatest of the Cartamandua line. He said our family would be powerful beyond dreaming." Dawning understanding knotted my hands and heated my cheeks. For a lifetime I had hated Janus de Cartamandua with every scrap of my strength. But he had given up his mind to the Danae, and in the throes of despair and weak-minded sentiment, I had come to believe he'd done it to protect *me* from harm. But now matters became clear. It was never for me—child or man. All was for the Cartamandua bloodline. "He must have thought staying free would strengthen my bent or change it in some way. He thought I would make our family 'magnificent.' "

"Would that we could question Picus. But not long after he and my father returned to Navronne, the monk vanished without a word to anyone. Come along." The prince motioned for me to walk with him. "What happens or does not happen on your birthday is not the only mystery to unravel. Would you like to hear what I know of your mother?"

"Very much." I needed to move, to walk if I could not run.

"Clyste was my father's foster sister, making you and me cousins of a sort. I hope that does not disturb you too awfully." We walked out of the garden, through the airy passages, and into a series of shuttered rooms. "She was daughter of the Danae archon Stian and beloved of every Danae for her joyful spirit and for the skill and glory of her dancing. When Clyste came into her season for her fourth change, the powerful Dané who had guarded the Well for time unremembered announced that he was tired and ready to yield his sianou to a younger guardian. All believed that the Well, a place revered among the Danae, had chosen Clyste. Kol told Picus that she brought an intelligence and a perfection to the Canon that the long-lived had rarely seen."

"Until Janus corrupted her," I said, near spitting gall. Anger burrowed under my skin and throbbed like a septic wound, poisoning the hard peace I had made with the old man on that last night in Palinur.

Osriel shrugged and strolled through a chamber littered with old paint splashes and stacks of canvas into a room hung with every size and shape of willow birdcages—all of them vacant. Someone of wide-ranging interests had lived in this house. But no longer.

"My father's failure to return to the Danae caused much

anger and grief, and as years passed, visits with Clyste and Kol and my father's other friends among the Danae grew rare. But on one night not long after I was born, Kol barged into my father's bedchamber. Bitter and furious, Kol told him that Clyste had been bound to her sianou with myrtle and hyssop, forbidden to take bodily form again. He left with no further explanation, and my father neither saw nor spoke to another Dané before he died."

I held back a curtain, and we passed into what must once have been a gracious library, its dusty shelves now holding only a few scattered volumes. I guessed that the rest now sat in the magical lighthouse.

"Clearly there is even more to the story than we know," the prince continued, "for one must ask: If the Danae knew Janus de Cartamandua had stolen you and punished him for it, why did they never claim you? It would have been no great leap of intelligence to see that the infant who appeared in the Cartamandua house at the very time of the theft must be the half-Danae child."

I caught his meaning. "Yet if they had known I was half Danae, they would never have tried to drown me in the bog along with everyone else."

"Exactly so. I believe that, of all the Danae, only Kol knows who and what you are. Clyste never told them that *Janus* had fathered her child."

Which meant that Kol alone had driven my grandfather mad and that it was unlikely that Kol had launched the owl to drown us in the bog. If he had wanted me dead, he'd already had ample opportunities.

"Had I known all this before Mellune Forest, I might have run into the wild and begged the Danae to make me one of them," I said, "assuming such a thing is even possible. But whatever their reasons might have been, to trick fifty people into drowning—without judgment, without mercy, guilty and innocent alike—is as despicable as the Harrowers clogging wells with tar in Palinur. To protect my friends, I had to become complicit in their evil. I won't do that again."

Perhaps it was my imagination that Osriel's complexion darkened. A perceptive man as he was would surely understand it was not only of *Danae* evils that I spoke.

I moved swiftly to make my intent clear. "I will uphold my oath of submission to you, lord—I'll not run—but I intend to stay out of their way until my birthday." I had no desire to live as a stone or a tree.

Our meandering path had led us back to the passage of shields and curtained doors. "Your position makes sense," he said as we neared its end. "But you have also sworn to serve the lighthouse cabal. As there seems to be no immediate danger to you from Kol, I must call upon your oath and bid you guide me to a place where I can try once more to speak to him. We must discover if the Danae know the cause of the world's sickness, and we must warn them of Sila Diaglou."

Bonds of oath and obligation, now made all the more repugnant by this deeper loathing, settled about my limbs. "But, my lord—"

"You'll not have to face him yourself. In the hour I stand in Danae lands—beside the Sentinel Oak at Caedmon's Bridge—I shall deem your present obligation to me and to the cabal complete, and you may choose your own course to face your past and future. Saverian will maintain her remedy for your sickness as long as you require it. You will be welcome to reside here or come and go as your health allows." His face—Gram's face—expressed his particular earnest sincerity that could persuade a hen to lay its neck beneath the ax blade. "After the solstice, the world and our place in it will be changed for good or ill. At that time we will renegotiate the terms of your service. So, are you willing?"

Free to choose my own course... how sweet those words, offering the one thing I'd ever begged of the gods. He was right. If Kol meant to hand me over to the Danae or drive me mad, he could have taken me at Clyste's Well or fifty different times back in Palinur. And the deed should be possible; I had seen the great oak where only a crude illusion should have existed, where nothing grew in the human plane. I could take Osriel there, then be on my way... search for Jullian. Once the boy walked free and Gildas had paid a price for Gerard's murder, all my oaths would be fulfilled. Free to choose... "My lord, yes. Of course I'll take you."

"Good. I'll have done with my thirsty warlords tonight. If you feel in anywise fit enough, we'll leave for Aeginea tomorrow. Time presses us sorely."

"I'll be ready."

I pulled aside the blue and yellow curtain and waited for the prince to enter my bedchamber, but he motioned me to go ahead alone, bidding me to rest well.

A wolf of hammered gold adorned the wall above the archway. Its garnet eyes gleamed fierce in the lamplight. Kindness, understanding, generosity . . . how easily Osriel induced me to forget my doubts. No matter my chosen course, this time I must not avert my eyes.

I took a knee and touched my forehead in proper obeisance, and rose at his nod. "Tell me, my lord," I said, as he turned to go, "if Brother Victor dies, will you take his eyes?"

The gaze he cast over his shoulder could have frosted a volcano's heart. "Yes."

I wanted Osriel to be worthy of his inheritance and worthy of my trust, but as the Duc of Evanore vanished down the passage, it felt as if he dragged my entrails with him. I needed to learn what Elene would tell me.

Chapter 10

Restlessness drew me out of my bedchamber before Osriel's footsteps had faded, and I paced the sprawling house as if paid to measure its myriad dimensions. In hopes of finding Brother Victor, I bypassed the domed garden, the painter's room, the scavenged library, and the other places I'd walked with the prince. Wisdom advised me to seek a confidant who did not transform my loins to fire and my mind to jam as Elene did. Loyalty bade me warn the monk of his peril. I could not believe he knew of Osriel's unsavory practices. I was already chastising myself for agreeing to my master's plan. Why did I trust him? He didn't even bother to mask his infamy.

Though dusty and deserted, the house was finely proportioned and lavishly ornamented with windows and murals, painted ceilings and rich hangings. Yet the farther I walked, the worse the stench: latrines, rotting meat, male sweat, candles, incense, and wood ash, mouse piss, boiling herbs. I'd always thought Moriangi houses the nastiest in the kingdom.

By the time I rounded a new corner only to find a corridor I had traversed three times already, I suspected some magical boundary kept me separate from the ailing monk. I touched the smooth tiles of the passage floor, seeking some trace of him, but as before my bent failed to answer my summons. Confessing defeat, I chose to retreat.

I could not find my bedchamber. My footsteps thudded on the tiles. The mice scuttling in the walls were surely the size of houses. Anxiety grew like dark mold in my lungs and heart.

Increasingly confused, I burst through a door I'd not yet broached. Tables jammed with neglected plants crowded the long room, and the glare of the westering sun through its three walls and roof of glass near blinded me. Eyes blurred, nauseated by the stink, I stumbled sideways.

An explosion of pain in my skull sent me crashing to the floor. I crawled into a corner and huddled quivering, arms wrapped about my head.

Running footsteps hammered the passage floor like the thousand drums of Iero's Judgment Night. With a hiss of disapproval, the newcomer wrenched my arms aside, pried my chin upward, and slapped something cold and round onto the center of my forehead. As worms burrowing into my flesh, magic flowed outward from the disk, gnawing skin, muscle, and bone, quieting whatever it touched before squiggling onward ... deeper ... farther ...

When the disgusting sensation faded, the world felt dull and distant, as if my entire body had been sheathed in silken hand bindings. "Could you not make this enchantment feel more like your fingers and less like maggots?" I said.

"My apologies, O Magical Being!" Saverian grabbed my hands and hauled me to a sitting position. The world spun only slightly. "What a fool I was to design this spell for your relief and not your pleasure."

"Mistress, I didn't mean—"

"Of course, had you remained where you were told, I could have renewed your shield at the proper time, and you would not have experienced the spell's less pleasant aspects so acutely. But then, the parts between your legs do resemble those of mortal males, so I shouldn't expect too much in the way of common wisdom." Her complaints were issued with the same ironical humor she had used to address the uncooperative logs in my bedchamber hearth. "And I dislike being labeled as anyone's mistress. My name is Saverian."

I rubbed at the crusted mess on my eyelids, hoping to regain my faculties now she had withdrawn her hand. Water sloshed and dribbled. She whispered, "*Igneo,*" and not long afterward, a hot damp cloth scalded my eyelids.

"Ouch!"

"*Must* you forever complain?"

Her blotting was indeed more satisfactory than rubbing away the grit of sweat and tears ... and blood, I noticed when she paused to rinse the cloth. My collision with the brick wall had split my head in more than my perception. But the sharp sting served as pleasing evidence that my senses now functioned in a somewhat normal fashion.

The physician had changed from her riding leathers into a skirt and shapeless tunic of dull green. A slim leather belt settled about her hips, more for the purpose of attaching a knife sheath and two leather pockets than any decorative enhancement of her spare figure.

"I was hoping to visit Brother Victor," I said. "He is a friend ... mentor ..."

"... and the prince told you, 'Not yet.' It might soothe your conscience to see the monk, but it would do *him* no good at all. His health improves. His injuries have challenged me, but will yield in the end."

She dropped a jingling something into one of her pockets and tightened the drawstring with a snap. Her insistent grip on my hand hauled me to my feet with astonishing ease. As I concentrated on remaining upright, she surveyed me head to toe and sighed heavily.

"Come along. Our doughty prince insists that you remain out of sight while he plays Evanori chieftain in his hall. He fears your presence would be a distraction. Nothing sets Evanori warlords slavering more than a tall, scrawny pureblood."

Untwisting my trews, I padded after her through another garden room and into the chilly corridor. My head throbbed, but only with bruising, not madness. "I'm no more pureblood than he is—or you are."

Saverian raised one instructive finger. "Ah, but Caedmon's holy blood flows in Osriel's veins, which means they will forgive him anything, and despite being a woman who prefers books to battle-axes, I can at least claim half an Evanori birthright. Were I in your place, I would certainly not attempt to explain to a hundred warlords come to the last night of a warmoot that, despite my Registry listing, I was not an Aurellian pureblood because my mother was an angel ... or a water sprite ... or whatever it is you claim. Of course, *I* say you can be damned and do as you wish, save that our lord has commanded me to see you obey him. And I *will* see to it. You must have peeved him something dreadful to put him in such a vile temper."

Her heavy black braid had been knotted at the back of her long neck and fixed in place with an ivory skewer. Easy to imagine that skewer stretching all the way down her spine. Half Evanori, half Aurellian—that likely explained her odd nature. Evanori hated Aurellians—and thus purebloods—with a passion wrought of gold, starvation, and survival.

After Ardra and Morian had fallen to the Aurellian Empire, and Caedmon had sent his infant son to the Danae for protection, the king and the remnants of his legions had retreated into the wilds of Evanore. Raiding, running, hiding in caves and corries, freezing and starving alongside his men, Caedmon taught the warlords to fight as one and helped them build impregnable strongholds to hold off the invaders and their cruel emperor, who lusted for Evanore's gold. When Caedmon fell at last, having earned their eternal loyalty, the Evanori held out a century more. Had they yielded their region's treasure, Aurellia would likely yet stand, and Navronne would yet be subject to an empire that built its strength on magic, slavery, and brutality.

Though feeling mostly myself again in body, my spirit remained tight wound. If Osriel meant what he said about my choosing my own course, I'd no mind to put off our coming journey into the Danae realm, no matter the state of my recovery. Thus, to learn what secrets Elene could teach, I had to see her that night. Which meant I had to find a way into the fortress. As a prison guard Saverian did not elicit the same unnerving fears as Voushanti, but she had shown power enough to make me wary, nonetheless.

"You seem excessively compliant for one who speaks of our master so slightingly," I said as she marched into the familiar passage. The hammered gold wolf with garnet eyes glared from the far end, guarding my bedchamber door. "Is it to benefit the lighthouse you do all this?"

She snorted. "I am Renna's physician and house mage, not a member of Osriel's band of merry monks."

"Your privileged position must shield you from his wrath. You don't seem to fear him as the rest of us do."

She waved me through the blue and yellow door hanging. "If you assume my familiarity with the prince buys me leniency from his strictures, I'd recommend you actually *use* these senses I'm protecting for you. Bear in mind, I've known him from infancy and have learned in what matters I dare cross him and in what matters I dare not."

I made as if to enter the bedchamber, but instead blocked the doorway. "Prince Osriel wishes me out of sight—fair enough. But might there be some hidden vantage from which I could observe tonight's events? I've no experience of Evanori customs, so I'm greatly curious. And, by every god in heaven, if I am left alone to parse my birth, my body, or my future for one more moment, not even your magics will keep me sane." This last came out sounding a bit more desperate than I liked.

She tipped her head to one side and pursed her thin lips into an unflattering knot. Her brow ridges were angled slightly downward from midforehead, giving her a forever-quizzical expression. After a breathless moment, she shrugged. "Why not? Let it never be said I granted Osriel of Evanore exactly what he desired on any occasion whatsoever."

I didn't think I'd ever met a person so unattached to human feelings. All the world seemed subject to her disdain. Recalcitrant logs or foolish sorcerers could cause her transitory annoyance, but I couldn't imagine what it might take to truly frighten her, or to please her, for that matter. At least she had no red sparks centering her pupils.

Saverian sat in my room for several hours that afternoon, writing in her journal, reading from several books, annoyed when I tried to talk or ask questions.

"Sleep, if you can't think of anything better to do," she said, after one ill-timed query. "I'm not here to entertain you. You've taken enough of my time over the past few weeks."

But my skin itched and my insides felt like a nest of ants. I could no more sleep than I could read her books. "What do you do with your time when not nursing twist-minds or demon princes? I've never seen anyone save monks or schoolmasters sit so long with a book."

"Books don't prattle. Books don't make demands. Yet they give you everything they possess. It's a very satisfying partnership."

I considered that for a while, as I watched her read. Annoyance vanished as the words absorbed her attention, replaced by a fluid mix of interest, curiosity, and serious consideration. Her brow would furrow; then she would write something in her journal. Once the thought was recorded, the furrow smoothed, and she went back to reading. Books supplied companionship, perhaps, but I doubted any words on a page could do what her hands had done for me as I lay in the doulon madness. "*Satisfying* doesn't sound like much to aim for."

"Enough!" With a spit of exasperation, she scooped all her belongings into an untidy armload and headed for the door. "I'll fetch you in time for the warmoot."

I spent the next few hours berating myself as an idiot. I hadn't meant to voice my musings aloud. At least she had given me something to look at beyond four walls and a bed.

One of her books had fallen to the floor beneath the table. I thumbed through it, picking out one or two letters that I knew, then watching them melt and flow into the ones next to them. *Gods, useless.* I threw the book across the room and went to sleep.

True to her word, Saverian returned just after a bristle-bearded serving man had lit the lamps. As I snatched a long black cloak from the clothes chest, I felt warmly satisfied that, for the first time in forever, I was both reasonably clearheaded and taking some action on my own behalf.

"You need to eat more than one bite of meat and a dried plum," said the physician after inspecting the food tray that had arrived an hour earlier. She stuffed a slice of oily cheese into my hand. "Eat this as we walk, and I won't find a reason to abort this venture."

I could make no plans until we reached the fortress, but

if I were to shake free of Saverian and find Elene, I would likely need magic more than nourishment. I obediently took a bite of cheese, then held out my fingers. "Can you unlock these, good physician? I feel a cripple without my bent even to know north from south."

Her dark heavy cloak made her look taller and more than ever like a stick. She shrugged. "You assign me more skill than my due. It's not your fingers, but only this house I've sealed against your magic—and that only possible because it is a peculiar house with a number of in-built protections already. I assumed you would be more in control of yourself by the time we took you out walking. Please tell me that's true."

"I promise I'm in possession of all the reason I was born with." I grinned and took another bite of cheese to please her. "Honestly, I do appreciate your care."

She blew a derisive breath and hefted a stout leather bag over one shoulder, the bag of the sort that Voushanti used to carry Prince Osriel's medicines. The outer doors waited in a pleasant vaulted alcove I'd not glimpsed in all my wanderings. The four broad panels of the twin doors had been painted to depict the seasons, the rich hues and intricate drawing giving the depth of truth to the design. Though stunningly beautiful, the paintings left a hollow in my breast. Each panel showed a pair of dancers, their pale flesh twined with designs of azure and lapis. We pulled open the doors and stepped into the winter night.

The cold snatched my breath away. Fine, sharp grains of snow stung the skin, the particles more a part of the air itself than anything that would pile or drift on the barren ground. Across the windswept slope, bonfires and torches lit the fortress gates and walls, orange flames writhing alongside a hundred or more whipping banners that flew from the battlements.

As we trudged down the path, thick darkness crowded the light-pooled fortress and the soft-lit windows of the house we had just abandoned, as if the mountains had drawn closer under cover of the starless, moonless night. I drew my cloak tight, grateful for Saverian's enchantment that tamed my senses. It must be that Evanore's violent history remained raw enough to taint the night with the anguish of its dying warriors and the wails of its starving children, for the wind bore grief and despair and anger on its back as surely as it carried shouts of greeting or the smells of horses and smoke. A harsh, dry land was Evanore. I would no more touch my fingers to this earth than spit on a grave.

From the battlements sounded the low, heavy tones of a sonnivar, the hooked horn that stretched taller than me when stood on end and that rang so deep and so true its call could be heard for vast distances through the mountains and vales, guiding Evanore's warriors home. Evanori claimed the timbre of each warlord's sonnivar unique, so that a fog-blind warrior could identify which fortress he approached from the sonnivar greeting alone.

A party of horsemen rode over the steep crest of the valley road and cantered up the gentler slope to the gates. Gruff voices carried across the dark hillside, shouting challenges and orders until the portcullis clanked and rumbled open and the party rode through.

"Pull up your hood," said Saverian softly, as if fearing that we, too, might be heard from afar. "And carry this." She shoved her leather bag into my hands. I hefted the heavy little bag onto my back, as our path joined the trampled roadway to the gates.

"The password, Saverian," said a slab-sided warrior standing to one side of the sizable detachment manning the gate tower and portcullis. "Even for you this night. And identify your friend."

"Pustules," said the physician. She stepped up close to him, as the sonnivar boomed again from above our heads. "Is your wife pleased with your renewed affections, Dreogan? Perhaps I need to reexamine your little—"

"Pass!" bellowed the guard. A snickering youth waited behind an iron wicket set into the tower wall. At the guard's signal, the youth unlocked the little gate, let us through, and locked it again behind us.

"You're on report, Dreogan!" Saverian called over her shoulder. "This is no night to be slack."

"Deunor's fire," I said, "has every man in the universe got crossways with you?"

"You've not seen me crossways, sirrah. Dreogan would kiss my feet did I but ask. More fool he."

More fool the man who imagined my companion a feeling woman.

The burly warrior's curses followed us as we hurried through a passage so low I had to duck and so narrow we could not walk abreast. The close quarters set my teeth on edge. Once through, we passed without challenge across the barren outer bailey and through the inner gates into the bustling main courtyard. Thick smoke rose from torches and warming fires, as squires and men-at-arms groomed horses, honed weapons, greeted friends, and shared out provisions. A burst of cheers and oaths pinpointed a dice game on our left, and whoops rose from the milling crowd when servants rolled three carts loaded with ale casks into the yard. We kept to the quiet perimeter, dodging several sighing fellows who'd come to the shadowed wall to piss or satisfy a lonely soldier's fleshly urges.

Naught fazed Saverian. She headed briskly for the northwest corner of the yard, where a tight stair spiraled up one of the fortress's barrel-like towers. The thick tower walls damped the noise of the courtyard until we emerged on a parapet walk. On one side we overlooked the noisy throng of waiting warriors, on the other a close, dark well yard. Two heavily armed guards, their heads wreathed in steaming breath, halted Saverian at a thick door of banded oak that led into the blocklike heart of the fortress. She complained of a sore elbow from riding and named me her servant, brought along to carry her medicine bag.

"I'm sure I needn't remind you to stay quiet and out of sight," said the woman under her breath once the guards passed us through the low doorway. "A warmoot is a sacred meeting between the warlords, their heirs, and their sovereign. It is closed to other Evanori no matter how favored, even wives or husbands, and most certainly closed to outsiders."

"But a half-Evanori physician is admitted?"

"Only if I remain out of sight and hearing. It is an ongoing argument between His Grace and me. He wishes no public reminders of his difficult health, yet he knows saccheria can flare without warning, so he tolerates my presence. Few know the truth of his condition: you, your fellow madmen in this monkish conspiracy, and those few who have served in Renna Syne—the 'window palace' where you're housed—since he was small. Even his royal brothers have it wrong. The cretins think he shapeshifts to disguise a crippled back."

"Does he?"

Her glance could have withered heaven's lilies.

Of a sudden the fine, graceful house set apart from the fortress made sense. Osriel had grown up here. Eodward had housed his pureblood mistress in Evanore, away from the Registry's interference, and he had named their child the province's duc, so that Lirene would own the bound loyalty of the Evanori, if not their love. The house protections used to damp my magic would be those of any pureblood home where the children had not yet learned to control their sorcerers' bent.

More anxious than ever to make sense of Osriel, I leaned in close and touched the physician's hand, hoping to soften her in the way I'd had success throughout the years. "I'll confess, mistress, Prince Osriel leaves me not knowing which ear to listen with. If you could but tell—"

"I am not your mistress, Cartamandua," she said with long-suffering patience. "I am a servant, as are you, and Renna's servants do *not* gossip about Prince Osriel. Best learn that." She removed my hand from her arm with a grip worthy of her warlord ancestors. Foolish to imagine my . . . natural skills . . . could lure *her* into anything she had no mind to.

Beyond a short vestibule, we came onto a gallery that overlooked a smoky feasting hall. Below us an elderly woman decried the depredations of a Harrower raid. Prince Osriel and a hundred or more warriors sat listening.

Saverian frowned speculatively when a grin broke over my face. The hall's arrangement reminded me of nothing so much as the refectory at Gillarine, with the monks seated according to seniority at long tables along the side walls, the abbot and prior at their head, listening to the day's reading of the holy writs.

Of course, rather than a splendid window overlooking

the cloisters and the abbey church, a solid wall of war banners rose behind Osriel's great wood chair. And rather than the tall glass windows of the refectory, only arrow slits penetrated the thick side and entry walls. Every other quat of wall space from floor to wood-beamed roof was given to a vast collection of war trophies: shields, weapons, bits of armor, several long oars and a carved wooden figurehead with snaky hair and peeling paint—evidence of Hansker longboats. A few dried, hairy lumps looked disconcertingly like long-dead squirrels . . . or scalps.

"No question where Evanori hearts find pleasure," I murmured.

Saverian folded her arms and gazed down on the panoply. "Indeed, the most welcomed entertainment at this gathering would be a Harrower raiding party storming the doors. What a collection of idiots. And the women are as bad as the men."

At least we agreed on one matter.

Despite the smoky heat, both men and women wore heavy fur cloaks over thick leathers, mail, and weapons. The only concession to ornament were the fine-wrought clasps, earrings, chains, rings, and bracelets—all gold—that adorned every head, neck, and limb. A gold band set with garnets circled Osriel's brow atop a soft hood that obscured his face.

Evidently Osriel had allowed Stearc to venture from Gillarine for this gathering. Elene sat just behind him on a bench against the wall, along with the other warlords-in-waiting, some young and blooming as she was, some older and as battle-worn as their sires and dams.

I examined our immediate surroundings for some way to slip the bonds of Saverian's custody. The featureless gallery where we stood stretched the entire length of the hall. I could imagine bowmen poised at the iron rail. Or musicians with harps and vielles—if Evanori subscribed to any display of the gentler arts. About halfway along the outer wall, I noted a narrow gap.

Leaving Saverian in the vestibule, I ambled down the gallery. A sidewise glimpse confirmed the gap was a downward stair. I squatted just across from it and peered through the iron railing, as if trying to watch the events below without being noticed. Clutching the medicine bag, I considered what excuse I might devise for a venture down the stair.

One after the other, the warlords took their place in the center of the room, gripped a staff topped with a wolf's head of wrought gold, and recited the incursions of Ardran or Moriangi raiders who scoured the countryside for food stores, or the vile deeds of Harrower burning parties who ravaged isolated villages and farmsteads on both sides of the border. I gathered this was the third night in a row they had recounted these same grievances, determined to implant them in one another's memory as if the offenses had been dealt against them all. When Thane Stearc took the staff, he told of the dog-faced man who led the Harrower pursuit on our journey from Palinur and how the pursuit had been thwarted only when his pureblood guide had tricked the Harrowers into a bog and drowned them all.

As always, reminders of events in the bog left me nauseated and uneasy. Reflexively, I glanced over my shoulder. Saverian was staring at me, her nose flared in disgust. Perhaps she had never heard the story, or had only now connected it with me.

During each report, the rowdy onlookers shouted confirmations or approvals, curses or reprimands for the speaker's tale. When a young thanea, sized like a brick hearth and clad in scarred mail, reported that she had dreamed of shadow legions overrunning Evanore, I expected derisive hoots and laughter, but the lords thumped fists on the tables and shouted that the time had come for Evanore's legions to take the field.

Prince Osriel listened to all without comment. Once the staff had passed through every lord's hand, the company fell silent. The elderly woman returned to the center of the room and began reciting. As her voice rose and fell in the fashion of talespinners, the torchlight dimmed.

The old woman spoke of Aurellian ships come to the river country in the north and Aurellian legions crossing the broad Yaronal from the east after discovering that the small magics they worked in their distant homeland took fire with power in the lands of Navronne. But they found this favored land ruled by a stubborn king . . .

It was Caedmon's story she told, tracing his lineage into the deeps of history and telling of his rise and fall. Her tale recalled the great window in the Gillarine Abbey chapter house. In jeweled glass it had depicted the sad and honorable king who had first united the gravs of Morian and the warlords of Evanore with his own kingdom of Ardra. He had made the disparate realms into something greater than the sum of its parts, only to see his beloved Navronne brought to heel by the predatory Aurellians. The storyteller painted her portrait with words, not glass, depicting the king leading the tattered remnants of his legions to the great bridge he'd built to link Ardra and Evanore.

Deep shadows enveloped the gallery. Saverian could not have seen my hand rummaging in her medicine bag. I snatched out a few items and stuffed them in my pockets.

When the old woman's tale was done, the lords began to sing. I stood up, fumbling the bag until I dropped it, spilling the loose contents on the gallery floor. *That* Saverian noticed. And came running.

"What have you done, fool?" she whispered, snatching up vials, packets, and tight-wrapped bundles of linen and wool. I held the bag open as she put the things away, sensing her itemizing each article, as I'd guessed she would. She patted the floor around us and hissed, "Three packets and two small jars are missing. Holy Mother . . ."

One of the lords took up another song—"The Lay of Groshug," an interminable recounting of a bloody boar hunt that I enjoyed only when I was roaring drunk. They'd be bawling it for an hour at the least. Saverian would not dare risk a scene. And I gambled that she'd not dare leave her post. Her first duty was to Osriel's health.

"I fear things dropped through the railing," I whispered. "I'm sorry . . . I'll fetch them." And before she could protest, I shoved the bag into her hands and darted down the stair.

The stair dumped me into a dark vestibule, crowded with two big tables, piled with empty tankards and dirty serving platters. A wide door led back into the hall. A narrower door led outside, where an arcade fronted the long side of the building. Accompanied by the lords' robust rendering of the chorus to "The Lay of Groshug," I sped eastward through the arcade in search of the *rock gate* Elene had mentioned.

The geometries of such a fortress were fairly simple. A cross wall joined a long barracks building to the Great Hall. The arcade tunneled through the wall and ended abruptly in an alley at the far end of the hall. Follow the alley to the left, and you would end up in a paved yard surrounded by kitchens and bakehouses and storage buildings. Go right ten paces along the east end of the Great Hall, and you ran straight into the mountainside.

No gate was visible where the blocklike hall merged with the rocky buttress, but I guessed that the perilously steep set of steps cut into the mottled gray and red rock would lead me there. As I half climbed, half crawled up the interminable stair, I blessed Saverian for clearing my head. With only the diffuse light from the hall's arrow slits to illuminate the rock, I needed all the acuity I could muster. My feet were bigger than the altogether too-slanted steps.

Elene awaited me atop the stair, like a warrior angel on a church spire. "I didn't think you'd come, not a day out of your bed and bound by Saverian's spellcraft."

"To meet with you, lady, I would even climb this god-cursed stair again," I said, gasping. "But by the Mother, do Evanori not approve of air?"

I bent over and propped my hands on my knees, coughing as the cold dry air rasped my heaving chest. I prayed I was not so sorely out of health as to be flattened by a hundred steps. But a squirrel could have toppled me.

"Renna is higher than Erasku. It's even higher than Angor Nav—the duc's official seat. Even I notice the sparse air here." Her face was only a pale blur in the night, but her pinched voice hinted at high emotion reined tight. "Osriel told my father you were taking him to the Danae tomorrow. Is that true?"

"That's what he wants," I said. "We've less than a month until the solstice."

"Come."

By the time I accumulated enough breath to ask where, she had pivoted sharply and marched into the night. I followed carefully. The stair had brought us onto a steeply ascending apron of rock that skirted a bulge in the massive ridge. I hugged the rock wall on my left, for on my right, tiny, winking blots of torchlight and bonfires in a gaping darkness marked the heart-stopping drop to the fortress. The irregular path canted outward, and my boots hinted that ice lurked in its cracks and crevices.

"I had decided to send you back to your bed," said Elene, little more than a formless darkness ahead of me. "To show you this betrays an oath I swore on my mother's memory, a villainous oath that should condemn me to the netherworld for the making, not just for the breaking. *He* chose it. Not I—stupid, mooning cow that I am to be so led into godless folly."

"What oath?" I caught up with her just as the path ended abruptly at an iron gate. The tall gate, anchored in the rock, blocked entry to a shallow breach in the ramparts of the ridge. "What folly?"

The gate rattled with Elene's violent application of her boot. "Papa refuses to come here with me or listen to what I say, because my showing him would break my oath and because the secret's owner is holy Caedmon's heir. I'd hoped one of the monks might listen, but I was never allowed to be alone with them. And I could never tell anyone outside the cabal. All I want is to stop this wickedness. And so this morning, seeing how you sensed his evil already—rightly so—and I was so angry, I said I'd bring you. Yet I would send you away ignorant even now if he'd not told you he was going to the Danae right away. He means to do this . . . to use their magic . . ."

She grasped the iron hasp, touched it with a gold ring that shot sparks like fireflies into the dark, and spoke a word I could not decipher for the half growl, half sob that accompanied it.

"Mistress, you must excuse my confusion. Who is going to do what? Osriel?"

Indeed, I thought my acuity must be impaired again, so little sense could I make of all this. The most daunting news I'd gleaned from her avalanche of words was that her fear outstripped her anger.

The breach in the rocks proved to be but a crumbling wash the width of my armspan. It rose at a shallow pitch, which my lungs approved, and wound between huge boulders that were easy to spot—a good thing, as the sky was as dark as tar. I wasn't sure how Elene could show me anything. Yet when we emerged from the gully atop the ridge, a livid haze lit the night before us, illuminating a scene of desolation.

For as far as I could see, the ridge top had been hacked away, gouged and broken into a shallow bowl a quellé wide, at least, seamed with trenches and pocked with dark holes. Broken troughs and sluices, iron wheels, and snarls of ancient rope rotted or rusted amid heaps of crushed rock. Chiseled slabs lay tilted and broken beside a monstrous quern and a cracked mortar broader than my armspan.

But it was not the ugly spoil heaps or grinding stones that colored my soul the same bruised gray as the unnatural haze and made me want to run far from this place. All the grief of Evanore lay here. All the anger. The pent emotions I had felt on the wind, and those I had sensed when first I looked upon Osriel's land, were but goosedown to the leaden weight of sorrow and fury that settled on my spirit. I could scarce breathe.

"What gold could be dug from Dashon Ra has been long carted away," said Elene, standing at my shoulder. "But he says the veins yet thread the earth like a web and extend throughout Evanore. He says they are like ring mail that strengthens our land, holding a power that fires magic. Come on."

She marched down the sloping side of the abandoned mine, hopped across a deep, narrow trench, and skirted the corner of a rubble wall—all that remained of a shed. The haze thickened, coiling violet tendrils about Elene's boots. I followed, wishing I had never asked her to show me this. Making Deunor's sign upon my brow and drawing Iero's holy seal upon my breast, I prayed that Saverian's spell would not fail me. This land held terrible secrets.

Down and down. Our boots slipped and slid on the loose tailings and patches of ice. Nearing the bottom of the slope, we ducked under an ancient leat, solid and unbroken, though only grit and gravel remained where water had once flowed. Beyond us lay the lowermost levels of the mine, a rectangular pit of iron-laced rock the size of Renna's Great

Hall, cracked and scarred by weather and men's work. Piles of rubble littered its floor. And across every handsbreadth of the rock walls, every protrusion, knob, or broken shelf held a vessel of carved stone, votive vessels as you would find in Deunor's temple or Iero's cathedral—hundreds of them, some the size of bread loaves or tabors, some smaller, palm-sized like oil lamps, like the calyx I had seen in Osriel's bloody hands in the abbey kitchen.

The bruised haze hung above the vessels as does the stench above a midden. Dread rose in my soul like fever. "This is where he brings them . . . the eyes of the dead."

"He seals each vessel with his own blood. When he brings it here, he unseals it and empties it into the earth. That dark blotch at the center is a bottomless shaft. Though the vessels are no longer needed, he names them sacred because of what they carried, so he leaves them here."

"Not sacred," I said, revulsion clogging my throat. "This is no holy place. No temple. It is a prison." As my gaze roamed the desolation, I clamped my hands under my arms as if some accident might make them touch this violated earth. I didn't want to hear those trapped here. I didn't want to feel their fury and confusion and hatred more clearly than I did already. Madness had owned me for too many days.

Elene scooped up a handful of crushed stone and dirt, then allowed it to rain through her fingers onto the dry earth. "He plans to work some terrible magic here. When he brought me here three years ago to show me—to end what we had begun in happier times—he said he hoped with all his being that he would never have to set his plan in motion, for it would be such a sin as would end his last hope of heaven. Truly, Brother Valen, it is not for his own glory, but for Navronne he strives, yet he does not listen that hope cannot be bought with sin."

The bilious light sapped all color from her warm skin. The tears rolled down her cheeks like gray pearls, and her palms pressed flat across her belly as if to shield the child that grew inside her. "I put *my* hope in Luviar and his noble lighthouse to show him the way of right. For one blessed hour on that same night you escaped from Gillarine, I thought his loneliness had led him back to love.

And though that hope proved false, I believed my dearest prayers answered when he told us of the Harrower hiding place you'd found, and that his brothers had agreed to join him to oppose Sila Diaglou. But a tenday ago, while you lay ill, reports came that Sila Diaglou had abandoned her hidden fortress and, at the same time, raised her own banner in Palinur alongside his brother's. A light went out of him that day. Within hours he left Renna with only Voushanti accompanying him. And since he's come back, he has not spoken to me, not looked at me, not told anyone where he went. I've begged him, yelled at him, pleaded with him to explain to the cabal what he plans next, but he refuses."

She waved her hand at the bleak scene before us. "Three years ago, he told me that his own power might not be enough to accomplish what he wants, and that the more certain way would be to ask the Danae's help to join their magic to his. And now you are to take him to the Danae. Whatever this is . . . he's decided to go through with it. By the Holy Mother, Valen, you're a sorcerer and his friend— the only one not blinded by fealty or awe or fear. Only you can stop him . . . save him."

I wanted to laugh at the idea of me stopping Osriel the Bastard, the rightful King of Navronne, the sorcerer who called up red lightning and performed rites that reeked of brimstone, from doing anything he chose. But Elene's grief and fear for the prince tempered my answer with sobriety, at least. "Lady, I cannot even begin to imagine what spells might be worked with . . . whatever lies in this place. And indeed the prince has good reasons to go to the Danae, the same he has stated all along. We must know what they can tell us of the world's sickness and its remedy. If he gives them warning of Sila Diaglou and Gildas, perhaps they will shelter our Scholar and give light to his lighthouse. It is his right and his duty to speak to them for us. But I promise you I'll do what I can to discover his plans and persuade him to some alternative."

I had no faith in my promise. Nor did she, though she thanked me and pretended it so. I took her in my arms as she wept, wishing naught but to offer comfort. For indeed the least significant, yet most painful discovery on this night of dread revelation was that I would willingly suffer any danger to serve Elene, though her heart was not—and had never been—mine to win. No wonder at her agonies if that ebullient heart—and the child she had conceived—belonged to the Duc of Evanore. And no matter the course of past or future, a love already tested by the trials of grim necessity, of denial and sacrifice, of illness, war, and unholy sorcery, was unlikely to be swayed by the fingers of a feckless vagabond, whatever the marvels of his birth.

Chapter 11

❖

Down, down, interminably down. The steep descent from Renna to the borderlands of Evanore in the driving blizzard was unrelenting misery. *Hold your seat. Keep your back straight. Legs forward. Trust the beast.* The distance was not so far, so I was told. Two days, three in such weather. But my backside was already hot and raw, and every other part of me was frozen, save two fiery strips on my fingers where the leather cinch straps, made into knife edges by the cold, had sliced my flesh. My back and shoulders ached ... as did my spirit, weighed to breaking with the memory of those thousand empty vessels.

I had spent the dreary hours speculating on how I could possibly accomplish what I had promised Elene. To set myself as intermediary between Osriel and Stearc's daughter was only slightly less witless than setting myself between my friend Gram and his dangerous royal self. What in the name of heaven did he think to do with Danae magic and thousands of imprisoned souls? And how could I possibly stop it? Elene had sorely misjudged my capabilities.

Stearc rode point, the dark expanse of his shoulders our guide staff through the world of white. Five of his own warriors rode alongside him. They were to escort him back to Gillarine and relieve the troop he'd left there, while Osriel and I hunted the Danae.

The prince and I followed close behind the thane. In the presence of Stearc's men, Osriel rode as Gram. He had insisted I wear my pureblood garb and return to pureblood disciplines, playing Prince Osriel's contracted servant sent upon a private mission. The mask and cloak felt odd, as if they belonged to someone else.

Voushanti guarded our rear, along with his trusted warriors Philo and Melkire. Just ahead of them rode Saverian, brought along to tend Osriel's health. She had been furious at the prince's insistence that she accompany us and had taken her vengeance by calling hourly halts and forcing him to drink her potions. Saverian reminded me of thyme or savory—useful in small amounts, but like to gag you in too great a quantity.

I'd no more questions about how to rattle her temper. On the previous night, when I had come round the end of Renna's Great Hall from the rock gate stair after bidding farewell to Elene, Saverian had pounced like a starved wolverine.

"Are you entirely without intelligence?" Clearly the question was not meant to be answered. She grabbed my cloak and dragged me past the doorway that returned to the hall, where Osriel's warlords were cheering. "Do you think me blind or just some thick-witted troll? What a striking coincidence that you dropped my things—which I had damned well better get back, by the bye—at exactly the same time the heiress of Erasku slipped out of the hall. I'm truly surprised not to find you naked again! Ah, yes, I forget: a Dané dances naked and reportedly can seduce a brick wall does he but sigh. So it is but your inborn nature to put the moon-mad little warrior at risk of a flaying from her father, and surely the annoying physician can fend for herself when the guards alert Prince Osriel because the woman's servant has gone missing at a warmoot!" Astonishing how she could raise such a lather in a voice that none could have heard five steps away from us.

We had returned straight on to Renna Syne. The walk seemed to cool her temper slightly, but upon our arrival, she made clear that I had exhausted what meager stock of forbearance she had vouched me as her patient. "I don't wish to be friends with you. I don't care to join monkish conspiracies to change the world. All I ask is civilized behavior—which means, among other things, that you do not put me at risk of losing my employment or my life."

When she had me sit on the bed and proceeded to drop a thin chain about my neck, I'd feared she'd decided to strangle me. But the fat little coin that dangled from the chain and weighed so heavily on my chest was, in fact, the gold medallion she used to tame my disease.

"When you feel your senses compromised, hold the medallion in the center of your forehead, infuse it with power until the world quiets, and do not beg me for any favors when it's no longer sufficient to the task."

With the remedy for my disease in my possession, I'd felt well rid of Saverian's attentions and gleefully anticipated setting out on my own business once my obligations to Osriel and Elene were concluded. But a night awash in sweat, plagued with doulon dreams and fits of the shakes, had stolen all the pleasure from my prospective independence. Eventually, I had squeezed enough use from the woman's medallion to soothe my night's ills, but I had sorely missed her hands.

Fingering the gold disk, I glanced over my shoulder. The prince was unrecognizable in thick layers of wool. Somehow I'd thought it might be easier to draw him into conversation with him traveling as Gram, but my every attempt had fallen to naught. In truth he had not spoken to anyone since we'd ridden out of Renna's gates at dawn, leaving Elene behind to tend Brother Victor in Saverian's absence. His visage reflected more of the hammered gold wolf with garnet eyes above my bedchamber door than my friend Gram.

Stearc's back vanished around a steep bank. The billowing curtains of snow had thinned, so that as we followed the thane around the prominence, the rugged borderlands opened to every side. Rival claims, blood feuds, and banditry had ever festered in this harsh land. A few Ardran manses, where villeins worked their lords' wheat fields, lay nose to jowl with Evanori fortresses and freeholds, where crofters kept flocks of rangy goats or coaxed rye and oats from the thin soil under the protection of their warlords.

A little past midday, the air grew thick with black smoke. Voushanti dispatched Philo to scout the road ahead and drew the little troop close around us. Swords were loosed in their scabbards. A flurry of powdery snow announced the warrior's return.

"Raiders burnt out Edane Godsear's villeins at sunrise this morning," said the ginger-bearded warrior. "Harrowers, not bandits. The village is ash. The women say their men were called to the manse, as it's burning as well, and they've seen smoke rising from both north and west."

"Is the manse still under attack?" asked Voushanti, who had come up to the front beside Stearc.

"No, lord," said Philo.

Voushanti and Saverian were of a mind to turn back. Had I not been accustomed to the monks' signing speech, I might have missed Osriel's gesture; as he adjusted his grip on his reins, one gloved finger broke out from his curled hand to point decisively forward.

"We've business west," said Stearc. "No rabble with torches and billhooks will hinder us."

We rode on. The Ardran village had comprised no more than eight or ten dwellings, huddled near the crossing of road and a stream. Naught but a clay baker's oven was left standing. Women stood paralyzed beside the smoldering ruins, children clutching their skirts. Plumes of smoke and billowing snow could not hide their smudged cheeks or the dull eyes that stared hopelessly as we rode past.

"Lord Stearc," said the prince softly, urging his mount up beside the thane. "We cannot just pass them by."

"We can do nothing for them, Gram. Godsear will see to their welfare. It's too dangerous to linger where raiders can hide so easily."

"They're stronger than we are and accustomed to hardship," said Saverian. "If they've no help for themselves, an hour's attention from us is not going to change their fate."

The prince bowed his head in deference. "You heard Philo's report, mistress. The manse itself is burned. We *must* stop."

And so, of course, we did. Osriel was the first off his horse. He engaged himself with one person, then the next, prodding each to move and think. "Goodwife, have you a place to shelter? Family? You must get out of this weather.

Gammy, have you a root cellar here? Or root crops under
the snow? Boy, use that fence pole to shove the embers together to make a fire. Then get your sister and bring the unburned beams to build a windbreak. Help your mam stay
warm through the night. Have you menfolk?"

Most of the women were lone—their husbands already
dead or gone with their lord to fight for the feckless Perryn, which they believed the same as dead. And rightly so.
The men called to the manse to help fight the fire had been
graybeards or cripples or boys under fifteen.

Saverian dressed burns and tended injuries, moving
briskly from one to the next. Our warriors offered packets of bread or cheese, sympathetic ears, and strong arms
to build shelters. The people gawked at me, wondering, as
if I might perform some magic to rebuild their lives. But
of course, they didn't know I was the most useless of sorcerers. I managed only to uncover their well with a minor
voiding spell, but I had no confidence they could survive
the frigid night.

"The new year will bring a new king," Gram told one
trembling goodwife. "Survive until then. Greet him with
your needs and sorrows. Those who have done this deed
are not messengers of great powers, but vile ravagers, and
your king will call them to account for this crime. Gods do
not begrudge you a roof."

After an hour, we rode on. Though our escort remained
alert, we encountered no Harrowers, only the path of destruction they had crafted. Every manse, croft, village, and
sheep shed we passed by lay in ruins, some already cold
ashes, some still blazing. We stopped wherever we found
people, whether Evanori or Ardran, whether villeins,
noblewomen bundled in charred furs, frightened boys, or
grizzled crofters with burnt hands. Some mumbled fear-
fully of the blind immortal Gehoum, afraid even to help
themselves. But more picked themselves up and set about
their own survival once they heard that a new king would
bring them aid with the new year.

As we rode past a ragged Evanori procession on their
way from their charred hillside to a warlord's hold, I moved
to Osriel's side. "Why, lord?" I said softly so that the soldiers
could not hear. "Why do you not reveal yourself to these

people? Not that you are Eodward's heir ... I understand
that. But how much more would their spirits lift if they
knew the one sharing his bread and blankets to be their
own duc? And how eagerly would they rally to his cause
when he *did* step forward to claim his father's throne?"

"Fear has ever been the Bastard's staunchest ally," he
said, hunching his shoulders against the bitter wind. "Hope
must stand aside and do its work softly until the day is won."
He kicked his mount ahead of mine and said no more.

Seeing the steadied shoulders, the firmer grasps, the
clearer eyes that Gram's care effected, I could not but remember Luviar's talk of the mystical bond between Navronne and its sovereign. *The lack of a righteous king speeds
the ruin of the land.* And so, perhaps, was the reverse true;
the ascension of a righteous sovereign might have consequences deeper than law or politics. I wanted Osriel to be
that king. I believed he could be. But the poisoned fury of
the dead that infused this land and hung like battlefield
smoke inside my skull made me fear that he was not.

For three days we pushed hard, fearing that a new storm
might leave the roads impassable. Late on the third day we
descended a steep pass between two spiny ridges only to
see a grand prospect opened before us, washed in the indigo light of snowy evening. From west to east the dark,
jagged gorge of the River Kay sliced the frosted landscape
of treeless terraces. Just below us the river plunged down a
great falls and veered northward through broken foothills,
where, freed from the confining rock, its character altered
into the lazy sweeping flow that fed the fertile valley where
Gillarine lay.

Bridging the gorge a quellé west of the falls was Caedmon's arch, its broken entry pillars on the Ardran side
resembling thick ice spears. And just north of the pillars
lay the crossroads where I had first glimpsed a Dané and
a tree that did not grow in the human plane. My stomach
tightened.

"Lord Stearc," I said, coaxing my balky horse up beside
the thane as the road wound downward onto the flatter approaches to the bridge. "Call a halt as soon as we're across.
I'll lead from there."

He jerked his head in assent. Before very long, Stearc passed over the bridge and between the broken pillars. He raised his hand.

"Saints and spirits," I mumbled, as I reined in beside him, gulping great lungfuls of Ardran winter. *Blessed Ardra*. The clouds seemed thinner this side of the bridge, the air clearer . . . cleaner. Only my own anxieties thrummed my veins, not the muted violence and suffering that had tainted my every breath in Evanore. I felt as if a mountain had rolled off my back.

"Are you ill, Magnus? It's been only a few hours since you renewed the damping spell." Saverian slipped from her saddle, squinting at me as if I were a two-headed cow. She'd not spoken three words to me all day. Only diseases piqued her interest.

"On the contrary," I said, wishing she weren't watching as I lifted my mangled bum from the saddle and dropped to the ground. I winced, but managed not to groan aloud. "Both health and spirits seem much improved now we're this side of the river."

"Except for the posterior." Her slanted brows mocked a frown and her small mouth quirked, as she cupped her hand beside her mouth and whispered, "However will you ride naked?"

Gods . . . A number of entirely crude retorts came to mind, but they would likely only encourage the creature. I vowed to ignore her and her odd humor.

Leaving the horses with Voushanti and the soldiers, we joined Osriel and Stearc beside Caedmon's pillars. Thane and prince were arguing quietly. ". . . But you have too few men to protect you, lord."

"Have the past three days taught you nothing?" snapped the prince. "You need to be out of sight. You carry the light-house ward. Remain at Gillarine until I give you leave to do elsewise."

The thane stalked away, threw himself into the saddle, and barked a command. He and his five men mounted up and soon vanished into the valley of the Kay.

"Are you ready to proceed, my lord, or do you wish to wait for morning?" I said, removing my mask now Stearc's men were gone. Voushanti, Philo, and Melkire had dismounted and were sharing a skin of ale with Saverian. The prince sat on a stained block of marble fallen from the shattered columns.

"We go now. I'd rather not push our luck with the weather."

"All I know to do is try to find the Sentinel Oak and seek a way to take us past it. I gather we've brought no nivat?" Though my voice remained determinedly neutral, conscience and resolution battled the guilty hope that he would contradict me. Would he dare tell me if they had it?

"No nivat." The prince rubbed his neck as if to ease the stiffness. "What need to lure the Danae into our lands, when your talents can take us into theirs? I trust we'll have no inflated illusions today."

Relieved, yes, truly relieved, I told myself, I sought some trace of good humor in this reference to my artful past. But none of Gram's wry humor or controlled excitement leaked from under Osriel's thick cloak and hood. He manifested only this passionless determination I'd seen throughout this journey.

Voushanti commanded Philo, Melkire, and Saverian to remain with the horses, while he, Gram, and I ventured onward. A few hundred quercae from the bridge, I halted. Time to keep my promise to Elene.

"My lord, perhaps we should discuss how we're to approach the Danae. If I could but understand the terms of your discussion, what exactly we are seeking from them, what's to happen on the solstice . . ."

"That is not your concern. The time for discussion has passed." And that was that.

I could have refused to take him farther, but I had no means to weigh the world's need against Elene's fears. If I postponed my leaving, stayed close if and when this meeting took place, then perhaps I could glean Osriel's purpose.

"It *is* my concern, lord, as your contracted adviser and as a fellow member of the lighthouse cabal. Eventually we must and will discuss it. For now, for the Danae's safety and our need for understanding, I'll fulfill our bargain."

I knelt and touched my hands to earth. At first I sensed nothing beyond the scrape of snow crystals on my wrists and cold grit under my palms. A momentary panic struck

me that Saverian's medallion had left my bent useless.
But she had insisted that it should not, and as distasteful
as her arrogance might be, she had convinced me of her
competence.

I closed my eyes and filled my lungs with the cold air,
imagining its pungent clarity sweeping aside all worries of
Elene and Osriel, of lost souls and abducted children, of
familial lies, gravid warnings, and looming birthdays. My
fingers prickled and warmed, and I swept my mind across
the frozen ground.

Beneath the wind-crusted snow lay a mat of yellowed
grass and dormant roots, clotted with damp soil and stones.
Sheep had grazed here along with deer, elk, and horned
goats come down from the mountains. The beasts left a
threadwork of trails down to the willow brakes and fens of
the Kay. Human hunters, trappers, and other travelers had
beaten two paths across the meadow—one leading down
the valley toward villages, abbeys, and cities, the other up
the bald rocky prominence to the thick-walled castle men
named Fortress Groult. At the conjunction of these paths
lingered the faint warm residue of sorcery.

Not much magical structure remained of my illusion—a
knotty stump magically inflated from an astelas vine, meant
to convince Gram and Stearc that I could read my grandfather's book of maps. Yet two months ago that cheat's ploy
had spanned the barrier between true life and myth, between the realm of men and Aeginea. On a meadow with
naught growing taller than my knee, I had glimpsed an oak
tree with a trunk the breadth of my armspan and a canopy
that could shelter a small village, and my companions and
I had encountered a Dané female with moth wings on her
breasts. I had yet to understand how I'd managed such a
feat, but I hoped to repeat it.

My magic enveloped the spot of warmth. Recalling the
great tree's particular shape and the wonder I had felt
upon seeing it, I sought some trace of a Danae presence
upon the land, some evidence of the juncture of two planes
that existed here.

The frozen world, the whickering horses, my companions, and my fears receded, and my mind filled with an
abundance of the familiar and mundane—the paths of an-

cient sledges drawn up the hill to build the fortress, the remnants of siege engines and destroying raids, the blood and
pain humans left everywhere they walked. Sounds, smells,
tastes echoed the richness of the land and its history. Trees
had once populated these terraced meadows: maples and
oaks, spruce and fir, white-trunked birch. I concentrated,
stretched, delved deeper . . .

. . . and came near drowning in music. A legion of musicians must have walked here, leaving behind songs in
varied voices . . . a pipe, a harp, a vielle, some instruments
unknown to me . . . everywhere random snips of melody
that on another day would fascinate and delight. But on
this day the pervasive music distracted me, and I pushed
past it . . . deeper yet . . . until I felt the weight of the land,
the slow-moving rivers of the deeps, the impenetrable roots
of the mountains.

Puzzled and anxious, I reminded myself to breathe amid
such ponderous life. Yet I sensed more in the deeps: heat . . .
circling movement . . . stone dissolved in eternal fire . . .

I backed away quickly. No beings left traces so deep as
this. No presence I'd a mind to encounter. I retreated to the
veils of music, each melody as rich and holy as plainsong,
of marvelous variety, yet not intruding one upon the other,
as if designed—

Understanding blossomed like an unfolding lily. Brother
Sebastian had taught me that plainsong was a medium
of prayer—bearing the petitions we would submit to the
gods—and also a mode of prayer—a state of mind that ex-
alted the soul and opened our thoughts to heaven. I focused
my inner eyes and ears upon the music as if squinting to see
differently or angling my head to pick up fainter sounds,
and I began to see and hear and feel what I had previously
gleaned in random glimpses and snippets. As blue sigils
upon smooth flesh, traces more numerous than the paths
of deer had been drawn on the land's music, circling, dividing, rejoining. The earth's music served as the favored
medium of the earth's guardians—their paint and canvas,
their clay—opening the mind and senses to the deepest
truths of the world. Danae shaped paths of music, imposing harmony . . . patterns . . . where they walked. No single
thread laid across the landscape, but many silver threads

that joined and divided and crossed one another. And now the path lay before me, I, Janus de Cartamandua's son, could surely walk it.

I jumped to my feet. "Follow me."

Mesmerized, I strode across the snow-clad meadow toward a spreading oak that had not yet shed its russet leaves. When at last I touched its bark, I marveled that the great bole's rugged solidity did not waver or vanish. Laughing as would a man freed from the gallows, I pressed my back to the trunk and peered at the hazy blue sky beyond the spreading canopy—no longer winter evening, but autumn afternoon. The chill that nipped my skin tasted of fruit and wine. Then was my attention captured by the prospect beyond the shaded circle.

Earth's Holy Mistress . . . Bathed in the steep-angled sunlight, the land fell away in the familiar giant's steps to the river valley far below. But here, the grass was not crushed with early snow. Rather it rippled in golden, ankle-high luxuriance. The great forests of the Kay, thicker, taller, stretched well beyond the boundaries I knew, so that swaths of red-leaved maples, of deep green spruce and fir and russet oak lapped even these upland slopes and spilled onto these grassy meads. A kite screeched and dived from the deepening sky, only to soar upward in an arc of such exultant grace as to bring a lump to my chest.

No evidence of the human travelers' road scarred the autumn landscape. No warriors' refuge had been hacked from the rocky pinnacle where Fortress Groult had loomed only moments before. I spun in my tracks. No human work existed anywhere within my sight, nor did any prince, warrior, physician, or beast.

"Lord Prince!" I called, hurriedly retracing my path toward the gorge, out from under the tree . . . back from golden afternoon to indigo evening and snow. When Osriel and Voushanti came back into view, standing not twenty paces from the barren crossroads, I grinned and beckoned, shouting as the wind billowed my cloak. "You'd best stay close!"

Osriel's eyes gleamed as hard as garnet. The deep twilight left Saverian, the soldiers, and the horses as anonymous smudges by the broken pillars of the bridge approach. "You've found your way, then? We lost sight of you."

"Ah, lord, it is a wonder ..." Osriel's somber visage stilled my desire to babble of music and sunlight. As did Elene, I feared his soul already lay beyond the rock gate without hope of heaven.

Reversing course toward the oak, I walked more slowly this time, relishing the passage, feeling the land and light shift all around me. I sensed a strip of woodland to my left before I could see it, smelled the intoxicating air of Aeginea while human paths yet lay beneath my feet. Voushanti's mumbling told me he saw the tree well after it had come into my view.

When we reached the tree, Osriel touched the craggy bark, and his gaze explored the spreading canopy. It grieved me that I could read no wonder in him.

"I would venture the opinion that we stand in Danae lands, Lord Prince," I said softly, as the dry leaves rustled in the breeze, a few drifting from the branches above us, "and that the meeting you have sought is at hand." For indeed another marvel awaited us.

Striding upslope from the valley were five Danae, their elongated shadows gliding across the rippling grass as if they flew. A big, well-muscled male led the party, his ageless face reflecting unbounded hauteur. A wreath of autumn leaves rested on a cascade of rust-colored hair that fell below his slender waist. A female walked alongside him. Though taller than most human women, she appeared but a wisp beside his imposing height and sculpted sinews. The skin beneath her blue sigils glowed the softest hue of sunrise, and a cap of scarlet curls framed her delicately pointed face. Her lean body spoke of naught but strength.

Slightly behind these two, almost as tall as the male, walked the disdainful female we had met here two months ago—she whose angular face was scribed with a coiled lizard, her flat breasts with intricately drawn moth wings. The Sentinel, Gram had named her. Woodrush and willow, mold and damp—did I truly catch her scent at such a distance or was it but memory?

These creatures value human life less than that of grass

or sticks, I reminded myself, summoning disdain and repugnance, lest the empty yearning of that magical night overwhelm me again.

Two other males trailed behind. They seemed younger, less ... developed ... than their leader. Or perhaps that was only my assumption as they had no sigils marked on their unsmiling faces. They carried bundles in their arms.

"Let us walk out, Valen. Best let them see us." The prince's command startled me, and my feet obeyed without consulting my head for a reason not. Osriel and I stepped beyond the oak canopy together, Voushanti so close behind I could feel his breath on my neck.

The five Danae halted ten paces away, wholly unsurprised, as if they had come here purposefully to meet us. The hair on my arms prickled, as my true father's warning crept into my memory: *Go not into their lands 'til thou art free ... not until eight-and-twenty.* My belief that Danae other than Kol did not know me dulled with the fast-failing sunlight, for it could not be mere imagining that five pairs of aspen-gold eyes had fixed on me.

"*Envisia seru, ongai ... engai.*" Prince Osriel inclined his head to the two in front.

"My lord," I said softly. "What is—?"

"So a human knows of manners ... and how to keep a bargain," interrupted the small female as if I did not exist. The breeze wafted the sweetness of white pond lilies. "Awe embraces me. But I cannot return thy offered greeting. The sight of thee doth *not* delight my eye, Betrayer-son."

"As ever, the long-lived honor their word," said the prince, nodding coldly to the Sentinel. "Thus I presume it is Tuari Archon"—he acknowledged the male—"and his consort, Nysse"—and the female—"who honor me with their hearing. I regret that my presence offends. My sire reverenced the long-lived and their ways, and rued the division that grew between him and thee. As do I. As thine eyes attest, and the call of thy blood will surely affirm, I have brought thee that which was stolen." His slender hand pointed at me.

No heat, no fire, no explosion of astonishment ignited my soul. Rather a deadly cold crept upward from my toes as floodwaters swamp a drowning man. This quiet betrayal should no more surprise me than should the sharp bite of Voushanti's dagger now threatening to pierce my spine. Would I never learn? *Ignorant, gullible, damnable simpleton.* My family … my true parents … Luviar … Elene … Gildas … Osriel … they were all the same. Only a sentimental fool could have imagined that Osriel the Bastard, master of secrets, might possess some trace of honor and friendship and set me free as he had promised. A prince who had used an innocent boy to gain my oath of submission would not flinch at using me to gain—what?

"What is my blood-price, Lord Osriel?" I snapped before they could complete their inspection of me. "Now you've had your use of me, you might as well explain. At the least may it be some magic to avert the world's end, for of a sudden I've lost all confidence that you are capable of illuminating your lighthouse for any Scholar. And I'd surely not wish my life to feed the evil that lies beyond Renna's rock gate."

He did not flinch. Neither did he offer me further assurances that my life was not at risk. "You will not be alone in your sacrifice," he said.

The two younger Danae had glided to either side of us, cutting off what escape paths did not lie through the Danae or Voushanti's knife. They laid aside what they carried—loops of braided rope tangled with some thick articles of wood—and stood alert. Watching me. Yet for that moment, as I met my master's hard gaze, bitterness outflanked fear. "Perhaps those who have no sorry history as liars and renegades will be given a choice as to their sacrifice—along with the grace of their lord's trust. Despite your dark mysteries … I would have served you willing, Prince, had you but asked."

At that, a tinge of color did touch his cheeks. But he did not waver. "Life is pain," he said. "Only movement—purpose—can make it bearable. As your life's path has now brought you here, I'd recommend you summon what resources you possess to meet your fate. You are not helpless."

He turned his back on me, opening his palms to the Danae in invitation. "Shall we proceed with our exchange? The day wanes. The world wanes. Our people suffer—both yours and mine. Our alliance promises hope for all of them."

Tuari opened his palm in acceptance. "Let us walk, Betrayer-son. You bargained news of the Scourge."

"There is a woman named Sila Diaglou," said Osriel, moving to Tuari's side. "She and her followers wish to return humankind to a primitive chaos . . ."

Heads together, the archon, his consort, and Osriel strolled into the evening meadow. Voushanti and the Sentinel trailed after them at a respectful distance. An owl soared through the air and settled on Moth's shoulder—an owl just like the one that had tricked me and my companions into the bogs.

The two young Danae stepped toward me. At once Janus's warnings took on a firm and terrifying reality. I'd come to Aeginea before turning eight-and-twenty, Osriel had mentioned sacrifice, and these two had muscles that looked like braided iron. No one was going to help me.

I bolted. I'd covered more than half the distance to the Sentinel Oak before one of them brought me down. Spitting grass and dirt, I slammed my elbow into the naked, wiry body on my back. He grunted, but did not let go. Writhing, twisting, I reached back in hopes of capturing the arm that was locked around my neck like an iron collar. I lifted my hip and bent my leg in unfortunate directions in an attempt to trap his feet. But my foot got tangled in my cloak, the Dané clung like a leech, and he caught my flailing arm with his free hand and pinned it to my side. His legs felt like steel ropes about my hips.

I wrestled my knees underneath my belly and prepared to lurch up and back, relishing the prospect of slamming him to the ground and crushing his balls. But as I rose, his friend pounced, and the two together flattened me again. Air escaped my chest in a painful whoosh.

While I fought to get a breath, the two Danae trussed my wrists and knees. Manhandling me as if I weighed no more than dandelion fluff, they dragged me toward the great oak on my back.

"Is this how the long-lived treat their kin?" I gasped as I bumped across the rocky meadow. The glowing pattern of oak leaves on one fellow's legs pulsed an angry purple in several spots. I hoped that meant they hurt.

"You're but a halfbreed," said the youth on my left as if I might have the intelligence of a stick. "Scarcely kin."

Entirely inappropriate laughter welled up from my depths. "Twice cursed!" Surely no man had ever been so afflicted with purulent family. Both branches of my ancestry grasped to hold on to a wretch that neither of them wanted.

When the dragging stopped, I assumed I'd be left until they were ready to take me wherever they thought to keep me. Did Danae have prisons? But the two uncoiled their loops of braided rope—vines, I thought—shoved me upright, and bound me to the massive trunk. I smothered a smile. No unspelled rope had held me for long since I learned how to make a voiding spell when I was eight. I just needed a little time and something to distract these two.

Yet as twilight dropped its mantle over this landscape, I could not focus on my spellmaking. Once they had secured my upper body to the tree, they spread my ankles apart and fixed them in place with loops of rope, a wooden block snugged firmly behind each knee.

"I would do this in thy stead, Kennet," said the taller of the youths, whose wheat-colored hair was braided with firethorn berries. "I'd not have thy gentle heart troubled by the deed."

The other youth, he of the bruised oak leaves, knotted the rope that fixed my thighs in place and looped it behind the trunk again. "I'd gladly give over the task," he said when he reappeared, "but I'd best not refuse Tuari. Give me leave to settle my spirit and strengthen my arm. I would make it fast and clean."

A third chunk of wood, long and narrow like a club—a very heavy-looking club—lay on the ground behind them.

A fluttering panic rose in my belly. "Great gods of mercy, what are you doing? I *can* be persuaded not to run again. Once sworn, I keep my word."

They wrenched the bindings tighter yet. I strained at the braided rope, but could shift neither legs nor torso so much as a quat. "What offense have I given? I've ever honored the Danae. I've left offerings even when I had naught for myself. Told your stories with reverence."

Their blue sigils glowed like traces of sapphire in the

lowering dusk. A last tweak of my positioning and the Dané with the firethorn braid picked up the club and moved to one side.

"I did not make my father lie with one of you," I said, panic stretching my voice thin. "I've done naught but be born!"

The other youth, Kennet, extended his hand upward as if to grasp a fistful of leaves above his head, then coiled his body into a knot close to the ground. As I watched, breathless with fear, he unwound himself, spun once, and leaped into the air higher than my head, legs stretched fore and behind, as light and quick as a frighted doe leaps a fence.

My heart leaped with him. For a moment the sheer power of his body's feat overshadowed my foreboding. But as he sank to one knee, took a deep breath, and stood up again, terror came rushing back. No time for pride. "Please, I beg you—"

"No deed of thine has brought this trial on thee," said the one holding the club. "Only the Law. Halfbreeds cannot be allowed to corrupt the Canon again. Thou must never dance in Aeginea. Thou shalt not."

"Dance?" My eyes latched on to the brutish stick of wood as he passed it to the dancer Kennet. "I don't even want to *stay* with you! I've no intent to dance anywhere . . . don't know how . . . save in a tavern brawl . . . crude stomping to pipe and tabor . . . nothing like what you do. I'll swear it . . . swear obedience . . . kiss your archon's feet . . . whatever you want. If you cripple me . . . gods, what gives you the right? If you do this, I'm a dead man."

I'd seen what happened to cripples in famine times. For a man who could not read, the only labors that might keep him eating required legs that worked.

"We cannot take the chance. No argument will change that. But be assured, once thou'rt recovered, we'll help thee make a useful life." When I opened my mouth to beg and curse him, he shoved a strip of leather between my teeth. "Bite down hard."

Kennet stepped toward me, the club poised on a line with my left knee. I slammed the back of my head against the ridged oak bark, squeezed my eyes shut, and all at once the sky fell and lightning struck . . .

Chapter 12

Stripes of lightning blazed on my breast. On the ground before me writhed a snarl of blue light... thumps, groans... quickly silenced. Beside me a dark shape yanked away ropes and my arms fell free. Dazed... confused... I spat out the strip of leather, but a hand clamped over my mouth, demanding silence before moving back to its other tasks. A whisk of cold steel sliced through the extra loops holding my thighs and knees, and I was free. My knees... intact. Of a sudden my every joint felt like mud.

My senses began to pick the truth out of the darkness. Blade strokes, not lightning strokes, had sliced through the braided rope across my breast. The spreading warmth dampening my shirt was my blood. And I had two rescuers...

Bright blue sigils faded to a dull glow, outlining my captors' sprawled bodies, then winked out. The third Dané, the one who had fallen... or jumped... out of the tree, fumbled at my arms. "How hast thou—?" Hissing enmity spewed through the night as if it were the glowing dragon on his face that spoke. "Who else walks here?"

"Stay away from him!" Saverian's brisk command whipped through the night as my ankles came free, the binding ropes hacked apart by her blade. "Run, Valen!"

Though I could not see the physician herself, her weapon—a dagger the length of my forearm—appeared to my right, reflecting the Dané's blue fire. I stumbled, weak-kneed, to join her.

"No!" Kol stretched out his leg and spun. The dagger went flying. He grappled with the shadowy figure, cutting off her growl of fury, and threw her to the turf. Then his iron hands clamped on to my arm and propelled me away from the oak. "Come with me, Cartamandua-son, or count thyself captive of the archon once more and be broken. The remedy I've given thy captors will not quiet them long."

"Wait! What have you done? The woman . . ." Recovering some semblance of strength, I wrestled free of him and returned to Saverian, relieved to feel the beat of life in her neck. "I'll not leave her." She had thwarted the prince's will and jeopardized his bargain with the Danae, and I trusted neither Osriel's mercy nor his friendship.

"The human is no concern of mine." Kol's voice shivered my bones. "She interfered where she had no business."

So did you, I think, uncle. Though not for love of me. The memory of his grieving at Clyste's Well remained as vivid as on the day I'd witnessed it. Duty, not care, had brought him to my rescue.

The Dané moved away, the words trailing behind him. "Stay if thou willst. Gratefully will I be finished with thee."

I had only a moment to decide. Kol seemed honest at least, both in his dislike and in his grief. He held out some hope of evading Osriel, whose perfidy had sapped all faith. No vow, no pledged service for whatever cause, should require a man be crippled. I scooped the limp physician into my arms, heaved her over my shoulder, and hurried after the Dané, praying the gods to forgive my presumption of divine benevolence in the face of my oath breaking.

We moved west on undulating ground, the river a constant rush on our left, and the bulge of land and rock that formed the pinnacle of Fortress Groult a swelling blackness against the starry sky on our right. I fixed my eyes on the blue-limned shape ahead of me, while concentrating every other sense and instinct on my footing. The Dané acknowledged my presence with neither glance nor speech, but the distance between us did not vary, no matter that I flagged under Saverian's weight on every uphill pitch. He could have vanished in an instant. I had no choice but to trust him.

The night deepened. My shoulders ached. The wind

grew into a constant buffeting, whipping my face with
the hem of Saverian's cloak and the flaps of her leather
skirt. The physical effort and the concentration required to
avoid a fall made thinking impossible. So it was only when
a sudden gust from my left staggered me that I noted the
change in the air. The wind smelled vaguely of fish and felt
odd—cold, yes, but heavy and sticky. A quick look around
staggered me as well. Not three steps to my left, the earth
plunged precipitously into the night. The far side of the river
gorge had vanished. And beyond those black depths . . . the
river's voice had changed into a rhythmic pounding crash.
"Kol," I called. "Where are we?"

He did not respond. I repeated the call several times,
especially once the path began a twisting descent that oft-
times seemed more vertical than not. Sand and gravel on
the path set my boots skidding and my heart galloping.
Immediately after one jolting slide, when only a nubbin of
crumbling rock had saved me from skidding off the path
and plummeting the rest of the distance to the bottom of
the cliff, Saverian began to squirm, mumbling something
about hands and castration. Her heavy cloak, leather over-
skirt, woolen riding breeches, and leggings were all in a
bunch about her thighs, half obscuring my vision.

"For the love of the Mother, hold still," I shouted, planting my heel in a crack well suited to a cliff swallow's roost.
"I've no place to set you down. And you don't want to see
where we'll land if you throw me off balance."

If she spoke I didn't hear her, but she did settle. The roar
of the sea grew louder, the scent of salt wrack affirming
the evidence of my ears. At a slight leveling of the track, I
risked another glance. A star-filled sky illumined the white
curls of breaking waves.

Ardra touched the western sea just north of the tin
mines and cliffside sea fortresses of Cymra. But to reach
the shore one must cross the wilds of the Aponavi, painted
clansmen who herded goats and crafted rugs and collected
heads for sport. To consider how far we might have traveled stretched my tired mind beyond reason.

Below me, Kol's fiery sigils vanished, and I hurried
onto the next downward pitch. My left boot slid sidewise
toward the void . . . *Concentrate, fool!* But my right boot

had no purchase on the skittering rocks, and I dared not trust it with our combined weight. Three quick steps at once brought me to another course reversal and an even steeper pitch. I dared not pause the entire last quarter of the descent, so that when I hurtled onto a shore of rippled sand I had difficulty persuading my feet to stop before they quickstepped right into the sea.

"Great Deunor's grandmother!" I said, dropping to my aching knees . . . my blessed, aching, unsplintered knees. A rush of gratitude led me to deposit Saverian onto the sand with far more care than my screaming shoulders would prefer. Then I sat back on my heels, gulping air. She sat up, pulled her half-unraveled braid out of her face, and gaped.

"You've infected me with your madness." Narrowing her eyes to slits, she rubbed her temples vigorously. "Else I've bumped my head, and all this"—she waved at the sea and sky and sand without looking at them—"is but my own mind's imagining. If you tell me it's neither, and that I've not just dreamed performing the single most appallingly stupid act of my life, I beg you snap my neck quickly."

"You saved my life, lady—you and he." I nodded a hundred quercae down the shore where Kol sat on a cluster of boulders, long arms wrapped around his bent knees, allowing the sea spray to shower him. "I could not leave you to reap Osriel's whirlwind for your kindness. But truth be told, I don't know as I've done you any favor. I've no idea where he's brought us . . ." . . . assuming Kol had *brought us* here at all. Just because I had managed to follow him didn't mean he wished us to be here.

She bent her head to her knees and beat her fists on her skull. Mumbled invective flowed from her like lava from a volcano. Her inventive mixture of human anatomy and unlikely violence altogether lifted my spirits.

The chill, damp wind flapped my cloak. Driftwood lay about the shore, tempting me to direct the prickly mage's attention to fire. But the luminous breakers, the wind-borne scent of unknown shores, and a heaven filled with brilliant stars of such profusion and arrangement as I had never witnessed reminded me that we were not in our own land, but lost in Aeginea.

I pushed up to my feet. "I must speak to him before anything. Find out where he's brought us and what he wants of me. You'll be all right for a bit?"

"On the day I require the protection of a lunatic, I'll snap my *own* neck. Yes, please go find out where we are, so I'll know whether I've a better choice to travel east to Estigure or west to Cymra to find a new employer." Her gaze, sparked with starlight, traveled up and down my height. "You're going to tell me we're in the realm of angels, aren't you? And that the naked man with the exceedingly odd skin that I've imagined seeing is some kin of yours?"

I grinned down at her. "My uncle. Though he's as loath as my every other kinsman to claim me. I'll be back as soon as I may, and I'd advise not burning anything right away."

I tramped the short distance down the broad tidal flats, finding it easier going than slogging through the dunes. Kol took no notice of my coming. Mustering every shred of graceful manners my tutors had beaten into me, I bowed and spoke the greeting Osriel had used. The Dané might not delight my eye, but my gratitude could not be measured. "*Envisia seru*, Kol. How may I serve thee in recompense for sound legs?"

"Be unborn." He continued to stare into the churning sea.

The rebellious ember that yet denied the story of my birth winked out of existence. Seeking shelter from the wind and spray, I squeezed between his waist-high perch and another slab, pressed my weary back to the damp stone, and sat.

"If wishing could accomplish such a thing, gods know it would have happened long before now," I said, twisting my aching shoulders. "My father's family wished it. Many's the time *I've* wished it—but that was before I learned that I had a kinswoman who could be spoken of as 'beloved of every Dané for her joyful spirit.' "

"Do not think to ingratiate thyself by speaking of her."

"I've no wish to ingratiate myself with any of your kind," I snapped, his arrogance a cold wash on my conciliatory sensibilities. "You have extended me favors I never asked of you and that are clearly at odds with your own inclinations. Thus I must assume it is your sister's desires you serve and that she wished us to treat each other with honor, if naught else. I offer no less than she would ask—and no more."

After a long moment, he jerked his head in agreement. "I retract my unworthy accusation."

Resisting the temptation to gasp in mock astonishment, I gestured at the desolate shore. "So, why would my mother want me here?"

"She chose me as thy vayar—thy teacher. The shores of Evaldamon provide a suitable place for teaching and are little traveled. Days pass slowly here. Yet were the days each the lingering of a season, the task is already impossible. I smell the remasti close upon thee. Once a body has passed the last remasti unchanged, naught can be done to alter it."

"The last remasti . . . my birthday."

He squeezed his eyes shut and ground his jaw. "Clyste trusted the Cartamandua to bring thee to me in the proper season—long ago. Despite what human lies tell, the long-lived do not steal human children away to Aeginea. Clyste's innocence burned as the stars; the Cartamandua's false promises stank as human dwellings do."

"So it was for one broken promise that you stole Janus's mind—stole his life." Kol's arrogance revolted me. "You mourn for my mother who broke your laws and sent me off with him. Yet for a failed human man, you alone issue a judgment that breaks all bounds of compassion. I've no desire for your lessons."

"Which is precisely why the teaching would be useless."

The Dané unfolded his legs, pressed the bottoms of his feet together, and drew his heels close to his groin. I squirmed as I watched, imagining the uncomfortable stretch. Clasping his hands together, he straightened his arms over his head, then slowly bent his body forward until his chest came near touching the surface of the flat rock. I hugged my knees tightly, as if someone might prod me to replicate his move.

The silence lagged. Already I rued my hasty retort. My life demanded answers. I needed to understand what I was and what I would be, come the winter solstice.

"You brought me here despite your belief that I could not learn what you would teach," I said. "She had some plan, didn't she ... my mother? She mated with Janus because she—"

"I will not speak of that joining." He sprang to his feet, his sigils pulsing, posture and voice articulating bald humiliation. "It is enough that my sister's blood flows in thy veins. She believed the Everlasting had accounted a place for thee in the Canon. This I cannot and will not accept. And if ever such a disordered event were possible, the season of its accomplishment has long passed. Yet even so late in this waning season I know what she would ask of me."

"The Canon. A vayar is—" I pounced upon the absurdity, astonishment ruining my intent to curb my tongue. "You don't think to teach me to dance?"

His face, long, narrow, and perfectly formed, might have been cold marble beneath his sigils. "No. But if I gift thee the separation gard, as if thou wert a nestling new released from thy parents' side, the Law forbids Tuari to damage thee without informing thy *argai*—thy eldest kin, who is Stian, my sire. The custom provides only a delay, shouldst thou be taken captive again, for the archon's judgment of a halfbreed will never be other than breaking. But it might give trustworthy companions a chance to protect thee." He jumped down from the rock, landing on his bare feet with the weight of thistledown. "If I can convince Stian to agree and gift thee the walking gard as well, thou canst move through the world with certain skills of the long-lived, which will aid thee in eluding capture. Clyste would wish these protections for thee, though all other wishes fail."

"The gards ... these markings ... the sigils of Danae magic ..." My hands crept inside my sleeves and rubbed my arms. Denial rose like bile in my throat. But a glance at the sea, churning a few paces from my boots where it had no business being, slowed my retort. The Danae could travel impossible distances ... vanish as if they had wings ... hide.

Twelve years I had hidden from the detestable life my pureblood birth prescribed for me. Lacking purpose beyond staying free, lacking skills beyond health and wits, I'd survived by embracing the chances Serena Fortuna had placed in my way. I had never turned my back on the divine damsel. And now matters were far more complicated.

I might be able to find a route out of Aeginea, but I could not imagine where I might be safe from Osriel's wrath *and* from these Danae who would maim me *and* from the Pureblood Registry, who yet believed me pureblood and would run me to ground without mercy did Osriel but hint that I had violated my contract. More important, a stolen child awaited rescue—so I prayed—and a murdered child awaited justice. I no longer had confidence that Prince Osriel would weigh their needs important beside this mysterious course he had chosen.

"So you could just . . . mark . . . me and I could travel as you do?"

"Not so simply as that. I would provide thee the necessary teaching."

"And the price? I understand that your . . . gifting . . . is to Clyste, not to me. But to gain these skills, surely I must be required to yield something. Janus warned me to stay away until I was eight-and-twenty . . . past this last change . . ."

"The Cartamandua never understood the remasti or the gards." Kol's tone made it clear that folk held higher opinion of crawling snakes than he did of the man who'd fathered me. "Janus believed a vayar imposed some alteration upon the body at the remasti, thus making it something other than ordained by birth. Even while promising to do as Clyste asked, he confessed his fear that I would make thee more our kind than his. To him birth was blood, and blood was all. But the change is already trapped within thee. Necessary, even for one with a human parent. Thy own skills and talents and practices determine the partitioning of thy nature—entirely of humankind, entirely of the long-lived, or somewhere part of each."

"So my father was wrong, and you, who despise me and my kind, will generously share your Danae magic with me." Kol's assurances sounded promising, but I could not bar Janus's wild eyes and drooling mouth from my memory.

Exasperation broke through his chilly reserve. "I shall not harm thee. Many easier ways could I damage thee, if vengeance were my intent. I could have left thee for Tuari to be broken. Do thou pass the time of the last remasti entirely unchanged, thy skin will harden into a prison and thy spirit shall die captive within it. To change, thou must yield only the desire to remain ignorant and incapable and incomplete."

Ignorant and incapable and incomplete ... my skin a prison. A pureblood diviner reading my cards could not have so captured the entirety of my existence. My gaze traveled the length of Kol's marked limbs. What did it feel like? Would my own human magic behave differently ... be lost? Great gods, did Danae eat? Make love? Well, of course ... I was evidence of that. But all I knew was fireside tales of beings forced to live as stone or trees, who died when trapped within walls. Different. Not human. I rubbed cheek and jaw, as if I might discover lines and sworls waiting beneath my skin.

Events were moving so rapidly. Gildas had taken Jullian to Sila Diaglou as a tool to manipulate me. Weeks it had been already. If she came to believe the boy of no use to her ... I could not allow that, which meant my time was short. Yet Danae magic might make all the difference, enable me to get him away, to learn and do the things I needed to do. The lighthouse must endure, no matter what wickedness Osriel the Bastard thought to work with solstice magic.

I blinked and gazed up at Kol. "How long would this take?"

He threw up his hands. "How long, how many, how far, how much. Hast thou no questions of substance?" He pointed to the rock where he'd sat. "If thou art here when the sun wakes from the cliff, I will begin thy teaching, as my sister would desire."

He turned his back and waded into the sea. Once the slack water lapped his thighs he dived into the rolling waves. Lightning the color of lapis and indigo infused the churning surf and then faded.

Snugged between the two chunks of granite, wavelets creeping ever closer to my toes, I tried desperately to think of some reason *not* to be here in the morning. But I could command neither mind nor body to any useful purpose ... what with the exertions of the day ... with this unknowable path beneath my feet ...

"You didn't ask him about a fire." Saverian's head popped up from the far side of Kol's rock, causing me to slam an elbow into the rock. My heart crashed into my ribs with the impact of the surf.

"Mother Samele's tits, do you forever sneak around and show up where you're not invited?"

"I've noted several nice-sized chunks of wood lying around. I can either set them afire so that you're not quaking like an Aurellian torturer on Judgment Night, or I can use them to turn your knees to powder as your other relatives proposed. And then I'll politely ask the naked gentleman to tell me where in the Sky Lord's creation you've brought me. You forgot to discover that, as well."

I *was* trembling. Fear had its part, no question. But the damp had penetrated my sweat-soaked garments, as well, and though in no wise as frigid as in Evanore, the wind cut through the layered wool like Ardran lances. "I'd say burn what you like. He's not going to be happy no matter what I do. Can you see where he's gone?"

Her gaze roved the enclosing night. "We should leave this place. Use your skills and get us away. Trusting a creature like that . . ." She shuddered. "His spirit is surely a glacier. He may have had feelings for his sister, but he has no feelings for you. He doesn't even hate. He exists."

"So speaks the woman who serves the Duc of Evanore."

She came round the rock and offered me her hand. "Osriel of Evanore is a human man of extraordinary discipline. His passions run very deep and sometimes lead him to ill choices. But I understand him."

"Explain the *ill choice* of crippling his friends." Weary to the bone, I accepted her hand—unusually cold on this night—and hauled myself up. We strolled down the shore, collecting the odd bits of wood thrown up on the sand. "Will he forgive what you did tonight?"

"Forgiveness is not Osriel's strength. He tolerates no weakness in himself, and while he does not expect the same of those who serve him, he *does* expect their trust. No matter how I argue with him, I've always given him that in the end."

"Even with whatever mystery lies beyond the rock gate at Dashon Ra?"

She halted in midstep. "If you ever whisper of that again, even in private, I'll unravel my spell and leave you gibbering until your mind is muck. Elene is a fool to have shown you." She snatched an arm-length branch from the sand. "*Never* misapprehend. I am Osriel of Evanore's loyal servant whether or not I dare stand in his presence again. As for tonight ... in no way was I prepared to tend horses while you and Osriel strolled into heaven or hell or wherever we are. And when their intentions became clear ... No worthy physician could stand by and see a healthy body damaged. But be assured I will always wonder what might have happened if I had let events play out as he planned. You would have survived without my intrusion."

So she knew at least somewhat of Osriel's plan for Dashon Ra. Unfortunately, as we wandered about the shore filling our arms, naught in her demeanor invited further discourse. At last we threw our bits and pieces into a pile, and I spread my arms so my cloak might block the wind as she arranged them and worked her magic. With her third snapped "*flagro*," the center of the little pile began to smolder. She broke off splinters of the half-rotted wood to coax and nourish the little flame.

"I should have you teach me how to do that," I said, stretching my hands toward the growing flames. "Probably more use than what Kol will teach me."

"You're going to allow him to work his wiles on you? Have you heard no tale of the Danae? Great Mother, preserve my reason, you *are* a fool."

"So, my wise physician, come up with a better suggestion before tomorrow—something that does not include mutilation, chains, or removal of my eyes. An innocent child languishes in captivity, his days short unless I show up to claim him, and another lies dead, and I'm the only one who seems to care anymore. Indeed I've done nothing of worth in my life, and see little prospect of it. But everything in this world has a purpose: clouds, thorns, fleas. Perhaps I'll do better as a ... whatever I am ... than I've done thus far, pretending to be human."

We sat in uncomfortable silence. Saverian's stomach growled. My own had near gnawed itself through, and we'd not a scrap of food or drink between us. Though her flames grew and bathed my front side in warmth, I could not stop shaking.

A soft slapping sound from the darkness to my left sent me to my feet like a whipcrack. A dripping Kol stepped into the ring of firelight, tossed two fish the size of my boot soles onto the sand in front of us, then walked into the night without a word.

"So, are you mad or sane this morning?"

Saverian's bent must signal her when a person's awareness returned, for I'd not so much as lifted an eyelid or stirred a muscle in my nest of sand. I managed only a grunt in reply. Such early questioning left a body no time to enjoy those few moments of uncomplicated, irresponsible satiation that occur between sleep and waking. It didn't seem at all fair.

Of course, I *had* waked her with my screaming in the middle of the night, convinced the sea's crashing signaled the world's end and that hurricane-driven knives were flaying me. I vaguely recalled her yanking the gold disk from my neck and wrestling my thrashing limbs quiet as it sent forth its maggoty magic to quell the onslaught. Humiliating. I'd been so sure I could control her spell.

"You've likely an hour until the sun's above the cliff," she said. "There's fresh water in the rocks down that way where the cliff's collapsed."

I rolled to all fours, spitting sand, blinking away sand, shaking my head to speed the shower of sand from my hair. The stuff had crept into my boots and my ears and every pore and crevice in between. As I stumbled through the cold gray dawn to relieve the pressure of food and drink, the grit abraded my feet, my eyes, my waist, and my groin.

I returned to our little camp clearer in the head at least. No matter what happened with Kol, if I thought to go anywhere and accomplish anything afterward, I needed Saverian's medallion back, along with better teaching as to how to use the thing.

The physician was cooking some eggs on the same flat stone I had used to cook Kol's fish. The lively fire and the replenished stock of wood testified she'd been awake much earlier than I.

"I hope you're not bruised," I said, squatting opposite her as she poked her eating knife at the eggs. "Thank you. Sorry for the fight."

"Having to deal with your illness was a good thing, I think. It made me forget what a puling coward I felt last night with all this ... strangeness ... and seeing Danae in the flesh and getting whacked in the head. I began thinking as a physician again."

Her admission startled me, but I detected no humility in her demeanor. She wrinkled her nose at the eggs as they quickly took on the color of dirt and the consistency of drying plaster.

"I considered what the Dané said about this 'change' being trapped inside you. Perhaps he holds the true remedy to your disease."

"I'd like to believe that. But clearly you've not met my mad patronn. Kol's work is not necessarily benevolent." I grimaced, as always, at the recollection.

"Osriel told me your history," she said. "I can't blame you whichever way you choose. But you can't go back to nivat, and I don't know how long the disk is going to help you."

"Your rock is a bit too hot." I offered her a flat piece of wood to use for a plate. If she didn't eat her eggs soon, she could use them to bandage wounds. My stomach growled and rumbled. "Were there more of those wherever you found them? Or did Kol bring them?"

"I've not seen him as yet this morning. And these were all I could find without climbing, so you might as well take half."

"I couldn't—"

"Would you stop being so polite? I've wiped up too much of your bodily fluids to like you, but I'm not prepared to let you starve or go mad, either one." She scraped the leathery mess onto the wood and ran her knife down the middle, dividing them precisely in half. "But I detest dirt and cold and sleeping on the ground, and as you see I'm worse than useless at cooking, so please just get this business over with and show me the way back to my own bed. I must get back to Osriel. His illness does not wait. I can resolve my difficulties with him."

She pulled a spoon from her belt kit and began eating. A bruise on my hip, caused when the two Danae had thrown me to the ground, was the only remnant of my own kit. Her dagger lay wherever Kol had kicked it, and I had carried no weapon since Boreas stole my knife all those months ago. I scooped the ugly little mess with my fingers and stuffed my mouth full. A fine time for my uncle to walk out of the sea with his hands full of green stuff.

With only a cool observation, he dropped the soggy weeds onto the sand beside us and strolled down the shore to the clustered rocks where we were to meet. His gards gleamed silver, scarcely visible in the sunlight. Instead of climbing onto the rocks to wait, as he had the previous day, he propped one foot on the rock and bent forward, leg straight, stretching his arms to touch his toes, his chest flat along his thigh. He remained there, perfect in his stillness.

"Do you think he's praying?" I said, wiping my sticky hands on my chausses and imagining the ache of such posture. It made the abbey practices of kneeling and prostration seem benign.

"Did you not observe the way the other fellow moved . . . danced . . . before he set to crush your knees?" said Saverian. "Evidently even a Danae body must work to develop that kind of power and forestall damage. The sea is cold, which tightens the muscles. He's loosening them again. I suppose he means for us to eat this green mess."

"You're welcome to all of it," I said, not so hungry as I'd thought.

Kol shifted his stance to the other leg.

I pulled off my boots and dumped the sand from them. Examining the brightening sky above the cliff top, I judged I had time enough to wash the gritty egg taste from my mouth. Naught was like to wash away the taste of fear or loosen the tightness in *my* back.

Leaving my boots by the fire to warm, I headed up the shore barefoot. As I strode away from Saverian and her fire, and Kol and his rock, doubts crept forward, whispering that I was a fool to consider Kol's offer. Saverian's leathery eggs had reminded me of days when I'd had naught so fat and filling. I'd never been greedy of pleasure, wealth, or happiness. I'd enjoyed my life—eating what I scrounged, drinking, singing, dancing, albeit in my own crude fashion. I'd shared delights with women and left them laughing and satisfied; I'd worked hard and walked the length of Nav-

ronne beneath the skies of summer and winter. I'd seen
marvels and talked of philosophy and nonsense with a variety of folk. What more did I want?

Education was truly a wicked thing. Ignorance had
served me well for seven-and-twenty years, and now these
monks, princes, and serious women and children had forced
me to take note of the world's trouble, and got it all tangled
up with honor and righteousness and good works. But I was
no grand thinker. No mighty warrior. No martyr or hero or
scholar. I had no plan for saving either Jullian or Navronne
from Sila Diaglou, and no twisting of my brain since my
recovery had devised one.

By the time I'd located the trickle of fresh water that
burbled underneath a collapsed segment of the sea cliff,
washed salt and sand from face and teeth, and swallowed
a few mouthfuls, I'd half convinced myself to run away. I
would persuade Saverian to return the gold medallion and
teach me how to control my disease. Kol had offered no
remedy to prevent me going mad from stinks and noises.

The Dané put himself through several more contortions,
sitting, squatting, bending, and stretching. The fellow could
not be built on bone. *Not human. Gods . . .*

I started back.

Kol positioned himself at the very brink of sea and
shore. Facing the sea cliff, he raised his arms straight over
his head, then allowed them to settle slightly lower, at an
upward angle with his shoulders. He paused there, face
lifted to the cliff top.

Without reason, my steps slowed. My breathing paused.
At the moment the sun nudged its rim above the sea cliff,
Kol ran five mighty steps forward and leaped into the air,
knees bent—one forward, one behind—lifting my heart
right out of my body. Music, some marvelous discourse of
pipe and dulcian, burst forth when his feet touched earth
and he began a series of impossible leaps and spins, linked
with sweeps of arm and hand, with slow turns and long ex-
tensions of leg . . . skyward, seaward . . .

Great gods have mercy! As the rays of morning light
touched my cheek, the earth shifted beneath my bare
feet . . . breathing . . . rejoicing . . . grieving . . . alive. I felt the
exuberant burst of its renewal, as I had felt my own upon

waking in sunlight through Osriel's window. And this . . .
the Dané's dance . . . had caused it to happen.

Down on one knee, chest heaving, Kol extended his
muscled leg and back and touched his forehead. He held
the position impossibly long until his breathing stilled, so
that one might believe him transformed into the very stone
statue I had seen in Osriel's garden. Perfect.

"Magnus Valentia!" Saverian called as I passed by her.
"We need—"

"Can't," I yelled over my shoulder, for of a sudden I was
running. Kol had risen, glanced at the barren rock, and was
walking away.

"Kol, wait! I want . . ." Breathless, I came to the rocks
and called after him, heedless of duty, fear, or pride. As if a
sword had opened my breast to expose a wildcat in place
of my heart, a lifetime's worth of dissatisfaction, of restless searching and unfocused longing made some kind of
sense. I had never imagined such possibility as my uncle
had just revealed. If I wanted to help my friends, I had to
live. If I wanted to live, I had to take this chance. I could
not let fear and caution make me run away—not this time.
"Please. Teach me."

Chapter 13

"Season upon season does it require to learn the dance. The fullness of a gyre at the least to grasp the very beginning positions." Kol's hands flew up in empty offering, demonstrating the futility of what I begged. His every word and gesture spoke the extent of his scorn. "For a body half human, unpracticed, grown fixed in its working, for a mind distracted by human concerns and unprepared even by the remasti, the breadth and extent of the Everlasting would not be sufficient."

Not even such denial could discourage me. Could I but find the proper words to describe this revelation . . . this certainty that lived in my very breath and bone . . . I could convince him.

"I am not wholly unpracticed," I said, following as he strode along the shore, incoming wavelets lapping at his feet. His gards shimmered palest silver in the cold sunlight. "I've run since I could walk, danced since I first heard a flute in the marketplace. And I've vigor and endurance beyond other humans—I see that now." My pleas sounded weak and pitiful beside a hunger that left the doulon but a passing whimsy. All my life's desires and longings had come together in those moments of Kol's dancing. Could I but grasp this purpose, surely all other matters—duties and vows and promises—would fall into a pattern I could comprehend. I was meant for this.

"To master the correct line of a jeque—the simplest leap—and how to balance, how to approach, how to land, how to shift weight and control the strength required while bringing grace and smoothness, takes practice—every day, every night, season upon season, constant work to develop the flexibility of the hip and the power of the leg and the understanding of how these work together. A sequence of three eppires—spins on one foot—happens not in all the seasons before a wanderkin becomes a stripling. And these are only the movements. The wanderkin and stripling study the land and seasons, the growing things, the beasts. Even more difficult . . . the maturing student must learn to work with the music of the Everlasting, so he may devise sequences of steps to conjoin all these elements, else the dance is but exercise with no effect. And once these are mastered, even yet must one learn the lore of the Canon and how to work a sianou. Thou art far beyond teaching, even were I willing to take on such a task." He had drawn his brow so tight his dragon's upper wing curled into a knot.

"A lifetime of practice . . . yes, I can see that. Like a swordsman's training. I could not do what you do in any matter of months or years. Even the moves that appear simple are built on layers of strength and precision. But the other learning . . . Music lives in me; I hear it everywhere . . . even across the years, when I use my bent. And I've not spent my life without eyes or ears. Likely I picked up much of the worldly lore in all these years. It's just the movements . . ." My limbs and spine longed to stretch and spin and soar. My heart and lungs ached to fuel such power as I had seen.

We rounded the curving end of the shallow cove and came to a point where sand yielded to a cobbled shore, carved with tide pools. White-winged gulls flapped and rode the wind, while bearded ducks and thin-necked grebes pecked at sea wrack abandoned by the tides.

Kol took out across the cobble, and I followed, abruptly aware of my bare feet on the cold hard knobs. The Dané halted and pointed at a crescent-shaped pool near the water's edge. One could not mistake the challenge. "Share your knowledge, halfbreed. Tell me what lives here."

Having worked for a time in the ports of Morian, I knew something of shorebirds and fish and shelled creatures. But to recite them as for a schoolmaster ... Kol's expression echoed my every childhood tutor's disbelief. *Ignorant* ple-beiu. *Stubborn, ill-mannered whelp who refuses even to try. Have you some disease, Magnus, that you cannot pick out one simple word from a page, or is this but the incurable hardness of your spirit?*

I forced past failures aside. This was the dance, life that linked sunlight and sea and earth. Even the Cartaman-dua bent could never again bring me to this crossroads of possibility.

Kneeling on the hard cobbles, I peered into the clear water, the sunlight dazzling my eyes. I saw little but rocks and a few sea plants with long stalks and filmy red leaves. One tiny fish darted into the rocky shadows. The carnage the hunting birds had scattered on the cobble told me more. "There'll be crabs and mussels here," I said. "Those bunched green fronds are a snake plant stuck to the rock, I think. When the tide goes out, it withers."

"But does it live or die? Guesses and simplicities hardly suffice." Kol stood straight as a post. What did he want? Such creatures as lived in pools hid among the rocks and weeds. Who could know them all?

Irked by his contempt, I plunged my hands into the pool. Perhaps my bent might reveal what passed here in the same way it allowed me to distinguish footsteps. Elbow deep, the cold water wet my sleeves and crept upward toward my shoulders as I loosed magic to flow through my fingertips. I listened, smelled, tasted, stretched my mind into the crev-ices and crannies. Slowly, I began to comprehend what my senses uncovered: threads of color, of stillness and move-ment, of life and death.

"Fish live here," I said. "Shannies and bearded rocklings—and tiny shrimp, almost transparent, and the warty yellow lump that is a slug, not a pebble. And this"—I touched a dark, twisted knot of a shell—"is a dog whelk that Hansker milk for purple dye. The strawberry growing on that bulging rock is no plant, but a tentacled beast that stings its prey—the smaller creatures who hide in these for-ests of leaves, like the glass shrimp brought in by the tide and the mitelings of the dog whelk ...."

I told him of death and birth, of how the whelk's tongue

scoops the flesh of the mussel between its closed shells, and how an entirely new creature can grow from the broken arm of the scarlet sea star that hid beneath a wave-smoothed rock. The pool was a world to itself, fed and ravaged by the god of the tide, as Navronne was fed and ravaged by our fickle gods.

When my hands grew numb from the cold, I had to stop. Bundling my fingers beneath my arms, I sat up, shivering and blinking in the watery light.

Kol sat on his haunches beside me, staring into the water. "As I have watched thee walk the land and sound the streams of the earth in company with humans, I assumed thy works a preening deception—the arrogance of the Cartamandua passed on in his seed. Again, I have erred." He shifted his gaze to my face as if he looked on me for the first time. "For a gyre—a full turn of the seasons—I studied this very pool, and only then did I understand so much. Thou hast a grace for seeing, *rejongai*. Did the gyres wheel backward, I would press thy sire earlier . . . convince him to bring thee to me for teaching, not wait, as I did, for him to fail."

He rose to his full height. "But no wishing can recapture lost chance. Clyste was wrong. Were all accomplished as she hoped, even then thou couldst *not* dance the Canon. Human blood flows in thy veins, and the archon forbids tainted blood nigh the dancing ground. Naught can change the lessons of the past. We will speak no more of the Canon. I can gift thee the gards of separation and exploration and the teaching of their use, as I said, and that only."

But the vehemence of his denial was no longer directed at me, but at himself. Pride had caused him to fail Clyste, a sister whom he loved. For the first time since I had seen him greet the morning, a spark of hope burned inside me. I would not push too hard. He would bend. Whatever the "lessons of the past," I believed as I believed naught else in this world that my mother had meant for me to dance.

"What must I do?" I shoved up my sleeves and stretched out my arms as if they were sword blanks to be heated, hammered, and shaped.

He motioned me to follow him back around the headland to the sandier shore. "As I said, each change lies buried within thy flesh already—the three suppressed and the great one yet to come."

"Then why didn't I change when the time was right? I suppose it's more difficult for ones like me. Halfbreeds. Which means this will likely be uncomfortable—" Memories of battle wounds came to mind, and those horrid birthdays when I'd gone half mad with pain and lashed out at anyone within reach, driven by an agonized restlessness that naught but violence or spelled perversion could still.

No matter my desires, dread shivered my marrow.

"It is neither fault in thee nor a factor of thy mixed birth that thou art unchanged. A remasti is impossible to accomplish alone. The vayar must guide the immature body to express its power, and the gards are the visible signs of its accomplishment. Other halfbreeds have taken the remasti without difficulty."

Kol motioned me to stand before him at the edge of the water, but I held my ground in the dry dunes. My nerves would not permit my mouth to be still. "What will I feel? What will change besides the . . . marks?"

As if even that alteration was a small thing! How would I walk the streets of Palinur again, with blue light glowing on my skin? "Surely it will be different for one who is part human."

"Certainly the result will differ." He visibly forced himself patient, closing his eyes, whose color had shifted from a deep sea green to aspen gold. "What hand or eye is entirely the same as any other? What walking step or standing posture is the same? The long-lived tread the path of perfection, but we each find our resting posture somewhere along the way, our own talents and our bodies' limits determining our place. Even tainted blood does not preclude one attempting the path. Now we must begin or even the slow days of Evaldamon will carry us to the Everlasting with thou yet unprotected."

I opened my mouth and then closed it again. Answers would come. With no more hesitation, I moved to the edge of the water. "Tell me what to do."

"We will begin by acknowledging our bond as vayar and tendé. Then, when I give thee a sign, thou must wash. Especially thy arms and legs. Sand is an excellent aid."

"Wash ... here? In the sea?" Water and cold, my two least favorite aspects of nature, and not entirely because a diviner had once named them my doom.

"Yes."

The wind had risen, frosting the waves with foam. A haze paled the sky and sunlight, and a layer of deep gray banded the horizon. No chance Kol intended for me to stay clothed. Gods, I was damp to the skin, and now he wanted that skin bare. However Danae managed to stay warm as they ran about naked in winter weather, I had not inherited that gift. I glanced along the shore and over my shoulder. A trail of smoke rose from our fire, but I could not see where Saverian had got off to. "All right, then."

Kol bowed with all the formality of a pureblood head of family, then clasped his hands behind his back. He dipped his head in approval when I returned the bow without prompting. "The season has long passed for thee to leave thy parents' side, nes—"

His dragon gard drew up as he cut off this pronouncement. "What name dost thou prefer? Thou art very big for such address as *nestling* or *wanderkin*."

This slight break in his formality nudged me toward an unlikely grin. Indeed, though he could likely break me over his knee, we were quite evenly matched in size. "I answer most to Valen. Is there some proper title I should use for you? I've no wish to be rude."

"Name me *relagai*—mother's brother—or *vayar*. To address an elder by name requires a harmony we shall never share."

I ignored his coldness and bowed to acknowledge his point. "*Relagai*."

He took up where he'd left off. How much "elder" was he? Likely centuries. Gods ... "Freed from thy parents' side, Valen, thou shalt have license to wander the world and learn of its wonders and its evils, to learn the names and natures of all its parts. I have accepted the duties of vayar given me by she who gave thee first breath and who nurtured thee for the long seasons of thy borning. I pledge with all honor and intent to provide thee truth and healthy guidance and to protect thee from harm to the limits of my being and the Law of the Everlasting. Come to me with thy questioning, with thy fears and troubles, with thy joys and discoveries, and I will hear thee ... without judgment ... and answer thee as far as I am able. Thy own part of this joining is but thy pledge to explore and learn and come to me if thou art troubled. If thou wilt accept my teaching, Valen, give me thy hands." He extended his own hands, palms upward.

I had not expected so solemn a swearing. The cost to his pride could not be small.

"Thy pledge honors me, *relagai*," I said, inclining my back in deference. "All the more for our disharmony."

At least my own part seemed uncomplicated—unlike the other oaths that bound me. I laid my palms over his, and the world—sunlight, colors, shapes, and outlines—dimmed and faded, as if reshaping themselves. Moments later, when he released my hands, the cast of the world returned to its normal state, as if I had but waked. He gestured toward the foaming sea. Time to wash.

I hesitated. It was not that I was shamed. Nakedness in the proper time and place was comfort and pleasure, not wicked. But somehow, when I glanced at Kol, I imagined myself as one of the transparent shrimp standing beside the scarlet sea star. And somewhere Saverian would be watching ... ready, no doubt, to catalog my lacks.

My vayar raised his eyebrows and inclined his head toward the water. Waiting.

Reluctantly I shed my layers and tossed them onto the sand above the tide line. My bare feet had become something inured to the chilly sand, but the cold wind stung, my manhood retreated, and my first step into the water was a badger's bite. By the time I'd submerged to the knees, my teeth clattered like hailstones on a tin roof. If I were to be done with this before my blood congealed, I'd best move faster. I lunged a few steps farther into the oncoming waves and sat.

"G-g-great Iero's m-m-mercy!" Unfortunate if some ritual silence was required.

Once sure my heart had not stopped, I scooped sand from underneath me and hurriedly scrubbed at my flesh. The waves slammed into my back and lifted me from the sea bottom, threatening to tumble me over, but I splayed my legs and dug in my heels. For the most part I managed to stay upright and keep the salt water out of nose and mouth.

After the briefest service to every spot I could reach, I floundered and lurched toward the shore, only to discover what I should have expected. Emerging wet into the wind felt far, far colder than sitting in the water. "C-c-could we be quick about this?" I mumbled.

A scowling Kol moved to my side and cupped his hands about my right shoulder. Warmth flowed from his touch and again the world shifted. The sunlight dimmed, and the shore receded as if a great fog had settled over it. I no longer felt the buffeting wind or the gritty sand, but only Kol's warm hands and the sea that crashed and gurgled about my ankles, tugging at me . . . breaking the bounds of my skin . . . pouring into me . . . filling me. Drowning me . . .

Do not be afraid, Valen. Kol's sharp command interrupted my growing panic. *To make this passage, we must step outside the bounds of bodily form. This sea is myself and will not drown thee.*

I lost myself—limbs and torso, head and privy parts dissolved. His hands yet anchored me—one solid point of heat, a tether to the world, all that stood between me and blind terror. All else was embracing water, as if I were the immortal sea star tucked securely in the tide pool, knowing that any broken part of me would form another self, and that the tide would bring me all I needed to live. I trusted Kol, and so I drifted . . . tasting salt and fish and sand. I smelled green sea plants, felt the tickle of wind on the surface and the great heavy urging of the god of tides— everything a curiosity. I wondered at the endless play of daylight in the shallows and shied from the shadows of the boundless deeps. Fish in silver armor darted past me . . . through me . . .

For a nestling, such life as this is the greater part of what he knows—the safety and comfort of a parent's sianou, its myriad parts, its voice and texture, and the elements that make it live. Kol's voice existed everywhere around me and inside me, though I could not say I *heard* him. *The remasti of separation shifts a nestling from an existence sheltered and constrained by sire and dam into one shaped by his*

*own body—a much greater change for most than for thee,
one who has lived across a multitude of seasons constrained
by flesh—however ill-fitting. Now, thou must choose to step
beyond this place and allow thy true nature to reshape thy
flesh. Let my hand guide thee.*

From the anchor point, warm strong fingers began to
re-create my invisible arm, moving down its length as a
sculptor's fingers might smooth his clay. Only *this* sculptor's
fingers left traces of fire and blade in their wake. Cutting,
burning, tearing . . .

Pain and panic bade me fight, but I could not locate the
rest of my body. Nor could I find voice in the sea to scream
or beg that he should stop before what flesh I yet owned
was left in tatters.

Be easy, Valen, he said, as he released the fingers of one
disembodied arm and shifted his touch to the place where
another ought to be. *I but release what is bound in thee. It
is so difficult, I believe, because thy true senses lie buried
deeper than those of a nestling. Be easy and dream of the
wide world. I shall not harm thee.*

Both arms now pulsed with agony. While the greater
part of me yet floated insubstantial in the gray-blue water,
I existed amid the frothing surf and freezing wind as well.
Great gray masses of cloud boiled on the horizon, reaching
for the sun.

Kol's hands left my fingers and began to sculpt a thigh.
Great gods among us . . .

By the time his hands released my second foot, I existed
wholly in the familiar world, sprawled on my face with my
mouth full of sand. Though fire raged in my legs, my arms
had fallen numb. I was afraid to move. I was afraid to look.

He relinquished my burning toes. "Stand now, Valen,
that we may end this passage properly. Thou art free to
wander Aeginea, and none may hold or hinder thee without our *argai*'s consent."

Entirely wrung out, I moved slowly to all fours. Every
quat of my length felt something different from every
other. Frozen or scorched or nothing. Worst . . . I could not
feel my hands at all. "What's wrong with me?" I croaked.

He offered me his hand, but I was loath to touch him
again. I stumbled to my feet and stared at my skin. My

chest and abdomen and groin remained as they ever had been, cold pale flesh and dark hair caked with sand, but the now-hairless skin of fore and upper arms, of hands and fingers, of thigh and leg and foot, appeared an ugly mottled gray. Dead. No pattern was discernible, and certainly no beauty or power. And as the fire of Kol's touch died, every particle of that flesh lost all sensation. I shook my lumpish hands, kneaded them, slapped my arms and dying legs with no effect. "By Kemen Sky Lord, Dané, what have you done to me? I can't feel anything!"

Knitting his brow, he reached out to take my arm. I jerked away and stepped back, wincing from the fire in one foot, stumbling over the deadness in the other. "Stay back."

"Does not the world speak to thee?" he said, puzzled. "Thy gards will clear as thy senses waken, and take on their design as you walk the days. Touch the wind, *rejongai*."

"I can't *feel* the wind, not with dead limbs! Is this your clever vengeance? What of Danae justice that punishes only the guilty?" I could not strangle his long straight neck, for my blighted arms could be used as naught but bludgeons.

"No, no. All was done as prescribed. Thou shouldst discern *more* than before. More intently. More delicately."

His conviction did naught but unravel me the more. My chest and stomach seemed stuffed with sodden wool that thickened and compacted with every breath. I dropped to my unfeeling knees and plowed my hands into the sand that might have been silken pillows or hot coals for all I could tell. Wrenching my focus tight, I sought magic, but no warmth flowed through my dead fingers. I sat back on my heels and roared in rage and frustration. "You've killed me, you cursed gatzé."

Kol crouched beside me, for once unwrit with scorn or anger. "This is not of my doing, *rejongai*. Why would I pledge thee care and teaching, and then set out to make my own words false? The remasti is a work of reverence for the vayar, a work that becomes a part of his kirani—the patterns he dances—as much as any jeque or eppire. No joy or use can be derived from such betrayal. It is why the long-lived fail in understanding of human ways."

"Then what's wrong?" I gasped, my chest laboring, my

throat swelling shut as if a door had closed behind my words. I was suffocating.

He reached out again, and this time I had no strength to resist. I watched his fingers touch my arm and trace my sinews, but I could feel naught of it. "I experienced resistance as I released thy change," he said, puzzled, "but I assumed it to be thy years of restraint and thy intractable nature. It felt as if some other skin sheathed thee."

His surmise stung me as a slap on my cheek. "Get the woman," I whispered. "Hurry. Please."

The daylight blurred and wavered. I did not see Kol move, for I curled into a knot on the sand and concentrated all my strength on drawing air into my lungs.

"All right, all right, you can let go of me. Am I to be punished for watching?" Her dry voice rattled like a stick in a pail fifty quellae distant. "Egad, Magnus, you look even worse close by. Is this part—? Gracious Mother, what's happening to you?"

"Undo your spell," I croaked. "It's stopping the change. Can't breathe."

Praise be to all gods, she did not hesitate. She ripped the delicate chain from her leather pocket and pressed the gold medallion to my forehead. The maggots crept outward, only this time they left life, not deadness, in their wake.

With a great whoop, I inhaled half the sky, clearing throat and lungs and head. When she took the disk away, I stretched out on my back and flung my limbs wide, reveling in the delights of properly working heart and lungs. "Mother tend you in your need, good physician . . ."

No more had I begun to speak than the wind caressed my arms and legs. Of a sudden I drowned in sensation: the overwhelming scents of the salt and sea wrack, and the lingering aroma of our cook fire, last night's fish, and the morning's ill-favored eggs. I smelled a distant winter—rank furs and damp wool, the smokes of burning coal and pine logs, the damp earth and scat and piss of animal dens, the dust of empty grain barrels, the ripe sweat of lust beneath old blankets. And from other senses . . . Not only did I hear the crash of waves and the gurgle of the slops between the rocks, but I perceived the rustling of the red-leaved sea forest in the tide pools and the rippleless darting of the shannies. Not only did I feel the salt in the wind, but I knew that in its wanderings the air had once kissed a church, drawing away the scent of beeswax and marble dust, the sweet smokes of incense and oil of ephrain, the pungent perfume of ysomar, used to anoint the sick and dying . . . And still there was more.

"Holy Mother," I whispered, wrapping my arms about my head to prevent its bursting, "how can I ever sort it all out?"

"Are you well, Valen?" said Saverian, sitting on her heels at my side, the gold disk clutched in her hand. "What's happening to you? I can moderate the spell if need be and re-impose it."

Unlike the experiences I had named a disease, this barrage of scents and sounds neither seared my nostrils nor made my ears bleed. Nor did my eyes revolt at the daylight's complex textures of gray, blue, and silver or the impossible shapes of distant rocks that would have been a blur an hour before. I could make no sense of much that I perceived, but none of it drove me mad.

"For now, yes, I'm all right. Thank you. I think—" I swallowed hard, took a shaking breath, and stretched my arms skyward so I could see them. The gray mottling had brightened to the same pale silver as Kol's gards, though that could be but a trick of the shifting light. I could yet discern no pattern to the marks. My stomach hitched, and I folded my arms across it and stopped staring at myself. "There's just so much."

"So your disease is indeed of your own nature," said Saverian, kneeling in the sand, as matter-of-fact as if on every day she witnessed madmen transformed into Danae children. "As I predicted."

"Thy perception is quite limited as yet," said Kol, looking down at me. His handsome face expressed naught but tolerance—no more of concern or bewilderment. " 'Tis the task of wanderkins to learn the source and nature of what they perceive and to extend the boundaries of their skills. As they learn to walk in quiet, layers unexpected reveal themselves. Having lived in the world so long, thou shouldst have an easier task than most."

"You mean, there could be more?" How ever could a child manage all this?

"Always more. Subtleties. Grand things that might once

have seemed whole display their sundry parts. The reach of thy experiencing shall widen from this small shore to distances and deeps. Wert thou a true wanderkin, destined to dance and live as one of us, such discrimination would be necessary to thy duties."

"And I'll perceive whatever exists in the human realm as well as Aeginea," I said, sitting up. Indeed, I was already experiencing many things far beyond this shore. No ale-sodden hunter lay snoring beneath fouled blankets anywhere near here, I'd guess. No wheezing practor in a freezing church anointed a woman dead in childbirth, unless . . . Perhaps those places existed as did Fortress Groult or the Sentinel Oak—visible in only one plane, though I could touch their very rooting place in the other.

His nostrils flared in distaste. "No. To experience the sensations of human works we must depart from the true lands and immerse ourselves entirely in the human world."

I glanced up sharply. "But I—" His certainty made me doubt. Perhaps my long-distorted senses were but remembering things I already knew. My finger crept up my ugly arms. The lack of hair was disconcerting, but I could not feel the marks themselves. I brushed at my skin, half expecting the pale mottling to fall away like dry flakes from a charred branch. Perhaps nothing at all had happened to me, save a blessed remission in my disease.

"A true wanderkin's primary tasks are exploration and the perfection of sensory knowledge." Kol took on his schoolmaster's aspect, as if I were indeed a new-changed Danae child. "I can teach thee closure . . . to silence one sense or the other . . . to quiet levels thou dost not wish to perceive. Control and discipline will ease thy confusion."

"Yes, I'd like that very much . . ."

Learning to manage this oversensitivity that had plagued me my whole life would be a grace indeed. But more awaited me. I was sure of it. My mother had believed that Kol could protect me from the Danae's crippling blows and instill in me what I needed to make sense of the world. If she knew Janus de Cartamandua at all, then she knew how unreliable his character. She would never have based her whole plan for me on his promises. I inhaled deeply, buried apprehension, and averted my eyes from my body.

"...and then I'd like— How soon can we move on to the second remasti?"

"When we move on." Kol strolled away toward the water.

Saverian rolled her eyes as if I were a lunatic. The burgeoning clouds released their burden, binding sea and sky into a gray eternity of rain.

Chapter 14

Saverian pressed herself to the cliff to shelter from the rising storm. I grabbed my clothing from the sand and joined her. But the rain drove straight in from the sea, a cold sheeting deluge that soaked us to the skin—not all that far in my case—chilled us to the bone, and made it impossible to think too much about what I had just done. Certainly the ugly change to my arms and legs did naught to keep me warm or dry. Naught that I could see along the strand promised better cover, and a fire was out of the question. We could not stay here.

"We need shelter," I shouted at Kol over the hammering rain, the continuous rumble of thunder and surf, and the maelstrom of sounds and smells that filled my head with more images than I could possibly sort out. "Humans die of cold and wet."

I saw no benefit in pressing the point. The Dané would choose to help or not. I believed he would. He had squatted ankle deep in the surf and spread his fingers in the incoming wavelets, as if ensuring that their texture met his expectations. Rain sheened his long back like a cloak of transparent silk.

"Thou shouldst not have brought the woman," he called back without looking up. "I could have taken *thee* into the sea again."

"Did he do that?" I asked Saverian as we waited and shivered. "Take me under water? I mean, I experienced *something*. Naught I'd want to do again." My antipathy for water was too deep-rooted. The gray waves churned and frothed in nauseating rhythm. "I felt as if I were dreaming of the sea ... of drowning ... of his voice. I didn't think it was real."

"Nor did I. When you came out from your w-washing, he grabbed your shoulder and led you right back into the water." The shivering physician grimaced and wiped water from her eyes. "The waves boiled bright b-blue around you. You both vanished. I've seen nothing like it ... nothing ever. How did you b-breathe, Valen? It was hours before he led you out again. Why aren't you d-dead?"

"Hours? That's not possible."

"I'm a good judge of time. I was beginning to think I would need to find m-my own way home."

I jabbed my fingers into my ribs. It hurt. "Well, I'm not dead. But I'm not going to try diving in on my own."

A reluctant smile teased at her mouth. "I'd planned to examine your new skin to see if you had scales or gills. But I've no paper or pens to record my findings. A poor practitioner to get caught without."

I could not but return her smile, grateful for her astringent practicality. Had she screamed or shrunk from me in disgust, the anxious knot lodged in my own breast might have unraveled into panicked frenzy.

Kol unfolded his limbs and struck out northward along the shore. His hand twitched in a gesture I interpreted as an invitation to follow. Saverian must have gotten the same notion. She sped after him like a constable after a thief. The physician might miss her bed or her books, but I couldn't imagine she would regret the absence of any *person*.

I used the moment's privacy to relieve myself and wrestle my ugly arms into my soaked wool shirt, hoping it might cut the wind and soften the impact of the driving rain. Then I set out after the others.

Saverian's time estimates could not be accurate. I could feel the sun hiding behind the storm. I could almost see it, in the way you see the rider in an approaching cloud of dust or envision a Syran woman's body within her cloud of drifting veils. And it had scarce moved from the cliff top since Kol's dance of greeting. As I marveled at this certainty, all out of nothing, a moment's flush left me warm and cold together. I tried to hold on to the sensation, but sounds and scents and images piled one up on the other like unruly children demanding my attention, and soon I was naught but cold and wet again. Strange.

Kol moved swiftly. Just past the slumped cliff where we'd found fresh water, the shoreline curved and took the two of them out of sight. I trotted a little faster and caught up with them just as the Dané started up a steep bank scored with rivulets of mud. The footing was tricky, and I was just as happy to be bootless, able to feel where rocks and rooted shrubs gave surer purchase.

Saverian climbed like a goat, but with far less grace. She was confident and fast, but grabbed on to every protruding rock and twig, and her boots slipped every other step. Her black braid had escaped its bonds and water cascaded from her straggling hair down her neck and the back of her cloak. When I came up behind her—by sheer virtue of my longer legs—she was mumbling through chattering teeth. "Wretched royal b-bastard. 'Leave your b-books and ride out with me,' you said. 'I need you.' Yes ... to be trapped in a city full of torch-wielding madmen, chased by Harrowers, saddled with a d-doulon-raving lunatic, frostbit, saddle-sore, bashed in the head, d-drowned, and now abandoned in a monsoon in company with said madman and a cold-blooded dancing g-gatzé. Never again, Riel. Enough is enough." She stomped through the mud as if it might be Osriel's face.

I scrabbled upward, wondering if she'd find it amusing if I accused *her* of whining. Likely not. "You've not traveled with the prince all that much, then? On his visits to Gillarine? Or to ... battlefields?"

Locked in her grumbling misery, she perhaps forgot what she considered my business and what not. "Stearc keeps him to his regimen when traveling. I give the thane spells and medicines enough to get Osriel home if he gets very bad. Of course, now Stearc's commanded to stay at the abbey, it's left to the dead man to see to Riel. The god-cursed fool oughtn't travel at all ..."

The *dead man* ... Voushanti? An extra chill raised my

neck hairs. Her commentary flowed like the mud around our feet, and I didn't want to interrupt it, but someday I'd get her to explain.

"...and certainly not in winter. The cold torments his joints, and swells his lungs and air passages. One day he'll fall off his horse and die, and *then* what of his grand plans? What of his father's wishes? What of his warriors and his subjects and his— The rest of them? Blasted, mite-brained, cold-blooded, soul-blind idiot."

The rest of *whom*, physician? Another question to save for a better time. "He told me that life is pain and only movement makes it bearable."

"Pssh." Saverian dispensed disdain as innkeepers dispense gossip. "His father spewed that drivel when Osriel was a boy and he was trying to coax the child out of bed on a day when every move Riel made was agony. He'd put Osriel on a horse or force him to run races with him. It wasn't fair. The child would do anything to please his father, though it caused his saccheria to flare and he suffered for days after, and King Eodward knew it. The king called this torment *love*."

"But Osriel got out of bed."

"He did. He does it every day. Honestly, I've no idea how. His father's *love* left his joints like broken glass and his soul a grinding stone." Saverian slipped again and only her grip on a pine sapling saved her from falling facedown in the mud. "The Mother spare me any such love."

I didn't think she had to worry. Loving the physician would be as rewarding as romancing the dunes we'd just left behind.

Mud squished between my toes as I climbed. I could well imagine robust, ruddy Eodward prodding his sickly child to be strong enough to survive in a brutal world. Yet I had received a privileged glimpse of the king's nature once when I was a young soldier under his command, and I surmised that the pain Osriel experienced on those hard days did not outstrip that his father felt at forcing him to it. Eodward had been rewarded by seeing his sickly child grow to manhood, an uncommon fate for a victim of saccheria. Saverian was right, too, though. Pain could change a man. Make him hard.

"Did you love the prince ... when you were children?"

"No. We were friends. Playmates. My mother was his physician." As if she realized, of a sudden, the personal turn the conversation had taken, Saverian tightened her jaw and hauled herself upward even more forcefully. "Where *is* this creature taking us?"

That, too, was a most interesting question, for a glance back over my shoulder showed naught but rain and a valley of trees. No sea, no shore. Even more unsettling . . . the sun, yet buried deeply in the clouds, now lay behind us, what my instincts deemed west, though our path had not turned and scarce an hour had passed from my recovery. What daylight the storm had left us was rapidly failing.

I pressed my hand to Saverian's back, hoping to speed her steps. The Dané would likely welcome an excuse to abandon us. When we crested the steep slope, Kol's sapphire gards were just visible through a scattering of saplings that bordered a darkening wood.

"Come on." I took Saverian's hand, and we pelted after him through the trees. The gloom of the deeper woodland enveloped us.

Saverian slowed. "Valen, look."

"Best keep up. He's using no track I can travel on my own." I tightened my grip on her wrist. What with the rain, tired legs, a head packed with fears and nonsense, and Kol's disconcerting route finding, the shifting of north and south, of before and after and here and there, was twisting my instincts underside up and forepart behind. Our every step moved across time and distance in ways not even a Cartamandua could fathom.

But the willful physician snatched her hand away. "Stop! Look at yourself, Valen."

"We daren't lose—" *Iero's grace!* I stopped. Threads of pale lapis-hued light snaked about my fingers and bare legs. I shoved one sodden sleeve higher. The light—some threads fine, some thick—shifted and blurred beneath the raindrops. The knot in my breast burst. A cold shaft of terror pierced me head to feet. I had become . . . other.

"What's happening? Is it uncomfortable? Pleasurable?" She made her odd little open-palm gesture asking permission, but touched my arm before I could refuse it. The traces sparked silver and blue under her fingertips.

"I'm— No. It just itches. Stings." As if a swarm of ants had taken up residence on . . . or inside . . . my flesh and took it in mind to bite me every once in a while.

"Do you feel it atop the skin or deeper? Perhaps it's like a lizard's coloring that changes with its surroundings." She bent my arm at wrist and elbow, which caused the marks to squirm and blur. "Look at that! If I just had my lenses . . . better light . . ."

Queasy and embarrassed, I jerked my arm away. The shifting marks seem to be connected straight to my gut. "We'd best go. He's waiting for us."

I stumbled forward, clutching my bundle of clothes and boots, unable to keep my eyes from the unstable patterns on my bare legs and feet. Saverian grabbed my sleeve and guided me around trees and stumps.

A flare of white welcomed us into a rain-swept circle of trampled grass amid the trees. A starlike cluster of twigs, the source of the pale, magical light, dangled from an overhanging branch, unaffected by the rain. The light revealed several ramshackle sheds and lean-tos nestled beside a thatch-roofed hut. Kol stood at the open doorway of the hut, engaged in conversation with a man in a dirty white gown and a brown— I wiped the rain from my eyes. Not a brown cloak, but a *cowl*, and a well-delineated tonsure that bared half his scalp. I was speechless.

". . . Well, of course, I've been gi'en to welcome the stranger, and to hear a voice of home would put me out of mind in heavenly thanks, though I've renounced all such. But a woman born . . . Brave Kol, could ye not ask me please to slash my throat or draw down the poison of the hemlock, but ye must put me in the way of my sin? Half a century's turn must I have fasted and prayed by now— not to say, great God of all, that I've complaints or believe by any chance that I've full expiated my guilt, for certain not"—he raised a bony hand to address this side comment to the heavens—"but to come to this moment to find myself in the full occasion of repeating my defilement—more likely, e'en, being half mad as I am—'tis a sore deterrent to hospitality!"

The white light bathed his face as he stuck his head around Kol's rangy form and squinted into the rainy night.

"Did ye not say ye'd brought two *human* folk? Or is it—?" As his examination took in my odd and soggy self, half dressed, legs flaring blue like miniature lightning, his own ruddy complexion lost all color, and he circled his breast with Iero's seal, completing the gesture by clutching his chest as if his heart might fly out of it. "Mighty saints protect me, Brother Kol, ye've brought me a halfbreed."

Assuredly his claim of fasting was no lie; the monk had scarce a citré's weight of spare flesh on him. But he had once been a robust man, perhaps a half head less than Kol or I, and his meatless bones were broad and thick. Gray-stubbled chin and tonsure appeared as ragged as his garb, and assuredly no cleaner. But despite his self-deprecation, his voice boomed clear and the pale eyes gleamed as sharp as a well-honed dagger.

"Is the woman also mixed blood?"

"Only the male," said Kol. "He is newly a wanderkin and cannot warm himself as yet. His companion has fallen afoul of Tuari, and the wanderkin would not leave her to the archon's retribution. She needs shelter."

"Ye've saved him from the breaking, have ye not, Kol? Put yourself in the way of burying, and if this girl aided ye in such an enterprise, then right and mercy it be to protect her. But how came ye to involve yourself with any human offspring, who've sworn never—?" The wide-eyed monk inhaled sharply. He stepped around Kol, and unheeding of the rain soaking his cowl and gown, grasped my arm and dragged me underneath the twiggy lamp. His fingers a manacle about my wrist, he swept my face as he might study his holy writs. "Merciful Iero, Liege of Heaven!"

"He is born of my sister," said Kol.

"The cartographer relinquished him at last?" The monk's fingers pinched my chin with the bite of a hungry dog on bloody meat and twisted my head side to side. "All count of human years has escaped me, but this one cannot have much time left before his maturing. Ne'er did I imagine your cruel penalty would budge the Cartamandua mule."

Kol stiffened. "Humans are not fit to judge cruelty."

"Strip off yer righteous skin, Brother Kol, and we'll argue it again," said the monk cheerfully, spinning about to face the Dané so quickly that his garb snapped my bare legs, causing a shower of blue and silver sparks. He tapped his own broad chest. "Would ye wrestle me to answer which of us has the One God's ear? I'm not what I was, but if blessed Iero doth keep this heart thuttering, a human sinner will yet crack your long-lived spine. Fasting and hard labor strengthens—"

"Janus did not send me," I interrupted, too curious to endure their jousting. "What, in Iero's glory, brings a Karish monk to Aeginea? You're not from Gillarine." The thread-bare brown cowl and white gown were not the black garb of Saint Ophir's brotherhood. A century's turn, he'd said. Names and faces, plots and schemes flew through my over-crowded head—the abbey, the lighthouse, the succession, Luviar, Osriel, Janus, Kol, Eodward . . . "By heaven, are you Picus?"

Then I, too, drew Iero's sunburst upon my breast, for to see a man two centuries old and not dead drew truths of dread mystery and mortality all too near. Caedmon had sent a monk to the Danae with his infant son, a man charged to educate young Eodward as befit a human prince. But the fellow had vanished mysteriously some few years after Eodward's return to Navronne, and only rumors had ever said where he'd gone.

"Picus?" Saverian tilted her head to one side, looking him over. "Osriel has a set of journals written by a man of that name. He was King Eodward's— Mother save us!" Even the cool physician could not contain her astonishment.

The monk's pinched face blossomed into such a joyful alignment as coaxed my own spirit to a smile. "I'm not for-got, then?" He quickly raised his hands as if to stay a legion. "Nay, nay, don't tell me. Be it honorable memory or ill re-pute, I must not care. Penance is a narrow road. But here we bide in the deluge, and this lady's lips blue as a wan-derkin herself! And the lad doth appear as he were a goat who's been witched into fasting. Prithee, come inside my cell and take what meager comforts I've to offer. Yes, the both of you. Should my weak character keep a drenched and freezing woman in the rain, 'twould be another sin to my account." Picus pulled back the hide curtain that served him as a door and waved us in.

"My gratitude, Brother," said Saverian as she hurried inside.

When I moved to follow the monk, Kol stayed me with a gesture. "Warm thyself, Cartamandua-son. I'll await thee, that we might advance thy teaching as the night settles in. If I can convince my sire of the need, I can gift thee the walking gard at next dawning, and so shall we be quit of each other the sooner."

"Tonight? Certainly . . . but . . ." I hadn't expected to go out again. Yet it was really just morning down by the sea. The rain pounded Picus's thatched roof, the tumbledown sheds to either side of it, and the thick mat of leaves beneath the bedraggled maples and copper beeches. "Won't you come indoors with us, vayar? I've so many questions. We could talk where it's dry."

Kol reached for a sturdy branch above his head, and in one smooth motion lifted his shoulders above the branch until he supported his whole weight on his stretched arms and hands. A graceful swing of his legs, a twisting motion, and he sat on the branch, knees drawn up in his encircling arms, perched as easily as a cat. "Thou'lt not be long inside."

Whether this was a statement or a command, I wasn't sure. Kol's manner was a bit wearing. If my mother was beloved of all, then surely her brother must have something to recommend him. I just hadn't seen it . . . save, of course, the grace to protect my physical well-being against Danae spite. From the sheltering doorway I watched him turn his face up, allowing the cold rain to bathe his face and stream his long red hair down his back.

"He is beautiful, is he not?" Picus stood at my shoulder, the ripe aroma of unwashed flesh and a diet heavy with wild onions souring the autumn pungency of old leaves and wet pine bark. "No Ardran rose was ever so lovely, no Morian stag ever so regal, no Evanori boar ever so stubborn as Kol Stian-son. Had he a soul, the Creator would not know whether to name him Archangel or condemn him to eternal fire for daring rival Him."

"Kol is certainly hard, but even I would not call him soulless." Not one who danced as he did, who grieved as he did.

Picus held open the flap of leather behind me. "Nay, nay. It is not a matter of naming. Have you ne'er been taught the holy writs, lad? The Creator gave the spark of life only to human creatures. Danae have souls no more than red deer or ash trees or the wind."

"Then what of those like me? Am I half souled, part tree, part man, destined for half heaven or half hell?" I tossed this out in jest, thinking he but carried on his sparring with Kol. But his prattle stilled long enough to disturb me. I turned and found his pale eyes picking at my face as if to search the darkest nooks and crannies behind my heart and ribs.

"I know not," he said softly. "There was a time when I believed the One God could not be so cruel as to beget a soulless creature upon a human parent. But then I saw evidence . . ." He switched his gaze back to the Dané in the tree. "Perhaps it is one by one He chooses."

I swallowed hard and hid my mottled hands in my soggy bundle of clothes. No soul . . . that was not possible. I shifted my shoulders as if to prove I had will and sense of my own, and I remembered Gillarine Abbey church and how I had felt uplifted there, and reverent—surely the sign of gods speaking to a *person*, one capable of repentance and service, one possessing life beyond the body's limits. But then, I had also felt uplifted when I saw Kol dance, when I had looked on Elene silhouetted in sunlight, and when I'd sat in Gillarine's refectory eating stewed parsnips. How would one ever know if one lacked a soul? Even Danae had thoughts and will, emotions and, at least in Kol's case, some sense of honor—not the marks of soulless beasts.

"Was Kol so fierce before his sister—my mother—was imprisoned?" Cowardly, I asked no more of souls.

"Kol hath ever a sober cast of mind," said the monk, palpably relieved at my shift of subject. "More than most Danae, and of a certain, more than Clyste—not that she lacked intelligence to accompany her cheery nature. He ever seeks perfection in his being—a hard road for any of God's creatures. But Clyste made him laugh and softened his eye, and my dear lad challenged him to find delight in brotherly friendship as well as duty. Twixt them both, held so dear by their love, Kol reflected Iero's light upon us all. But I fear his joy has died with them."

My dear lad . . . It took me a moment to realize the monk spoke of Eodward.

"Come inside, lad, and relieve thy chill." The monk's hand gripped my shoulder kindly, even if his offer was wholly nonsensical. Naught could relieve the chill he had just laid on me. For a being without a soul, death became the end of all.

Moist heat slapped my face as I ducked and stepped into Picus's round hut—scarce eight paces across. Saverian knelt by a small fire pit in the center of the dark room, stretching her cloak to help the thick layers to dry. I needed no polite encouragement to sit on the hard-packed dirt beside her. Not only could I not stand upright without cracking my head on the low slanting ribs of the roof or poking my eye on wayward thatch, but I could scarce see or breathe at that height. If the monk had a hole in the roof to draw out his smoke, it was wholly inadequate to the task.

Picus let the door flap fall behind us. Quicker than blinking he had coaxed his fire brighter, set a clay pot of water over it, and snapped sprigs from a dry bundle dangling from his roof alongside a skinned rabbit, several woven nets bulging with pale, dusty vegetables, a variety of tools with leather-wrapped handles, and a pair of snowshoes. He settled cross-legged across the fire from me and Saverian and crushed the leaves into a clay mug and bowl. "We'll have a bracing tea anon. 'Tis such pleasure to have company, I scarce know up from down—not seen a human person in much longer than you'd want to account. I'm flummoxed that I can recall how to speak, so you must command me stopper my mouth when thy ears protest. Kol comes to check on me now and again. Tends my garden or brings me a fish or a bag of apples, and in return I deluge him with human words, poor fellow, the last thing he cares to hear. Which recalls . . ."

He sprang to his feet and poked his head through the door flap. "Kol, as thou'rt waiting . . . my turnips suffer black mold, and the onions pull up soft and slimed, scarce a layer fit to eat. I fret this rain will finish them. The spelt in the far mead has no ripe heads, and frost nips the dawn. I know it's been scarce a month since you've tended it, but if thou wouldst have mercy upon my poor plot, I'd be most grateful."

I tried to hear Kol's response, but I could not distinguish it from the sounds of snapping fire and rain rustling on the thatch, and the thousand other noises of storm-racked forest and distant sea vying for attention in my head. Overwhelmed with mystery, I could not even imagine what Picus required. I doubted Kol would set to work with rake and hoe. Another question to add to my growing tally.

I held my hands near the fire, but instantly withdrew them before my skin blackened like scorched paper. The shifting blue marks had faded to silver. I wrapped my arms around my unsettled middle and hoped the steam rising from my sodden shirt would suffice to calm my shivering.

Picus closed the flap again and lowered himself to the dirt floor, scratching his grizzled chin. " 'Tis a wonder Kol comes here. The land grows ill. Will not stay healthy no matter that he puts it right. And my company is no pleasure to him. Though, indeed, he's exiled himself from *their* company, save when he is summoned to the dance. Even his sire is near a stranger to him since Clyste's fall."

I believed I knew why. "None but you and he know that Janus fathered Clyste's child."

Picus nodded. "After Clyste's prisoning, I saw that Kol bore some weighty burden and seemed like to shatter with it. So I baited him into a fight—not so difficult to do, as you see—and goaded forth his secret. Took me a good trimonth to walk without those bruises squalling, and I've ne'er regrown the teeth."

He kneaded his unshaven left jaw for a moment, his attention suddenly far away. But then he scooted around and rummaged in the dark behind him, pulling out two irregularly woven blankets that might once have had some color. He gave one to each of us. "Come, thou'rt a soggy pair. Bundle up and get warm, mistress. I'll leave thee lone here in the house and take me to the shed when sleep time comes so ye can do what women must. And I'll not even think on it, I promise, or if I do, I'll perform my most rigorous spiritual exercises or even hike me down to the sea and douse my head, though I could wish for better weather or at the least Kol to take me down a shorter path. The determination to penance can take a man only so far until it falls into the sin called 'pride of mortification,' if thou'rt familiar with Karish vice and virtue."

"Good monk, you've no need to give up your bed," said Saverian. "I'm a daughter of Evanore and our customs see no wrong in stalwart women sheltering with honorable men." She was being exceptionally polite. She didn't correct his use of *mistress.*

Shaking his head sadly, Picus poured the simmering water over his herbs and handed the mug to Saverian and the bowl to me. "Ah, mistress, hope of heaven and true repentance bids me warn ye that I am no honorable man, but abjectly fallen. Though vowed chaste at fifteen, and gi'en naught to suffer in this life but a surfeit of adventure and the joy to serve the fairest prince the One God ever sent to humankind, I succumbed to the Adversary's assault and broke my vows and the most solemn responsibilities of a teacher to lie with a woman. None should trust me."

A long pull on the steaming tea seemed to restore the physician's ironical humor. She tilted her head and examined the monk, as he opened a flat wood chest he'd dragged from the same dark corner where he'd found the blanket. "So you what ... consummated an attraction ... kept a female companion ... in two-hundred-some years ... a healthy man who lives among beings who go about unclothed? I've little understanding of Karish ways, despite my association with Brother Valen here, but I hardly see the difficulty. If you are indeed this Picus ... a man of such advanced years ... I would think the continuation of a young man's animal urgencies would be more reassuring than problematical—mayhap a sign of your god's favor." She sounded little short of laughter, which I feared must surely wound a monk so determined to penance, no matter how foolish we judged his rigor.

"The structure of virtue was the last lesson of my novitiate, Saverian," I said, "though I scarce got beyond naming the seven great virtues and the twelve great vices. But pride of mortification made sense to me—the vice of those who aggrandize themselves by the extremity of their pen-

ance rites or humility. Clearly Brother Picus heeds the first
duty of the sinner—to sincerely balance his reparations
with his clearest assessment of the severity of his sin. We
must honor his judgment, while welcoming his willingness
to allow us to intrude upon his solitude."

Picus looked as though the portal to heaven had opened
in front of him. His rounded mouth opened and closed
like that of a fish. His hands, one holding a rank-smelling
onion and the alter holding a leaf-wrapped bundle that
smelled fishy, dropped into his lap. "Novitiate?" he stammered. "Thou art Karish, then, a monk vowed, as well as
the Cartamandua's halfbreed son who has begun to take
the Danae passages. How comes that—?" Pain etched his
fleshless face. "Ah, great Iero's heart, I must not even ask. I
have *renounced* the world."

"I did take novice vows, but my abbot sent me back
into the world. The story is very long, Brother Picus, and
not half so interesting as your own, which we would relish
hearing."

This man had known King Eodward ... and Caedmon
himself. He could tell us of the Danae ... of Kol and his
disaffection from his own kind ... of my mother and her
plan ... perhaps even something of the world's grief. A
guilty fear gnawed at me that the archon would be so an-
gered by my escape, he would refuse to tell Osriel what
they knew of the failing world. If I could learn from Picus,
perhaps I could make up for it. Once Kol set me free to go
back to the human world in safety, I could send what I'd
learned to the cabal, thus keeping my vow to Luviar. As for
Osriel himself, I felt no pity. Likely they would not cripple
him for their own failure to hold on to me.

"Thou must tell me thy names, at the least," said Picus,
as he busied himself with his pot and his bundles, "and
some small summary of thy purpose in Aeginea, lest I go
mad and forget even my devotions. If the Cartamandua
did not send thee to Kol, then how come ye here? Kol's
pride would never allow him to fetch thee. Didst thou not
know what breaking awaited a halfbreed, boy? I fought to
convert the long-lived from all their heathenish ways, especially from such cruel abuse of their own children"—he
clutched his hands to his chest for a moment, closing his

eyes and looking as if he might choke—"but their terror
of Llio's curse ever drives them. And you, lady, so wise and
gentlewomanly . . . an Evanori warrior? Stalwart, I'll vow,
but not half so ferocious as the warlords I remember, who
painted their faces with blood and brought Hansker scalps
to lay before King Caedmon. How come ye here with Janus's son?"

As his stream of words bounded and flowed like an exuberant watercourse, the monk dropped the leaf-wrapped
bundle into the blackened clay pot and whipped a knife
from the folds of his robe. Though the blade was worn
near the slimness of a stiletto, he proceeded to slice the
onion into the pot, as well, tossing the moldy outer skin out
through the dripping door flap.

"My name is Valen," I said. "I've come here to learn of
the world. Tell me, what is this Llio's cu—?"

Of a sudden, I was not sure I could sit still to hear
the secrets of heaven, much less whatever tidbits the monk
could reveal. Picus's pot belched steam, smelling strongly
of fish and onion. The smoke filled my lungs, and the rank
smell curdled my belly. My skin itched. My foot tapped the
dirt floor uncontrollably. So little air.

I waved at the physician to take up the conversation,
while I downed the lukewarm tea—mint and elderberry—
and appreciated its spreading comfort. An unlikely sweat
broke out beneath my wet, scratchy shirt.

"I am Saverian, physician and student of natural philosophy, house mage to Osriel, Duc of Evanore, Prince of
Navronne. A daughter of warriors, not one myself."

Picus's expression blossomed with wonder. "You serve
my king's son? What a fine man he must be. I had warned
Eodward that the One God disapproved using holy marriage for wartime alliance, but the Moriangi grav and his
men knew of ships, and when we drove the Aurellians to
the sea, 'twas the grav who crushed them. And the grav's
daughter produced such a robust babe. I knew him only as
a motherless boy, of course, rough mannered and interested
in naught but fighting. I tutored him in combat as I had
his father. I tried to introduce book studies as well, but the
fighting was heavy in those days, and we were constantly on
the move, so we'd no time for it."

Saverian nodded. "You speak of Bayard, the eldest of Eodward's three sons. When times were more settled, another son, Perryn, was born to Eodward's second wife, an Ardran ducessa. My master is the third and youngest, born to his pureblood mistress. You *do* know of Eodward's fate, Brother?"

"Do I know he is dead? Aye. Even I, whose eyes remain steadfastly human, saw the sun dim on that day. Kol came to break the news and invite me to share his kiran, but I could not, though I knew it would be such a glory as I had not seen since he danced for Clyste. I sent him away, that a heathen creature would not witness a monk's blaspheming, for I had always believed merciful Iero must surely bring my lad home before the end. Whate'er his sins, as any king must commit in carrying his office, they could not be so dread as to forbid him one last glimpse of the Canon after so long away. Once thou hast seen it . . ." The monk dashed a hairy knuckle at his eyes, as he stirred his pot with a wooden spoon. "Three sons left. A mercy in that at the least."

A mercy only if we did not tell him of the princes and their war. Though Picus's talk touched on old mysteries, like the Canon, and new ones like this *Llio's curse* that caused the Danae to cripple halfbreeds, and *kirani* that seemed something more than mere dancing, it was an effort to concentrate on the conversation. I hunched deeper into myself, cold and hot together, ravenous, yet unsure if I could choke down this mess he stirred. Something was definitely wrong with me. When had I ever found aught I would not eat? The light had gone completely from my gards, leaving my skin purplish gray and leprous in appearance.

"Why did you abandon King Eodward, Brother?" said Saverian, a physician setting out to diagnose the world's ills. "You vanished without a word to the king or anyone else. You were seen leaving Palinur, but no evidence of mishap or treason was ever found. Even the journals you left behind told Eodward nothing of your fate. The prince says his father died yet grieving for your loss, chastising himself for some unknown failure that drove you away. Surely your god would agree that service to Navronne's king supersedes any personal penance, especially for minor transgressions of the flesh."

Picus squeezed his broad brow tight as if to force aside the sentiments that had bubbled so near his surface. "One night's fall from grace drove me from my lord's side. I had long renounced the woman and thought I'd made amends. But when I was confronted with the lasting evidence of my wickedness and shown how it contravened everything I loved, everything *he* loved, I knew no man had ever so abjectly failed his god or his lord. Ronila said that to cleanse my sin I must bleed, suffer, and die by my own hand or hers. But the One God forbids self-murder, and I would not add to my soul's debt by allowing her to take my blood on her own hand. So I swore to her on Iero's name that I would die to the world—leave my prince and all my friends and holy brothers without apology or explanation, and live henceforth in solitude, penury, and repentance for as long as the streams of time might carry me forward. She knew me and believed I would keep any pledge so sworn. And so I have, save for these few untimely lapses, when I am out of measure surprised."

"Ronila?" said Saverian. "The woman you lay with . . . who must have been a student, if you betrayed a teacher's trust. But I thought your only student was Eodward himself."

I glanced up from my knees where I had focused my eyes to get control of my stomach. The dim smoky room swirled unpleasantly. "You mentioned Ronila in your journal—a disaffected halfbreed girl who left Aeginea after making her third change."

Picus wagged his head. "We witnessed her knee-breaking, my prince and I. A golden child of an age ye would judge fourteen summers. 'Tis after the child passes the second remasti they do it. She screamed and begged us to save her from crippling, but we could not. My prince was naught but a tender seven-year-old, and I God-sworn to protect him above all things, which meant honoring Danae customs. So much pain . . . After, I thought to give her something back to redeem her suffering, something the others would not have and could never take from her. The long-lived claim to bear no grudge against a broken halfbreed, but of course they do. They seek perfection in their arts—which are firstly their bodies and their use of them—and thus treated her

with cruel disdain. She was clever at numbers and had such
a vivid imagining that she devoured all I could teach her of
Navronne, of natural philosophy, of human history and warfare, of moral philosophy and the teachings of Karus. Every
afternoon when she had completed her tasks of the day—
making baskets or weaving spidersilk or gathering apples
or mushrooms—she would hobble to my canopy for teaching . . . Ah, I babble on too long. I sinned. I renounced that
sin. But I will pay the price of it until my bones are dust."

He tightened his mouth and would not speak more
for a while. He broke pinches of herbs from his dangling
bundles and threw them in his pot, each breaking an explosion of fragrance. The scent of dried mushrooms, damp
earth, and moldering leaves left the memory of nivat on
my tongue. Sweat dribbled down my sides. My left thigh
muscle cramped, and an ember burned in my gut . . .

No! Nivat no longer had power over me. I forced my
thoughts away from my body. So the celibate monk, exiled far from home and holy brotherhood, had seduced a
half-Danae girl. Or had she, a lonely outcast, enamored of
a kind, virile young man, used her Danae wiles to tempt
him? Yet more troubled me than such common failings as
lust and seduction. Something in the telling of his story . . .
something in the words . . . had touched off a bone-deep
revulsion, but I could not capture it. Wit seemed to have
drained out of me, along with the myriad telltales of my
senses that had been with me since the remasti. This win-
dowless room. So small. So close.

"Here, give me thy cup, good Valen, and we'll see thy
belly filled."

I looked up and Picus's grimed face leered huge and
grotesque in the garish firelight. The encircling walls of his
hut bulged inward, threatening to squeeze the breath out of
me. Heat seared and scoured my limbs. Of a sudden I was
back in my bedchamber in Palinur, my skin on fire from my
father's leather strap, panicked, cursing, screaming, beating
on the door barricaded with sorcery as the walls closed in.
The firelight wavered . . . darkened.

"Excuse . . . must go." Gasping for air, I scrambled to my
feet, knocking my forehead on the roof beams, and escaped
into the night.

Saverian burst through the door flaps while my hands were yet propped on the outer wall of a lean-to filled with wood, and I was gulping great lungfuls of cold air. "Do you need the medallion, Valen?"

"Just air. So hot." I fumbled at the laces on the scratchy shirt and ripped it over my head, allowing the cold rain to hammer and scour and revive every part of my skin. My senses quickly regained some balance. "Sorry. Rude of me."

From her shelter in the hut's doorway, she held out her cupped hand, overflowing with tangled gold chain. "Perhaps you should wear this."

Shaking my head, fighting to shed the oppression of panic and suffocation, I turned around and leaned my back against the woodshed. The sodden shirt wadded in my hands preserved a bit of propriety. "I'll be all right. You may write this in your notes: Danae halfbreeds sicken within walls."

Kol had known what would happen. The Dané no longer sat in the tree, but music had joined the clamor in my head, and I glimpsed blue flashes among the trees. "It must be time for my lessons. You'd best stay here, unless . . ."

I beckoned Saverian urgently. Without hesitation, she darted across a muddy strip and sheltered under the lip of the shed.

My finger on her lips silenced her question, and I dropped my own voice to a whisper. ". . . Unless you're afraid of the monk."

She yanked my hand away and took on such a look of scorn as would chill a salamander. "Afraid of the chance to converse with a man two hundred years old? I'd barter my maidenhead for the chance, and here it is laid in my—" Of a sudden the fireglow of her damp cheeks outshone the white light from the twiggy lantern. "What are you smirking at? That I happen to find many amusements more enticing than rutting like an overheated dog? Study the human body and its lamentable urges, and you'll see it is an altogether ridiculous object."

"Bless me, gods, that I remain an unstudious man!" Not even her sour expression could restrain my laughter.

But now that the rain had reawakened the chaotic information of my senses, I could give thought to the serious matters that had gathered with the deepening night. So I stifled amusement and quieted my voice. Despite her peculiarities, Saverian was a woman of sense and intelligence. I could not stay here to learn what I needed, but perhaps she could.

"Saverian, if you would, I beg you discover what you can of this Llio's curse—this Danae fear of halfbreeds. My mother conceived a halfbreed apurpose, knowing what her people would do to me if I was caught. Why would she do that? Kol says that she believed I belonged in the Canon, which makes no sense at all. The mere consideration appalls and disgusts him, and I've no faith that I can budge him to tell me more. And there's something else ... something in the monk's story ... that sets off warning trumps in my head. Truly I'm half knob-swattled with this day and cannot capture it, yet every bone in my body screams that all this is connected: Eodward's history, Danae intransigence, my birth, the wretched weather, and the sickness of the world, the Harrowers and their poisoning of the Danae."

A thought darted past like a firefly, before being swallowed in an assault of scents reminiscent of a town marketplace: baking pies, roasting meat, leather goods and perfumes, herbs, vegetables, and scented oils, horse manure, pigs. I prayed that Kol could teach me what to do with all of it.

"Even if you care naught for Navronne, you're Osriel's friend and servant," I said. "What we learn here could be the keys to his future."

"Osriel betrayed you. Why would you care about his future?"

"You've witnessed the havoc the Harrowers wreak in Navronne. And I promise the damage is much deeper than that you saw. Surely you saw, too, the hope he brought them, almost without trying. People wiser than me have entrusted Navronne's salvation to Prince Osriel's hand—but I fear that trust has been misplaced unless we can find out the truth of all this before he takes a path of desperation. This thing you will not speak of. This thing he hopes to fuel with Danae magic. I have this notion I can help him, but only if I learn enough."

What wastrel fool had ever made so pompous a statement? But I *did* feel it, however foolish. If I could only see the way.

Saverian nodded slowly, her clear eyes as lustrous as jade in the white light. I had never noticed their color. "I'll learn what I can." Then she lowered her lids halfway and snatched the wadded shirt from my hand. "Meanwhile, I'll dry this out. I doubt you'll need it for a while."

I grinned as she threw it over her shoulder and ducked into Picus's hut. Then I set off into the trees to find Kol. Amid the cascading telltales of hunting foxes, nervous deer, and mice and moles that burrowed through leaves and earth, I heard Picus greet Saverian with concerned questioning. She reassured him as to my health. "Ah, for certain," he said. "I'd forgot how the walls torment the odd creatures . . ."

Creatures . . . beings that had no souls. My smile faded.

Chapter 15

———◆———

Kol crouched impossibly high in the limbs of a leaf-
bare ash that bordered a swath of open meadow.
The wind rustled knee-high grass and faded leaves,
and the rain outlined odd dark shapes, barriers of timber and
tied brush set at angles across the meadow. I blinked, astonished that I could see so much as that on a starless, moonless night. The air smelled of must and soured grain, of soggy
earth and the small stream that bisected the gentle slope,
and of a thousand other scents that had naught to do with
this meadow. A wolf's howl sent chilly fingers up my bare
spine, hinting that even the magics of Aeginea could not
hold back this foul winter. Naked in the night wood . . . I'd
never felt such an idiot.

As I opened my mouth to call him, the Dané rose from
his crouch and brushed bits of bark and leaf from his skin.
Angling his feet, as if for proper balance on the branch, he
stretched his arms skyward. His gards brightened to the
cold blue of a mountain winter sky. Somewhere—in my
head, in my heart, in my imagining?—music swelled. The
sweet clarity of a rebec's bowed strings twined my over-
crowded thoughts in a single long note that stretched my
nerves taut . . . and then Kol launched himself from the top
of the ash.

My heart near stopped until his feet touched solidly to
the grass, and he began to whirl and spin and leap through
the meadow, a glory of power and strength, raising one and

then another thread of melody to join in a driving gigue. Danae danced to the land's music—or made it.

Determined to understand what he did, I pushed aside the wet leaves and pine needles at the edge of the wood, pressed my fingers into the mud, and released magic. As if lightning illuminated the symbols on a fiché, I glimpsed rowed turnips, carrots, and onions slimed and rotting underground, a plot of stunted wheat across the stream, and hungry moles panting as they excavated tunnels underneath it all, their fur patched with disease. My spirit choked at the suffocating sickness. Kol's exuberant feet scribed silvered traces across the unhealthy landscape, his every bend, dip, and spin bringing new complexity to his insistent melodies.

I could have watched him dance until the end of days. Every note perfect ... every step exquisite ... exhilarating. Even when I knelt up, allowing the rain to rinse the mud from my hands, the magic he raised in Picus's garden meadow enfolded me in such beauty as would draw a stone's tears.

The music reached its whirling climax, and Kol stretched legs and arms to leap in one great arc across the stream, streaks of blue trailing behind him as if his gards were threads of silk, whipped to frenzy by the wind of his passing. Above and below and around me an explosion of color washed the landscape like watered ink. The healthier humors of a nearby forest glade flooded the diseased plots. Owl and hawk rose up from the wood, dark shapes diving and soaring to purge the pests, while other creeping creatures deep buried in the soil, too tiny for a human eye to see, woke to cleanse and nourish roots and stems. The waterlogged soil released its burden, riddling the undersoil with new channels to the stream. When the spinning Dané took a knee, aligning his back and outstretched leg in the position I'd come to know as completion, it seemed as if the earth gave a great sigh of contentment, while I was left roused and aching with unspent desire.

Kol held his position for a long while, and when at last he stood, his posture bespoke a man completely drained. His head came up, expression vague and lost, his sculpted features sharpening only slowly when he caught sight of me. He heaved a sigh, kneaded his neck, and started up the gentle slope, following the path of the stream. A slight sweep of his right hand commanded me to follow.

I joined him, padding through wet grass while he strode on a game trail that bordered the stream. "How do you do it?" I said, when it became clear he had no plan to initiate conversation. "Draw the music from plants and beasts and dirt clods? Use your body . . . your movements . . . to join all the parts together? Is the Canon something like this?"

"I am not here to teach thee of the dance. I'll not speak of the Canon. Nor will I guide thee through the remasti of regeneration. No use in developing skills . . . and hungers . . . thou canst neither use nor satisfy." He swept his dripping hair back from his face, squeezed water from it, and tied it into a heavy knot at the back of his neck.

"Regeneration," I repeated. Osriel had said the third remasti was the passage of regeneration, when Danae first experienced the hungers of fleshly love . . . when they became both capable and desirous of mating. "*That's* what you did to this field. Your dance healed its sickness as a human physician heals a body, diagnosing its ills and applying the proper remedy. You called forth creatures to cleanse and nourish it, changed its makeup in subtle ways to leave it healthier. But the way you accomplished it was more like mating than healing. The dance this morning touched my spirit, but this . . . I was honored . . . humbled . . . to witness it, *relagai*."

Kol cast me a sidewise glance. Suspicious. "Thy gards tell thee these things?"

I looked down at my mottled arms and legs, so pale and ill-defined beside the brilliant clarity of his dragons, reeds, and heron. My marks no longer flashed or swirled. I doubted a human eye would even notice them were I ten paces distant. Yet though the wind had picked up, and I felt its bitter edge, the cold no longer penetrated beyond my skin.

"No. Not the gards . . ." I stumbled a bit, as the truth of my change settled even deeper in my gut. "I saw, or well . . . rather, it's something like seeing. When I touch the earth and use my magic . . . my Cartamandua bent . . . an image of the surrounding land forms in my mind, in my senses, so I see and hear and smell what's there or has been there in the past—plants, beasts, humans, the paths they've left. And I can explore the image—look deeper, learn how it fits together, as I did with the tide pool. It's difficult to describe."

"Thy *senses* comprehend the particular changes I brought to this land?" Surprise and skepticism boiled out of him like seepage from a wound. "Without study or examination or practice?"

"The changes—the hunting birds you called forth, the water channels, the rest—yes. The paths of your movements that link them all together appear to me as threads of silver across the landscape. I can see the threads even as you draw them, and those of other Danae from earlier times."

He halted in midstep and glared at me, his aspen-gold eyes like flame in the darkness. "Thou canst see the *paths* of the kiran—the patterns left behind from the dance?" His tone dared me to affirm it.

"I could walk them as you do this track under your feet."

He clamped his mouth shut and stomped faster up the path. When a dead limb blocked his way, likely fallen from Picus's fence making, he snatched it up and threw it farther than even my improved eyesight could make out in the middle of the night. Had it struck a fortification, even at such a distance, I would wager on the stick to penetrate the stone, so vicious was its launch. I'd thought he would approve my increased understanding. Perhaps I had trespassed some protocol by observing Danae mysteries or speaking of them. I trailed along behind him, my bare feet tormented with sticks and rocks, narrowly avoiding wrenching my ankle in some burrower's entry hole, and near giving up on comprehending my uncle.

As the vale sloped upward, the land grew rockier, so my battered feet could attest. The path soon vanished, as did the stream, replaced, almost before I could imagine it, by rills and rivulets that trickled across the hillside from thick forest on either side of us. The soil beneath my feet thinned. At least the rain had slackened, holding somewhere between a drizzle and a mist. Kol's gards flared brighter.

Of a sudden, I realized that we had traveled farther from Picus's meadow than our steps could justify. Alert now, I began to feel a shifting when Kol invoked his magic—when the path took a sudden turning or broke dramatically uphill. When the scent of pine and spruce entirely supplanted the scent of oak and ash and hawthorn in the space of twenty paces. When the air grew sharply colder and very dry.

"Your gards carry power that enables you to move from one place to another," I said, pushing my steps to keep up with the fast-moving Dané.

"Aye. After the second remasti, the stripling's growing familiarity with the world becomes a part of the walking gards and can be called on as desired." The brisk walk seemed to have restored his calm. "The particular slope of a grass-covered hillside recalls that of a mountain meadow. The sound of one stream echoes another that happens to feed a mighty river. Just here"—he pointed to a stand of evergreens—"the odd shape of that tallest tree's crown recalls to me the outline of another tree against a different sky, thus forms a path from this place to the next. I can walk there if I will. It is all a matter of similarity and recollection, for all places are bound one to the other in ways a human—most humans—cannot perceive."

"Sometimes we do," I said. "We come to a new place, yet feel as if we've been there before. Or we meet a stranger and feel as if we know her already."

"Perhaps." A grudging admission.

By the time I wrenched my eyes from the fork-tipped fir, disappointed it had not belched fire or displayed some other obvious magic, we walked a slightly steeper path amid widely scattered trees. My breathing labored. Around another corner and we were traversing the shoulder of a conical peak outlined against a star-filled sky. Mist floated like a gray sea below us.

A half hour's hard climb and we had left the last stunted trees behind. We came to a rocky prominence—a thick slab of pale stone, some twenty quercae in height, that poked up in gloomy isolation from the mountainside. Kol propped one foot on a broad flat shard, long split off from the standing rock and toppled to the grass.

"We begin thy teaching here," he said. "Thy gards draw

in the sights and sounds, tastes and smells from forest, vale, and shore, as well as the dust of Picus's foolish babbling and the stink of his dwelling place. No doubt remember-ings of thy usual days intrude upon thy perceptions, as well. Likely it is some confusion of these impressions with the observation of my kiran that caused this *seeing* thou hast reported."

So he had not entirely dismissed his disturbance at my claim. "Yes, my eyes, nose, and ears are overwhelmed, but what I saw back there, the silver traces—"

"Thy task is not to think or speak," he snapped. "I'll give thee ample opportunity to question. 'Tis the deeps of the night here on Aesol Mount, the time when the world is qui-etest. Best for listening to voices that cannot be heard in the day. Best for learning control."

I shut my mouth, suppressed my resentful urge to kick him, and bowed. I needed to learn.

As before, the politeness seemed to take him a bit off guard. "I should not have taken the time to shape a kiran for Picus's plantings. Thou didst not linger within his walls as long as I thought a halfbreed might, thus my hurry opened the way for this misunderstanding. So, no matter." He waved as if his willing could dismiss my beliefs. "A wan-derkin's task is learning of the world, thus the separation gards are the most sensitive and most subject to confusion. Thou must seek perfection in their use, as in all things. For now, I promised to teach thee closure and control. Sit be-fore the rock"—he pointed to the featureless slab—"and listen. Stone speaks softly but with utmost authority. Seek its voice. Listen for it alone, and it will root thee firmly. Once thou canst hear the speech of stones, thou shalt begin to understand closure."

Were he anyone else, I might discount such instruction as lunacy. But the man who had made love to Picus's garden, tending it, infusing it with life, must be granted trust despite our other disagreements. The effects of his work yet fired my blood. Feeling exceedingly awkward, I sat cross-legged on the damp ground facing the rock and reached out.

"Do not touch the rock!"

I snatched my hand away.

"Our purpose is to develop and exercise thy control

of the gards. Human tricks have no place here. Heed the stone. Work at it."

Balls of Karus, the man is difficult! The task seemed impossible with him standing not two paces behind me, with the riot of smells, sounds, and tastes from my senses swelling my skull to bursting. The traveling had, at least, reduced the uncomfortable involvement of my privy parts, but had presented its own myriad questions. And somehow in this clean and pungent air, my charge to Saverian kept repeating itself in my mind . . .

I needed to understand Llio's curse, which condemned halfbreeds to crippling. My sudden conviction that my own existence was intimately entwined with the fate of Navronne had surprised even myself. But surely my life had taken no random course—not from the day I was conceived, not from the day I happened upon the book of maps, not from the day three months past when I lay bleeding in a ditch, only to stagger, blind and ignorant, straight to my mother's sianou, where a Karish abbot had built his lighthouse. Clyste, a dancer so powerful that the earth itself had chosen her for a guardian, had laid the preservation of the lighthouse . . . of Navronne . . . at her son's feet. My feet. Of a sudden that seemed so obvious. And terrifying.

Listen for the stone. A hand clamped my bare shoulder as a dog's jaws grip a bone, infusing my body with my vayar's will. I had to learn before I could act. And so I shoved aside fear and looming destiny for the moment and set to work.

How would one recognize the voice of stone? First concentrate on hearing in preference to the other senses. Dismiss colors, images, tastes, and tactile sensations. *Soft*, Kol had described it, and so I dismissed the noisy, loud, and brightest sounds, the florid trumps and horns, the bawling of donkeys, the screams of prisoners, and cackles of madmen. *With utmost authority*, he'd said, and so I dismissed the quiet nattering of birds and insects, the trivial speech of gossips, and the soft mouthings of lovers, the pale colorings of everyday living. As if the entirety of my perceptions were bedcoverings, I peeled away layers, hunting a voice of solidity, of weight, of dense, slow changes . . .

Saints and angels, this is impossible! As if slogging through desert dunes hunting for one particular grain of sand, I would push one thought aside only to feel five thousand more cascade into its place. But in the end, when all else was stripped away, a soft word rumbled through my spirit like distant thunder, like the shudder of an avalanche halfway across the world. A burden settled on my shoulders ... ponderous ... immense. *Hold.* And some interminable time later came another. *Forever.*

This was no dialect a mouth could imitate. Truly I *heard* no speech at all—no sentient mind produced such words. Rather I experienced an expression of unyielding heaviness and stalwart density, stiffening my back and chest, forcing thigh and shoulder taut. Unmoving. Unshakable. Just as I was about to release my concentration and declare victory, for of a certain no entity but a mountain itself could speak with such weight, another word boomed from a wholly different direction. *Crush.* I held breathless, as if the massive boulder and its fellows were grinding *me* to powder. *Pound. Squeeze.* This voice drummed cold and harsh. Then came another voice—smaller, lost. *Deep. Tumbling. Diminished.* Dizzy, I imagined smooth rounded stones washed endlessly in a mountain river, their substance ground inevitably away.

Fascinated, I sorted through the slow-moving litany, seeking the voice of the particular rock before me, for the words came one and then the other with great gaps in between. Was this a conversation? I decided not. A foolish notion, and yet what would I have said a few days previous to anyone who told me I would hear words in the voices of stone?

Shattered. Waves of blazing heat rolled over me, and more of wet and brittle cold, an uneasy pressure culminating in explosive power and breaking—*this* rock, whose fractured shoulder lay prostrate beside it, whose enduring memory spoke destruction and ending.

I'm sorry, I answered. Not that I believed the slab could think or understand, only that its overwhelming desolation required some response.

Satisfied and weary, I released the sensory textures of the world to intrude once again. How small and weak they seemed. Not trivial. Not unimportant. But eminently controllable. This must be what Kol wished me to understand. Closure.

Excited, I nudged and poked at the clutter, recalling the depths to which I'd gone to hear the stone. The act cleared a small space where I could have a thought without intrusive clamor. Of course, my newfound order quickly collapsed into confusion again. This would take practice. I gave up and opened my eyes.

Mist had crept up the mountain and enfolded me, soft and damp. The bulging moon hung in the sky, thinly veiled like a pureblood bride. A rush of air overhead marked a hunting eagle's quiet passage.

"This rock misliked its breaking, vayar," I said, grinning as I straightened my back and twisted my neck, stretching out muscles too long still. Had someone told me I'd sat before the confounded rock three nights in tandem, I could have believed it. I needed a piss so badly, I felt like to burst.

No one answered. And I felt no presence behind me. I peered first over my shoulder and then around the rock.

Kol stood slightly higher on the slope, conversing with another male of his kind, this one shorter and wider in the shoulder, though yet lean and tautly muscled. The moonlight-illumined moon-white hair, bound into a long tail tied every knuckle's length with scarlet. The gard on his broad back—a twisted pine as you might see on a mountain crag—gleamed a sharp and vibrant cerulean. The two of them were arguing and did not glance my way.

I shifted my position slightly, so that I could observe the two less obviously. Clearing away the clutter inside my head, I picked out Kol's voice.

". . . told the tale of my kiran as if he had himself designed it. He touches the earth to know these things. He *saw* my changes, Stian. He claims to see the kiran patterns themselves." Kol's voice rang tight. Anxious.

Stian . . . my Danae grandfather. The eldest of my family. Wonder held me speechless.

"And this is the same sorcerer who brought death to Aniiele's meadow? Who violated Clyste's sianou so that now thy sister, too, lies poisoned by the Scourge? How canst thou look upon a human without loathing? How canst thou ask me to approve a halfbreed as my charge?" The elder crouched beside a cracked slab of rock and picked at a tangle of vegetation, tossing aside dead leaves and stems. "The Cartamandua . . . healthy for them both thou didst hide this history from me. Humans are a breed of vipers."

I held my place behind the rock, excitement quenched. Fortunate that experience had given me no expectations of warm family welcomes.

Kol stood his ground above the older man. "Indeed, this Valen broached Clyste's sianou, but only his companion sullied the water that day. And I've told thee repeatedly that he *saved* Aniiele, though I did not understand how so at the time. The hands of the Scourge had struck down the victim and left him to bleed. But this sorcerer gave back the victim's choice as to the manner of his passing, and so, at the last, the victim's blood was freely given. Aniiele lives, Stian *sagai,* by virtue of this man's deeds."

Great Iero's heart . . . Kol had watched me murder Boreas! That terrible night had etched a vivid horror on my soul: the black, blood-smeared lips of Sila Diaglou and her henchmen; my old friend captive of agony and despair; the sweet meadow that had felt as a part of heaven stained in so vile a fashion by his blood and torment. *Blood freely given . . . Aniiele lives . . .* Though naught could cleanse the blood from my hands, Kol's words brought a measure of comfort I had never expected.

"I have tried to dismiss him," said Kol. "But he sticks to me like thorn. I have named him as insolent as his sire, yet he sounds the streams of earth with reverence and respect, using skills unknown to our kind. He hungers for learning and does not hold back. He led me to the poisoned Well, and I danced beside it. Had my kiran not been flawed with anger and grieving, I might even have reclaimed the Well. And Clyste . . . Thy daughter was no birdwit child, Stian, tricked into mating with a pithless fool. The Well chose her as its guardian, and she chose the Cartamandua as her child's sire. She never explained her choice even to me, but just this day I've wondered— Feel the waning season, *sagai.* The true lands are dying. Just this morning I've had to reclaim yon garden vale yet again. The Well and the Plain are lost, and my heart speaks what my mind cannot grasp—that the Canon is diminished by far more than we can remember. If this halfbreed's claim is true, if he can see the patterns, might he be—?"

The elder burst to his feet and shook his finger at his son. "*Thou* art our answer, Kol, not a halfbreed Cartamandua. Each season brings thee closer to perfection. All recognize it. Thou shouldst dance the Center this season. But thy petulant exile sours the archon and the circles, and as a storm wind among roses hath thine errant rescue of the halfbreed pricked Tuari's wrath. He would see thee bound and buried for the shame thou hast brought on our kind before Eodward's son. Only thy irreplaceable ability keeps thee free. Break the halfbreed. Give him over."

"Have I shamed *thee*, Stian *sagai*?" Kol's words cracked and snapped as does a frozen lake.

The white-haired Dané clasped his hands behind his neck and pressed his arms inward, as if to squeeze out the thoughts Kol had implanted in his head. Only after long silence did he release his grip. Tenderly he drew his fingers along Kol's hard cheek and tucked stray red curls behind the younger man's ear. "Nay, *jongai*, never shame," he said softly. "It is only . . . for good or ill, the archon's word speaks our Law. My human son has met his mortal fate. My daughter ne'er will dance with me again. I would not lose thee, too."

"Then do not allow Tuari's blind hatred to speak for thee. This halfbreed is born of Clyste. *Her* choice. Grant him the walking gard to keep him safe."

Stian dropped his hand heavily, leaving three small flowers twined in Kol's hair. "Bring him."

The true lands are dying. So simple a phrase to leave my heart hollow. Did no one know the reasons? Were even the Danae, who could reshape the earth and command its creatures, confounded by it? What did that do to Osriel's hope? Navronne's hope?

Kol tramped and skidded down the slope toward me. Wary of this elder who spoke so casually of breaking halfbreeds, I chose not to let them know I'd overheard. I sprang to my feet and shouted louder than before, "I've heard the stones' voices, vayar. This one is most unhappy."

"Thou hast heard—" Kol stopped halfway down the

slope and shook his head as if to clear it. "Come up, *re-jongai*. We will talk of stones' voices later. Stian summons thee."

When I reached Kol's side, and we climbed slowly toward the waiting elder Dané, he spoke softly. "Thou hast shown reasonable manners thus far, Valen, and I would caution thee to continue. My sire hath only tonight learned of thy parentage . . ."

". . . and he is no happier than I was."

For the first time I glimpsed amusement twitch Kol's fine mouth. "Thou hast no measure of his unhappiness, wanderkin. And Stian's skills make my own appear but a nestling's tricks."

I doubted that, having heard how Stian spoke of his son's talents, having witnessed those talents summon the earth itself to his service.

"And mention *not* thy female companion or the monk."

No, Stian would likely have no kind feelings for Eodward's tutor or a human stranger, however unlikely that Saverian and Kol would repeat my parents' folly. Indeed, the consideration of a mating between Stian's son and the physician conjured a delightful image—something like the conjoining of a swan and a woodpecker. A virginal woodpecker.

I smothered a grin. "Aye, *relagai*. No mention of distracting humans."

The elder Dané awaited us where the rolling meadow formed a shallow bowl, choked with dead willows and matted vegetation. His fingers stroked the blades of brittle grass that had once stood as tall as my hip.

"Stian *sagai*"—Kol bowed gracefully before his father—"I present a wanderkin of our blood-clan. I have accepted the charge of his dam to stand as his vayar. He hath pledged himself to explore and learn, and I judge that his talents and experience have given him knowledge sufficient to accept his walking gard. He answers to the name Valen."

Stian rose. A snarling cat graced the brow and cheek of the broad-shouldered Dané, its long tail twined about his neck. The gards that marked his flat belly, broad chest, and muscled limbs spoke of jungles and hot, languid pools. Despite his white hair, he appeared no older than Prior

Nemesio. A man in his prime, with spring-green eyes that scoured me.

"Scrawny. Thick-boned. Weak." I might have been a cow. An ugly cow.

Kol answered coolly. "Valen followed me from the Sentinel Oak to Evaldamon without rest, *sagai*. Even so, his strength or endurance is no matter. I seek thy consent only for the walking gard, that Clyste's child may have skills to elude those who would break him . . . to our shame. His use of those skills shall be his own burden, not thine or mine. He is not to dance."

Stian's lean face resembled Kol's. The father's chin sat squarer. The son's eyes sat deeper. Stian reminded me of the first stone whose voice I'd heard. Unyielding heaviness. Stalwart density.

The elder's arched nose flared in contempt, and the creases about his eyes deepened. "The Cartamandua bragged that he sowed his seed across the lands and seasons and taunted his kin with his scattered offspring. That such a preening rooster laid hand to Clyste . . . that she chose prisoning to protect him . . . Pah!"

"When I was a boy, Janus named the Danae glorious, generous, and hospitable," I snapped, anger banishing caution. "I refused to believe him, madman that he was, preferring the common wisdom that the long-lived are spiteful, petty, and cruel. A child's insights can be astonishing, can they not? For even then, I did not know that a Dané had stolen Janus's wits over a broken promise. Nor had I been ensnared by Danae trickery designed to murder other humans. Nor had I yet experienced the Danae welcome for their imperfect kinsmen. Is your hammer ready?"

"*Rejongai!*" Kol barked.

I pivoted to face my uncle squarely and bowed. "Teach me, if I have erred, vayar. I assumed that frank speech must be expected between elders and wanderkins. Or perhaps it is believed that halfbreeds do not hear when their lacks and parentage are so unkindly discussed, which, of course, must make it proper to cripple such a flawed being."

Stian's complexion darkened. He stepped forward, his fingers splayed in some fashion that caused sweat to bead on my brow and back.

I did not retreat.

"Stian *sagai!*" Taut as a maid on her virgin night, Kol stepped between us. "I am his vayar. Thou canst not touch him without first touching me."

"Give him passage, Kol," said Stian, snarling and pointing to the fractured rock. "I consent. But do it here. Without sparing. Then keep him forever from my sight."

Chapter 16

W hile Stian reclined on the fallen slab, glowering at us, Kol led me up the jagged southern face of the rock. Once we had left the ground behind, Kol's muttering never ceased. "Thou hast the thoughtfulness of a badger, Valen. Did I not warn thee of his temper? Did I fail to mention that this is the same Stian who must be consulted as the archon prepares to break thy knees? For a passing satisfaction, thou hast forfeited every benefit of his tolerance."

"What hope has any halfbreed of his tolerance?" I called up to my uncle, whose feet dislodged sharp slips of rock that peppered my face. My blood yet ran hot, as well, though it was cooling rapidly as the distance between my feet and the hard ground increased. Why did words bother me so?

The uneven steps, created by long-ago fracturing and smoothed by centuries of wind and rain, grew narrower and impossibly farther apart as we neared the top. I squeezed my fingers into a crevice, even as a fierce wind threatened to rip them out again. Praising Kemen Sky Lord for his moonlight, I gripped with toes curled as if they might hold me to the rock.

"Stian bears no inborn hatred for humankind," snapped Kol. "He nurtured Caedmon's son against all custom. Never did he fail in love for Eodward, even when my mortal brother broke his promise to return—a betrayal that cost my sire the archon's wreath and brought to power those who despise all humans and their works. Never did he fail in love for Clyste, though she tore his heart by refusing to explain who had fathered her child and who had taken the babe away, though it meant he watched her unmade and bound to earth."

With a last smooth effort Kol stood atop the rock looking down. Wind gusts snatched his hair from out its knot and threatened to tear me from the wall. Every scrap of my will was required to loose my fingerhold and follow him.

"Nor did Stian fail in love for me when he saw I knew Clyste's secret and would not yield it. When my sire takes his season in this mountain, he feels the dying of the earth and believes some failing of his has left us helpless to change what comes. Thou knowest not of tolerance."

Of a sudden, my personal grievance seemed petty. Kol's passionate avowal touched the very heart of my purpose. Out of breath, heart galloping from the climb, I crawled over the rim of the rock. "Kol . . . *relagai* . . . why is the earth dying? In the human realms, matters are far worse than here. Our weather, our crops and herds—"

"Such matters weigh too grievously to be spoken of in passing, and we must begin the rite. I had planned more teaching, but Stian could withdraw his consent as sudden as he granted it. Get thee to the center spire."

The flattish summit of the rock encompassed only a few quercae around, and most of it comprised the jagged edges of great fractures, impossible to balance on. Even the more solid center was laced with cracks. Deep inside the rock, the rain froze and melted and froze, threatening to splinter it yet again—to its grief, as I had learned not an hour since. But as a spear thrust into a body's heart, a slender spike of harder stone protruded above the surface to the height of my shoulder.

Kol, of course, reached the spike in two easy leaps. Filled with misgivings about rites that took place atop such perilous perches, I stepped after him, only to wish fervently that I had remained on hands and knees. Every step across the gaping blackness of a crevice sent my stomach plummeting, no matter that most were narrower than my foot. Time and distance reshaped themselves in Aeginea, why not length and breadth as well? Had a crack yawned and swallowed me whole, I would not have been surprised.

Once I joined him, Kol whipped out the length of braided thong that tied up his hair and bound one of my wrists to the narrow column. "Hold up," I said. "What are you—?"

"The binding is to keep thee safe, *rejongai*, lest thou shouldst move untimely and fall. Stian insists we work thy remasti here, and not *solely* that the exposure might discomfort thee. This rock is called Stathero and plunges deep into the heart of this mountain, which is his sianou. Stathero hath a mighty presence, and wind is necessary for this passage as water was needed for the first. But thou needst not worry. I made my own remasti here and emerged unbroken."

Stian's sianou. I was not soothed. Stian *valued* Kol.

My uncle motioned me to stand straighter. "We must imagine that the rain hath sufficed to cleanse thee. I understand this passage comes hard upon thy first. Thy separation gards have not yet settled into their pattern, and thou hast much to learn as a wanderkin. Yet thou art full grown already and resilient, I believe, thus new changes should not daunt thee. Art thou willing to continue?"

I nodded, but kept my mouth closed lest my stuttering resolve declare this lunacy gone far enough.

He inhaled deeply and bowed. I returned the formality as best I could, tethered like a wayward goat. But then a blast of wind staggered me. My fingers closed around the black spire, and my free hand as well, and I wished heartily for a thicker leash.

Kol briefly touched his hands to my shoulders. Then, impossibly, he began to dance. His unbound hair billowing wildly in the wind, he spun on his toes about the perimeter of the rock. One misstep, one miscalculation, and he must crash to earth. No winged angel, he had *leaped* from the high branches of the ash tree, not flown, and Stathero reached more than three times the ash tree's height. In fascinated horror I watched the stars grow hazy and the moonlight dim, and I heard no music but the howl of the wind. "Kol, do have a care."

By the time a breathless *Do not be afraid* appeared in my head, I could not heed it. The bluster atop Stathero had grown to a shrieking gale, tearing at my hair and rippling my skin, lashing me with particles of ice and whips of cloud.

Had I the benefit of clothes, they would have been torn away. My own gards pulsed a dull gray-blue, yet all perception fled as if the south wind blew straight through my head to empty it of thought, of prayer, of memory, of identity, and the north wind reached deep to snatch the very breath from my lungs. The world shrank to a roaring knot of black and gray, threaded with the blue lightning that was Kol. And then the lightning struck and set my back afire.

Somewhere Kol's voice called to me, but I could not heed it for the burning. The wind tore my free hand from the column and raised me in its giant's grip. Bound only by Kol's tether, I fought the wind, drew in my limbs, and crouched lower to find purchase on the rock. I touched my hand to the cold surface and released magic, but I could summon no thoughts save *Let me be somewhere else than this* and *Please don't let it blow me off the edge* and some fool's apology for causing such chaos atop the broken rock. Roaring, devouring, the lightning reached over my shoulder to fire my breast, and I closed my eyes and screamed . . .

"It is done, *rejongai*. Thou art—" The hands that had untied my wrist and now rested so gently on my scorched shoulders withdrew abruptly. "Stian! *Sagai!* Come up, quickly."

I was far too weary to heed unexplained urgency. My head rested on my arms. When had I last slept? The bitterly cold world whispered hints of rose-colored light around my eyelids. The wind had settled to a modest bluster, but something blocked it, so that it touched my face only now and then. My legs felt odd. Kneeling. Cold. Heavy. I didn't bother to look. Moving, thinking, choosing what to do next . . . those tasks waited far beyond me. I craved sleep.

Approaching voices. ". . . never seen such . . . not precisely a hole, but a niche . . . to fit . . ."

". . . some error in thy kiran . . ."

"My kiran intruded not upon this rock, *sagai*." Kol stood over me as he pronounced this chilly conclusion.

I wished they would take their bickering elsewhere. A sunbeam touched my cheek, a lancet that pricked my veins, infusing warmth and light, as if I had drained the Bucket Knot's prize butt of mead. The fond memory of my favorite sop-house roused such a prodigious thirst as no man had ever suffered. The wind and lightning had surely burned out every dram of moisture in my body, and I would lick old Stian's toes did I imagine he had brought a wineskin with his grim company. As I had no wish to be subject to further insults, I kept my heavy head where it was.

"Didst thou sense a breach, Stian? What does it mean that he could do this?"

"No. And I cannot—" The elder Dané bit off his words. Did I not think it ludicrous, I would have called him frighted. "Get him beyond my boundaries, Kol. But let him not stray from thy sight until I come to thee."

The knots in my burning back did not relax as Stian's angry presence receded and vanished.

"Come, get up, Valen," said Kol, tugging on my arm. "Thou'lt have to extricate thyself."

I lifted my boulder of a head, stared at the Dané's toes, and realized my eyes were *below* the level of his feet. So the rest of me . . . I blinked, squinted, and peered downward.

I sat in a hole—actually more like a small, dark cave hollowed from the surface of the rock. My legs were tucked around a small protrusion, preventing Kol from pulling me straight out.

I looked up at my uncle, whose face was shadowed against a brightening sky. "This isn't usual, is it?"

"No. This is not usual," he said, dry as sunburned leaves. "Somehow your remasti has caused an unnatural change in Stian's sianou, one of the most stable locales in all the Canon."

"The wind," I said. "Never felt such a wind. And lightning."

He gave me his hand, and I untangled myself from the rock that appeared to have melted and hardened again in just such a tidy nest as to hold me. "The wind did not do this, *rejongai. Thou* hast done it—and if by accident rather than intent, that is perhaps worse. Assuredly were this known among the long-lived, knee breaking would be the kindliest remedy proffered thee."

I did not want to imagine consequences worse than crippling. Nor did I want to remember my prayers for shelter or think of what power might shape rock. Such wonders could have naught to do with Valen the Incompetent. I stepped out of the little bowl. Movement and the resulting sting front and back reminded me of the occasion for my presence atop this hellacious boulder. Apprehensively I glanced down. *Gods among us . . .*

A tangle of fading sapphire traces marked my breast and belly. Kol stepped back and cocked his head to one side, then walked around behind me.

"Stathero hath taken no offense at thy intrusion. Its likeness forms the gard on thy back, and here"—his finger traced an outline on my breast—"I have a thought we may find a sea star, a dog whelk, perhaps other beings from my own sianou." He sighed, and rueful resignation scribed his face as clearly as his dragon. "To carry so clearly the markings of the places thou hast touched . . . and so early . . . those things, too, are not usual."

Twisting my head in an attempt to see my back near broke my neck. That the marks faded into silver as the sun rose higher did not help. I closed my eyes and pretended I did not feel like some marketplace oddity come from savage lands to swallow fire and juggle hoops.

"Come, Valen. Thy tasks and lessons have scarce begun. And we must leave my sire's sianou that he may examine this night's work in peace. Thou'lt come to envision thine own gards, as their use becomes a part of thy nature. If thou art fortunate, their line and color will please thee."

We began the long climb down Stathero's jagged south face, a matter that consumed all my attention. *Down*, even in daylight, was at least as terrifying as *up* in the dark. Yet from the number of questions that tumbled out of me when my feet at last touched the ground, at least a bit of my mind had been working.

As we hiked down the mountain, away from Stathero and Stian, Kol responded to my barrage of queries with studied patience.

"The gards fade naturally in sunlight, save when we dance or otherwise focus our needs upon them. Once fixed in design, they do not change. Some believe they express a truth about the spirit who wears them . . .

"Wearing coverings, such as human garb, that hide the gards inhibits our use of them and the power they carry. Excessive covering and lack of use will weaken them. To travel the paths of linked remembrances requires full use of the gards . . .

"Males with maturing bodies oft bind their loins for dance training to ease soreness, but they cannot persist in it too long else they'll not progress as they should . . .

"Yes, we sleep and eat and drink, though not so frequently as humans. Of course we enjoy it. We do not understand why Picus's 'one god' prizes dirt and hunger. The sea doth not starve itself of rain to satisfy the requirements of the Everlasting . . .

"We do not understand human gods at all, though every human tries vigorously to explain them. The long-lived, as all things—sea and sky, humans and beasts—are both subject to the Everlasting and a part of it. The Law of the Everlasting has charged our kind to tend the land and sea. Thus in our work we seek beauty, balance, vigor and harmony to match that we see in the Everlasting. But even among the long-lived lie disagreements as to the exact nature of the perfection toward which we strive . . .

"No! As vayar I pledged to answer thy questions as far as I am able. But I cannot and will not discuss the Canon with a halfbreed stripling, though you were to stand twice my size or manifest talents to make your present ones seem small. Thy tasks are other and will never be concerned with the dance."

And this last answer drove me to distraction. "You've told me the world is dying," I said, as we trotted down the mountainside, "and I believe you. I've seen it. My prince, Eodward's son, a man who studies and reveres the Danae, has brought your archon news of those you call the Scourge—the Harrowers. We fear the Harrowers have some larger plan that threatens your kind. Ignorant as we are, we cannot guess what that might be or what must be done about it. That is what he hoped to learn from the archon . . . the reason he gave me up to them." I told myself that knowledge was Osriel's aim, not solely the power to aid in his unholy mystery, as Elene feared.

Kol listened carefully, gravely, his body poised in interest. But his response, when it came, remained unchanged. "Humans can do nothing. Nor can halfbreeds. I will *not* discuss this matter with thee." Which declaration, along

with his troubled expression, told me that all of this most
certainly had to do with the Canon, and that no matter my
wheedling or pleading, he would not budge. All I could do
was stay close and hope to change his mind. Perhaps Saverian would have more luck with the monk.

"Attend, stripling!" As we descended into the forest that
wrapped the lower slopes of Aesol Mount, Kol broke his
broody silence. "If thy walking gards are to be of use, thou
must learn. Unless . . . Perhaps thy human half flags?"

His scorn grated, especially as it reminded me how long it
had been since my restless night on the sand and Saverian's
lusciously fat and gritty eggs. "I'm here to learn," I said.

He acknowledged my declaration with a jerk of his
head. "Recall the crowned fir I showed thee. Dost thou
see something like here in the daylight? Yes . . . there.
Now consider the one that stood on the ascent from the
meadow—the same in its shape against the sky, in its smell
and taste, in its presence in the wood, though its location
differed greatly . . ."

As dreams of food and sleep crept into my bones with
the allure of nivat, Kol forced me to dredge up every recollection of the path we had been walking when I had asked
about his mode of traveling—the slope of the land to either
side as well as what had lain under our feet, the configura-
tion of the stars, which I could not remember, and the taste
of the air, which, to his surprise, I could. And then he bade
me close my eyes and consider the new marks I wore, explaining that it was easier to begin this teaching while I yet
could feel the burning of their newness.

"I've no expectation that thou'lt accomplish a shift so
soon. Subtle moves give always the most difficulty to a
stripling. The touch needed is not a grand jeque, but only a
small leap from one manner of thinking to another. Haste
leads to error. Thou must remember to—"

"Just so. I understand." Impatient with his tedious
schooling, I glared at the treetop. I was accustomed to
wielding magic, and the memory and instinct he described
as bound into my new markings were but another form of
it. My mind held to the recollections and reached into the
faint blue aura that I envisioned near my heart, grasping
the power I found there . . .

. . . and I was tumbling head over heels down a steep gully, snagging limbs and hair on rocks, wild raspberry thorns, and rotting timber. My sublimely graceful vayar, gards gleaming silver in the morning sunlight, stood on the path at the verge of the gully, one arm wrapped about a stately fir, laughing at me. It was worth the uncomfortable exercise to see him laugh. If his grieving made the mountains weep, Kol's merriment made the sunlight shimmer.

"Another lesson, my cocky stripling," he said, once on the near side of sober again. "One must remember to decide a position for one's feet, else one may topple from a mountaintop, step into a lake or tar pit, or slide . . . most wretchedly . . . into a ravine."

I struggled helplessly in my nest of raspberry thicket and rotted hawthorn, laughing, too, despite my humiliating display, the painful scrapes and bruises atop my already tender skin, and the long, steep climb awaiting me. Even beings of legend could not always get things right.

When at last I climbed onto the path, I stretched out my blood-scoured arms. "Tell me, vayar . . ."

"The gards survive all but the most violent wounding," he said, all seriousness again. "On our way, we shall practice closure. Clearly thou didst not find true closure at Stathero, if thine ears yet reported sound. Stone hath no voice."

"Nay, vayar, I heard them, even Stathero . . ."

Kol refused to believe my claim to have heard the speech of stones. Evidently the exercise was supposed to result in the silence I ultimately found. He set me other problems as we walked: to describe the scent of thistledown from one particular withered plant along the path, to isolate the feel of salt spray on the wind, carried from the northern sea. Some I managed, some I did not. But I felt more in control of my senses, and came to believe I could learn to pick and choose what I saw and heard.

"Control and discrimination must become as natural as breathing," said Kol. "With practice, it will."

He jumped from a steep hillside, where he'd had me examining the movement of the soil sifting ever so slowly downward, and landed softly on the path far below.

I flattened myself to the scrubby ground and crept

downward, my tired feet skidding—speeding the hillside's centuries-long collapse.

When I joined my uncle on the path, pleased I had not slipped and broken my neck, he huffed scornfully. "Thou hast the capacity to jump as I do, if thou'lt but try. Drive thy spirit upward with the leap and hold it firm and soaring until thy feet touch solidly. It is will that counters the forces that draw us to earth." Without waiting for me to so much as catch my breath, he marched down the path. "Next task: Tell me which elements key our shifts on the way down. Be attentive."

After some half quellé of rocks and roots enough to make a goat stumble, Kol halted and asked me how many changes we had made since he had jumped from the hillside. The shifting exercise and the downward climb had sapped nearly the last of my endurance, and the wintry air had begun to penetrate the shield of warmth I had enjoyed since leaving Picus's house. Unable to summon words enough to describe or even count what I'd seen, I sat on my haunches, cleared away the leaves and debris from a square of earth, and sketched out a map in the soft dirt.

The exercise helped refresh my mind. I pointed to an angled square that signified a rock. "You shifted here, where that squarish boulder hung out over the path. Again here . . . I think . . . where the pond was choked with dead leaves. And here"—I pointed to a split in the path—"or just beyond . . . I'm not sure. Here, perhaps?"

Kol looked from my face to the sketch and back again. "Dost thou mock me?" he said stiffly. "Thinkest thou my object is to shame thee, that thou must attempt the same?"

I blinked, entirely confused. "No . . . I'm sorry . . . what is it? You asked how many shifts. My head is too tired to think. I drew the map so I could show you."

"Thou canst untangle such markings?" he said. "Like Janus's papers? Picus's books?"

"Read? Not words, no. I've never—" As the underlying sense of his question struck me, I understood his surprise . . . and his offense. I was *both and neither*, Osriel had said. "I cannot read words . . . books . . . the writing on pages as humans can. They appear naught but blotches and a jumble.

However, the lines and patterns of a map, the pictures and symbols, those make sense to me. But you . . . and the others of your kind . . . can't sort out those, either?"

"We see what lives. What moves. We understand bulk and shape and eating and purpose. Scratchings on beast skins or wood chips or dirt have no meaning to us."

"And yet, your eyes can interpret these." I held out my arm where pale fronds of sea grass twined my fingers.

His eyebrows rose. "Thy gards live—a part of thee, as mine are a part of me."

I bowed to him in sincere apology. "Forgive me, vayar. I did not understand. Another lesson learned."

He jerked his head and walked ahead. "Attend, *rejongai . . .*"

Feeling as lively and attentive as a post, I stayed close enough to follow Kol's shifting paths the rest of the way, but was incapable of analyzing his moves or the terrain. When the woodland and Picus's little garden vale came into view at last, I had fallen considerably behind.

Kol halted a little upstream from the monk's tidy plots, and by the time I joined him, he had plunged his hand into a reed-shadowed backwater and pulled out a plump silver fish. As he stilled its flopping distress with a rock, I knelt beside the pool and plunged my head into the water. Though chilled already, I hoped the icy bath might set my sluggish thoughts moving again. I had so many questions I needed to ask, so many lessons to learn. I could not allow him to think me weak or foolish.

But when I sat up again, all I could think was how fine the sun felt on my back, and how soft the earth under my knees, and I could not help but sag into a formless heap on the stream bank, mumbling something to Kol about taking just one moment to consider all I'd learned.

Rosemary and basil. Fish. My stomach near caved in upon itself at the fragrant wood smoke. I blinked and stirred, grimacing at the twigs and pebbles embedded in my ribs. One numb hand prickled painfully as I raised my head. An odd coating of ash dirtied that hand, and I tried for a goodly while to brush it away before remembering that the livid marks were a part of me. I sat up quickly.

Thin blue smoke rose from a patch of sandy stream bank a few paces from my feet and dispersed slowly above a sea of yellow grass and the green islands of Picus's garden plots. A bundle wrapped in blackened leaves sizzled in the little fire—the source of the savory smells. Though steep-angled sunlight sculpted the nearby slopes, deepening the colors of the meadow to ocher and emerald and highlight-ing the splash of dark trees to either side, iron-gray clouds obscured Aesol Mount and all else to the east and south of us. I stretched and shivered, then stepped closer to the little fire and sat on my haunches.

Kol danced in the yellow grass, or rather practiced, I guessed, as he repeated a particular spinning leap for the fifth time. I felt no stirring in the earth or magic in the still, cold autumn afternoon. He stopped, stretched out first one leg behind him and then the other, bent himself in an im-possible arc to one side and then another while clasping his hands at his back. Then he began again. Arms set in a graceful upward curve, now step, leap into the air higher than my head, spin with legs straight together, land like a settling leaf. Shake out the tight legs. Step back. Pause. Arms up, step, leap, spin. Step back ... Whatever difference might exist between one exemplar and the next was far too subtle for *my* judgment. How could a man force his body into such feats?

I rose onto my toes, then bent my knees and jumped as high as I could, doing my best to turn but halfway round as I did so. My leap might have cleared the height of a small dog, and my feet struck earth so hard I rattled my teeth and came near falling in the fire. How could one even begin without music?

I squatted and touched the earth, not seeking, so much as wondering ... and laughing a little ... at what strange byways my thoughts traveled nowadays. Not so long ago my mentor was tidy Brother Sebastian, and my worst trouble the good brother's scolding me for a dirty cowl or discovering my inability to read. Danae did not read. Danae danced, healed, and moved, soundless and graceful, through the world like the bird that glided in circles high above the meadow.

"Hast thou failed in attentiveness and burnt my fish,

rejongai?" Somehow Kol had come up behind me without my knowing.

I jumped up, my face blooming hotter than the coals. "I didn't know you intended me to—"

But the arch of his eyebrow and a particular compression of his lips gave me to believe, of a sudden, that I had no need to defend myself against his charge. And in the moment I comprehended that, I understood a number of other things.

"You have bested me, uncle, I'll confess it. All my claims of strength and endurance and learning crumbled at your assault. I suppose I'm fortunate that I didn't step off a cliff. I could neither have walked one more step nor imbibed one more lesson, which, I'm coming to think, is one of those very lessons you wish me to learn. And if you truly relied on me to heed your cooking, you're neither so wise a vayar as I'm coming to suspect nor so vigilant a guardian."

"To recognize a body's limits is surer protection than gards or human magic. I have pledged to ensure thy safety. The lesson had to be taught." He retrieved a stick and arranged the coals piled about his wrapped fish. "In truth thou didst surpass every boundary I foresaw. And I am not sure what to do about that."

My hopes, despite the tempering of truth, surged anew. His manner invited me to broach the most important topics again. "*Relagai . . .*"

The sunlight vanished. I shivered and searched for words sufficient to express my need. Snowflakes drifted from the overripe clouds. A red-tailed hawk circled lazily above the meadow. Kol turned his fish with a stick, frowned, and glanced upward. He sat up sharply.

"Valen," he said, eyes fixed on the bird. "Canst thou find Picus's house, by gard or eye or thy human magic?"

Of a sudden, the air thrummed with danger. My gaze swept the forest edge and the ash tree where he'd sat when I joined him in the night, then shot up to the bird, which had completed a loop and now arrowed toward Kol. I had walked here from the hut without any magic. "I believe so. What's wrong?"

"Kneel and bow thy head so the bird cannot note thy unmarked skin. Do it now." His command brooked no question. "When I leave the meadow, be off to Picus and await my return. Or Stian's. Do *not* walk the world unguarded."

I did as he said, extending my legs and bending over them in one of his stretching postures. The only reason to hide my unmarked face and groin would be to pass me off as a mature Dané. Which meant that someone—the bird's master?—must be watching. "Who's coming?"

"Hush." He tossed his stick into the fire and rose. Wings ruffled. "In the Canon, bird, and honor to thy master and mistress." I felt no presence save Kol and the bird. "Fortunately I've completed both work and practice this day, thus can answer their summons promptly."

No one responded. My uncle's chilly declarations seemed directed solely to the bird.

"I prefer to travel uncompanioned, as you know, but of course, I cannot prevent thee. Wait . . ."

Kol's hand rested lightly on my back for a moment. "It seems Tuari and Nysse require my presence, Jinte. Keep thy spine stretched and loose until the finger numbness subsides. 'Tis the surest method for relief."

I waved a hand and shifted my position slightly as if heeding his advice . . . as if the bird might remember my false name or how I had responded to the prompting. The evening's chill settled deeper.

The wings ruffled again and flapped, and after a moment, a sidewise glance showed Kol striding down the meadow and the hawk gliding in lazy circles above him. Once they had vanished into the evening, I jumped up and raced into the wood in search of Picus and Saverian. Kol's abandoned fish had charred to ash.

Chapter 17

"The messenger bird is like to be a friend of the archon, one who failed to make the fourth passage." By the light of the twig lantern, Picus picked bits of leaf and thorn from a sheep's skin. " 'Tis the common fate of those who cannot dance their Danae magic well enough or learn the skills required of them."

"They're forced to become *birds* if they fail to make the fourth passage?" Saverian paused in her frenetic pacing to gape at Picus as if he'd said Magrog himself would sit down with us to dine.

Saverian's relentless urgency had me gobbling much too fast. The woman had come near taking off my head with an oak limb when I refused to leave straightaway to take her home to Renna. The woman and the monk were bundled in cloaks and blankets, while I sat comfortably on the snow-dusted ground in shirt and braies, sopping up Picus's boiled turnips with a wad of doughy bread. Though I mourned Kol's fish, I would have relished far worse than the monk's meager fare by this time. Evidently two full days had passed since I'd gone off with Kol.

"None are *forced* into bird form," said Picus, scratching his arms thoughtfully before returning to his wool picking, "unless they've sore trespassed their Law, in which case their new form would more like be stone or snake. The alter choice for failure is to live on as a hunter, artisan, weaver, or some such like, and such is not a happy life for a Dané. While their fellows dance, their own bare

faces wrinkle and their bodies fail near quick as us human
folk. Without a sianou they will ever feel rootless and
lost. Most prefer inhabiting bird or beast to such shame,
though I've always been of a mind 'tis a perversion of
the *ordo mundi* as if 'twere *I* had walked into Navronne
as king instead of my good prince. But at the least, they
choose it for themselves."

My hand paused twixt bowl and mouth, soup dripping
from the bread onto my knees. "The hawk was a *person*,
then, thinking and listening . . ." Which explained Kol's little deception. A person . . . trapped in that feathered body.
And in Moth's owl, too. I had already decided that Moth,
not Kol, had led me into murder in the bogs. I shuddered.

"Nay. No *person*. 'Tis said they lose most faculties, retaining only what wit their companions especially nurture."
Which made sense if the person had no soul to begin with.

I stuffed the bread into my mouth, making sure to savor
every morsel. I'd sworn not to think of souls. I'd plenty more
worries closer to hand. "Why would Kol be summoned so
abruptly? He seemed wary, but not afraid."

Picus shook his head. "Tuari hath neither favor nor use
for Stian or his kin. If the archon has staunch witnesses to
thy rescuing, he'll happily bury Kol."

"Bury . . ." Of course, that's why Kol had said Stian might
come for me, if he could not. The gummy bread clogged my
gullet. "Iero's grace, I must go after him . . . save him."

"Fie on that, lad. Ye'd make his good deed a waste and
end up broken and prisoned alongside him. None's so
clever as Kol, and he'll not be easily locked away. They
need him."

I recalled Stian's words. "Because of his dancing."

"Because his line is fertile!" Saverian's declaration burst
out like floodwaters through a breached dike. "Picus says
the Danae have always been slow to reproduce—likely
a matter of their long lives—but the problem has grown
worse in the years since Llio's curse. Children have grown
so rare among them that these Harrower poisonings are
devastating. They can't replace those lost. For a Danae
coupling to produce *two* offspring, as Kol and Clyste's parents did, is unheard of. That's why they were enraged when
Clyste's child disappeared. To learn that she *wasted* her fer-

tility on a human mate has surely infuriated them all the more."

"Aye," said Picus. "They're sore diminished from their greatest glory. Tuari blames humankind for all their ills." The monk's big hands fell still, and he closed his eyes as if praying. "Sin begets sin."

"Fear for survival will drive a species beyond custom and boundaries, Valen." The physician crouched at my side, her jade-colored eyes drilling holes in my skull. "Picus says that this Tuari's despite is so great that any bargain worked with a human—especially one of Eodward's kin—is surely devised to turn upon the human party . . ."

. . . and Elene believed that Osriel had come to Aeginea to bargain for power—a magical alliance to fuel the dread enchantment waiting at Dashon Ra. I could not imagine the magnitude of the working Osriel planned. But surely a backlash from its failure would be his ruin . . . and Navronne's. No wonder Saverian was agitated.

The monk filled my emptied bowl from the ale crock at his elbow, glancing from one of us to the other, his eyes sharply curious. "What troubles thee, friends?"

I took a swallow of thin ale. "Good Picus, I must get this lady home. She guards Prince Osriel's health and has been from his side too long. As Kol can care for himself, I'll see her safely back to her duty. We'll need a few provisions for the road, lest my poor skills delay us."

"But ye said Kol told ye to bide." His sheepskin dropped into the mud, and his broad brow knotted in concern.

Who knew how many human days had passed since Osriel had given me up to the Danae? Instinct told me that the winter solstice raced toward us with the speed Nemelez drove her chariot of ice through her demonic lover's fiery kingdom.

I drained the bowl and returned it to the monk. "We dare not wait. Tell Kol I'll return here as soon as may be."

We took our leave within the hour. Now I'd had a little rest and food, the cold did not bother me so much, but we bundled my thick hose, winter tunic, belt, boots, and pureblood cloak with Picus's dried fish, a skin of his ale, a clay bowl, and the remainder of his bread. Picus insisted Saverian keep the blanket he had lent her. "Best I not inhale the scent of a woman lest my dreams illustrate the sins I've banished from head and heart."

I bowed deeply, crossing my clenched fists over my heart—Gillarine Abbey's signing speech for farewell and a reminder to remain staunch in one's vows and devotions. Picus, eyes bright, returned the gesture solemnly. "I shall sincerely try to hold fast to my tottering virtue, Brother Halfbreed. But if a word as to the meaning of this haste should fall upon mine ear at thy return, I do not think Iero would grudge it."

"When I can, Brother. When I can." I grinned and waved as we headed into the chill autumn night.

At every step of those first hours, Saverian and I worked at cross purposes, my long gait unaccommodating to her quick, careful steps, my inclination to go over obstacles while she preferred under or around. And though I could not see well in the thick dark of the woodland, I could rely on my bent. She could see nothing at all. After she stumbled for a third time, near breaking her skull, I took her arm to steer her between the bare limbs and woody underbrush that snagged her cloak and skirts. That only made our disparities more awkward.

Before long, she sputtered and shook off my hand. Waving me to go on ahead, she snatched up a dry limb and set it gleaming with yellow light that had naught to do with fire. "I'll see to my own feet, thank you. By the Mother, how ever does a blind person manage without going mad?" She dogged my steps, tight-lipped save when urging me to go faster.

Happily, we soon emerged into the open, gently rolling country to the south. I knelt and sought a route to the Sentinel Oak, the only way I knew to get us back to the human plane. As in the garden meadow, the landscape took shape upon my mind's canvas in a single grand leap of understanding, rather than the slow building of the past. A confusion of tracks sprawled before us—migrations of great herds of elk and wild horses, footpaths of deer and Danae folk, and a great blight of blood in some past epoch—but no settled roads. And, unfortunately, the oak lay hundreds of quellae to the southwest, beyond expansive forests, a sizable rise in elevation, and at least two major river crossings. To travel the distance afoot would take us more than a month.

"But you've learned to journey as Kol does," said Saverian, when I announced this unhappy news. Like a fine hunting hound, she seemed poised to charge off in whatever direction I pointed.

"Only once," I said, sitting back on my heels and scratching my head. "And yes, I ended up in approximately the correct location. But I've too little familiarity with Aeginea to know many landmarks to use for shifting. Danae wanderkins are supposed to explore for years to learn the landforms and plants and trees and such."

Snowflakes flurried from overburdened clouds, melting quickly on our cloaks. A frost wind from the south had whipped the woman's deep-hued cheeks to a rosy brown. I'd been so sure I could get us home. *Cocky wanderkin*, Kol would say. *Recognize thy limits*.

Saverian was not so easily discouraged. "Osriel says that human lands and Aeginea are actually the same; we just experience different aspects of them in the two planes. You've traveled all over. You know *Navronne*."

"But no Navronne cities exist in Aeginea, no roads, no houses. The trees and forests are all grown up differently ..."

Yet she was right. The terrain should be the same. Since I had walked into Aeginea, I had seen the chasm of the River Kay, the familiar climb from the valley of the Kay toward the mountains, and the rock of Fortress Groult, even though the fortress itself did not exist in this plane.

"Come on." I made for the top of a rocky little knob half a quellae ahead, stopping only when I reached its crest. Squinting and puzzling at the landforms, I reached up to clear the melted droplets from my lashes, only to see a sickly thread of pale blue snaking about my fingers and up my arm into my sleeve. Laughter welled up from deep inside.

"The humor in this situation entirely escapes me," said Saverian, heaving and gasping as she finished the sharp little climb and halted beside me. Her magelight had paled to the color of cream, and breath plumes wreathed her head. Her vehemence triggered a bout of coughing, aborted by a great sneeze.

"Are you all right?" I said. Her flushed cheeks flared brighter than her magical light.

"Well enough, considering I'm hiking into nowhere with a man whose walking pace is a modest gallop. Is *that* the joke?"

"I knew you'd wish no coddling," I said, shoving my bundle of clothes and provisions into her hands. "You should have yelled at me to slow down."

I unlaced my braies and shirt. She stared as if I were a lunatic. Which I believed I was. "Indeed, physician, *I* am the great joke. Here I've been so preoccupied with Danae secrets, princely deviltry, Kol, Elene, and what in Iero's name will happen to the lighthouse, not to mention this confounded route finding and the nature of Aeginea, that I've completely forgotten my lessons. If you'll pardon my boldness, I am going to remove my clothes just now and attempt to do as you suggest—see if I can make some use of this motley collection of strangeness that is my body. Yell at me if you see anyone coming."

She held out her hand to take my shirt, a smile tweaking the thin lips into something altogether more pleasant than their usual sardonic set. She waved her hand at my disrobing. "Please. Do whatever you must to get me home."

I grinned and left the rest of my garb in her custody. For certain she was no wilting ninny.

Sitting cross-legged atop the little knob, I listened for the voices of stone. It seemed to take quite a while—or rather I managed it only after setting aside all fretful sense of time. Once I had rediscovered that quiet place where only a few faint declarations of *Forever* and *Grind* intruded, I allowed my Danae senses free rein and used the cascade of sensation to expand and deepen my Cartamandua seeing.

The cool dry air of summers past, along with the sharp blasts of past winters, teased my skin. The rich scents of soil and the buried roots filled my nostrils. I experienced not only the sounds and smells of wild Aeginea, but those of human habitation as well: sod houses, flocks of grazing sheep, the sharp bite of axes and tools. The blight of human blood and death near choked me. I explored deeper. Farther.

Were we walking the lands of Navronne, I would declare our location to be the upland moors of far northeastern Ardra, a long-settled expanse of sheeplands, grouse, and heather, whose streams and springs fed the riverlands of Morian. Indeed I had marched through those very moors with King Eodward's legions, camped and foraged on that land—this very land—fought a great bloody battle here with the Dasseur, the barbarians who had stripped the Aurellian Empire of its northwest territories. Eodward had triumphed in that battle, making his stand on a dimpled fell that was the highest point of the region. Even then the barren mound, shaped so like a young girl's breast, had reminded me of Mon Viel in the hills of southern Ardra, a region as familiar as my hand.

Carefully I shuffled through the cascade of impressions like a gem merchant through a bag of rocks, choosing only those that came through my eyes, while silencing all the rest. Then I stood up and peered again into the night.

As had happened on that strange night of my nivat madness, when Osriel and Voushanti and I had tracked Gildas's flight from Gillarine, the landscape gleamed of its own pale light. The route my Cartamandua bent had prescribed stretched south and west across this luminous terrain as if a giant had unrolled a spool of gray floss and left it behind to guide us. But it was the landforms I examined.

"There," I said, pointing to the gentle mound that sat in the center of the blood-tainted ground between us and the southern horizon . . . and, at the same time, far past it to that other swelling prominence some two hundred quellae to the south, known in the realm of humankind as Mon Viel. Reveling in the success of my combined Danae–human magic, I was already recalling the feel of the springy turf beneath my feet, the scents of wild lavender and lemon thyme, the calls of meadowlark and blackthrush that spoke freedom to a child run off from home in stinking, noisy Palinur. "We're going there."

*   *   *

Ignorance and inexperience put a quick damper on my satisfaction. Each leg of our journey took longer than it should. We had walked halfway to the horizon before I could join the knowledge of my senses with the power of my walking gards to make the shift southward to the slopes of Mon Viel. We were yet in Aeginea, of course, for the nearby heights where Caedmon's royal city ought to rise in all its glorious might sat dark and bare.

Next it required three false starts before I gave up trying to use a rocky little grotto to walk into a similar nook I remembered from my journey in Mellune Forest. Perhaps I recalled too little of the snow-drowned nook's scents or actual conformation to make the Danae enchantment work.

And then I discovered the risks of impatience when I tried to use a boggy spring surrounded by dry vineyards to plant us in the vastly different boglands of the River Kay. Saverian and I both spent two hours spewing our last month's meals from fore and aft into the muck and praying we would expire before we drained ourselves to raw husks. Human bodies—even those half Danae—were evidently not meant to move through the world so abruptly.

Subtle moves, Kol had told me. I now understood that he'd not meant subtle in distance, but in distinction. To shift from one steep, shaded mountain path to another so much like it was easy, even were they a hundred quellae apart. To shift from a puddle among barren hills to a forest-bounded bogland was possible, but would wring a body inside out. At least I had remembered to "place" my feet, so that we writhed and retched on mostly solid ground and not neck deep in mud.

"If you can find anything to burn, I can spark a fire," said Saverian in a croaking whisper. "Tea will get us on our feet again."

She sat halfway up the steep little bank, her head resting on our provision bundle nestled in her lap. A seep around the woody roots of a larch had induced her to crawl up the bank to clean her face and hands. That she could consider doing more stoked my admiration. I yet wallowed in my own stink half in the mud, half out, thoroughly humiliated, exhausted, and shivering. I wasn't sure anything could help.

"I'll find something," I said, dragging myself to my feet. This bog was the last place in the world I intended to die. Did I touch this muck with magic, I was certain I would hear the wails of drowned Harrowers, even across the barriers of the human plane and Aeginea.

I dragged handfuls of dry sedge and leatherweed and a few dead alder saplings from high on the bank to Saverian's feet, and tore open cattail pods to provide tinder. Half an hour more and we sipped lukewarm tea made from Picus's blessed herbs.

"I'm sorry," I said, clutching the bundle of clothes in my lap, my throbbing head propped on one hand. "I need a bit more schooling."

"You should put on those clothes," said Saverian, ever the physician, as she passed me the blackened clay bowl. "Your lips are blue, and not with Danae sigils, and I can walk not one quat farther tonight. Assuming this is night."

I gazed dully at the sky. Though it had gleamed azure in the wintry daylight at Mon Viel, it now glowered with the blue-black sheen of a magpie's wing. I could not sense the sun anywhere. Snow dusted the landscape, and wind moaned over the bog, rattling the leafless willows.

"We can't stay here," I said. "This is Moth's sianou. She hates humans—and has proved it. Would as soon drown us all as look at us. We can walk all the way to the oak if need be. Rest, get your legs back, and then we go."

I downed a swallow of the rapidly cooling tea and passed it back. The pulse and twitter of a curlew echoed through the morbid stillness, reminding me of the deserted mine above Renna. "When are you going to tell me what Osriel plans?"

"I will not. I cannot." She threw a rotting limb on the fire, and a veil of sparks spurted upward.

"Have you seen the place where he imprisons the souls? Have you felt them? It's wrong, Saverian. Evil. They are so angry, so terrified, filled with hate. I've never felt the like."

"Impossible. Those people are dead. Emotions are created by the living body and mind in response to changing circumstances. They are no more than the body's humors infusing the blood, like the tincture in an alchemist's vial.

There is no such thing as a soul." Her utter conviction was tinged with a bleak and weary sadness that surprised and grieved me. What had happened to her to cause so sere a vision of life?

"Then what does Osriel capture when he seals a dead man's eyes in a calyx?"

"Waste. Dust. Echoes of life."

"So why not tell me what he thinks to do with his nasty treasury? Certainly it's not too dread to speak of, if he but plays tricks with dust and waste."

"He is my lord and my friend. I will not violate his trust."

I wished I had the wit to argue with her. So sharp and scholarly a mind as hers should not be burdened with so barren a philosophy. She was no alehouse philosopher, taking a position for the sake of argument. Yet having so recently examined my own state and come up with no conclusive evidence of a soul, I had no weapons to bring to a joust about the rest of humankind. And while I remained firm in my belief that the essence of a *human* person lived beyond the last breath, I certainly didn't want Saverian providing sensible evidence to crush my own hope for the same.

As the last of our pitiful lot of fuel fell to ash, I stood up, slung the bundle over my shoulder, and pointed south along the bank, where in the other realm so like to this, Thalassa had escorted me toward Gillarine. "Let's go."

Saverian wasted no breath on conversation along the way, so I amused myself imagining what various monks would say did I come striding through their gates clad only in blue fire. And then I thought of Thalassa, and, for the first time in my life, found myself wishing I could talk with my sister . . . half-sister . . . no, half-niece . . . now. A priestess of the Mother, she could tell me of souls. It might be easier to hear the truth from her than from Picus or Saverian.

We left the treacherous bogland and soon trudged across the river-looped valley floor where Gillarine ought to lie. Clumps of slender beeches dotted the grassland, their trunks split and peeling. The limbs of scattered oak scrub curled like the legs of a dead spider. And everywhere patches of blackened, slimy grass testified to the land's death—to my mother's death and Gerard's death—to poisoning by people who stole innocents like Jullian and slaughtered bold and noble spirits like Abbot Luviar.

I knelt and touched the damp earth, snowflakes melting on the back of my blue-scribed hand. The land's sickness coursed through me like a river of sewage, bearing the stink of betrayal, mindless ravaging, and death. I welcomed it, allowing it to fuel anger and temper the steel of my resolve. Whatever I had to do to stop this, I would do.

"We need to move," said Saverian, tapping a cold hand on my shoulder. "This place is too open. Someone . . . something . . . unfriendly lurks here."

"Did you not say such feelings are but a body's humors mingling?" I said, bitterness overflowing. "You are part alchemist, Mistress Mage, so repair them yourself." But I rose and led her southward.

Recovered equanimity told me when we passed beyond the boundaries of my mother's poisoned resting place. The gloom lightened a bit. I could sense the sun nearing the zenith behind the layered cloud. "I'm sorry," I said. "I was feeling a bit useless earlier and should not have taken it out on you."

"We could both use a real bed." Save for a fleeting smile, her expression was etched with determination. What drove her? Never had I known a woman so complicated. Strong, though. And honest. I could understand why Osriel trusted her with his life—and why he valued her prickly company.

"You never told me what you learned of Llio's curse."

She hitched her cloak about her shoulders. "It's difficult to know what to believe. Picus swallows every tale and grinds it in the mill of his faith. Simply stated, Llio broke the world. Somehow. Picus says that Danae speak of four sacred places, the first sianous where the first four of their kind were born of the Everlasting, brought to life and given bodily form. These four are the Mountain, the Plain, the Sea, and the Well."

As always, the mention of sianou joining made my skin creep. "My mother's Well."

"Exactly so. The guardians of the Four are always exceptional dancers. Llio, the halfbreed son of a Dané named

Vento and a human woman, became the chosen of the Plain. Among his many couplings—it seems most Danae are not singular in such matters—Llio mated with a human woman named Calyna, and got her with child."

Saverian warmed to her storytelling, as we ascended the terraced foothills that would lead us to the Sentinel Oak. The snow swirled thicker, and the wind blustered as we came out of the valley.

"On the spring equinox, Llio attacked another Dané during the dancing of the Canon, and in the ensuing struggle, Llio died. From that hour the Plain was lost to the Canon. Picus does not know why or how—he babbled about human legends and the lost city of Askeron. But the Danae blame Llio's half-human temper for this great breaking and their decline in fertility that followed. They vowed that no halfbreed would ever dance the Canon."

"Thus they break our knees."

"That's only the beginning of the deviltry." Saverian double stepped to catch up with me again, and I tried to slow my pace to accommodate her. "Llio's father, Vento, held Calyna captive until the child was born, then drove the mother from Aeginea, while keeping the infant. But Calyna knew of the Danae's weakness—this bleeding rite they call the Scourge—and she bled some poor human to poison Vento's sianou when he took his sleeping season. As it happened, Vento also had a full-blooded Danae elder son, none other than Tuari, the present archon. Tuari used the child to trick Calyna to fall off a cliff! He claimed he did it to prevent Calyna telling other humans about the Scourge. But Stian, who was archon, believed Tuari did the murder from shame and vengeance, and he condemned Tuari to take beast form every summer until Llio's child reached maturity."

"So Llio and Tuari were half-brothers," I said, astonishment stopping me in my muddy tracks. "Saints and angels, no wonder Tuari has no use for human folk. Or for Stian's family either."

Saverian bobbed her head in a most satisfied manner. "Humans are not the only fools who cripple themselves with lust. Sin begets sin. And did you guess? The child of

Llio the halfbreed and poor murdered Calyna was the same crippled halfbreed girl Ronila who stained Picus's virtue!"

"Gods!"

As all these threads raveled and unraveled, our urgency redoubled. We hurried through the chilly gloom, wondering what it meant that the Danae had now lost two of their four holiest places. And we speculated about Ronila's *evidence* that had driven Picus to such extremity as deserting Eodward and living out his life in penance. Saverian said the monk had refused to discuss the woman.

At last, weary beyond bearing, we dragged ourselves up the last steep rise. Across the rock-laced meadow stood the Sentinel Oak. Saverian leaned heavily on my arm, no longer reluctant to accept help. "Too much to hope that Osriel is camped at Caedmon's Bridge," I said.

"He told me he intended to return to Renna straightaway from Aeginea. But then again, he didn't mention he planned to leave you tied to a tree with broken knees. Damnable prick."

Smiling at her vehemence, I knelt and touched earth. I needed only my Cartamandua bent to find my way back to the human realm from here.

The patterns of the Danae were scribed everywhere upon this land—the fine sprays of silver, whorls and roundels, ovals, spirals, and multiple sets of straight lines that crossed to form gridlike shapes. What marvelous patterns must radiate from the four great sianous, the oldest, the first.

Though, for the first time, I felt close to answers, I'd no time to consider the earth's mysteries. We needed to find our prince and prevent him using whatever grant he had bargained from the Danae, lest the backlash of Tuari Archon's hatred make our problems worse. Magic flowed through my fingertips as I held in mind Caedmon's Bridge . . . the grim verges of Evanore . . . the snow-buried barrens we had left behind . . . every edge and sweep etched on my memory. And instinct led my eye to one bright track leading into a thicker night and deeper winter—into human lands.

"Valen!" Saverian's tense whisper brought my head up. She crouched beside me, pointing to the Sentinel Oak. From beneath its bare canopy three Danae moved deliber-

ately toward us. Likely it was my imagination that told me
two of them carried wooden clubs.

I grabbed Saverian's hand and bolted. The guide thread
led us straight toward the spot where Caedmon's Bridge
should span the Kay, and I dared not deviate from it in hopes
I could take us to the human realm some other way.

The Danae changed course to intercept us. We had no
hope of outracing them, and naught would prevent them
following us into the human plane. I needed to shift us far
from this place.

As we sped across the hillside, I focused on the great
rocky pinnacle that overlooked this mead and recalled another rocky peak that overlooked a barren hillside. Both of
them should house a fortress. "Physician," I said, breathless.
"Pin your eyes straight ahead. Yell at me the instant you
glimpse Caedmon's Bridge."

She jerked her head. The blood pounding in my ears
near deafened me, as I concentrated on the fortress rock
and the thick straight walls I knew existed atop it in the
human realm. At the same time, I built the image of the
second fortress: its rarefied air, its looming mountain neigh-
bors, its thick, safe stone, the smell of warriors' piss along
the inner walls, the welcoming fire of torches and the boom
of the sonnivar, pitched to match no other in any world.
Not at all a subtle leap.

The Danae cut a swath of sapphire through the snowy
night. Moth wings gleamed upon a female's breast and
brow. I gritted my teeth and dragged Saverian faster, gripping the dual images of the fortress. This *would* be enough.
It had to be.

"The bridge!" gasped Saverian at the same time a killing
frost enveloped us.

Trusting her word that we had entered the human plane,
I shifted course abruptly, angling back across the hill toward the rocky summit of Fortress Groult, putting us directly on a course for the closing Danae. Then I reached
into the blue fire that raged from my own breast and drew
forth magic . . .

Harsh breath crackled and froze the hairs in my nose.
My bare feet skidded on a patch of ice, and as Saverian and
I crashed to earth, I whooped in exultation. We lay tangled

in a heap at Renna's gates, and the Danae were nowhere to be seen.

Even the blinding pain in my head and the wrenching spasms in my empty gut could not damp my good humor. I had seen across the boundaries of Aeginea clearly enough to build the shift—a work of the senses that Kol had said was impossible for his kind. My every instinct insisted glee-fully that I could have worked the shift directly, before we had even crossed the physical boundary between Aeginea and Navronne.

Arms and elbows dug in my gut. Boots scraped my legs. My throbbing head slammed abruptly into the frozen ground. "Gods, woman"—I pressed the back of my hand to my mouth to hold back the surging bile—"give me a moment's peace."

"Put on this cloak, fool." Even sick and frozen, Save-rian could pierce a man's craw with her disdain. She threw something scratchy and wet over me. "You don't want any-one to see you . . . like *this*."

I thought at first she meant heaving, but when I drew my hand away and glimpsed the delicate outline of a dog whelk nestled in fronds of sea grass that twined my fingers, I understood—and blessed her practical wisdom. The bright-ness of my gards near cracked my skull. I closed my eyes and pulled the cloak around me. "Need to find my braies and hose."

By the time Saverian screamed out her name to the sentries, most of my gards were covered, and I had even donned the pureblood mask I'd found in the pocket of my cloak. Saverian and I stood in a delicate balance, support-ing each other, but if someone didn't open the gates soon, they would have to drag us in by the heels.

The gates ground open with a soul-scraping cacoph-ony. A torch flared the dark tunnel, searing my eyes, but I could not mistake Voushanti's bulk in company with the soldiers.

"We need to see Prince Osriel as soon as possible," said Saverian.

"Unfortunately His Grace is not in residence," said Voushanti. "Dreogan, prepare to close the gates. Muserre,

Querz, wake Mistress Elene and tell the steward to prepare hot food and wine for the physician and the pureblood. I'll escort them in."

"Where in the name of all holy gods is he?" I said, unreasonably irritated, as my bowels churned.

Voushanti waited until the three warriors had left us. Then he turned his gaze our way, the red centers of his eyes flaring savagely. "Our master has been taken captive, sorcerer. He lies in the dungeons of Sila Diaglou."

PART THREE

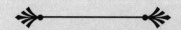

Ever Longer Nights

Chapter 18

"How did this happen?" I said, rubbing my head to keep my sluggish blood flowing. I would need to sleep soon or I'd be gibbering. But not yet. Not until I understood the magnitude of this disaster. "You're sure the witch doesn't know his true identity?"

"We have no reason to believe she knows he is the prince," said Voushanti. The mardane stood stiffly at the door of Elene's retiring chamber. He had brought Saverian and me straight from the gates. "My lord's saccheria struck him hard just as we left the Danae. In the physician's absence, he chose to ride on to the monkhouse, where Thane Stearc would be able to care for him."

"Papa always keeps a supply of Osriel's medicines," said Elene, her circled eyes speaking raw grief and desperate worry. "Saverian sees to it that he knows what to do for every variant of the disease. He had to ride as Gram. No one remaining at the abbey knows him as anyone but Papa's secretary."

Saverian huddled by the hearth wrapped in a dry blanket. Barely controlled fury had sealed her lips since she'd heard that all her worst fears for Osriel had come true. She clearly blamed herself.

I perched on a window seat, pretending I was not within walls. As long as I could see the sky, my lungs did not feel quite so starved or my stomach quite so certain it was going to turn wrong way out.

Elene, flushed as summer dawn, sat in a padded armchair, a bright-colored shawl covering what her shift and hastily donned bliaut did not. Sleep had left half of her short bronze braids unraveled, the others matted or sticking every which way. Heat rose from her as from a smoldering bonfire. "Sila Diaglou and a small force lay in wait at Gillarine for Papa to return from the warmoot. Before the priestess could remove Papa from the abbey, Osriel walked through the gate and right into her arms."

Anger and resentment bulged Voushanti's fists and twisted his scarred mouth. "My lord insisted I return to the bridge with my men as soon as we sighted the monkhouse gates. He did not permit disobedience."

I squirmed at the remembrance of Voushanti's battles of will with Osriel. Their hellish link of enchantment and submission still confounded me.

Elene beckoned me to her side and thrust a crumpled parchment into my hand. "The witch dispatched two of the monks to carry this message to Renna. Can you fathom her insolence?"

The precisely formed letters flowed into their usual incomprehensible blotches. My own cheeks hot, I shoved it back at her and returned to my window. "So tell me, what does it say?"

Elene frowned for a moment before her expression cleared in understanding. "Forgive me, Brother. Here, I'll read it . . ." She smoothed the page and began, her voice swelling with repressed fury.

Osriel of Evanore,
    Believing our partnership holds more promise for Navronne's future than our enmity, I extend to you my sisterly goodwill and offer an exchange of benefits. Our purposes do not and cannot coincide. I serve Powers beyond the ken of any mortal born, while you serve your own secret pleasures of a diabolical odor. Yet our interests may not conflict in every instance.
    You hold an injured monk, the chancellor of Gillarine Abbey, known to be involved in this Karish lighthouse foolishness. As your deeds exemplify no maudlin sympathies for Navronne's peasants, I cannot

conceive that this errant project holds any innate value in your estimation.

On the other hand, your position as Evanore's lord makes your defensive strength dependent on a handful of ancient families who demand certain strict loyalties and protocols. Unfortunately, one of your warlords seems to have connived with these Karish librarians, and I have caught him at it. But he has convinced me he cannot work magic.

Perhaps you are strong enough to control your clansmen even while abandoning one of them to your adversaries. But if you prefer to avoid a disruption among your supporters, I can offer you this bargain. I will return your errant Thane Stearc in exchange for the monk Victor. To sweeten the offering, I will include your pureblood's catamite. I doubt your warlord's diseased scribe could survive the journey, but if you prefer him to the boy, you may have him instead. I believe we shall both be well pleased with the outcome of the trade, and our relative strengths will remain in balance.

I require this bargain be completed before the solstice. Do you agree to it, take the monk to the crossroads at Gilat on the Ardran High Road and send word to me at Fortress Torvo.

In the glory of the Gehoum,
Sila Diaglou

"Damnable . . . vile . . ." Rage threatened to cut off what remnants of use remained in my exhausted brain. "Gods ship them all to the netherworld!"

"Does anyone else find this letter's language odd?" asked Saverian, her fiery anger banked by curiosity. "I thought the woman disdained learning."

"She didn't write it," I said. "Gildas did. Who else would slander a child?" I pressed the heel of my hand to my forehead as if it might prevent my skull's imminent disintegration. "Why would they trade one for the other? Stearc can open the lighthouse as well as Brother Victor, right?"

"No." Saverian returned to the hearth stool. "The open-

ing requires *two* paired warders—one embodying the unlocking spell, one with power to release it."

"And Gildas knows this?"

"Not unless they've tortured it out of someone," she
said. "Until this hour, I've been the only person outside the
four warders themselves who knew. Luviar and Brother
Victor were one pairing. Stearc and Osriel the second. The
priestess and her monk don't understand what they have."

"Neither my abbot nor I revealed the secret." An ill-
favored little man wearing a black cowl and an eye patch
shuffled through a side door not three paces from me, leaning heavily on a cane.

"Brother Victor!" I popped up from the window seat.
Only fear of crushing his fragile bones kept me from embracing him. Which would have been an entirely unseemly
greeting for the chancellor of Gillarine, and an act I would
never have contemplated when I lived there. But I could
not help the surge of pleasure as I bowed, cupping one
palm in the other and extending them in an offering of
Iero's blessings.

He smiled back, stuffing his cane under one arm long
enough to return the blessing. "Dear Brother Valen, one
of my three blessed saviors"—he nodded graciously to
Voushanti and Saverian. "It is a grace to see you returned
safely to our company. Though, as always, you present
yourself at inconvenient times."

As I helped him settle gingerly into the chair beside
Elene, he glanced curiously at my hands and then quickly
to my face. I snatched my hands back under my cloak, hiding the marks that had paled to silver. I'd not told Elene or
Voushanti of my own particular adventures in Aeginea as
yet. Osriel's predicament preempted every other concern.

"These secret pairings ..." I began, returning to the
lighthouse secret. Elene could not work magic, but Brother
Victor was a pureblood sorcerer. The puzzle pieces shifted.
"So, Mistress Elene, Osriel didn't send you back here to assume Brother Victor's burden, but to *partner* with him. To
take Luviar's place."

She dipped her head, tears brightening her eyes. "We
dare not leave my father and Osriel there together. Sila
Diaglou will give them up only so long as she believes that

only one warder is necessary. A pureblood warder. Dear, brave Brother Victor has agreed to the exchange."

"Brother!" Saverian looked up in shock. "You can't. You're scarcely walking!"

"And what of Jullian?" I snapped. "You don't think the priestess will notice you choosing to retrieve a sick man over a healthy, innocent boy?" That no one seemed concerned over the boy made me irrationally angry. I had yet to admit that Osriel's life was worth the saving.

"If there is the slightest hope to rescue our prince, I must do it," said Brother Victor. "I can transfer my wardship to another. And we must certainly do whatever we can to retrieve young Jullian as well. Perhaps I can speak to Gildas's conscience . . ."

Perhaps they hadn't told Victor about Gerard. "Gildas owns no conscience," I said.

"The priestess will never yield a living captive." Voushanti's opinion interrupted the discussion with the subtle grace of a crossbow bolt. "Go through with this exchange and you but confirm she has a prize in hand. Then she will redouble her efforts to extract the truth from Thane Stearc. Whether or not he tells her what she wants to know, Thane Stearc is a dead man. His endurance is all that stands between Prince Osriel and Sila Diaglou's questioning." He glared at Saverian as if it were her fault Osriel was taken.

Voushanti's reasoning—and its implication that Osriel was as good as dead, too—silenced us all. Elene closed her eyes and pressed folded hands to her mouth.

There had to be some other way to save three lives than to send this good man to certain death. I rolled the priestess's message over in my mind. With every skill of memory I had developed through the years, I reviewed the exact phrasing, my thoughts focused as if heeding the whispers of stone. "She wants to have it done before the solstice," I murmured.

Then truth struck home like a cudgel to the knees. "Of course!" I blurted out. "Max has settled her bargain with Prince Bayard!"

Saverian and Victor had not heard the details of Osriel's meeting with his two half-brothers at Gillarine. Thus I had to explain Osriel's agreement with Bayard to join him in confronting the Harrowers, and how my brother Max, as Bayard's negotiator, had been charged to drive a false bargain with the priestess over her demands for control of Evanore, the lighthouse, and me. "... and so Prince Osriel told them that either the joined might of Eodward's sons defeats Sila Diaglou on the winter solstice or the world we know will end."

"By the Mother, Riel!" Saverian's harsh whisper split the despairing silence.

The problem, of course, was that without Osriel, his plan, whatever it might have been, collapsed like an empty sack. What hope had we of preventing Sila Diaglou from doing whatever she wished on the solstice? She could make Bayard her puppet king or crown herself. As long as she possessed the book of maps and the traitor Gildas to use it, she could eventually find every Danae sianou and work her poisoning, further corrupting the Canon. Harrowers would lay waste to Ardra. The warlords might hold Evanore against the combined legions of Harrowers and Moriangi, but what light would ever draw them from their caves as night and chaos drowned Navronne? No more savior princes waited hidden in Aeginea.

"Osriel commanded the warmoot to muster at Angor Nav on the solstice," Elene said numbly. "He promised they would ride for Palinur the next day to enforce his claim to Navronne."

No need to remind us that Angor Nav lay more than eighty queliae from Caedmon's Bridge or to state the logical conclusion that Osriel had no intention of confronting Sila Diaglou with his Evanori legion. The prince had believed victory lay in the deserted gold mine of Dashon Ra, and if any knew what that dread solution entailed, it was Saverian. She looked as if she could snap bone with her teeth.

"Our first responsibility is to preserve the lighthouse," said Brother Victor, always a man of practical reason. "Whatever plan Prince Osriel formulated and whatever he learned from the Danae that might aid him are imprisoned with him. So we must devise a new plan on our own."

"Unless *you've* learned what we need, Valen," said

Elene, forcing her voice steady. "Perhaps he told you his intent before you were taken? Or perhaps you heard what he learned from the Danae?"

I heard her truer inquiry. Had I kept my promise to learn of Osriel's dire enchantment and dissuade him from it?

I met her gaze and shook my head, then spoke to all. "We learned nothing from the prince or his meeting. But Saverian and I did learn that the Canon has been broken for a very long time. The Danae themselves are in decline and have found no answer for it. With each Harrower poisoning—what they did with Gerard and tried to do by killing Brother Horach—another part of the Canon is lost."

Even as I spoke, many things seemed clearer in my own mind. On the day we retrieved Gerard's body at Clyste's Well, Kol, in his anger, had handed me the first clue. *You lead me here, cleanse the Well so I do not sicken, return it to my memory so I cannot escape knowing what is lost— though I must lose it all over again.* And Picus's failing garden had given me the second.

"Once a sianou is poisoned, they can't find their way there anymore," I said. "And the rest of the land, despite their care, keeps failing. I saw what they do, what they fight, and I would wager on my hope of heaven that this failure is the root of our plagues and pestilence, our weather disturbances, too, for all I know. Prince Osriel went to the Danae hoping to gain use of their magic on the solstice, and we've no way of knowing what answer they gave him. But what Saverian learned is that no matter what they promised the prince, the archon's enmity for humankind is so deep-rooted that trusting the Danae in any matter whatsoever *increases* our peril."

As I laid out these truths, I saw no hope for Osriel or Stearc. Even if the thane had endured Sila Diaglou's torments thus far, in the moment the priestess paraded her prisoners before Bayard, the game would be up and Osriel would die. It was only a matter of time.

"How long have we been gone?" I said. The confusions of Aeginea had destroyed my concept of time. Were we but a day or two from the solstice, I could see no course but to hide Elene and Victor and whatever monks we could salvage from Gillarine. Unbreached, the lighthouse might survive. But if those who could read the books and work the tools fell to Sila Diaglou's holocaust, what matter if the priestess took her time to find her way inside? On the other hand, had we a sevenday, something more might be done, though I had no idea what.

"Six days have passed since you were taken." Voushanti's harsh intrusion grated on my spirit. "His Highness was made captive that same night. I returned to Renna only two days since."

I spun to Saverian. "Only six! How could that be right?"

"Picus explained that it is not the days themselves, but the spending of human life that slows seven for one in Aeginea," she said, with only vague attention. "Though time itself is fluid there, as we saw, the years pass side by side in the two planes, the sun's passage marking the season's change at the same hour."

Saverian fell back into her own silence, distracted far beyond the matter of dirt and dishevelment and exhaustion. Her eyes flicked now and then toward Voushanti. But I accepted her word. Osriel had said something much the same.

Only six days . . . Perhaps we had a little time to work after all. "We've yet a fortnight until the solstice," I said. "When is the anniversary of Eodward's coronation? Has it passed? The prince was supposed to send to Bayard on that day to confirm their agreement."

"The anniversary is three days hence," said Brother Victor. "Mistress Saverian, did you say *Picus*?" She didn't look up.

"A small, fast force might be able to intercept the priestess between the monkhouse and Palinur," Voushanti broke in, his mailed bulk seeming to grow and fill the door. "One word and I can have the prince's elite guard riding."

"You will do nothing without my leave, Mardane," said Elene harshly. "Renna is the gateway to Evanore. I'll not leave it defenseless. As Prince Osriel's appointed castellan, I command you stay here until Thane Boedec and Thanea Zurina arrive."

"You cannot travel, Mardane," said Saverian. "You know it."

Voushanti folded his massive arms across his chest and looked away. I blinked, rubbed my own arms, and reached for better control of my wayward senses, for it seemed, just for a moment, that the edges of his flesh rippled like the surface of a wheat field. Though none acknowledged her comment, everyone looked as if a foul odor had wafted through the chamber.

"Sila Diaglou has several days' head start and can call up remounts and reinforcements throughout Ardra," I said, impatient with their secrets. "She's likely back at Fortress Torvo already. We'll have to take the prince from her there."

My vow to preserve the lighthouse demanded Osriel's rescue, no matter my grievances with him. And my vow to Jullian demanded my participation, for I could rely on no one else to protect him.

Brother Victor tapped his walking stick on the floor idly. "We would need to be sure Osriel and Stearc are inside the fortress. We've heard that Palinur is in confusion. Perhaps we could send in a small party, shielded with enchantment. Strike quickly."

Elene's head popped up. "*You* could locate them, right, Valen? Your magic . . ."

"Of course . . . yes." I knew Jullian and Osriel well enough that I could locate them if I had a clue where to start.

Yet a direct assault on their prison was out of the question; the ancient fortress where Luviar had bled out his life sat in the heart of Palinur. And negotiations of any kind could allow Sila Diaglou to discover the prize that lay in her hand. Our plan must use stealth. Something unexpected . . .

"As for getting inside the fortress . . ." A fearful, horrid idea began to take shape in my head. "There's a possibility I could do that, as well. Max has negotiated this solstice bargain between Bayard and Sila. If I were to go to Max . . . find out the terms agreed to . . . make sure they've no inkling of the prince's situation, I could likely get inside." As long as the priestess still wanted me. Getting four of us out would be another problem, unless my Danae skills could suffice.

Saverian threw off her blanket abruptly and kicked her hearth stool aside. "Your health is unstable, Valen. Someone should go with you."

"No choice," I said, shaking my head. "I can get to Max. But without a lot of awkward explanations, none of you would be admitted into the place I'll have to meet him. Once we've spoken, I'll return here, and we'll decide how to proceed. Unless someone has a better idea?"

I expected at least Voushanti to argue, but he merely stared at me, his hand caressing his battered sword hilt.

Elene looked bewildered. "But your brother is in Palinur with Bayard! That's weeks of traveling! We can't afford—"

"Our sorcerer has acquired new skills, lady," said the physician.

Brother Victor glanced between Saverian and me. "What's happened to you, Brother Valen? There's something very different about you tonight."

"Perhaps Saverian could tell you some of it tomorrow, Brother. Just now . . ." Somehow deciding a course of action had released my weariness to settle on my shoulders like the gods' yoke. And I would need all the wits I could muster where I was going. "I don't know about the ladies, but I can't promise one more sensible word until I find a bed. Mardane, if you could . . ."

"Excuse me, good Saverian," said Brother Victor, insistently, "did you say *Picus*?"

Voushanti, with as much curiosity as I had ever seen on his scarred visage, motioned me toward a side passage and a stair. When he showed me a small tower chamber, I almost wept at the sight of the plump pillows and folded blankets piled on a bed. Dané or not, world's end or not, walls or not, I had to sleep. "Four hours or morning, Mardane, whichever comes later."

Voushanti jerked his head and left. I drifted off still piecing together the puzzle of the Canon, the Danae, the Harrowers, the world's end—why had I not asked Kol about the damnable weather?

The ancient wall embedded in crumbling earth . . . pebbles and mud washed down to the road at its base, crusted and

frozen in this early morning. A gentle rightward curve . . .
dawn smells of roasting meat, of baking bread, of damp
earth . . . And around the next corner the sound of dribbling
water—here melting ice dripping into the cistern, there the
font that never froze or dried. Scrawny trees grew sidewise
from the bank, branches heavy with snow drooping over
the road . . . in my face . . . tickling, scratching, freezing . . .
the smell of burning from the lower city . . .

I walked around the corner, and in less time than it took
to think it, the narrow alley that squeezed between Renna's
kitchens and an ancient fortification built into an Evanori
mountainside led me straight into the narrow lane in Palinur, more than two hundred quellae distant. The stare of
an Evanori guardsman, flummoxed at the sight of an oddly
naked man in the kitchen alley, now came from a ragged
woman using water from the Aingerou's Font to wash
vomit off her boy child.

The boy pointed at me and cried out weakly, "Mama,
look! He's on fire . . . an angel . . ."

"Not so!" I whispered, embarrassed. "Sorry! Shhh!" But
the lad's thready cry bounced through the lane like a child's
ball, from one hushed voice to the next, for a beggars' city
jammed the lane that ought to have been deserted.

In the past, this favored quarter of Palinur had escaped
the untidy truths of hard living. Evidently that was no
longer the case. A few small fires smoldered here and
there among makeshift tents and crude lean-tos, built from
branches cut from the overhanging trees. Fortunately most
of the crowd still slept.

I jogged down the crowded roadway, jumping over
pools of filth, bundled possessions, and sprawled bodies,
then dived over the low wall into a crusted snowbank and
scrambled well away from the lane. Thanks to half a night's
rest and enough roast venison and jam tarts to breakfast a
legion of halfbreed Danae, the cold did not bother me. All
the same, best not dawdle. Fine houses, like those around
here, would have pureblood guards and magical wards.
Staying hidden in the straggling shrubbery, I donned my
silk and satin finery.

Elene had somehow managed to get my pureblood
cloak and mask cleaned by the time Voushanti woke me

that morning. She had brought them herself, along with her thanks for my venture. "We all knew you were extraordinary, Valen, even when you were playing monk," she'd said, touching the gards on my hand. When I inquired about her health, her courage came near breaking. "He doesn't know," she'd whispered, crossing her arms on her breast. "He could die this very day, not knowing of his child."

I'd had little comfort to offer. The remembrance of her grief and the weight of her head on my chest ached like old wounds, as I slipped on my mask, hopped over the wall, and hurried up the lane. A cloud of yellow smoke and frost haze masked the lower city.

I had not expected ever to walk this particular lane again. But a pureblood head of family had the authority to summon each of his children to the family home without specifying a reason. If I worked matters right with Claudio de Cartamandua, he would arrange my meeting with Max.

"Best run, pureblood," snarled a woman who was skinning what appeared to be a cat. "Orange-heads drove out a number of your kind just yesterday. We'll see purebloods plowin' come spring. Your pretty fur cloaks'll ne'er keep ye warm in the mud."

A few others joined her taunts. For once I was happy to see armed warriors in Registry black and red patrolling the upper end of the lane. They rousted a few sleepers who had wandered too close, but did not challenge me as I strode past them to the iron gate with the bronze gryphon.

How truth can change everything. Unlike the last time Serena Fortuna had brought me to these gates, my gut did not seethe with fear and loathing, nor did my skin blanch at unwelcome memories. None of the past had been my fault. Claudio and Josefina de Cartamandua-Celestine were not my parents. As I touched the lock and assembled my favorite spell, it occurred to me for the first time that Claudio, not Max, was my brother—and only half a one at that. Laughing, I fed magic into my spell, and the familiar lock shattered in a fizz of gold sparks and twisted bronze. Then I yanked the bellpull to wake them up and walked in.

Chapter 19

F ive heavily armed guards met me in the entry court,
  blocking the gap between the iron lampposts and
  the lily-shaped brazier dedicated to Deunor Light-
bringer. Their challenge died upon their lips as I removed
my mask. They could not fail to recognize me or recall the
dread prince who owned my contract.

"Announce me to Eqastré Cartamandua-Celestine," I
said with true Aurellian arrogance, while gloating childishly
inside at naming my erstwhile parent as an equal. Truly this
pureblood lunacy brought out the worst in me.

I did not wait for their return. Rather I strolled into the
columned reception room, where my family had sold me to
Prince Osriel. Naught had changed there, from the richly
colored floor mosaics that displayed the order of the plan-
ets to the marble statuary, gilt caskets, tapestries, and urns.
For generations, pureblood families had profited from Navronne's hunger for sorcery. My family had been particularly
successful at it until I'd come along.

". . . impossible! Where is this visitor?" Claudio strode
into the room in the company of the guards, as well as two
gentleman attendants of exceptionally sturdy physique. He
halted when he caught sight of me. "Magrog's teeth!"

"Patronn." Maintaining protocol, I sank to one knee
and touched my forehead with my gloved fingertips. His
servants were present, and I was not yet ready to proclaim
my true heritage. Proof of one member's tainted blood
would call into question the lineal purity of every member

of the family. I could ruin this house by removing one of my gloves.

For fifteen years this stocky, black-haired man adorned in red and green velvets and a fox-lined pelisse had been the bane of my life, unrelenting in his despite, deliberate in his cruelty. For twelve years more, I had struggled to survive in alleyways and battlefields, choosing poverty, abasement, and danger in preference to his sovereignty and the life it prescribed. Today, as I rose from my brief genuflection, I looked Claudio de Cartamandua-Celestine in the eye and smiled.

His glare of malice shifted to uncertainty. His eyes narrowed, and his powerful fists began to quiver. "Insolent . . ."

Protocol forbade him to touch me. My contract permitted only Osriel to do that. I longed to tell Claudio I knew his dirty secrets, but what I needed today was for him to summon Max. In no wise could I expect willing cooperation, and it was not yet time for threats, which meant I had to proceed very carefully.

"Please do not trouble yourself with the conventions of refreshment or pleasantries, Patronn. I am here strictly on business, and must make speedy work of it. My royal master bids me—" I twirled a finger to indicate his retinue. "Ah, I really must present his request in private."

Though he would clearly prefer to strangle me, Claudio motioned his attendants to the corners where they could not hear us, and then seated himself in a delicate armchair. He left me the choice to remain standing, drag another chair to his side, or sit on the floor—any one of which would be demeaning to a pureblood. As he intended. He was a bit discomfited when I chose to perch on a marble table a few steps away. My position only emphasized the difference in our height.

"You look well, Valen," he said. "Does submission to the Bastard suit you, then?" Curiosity poked through his studied calm like a kitten's sharp claws through silk.

"My master believes in strict discipline, as you warned me." I folded my gloved hands in my lap. "And he has schooled me quickly in his requirements. Fortunately, he is pleased with my talents. So much so that he is interested in pursuing a contract with another of our family. In short, he desires a cartographer to map the new bounds of his kingdom. My difficulties with written language preclude such service, of course. But what prince would consider other than a Cartamandua to make him maps?"

"His *kingdom*? You're saying Osriel the Bastard intends to claim the throne?" His dark eyes raked my face, hunting signs of the mockery and lies that had passed my lips far more often than serious discourse.

But thanks to this man, I was well practiced in deceit. I only smiled again and shrugged. "He has his plans. As you might imagine, I tried to divert his attention to other mapmakers, but he would have none. He bids me insist, and I do *not* disobey. I am to remind you that Evanore's gold could ensure our family's fortunes for decades to come."

My father sprang from his seat, walked away a few steps, then spun to face me, calculating. "You cannot be serious."

"I told him it must be Max or Phoebia, as Nilla and Thalassa have taken the Celestine bent instead of yours. Janus, of course, is out of the question. And you . . . well, you are head of family and could not possibly leave Palinur. My master will not be denied, Patronn."

There passed a long silence. He chewed on his lip and did not take his eyes from me. I strove to remain neutral in expression.

He lowered his brows, pursed his lips, and glanced at me sidewise. "Phoebia has decent skills. Max's are better, if he would only get off his horse and use them, but he is contracted to Prince Bayard."

I swallowed my disgust at his connivance. "I need to speak with each of them, of course, to form a better estimate of their experience with such work and their degree of willingness to cooperate with a demanding master. Once my lord has my report, he will send Mardane Voushanti to negotiate terms. He doesn't quite trust me to do that as yet."

Yes, that last point made him relax a bit. That any master would trust *me* was the most difficult of all these matters for him to believe.

"Phoebia is easily available," he said, "and Max . . . fortunately he is in the city just now. I can send an official summons as head of family, which requires no explanation to his master." He rubbed his chin in a mockery of indecision. "But, of course, to release him from Prince Bayard's contract . . . that would cost a great deal of money."

Somewhere in our family veins must run a river of lies. Had Max not complained to me of how our family's contract value had waned due to my rebellion and long disappearance, I would have believed his last concern.

"Understood," I said. "Now, I shall require privacy for the interviews. My master would not wish his business to become public prematurely. I've certainly no fear of anyone in the family speaking out of turn, but servants . . ." I shrugged again. "And you have frequently expressed your disinterest in anything from *my* lips. Unless that has changed?"

I thought his teeth might grind to powder. Mighty is the power of fear and gold to a pureblood. But Claudio's pride and hatred won out. He spread his arms. "Wherever you like."

Despicable gatzé! What kind of man would even consider pledging his young daughter to a master of Osriel's foul repute—a daughter who had amassed no history of violence or disobedience as I had? Even Max, though arrogant beyond bearing, had been the most dutiful of sons, deserving no such fate.

As I waited for Claudio to summon my young sister, I tried to think what to say to her. Bringing Max to the neutral ground of our family home, out of his master's hearing, had seemed a more reasonable course than tracking him down myself in war-ravaged Palinur. I had foolishly assumed Bia's father would wish to shield her from a monster, making this bit of playacting unnecessary. On the other hand, I wished again that I had some excuse for speaking with Thalassa, but this lie was elaborate enough without working Samele's high priestess into it.

Footsteps hurried through the tiled passages of the family wing. As I stood, the walls of the room wavered and bulged. I closed my eyes for a moment, breathed deep, and blessed the potion Saverian had offered me that morning to tame my nausea at sitting indoors. The insidious panic of collapsing walls, I had to manage for myself. The symptoms seemed much worse since taking on my Danae gards. Or perhaps it was only my approaching birthday.

"*Serena pauli*," I said, offering a shallow bow to the young woman who appeared at the door, her arm firmly in Claudio's grip. I motioned a servant to bring her a chair, and then waited as Claudio dismissed the servants and guardsmen. When he saw I was not going to begin until he'd followed them, the glowering Claudio whirled and withdrew.

My younger sister Phoebia, a plainer, less womanly version of her mother and elder sister, wore her heavy black hair wound about her head in tight braids like a warrior's helm and resentment about her shoulders like a mantle. She had been so young when I left home, I did not know her well enough to read beyond her sullen facade. The only time I'd seen her since my recapture, she'd spat on me.

"Our conversation will be private, Bia," I said, drawing my chair close so we would not be overheard. "Patronn told you why I've been sent here?"

She jerked her head in acknowledgment. Her knuckles were bloodless, and a thin film of sweat sheened her copper-colored skin.

"You've naught to fear from either me or my master," I said. "He is hard, and a man of fearsome mystery, but fair to his servants who carry out their duties . . ." We spoke for more than an hour of the tasks she performed for the family—coloring Claudio's maps, inking lists of place names and distances, using her Cartamandua bent to smooth curves and add in details he thought too unimportant for his particular attention. She did not travel, did not publish maps of her own, and had attracted neither a contract nor an offer of marriage. She blamed her sorry lot on me. I could not deny the responsibility. Despite my rehabilitation by the pureblood Registry, my years as a *recondeur* had made alliance with our family a risk for other purebloods. Petronilla's beauty had caught Bia's twin a lucky match, and Max and Thalassa had the talent and determination to gain them favored, if not excessively profitable, contracts. Which left Phoebia alone with a despicable father and a drunken mother.

Though she did not warm as we spoke, her fists unclenched. In the end, I felt sorry that I had no contract to offer her. When I heard the bustle of an arrival from the front of the house, I stood and, to her astonishment, kissed her hand. "I doubt my master will take you on this time, *serena pauli*. Right now he needs particular skills. But if this succession is settled favorably, he will have need of many services."

She touched her fingers to her forehead, then wriggled those I had kissed, examining them as if half expecting they might break out in a rash. "The city . . . out there . . . is very bad, is it not?"

"Yes."

"I've heard that Harrowers burn books, so I would guess that they'll have no use for maps. And they despise purebloods."

"All true."

She looked up at me, her dark eyes troubled. "What should I do, Valen? Matronn warns of this danger—a dark veil, she calls it—that is coming down on Navronne. She sees purebloods sent into the countryside to dig and plant . . . to labor in the fields like villeins. Patronn refuses to listen. He calls me stupid to worry."

I shivered. Josefina de Cartamandua-Celestine's divinations invariably made me shiver.

"You are *not* stupid to worry," I said, touching Bia's shoulders, wishing I could do more for her. "Go to Thalassa. Patronn can't stop you going to temple. Temples are little safer than anywhere else, as it happens, but Lassa understands what's happening in the world as well as anyone. She'll see to you."

Bia didn't question how I knew all this. I was no diviner. But she ducked her head and hurried out of the room a great deal livelier than she'd come. Then Max strode through the doorway, leather and steel gleaming from beneath his cloak, and I could think no more of frightened little sisters.

"What in the name of the blistering bawds do you think you're doing?" he said through clenched teeth, as he whipped off his mask. "If one word leaks out linking Bayard and Osriel, this little game is up. Are you as mad as your prince, or is this *his* imbecilic idea?"

"Sit down and speak normally," I said, as I bowed and

touched my forehead. "Patronn believes I'm here to discuss a possible contract between you and Prince Osriel, and we would not wish him to learn differently. Hear me out, and all will become clear."

Though seething, he greeted me properly and lowered his compact bulk into the chair. "We are involved in no alleyway scrap, Valen. The witch has left Grav Hurd, her favorite ax man, here in the city. He's pushing Prince Bayard to close the temples and alehouses and ship any man, woman, or child convicted of crimes into the countryside where they can 'heed the voice of the Gehoum.' He threatens to bring down the Registry tower. We are drowning in madmen."

"I understand," I said, leaning back in my chair as if settling in for a long interview. "Prince Osriel has sent me to hear the terms of the solstice bargain you've worked out with her."

He leaned back, twisting the corner of his thick mustache where it tangled in his well-trimmed beard. The beard was Max's only true rebellion of his one-and-thirty years. Claudio hated it. "Why now?" he demanded. "It was your master who chose to confirm the agreement on Coronation Day."

I'd never seen Max so serious. His private face had always been a snigger, and he met every circumstance by boasting of some way to turn it to his advantage. Only a few short weeks ago, he had twiddled magical dust from his fingers and joked how sorcerers would be exempt from any harsh future by virtue of the awe in which we were held. Yet, in a way, his sobriety might make my task easier. I quickly rethought my approach.

"Prince Osriel is a hard master, Max, and more clever than you can imagine. He will do *anything* to accomplish his purposes. He's told me I need to prepare—" I leaned forward and dropped my voice even lower. "Great gods, Max, tell me that you've talked the priestess out of having me."

His black eyes sharpened. "Why would you care? I assumed from all he said that this bargain was but a feint as long as we got Sila into Evanore by the solstice."

"It is and it isn't. He wants her focused on the solstice

and will do whatever is needed to convince her that she's won. Indeed that *is* the night that will prove who holds power in Navronne. But he also wishes—" I stopped. "Tell me the bargain, Max."

"One honest answer first. Did Osriel send you to me? Here?" He watched me unblinking, his every sinew like stretched wire.

I shook my head and felt him relax.

"All right, then. You'll be hearing the terms soon enough." He rested his thick forearms on his spread thighs and clasped his hands loosely. He was already gaining confidence ... recognizing advantage to be won. "I met twice with this Grav Hurd—a smart devil, tough as a spire nut—and once with the priestess herself, to wring out the final changes. I tell you, Valen, these people make Patronn seem as charming as a courtesan. But we came to agreement, signed and sealed. It states that as of midnight on the winter solstice Sila Diaglou will reign sovereign in Evanore, subject only to Navronne's crown. She will administer Evanore's gold, but will pay the crown a twice-yearly tithe of no less than ten thousand solae—and don't ask me who will collect it. Prince Bayard will not release Prince Perryn into her custody, but agrees to parade him in chains through the streets of Palinur on the first day of the new year and allow the priestess to conduct a rite of purification for him. Perryn's life will *not* be forfeit—though I would not stand in his boots that day for all of Evanore's gold. As for the lighthouse ... she dropped the demand for its location, indicating that it was no longer of immediate concern. But you, little brother ..." He paused for a long moment in this impressive recital, gazing at his boots and shaking his head, near smiling when he raised his head and took up again. "On your contract she would budge not one quat. And no matter how I strutted or wheedled, the witch would not tell me why. So ... Prince Bayard agreed that you are to be turned over to her on the solstice."

I should have been happy to hear this. My hope to get near Osriel and Stearc and Jullian relied on Sila Diaglou's intent to have me. It fit with my odd, unlikely belief that my personal mystery was fundamentally entangled with Navronne's doom. But all I could feel was hollow and clammy ... the dread of being locked in a tomb while living ... the dread of facing Judgment Night and seeing the One God point to the downward path. What did a priestess who found joy in bleeding miscreants and innocents want with me? I just had to believe she didn't want me dead.

I mustered a voice. "What of my master? What do they propose to do about him as they apportion his demesne?"

"Ah, yes ..." He tapped his fingertips together for a moment, then shrugged. "If the priestess captures him on the night of the solstice, she may keep him, but he will neither be publicly punished nor publicly displayed. He will disappear."

"And if he were to end up in Prince Bayard's custody?"

Max shrugged and grinned. "Well, for the purposes of the agreement, we implied the result would be the same ... Osriel would be neither seen nor heard from again ... which *could*, of course, mean private retirement or exile. But, of course, Bayard believes that our joined might will defeat the witch and that Prince Osriel will come to an equitable and honorable agreement with his elder brother as to Navronne's ruling."

"Yes. That is certainly the intent." Though, after Osriel's betrayal in Aeginea, I had no more certainty of his true intent than I did of Bayard's.

Max leaned close again and his smile vanished. "Now, why are you and I discussing what must be laid out again three days hence for your master's messenger?"

"He desires for her to have me before solstice night, Max. She has a Karish monk in her party."

"Her pet monk ... yes, I saw him. Smug kind of fellow, always whispering in her ear. I never trust a man who shaves off all his hair."

"That's him—Gildas. The monk owns some secret ... gods, I don't know what." I rubbed my head and kneaded my neck. The wavering walls left me dizzy and sweating, like a prisoner awaiting the hangman. Did I appear as ill as I felt, Max would certainly believe me frightened—as I hoped for him to do. "So Osriel is sending me to Bayard. He's going to let you turn me over to the priestess as a pledge of good faith, as if you'd caught me by good fortune. And then ... he's commanded me to kill Gildas. I've no

qualms about that. We've no love between us, Gildas and I.
That he serves the priestess is reason enough to condemn
him. But my master's given me no way out. Just says that
he'll *see to it* as he's no intention of forfeiting my contract.
He says that all will be sorted out on the solstice. Max, I've
seen what Sila Diaglou does to those who displease her.
But if I disobey the Bastard . . ."

He settled back in his chair, tilting his head, saying nothing. It took no Danae senses to feel his mind racing.

I stood up abruptly. "All right, then. Thank you for sharing the information with me, *ancieno*. I'll figure out something." I hurried toward the entry court door, listening . . .

"Wait!"

Closing my eyes, I promised Serena Fortuna a grand li-
bation. I swung around slowly.

Max waved me back to my chair, and when I was
seated, leaned forward as if to hold me there with his authority. "I know exactly what solution you'll 'figure out,'
little brother—the same as always. But running away will
not save you this time. Despite Grav Hurd's best efforts to
drive all purebloods out of the city, the Registry is like to
be the only power that survives this war—and once they
find you again, they'll bury you so deep, you'll remember
this house as heaven and beg for Patronn's strap in preference to their gentle hands." He smoothed and straightened the front of his pourpoint as if he were a caring elder
brother. "And, of course, you would destroy the family
along the way, not to mention laying waste all this delicate negotiating—for which I have pledged every minim
of my own future."

No matter that I had expected this response from him—
no matter that I had come here rejoicing that I no longer
accounted these people the whole of my kin—I could not
stifle the rage his calculation roused in me. I let him see it.
"And why would I be willing to suffer either Sila Diaglou's
fury or Osriel the Bastard's to preserve this misbegotten
family or this misbegotten kingdom?"

"Hold, little brother. I am not suggesting you sit back
and accept your dismal lot." He smiled in the very same superior manner he claimed to detest in Gildas. "I owe you a
debt. You gave me this chance for advancement when you

stood up for my honor in front of your prince and mine. Even you know the importance of honor and trust to those of us who actually believe in pureblood contracts. So perhaps you and I can come to an accommodation ... help each other ..."

"Max will see no advantage to warning Gildas of my murderous intent. He'd much rather have Gildas's secrets." I dug into the platter of roast pork under Saverian's watchful eye. The two of us sat in the courtyard at Renna Syne two hours after my return from Palinur. "I'm not leaving Max personally at risk. He won't even know I was actually after Jullian, Stearc, and the prince until we're safely back here. All Sila's anger and Bayard's will fall on me and through me to Osriel. Bayard is conspiring against the priestess already, and I've hopes our prince will forgive me for saving his neck."

"But you trust Max enough that this weapon he promises to supply is your only sure defense and this escape route he gave you is your only way out?" Saverian's skepticism could have eroded Renna's cliffs, so it did no good at all for my fragile confidence.

"In the best case, I won't need to rely on either one. I've size, I've magic, and I've surprise to wield. Surely something in Fortress Torvo will remind me enough of something here that I can shift the four of us straight back here. And yes, before you ask again, I'll not let Max turn me over until I've made sure the prisoners are actually *in* the fortress."

The physician poked at the blaze in the fire pit. The serving man had thought she was mad to have wood hauled into the sunny courtyard of the window house. He was not present to note the greater oddity when I stripped off my cloak, tunic, and shirt as I ate, basking in the frigid air as if it were a river of mead, while Saverian huddled next to her blaze. Only a few hours remained until sundown, when Voushanti was to deliver me to Prince Bayard. Every time I thought of it, my gut tied itself in knots and my head got woozy.

"I won't argue that we've much choice in the matter," said the physician, "but your plan is madness. You've no idea what Sila Diaglou thinks to do with you. Do you actually believe she'll allow you to roam free and abscond with her prisoners?"

"In the best case, I'll have the three of them out before she can get over the surprise. In the worst case, well . . ." The worst cases were innumerable, and I couldn't bear thinking about them. We'd no time to plan more intricate ploys. ". . . I'll just have to lie a bit more. It's still my finest talent."

I had exercised that skill in plenty since I'd returned from Palinur, pulled on the damp clothes I'd stashed behind a water cask in Renna's back alley, and rousted my fellow conspirators from their afternoon's business. I had told Elene I had no reason to fear Sila Diaglou's custody, as the priestess had made clear she wanted me alive. I had promised Brother Victor that no amount of intelligence and clever deceit could give Gildas the power to match a half-Danae half sorcerer. I'd assured all of them that my new skills could certainly get me and the prisoners out of Sila Diaglou's house and back here in good order. I had even asked Elene to show me Renna's dungeons so I could impress their complete image—the stink produced by the three drunkard prisoners, the chill, the taste and smell of iron and damp and enclosing walls—firmly on my mind. I had insisted that she needn't worry about my pallor as I followed her through those dank passages, and when we'd come out into the wintry sunlight, I distracted them all from my sick fear and sketchy plan by showing them the fronds of sea grass that marked my hand with pale blue and silver light.

Saverian knew better. I appreciated that she didn't contradict me until we were alone. While Elene, Brother Victor, and Voushanti prepared a letter in Osriel's name, confirming the solstice plan and offering me to Bayard as a "gift of good faith" to hand over to Sila Diaglou and close their bargain, the two of us had hiked over to Renna Syne. Along with some of the wardrobe Osriel had provided me, Saverian had supplied food, medicine, and her own astringent honesty.

"This Gildas will suspect you're there to take the boy and the others. He knows about your problem with nivat. That should worry you. One wrong word from Max and he'll pounce."

It *did* worry me. And then there was the matter of being staked bound and bleeding over some Danae sianou. Alone and dying slowly ... great gods, what end could be worse than that? Especially when all assurance about what might come after my death had been upended. Saverian's marrow-deep scrutiny had surely uncovered this fear, too.

"Yes. Yes. And yes," I said. "It is a demented plan. A thousand things can go wrong. But from the beginning Sila has said she wants my *contract*, not just me. She has some use for me, Saverian. She's not going to kill me or let Gildas do it. And if she has some use for me, then I have leverage. I won't be shut up in a box. As for the nivat ... I'll be wary. At the first whiff, I'll shut down my sense of smell—Kol taught me how to do that. Yes, I could be horribly wrong about all this, and if you think I am terrified, that's not even the half of it. Gods, I'm no strategist. This is all I can think to do."

I stuffed down more food, not knowing when I might get to eat again. I had to stay warm. I had to stay sensible. Saverian was too good at making me think, however uncomfortable. It was certainly possible that my connection with Osriel might lead Gildas to suspect that Osriel and Gram were the same man. In that case, the game would be up before it had even begun.

"You should get the others to prepare for the worst," I said. "They respect you, listen to you. They know about strategy and tactics and all those things I've no head for. They must know some way to call in Osriel's warlords. So use it and persuade the lords to defend Caedmon's Bridge on the solstice. Stash Gillarine's monks in the highest mountains of Evanore."

"What if you're wrong about bigger things, Valen?" said the physician softly. "What if your importance to the Danae is more critical than saving Osriel or Jullian or this lighthouse? Your mother had some plan for you."

That argument, of course, I had no possible way to rebut, so I tried to explain the course that spirit and instinct had chosen for me. "Jullian is my friend and my sworn responsibility. Stearc is an honorable man and beloved of my friends. Though Osriel betrayed me, though he terrifies me, he is my lord and rightful king. He wants to do right for Navronne, even beyond his own life and honor and future—I can see that much. My mother told no one her plan, so I can't see what would be so important that I must let my friends and my king die. And no one else has the skills to save them. I might. So, physician, steer me a better course."

"Kill Voushanti."

"Spirits of night!" I said, near choking. I dropped my eating knife into the platter as if it had given her the macabre idea. Had I not already closed down the rattling abundance of my senses, I would have been sure I had misheard. "Why, in the name of the Mother—?"

"He is already dead. Has been for over ten years. And if no one steps forward by tomorrow night, he'll die again, this time with no coming back. To continue breathing he must be blood-bound to another living person. Osriel and Stearc are not available. Elene will have naught to do with the business. The monk is too weak. I can't do it myself if I'm going to work the spell, not that *I'm* interested in having so close an attachment to him, either. He is brutish and bullheaded, frightens most of my patients, and has no respect for women, especially those who aspire to studies. I could perhaps persuade Philo or Melkire to the task—they respect him and are not so afraid as everyone else—but Osriel has given me no leave to tell anyone else of this."

I worked to take in so much information. "But you're telling *me*."

"I believe the prince would trust you with the knowledge. In the days ahead, you might need someone who is bound to your will and devoted to your service . . . at least until Osriel can take on the burden again. It won't improve your crazy plan, but it might give you and Riel a better chance of surviving it."

She spoke as seriously and reasonably as Brother Sebastian explaining the structure of virtue. But the little lines atop the bridge of her nose had deepened to little ravines. Slowly I wiped my greasy mouth on my shirttail, startled as always to see the silvery gards gleaming from my hand. I swallowed. "Are you planning to explain more or do you expect me just to agree to such a mystery at your suggestion? Which I won't."

She shoved the plate of meat back toward me and refilled

my cup with Evanori ale that tasted as if it had been made from discarded boots. "Keep eating. You don't have much time, and if we're to do this, we'll need to do it soon."

I just looked at her with the kind of expression such a ridiculous suggestion deserved.

She sighed and rested the ale pitcher in her lap. "Voushanti was the third son of a minor Evanori family, a veteran, competent warrior. When King Eodward moved his mistress to Renna to get her away from your hateful purebloods, he sent Voushanti along as her bodyguard. Voushanti was arrogant and silent and not particularly happy at being shoved off to watch over a woman. Everyone here was a bit afraid of him. And then Lirene died."

The physician took on her most argumentative expression, but her eyes were focused on the past and not on me.

"You have to understand how Osriel adored his mother. She cared for him through so much pain and sickness, sang to him, bathed him, held him through long, dreadful nights. He was only seven when a sudden fever took her. He truly believed he would die without her. Evanori have stories . . . well, all warrior people have stories, I'm sure, about heroes that live beyond death. On the day of Lirene's funeral rites, Riel told me that his magic was going to bring her back. Voushanti heard him say it, and called Osriel a blasphemer to so question the laws of the gods and insult the memory of true warriors. Osriel hated Voushanti from that day."

"He planned to bring his mother back from the dead," I said numbly.

"Osriel read everything he could find about Aurellian sorcery, and he questioned my mother and his father's other purebloods until their ears blistered. He studied and followed my mother about as she worked with the sick. She said Riel could have been a healer himself were he not a king's bastard, required to study politics and war. Everyone believed Osriel sought a cure for saccheria, but I knew what he was looking for. At twelve, when his father took him to Ardra for the first time, he brought back a wagonload of Aurellian books, and in an old book of herb spells, he found the key."

Saverian's long, capable fingers were tangled in a knot, pressed to her chin, and she kept her eyes averted as people do when they tell stories they believe they should not.

"At fifteen, he showed me how he could smother a frog and set it breathing again. A few months later, he claimed to have touched the living soul of a villein who had been kicked by a horse, though the man's soul escaped him before he could catch it. By this time he had accepted that his mother was gone, but he could not stop." She paused, pressing her lips together.

"And Voushanti?" I said, urging her on.

"From the day Lirene died, wherever Osriel walked, sat, studied, or slept, Voushanti stood by. Riel hated it. He called the saccheria his prison, and Voushanti his warder. When he was small, he cast magical curses at Voushanti— little flaming, stinging things—and his father chastised him sorely for it. By the time he turned sixteen, he merely lived as if Voushanti did not exist.

"One winter afternoon, Osriel was sitting in the old library of this house, studying. He was feverish again, his joints so swollen that any movement was excruciating. He was practicing fire work, smothering the hearth fire and starting it up again with pure magic. Voushanti warned him repeatedly to stop, for the steward had reported the library chimney clogged. Voushanti stood directly in front of the hearth . . ."

I needed no more words to see what happened—a frustrated, angry, pain-racked youth flaunting his talent before his jailer, casting a great flaming spell toward the hearth.

Saverian stopped and drank from her ale cup. I was so caught up in the story, my own remained untouched. "Voushanti saved him from the fire," I said.

Saverian drained her cup. "The place burned like dry wheat. You can still see the ruin out behind the west wing. Voushanti took the full brunt of Osriel's fireburst and the eruption of the chimney, yet he carried Osriel out, completely shielding him from the flames. No one could have survived such injuries as the mardane bore. My mother pronounced him dead within the hour."

Like the tides of Evaldamon, cold dread swept over me again. "But Osriel . . ."

"He demanded servants carry the body into his private study. Almost a full day later, Riel summoned my mother to tend Voushanti's burns. Lungs, heart, all his organs were functioning, though his burns remained savage. Voushanti lived again."

"You say this has happened more than once ... his dying ..."

"Three that I know of. One that I saw, when Riel was too sick to complete the spell and called me in to help. Severe wounds can stop Voushanti's heart, but he can be brought back if the enchantment is renewed immediately. Time can stop his heart if the enchantment is not renewed at least once in a sevenday. But the one whose blood seals the enchantment on the mardane's lips is bound to him, able to command Voushanti to his service. Unless you force him elsewhere, Voushanti will not leave your side. He will sense your presence, know when you're in trouble, and he fights like a man who has nothing to lose. He could make the difference between your venture's success and failure."

"What of his soul?"

"I don't believe in souls."

"What does the prince say?"

She folded her arms tight across her breast and hardened her mouth as if expecting me to assault her. "He says that Voushanti's soul and body are fused, and that when his body dies at last—truly and forever—his soul will die with it. Osriel bears some dreadful guilt over the whole thing, which is ridiculous. The magic is truly remarkable."

I would have given my teeth to have more time to consider what Saverian had told me, for in her story of Osriel's bold sorcery lay the truth about dead men's eyes and votive vessels sealed with blood and what Osriel intended to do with them. I had assumed he planned some great enchantment, built with the substance and energies he had stolen from dying men. But now ... It came to me that the Bastard thought to ensorcel himself an army.

Chapter 20

"Who gave you leave to speak of these matters?"
The red centers of Voushanti's dark eyes gleamed
with fury. "The prince will have you flogged."

Saverian stepped closer to my side, as if together we
could withstand his wrath. I wished I was far from Saverian's meticulously ordered study.

"The prince commanded me to do what was necessary
to give you a full span of life, Mardane," said Saverian.
"You owe him your obedience, as I do."

"Him. Not you. Not this fey sorcerer."

"Then do as he would command you. If you have another partner in mind, perhaps Magnus could fetch him."

Cream-colored light streamed from a lamp of the magical variety that lit Renna Syne, illuminating shelf upon
shelf filled with books, beakers, bottles, and jars. Two well-scrubbed tables laid out with brass implements, mortar and
pestle, pans, and balances furnished one end of the room. A
chair, side table, and footstool held the opposite end, with a
variety of stools and benches in between. The physician had
failed to mention the chamber's location in the bowels of
Renna's fortress or its lack of windows. Evidently she disliked being bothered by household noise, outdoor views, or
air as she worked.

When I had said I would consider doing as she suggested,
Saverian had bustled me here immediately. "What of your
scruples?" I'd asked her, as we traipsed across the dry hillside

between Renna Syne and the fortress. "You once told me that 'no worthy physician could stand by and see a healthy body damaged.' "

"To cause death deliberately violates every principle of the healer's art," she had said. "And to keep a body alive by enchantment violates the good order of nature that stands before any god in my esteem. But if I refuse to perpetuate Osriel's ugly mistake, then I have destroyed Voushanti just as surely and far more permanently. He *will* die unless you and I do this." That was the point I could not argue.

Then we had arrived and Voushanti had been waiting for her. And before I could say yes or no, she had told Voushanti I would be his new partner in this macabre business. Since then he had been circling the workroom like a trapped wolf.

Saverian continued to speak calmly. "It seems unlikely that the prince will return in time to perform this service for you himself. As you are accompanying Magnus to Palinur to effect our lord's rescue, it would be most inconvenient if you were to die in the midst of it. This seems a reasonable solution to your problem."

"Reasonable?" There ensued one of the most horrible sounds I had ever heard—a strident gargling bellow that might have emanated from one of the nearby dungeons. The accompanying jerk of Voushanti's shoulders and the spasm of emotion that crossed his scarred visage gave me the unlikely idea that he was laughing. "You cannot even tell me how this one's fey blood might affect the enchantment. Would I had a tankard, physician, that I could raise it to your twisted notion of *reason*."

Saverian, unfazed, pointed to a long low bench. Scuffed leather covered its thin padding. "I promise you will be no more dead using the sorcerer's blood than you will be without it. You've an appointment in Palinur three hours hence, Mardane, which means you've little enough time for recovery. If we're to do this, we do it now."

Events swept past and over me like a flock of startled crows. Abandoning me at the door, where I held a drowning man's grip on a much too low lintel stone, Saverian dragged a stepstool to one of her shelves and retrieved a small enameled canister shaped like an angel. She set the canister on a knee-high table in company with a silver lancet, a square stack of folded linen, and a bronze basin with an extended lip like that of a pitcher.

"Slitting your heart vein will be quickest, Lord Voushanti, though the blood loss will likely leave you weaker than you would prefer," she said. "But delivering Magnus to Prince Bayard should not entail a fight, and the journey ... you will marvel at its ease and, in fact, decide that you have bound yourself to a fine racehorse. We'll hope he keeps his pace *reasonable* in deference to your recent demise."

Like dust motes floating on the light, her macabre humor failed to settle. Voushanti's pacing slowed. Perhaps he might refuse the enchantment ... which seemed a vile and wicked hope.

Saverian paused in her preparations. "Do you wish a sleeping draught? I know Prince Osriel does not offer, but I could—"

"No!" None of his answers had approached the ferocity of this one.

Without further argument, the seething warrior removed his leather jupon, gray tunic, and wool shirt, exposing broad chest and shoulders mottled with ugly red burn scars, old battle wounds, and patches of black and gray hair. He laid his garments on Saverian's chair and reclined on the leather bench.

At Saverian's direction I moved to Voushanti's side. He averted his face, and neither twitched nor fidgeted.

With a flurry of brusque steps and clinking glass, Saverian added a few vials, tapers, and small dishes to her supplies. Then she doused the magical lamp and brought a lighted candle to her table. Drawing her stool beside mine, she thrust a stained but clean wadded sheet into my sweating hands. "Be ready with this," she said softly.

I could not think what she meant, but didn't ask. My eyes would not leave the wide flat handle of the lancet that lay snug in her hand.

"Mardane Voushanti, is it your will that I take you past the brink of unlife and work this magic to restore your breath and blood?"

He jerked his head in assent, but fixed his eyes on the far wall.

"*Speak* your will, or I'll have none of this," she snapped. "No man will say *I* chose this way."

Voushanti swiveled his head to glare redly at the both of us. "You've not bound me to this bench. Obey our master's will. Take this life and give it back."

He turned away again. Saverian probed his neck with two fingers and without hesitation jabbed her lancet in between.

Blood spewed from Voushanti's wound like the liquid fire Aurellians discharge from their warships to set their enemies ablaze. Only by fortunate reaction did I hold up the wadded linen to catch this monstrous volley. Voushanti jerked and gripped the edge of the bench, emitting only a grunt.

Saverian, her hands gloved in gore, snatched up one of her smaller folds of linen and held it to the surging flow, channeling it into the long lip of the tin basin, a river of red that threatened to overflow the vessel. The chamber fell silent, save for Voushanti's rapid, shallow breaths.

I rubbed my arms through the thin shirtsleeves, afraid to let myself feel anything. I had experienced a man's death once. Saverian must wear steel beneath her plain garb.

As the pulsing flow of blood dwindled, Voushanti's breath began to labor. The half of his face we could see was a morbid blue-white and sheened with sweat. His hands that had gripped the bench now lay flaccid on its cracked leather.

Saverian had me set the heavy basin aside while she wiped her hands clean. Then she turned the warrior's head to face us and slipped another square of folded linen under the wound to absorb the waning trickle of his life. His scarred face was slack, his stare dull, even as his chest strained and heaved to draw each breath.

I labored with him. The walls bulged and writhed around us. The flat iron stink of blood wakened reminders of battlefield nights, of wails and screams and dread visions. The physician dipped a finger into a small jar and dabbed a yellow ointment on Voushanti's eyelids, flooding the thickening air with the pungent perfume of ysomar that the Karish said would summon angels to carry the soul to heaven, and the Sinduri claimed would call the

Ferryman to the earthly shore to transport the soul to the Kemen Sky Lord's feasting halls or Magrog's land of torment. But what if a man's soul was "fused to his body" and could not journey onward? What if a man had no soul?

I had stabbed Boreas for mercy, drowned a pack of Harrowers to save other lives, and slain Navronne's enemies for my king. None of these deaths rested easy in my mind, but at the least I had believed that those victims would be granted some existence beyond this life. Every god I knew promised a continuing for those who had a soul, so I'd never imagined I was sending them to endless nothing. But this . . . what was this we did here? A certain horror gripped my breath and bone. I could no longer sit still.

Grabbing Saverian's arm, I yanked her off her stool and dragged her away from the couch so Voushanti could not hear me. Scarlet cheeked, she wrestled to get free. "Are you mad?" she spat. "I need to watch him."

"Is there a chance this spell won't revive him?" I said, harsh and quiet. "Have you done it before . . . you yourself?"

"I've seen it done. I know what to do."

"But is there a chance? Could he not revive?" I shook her, unwilling to release her until I heard *yea* or *nay*.

"No spell is proof against failure," she said. "I'll do my best, which is better than most. Now let me go, lest his heart stop for too long, for then the magic *will* fail."

I let her go, and she hurried back to her work, examining the blood that dribbled slowly from Voushanti's neck. Briskly, she sprinkled herbs and powders from her vials into three glass dishes and used a thin brass spatula to dip blood from the basin and drip some on each dish. With thumb and forefinger she used one mixture to draw sigils on Voushanti's forehead and cheeks. With another, she marked spiked crescents under her own eyes.

Wiping her lancet clean on another folded square, she beckoned me back to my place. "The time approaches. Stop now, and *you* murder him."

Furious at myself for not questioning earlier, furious at Saverian, at Osriel, I returned to my stool. We might have already sent this man to his end. Alone. Before Saverian could stop me, I laid my hand on Voushanti's spasming breast.

"Valen! What are you doing?"

So near, linked by touch and his blood on my skin, I existed with and in him. I opened my senses.

The cold of Navronne's untimely winter was as nothing to the bitter hour of Voushanti's dying. One gouge of fire seared my neck ... one grating burn marked agonized lungs ... elsewise, waking mind hung suspended in a world of freezing black. Utterly alone. Anger rumbled faintly in the dark like retreating thunder. No fear, though. No grief. Not his, at least.

One more straining breath and the body could do no more. The candlelight retracted to a pinpoint, only bright enough to serve as a reminder of loss. And as light and pain flared and faded, Voushanti and I shared one silent cry of such piercing hunger as tore the fabric of the descending night ...

"Valen! Give me your hand. Now!"

I gasped, blinked, and snatched my hand from the clammy, flaccid body. Shuddering, wagging my head, I tried to clear out the morbid darkness, but patterns of light and shadow, more than could be explained by one small candle, shifted and wavered on the walls and in the very air itself, overflowing that chamber as the mardane's blood did the tin vessel. Saverian's cheekbones, flushed under the blood marks, and her green eyes, fiery with purpose, supplied the only sparks of color. The angel canister stood open on the table, whatever enchantment it had contained now released.

Murmuring words I could not distinguish, Saverian scooped a fragrant green liquid from her third glass dish and traced patterns on my cheeks and forehead. Then her warm fingers clamped my wrist and pressed the back of my hand to a leather cushion that rested in her lap. Quick as lightning, her sharp little blade scored my thumb. Pain far beyond the wounding shot through my hand and up my arm as if traveling through my gards.

She pressed my bloody thumb to Voushanti's lips, crying out in Aurellian, "Rise and live, mortal man, all desire and worth bound to thy master's will until heart stops, bone crumbles, and breath fails." Her marks on my face grew hot, as if Kol were at his work again, and I felt the varied parts of the spell engage, as if they were the shafts and cogs of a mill wheel.

Shadows whirled over our heads, raising a wind that flapped book pages and rattled the shelves. Glassware tumbled to the stone floor and smashed alongside metal containers that clattered and bounced. The candle winked out. And still the physician held my bleeding thumb to those cold lips.

Then, of a sudden, Voushanti's head jerked beneath my hand, and a shaft of red lightning shot from his dead eyes straight into my own head. For one soul-searing moment, I could not look away ... and then it was over. Darkness engulfed us again, the quivering excitement of air and life that signified enchantment vanished. Saverian released her grip.

Blind in the absolute blackness, I cradled my cut hand to my breast, hoping to ease the pain in my arm and in my soul. The marks on my face cooled quickly, and the rattles and clatters ceased as the whirlwind dissipated. A choking noise came from the bench in front of me.

"Come away," whispered Saverian in my ear, drawing me up and away from the muffled sounds. "Careful. Mind the lintel."

I shuffled my feet to keep from stumbling over the debris and extended one hand at head height. Just as my fingers encountered stone and I ducked my head to clear the doorway, a pale light burst out behind me, illuminating Saverian's face and hands. Two fingers of her right hand were pointed at a lamp in the room behind. I turned to look, but glimpsed only Voushanti's back as she pulled the heavy door closed.

"He prefers to be alone as he recovers," she said. "It takes him an hour or so to gather himself, somewhat longer to heal from whatever has brought him to the point of death. He likes it quiet."

Not quiet, I thought. *Private*. I could hear the groans of pain and despair that burst through his choking silence, only to be buried in his thick arms and in layers of bloody linen and leather.

"I need to get out of here," I said, as the torches that lit the long passage swelled into glaring banners of hell. The entire weight of the fortress pressed upon the back of my neck.

"You did well," said the physician, hurrying her steps and pointing to a stair that I knew led to light and air. "I was worried about your tolerating the chamber. But for me to attempt such a working anywhere else would have been—"

"Never again," I said, taking the steps three at a time, leaving her behind. "No matter who commands or who begs, I won't be part of that again." The enchantment clung to my spirit like dung to a boot. I had touched earth with magic and glimpsed its patterns of life and death and growing. Nowhere in that grand display was there a place for what I had just experienced.

Saverian rejoined me in the well yard where I sprawled on the dry grass inhaling great gulps of air and sky. Despite the hazy blue overhead, evening had already come to the little garth and the stone-bordered well, enclosed as they were in the heart of the fortress. "Osriel and his magics seem to have that effect on everyone."

"Are there others like Voushanti?" I said.

"Osriel says Voushanti is the only one."

"Is this what he plans for the solstice, Saverian?"

"That's impossible," she said, averting her eyes. "Osriel does not collect bodies. This enchantment cannot be worked on those dead more than a few hours."

But the weakness of her denial only made my conviction stronger. I rolled up to sitting. "I've little enough knowledge of sorcery or natural philosophy. But I know that such magic as we just aided will not repair what's wrong with the world. I won't let him do it."

Her color flamed like a bonfire. "You cannot leave Osriel with Sila Diaglou! The danger, if she identifies him . . ."

"I've said I'll do my best to get him out. But if none of you will explain what he plans, then he'll have to tell me himself, and I'll be his judge before I set him free to do it."

What if Sila wanted to bleed him? Osriel had said that sacrificing a body consecrated to Navronne might have consequences beyond the poisoning of one sianou. I needed to ask Kol if that was true.

Of a sudden my chest tightened with a longing that left

me breathless, a wrenching ache I had known since child-hood, never able to name its cause or its object. I had be-lieved it only another symptom of the insatiable disease that drove me wild. But now images raced through my mind: of my uncle's grace and beauty as he strode through bound-less vistas of earth and sky, forest and sea. Of the power he had brought to healing one small garden meadow. Ah, gods, I wanted to be in Aeginea dancing and not setting out to war.

"Valen, are you ill?" Saverian seemed to speak from a vast distance, as if the few steps that separated us were the Caurean Sea. "What's wrong?"

"Naught," I said, blinking rapidly and stroking the blade of healthy winter-dry grass that grew in this little yard. Tears were surely but stray remnants of my long madness. "Naught."

From Renna's walls the watch called the second hour past noonday. So late in the year, sundown would follow in little more than two hours. Time to be traveling.

I left Elene's retiring room bearing a small case with my extra clothes, the vials of Saverian's potions—some for me, some for Osriel, some to use as weapons should the oppor-tunity arise—and the fervent prayers and good wishes of Elene and Brother Victor.

The lady and the monk had read me the letter to Bayard they had composed while Saverian and I had been engaged in murder and resurrection. Had I not been so disturbed at my own part in Voushanti's ordeal and this entirely lu-dicrous bout of homesickness for Aeginea, a home I had known but a few hours, the scroll's contents might have given me a laugh.

I have enjoyed controlling Magnus's infamous streak of rebellion, but find him much less interesting with-out it. His myriad lacks—reading, writing, education, combat training, and even rudimentary sorcery— leave him somewhat bored and lacking purpose. As I cannot imagine what use the priestess has for him, I have decided that his best use might be to discover her intents.

Though my life's purpose remained determinedly unclear, the past few weeks had been anything but boring. Elene and Brother Victor had sealed this missive with Osriel's signet. I wondered which of them had come up with the wording.

I hurried along the Great Hall gallery, where Saverian and I had spied on the warmoot. The hall sat dark and deserted, smelling of old smoke, old ale, and the old wood of the massive ceiling beams.

Our ragged little cabal of three had agreed that Elene and Brother Victor would send a long-planned alarm to Prior Nemesio at Gillarine. The coded message would bring the prior and his flock to shelter at Magora Syne—Osriel's most remote stronghold, deep in Evanore's mountains. A sevenday without word from me, and they would command Osriel's warlords to muster at Caedmon's Bridge on the winter solstice.

I had insisted that Elene and Brother Victor, as the last lighthouse warders, should not attend that solstice confrontation, but retreat to Magora Syne as well. "You guard Navronne's future in many ways," I said. "You must keep Saverian informed of all circumstances . . . see that she goes with you." I made sure Elene met my gaze and caught my double meaning. Should Osriel fall, she carried Eodward's rightful heir.

My footsteps clattered and echoed on the downward stair, and I emerged into late afternoon. Wind whined and blustered about the fortress arches and towers. Despite the hazy sunlight, the smell of the wind promised snow before morning. Halfway along the covered walk that led past the Great Hall to the kitchen alley, I switched the small, heavy case to my left hand, as it was irritating the cut on my thumb.

"I can carry that, sorcerer." Mardane Voushanti appeared at my left side, matching me step for step. Impeccably garbed in a spruce green cloak and a silver hauberk blazoned with Osriel's wolf, he kept his gaze straight ahead as he held out his hand for the case.

"That's not necessary."

I did not slow my pace and did not stare. I'd not quite believed he would meet me here as Saverian had promised when she left me in the well yard.

"You should take this, though." I passed him the scroll bearing Osriel's seal. "Max—Prince Bayard's pureblood—will meet us at my family's house with a small escort. If you sense anything amiss, we'll turn right around and come back here."

"And once you are in the custody of Sila Diaglou, I am to wait for some signal from you—a bonfire or magical explosion—at which time I am to charge into Fortress Torvo and pull you out. That is, unless you have burst from her dungeons with the prince and the thane or crawled out along some escape path given you by a generous not-brother who has always loathed you. That is a fool's plan . . . no plan at all."

If it *sounded* ridiculous, it *felt* impossible. "I believe I can do this," I said. "But I've no idea how long it might take to discover where Jullian is or to find the opportunity to get to the others. If I think of anything else between here and there, I'll be sure to tell you. Just stay close and be alert."

The mardane halted. I kept walking. "I'll give you two days," he called after me. "Mistress Elene has given me a well-filled purse. Bring the prince out before midnight two days hence, or I'll buy me some fighters and come in after you."

I stopped and looked back at him. The scarlet centers of his eyes had heated in defiance, but I had not even asked Saverian how to call up the power I had over him. I had no desire to wield Osriel's red lightning. "*Three* days," I said. "But buy your fighters and have them ready beforehand."

"Done." He jerked his massive head and caught up with me. The unscarred half of his face was the color of chalk. We resumed our walk and rounded the corner into the alley that so resembled the lane in Palinur. "You *will* abandon me and get the prince straight back here if we cannot rendezvous," he said.

"I will. I assumed that's what his sworn protector would wish."

When we reached a certain dark little gap between two deserted storage buildings, I stopped and set down my case. "If you'll be so kind as to keep prying eyes away, I need to . . . uh . . . change my clothes."

Perhaps Saverian's summary description of my new talents had not included the required livery, for Voushanti's startled visage hinted that he'd not expected me to emerge from the gap lacking all accoutrement save light-drawn rocks and sea creatures.

"Strange, are they not?" I tossed the bundle of wool and velvet atop the case and stretched out my arms. With every passing moment in this shadowed alley, my gards brightened and their color deepened. Somehow the sight of them . . . or perhaps the gards themselves . . . left me feeling stronger, less battered by the wretched day, and if not exactly warm, somewhat warmer than my state of undress would promise. "Can't say I know what exactly they are. But they don't work if I keep them hidden."

His terrible eyes traveled up my body until they locked on my own. The red centers pulsed faintly, very like his blood as it had leaked out of him. "We are two of a kind," he said, his mouth twisting in his grotesque semblance of amusement. "Neither here nor there."

Squirming inside, I picked up my case and my clothes bundle. "We'd best move. Wouldn't want to be late." The ways in which I did *not* wish to resemble Voushanti were beyond numbering.

Shoving worries and plans aside, I stepped forward, my eyes on the stone walls and banks, on the overhanging trees, my ears on the dribbling conduit that piped water from the well yard. I inhaled the scents of the fortress cook fires and refuse heaps, and recalled the stink of fear as the ragged folk gathered on the hillside lane near the Cartamandua house. The air would be thicker in Palinur . . . and a wetter cold than here . . . with more snow on the ground—old, wet snow, freezing as the night approached.

We walked slowly along the alley. At a particular well-shadowed length of the wall, I threw my bundles over and climbed up the old stones . . .

. . . straight into the brushy, snow-clogged beech grove in Palinur where I had undressed on my way back to Renna earlier in the day. Voushanti topped the wall and immediately spun in his tracks, for the babble, clatter, and stink of the beggars' encampment fell on our heads like a bludgeon. Fires had driven more people into the purebloods' lane. Enchantments vibrated on every side of us, shielding the fine houses that stood back from the lane.

"I'll be ready to go in just a moment." As I bent down
to retrieve my clothes, my foot broke through the crusted
snow, scraping my ankle and shin. A youthful voice cried,
"Mam, it's the angel come back again!" And Saverian
climbed over the wall.

"Gods' teeth!" I said, as running feet crashed through
the underbrush from farther down the lane, and bodies
gathered just at the point we'd topped the wall—cutting off
my return route. We had nowhere to run. This particular
grove crowded between my family's garden wall and the
lane. I shoved Voushanti and my case behind the largest
tree, then grabbed my cloak and Saverian and dived into
the underbrush. "What the devil are you doing here?"

Saverian crawled on top of me, spreading her own cloak
wide and enfolding me in her arms. "Just be still," she whispered. "Your gards shine like a watch fire." I drew my legs
up under her, while she proceeded to tuck all the straggling
bits of me and my distinctively colored cloak out of sight.

"Over there in the trees," piped the child. "By the saints,
I swear it. Knew he'd come back!"

" 'Tis a sign! The god's not forgotten us." Murmurs
swelled from the lane beyond the grove. "He sends his holy
legion to drive out these Harrowers!"

"Blue fire, ye say, child?" said a man with a voice like
gravel. "My gammy told me of those who wear naught but
blue fire . . ."

"And wings, boy, did ye see wings or no?" Boots and
bodies crashed through the dry brush.

Saverian hissed. "Do something, sorcerer. Move, else
they'll think we're dead and not just preoccupied."

The warm weight of her body pressed my bare backside
into the twigs and snow. How like Saverian to lie close in
a thorny bed . . . which thought led me to remember *Elene*
in my bed, sunlight bathing her golden skin . . . which led
me to recall Saverian's capable hands, guiding me through
my nivat madness . . . touching me everywhere . . . Of a sudden, fear and strangeness and this ridiculous situation, lustful memory and a barrage of sensations—earth and snow
and woman and oncoming night—enveloped me in such a
fever, I could not control it.

"Deunor's mercy, mistress," I choked, "I dare not move."

But I did. Safely hidden beneath her cloak, I snaked my arm up her back. Fingering her neck, I pressed her head gently downward, until her face rested in the crook of my neck and shoulder. Her breath so warm . . . so inviting. Her bones so firm and straight. My alter hand stroked her rigid spine to yielding . . . then found its way to her backside, while my knee drew up between her legs and nudged them apart . . .

Her head popped up. "Villain madman!" A sharp blow stung my cheek . . . and waked me from my fog of lust to shuffling bodies and laughter all around our ungainly heap. "Get your hands off—"

I pulled her head downward, crushing her lips against mine. Her hands scratched and gouged my arms and pulled my hair as she tried to wrestle away. Scrabbling, wriggling, she drew her knee up sharply, and I shifted to preclude disaster, praying her cloak would not fall aside and display my glowing feet.

"No angel here, young Filp," said the gravel-voiced man. " 'Tis only ones searching for a bit of heaven fallen in the midst of hell."

"Could ye not give a man a quat to 'imself?" I shouted, squeezing Saverian's face to my shoulder before she bit my lips off. "Yea, laugh as ye will . . . get ye all to Magrog's furnace and take all pinchy wives with ye!"

The men shoved the pale-haired child behind the women. Ribald comments all around and they decided the fun was over. Murmurs and laughter faded into the evening noises of the lane.

"I'm sorry," I said, still muzzling the squirming physician. Torn between annoyance that she had intruded her peculiar self into an already precarious activity and a fear that I'd committed an unpardonable sin and forfeited her skillful and sensible aid, I couldn't stop talking. "My head just went off . . . well, not my head exactly . . . but it's been a long, weary autumn . . . yet I meant no ill to you. I would never— Well, I don't think I would. I do appreciate your hiding me—damnably awkward to light up like

this when I can't afford attention. Though one might say
you invited this problem by coming along where you were
not expected—though certainly you did *not* invite my inappropriate reaction—but I've no idea what we're going
to do with you or how we're going to keep you safe when
you cannot possibly go with us. What the devil were you
thinking?" Hoping she had enough fodder for conversation
beyond withering my manhood, I released her.

She climbed to her feet without the least care where her
elbows, knees, and fists found purchase. Were her discomfiture a bit more intense, her complexion might have lit sigils
of its own in purest scarlet.

"I *thought* that the people who were most likely to need
my care happened to be in Palinur—three men with somewhat specialized needs that no hedgerow leech or back-
alley surgeon is capable of tending. I *thought* that you and
I had come to some kind of mutual respect, untainted, for
the most part, by the brutish instincts of those who prefer
action to reason."

"Well, of course, we—"

"As for my safety, you are most certainly *not* responsible
for me. Nor is anyone but myself. After a discussion with
Brother Victor, I decided that I might better be close by
as you attempt this rescue, and that as long as I was here,
I could bring news of these ventures to your sister, the
Sinduria, who seems to care what becomes of you, though
she's not yet been informed that she is *not* your sister. And
I brought these." She pulled a vial and a scrap of stained
canvas from her pocket and shoved them into my hand.
"Elene told me that touching blood enabled you to track
a person more easily—a detail that you failed to mention
to me. While you and Mistress Moonhead exchanged your
overwrought farewells, I was retrieving a sample of Prince
Osriel's blood, which I keep on hand to formulate his medicines. I also managed to acquire this scrap cut from one
of Thane Stearc's old jupons, though I don't know that
dried blood has the same useful properties for pureblood
magic."

"Blood . . . gods, yes. It makes tracking much easier. I
just never imagined anyone would have any." Thickheaded
and embarrassed, I brushed twigs and ice crystals from my

skin. "And, yes, Thalassa should be told. All right ... yes, that would be kind of you ..."

Happily for me, Voushanti joined us before I could get too tangled up in words or recollections of the sensation of Saverian's breath on my skin. The sun was sinking. I turned my back to her and donned my finery as quickly as I could. Nothing like the luxurious restriction of buttons and laces for taming lustful mania. Gods, Saverian ... of all women in the world ...

So do as she says, fool. Attempt to reason, instead of acting blindly. I fastened my cloak with the ivory-and-gold wolf brooch.

"You can't traipse alone through Palinur, mistress physician," I said, tugging the mask from my pocket. "No matter how easily you can ensorcel those who aim to harm you, it's too dangerous. I wouldn't let *any* friend of mine do so. I'll come up with some explanation for Max, so Voushanti can deliver you to Thalassa."

Voushanti, his own attire impeccable despite his sojourn in the shrubbery, glared at me as if I were a particularly stupid infant. "To change your arrangements this late risks the entire plan, such as it is. And I must follow you to the Harrower priestess, so we'll know where you and the prince are held. I've no time to coddle foolish women."

"I'm not an idiot," said Saverian, her dignity regained though her skin retained a rosy hue. "I'll wait here until Magnus is delivered and transferred. Once you know his location, Mardane, you can return here for me. I would welcome your escort on my brief visit to the Mother's temple."

"Leaving the scene will jeopardize the prince's rescue," snapped Voushanti. "You have blood-bound me to this man, but I cannot read his thoughts. With no means of contact between us, I must be available at whatever time he chooses."

"No means of contact?" Saverian raised her eyebrows, quite smug. "You gentlemen really should have said something earlier. I can, of course, work a small enchantment ..."

Stupid not to think of it. My sister Thalassa had once worked a word trigger with her favorite insults, so that anywhere within ten quellae, I could hear her address me as *fiend heart* or *iron skull* did she but feed magic to the words.

Voushanti and I left the beech grove tight bound with the names of *dead man* and *bluejay* and a few specific signals for special circumstances. If he didn't hear from me in three days, he would force his way inside Fortress Torvo. As we picked our way through the crowded lane to our meeting with Max, my hearing picked Saverian's laughter out of the noise. I smiled as I remembered the warmth of her breath and the feel of her firm flesh and slender bones crushed against my skin. What an extraordinary woman.

Chapter 21

❖━━━━━━━━━━━❖

"See the iron grate over the drainage canal? That's where you'll come out. You *can* still quicken a spell, yes?" Max spoke using only the half of his mouth beneath his mask. As protocol required refraining from conversation in the presence of ordinaries, every pureblood youth developed the skill early on.

"Yes." I mimicked his trick. Though I stood slightly behind him, I was enough taller that I could easily be observed by either the spear-wielding Harrowers guarding Sila Diaglou's gates, the bowmen on the barbican above the gate tunnel, or the five of Bayard's warriors who surrounded us protectively, while their captain identified our party to the gate commander.

The knee-high grate to which Max referred blocked the only breach in the thick, ugly walls of Fortress Torvo. The canal had once drained water and sewage from the fortress, but that function had likely been relocated as the city grew up around the place. Weeds, dirty snow, and broken paving choked the old ditch, which disappeared into the squalid houses and snow-clogged ruins that crowded this miserable square. Riie Doloure. Last time I had been here, Harrowers had been throwing severed heads from the battlements down to their rioting fellows and fire had raged in the tenements. On that vile morning, men and women had been screaming from behind those walls, one of them Abbot Luviar, as his executioner exposed his bowels and set them afire.

Another wave of the sweats dampened my skin, my

hands trembled in their bonds of silk and steel, and my own bowels threatened to betray me. What kind of idiot would broach Sila Diaglou's fortress in shackles? And Gildas would be here. Gildas, who knew all my weaknesses.

The plan we had made over the past day had gone smoothly thus far. Max, Voushanti, and I had made a show of my resistance in front of Prince Bayard, enough to make Bayard think me cowardly and not worth keeping for himself. Sila Diaglou had accepted Bayard's request for a meeting. Now it was up to Max to convince her of our story, and it was up to Max's spy within Sila's entourage to provide me a blade. With a weapon and a smattering of luck, I could get out of a warded cell. Outside of a cell, I could use magic to free the others. Somehow. That was the plan. As with most plans, it seemed far less plausible in daylight.

"Forward," ordered Bayard's captain upon his return from the gate. "Lower arms."

He pivoted smartly. We marched briskly past the gate guards, under the raised portcullis, and into the gate tunnel. I resisted the urge to look back at the burned-out tenements where Voushanti and Saverian were to have set up their watchpost by now. Rather I gave thanks that my hands were silkbound and that Max's hand gripped my arm to prevent my stumbling in the dark. I did not want to touch earth and sense the horrors that had gone on here.

The dark-stained gallows, the judges' platform, and the prisoners' cage stood vacant in the outer bailey, like the bones of some vicious monster left to rot in the weak sunlight. As we were hurried across the yard and through the inner gate, I noted the rubble-filled drainage channel. Another grate barred its passage through the inner wall. If I could find no promising venue to key my Danae shifting, I might be forced to use Max's route to the outside. Naught of this executioner's yard recalled enough of Renna's baileys that I could take us from one to the other by Danae magic.

Sweat dribbled down my back. I could not retreat now. They were here—Stearc and Osriel at least. One touch of the blood samples that Saverian had brought had told me that much. But I could get no better sense of their exact location until I was inside.

We proceeded up a narrow ramp, overlooked by the inner wall walk, two flanking towers, and the arrow loops of the blocklike keep. What remained of Fortress Torvo's conical roofs stated that this small fortress had been here long before the Aurellian invasion, long before Palinur had grown into a great city.

A barren courtyard awaited us, and more Harrower troops—some in the shabby cottes and braies of townsmen or the shapeless tunics of villeins, some in sturdier padded leather jaques with metal plates sewn on arms and breast. But all of them wore orange rags tied about their necks or arms or trailing from their hats. At the head of a wooden stair, two Harrowers opened the iron-bound doors of the keep.

Max released my arm and smoothed the wrinkles his fingers had made in my velvet sleeve. His dark eyes glittered. "Well done, little brother. I doubted you'd balls enough to make it so far without bolting. Are you ready?"

Who could be ready for the things Sila did? I ducked my head, rather than embarrassing myself by choking within his hearing. The priestess wanted me alive. She had some use for me. I had to believe that.

Max grinned and flicked a finger at one of his men, who quickly knelt in front of me with a weighty set of shackles. I lashed out at the soldier's head with my bound hands and twisted away as if to bolt. But as Max and I had planned, a few wrenched muscles, bruising holds, and snarled curses later, I was well subdued and stumbling up the steps in chains.

Max gripped my arm with one hand. "After you." Then he added so that none but I could hear, "May Serena Fortuna smile on our first fraternal venture. My spy will use the password *brethren*."

Inhaling a last breath of the open air, I stepped inside.

No dais or grand chair marked Sila Diaglou's barren hall. No tapestries covered the smoke-blackened walls. The old fortress was well suited to a temporary military headquarters—the best-fortified position in the city outside the royal compound itself, plenty of space for bedding down men and animals. Splintered remnants marked where wooden walls had once divided the long chamber into three. Where the roof had leaked at one end of the hall, the rotting roof beams sagged ominously. Harrower fighters drifted in and out of the hall, warming themselves at the cookfires scattered across the cracked stone floor. I doubted the drafty ruin ever got warm.

Leaving our escort at the door, Max led me confidently through the busy chamber, past five or six warriors arguing across a broad table propped up at one corner with stones. A troop of perhaps twenty—a mix of poorly turned out swordsmen, ragged townsmen, and several sturdy women—stood attentively as an officer gave them orders to raze a mill outside the city's southern gates. Women and boys served out the steaming contents of copper cauldrons to the milling fighters.

At the far end of the hall, a group of ten or fifteen split and moved aside at our approach. Sila Diaglou stood in the center. Warrior's garb of steel-reinforced leather rested as comfortably on her tall, slender frame as on any man's, while her flaxen hair, cut short since I had seen her preside over Luviar's execution, now curled about her pale, imperious face like the fair locks of painted cherubs. Here in the ruddy light of cook fires and torches, the murderous witch appeared little older than Elene.

A tall, elderly woman in shapeless brown leaned on Sila's right arm. Though the wisps of white hair escaped from her wimple seemed oddly out of place in such a company, the old woman's narrow eyes gleamed as sharp as an Aurellian poniard. Beside her stood a beardless man with a needle-sharp chin, a small, copper-skinned young woman with great brown eyes, and a soft-looking man with oiled black curls and an ear that was split, gnarled, and bulging like a chestnut canker—Sila's accomplices in slaughter.

But it was the youngish man on Sila Diaglou's left who spurred my deepest revulsion. Though he had traded the black gown and cowl of Saint Ophir for gray tunic and black braies and hose, his hairless skull, the solid line of black eyebrows, raised in surprise, and the deep-set eyes and well-drawn mouth, so quick to take on a grin, marked him as Gildas—child stealer, liar, and traitor to all he professed.

"Holy one," said Max to the priestess, touching his fingers to his forehead in respect, "I bring greetings from His

Highness Prince Bayard and a gift to serve as proof of his sincerity and good favor. Have I your leave to tell the tale?"

"Speak, pureblood." Sky-blue eyes stared coldly from beneath Sila Diaglou's intelligent brow. Her face, square cut like a faceted gem, was flawed only by the diagonal seams on her cheeks, carved by her own hand on the day she had publicly abjured Arrosa and the rest of the elder gods. As a girl she had pledged service to the goddess of love, so I'd heard, but only a year out of her novitiate, she had claimed Arrosa's temple corrupted, its priestesses little more than whores for wealthy donors, its rites a mockery rather than a celebration of fertility and renewal. How her indignation had translated to leveling civilization I had yet to comprehend.

Max inclined his head. "Early this morning, I was summoned to my father's house on urgent family business. Unlikely as it seemed, my brother had arrived, ostensibly to seek my young sister's contract for a mapping project desired by his master, Prince Osriel. Further questioning revealed that he had, in fact, approached us without the knowledge or permission of his fearsome lord and sought our aid to escape his burdensome contract on the grounds that his master had threatened his immortal soul. Of course, revoking a contract is impossible without the Registry's consent, which will never be granted in Valen's case. But I, ever mindful of the gifts that fate lays before us, agreed to allow my foolish brother to plead his case before Prince Bayard."

The priestess scrutinized Max as if she were a gem cutter examining the facets laid bare by her work. Her attention did not waver, even as Gildas murmured into her ear.

"Speaking frankly, holy one, this put my lord in a difficult position." Max, the consummate performer, stood with his hands clasped behind his back, well away from weapons, his feet widespread, back straight, and voice casual and confident—postures taught us early to put ordinaries at ease. "Until the day he assumes his rightful crown, Prince Bayard must obey the law of the land, which demands he return a *recondeur* to his contracted master within a day. But my master, also ever mindful of the gifts that fate lays before us, understands that *you* do not recognize the authority of the Registry, and that this brother of mine is the very pureblood whose submission you desire. In short, lady, Magnus Valentia de Cartamandua-Celestine is yours to do with as you please."

Max sounded altogether too pleased with himself for my comfort, though I had devised this story and put it in his mouth. He stood to gain in everyone's favor. We had ensured that he remained entirely within pureblood discipline. The only untruths he told were those he had agreed upon with Bayard for the purposes of his bargain with Osriel.

"And what change does Prince Bayard seek in the terms of our agreement?" asked the priestess.

"My master concedes that you have been most generous in our negotiation, holy one, and asks only your continued assurance that once you and he have subdued the Bastard of Evanore, you will take a knee at my lord's coronation on the first day of the new year, then sit at his right hand as his most valued friend and ally."

An old comrade of mine, a veteran of the Hansker wars, had once pointed out that only the most assured of commanders would approach a subordinate or prisoner of greater height while in the presence of other subordinates. I had observed the rule proven time and again, and this occasion was no different. Despite my topping her by a dozen quattae, Sila gave her elderly companion's arm to the doe-eyed woman and came forward to take a closer look. She appeared supremely confident, as only those who hold the leash of heaven can.

She touched the ivory-and-gold wolf brooch on my breast, then lifted the front laps of my cloak and tossed them over my shoulders. Folding her arms, she walked around me, her face unexpressive as she examined the fine embroidery and ivory buttons on my doublet, my gold-link belt, and the pearl trilliots sewn on my green satin sleeves. She even crouched down to examine my shackles and ran her fingers over my fine leather boots.

At such close proximity, I expected to see lines and weathering in her cheeks, signs of her age that I knew to be past forty. Yet save for the dual scars, her skin shone as flawless as that of a healthy child. Cold, though. Great gods, the air around her felt colder than the winter sky, so cold I could neither smell nor taste her scent. I could sense nothing of her at all. Perhaps I'd worn clothes for too long.

She straightened up again. "No weapons save these," she said, touching my silkbound hands. "I had understood his poor skills warranted no such restriction."

I had persuaded Max to allow me to keep my gloves on beneath the cord bindings, as the weather was so bitter. Though my sweating palms had dampened both gloves and silk, my gards remained hidden. The longer I could conceal them, the better. I had few enough surprises to spring on Gildas.

"The binding is merely a formality, holy one," said Max. "My brother is adept at lock breaking and crude illusions, but little else of sorcery. But what gentleman would lay an unsheathed knife in an ally's hand, though the blade be dull as lead? The shackles . . . alas, I must warn you that it is only with great . . . firmness . . . that my lord and I have persuaded him of his limited choices. He will likely walk gingerly for a few days. He has a nasty habit of bolting his responsibilities."

"Indeed, he shall serve for much more than lock breaking." The priestess's blue gaze met mine . . . turning my bones to ice. With a firm finger, she traced the line of my mask down my brow and nose, coming to rest on my lips, her touch so charged with heat and light, it sent waves of urgency straight to my groin.

"I accept the gift," she said, breaking away briskly. "Tell your prince that I find it most pleasing. If all falls out on the solstice as he has promised, he need have no fear of my defection." Which sounded no firm assurance to *me*, though, in truth, my head had emptied of all save an ill-defined dread that fell far outside the bounds of my expectations.

"Then I shall take my leave of you, holy one. May your life and health prosper." Max signaled one of his men to hand over my case and left the key to my shackles with one of Sila's guards. Then he stood at my shoulder, straightened his back, and touched fingers to brow. As he spun around to go, his cloak flared. Under its cover, where Sila Diaglou could not see it, his hand squeezed my arm.

Still dazed, I met his gaze and caught a quick wink. Then he was gone. I had not wits enough to decide if his gesture was reassurance or apology or merely Max's usual self-indulgent humor, combining the concern of a proper brother with a taunt. All I wanted to do was run.

"Falderrene, Jakome, take him to the chamber we have prepared for this day." As she issued this unsettling command, the Harrower priestess had already turned her back to me.

She spread her arms as if to embrace the rest of the company. "My beloved companions, have I not assured you that our dedication and righteous service will force the world into its proper order? Destiny has laid a treasure in our hands—one I have long sought. The future proceeds as I have spoken!"

Addressing such a multitude did not coarsen the priestess's voice. Though speaking in such a cavernous space, her tone maintained a certain intimacy, as if she spoke to each of us alone. Every conversation ceased. Every face turned toward the woman, as if she were the divine prophet Karus, come back to life clothed in the sun.

"The last walls shall crumble!" Triumph ... exultation ... joy ... her song without music rang from the rotting rafters. "The mighty shall be brought low, no being that breathes the air of this world set above another. No cache or hoard shall remain unopened; no treasure be locked away whether in vault, veins, or marrow. Burn, harrow, and level this blighted land! Let all who stand in our way feel our knives, our spears, our claws that in the future we shape, all may be one in awe and service before the mighty Gehoum!"

Cheers shook Torvo's foundation. Ferocious. Wild. Terrifying. As if there were seven hundred partisans in the hall and not seventy. The only one who did not cheer was the old woman in brown.

As the cheering throng swarmed Sila Diaglou, Falderrene, the murderous minor noble with the malformed ear, and a bony pale-haired young man she had named Jakome led me briskly toward the corner where the rectangular hall butted into one of Torvo's massive towers. A third man followed with my case. To my surprise, once we passed through a low arch into the tower, they shoved me onto the *upward* stair.

My escorts did not speak, save for whispered watchwords for the guard at each landing. Shaken by the intimate intensity of Sila's touch, appalled at the power of her conviction, and alarmed at the mysterious connection of such ferocity with me, I felt what small confidence I had brought with me seep away. As well I did not know what to think, for getting my shackled feet up the tight, narrow stair without hands to grip or balance proved a challenge. I listened for any hint of my friends or the prince along the way, but the fortress walls were so thick that a hundred muted conversations sounded no different from scuttling rats.

Our destination lay at the very summit of the stair, where the tower roof of layered wood, earth, and lead pressed so low I could not stand straight, where the steps were so impossibly shallow, only the toe of my boots could fit, where the only light was an arrow loop. No matter Saverian's potion, I pressed my bound hands to my mouth to keep from heaving as I waited for my escorts to unfasten the latches of a solid iron door. Surely I would die in such a prison.

The door swung open with a metallic screech. Blessed cold air bathed my feverish face, and the last rays of sunset, arrowing beneath a thick pall of clouds, near blinded me. All gods be praised, the chamber was open to the sky.

"In with you." Falderrene motioned me forward.

I ducked my head lower and stepped in, astonished to discover I could stand straight without touching the ragged timbers of the ceiling as it swooped upward to its conical peak. Not one, but five tall windows opened onto the settling night. Though defensive iron grillwork yet guarded the window openings, only rusted hinges remained of their wooden shutters. A laugh bubbled up inside me, withheld only by my silk mask. Did they think to torment me with exposure to the elements?

Falderrene unhooked a jangling ring from his belt and dangled it in the air. "Shall we toss a coin for who plays nursemaid tonight, friend?"

The pale-haired Jakome snatched the keys and twisted

his whey-colored face into a bitter snarl. "I've a personal interest tonight. The holy one forbids me interfere, but I'd stay close. He is an animal."

Falderrene grinned unpleasantly and swept an oily lock behind his malformed ear. "As you wish. Might as well remove his shackles. Not even his gatzé master can retrieve him here. He'll not escape lest he can fly. I'll wait on the stair lest he give you any trouble."

As the pale-haired Jakome bent to unlock my ankles, a survey of the chamber's furnishings revealed comforts not usual for a common prisoner. A small cabinet held a painted washing bowl, night jar, and neatly stacked towels. The bed, piled with thick quilts, was a rarity—built long enough to accommodate a person of my size. And though the crumbling hole in the center of the stone floor had not held a watchfire for many years, a lamp with a glass wind shield sat on a small round table beside a bowl of apples.

The chains clanked and rattled as my bony jailer stood up again. I shook out my legs, relishing the lightness.

"A meal will be brought shortly," said Jakome. "The same as we all eat. Though the chamber's open to the weather, you've been left blankets enough. This is no pureblood palace, but Sila Diaglou has no wish to starve or freeze you."

His wish, though . . . His face told me that his wish was different and had a great deal to do with sharp knives and stakes through the gut. Would that I could shove the man and all his fellows down the stairs and burn this maniac-infested den until the lead roofs fell in on them all.

The ragged guardsman had carried in my case and set it beside a plain wood chest. Jakome yanked open the case and threw my silks, velvets, damasks, and linens onto the stone floor, searching them briskly. Looking me straight in the eye, he hawked and spat on my spare mask, wadded it up, and threw it atop the pile of clothes. "We'll see you get proper clothes. When all are brought low, such pureblood fripperies will have no use."

No use mentioning that I'd done my best to forgo pureblood frippery for most of my life.

He turned the emptied case upside down and shook it. Naught fell out. "That's it, then," he said as he stood up again. Tossing the case onto the pile, he waved the guardsman toward the stair. "Get on. Tell Falderrene I'll set the locks and meet him below."

Once we were alone, Jakome's colorless lips curled into a toothy grin. He pulled out his knife and twirled it in his fingers. "I've heard you have need of a knife. Heard it from my *brethren.*"

"Saints and angels!" Surprise and relief turned my spine to jelly. "Do you ever need a recommendation for an acting troupe, say the word! Can you get me out of these?" I held out my bound hands.

"Aye, I can and will. But you must kneel first, pureblood." His bony chin indicated the floor.

"Why so?" I was already spying out places to hide the weapon.

"Because I'm still thinking whether or not to give you what was promised. Matters have changed." Venom laced his tongue. "Do your knees bend? I've ne'er seen a pureblood kneel."

I knelt, my spirits plummeting. I knew this kind of man. Give him the deference he wanted and he might relent. He couldn't have much time until he was missed. "Come," I said, wheedling, "you were trusted . . . well paid . . ."

"Shhh." He pressed the knifepoint to my lips, unmasked rage and bloodthirst reddening his white skin. I held my tongue and gave up hope of the knife. Keeping blood and breath would be enough. "The thing is, I was paid to give you a knife if I could manage it without being caught. But if I've decided I can't manage it, who's going to hear your complaint?"

He spun the weapon in the air and snatched the hilt, then waved the weapon slowly side to side as one might try to mesmerize a dog. "You're being given what you don't deserve, as pureblood pups are always given what they don't deserve. It would please me to carve your throat out."

I maintained discipline, keeping my shoulders relaxed, my mouth shut, and my gaze somewhere neutral, even when tiny flames rippled along the edges of his blade. The fellow must have a trace of sorcerer's blood, at the least.

After a few uncomfortable moments, he exhaled in disgust and let the flames die, then began to cut away the silken cords that bound my hands. "Fortunately, you've worse to come than I could do to you."

"Ouch! Careful!" I snatched my hands away and shook off the remnants of the bindings. His last cut had slashed through cords and glove alike, leaving an ugly red smear on his dagger and a fiery laceration at the base of my thumb. "Are you wholly an idiot as well as a scoundrel?"

"Not I, pureblood. Not I." Sneering, Jakome left the chamber, slammed the iron door shut behind him, and shot the noisy bolt.

Breathing raggedly, I sagged back onto my heels, bent my head to my knees, and tried to slow my hammering heart. When my refocused senses told me that no one remained outside the door or on the stair, I pulled off mask, cloak, and gloves and got to work. Without a weapon I would have to find another way out of this prison. And if Jakome was going to report Max's bribe to Sila Diaglou, I'd best get out of here fast.

First, test the door. I structured a voiding spell. Releasing magic into the spell, I traced an arc at the bottom of the iron door. The iron remained cold and inert. Neither did the locks respond to my best probing with so much as a spark. Disappointing, but no surprise. I had assumed Sila would have my prison warded to preclude all common spellwork. Jakome had worked his little fire magic with the door open.

I retrieved my leather case and ripped out the false bottom Saverian had cleverly disguised so that I needed no magic to open it. I pulled out her three vials of medicines—blue for me, amber for the prince, clear for the tincture of yellow broom—a useful common remedy that could ream a man's guts. I had intended to carry these in my pocket once I had been searched, but after Jakome's words about new clothes, decided I'd best find a place in my cell to stash them. With the open windows, perhaps I wouldn't need my own remedy.

The clothes chest had no pockets or drawers, but a wooden tray, half its length, had been crafted to sit in the top of it to hold buckles or belts or other oddments. Several objects sat in the tray already: a dice box, a canvas bag of knucklebones, a long narrow board pocked with egg-shaped hollows for playing armaments, and a set of ivory and jet pebblelike game pieces. I emptied the canvas bag, dropped the vials into it, then replaced the bones. I had always been luckier at knucklebones than dice.

Games. From the look of it, they intended to keep me here a while. Which made no sense at all. If Sila and Gildas didn't want my bent to lead them into Aeginea . . . or anywhere else . . . then what, in Iero's heaven, did they want with me?

Now to test the greater magic. Common wards laid to prevent spellworking could not disrupt the bent—the inborn talents of a pureblood. Most talents prescribed by a pureblood bent had naught to offer in the way of escape routes or weaponry and posed little risk to a jailer.

I loosened my belt and fumbled beneath layers of pourpoint, shirt, and tunic to find the upper hem of my chausses. Two scraps of stained fabric lay hidden next to my skin— one, the bloodstained canvas from Stearc's jupon, the other a square of linen Saverian had dipped in the vial of Osriel's blood.

Best not think too much of what I had to do. I laid the scraps on the floor, pressed my hands atop them, and closing my eyes, poured out magic enough to search Fortress Torvo. Indeed, naught prevented me . . . though I came to wish it had.

I cursed. Swore. Eventually I crawled away, buried my face in the bedclothes, and screamed out a monumental rage. Had any other edifice this side of hell seen so much of torment? The Harrowers' self-righteous slaughter was only the most recent depredation. For decades this ruin had been a secret prison, used by nobles who took pleasure in meting out punishments in cruel excess of those mandated by Eodward's ideals of justice. Men, women, children, noble or common . . . none were exempt. Before that, the fortress was used similarly by the Aurellians, a race whose delight in torture reached levels of depravity that counterbalanced every glory of their arts and every marvel of their building. And in ancient Ardra, before the rise of the enlightened Caedmon, Ardran nobles had lived in constant war with one another, as well as with the Moriangi Gravs to the north—and they had locked their rivals and their families here to starve. Every wail and scream and bloodletting had left its mark upon this stone. Despair had become its mortar.

But my uncomfortable exercise had repaid me. Osriel and Stearc were held straight down below me, six levels, at the least. Both men lived—that the magic had worked told me that much—but I could discern naught of their condition. I fixed their guide threads in my mind, the route of steps and passages through layer upon layer of blood-woven history, a trail that would lead me to them as soon as I could manage it. Some of the blood and pain I felt was surely theirs.

But what of Jullian? I had no blood to trace him. Of all the prisoners who had trod these vile halls, far too many had been boys. Three days ... most of this one gone already.

The sun had gone, leaving the night beyond the windows black as pitch. The wind whistled through the window grates, as I yanked and twisted each one. Many of the bars were loose in the weathered stone facings; some were rusted through, some missing altogether. A little brutish work would allow me to crawl out. But one glance down into the blackness showed the pinpricks of light that would be torches at the gates. As far as I had learned, Danae did not fly, and surely even Kol could not survive so great a leap. Damn the cowardly Jakome to the nethermost regions of hell!

Of a sudden I heard murmurings outside my door, and the bolts and latches scraped. By the time the door swung open, I was seated in one of my two chairs, feet propped on the table, and my gloves covering the blue telltales on my hands. I snatched up an apple and started munching. The taste of the fruit and the scents of porridge and wine waked an appetite I'd thought ruined by my searching.

"Good evening, Magnus Valentia." A small woman hurried past me and set a loaded tray on my table, as an invisible companion closed and locked the door behind her. "A simple meal, but nourishing. And hot, if we partake right away."

The soft-voiced visitor, barefoot and clothed in a plain white shift, was Sila Diaglou's young devotee, the copper-skinned young woman with the earth-brown eyes. Thick hair the color of walnuts hung over her shoulder in a single plait, as if she were on her way to bed. Any man would find her alluring did she not have a habit of smearing her victims' blood on her full lips.

"I do not sit down with murderers."

She wrinkled her brow as if pondering the course of the universe. "But you've broken bread with other warriors, have you not—your comrades-in-arms in Prince Perryn's service? War is dreadful, but when the world's need demands it, all must serve. Some by killing. Some by dying."

"My comrades took no pleasure in their deeds. They did not slaughter innocents or lick their blood." Yet Boreas had notched his spear whenever he skewered a beardless Moriangi, saying he'd "keep the river dogs from growing up another warrior from a whelp." And Boreas was not near the worst of those I'd called comrade.

"Some kinds of killing cannot be justified by war," I said. "Unclean killing. Children."

"If the war itself be noble, then I can't see how one death be different from another. Please, let us not argue this evening. You should eat." She had set out two deep bowls of porridge, a small plate of butter and bread, two spoons, and a steaming pitcher, and now poured wine into two waiting cups, sloshing a bit onto the table. The stout fragrance of wine and cloves filled the room, swirled by the chill breeze, setting up a raging thirst in me. Of a sudden I was sweating.

The girl perched on the second chair, tucked her bare feet under her robe, and dipped her spoon. "Will you not tell me more of yourself, Magnus?" she said between bites. "Then I'll do the same. My mistress would not have us enemies." Her great eyes gleamed in the lamplight, no hint of guile. Indeed they were empty of anything save eager curiosity and a certain sincere . . . appreciation.

I looked away. I did need to eat. Even more, I longed for the wine. It was a mercy that only this girl had been sent here. I was much too tired to spar with Gildas or Sila herself. Yet I would need to have a care. This girl was little more than a child herself—sixteen, seventeen—but a child who collaborated in murder. I dared not forget that.

I swirled the wine in the wooden cup, inhaling. Bless all gods, no lurking scent of nivat or anything else untoward wafted from it. Cloves certainly . . . a touch of cinnamon. Sweet Erdru, the aroma itself could get me drunk. All the better to sleep and forget what my bent had shown me.

I touched my tongue to one drop left hanging on the rim. Warmth spread from toes to eyebrows in less time than a flicker's peck. No nivat. No lurking trace of herbs or potions. But the wine itself was disappointing, heavy on the tongue and tasting as if it had been kept in a cask of iron instead of oak. No use risking a muddled head for spoilt wine.

Unable to stomach sitting with the girl, I left the wine cup on the table and perched on a window ledge with bowl and spoon. Perhaps I could induce her to tell me where Jullian was kept or discover a way to get out of this room. The cursed Jakome's treachery had been a sore blow.

"You speak first," I said. "You likely know a few things about me already. What is your name?"

"Malena."

An Aurellian word. *"Goddess's treasure."*

A pleasured flush deepened her already richly colored skin. "That's right. I was a third daughter of a third daughter, so my parents gave me to the temple in Avenus when I turned five. They'd no coin for the fee, so I was put to work in the temple baths—scrubbing tiles, fetching water or towels or candles, waiting in corners till I was needed." She popped a bite of buttered bread in her mouth.

"Arrosa's temple, then." Only the goddess of love required baths in her temple.

"Mmm." She nodded and swallowed her bread. "I was lucky to serve and not take vows, though I didn't know it then. I didn't understand what I saw—the wickedness what took place in the baths."

She licked the butter off her small, delicate fingers.

"Copulation ... mating ... is no corruption," I said. "Arrosa blesses earthly love, makes it divine, if pleasure is shared freely." The qualifier was not widely preached, of course, but its truth had become apparent to me early on, and no woman I'd had since had ever disagreed.

"Well, of course we're meant to join and make more of us, and if we can take comfort in it, all the better." A sprightly smile illuminated her round cheeks and pointed chin, then faded as she knit her brow. "But in the temple, pleasure was *not* offered freely. Novices younger than me were used by whatever great lords and warriors took a fancy. I heard them screaming from the bath, saw them thrashing in the water when the lords forced them down on their . . . laps. And I had to bring towels to wipe the girls' blood, and oils to anoint their skin, so they could be sent into the bedchambers to *glorify Arrosa* through the night."

I well knew such crimes happened. I had warned Jullian of them, sworn to protect him. I wished she would speak of something else. All manner of unseemly urges seemed waked in me this night.

"One night when I was ten, a lord tired of the priestess who serviced him in the bath. He bellowed that he preferred a younger body. He saw me hiding in the corner and demanded me. And he got me. For a sevenday. Even though I could offer him no temple blessing. Even though I could not read to him from the temple writs or recite the lays of love."

Her simple statement of evil gave weight to her story that indignant diatribes could not. I believed her.

"Afterward, I ran away. If I had taken vows, like Sila, they would have come after me, and I would have had to cut myself as she did to undo the swearing. But I was just a bath girl . . ."

". . . Yet your parents refused to take you back—their gift to the goddess." No need to ask what had happened to her after. I had been fifteen when I ran away, and the ways to feed oneself so young were very few. "I'm sorry for what happened to you, but it does not . . . cannot . . . justify—"

"But I am *not* sorry! Don't you see?" She twiddled with the lamp, retracting the wick so its fire dimmed, confining the pool of light to the table and her red-gold complexion. "Had I stayed a bath girl at the temple I'd not have met Sila. I'd not have learned of the Gehoum, and how we must make ourselves humble before them. I'd not understand the need for cleansing and repentance or to tear down the false structures of learning and privilege that make one man's will more powerful than the purity of a girl."

I had learned long before that when a certain note crept into an otherwise reasonable argument, it paid a man naught to continue. The fanatic's gleam shone in Malena's soft brown eyes, and she was never going to agree that her slaughtering children in the name of her uncaring Gehoum was no holier than a lord's raping children in the name of his own pleasure.

"I've eaten all I can bear," I said, setting down the tasteless porridge. I wanted this woman out of here. Long-buried memories of drunken soldiers and their rough, fumbling hands, of filthy alleyways and painful humiliations, had gotten tangled with images of bath girls and swimming brown eyes and soft copper-hued limbs. "Tell your mistress and her monk that sad stories and beds with quilts will not make me their willing captive. Let them come and tell me what they want of me."

I saw no use in pretending cooperation. Gildas knew me too well. I just needed to keep their eyes on me and away from the captives down below. But what if I found a way to get Osriel out of here, yet had not secured Jullian? I shoved the thought away as soon as it appeared. I had two more days.

Malena set down her spoon, picked up my wine cup, and joined me at the window. Her round cheeks bloomed with health. "Dear Magnus," she said, pressing the cup into my hand. "The holy one has sent *me* to tell you what she wants of you."

Her lips parted slightly. Soft. Waiting. I drained the cup in one gulp, and her smile blossomed in fragrant sweetness like moonflowers. A gust of wind whistled through the iron grate, and she shivered.

"And what is that?" I said, relishing the potent richness of the wine. Malena was so small . . . so fragile in the thin white shift that fluttered in the wind, giving shape to the ripened form beneath. I wrapped my arms about the trembling girl to shield her from the cold.

She wrapped her arms about my neck and pulled my head down so she could whisper in my ear. "I am your chosen mate."

Chapter 22

"Chosen mate?" Increasingly thickheaded, as if I'd drunk a vat of wine, I could not seem to grasp her meaning.

"Mmm. The world shall be renewed." Her fingers stroked my neck and teased at my ears.

My body swam with lust. My mind swam with the wine and unfocused danger, and I knew I should stop what I was doing. I just could not remember why. Even as I voiced the question that might elaborate the risk, my gloved fingers found the ties that held her flimsy shift closed, and I pulled.

Goddess Mother . . . Her breast tasted of ginger and honey.

"I am the holy one's gift to you ... prepared ... purified ... ah ..." The soft catch in her throat as I pushed the gossamer fabric downward and shifted my mouth from one sweet curve to another drove me out of my senses. I drew her to the bed and lay beside her. As she unfastened my buttons and laces, I imagined vaguely that I should stay her hand. But instead I loosed her hair, inhaled her rising scent, and traced the line of neck and jaw and mouth with kisses, inhaling her sweetness as a starving man devours the first spoonful of sustenance.

"Why would the goddess send a gift to me now?" I whispered, my words buried in Malena's smooth belly, as somewhere above my head her trembling hands unbuttoned my gloves. "I've failed to honor blessed Arrosa for far too long, though I am ever her servant in mind."

The girl's laugh echoed the song of larks, until she freed my hands and gasped again. I took full advantage. My fingers explored silken breasts, smooth flanks, and swollen lips, while my mouth continued its downward trek. "Careful, lady," I mumbled, as her quest to strip away my layered garb grew insistent enough to tear skin along with fabric. But I was as eager as she. More.

"Ah, Magnus, they told me you might— But I never—" Her voice quivered . . . caught in a sob . . . as her fingers traced a path on my naked back. "They are so beautiful. *You* are so beautiful . . ."

Of a sudden my back bloomed in exquisite fire. Her fingernails had transformed to steel blades that slashed a path of agony across my skin. The pain drove me into frenzy.

I buried myself in her. Heedless . . . mindless . . . I strove and thrust and drowned in sensation that sent coils and spirals of lightning to every quat of my skin. Were the dissolution of the world appointed for the culmination of my act, I could not have stopped. And the explosion, when it came, had naught to do with sweetness or shared pleasure. Only need.

Laughter eddied about my head, swirling, dipping . . . changing pitch from low to high and back again. Sluggish, sated, incapable of movement, I sat with my fire-scoured back against the curved wall of my tower prison, my head on my knees. Wine lay sour on my tongue, though I could remember only one cup.

"Well done, child." The higher-pitched voice. Sila Diaglou. She had said this three times. I couldn't understand it. Why weren't they angry?

The two of them—priestess and monk—had burst through the door and pulled me off the girl. Was it Malena's strangled cries and strident weeping had brought them or was it my bellow of completion? They were gentle enough, supporting me stumbling toward a window and lowering me to the floor. But since then, my head had grown so heavy I could not lift it. Nor could I persuade my tongue to speak such apology as I wished. *Sorry . . . sorry . . . sorry. Never do I take without giving . . . or so I intend . . . never, never would I take pleasure in forcing . . . in injury . . .*

The tide of shame drenched me yet again, swirling my meager thoughts into confusion. The girl had screamed and wept and begged. How could she not be injured? Why did they laugh? Gildas's robust chortle was unmistakable. Even Malena's moans and whimpers had yielded to girlish giggles.

A bitterly cold wind raked my naked skin. Sapphire light danced beneath the flutter of my eyelashes. My gards entirely visible ... I tried to draw in my limbs ... hating to be so exposed ... hating for them to see. But I could scarcely twitch my fingers.

I had felt washed clean in Aeginea—the gards a sign of renewed purpose, a hint of a joy that I had not believed existed in this life. No more of that! I had proved myself an animal, a damnable, brutish thug who had so pompously called judgment on men who corrupted children. What had come over me?

Someone new arrived, cursing under his breath, his malevolence hammering at me.

"Get her up," the priestess commanded. "Carefully, Jakome! Do not drop her on the stair. Stay abed and still until I come to you, child."

Feet shuffled and scrambled. "*Kasiya Gehoum*, mistress. *Sanguiera, orongia, vazte, kevrana.*" Bleed, suffer, die, purify. Malena's cheerful invocation of blood and suffering only worsened my confusion. *Your chosen mate* ... not chosen by Arrosa, but by Sila Diaglou. They had used the girl—a willing girl. And used my cursed weakness for pleasuring, for wine ...

"Did I not tell you that his appetites would be his leash?" said the monk, as if in echo of my self-condemnation. The syllables grated on my ear like steel on glass. "A little wine, a fair young body ... and so much easier than reasoning with him or putting him to the question. He will be everything you wish. Pliable. Controllable. One taste of decadent pain and pleasure, and he is yours."

How did the priestess bear his patronizing manner? How had I ever mistaken it for brotherly mentoring and friendship?

A finger began tracing the patterns on my back. The priestess's, I knew, from the heat. At least her touch did not sap my wits this time, as I had so little remaining. Her exploration, though not purposefully brutal, did not avoid the lacerations that dribbled warm blood down my flanks. That I flinched each time she encountered one did not deter her. The blade had been no lust-fueled imagining. They must have hidden it beneath the palliasse.

"What does it mean that he displays Danae markings, Gildas? You said he did not know what he was."

"It would appear he's found out. We can ask him, as soon as he recovers enough to speak, but I would not count any report he gives as reliable. Not yet. He has no fond feelings for either of us, and you've heard his history of lies."

Recovers . . . Like a sleeping lion, mortal dread raised its head and set me screaming inside. *Wake up, fool. Wake up.* But I had smelled the wine, sampled a drop before drinking. And porridge could not mask poison.

"We must ask the old one what the marks signify and what powers they give him."

Unnamed panic threatened logic. How was it possible they knew of my mixed birth? And what *old one* could they ask? Not Stearc or Osriel. The image of Picus flew through my head, but he had no intercourse with Navronne. Why could I not lift my head and ask them?

This leaden indolence, this sodden paralysis that left me near incapable of reason . . . I had not felt the like since the morning Luviar died, the last time Gildas and I had spoken, when I yet believed him my friend . . .

And then as words and events settled like a silken shroud, giving shape to those things beneath, the simple truth came clear. Fear robbed me of breath. *Pain and pleasure* . . . Gildas knew all my vices.

Of course, I'd not smelled nivat in the wine. The heat of enchantment burned away the scent of blood-spelled nivat. They had laced the wine with doulon paste. Never had that possibility crossed my mind. Gildas was no sorcerer; he would need my blood. And now, too late, I remembered Jakome's knife and his smirk as he had slashed my hand. I had been lost the moment the first droplet of tainted wine had touched my tongue. Saverian had warned me. *A fool should know what his stupidity has cost him.*

Sila Diaglou knelt on the floor beside me. Her breath

smelled of anise, and her hand stroked my hair and the back of my neck as if I were a favored hound. I would have given an arm not to shiver at her touch. I would have given both legs to believe they had not infected me with my old sin.

The woman gently blotted the blood dribbling down my back, and in a flutter of panic, I wondered if she licked it from her fingers. "They truly find pleasure in the wounding . . . during the carnal act? I'd never heard that. It seems depraved."

"Dear Sila, in these few matters . . . especially in regard to the male response . . . how could you know . . . how could even the old one know? The journals of Picus recount the Danae male's need for pain during copulation."

For one brief instant, the world grew quiet, as if I had closed off my senses to heed a stone's cry. Gildas lied. Saverian had told me the journals did not speak of nivat. And in this lie did I sound a gulf between the monk and the priestess. *Great Iero, mighty Kemen, give me strength and wit to fill that gap with liquid fire and shatter their unholy collaboration!*

"Your plan is sound, mistress. The pureblood stranglehold will be broken. The long-lived will infuse your people with strength and endurance beyond human understanding. Navronne will be brought to its knees, groveling before the Gehoum for generation upon generation." His passion sounded convincing . . . except to one who had heard this same passion for the lighthouse and its learning, for friendship and holy brotherhood.

"I must see to Malena," said the priestess, rising from my side. "That we could have a catch at first mating is presumptuous, but failure shall not be accounted to any lack of diligence on my part."

Infuse your people . . . a catch? They wanted me to breed a child on the girl . . . Harrowers and Danae and Aurellian sorcery. My spinning head came near flying off.

Gildas chuckled. "I yield to the students of Arrosa's temple. We were not taught of such women's matters at Gillarine. I'll put this one to bed. I doubt my old friend will be lucid before morning. To get him drunk loosed his true nature."

"Bring him to me as soon as he wakes tomorrow. As yet we've had no response from Prince Osriel on our offer to trade these useless prisoners for the monk. The Bastard is the last obstacle on our road. If Magnus can unlock his plots and mysteries, our war is won."

"As you command, priestess. A peaceful night to you."

"And you, Gildas. Well done."

Osriel the Bastard ... the King of Navronne. The lord's secretary who lay ill in their dungeon. They didn't know! This reminder of my purpose gave me an anchor. They must not find out.

The door opened and closed. Someone set the lock. The wind howled and swirled, rattling the loose bars. In the lulls, I heard Gildas's breathing as he waited, and I smelled the taint of nivat on him. Had I thought it would do any good, I would have stuck a finger down my throat to purge the poison I had downed so blithely. Naught could purge the evil if I had planted a part-Danae child in Sila Diaglou's hands this night.

"So, friend Valen, do you appreciate your lovely open chamber? What captive in all Navronne has a cell so suited to his nature? You can thank me for that. I'll confess I did not at all expect to see you marked, but then, Stearc and his tidy Gram were always parsimonious with details from old Picus's journals. Did the Bastard whip these sigils out of you, or is it something like a boy's night spew that comes upon one like you at the proper time and season? And you ran away from Osriel—no surprise that—but to your family? That is perhaps the most difficult of all these manifold mysteries to comprehend." Gildas's questions were like a sea creature's tentacles, touching me lightly on every side, exploring, distracting, any one of them capable of stinging me to death.

"So am I to be kept here like a stallion until I breed true?" I said, summoning control enough to lift my head. Gildas sat across the chamber, his feet propped on the clothes chest. The faint azure glow from my gards, our only illumination, kept him a dark outline.

"I suspected you were more wakeful than you showed," he said, white teeth gleaming. "It saves me a deal of explaining. And the answer is yes, at least until the balance

of power shifts on the winter solstice. The lady thinks to
create a new world, where the boundaries between purebloods, ordinaries, Ardran, Moriangi, and even your dancing kinsmen are erased. You are to be—excuse the crude
expression—the seed and root of that new world. Half
pureblood sorcerer, half Danae. My reports of you had
already intrigued her, but when I informed her of your
unique bloodlines she came near rapture. We have no evidence of another Danae–pureblood mating in the history
of the world."

My mind stuttered over the simple immensity of what
he described. Somehow I had always dismissed Harrower
rants as ploys to attract the gullible. I'd never imagined the
priestess *believed* what she preached. "She would destroy
pureblood sorcery?"

"Certainly the end of pureblood breeding laws will di-
lute the Aurellian bent. But it will take on a new life and
character by the infusion of Danae blood—so Sila imagines.
From the long night of the great Harrowing shall rise a new
race of men and women—robust in health, what remains of
the world's magic held captive in their veins, with no need
for books or gods or kings or anything else that might el-
evate one above another. A seductive vision, is it not? She
sees you, the Danae-bred Cartamandua *recondeur,* as the
exemplar of her new world."

Seductive . . . deeply, intelligently seductive. Magnificent.
Surely it was my addled state that came up with no answer
to it. How could I argue against breaking down barriers
of birth, a man who had rebelled against the strictures of
breeding my entire life, son of two people who had done
the same?

"How did you guess what I was? How could you possibly
have known?" I had more pressing questions, but I needed
time to think. Gildas lived by his cleverness. If he kept secrets from Sila Diaglou, then he likely had no confidant
among her company and might enjoy a bit of boasting.

"I put it all together when you refused to walk into the
Well grotto. The place profoundly affected you—as if you
could feel the myrtle and hyssop that bound its guardian—
and yet you had taken on the search eagerly and actually
found the Well when no one else could do it. You could not

have used the maps, for I had long discovered your inability to read. But the possibility that you were a Cartamandua simply did not occur to me. You are so unlike the rest of them."

"I'll thank you for that, at least." I pressed the heels of my hands into my eye sockets, trying to squeeze out the muzziness. Beyond Sila Diaglou's seductive vision lay her murderous war to implement it. I needed some way to free my friends.

Gildas continued eagerly, as I had known he would. "You'd had me curious from the night I submitted to Sila's whip—proofs of devotion are a dreadful bother. You located me despite a barricade of magic, and our companions told odd tales of ghostly apparitions that night. As I asked myself why visiting the Well would affect you so strangely, I recalled your collapse on that very first day I took you into the cloister garth—the residue of the Scourge clearly affects you, whether the rite succeeds or no. And, of course, I had witnessed your uncontrollable aversion to captivity. I could find only one explanation to encompass all these things. Days later, when Gram told me of your emotional response to seeing a Dané, I was sure of you. Truly you had me coming and going when you were exposed as a pureblood."

I blurted one cheerless guffaw. "And then I begged you to bring me nivat. You must have been beside yourself." I had handed him the very leash that would bring me to heel.

His white teeth gleamed in the dark. "The tainted water was the final test. By that time I could see that your Danae characteristics were tempered by your human heritage, so I trusted you wouldn't die from a few drops of blood in the water."

Damnable savage to so callously dismiss a boy's torment! "Do you long for hell, child murderer? For I swear by every god and demon, you will meet the Tormentor himself before another season passes."

"You will do nothing to me." He jumped up from his chair, his playful drawl abandoned. "Claudio de Cartamandua did me a great service when he made your childhood a misery. He left you weak. A penchant for unsavory pleasure rules your flesh, and this maudlin sentiment with regard to children rules your wit."

My loathing for Gildas eclipsed every hatred of my life. "If you've touched him, Gildas—"

"I've kept young Jullian safe. Intact. Healthy. He begins to understand that men of exceptional mind must lead the world out of its morass. If I choose to complete his education, he will serve as a fine acolyte in the new order. Indeed, friend Valen, I hold *everything* you want and need."

A soft clicking sound came from his direction, almost like a shower of raindrops... or nutshells shaken in a bag... or seeds... The earth-ripe scent that accompanied the sound constricted my lungs and clenched my gut. With every breath the craving spread its spiked tentacles through flesh and bone. The same paralyzed incapacity that prevented me from shoving Gerard's murderer through the iron bars into eternal night was all that held me back from snatching away his hoard. His soft chuckle said he knew that.

My hands trembled like a palsied beggar's. I needed to drag my mind away from nivat and the hellish cost of deeper enslavement. Saverian... great heaven grant that she would help me again. For now, I had to live with it and find a way to damn Gildas to eternal fire.

Somehow thoughts of my astringent angel affected me as might an icy plunge, for it occurred to me that Gildas's lie about a Danae predilection for pain meant that he had not told Sila Diaglou of my problem with the doulon. Harrowers despised twist-minds, and burnt or bled them. They did not use us to breed favorites. Which meant that Gildas intended to hide his deepest hold on me. Which meant that he had plans beyond those of Sila Diaglou, and it would best serve my interests if I learned of them. So let the arrogant gatzé believe he owned me.

"Indeed, it seems I am your thrall." It took no effort to mime a doulon slave with an aching head and resentful soul. "How much did you give me that morning you betrayed Luviar? I lost the rest of my supply on that day's adventure, and you've no concept of wrath until you try telling Osriel of Evanore that you're no good to him unless he feeds you nivat every five days."

"Every *five* days?" Gildas chortled. "I'll confess I gave

you most of what you had in hopes you would lose track of the day's events. And I knew it would accelerate your cravings, a matter I thought might be useful. But I'd no idea it would compromise you so sorely. I am *sorry* for that. Truly I bear you no ill will. Tell me, what use did Osriel have for you?"

This casual inquiry bore all the power of his considerable intellect and will. The answer would take some care.

"What do you think? The Bastard wanted entry to Aeginea." Summoning every reserve of will, I reached a hand behind me to the window facing, hauled myself to my feet, and rested my ponderous head on the iron grate. "I refused to take him, and he did exactly what you will do. I held out for three days from the onset of my hunger. Remind me not to do that again, Brother."

"So you took Osriel the Bastard to Aeginea." Gildas hated that thought. "What did he learn? Who did he see? What was it like?"

"I've no idea. He waited until I was near my time again. I led him past the Sentinel Oak and promptly lost my mind. But somewhere along the way, he sold me to a clutch of the blue-marked gatzi. One of them did this"—I swept my hand across my pulsing sigils—"which makes the entire world into a madhouse. Then someone tied me to a tree and said he was going to break my knees. Gods . . . I went crazy. Broke the bindings and ran. I hope they killed the Bastard. I hope they died doing it."

"And you ran to your family. Astonishing . . . and yet your family is a strange mix. What could exemplify it better than your brother's clumsy attempt to bribe a weapon into your hand after serving you up to Sila Diaglou?"

I sputtered in disgust. "I needed money. I needed nivat. I needed a roof and walls to protect me from this rabble you've joined. That Max betrayed me to Bayard Slugwit was no surprise. And only a doulon-crazed fool would believe he'd help me out of this madhouse. He likely paid your whey-faced lout to taunt me with the knife, not give it." And more clearly than ever, Jakome was *Gildas's* whey-faced lout, not Sila Diaglou's. Jakome had taken my blood for the doulon.

"So, tell me, Brother Gildas, if the mad priestess plans

to create a new world from mingling my blood with that of her mad followers, what is to be your place in it? Chief Corrupter? The Baron of Books?" And here I took the dangerous leap. "Or are your aims, perhaps, different than the lady's?"

He strolled across the room and halted just behind me. I gripped the iron window grate, straining every sense to decide if cold steel was aimed at my back. But instead, he spoke softly over my shoulder. "You know I cannot trust you, dear fellow. You have made clear that you have no use for practical, unsentimental men. Know, too, that I have given the priestess everything she has demanded of me. She is fiercely loyal and will believe no slander—especially from a renowned liar. And she relishes bleeding doulon slaves to poison Danae sianous. But I will also tell you this, my friend: Heed my direction, and one day soon, before these cretins wreak heaven's wrath on the winter solstice, you and I will exchange favors. You would like to keep your mind and be free of this madhouse and a future impregnating Harrower broodmares. I would like to spend the next few hundred years in Aeginea. I believe I've knowledge enough that I can buy the archon's good will, but alas, your book of maps does not suffice to get me beyond their borders."

Inside, I smiled with grim satisfaction and chose to take one more risky step. "Give me Jullian along with the nivat, and all my skills will be at your service, Brother Treacher. The boy stays with me until we go, and I breathe no word of your plan to him, to Sila, or to anyone. Sentiment and pragmatism will walk hand in hand."

His breath moved on my back, fast and hot. My own breath held still as my mind raced over everything I'd told him—where I might have yielded too easily or pushed too hard.

"Done," he said at last, clapping a hand on my bare shoulder, his forced joviality reopening one of Malena's lacerations. He snatched up the bloody rag from the floor and blotted the wound.

I did not allow him to see my fierce hope. If I could truly persuade the blackguard to give me Jullian, I would tear down these walls with my toes if need be to get us out.

"The diviners have foreseen the fall of humankind,

Valen. It is up to each of us to find our way through it. Follow my lead, and you will survive as you have all these years." He dropped something onto the table and tapped on the door. The door guard let him out and set the lock.

His parting gift comprised a small canvas bag holding a silver needle, a linen thread, a finger-length rectangle of mirror glass, and three nivat seeds—far too few for one doulon spell, but sufficient to rouse my hunger. I clutched the bag to my chest and told myself that I dared not risk my pretense of cooperation by tossing the seeds from the window.

If I were actually planning to deliver Gildas to Max, I could save my brother the work of interrogation and tell him Gildas's secrets, writ as plain as my own on this night. Instead of serving as the lighthouse Scholar, vowed to teach the world what might be forgotten in the Great Harrowing, Gildas planned to keep his treasury of knowledge all to himself. Instead of watching magic that he himself could never possess become every man's birthright, he could astonish the ignorant by fashioning a spindle, by predicting the sunrise or the change of seasons, by working the magic of fire by striking flint to steel or the magic of life by suturing a wound. Gildas fancied himself a prophet, an alchemist, a sorcerer. The weary survivors of the world's chaos would name him a god.

Chapter 23

⫸━━━━━━━━━━⫷

Lust and nivat plagued my dreams. I was out of bed and pacing my tower cage well before what passed for sunrise. I donned my shirt and chausses, unable to bear the thought of my captors gawking at the mystery of my gards, and hoping that clothing might quench the dual fires that plagued me with fits of the shakes.

Trying to recapture some use of my senses, I examined the inner side of the door locks, peering through the seams of the door, tapping, shaking, rattling. The exercise revealed little. I needed to be out of here.

When Malena brought ale and bread, I could not eat. I could not speak. I could not look at her without wanting to tear away her gown—stitched of common russet, buttoned tight across her breasts to reveal everything of softness and curves. I hated myself for it. I hated those who tempted me to it. I didn't understand it. In the past, the doulon had quenched all fleshly desires, not driven them. I donned my pourpoint, thinking to put another layer between my skin and temptation.

The girl played the good wife, commenting upon the weather and the food and did I wish for a heavier cloak to wear over my garments. She folded the clothes still scattered on the floor and laid them in the clothes chest. She even began some apology for serving me wine laced with "vigger's salt," which was the common name for saffron that alley witches swore could inflame a man's flagging prick.

I choked on a miserable laugh, closed off my hearing, and clung to the window bars. Saffron was more expensive than nivat.

Though I did not suffer from the cold, the morning was bitter. Ice crystals whipped through the barred windows, swirling on the floor and settling like dust in the cracks and crevices on either side of the door. In the mottled gray of storm and smoke, Palinur spread below my tower like a battlefield, its streets and houses like fallen soldiers—some of them charred ruins, half buried in mud and blackened snow, a few still displaying life and movement. Somewhere out there, Voushanti and Saverian awaited my call.

Considering the two of them gave me extraordinary comfort. That a dead man with a mote of hell in his eye and a physician with a desert for a heart seemed like the world's finest companions told me what a nest of lunatics I'd come to. And I was as bad as any of them. The moment I had Jullian at my side, we would find a way through this damnable door, down to the prison level, and out of this cursed place.

"Dear Magnus, the day is so very cold." A weight pressed softly against my back and Malena reached her arms about my waist. She was shivering, and my arms ached to enfold her. "Could we not begin again? If we learned more of each other, we could be friends." Her fingernails were chewed and broken, ridged with black dirt and a rusty residue that could so easily be old blood. *Saints and angels!*

I grasped one of her hands as it snaked toward my groin and twisted her arm as I turned, using it to force her back toward the door. "Let us learn more of each other, Malena. Shall I tell you stories of my friend Gerard, of how he loved to watch the wall of light move across the refectory or how he named all the abbey's goats after holy saints or how this boy, who blanched at butchering a chicken, sat bravely on a wounded soldier, singing of hearth and home, as our infirmarian sawed off the man's leg? Tell me, Malena, did you cut Gerard at the Well? Did you drive the spikes that held his hands to the rock or taste his blood? You will need more than vigger's salt to make me lie with you of my own will."

Even as I spoke these things, my body craved her. Revolted, I shoved her against the wall and returned to my window. I would bind my hands to the bars before touching her again.

"You speak bravely in the light, Magnus," she said, all sweetness foregone. "But when I come in the night, you shall bend as the earth must bend before the power of the Gehoum. They care naught for one boy, naught for you, naught for me, but only that the land and people be subdued and humble and made clean. Your body speaks their will. Look at your hands." Indeed my shaking dwarfed her shivers.

She rapped on the door and was released. I wondered if the unhappy Jakome was forced to deliver her to me. I hoped so. I wondered if she had "caught," and near screamed at the thought of a child given life from a doulon-fed frenzy and in such a creature as Malena.

The morning was quiet so high in the tower. I fidgeted and paced. I sipped Saverian's potion, hoping it might quench these other uneasy sensations as effectively as it controlled my stomach. After my outburst at Malena, I might find myself in the dungeons by midday. I touched the stone floor and, for the tenth time that morning, verified that the guide threads I had established the previous night were still intact. Somewhere far below me, Osriel and Stearc yet breathed.

I had just emptied the ale pitcher out the window without tasting its contents, when the bolts and latches rattled again. This time I heeded every snick of pins and levers in the locks. My visitor was Gildas.

"You've distressed our little wench this morning, Valen."

"As long as I've a mind to choose with, I choose not to dance to Sila Diaglou's music," I said. "Which leaves me perhaps two days until I succumb." I prayed I was misleading him. The more preoccupied I seemed to be with my cravings, the less cautious he might be.

"I am to take you to the priestess. Alas, good Jakome is required to bind your hands against the chance of some magical escape. Do I need to call for shackles, as well, or ruffians with blades?"

Lifting the hems of pourpoint and shirt, I showed him

his little bag tied at my waist. "Your leash is quite strong enough, though it's mostly promises as yet; three seeds get me nowhere but sick. Nor have I seen my young friend this morning. And all bargains are moot, if the priestess thinks to bleed me."

Gildas grinned. "Sila much prefers you alive ... as do I. I discussed Jullian with her last night, suggesting we entrust the boy to your care. I proposed that he could relieve Malena of serving your meals. Thus reassured that we mean well, you might be more attentive to the young woman's charms." Sila seemed receptive. Perhaps you could set her remaining doubts at rest during this morning's interview. Each hour you behave well will add weight to your nivat bag."

Gildas admitted Jakome, who carried a grimy wad of silken cord. The silkbinding took an extraordinarily long time, for Jakome wasn't particularly good at it. He bound the cords tight, but uneven. And unlike pureblood guards, whose skilled binding left no bit of flesh exposed and not the least possibility of movement, Jakome failed to keep my fingers properly clasped and tucked as he worked. With a little time, I might be able to wriggle my thumbs loose and poke them through the coils of cord. The bony man completed the tedious task by spitting on the already filthy wrappings, evidently his idea of a proper torment.

Gildas led the way down the tight coil of worn and broken steps. Jakome followed behind me.

Once free of the wards on my door, I snatched the opportunity for spellwork. *Dead man. Fallow.* I closed my eyes and fed a bit of magic into the words. *Fallow* would inform Saverian and Voushanti that I was alive and safe enough for the moment. I strained my inner ear until I heard the echo. *Bluejay. Fallow.* In heart and head I thanked Saverian for her cleverness and skill.

How different from this doulon-fed frenzy had been the forces that heated me as I lay with Saverian in the shrubbery. I needed to hold fast to that memory ... which made me smile at what Saverian might say to my using carnal thoughts of *her* to shield me from unsavory lust.

Three landings down, a doorway opened into a long, wide passage. Embrasures along the left-hand wall admitted smoke and dusty light. A purposeful stumble allowed me to sneak a glimpse through one of them. The passage was actually an enclosed gallery that overlooked the long hall where I had been delivered the previous afternoon. Observers or bowmen could lurk here, completely hidden from below.

Opposite the embrasure wall, dim chambers opened off the gallery, appearing, for the most part, to be but habitat for spiders. But Gildas stopped at one doorway hung with a blanket. He held back the dingy wool, and Jakome shoved me into a cavelike chamber.

No windows graced this room. Arrow loops on the outer wall admitted bitter air and threads of wan daylight that scarce sufficed to keep me from colliding with Gildas. The now-familiar pressure of walls grew as I stood in the close quarters, but my stomach stayed in place, and again I blessed Saverian for her potion.

"Sila should be here by now." Gildas's voice dripped annoyance.

The sullen Jakome fed and stirred coals that smoldered in a rusty brazier. The rising flames pushed the darkness back a little.

The long, narrow chamber appeared to be a soldier's billet, or more properly, a commander's billet, as I saw no sign that more than one person slept here. Wool blankets were folded neatly atop a rolled-up palliasse. A folding table and several stools leaned against one wall, alongside a pile of leather saddle packs. For the most part the accumulated dust, dried mud clots, ancient straw, stone flakes, wood chips, bark, and ash that grimed the chamber and hearth had been left where they lay. But the end wall closest to me, where the firelight shone brightest, had been swept and scrubbed clean before someone mounted a map of Navronne. Only in my family's home had I ever seen a map so large—fully twice the width of my arm span and almost as high. Janus de Cartamandua had drawn both of them.

Jakome took up a guard stance at the door. Gildas had begun to pace, glancing constantly into the shadows as if expecting gatzi to pop out at us.

I could not take my eyes from the map, noting the bold arcs of Janus's roads, each drawn in one stroke of his fa-

vorite pen, the particular feathery gray foliage of his trees
that no artist had ever been able to duplicate, the oddly
individual faces he gave to the birds that inhabited the map
borders. Heaven's mercy, had he known what happened to
failed Danae?

Gildas glanced from me to Jakome. "Something's off.
Don't let him out of here."

The monk pushed through the hanging blanket and disappeared. Jakome drew his sword and blocked the doorway behind him. His mouth twisted upward and his sharp
eyes fixed on me, as if he hoped I would challenge him.

But it was the map that drew me, not the prospect of
being skewered trying to escape while my hands were
bound. Jakome made no move to stop me as I strolled
across the room to an arrow loop and peered down at an
inner ward littered with broken masonry and fine rubble.
Several corbeled privies had collapsed, tearing down half
of a sewage-stained wall. After a short time, I drifted idly
toward the map.

Something struck me as odd beyond its grand scale, but
I couldn't decide what it was. The borders and compass
rose were grandly decorated. The firelight sparkled from
flecks of gold that had been mixed with some of the inks.
It was certainly very old. A Cartamandua map never yellowed or cracked, but rather took on a certain luster, as if
the lines and colors, the drawing and the magic had blended
and transformed it into something richer and deeper than
its parts. This one seemed near as deep as it was wide. The
ink washes were curious—only two colors, green and ocher,
spread across irregularly shaped areas that corresponded
to no other boundaries. Yet there was something more ...

Uneasy, I glanced over my shoulder at the bored Jakome
and at the far end of the chamber where the darkness hung
so deep, unpenetrated by flame or thready daylight. Then I
peered a little closer at the map.

Increasingly frustrated, I tapped my silkbound hands on
my mouth and chin, rested them on my head, and dropped
them down again. My fingers itched to trace the web of
paths, like those through Mellune Forest, where I had misled the pursuing Harrowers. They ached to touch the fine
details, such as the cairn that marked the split in the track

leading to Caedmon's Bridge and Fortress Groult. In satisfaction I noted the vast distances Saverian and I had frog-leaped from the rounded hills of northeastern Ardra to the hills of Palinur, to the bogs, to the cairn, to the Sentinel Oak—

I blinked. I would have sworn I had seen the faint shape of the Sentinel Oak depicted beside the cairn near Caedmon's Bridge, but now I stared at the spot directly, I saw only the cairn. I angled my head to the side, and again glimpsed the tree.

Shifting my examination westward, I scanned past the limits of civilized lands, across the wilds of the Aponavi, to the shores of the western sea that separated Navronne and Cymra from the uncharted lands beyond. Under a wash of green, the coastline jagged and curved, and I wondered which curve might be the shore of Evaldamon—Kol's sianou, where the days passed more slowly than elsewhere in Aeginea. Somehow I felt that if I could touch the map, I would know such truths—as if I were a blind man touching his lover's face.

Of a sudden, I caught my breath—that's what it was. This map had no words! Not one anywhere.

"Wait outside, Jakome." Sila Diaglou's cool voice spun me away from the map. "And you, dear Gildas, I wish you to take our provisioning in hand. Hurd's fifth legion, the last of our assault force, marches for Evanore this afternoon, and Falderrene has not the cleverness to see it done properly. The Grav has been so busy rousting purebloods, he's had no time to see to it himself."

Sila swept through the door curtain. Gildas followed close behind, protesting. "But, holy one, I was to be here—"

"I prefer to interview Magnus alone. Remind Jakome that no one interrupts me. And take the book—I want another site before tomorrow."

"Of course, holy one." Gildas, flushed the hue of poppies, rummaged in the piled baggage and pulled out a thick square of brown leather, then inclined his back and left.

I stared after him, ready to bash my head against the wall in frustration. Perhaps Sila knew Gildas was not entirely committed to her purposes. Perhaps not. But she had just sent him away with my book of Cartamandua maps. I had not been certain it yet existed.

Once we were alone, the priestess moved briskly to retrieve a soiled cloak from the piled baggage. She fastened it about her shoulders and drew it close, giving an exaggerated shiver as she moved to the hearth. The action made her seem almost human.

"The cusp of autumn arrives untimely." She gazed into the leaping flames and spoke in a dreamy singsong voice. "Dun haze. Tarnished gold. Leaves ... glory dulled ... whipped from their branches. Wolves gather, howling, gnawing the light. No more the culmination of summer, but harbinger of bitter blue days and ever longer nights. The dance is finished, and my heart aches for the waning season."

She looked over her shoulder at me, her eyes narrowed, judging. "My grandmother taught me that when I was very small. It's supposed to be sung. Have you heard it?"

"No," I said, mystified, wary.

"She called it 'The Canticle of the Autumn.' I'm sure there once was a canticle for each season, but she never sang any but this one. Autumn is a sorrowful season. A dying season."

Somehow such flat pronouncement raised my dander. "This autumn, yes. But a rightful autumn is golden and fruitful, a worthy celebration of summer's labors."

"And so you would say, too, that winter is not death."

Who could argue that the winter that held Navronne in its grip was not death? Not I, who had always envisioned the netherworld as a dungeon of ice.

Turning back to the fire, she drew a greasy packet from her cloak, unwrapped it, and pulled out two flat strips of dried meat. She tore off a bite and closed her eyes in the way of a soldier who has been too long in the field and savors his meat as a sign he yet lives. Wordless, she offered me the second piece. I shook my head, and she devoured it, while I repeatedly rolled one thumb against the other in an attempt to free them from their bindings. I hated feeling so helpless in her presence.

When she had finished the meat and wiped her hands on her breeches, she drained a small flask rifled from the depths of her cloak. Then she sighed and tossed another stick on the fire. "I apologize for your hand bindings, for your confinement, and for last night's ... coercion. You showed up at my door so unexpectedly. Though I believe you will eventually grant me your willing cooperation, events leave me little leeway for chance, and I must seize opportunity. Malena happens to be fertile just now."

"I await your explanations, madam." Though expert at lies, I had never been very successful at feigning cooperation with those who restrained me and pretended they were doing it for some greater good. Yet I neither spat at her nor cursed her soul to everlasting fire as I would like to have done. If I were to save my friends, I needed to find some common ground with this woman.

"You were examining my map," she said, ignoring my abruptness. "It's a Cartamandua map, as I'm sure you can tell—an unusual one."

"I've seen only a few so large." Perhaps she would tell me what *she* thought was unusual. No words ... I'd never seen a finished map lacking written names and keys. Janus had not made it for me; it was far too old. Yet naught gave me indication that it was incomplete. His own gryphon mark was scribed at the lower right corner. The cartographer's mark was always the last thing added.

"You may study it sometime, if you wish, before I destroy it." No gloating or cruelty or irony accompanied this offer. With the same casual sincerity that Picus spoke of forsaking the human world to live in penitence, she spoke of destroying a work of incomparable magic, artistry, and breadth of knowledge. It must have taken Janus more than a year just to render it, and untold years of travel and study to gather the material for the early sketches. Saints and angels, the vellum itself was priceless without accounting for the map. Only a few sorcerers in the history of Navronne had been able to transform sewn vellum into so large and seamless a whole.

"Why would you destroy such a marvel?" I said, the tantalizing mystery overwhelming my wish to let her lead the conversation. "What god could possibly wish it? Surely to know the size and variety of the world can but glorify whatever powers rule it."

Sila nodded, as if expecting that very question. "The map, like those things hidden in the Gillarine lighthouse, is an artifact of corruption. Until we have lived through the age of breaking and repentance, we have no need for such knowledge. Until we have destroyed the barriers that separate those who can make such a thing from those who cannot, we have no right to it. We shall drive the purebloods from their comfortable walls and squeeze the long-lived from their hiding places, breaking down the boundaries of birth and blood that hoard their gifts from humankind. When my use for this map is done, I'll burn it. I don't expect you to grasp everything right away."

Right away . . . So she expected me to live beyond the moment, at least. "Do you truly believe that mating me with your illiterate handmaiden will enable every man and woman to create such a work as this?"

"If not, then we have no need of such works." Always simple answers. Of all the things I had learned in my life, nothing was so simple as fanatics imagined.

"I don't understand any of this," I said. "I very much dislike being used for *anyone's* breeding projects."

Even from the side, I could see her smile blossom. The curve of her lips dimpled her left cheek just below the terrible scar, completely transforming her. She would never be a transcendent beauty like Elene, but when Sila Diaglou turned her smile on me, it felt as if Navronne's winter had yielded to such a glory of summer as I could scarce remember. The world and all its troubles receded into dim anxiety beside an urgent need to touch her cheek. *Great merciful Mother!* Was my entire being reduced to naught but my treacherous prick?

"I fully expected such rebellious sentiment from you, Magnus. Your indignation but confirms that you are meant to stand at my side and lead our people into a new age."

"*Lead?* At your side?" No beggar presented with a crown of rubies could be more astonished or more skeptical.

She rose and joined me at the map, smiled again, and with one finger gently closed my mouth. "Who else could I trust to see both the wisdom of the future I propose and its dangers? Your life will stretch long enough to ensure we move past our time of suffering and penitence and into the new order"—she touched my wrist, setting my skin afire where a streak of pale blue peeked out between the silkbinding and my sleeve—"longer than I first imagined, longer than my own. Your unique magic will grow in these stretched years, serving to keep you safe and strong enough to lead. And your moral stature will shield the remnants of the old races from oppression as they die away."

I had expected to find Sila Diaglou evil incarnate, a leering devil who relished blood, or perhaps a drooling madwoman who saw macabre visions. What was beginning to disturb me most were these times that she seemed halfway reasonable. She shivered in the chilly fortress, relished her supper, had a grandmother who taught her songs. She worried about moral stature and oppression . . . which made her act of stabbing a spear through Boreas's gut to pin his bleeding body to the earth all the more horrific. I would not allow myself to become one of her besotted sheep.

I wrenched my attention from her face before I was completely undone. Behind her, the hanging blanket that covered the door to the gallery swayed, as if just dropped back into place. Despite Jakome's wards, someone had been standing there, listening to what she had just said. Or perhaps I was merely twitchy because Gildas's danger loomed so large. The last place on earth I dared stand was on some pedestal Gildas desired for himself.

I stepped away from Sila. If she viewed the move as a retreat, so be it. "Madam, I claim no unique magic and no moral stature. Indeed I think you mistake me for someone entirely different. But even if I were as you say, and even if I espoused your goals—which seem so grand as to be impossible—how could a person of any 'moral stature' countenance your tactics? These rites of blood, these burnings, and spreading fear . . ." I dared not mention the Danae. Not until I understood more. "I don't believe in your Gehoum."

"Your feelings are but confirmation of my judgment," she said without the least trace of rancor. "They do you credit. But you must abandon your childish views, these notions of benevolent mother goddesses, compassionate father gods, and nurturing Danae guardians. No one tends this world. The universe is not benevolent. Look upon the stars—equal in their clarity, undivided in their brilliance—and the harsh truth of the universe becomes clear. I name this truth *Gehoum* that my followers might grasp it. It prescribes simplicity and demands order, and we who see the rancorous division and greed our ancestors have wrought upon the world, the corruption, this hoarding of talent, wealth, and privilege, the cruelties of war and servitude, must accomplish its return to purity. To me falls the dread task of cleansing, to you the task of regeneration. Our destinies track side by side, but shall never . . . *marry*." Her apologetic smile ravished my wits.

Of a sudden, wood rapped on stone from the gloom at the far end of the chamber. "*Regeneration*? Fool of a girl! Didst thou think I would not learn of this connivance?"

"Grandam! Why are you hiding here?" Sila grabbed an unlit torch from the sconce by the door and shoved it into the brazier. Once it flared, she raised it high.

The shadows fled to reveal a person sitting in the room's farthest corner. Shapeless robes and wimple hid all but her face and the walking stick she rapped angrily against the floor.

"I seek to understand why my dearest girl has not brought me this perverse creature fallen into her grasp. As she does not see fit to confide in me, I must resort to devious means."

The pale-complected woman who voiced this harsh complaint was the ancient I had seen with Sila in the hall the previous day.

"Have you learned no lesson I've taught you, girl? The long-lived are a wound, festering with pride and corruption. They serve no purpose and cannot be made clean. And these Aurellian magicians dare set themselves above the rest of us. The world must be purged of them both, along with Caedmon's prideful get. This halfbreed is abomination, yet you think to breed him and make more?"

"I will not bend just because you and I disagree, Grandam." Exhibiting her coldest self again, Sila set the blazing torch in its sconce and knelt beside the old woman to kiss her cheek. "You would chastise me did I betray my convictions for sentiment, would you not? Thus I chose not to distress you with my decision."

"But what is this breeding plan but sentimental attachment to corruption?" No excess affection displayed itself between Sila and her elder as they argued the merits of the world's ruin.

Momentarily abandoned, I shook off my fascination with Sila Diaglou's family disagreements, and stooped down as if using my bundled hands to adjust my boot. A little more wriggling and my thumbs poked through the layered cords and touched the floor. I poured out magic, searching for the threads of life I had created the previous night. Gods, I was halfway to the prince and Stearc.

"Magnus?" Sila's hand touched my shoulder.

I blinked and looked up. "My boot . . ."

The lady's laugh bit flesh as fiercely as Malena's blade. "Do you think I don't know what you do when you touch the ground? Gildas has told me of your Aurellian bent—and of your fondness for the Karish boy. Truly I have no wish to do him harm."

This gentle declaration appalled me. She did not see what she had done to Gerard and Jullian as harm. How could a flesh-and-blood woman feel *nothing*?

One by one my secrets had fallen open to her, but anger hardened my resolve that she would *not* learn the rest. "You are most gracious, madam," I said, bowing my head and climbing to my feet with as much dignity as bound hands allowed. "This child . . . I'll confess I am preoccupied. He saved my life. Such a debt must be repaid, else a man's life never comes into balance. With my own fate so little in my control, my concern for *his* rules both head and heart."

"You must tame such weakness that your mind may be devoted to the greater good, Magnus. So my grandmother taught me." She beckoned me to follow. "Come, she asks to meet you."

Dutifully I stood before the old woman—older than I had thought from a distance. Framed by veil and wimple, her brow was high and her cheeks taut over square-cut bones like Sila's, her dry skin finely checkered, like linen washed too many times and shriveled in the sun. Yet her turquoise eyes were astonishingly unclouded by time. They could have looked out at me from the face of a maid of one-and-twenty, save for the layer upon layer of despite in them. No few decades could have accumulated the depth of malice written in this woman's face.

"Tell me of your parentage, abomination," she said, wasting no time on pleasantries.

More than Gildas, more even than Sila, this woman incited me to caution. Her intelligence and festered grievance were so closely twined, opening anything of myself to her felt akin to spreading the lips of a wound and asking for salt. "I believe your granddaughter thinks bloodlines important only in their purposeful unraveling."

She leaned forward, her invisible hands propped on her stick, her body formless beneath the heavy robes that draped her head and spilled from her shoulders. "Call it an old woman's curiosity."

Years … malevolence … somehow the pressure of her scrutiny squeezed an answer out of me. "My father is Janus de Cartamandua-Magistoria, a pureblood who languishes in drooling mania for his sins. I did not know my mother, and he did not tell me of her. I was raised as human, only learning of my dual heritage these past weeks."

"Son of the pureblood who returned Caedmon's spawn to Navronne." Hatred poured out of the old woman in a poison spew. "That itself is enough reason to drain thy blood. Who told you of your unnatural birthing if not the animal who caused it?"

No difficulty in framing this answer. Truth would suffice. "My master, Prince Osriel, is an uncommon mage. He suspected the truth—using much the same evidence as Gildas, I suppose. Once his theory proved correct, he discarded me in some bargain with the Danae. Osriel explains neither his methods nor reasons."

"And now you have passed two of the remasti while out of your head. How is that possible? The dam directs such matters. Yet she has clearly been uninterested all these years, and who else of the long-lived would bother to force a human-raised halfbreed through the passages? And why?"

The old woman held me paralyzed with her attention— a much more fearsome scrutiny than Sila's. I dared not answer. I dared not meet her gaze. Surely she could read my flesh and bone. Sila saw people as clay to be molded to her will. This woman viewed us as prey.

"I desire to look upon his gards." The old woman's crackling voice rose a note. "Perhaps they are but pureblood enchantment designed to deceive, some play of this cursed Osriel. Have him show me, Sila."

"This serves no purpose, Grandam. His marks are not spellworked." Sila's impatience scraped my nerves, creating noise and distraction when some insight waited just beyond my grasp. How did the old woman know so much of Danae?

As much to quiet the argument as anything else, I stuck my bundled hands in front of the old woman's nose. "Look as you please, gammy. The god-cursed Danae did this thing to me. For all I know, they were trying to drive me as mad as my father."

With a sigh of exasperation, Sila yanked my sleeve upward as far as it would go, exposing my right wrist and half my forearm. The gards had paled to silver, faintly tinted with blue. The old woman bent her head over my arm. Her breath seared my skin, as if hellfire burned within her withered body.

She slumped back into her chair. "The gards are true," she said, her venom muted.

"As long as you confess their validity, then tell me what skills they give him, Grandam."

The old woman averted her face. Had I not been cranked tight as a crossbow, I might not have noted the alteration in her expression—a closing, as if she had determined not to share what she had seen. "After taking the two remasti so short a time ago? Nothing of import. He experiences the world as unending noise and confusion. If you want to keep him living, lock him away where he can touch the wind and breathe. I am surprised he is not slamming his head against these walls. I am *not* surprised you find him pliable to breeding lust. He has completed only two changes. The third awaits."

The third remasti—the maturing of fleshly desire—was that what was happening to me? How did she know?

Frigid as the coming night, Sila glanced from her grandmother to me. "And one more question . . . Gildas says that Danae males need pain to quicken their seed. You never told me that."

The old woman snorted, an amusement that sounded like cracking wood. "I'm sure he must be correct," she said. "Gildas knows everything. My small experience is of *human* males, and that is quite revolting enough. Do not fear, granddaughter, this one shall become everything you wish."

"Who are you?" I whispered.

The old woman merely bobbed her head while staring until I felt naked.

Sila grabbed two of the folding stools and beckoned me to the brazier, leaving the old woman hunched in her dim corner like a mother spider. Relief warmed me more than the flames.

"Do not expect me to apologize for my grandmother's plain speech. Grandam has a gift for seeing through all the world's masks, and she has taught me to do the same. We speak as we find. But my experience out in the field, seeing the cleansing as we accomplish it, has caused my vision to expand beyond hers. Once the harrowing is done, something will grow; it can be weeds or it can be wheat. I have great hopes for you."

She beamed, and I began to understand why men and women destroyed themselves for her. Her beliefs permeated her being—flesh and spirit indistinct one from the other and exposed for all to view. She stood as an exemplar of truth, naught hidden, naught sly or deceitful. She wore no mantle of ambition or greed. No petty grievance sullied her mission. No wonder the battered poor overlooked her ruthless strikes against their own interests. They *believed* her.

I could not succumb to fascination. For every answer I gleaned, two more questions arose. "To learn more of this vile"—I gestured toward my body—"*state* I have been left in would be a boon. *Noisy* is a mild description of what they've done to me. How does your grandmother know these things?"

"She has lived a long time. And now, dear Magnus"—she leaned forward, hands folded—"I must know about Prince Osriel."

For near an hour, she questioned me, precisely and specifically, about Osriel's magic, his fortresses, his legions, and his gold. The intriguing map loomed over us, yet I could spare no thoughts for it. The interrogation justified the prince's close grip on his secrets, for I had scant need to lie or hide anything. I spoke of his cruel and varying humors, of his disdain for friends and confidants, and his callous use of Jullian as hostage. Without mentioning gold mines or walking dead men, I spoke of my certainty that Osriel dabbled in vile and wicked sorcery, developed through long study. I described in gruesome detail the scene in Gillarine's kitchen when he took the dead messenger's eyes, while disclaiming any knowledge of what he did with them. When she asked me what I could tell of his military aide, Mardane Voushanti, rumored to be under diabolical influence, I said only that the man was a formidable warrior and shared his master's scorn for unskillful pureblood vagabonds. And I could certainly tell her nothing of Osriel's bargain with the Danae.

When she questioned me of Evanori military strength, I gave her modest estimates of the warmoot and vouched the warlords' loyalty was for Caedmon's kin and no love for Osriel himself. And when she probed to discover his plans, I said only that I had been discovered and tossed out before I could hear the prince's charge to his warriors. The Bastard believed his brothers weak and untrustworthy, I said, and Sila herself to be his only worthy rival. All his machinations were to defeat her—but I swore I could not tell her what those strategies were. "He never trusted me."

While displaying reluctance to aid her cause, I let her tease out this information. And I focused my answers through the prism of Osriel's betrayal, allowing my rage to surface and taint every detail of my experiences with the worst possible interpretation. And as I spoke, I gave full rein to my body's certainty that the arrow slits in her walls were closing and I would soon be dead of suffocation. Sweat beaded on my forehead, and I twitched and fidgeted. Her grandam should be well pleased that I was half a lunatic.

"What of this Stearc of Erasku?" she said, after I repeated my claim that Osriel favored no Evanori lord above another. "Your friend from the cabal? And his secretary and his charming *squire*? How does Osriel view their activities?"

I croaked a laugh. "Friend? The thane damned me as a coward from our first meeting. And I don't believe he changes his mind. The only time I saw Stearc at Renna was on the night of the warmoot, amid the other lords. I glimpsed Gram—the secretary—only briefly on that visit, but was not allowed to speak with him. I doubt the prince takes notice of secretaries. As for the girl, she near fainted from fright when I once mentioned Osriel's name. I gathered she believed he would flay them for their activities."

"Why did you help the cabal? Gildas could not explain why you would endanger yourself for those who want to preserve their superiority over common men."

"I was looking for advantage," I said. "If they had found out I could not read, they would have thrown me out of Gillarine. I had no intention of starving." As I said this, it came to me that this crass rendering was naught but truth. Yet even if I had dared explain to Sila Diaglou how my motives had changed, she would not have understood. *Faith* was not a word she had use for.

"So what of the monk you saved from my hangman—the chancellor Victor—what happened to him?"

"Osriel never permitted me to see him. He claimed that his house mage had put Brother Victor into a healing sleep to recover from his wounds. I didn't particularly care. Save for Jullian, the Tormentor can take the whole lot of the cursed cabal—including your pet monk, Gildas. They thought to use me, just like every other person in my life has sought to use me, and when they had squeezed the use from me, they threw me to the dogs. The boy was the only one of the lot who tried to teach me how to read their fine books."

"Loyalty is a great virtue and should be rewarded." She stood and motioned me toward the door. I prayed I had not given her anything of value, nor condemned myself with some contradiction of Stearc's testimony.

"Jakome!" The guard came running. "Return Magnus to his chamber and unbind his hands. Then inform Gildas that, at his convenience, he may release the boy to our guest's protection."

She held my wrists and smiled, sending spiders' feet creeping up my back. "Sleep well, and do not think to deny Malena again. She is strong and faithful, and it is my will that she catch your seed."

Chapter 24

Leaving Sila's chamber felt like crawling out of a grave. Jakome led me to the tower stair, only to have Sila call him back to her door for one more message—a summons for Gildas to join her for the evening meal.

As I awaited my jailer's return, the downward stair gaped dark in front of me. I wished an apology to those who languished below. *One more day, Lord Prince,* I said. *One more day, Stearc. Let me get Jullian and then I'll find a way down to you.* More than any bloodline, book, or tool, this world needed something of innocence preserved.

"Come, Grandam. I will take you back to your room." As Jakome sauntered back toward me, Sila led her grandmother down the gallery. The old woman moved in a halting, rolling gait, leaning heavily on Sila's arm and a walking stick. Surely some cruelty had blighted her life to nurture such malevolence.

Of a sudden, the world held its breath ... as bits and pieces of our strange interview peppered my thoughts like wind-driven sand. "What's wrong with the old woman?" I whispered, not expecting an answer.

"Move along or I'll see you walk the same as she," said Jakome, snarling and shoving me roughly toward the stair. "Even crippled, you can still service a quenyt."

I balked, staring at the two receding backs. "Sila's grandam ... her legs are crippled ... or is it her knees?"

"What of it?" he said. "Now get on with you."

The *old one,* they called her, the venomous old woman

who knew the lore of Danae. A woman bitter at humankind and the Danae and Caedmon's line alike, whose shapeless garments hid hands and feet, arms and crippled knees . . . and what else?

"What do you name the old woman?" I said, as I stumbled numbly up the stairs and through the door of my tower chamber.

"She gives no one her name," said my jailer, unbinding my hands. "She says we're to call her the Scourge."

Surely breaking a girl's knees at fourteen would sow hatred enough for a lifetime of bitter harvesting—especially in a girl whose half-Danae father had broken the Canon and whose human mother had murdered her kin. Especially in a child who had been taunted and shunned and used to trick her own mother to her death. Ronila.

The one person who had ever been kind to her—a human man vowed to chastity—had tormented himself with guilt after lying with her. And even Picus had turned away from her, choosing to hold to his monk's vows and stay with his young prince while Ronila fled to the human world, bringing with her knowledge of the Scourge—the Danae vulnerability to tormented death.

Wind howled through the window bars. I had neither eaten nor drunk since the previous night, and the hunger and chill crept into my bones. I wasn't sure whether I needed to crawl under the quilts or take off my clothes.

Jakome slammed the door and shot the bolts. I sank to my bed and imagined what might have gone through Ronila's mind when Eodward and Picus had returned to Navronne. An old woman by then, she would have seen Picus still in his prime, reflecting his prince's glory. Five short years after their return, Picus had vanished—after Ronila had shown him evidence that the offspring of Danae–human mating had no souls, a grandchild, perhaps, nurtured and tutored in the ways of hate, a granddaughter who saw no crime in slaughter, who believed that art and beauty, learning and faith were corruption and that the earth must be wiped clean of gods and Danae, monks and kings—everything Picus valued. Even in his despair, he could not have imagined what she would grow up to be.

Now I knew what had nagged at my head when Picus

recounted Ronila's accusations. The halfbreed girl's condemnation had reflected the words of the Harrower blood rite—*sanguiera, orongia, vazte*. Bleed, suffer, die. Ronila, the Scourge. Sila Diaglou, a mixed-blood Dané.

No wonder Sila used a wordless map. She could read words no better than I could. No gards marked her hands—not even the pale silver of gards too long hidden. So she had not passed even the first remasti. My experience was so different—being half-Aurellian sorcerer already—I had no idea what power Sila might have. Was it her Danae blood that enabled her to mesmerize a crowd, to make women weep when they saw her scarred cheeks, to make men believe that they should tear down their cities and burn their fields? She had said her grandmother had taught her to control her heart and her body, so she must be unmatched in discipline ... but then, the world knew that already. And she would not be easy to kill. Gods, the others ... the cabal ... Osriel ... needed to know this great secret.

I crouched beside the door and ran my fingers over the lock. The warded iron was no more yielding of its secrets than earlier. Nonetheless, I pulled one of the pebblelike armaments game pieces from the clothes chest, examined it carefully, and used its likeness along with my experience and estimates of this type of lock to lay the rough groundwork for a spell.

Once I had done what I could—without a better idea of the lock or magic to feed the spell, that was not so much—I shed my outer layers of pourpoint and boots, hiked up my shirtsleeves and unlaced the neck, and sat against the wall under the middle window. As sheltered from the wind as I could manage, I hoped the bit of exposure might strengthen my gards without giving me frostbite. I practiced closure and control, listening only for footsteps on the stair. Ready.

Next time the door latches rattled, I was able to visualize the snap of the bronze levers and the draw of the lock pins. By the time the door opened to Gildas, I had refined my internal image of the lock.

"Whoa, a dismal, blustery afternoon," he said, standing in the doorway and holding a small lamp. "Is the coming storm too stout even for a halfbreed Dané?"

"Where is Jullian?" I said, without moving. "The priestess gave her permission for him to stay here."

"Jakome brings him. I wanted to make a few things clear before his arrival."

Gildas wrenched a balky handle on the outside of the door and shut the door firmly behind him. The pins and levers moved—slight differences this time with the latch already set. I refined the lock's image yet again.

Suppressing a smile, I opened my palms in invitation. My gards wreathed my fingers in sapphire light.

He used his small lamp to light the larger one on my table. Then he squatted beside me and reached for my right arm, hesitating only at the last moment. "May I?"

In the interest of our partnership, I suppressed my revulsion and allowed him to take my arm. He peered at my wrist and turned it over. "It seems you have powerful kin, Valen, and we don't quite believe your claim that these marks happened by chance."

I followed his gaze. The grass outlined so delicately on my forearm and fingers might have been sea grass as I assumed. But among the fronds that curved along the inside of my wrist, where I had not seen it before, stretched a long, lean cat with a snarling face. I thumped the back of my head against the wall. Ronila would surely know Stian's mark.

His long brow drawn tight in consideration, Gildas released my arm and returned to the vicinity of the door. "Something is not right about your presence here, friend. I am told that you may have acquired certain ... capabilities ... along with these Danae markings, skills that might contribute to an escape. We can't have that."

"Did you forget your leash?" I said bitterly. "You own me now."

"I've not forgotten." Leaning in deceptive ease against the door, he tossed a fist-sized pouch across the room. It landed heavily in my lap. The smell near set me howling. "Because you lied to me, I think we must restructure our agreement slightly. I want you to work your nasty little enchantment this afternoon."

A stray wind gust snapped my hair, stinging against my cheek. "But it's not time yet. If I do it between times ..."

"... your need will grow stronger and demand to be serviced more often. Alas, that's true." He cocked his head. "But it only accelerates a condition that exists in you already. Do it now, or Jakome will introduce our young friend to the doulon."

I stared at him in disbelief. "Iero's holy name, Gildas. You would not . . ."

But whyever would I imagine that he would balk at this depravity? No one would ever fault Gildas de Pontia for failure of insight. His very posture, so like a strutting rooster, told me he knew that of all the torments he might promise, this one I could not abide.

Rage and hatred only fueled the need lurking in my veins. I struggled to form a plan. To attack him. To delay. To run. But each solution would forfeit lives more important than mine. One more doulon would not kill me, only embed the craving deeper. What did he plan that called for so strong a control of me?

"You lied to me, as well. You've Ronila to take you into Aeginea. Why do you need me?"

"So the clever sorcerer has guessed the crone's name," he said. For one moment I glimpsed the true man—greedy, prideful, jealous—the man who had grown up shamed by his poor and ignorant family. Then he slipped on his smiling mask again. "Let's say I enjoy watching you grovel. Do it now, Valen. And don't think to throttle me or toss the bag through the windows. Without my password, Jakome will not open this door. When he informs Sila, you will bleed out your remaining life in ways most unpleasant. And then he'll see that Jullian loses his soul to this perversion." He shrugged and screwed up his mouth in distaste. "You must understand, I intend to live in this world on my own terms or none, and you are necessary to my plan. Do as I say, and Sila will not know the ugly truth about the abomination she has chosen to . . . plow her fields. We shall merely proceed with our bargain as before."

I knew well the determination to find something better than the life one was born to. Not even Voushanti would be so dangerous a foe as Gildas. I wanted to tear out the blackguard's heart.

Hands shaking, I set out the needle, mirror, and thread and spilled out a pile of hard black seeds beside them. I was a doulon slave already. Gildas and Jakome had but fed tinder to the coals that Saverian had warned would ever burn in me. To do it once more ... truly it could not make ridding myself of the doulon's yoke worse than what I'd gone through after twelve years' enslavement. I just needed to retain as much sense as possible. Control it. And before they could force me to do this a third time, Jullian and I would be away from here.

Gildas watched from the doorway. Using my arm to shield the work from the wind, I crushed the seeds with the bottom of the wooden cup. I tried not to inhale as I worked, but by the time they were powder, my heart was galloping. I dragged the lamp close.

"Wait," he said. "Before you begin, double that amount."

I stared at the pile of seeds in horror. Double ... never had I known any doulon slave who used so much at once. "Fires of Deunor, Gildas, you'll leave me no mind! I've told you I'll do as you wish."

"I want this leash secure." Why would he doubt? Unless Ronila had told him something ...

I recalled his anxious glances into the corner when he took me to Sila's room ... his annoyance that Sila was late for the meeting. He had known Ronila was there. The old woman had not contradicted his pronouncement about Danae males and their need for pain, though she had grown up in Aeginea and knew better.

I poured out more seeds, crushed them, imagining each as one of Gildas's bones.

Ronila had no use for Sila's vision of regeneration and neither did Gildas. At least for the moment, they were allies.

I pricked my finger with the silver needle. It was not so insulting a discomfort as Jakome's knife, but the pain of this exercise ran much deeper than my skin. I would give much to believe that the remasti had given me a higher tolerance for the perverse enchantment.

My blood dripped into the crushed nivat, the scents mingling. Desire crept upward from my toes, inward from my fingers. "Gildas, please ..." My voice was already hoarse with need.

"Remember, I've watched you do this. I'll know if you don't complete it correctly."

I held the little mirror glass upright, angled so that I could see the fumes rise. Between two fingers of the alter hand, I gripped the length of linen thread, dangling the end into the sodden little heap. Gildas would expect that. But he didn't know why I used the thread. Thus he didn't stop me when my last two fingers made contact with the mound. To touch the paste as it heated drew off some of its potency, spreading the infusion over the preparation time. A small difference only, but perhaps enough to keep me sane. I released magic to flow through my fingers and down the thread.

My gaze fixed on the ensorcelled mirror, as the otherwise invisible fumes rose from the bubbling black paste. Wind doused Gildas's lamp and threatened the shielded table lamp. Sweat dribbled down my cheeks, down my spine, as dark fire prickled my hidden fingers and surged up my arm. The locks snapped on the door.

Ought to look. Ought to listen . . . to refine the lock spell. Ought to stop . . . But I had gone too far. Even when the damnable mirror glass reflected the ruddy young face and the widening eyes of Ardran blue, I could not stop.

"Your protector is occupied for the moment, lad," said Gildas. "Did you not know of his little problem?"

"What does he, Brother? Is it some pureblood magic?" Innocent still.

Had I owned a mind or conscience just then, I would have wept at Jullian's wondering stare. As it was, my arm quivered with the doulon's burning, and all I could think was, *Please, gods, make it hurt more.*

Gildas chuckled. "I'm sure he'll explain when he's done. Tell him that Malena's forked blade can seal the spell, if he can but wait till nightfall to soothe all his lusts together. Then the priestess and I will both be happy."

His voice swelled in my ear. "You will be *my* slave, half-breed, and I will not be a kind master."

Whispers and laughs faded. Friends . . . concerns . . . dangers faded. The world faded. Eventually the fumes ceased their rising, and I let the mirror glass fall. As my fingers scooped the hot paste onto my greedy tongue, my other hand groped about the table as if it had a mind of its own. *Glass will cut . . . hot oil will burn.* I needed pain.

The doulon itself carved paths of agony from eyes to heart to limbs. My vision blurred. My back spasmed as if an Aurellian torturer had hung me from his hook and dragged me behind his chariot. Every nerve stretched taut and snapped like drawn bowstrings, launching nets that encompassed every part and portion of my body.

Not enough. Not enough. Gods . . . I did not want to be this thing.

I swept my arm across the table. The lamp crashed to the floor; the oil pooled and flared. The black paste clogged my gullet, slid downward, and seared my empty stomach. Still the enchantment would not resolve, but kept building . . . waiting. I choked and gasped and shook, hammered my fists on the table, then gripped its edge as if to snap the oaken plank in twain. I needed more.

"Brother Valen? What's wrong? Why do you look like that?"

"Strike me . . . please . . . use anything!" Lest I be driven to roll in burning lamp oil or gash my hands with shards of glass, damaging myself beyond recovery.

Wind tearing at his hair, Jullian backed away and pressed himself to the door.

"Do it now, boy! Make it hurt!" My heart rattled my ribs, threatening to burst. My lungs strained for air enough to feed the raging power of enchantment. I screamed at him. "By holy Iero's hand, strike me! I beg you!"

His twelve-year-old limbs had done their share of labor around the abbey. He broke the second chair over my head. It was enough.

A bolt of joyless ecstasy shot through my head and heart and gut, wiping clean the canvas of agony, settling the shards of life and mind into their proper places. I roared in release and rapture.

As ever, the sensation abandoned me as quickly as it had come, and I collapsed across the table, dull, lead-limbed, sick. Only this time my head and shoulders felt as if I had rammed into a tree. And this time it was Jullian weeping.

Though I could not lift my head from the table, I clung to conscious thought, heeded the crackle of dying flames, the smoky stink of cheap lamp oil, the blessedly cold wind—anything to keep me sensible for one moment. The two gatzi had left the boy and me to enjoy this vileness alone.

I stretched out my hand across the table, palm up, and beckoned him nearer. "It's all right, Archangel," I croaked, near weeping myself when I felt him step closer. I did not deserve such trust. "You did well. Thank you. Just . . . give me a little time."

He tiptoed across to the bed and sat, and I fell into blackness.

"Brother Valen." The whisper came from a thousand quellae distant. From another world. I turned my back on it and slipped again into my sinful dreams.

"Brother Valen." The whisper touched me again, like the soft pecking of a chick.

I reached for my wits, caution nagging that I had been unconscious much too long. Mud clogged my veins. Every pore and sinew begged for sleep, and I longed to drag my leaden limbs into a badger's burrow and hide. From what?

"Brother Valen." Quiet. Patient. Terrified.

Like a rain of sewage, the abasement of the day fell on my head. I located my hand and raised it, hoping he would see I was something awake. Then I turned my face to the windows, inhaling wind and cloud and winter to sweep away the detritus of sin. The sun, fallen far into the west, hid deep behind Navronne's shroud of storm. I willed it to sear away these aches and guilts as if it were a cautery iron.

I had no more time for sleep. Soon would come nightfall and Malena. Goddess mother, even after all this, the passing thought of the hateful wench . . . so ripe and willing . . . heated my core. I had no time for that either.

I raised my head a quat or two. Blotted my mouth on the back of my hand so as not to drool before the boy. Which seemed a silly matter now he'd seen my worst. "Are you well, lad?"

"None's harmed me." The terse declaration spoke more description than a warmoot's worth of tales. Jullian, the scholarly boy who read books I would never comprehend, had no words to explain what his captors *had* done. What *I* had just done. *So, Valen Lackwit, let anger banish lust and shame.*

"Sorry I took so long to find you," I said, shuddering as a howling gust billowed the shirt on my back. "Not much of a rescuer, eh?"

"I knew you'd come."

Needing to be still before my skull cracked, I lowered my head onto my hand, where a sea star nestled in the grass. "A few matters came up along the way. Some ugly . . . like what you just saw. Some wondrous . . . unexpected."

"Guessed that." The bed creaked. His sandals scuffed a step or two in my direction. I felt his eyes on my glowing arms and feet. "Are you a demon?" he said softly.

"Great gods, no. Or . . . I believe not." I grinned into my hand. "I'll show you later. Just now"—I opened my ears; no one on the stair as yet—"we need to prepare for visitors. In the chest, there's a bag of knucklebones."

He scrambled to the task. Before I could lift my head up again, the canvas bag sat in front of my nose, alongside Gildas's small lamp, relit from the dying flames of the spilled oil. "Do you know about the others held captive here—Thane Stearc and Gram?" he whispered over my bent back. "They need rescuing more than me. When I heard you'd come, I thought . . ."

"Aye, I know of them. We're all getting out."

"I don't think—" His breathing came heavy and fast. "I don't think they could possibly— I've heard Thane Stearc since they brought him here. Why would they do that to anyone? They've kept me just down the passage from his cell. They wake me so I can hear. I pray . . ." His voice quivered. "I pray for him to die."

"The pr— Gram. Have you heard him, as well?" Jullian did not know Gram's true identity.

"Coughing. Crying out. Mumbling madness like with a fever. Gildas complains he's dying and can't tell them what they want." Good to hear the boy's touch of anger. He *should* be angry. "Gildas says Stearc will open the light-house or they'll burn off his—"

"Doesn't matter what the gatzé says, Jullian. We'll get them home." I ignored the way the room sloshed like the waves of Evaldamon and lifted my head higher where I could look at the boy, so he might believe. His aspirant's gown had been replaced by scraggly leggings and a thin yellow tunic, belted with rope. Dirt and grease matted his red-gold hair, and his ruddy cheeks were pinched with cold and fear. But his hands held steadier than mine, and his slender jaw jutted firm, willing to work with a demon to free his friends.

"Father Abbot would be proud of you, Jullian. There's naught you could have done to help Stearc. Stearc himself would tell you that. The god knows it, too."

I had once imagined Jullian to be Eodward's youngest bastard, a Pretender to the Navron throne, hidden at Gillarine until his majority. Though I knew better now, he was well worthy of it—likely more so than any of the three men who stood in line.

"Gildas said I would stay here with you from now on, save when your . . . woman . . . came."

"We've a thing or two to teach Brother Gildas."

I fumbled Saverian's vials from the knucklebone bag, wishing one of her medicines might help what was most wrong with me. I drained the blue vial. If we were going to be rousting dungeons, my stomach would need calming. The prince's vial I stuck in the pouch at my waist, along with the vial of yellow broom. On the floor the silver needle gleamed in the lamplight, and beside it lay the little mirror, cracked through the middle. The nivat bag lay soaking up the unburned lamp oil. Even shamed and sickened, I dared not touch them.

"Those things I was using . . . toss them through the window bars. Quickly, before I tell you different."

"What are they?" he said, retrieving them gingerly. "I thought you were working some powerful sorcery. Or dying."

"Something of both."

"While I waited . . . I touched you . . . to make sure you were breathing." Gods, he was apologizing.

"The enchantment is called the doulon, Jullian. It is a sinful weakness, a poison that enslaves the mind and body. When I was scarce older than you, I used it to run away from terrible things. But the doulon itself is more terrible than any of the things I ran from. Someone may tempt you to it some day. Gildas may. But don't allow it. Not ever."

I did not watch as he disposed of the implements of sin, lest I grab them away. Instead I pressed my eyeballs back into their sockets and tried to think how to go about what we needed to do. Last time Gildas had given me an excess of nivat, I had experienced recurring attacks of thick-headed confusion for most of a day. Abbot Luviar had died because of it. I could not allow that to happen again.

"Gildas says you're to be his slave," said the boy. "I didn't see how he could force you."

I shoved myself to my feet. "He won't. Help me with this palliasse."

Using the lamp flame to burn through the rope webbing, we unstrung half the bed and ended up with several moderate lengths of rope. I had Jullian pile the palliasse and quilts back over the half-strung frame, using the broken chair to create a hollow like a badger's burrow at one end, while I rested my woozy head between my knees. Great gods how was I ever going to accomplish anything?

"Can you tell me what guards watch Stearc and Gram?" I asked from my odd position.

"There's always one or two in the passage except when they all go down to beat Thane Stearc in the morning and when they . . . hurt . . . him in the evening. Nikred or Crado mostly. Both of them in the day. At night they take turns for rounds, changing at Matins and Lauds and again at Prime." Matins—morning at midnight. Lauds was third hour, Prime sixth—the dawn hour in summer. "I try to keep the Hours here. I thought . . . I hoped I might help him."

"And this torturing happens the same time every night?"

"Between Vespers and Compline . . . when they call the last watch but one before Matins. Crado says they like him to know when it's coming."

"All right." Slowly I sat back onto my heels. The boy perched on the rumpled bed, two or three steps away, his body a wiry knot. "So tell me how the cells are laid out, if you can."

In moments he had sketched an outline of the prison

block in the sooty remnants of my lamp. I planted the image in my head, then had him rub it out with his boot. "Clearly you're a good observer. So did you happen to note the guards when they brought you up the stair earlier?"

Though his eyes flicked between my face and my glowing hands, he did not falter with his answers. "One at each level. Sometimes when Gildas brought me to walk in the inner ward or to study the map, I'd see two at the hall level."

I popped my head up, blinking until the windows took their proper places instead of whirling one atop the other. "To study the map—the big one in Sila's sleeping chamber?"

"Aye, that's it. Gildas doesn't understand what she does with it, so he studies it when she's not there, and he has me study it, too, so I can remind him of details he might forget. It maddens him that no paper or pens are allowed here, save the map, your grandfather's book, and the Aurellian book he uses to interpret the maps."

The great map . . . its luster of age and art and magic . . . its shifting images . . . had captured my imagination. I closed my eyes and envisioned the green and ocher washes over the wordless fiché. Made for those who could not read words—Danae, then, or halfbreeds like me and Sila. Just as in the book of maps, Janus's secrets lay exposed for all to see, if only I knew how to look at it. "Does Gildas say what he suspects about the map?"

Jullian shook his shaggy head. "Only that the features change over time. He thinks the old woman knows a secret about it that even Sila doesn't know, and that bites him sorely."

A map made for the Danae . . . but Kol had shown me they could not interpret maps, even ones without words. What would prompt Janus to make them a map—a map that Sila found use for and that held place in the gap of secrets between Sila and Gildas and Ronila?

I felt the sun slipping lower. Both enlightenment and vengeance must wait, for I'd yet to come up with a route out of Fortress Torvo. "Where did they take you to walk?"

"Gildas would walk me in the inner ward—"

"—where half the north end wall has collapsed? Piles of rubble all around?"

"Aye." Wind rattled the window bars. Jullian scrambled back onto the bed, shivering, burrowing slowly into the quilts.

I pushed myself up to a squat, summoned all my resolve, and stood up. In hopes that movement might shift the clay in my limbs and rouse some insight, I crossed the room, raking fingers through my hair, trying to reconstruct the scene I'd glimpsed through Sila Diaglou's arrow loops. "The broken wall once supported a row of privies hanging out over the court. Do you recall seeing a drainage canal on that end of the yard? It would only make sense . . . the sewage draining out of the privies into the canal." Unless the privies had been put in after the canal was rerouted, or no one had considered draining the muck from an inner court that was naught but a well in which to trap one's enemies and pour down death on them.

"A cistern sits in the middle of the court, but I didn't see a canal. If it's there, it's full of rock."

I grabbed my heaviest wool shirt from the clothes chest, convinced my leaden feet to carry me back to the bed, and dropped the shirt over Jullian's head. Then I took myself to the window, bathing my skin in the cold afternoon. "Did you notice any grates around the walls? Something as tall as my knees?"

His head popped through the shirt's neck hole, his eyes curious. "Aye, I saw a rat squeezing through a grate . . . just south of the broken wall . . . at the ground where a canal *might* run . . ."

I grinned as he wrestled his arms into the warm gray shirt and retied his rope belt to tame its bulk. "I know going inward seems an unlikely route to the outside, but it might serve if we can find no better. You *can* find the way to this yard in a hurry?"

He gave me his most scathing look. It was all I could do to keep from ruffling his filthy hair.

Footsteps echoed on the stair. I knelt in front of Jullian and took his cold hands in mine. "A woman is going to come here soon. You must hide in the burrow you made, and make not a sound, not a sneeze, not a prayer, no matter what you hear or think you hear. You'll come out only when I tell you."

He nodded, solemn faced, curious, but not so frightened anymore.

"Gildas thinks to torment me by prisoning us together, knowing you'll see what this vile enchantment does to me and what Sila Diaglou intends for me to do here every night. But then, he doesn't believe in angels or aingerou or any other blessing that a god might send to sinful men. We're going to show him different."

Chapter 25

Malena arrived with the early nightfall. I waited behind the door. In the instant the door opened, breaking the barrier ward that bound the room, I touched the lock and quickened the spell I had built throughout the day. Anticipation held my bones rigid . . . with so much depending on a blindworked spell in an unfamiliar lock . . . and every alternative sure to draw blood.

As the girl crossed the room with a supper tray, I buried my face in my hands, listening for the latch. The guard on the stair pulled the door shut. The pins and levers moved . . . and stopped short, as if a small clot of dirt, oil, and bronze shavings, about the size of an armaments game piece, had slipped into the works and prevented them seating properly. I smiled into my fists.

Again Malena wore naught but flimsy shift and braided hair. Again she set out warmed wine. I had eaten nothing since the previous night, and even the prospect of maggoty bread would have set me ravening had I not spent the last half hour practicing what Kol named *closure*, attempting to subdue every sense to my will. Three times in the past hour echoes of the doulon had threatened to unhinge me, wreaking havoc in my head and shooting spasms of pain and desire through breath and bone. But I had cut them off like rotted limbs. No matter desire, no matter temptation, no matter perversion, neither Gildas nor Sila Diaglou would control my deeds this night.

"Where is the boy?" said my chosen mate, forgoing all

pretense of holy ardor. "I was told he would be here. We're to send him out to Jakome when the time comes, unless you wish him to watch."

"Gildas took him," I said. "They fed me extra vigger's salt this afternoon and I got a bit . . . tightwound . . . waiting for you." I shrugged and pointed out the broken lamp, the rumpled bed and scattered cups.

She pouted a bit, as if she had been looking forward to the extra company, then watched in puzzlement as I tied my spare hose over my feet like soft slippers, hiding my gards. The hose would be easier than boots to remove if I had to bare my gards in a hurry. "Cold feet," I said.

She retrieved the wooden cups from under the clothes chest where I'd thrown them. "Do you wish to sup first or shall we do our mistress's bidding so I can be away from here the sooner?"

"Our mistress has explained her remarkable . . . glorious . . . vision," I said. "And I understand a great deal more about what we must sacrifice than I did this morning. But I've not eaten all day, and I'd not wish to fail in strength or endurance tonight." I smiled and tugged at the lace that bound up her braid.

I did not want to tip my hand by rushing. The call of fifth watch had not long passed and Stearc's punishment would not begin until sixth.

Malena did not seem mollified. She dragged a quilt from the bed and wrapped it around her shoulders. Blessings to Serena Fortuna, Jullian's hideaway was not exposed.

I took possession of the remaining chair, poured the wine, and offered her a cup. As she drained her cup, I swirled my own and sniffed it. Though I doubted Malena was a doulon slave, and I didn't think Gildas would risk a second doulon for me in the same day, not after the pile of seeds he'd had me use, I dared not taste it. I did devour the porridge and bread, and when Malena said she had already eaten, I ate hers as well, praying with every bite that nourishment might put some bone in my knees and wit in my skull.

I was not halfway through the second bowl when my body spasmed with a burst of heat that shot me to the verge of ecstasy only to send me earthward again, as if I plum-

meted from Stian's rock Stathero. Breathing hard, trying
not to lose what I had already eaten, I pushed the porridge
away and told myself this was but an echo of the doulon as
I had experienced before when I had used too much nivat.
Keep moving. Hold fast. Men will not *die today because of
your weakness.*

"What's wrong?" said Malena, from her perch on my
clothes chest.

"Naught," I said. "I just— Birthing a new race is a great
responsibility."

I beckoned the girl to my lap. She had refilled her cup,
and a droplet of red hung at the corner of her mouth. It
sickened me.

"A cup of wine can smooth over many a grievance," I
said, and traced my fingers about her face. Her body softened in my arms. When I touched her lips, she nipped my
finger and smirked. A few kisses and I set her cup aside,
gathered her in my arms, and carried her to the bed. She
did not protest at its sagging middle nor did she argue when
I took both her wrists in my left hand and drew them up
over her head, kissing her neck.

"Shhh," I said, as I pulled out one of the lengths of rope
from the side of the bed and tied her wrists. "There are many
variants of pleasuring, Malena."

Her eyes grew very wide. She licked her lips and attempted a smile. Only when I snatched my mask out from
the same hiding place and stuffed it in her mouth did she
understand. She growled and struggled, drumming her feet
on the palliasse, squirming and writhing to get out from
under me or at least get a knee where she could do some
damage. But I had very long legs and arms and the memory
of Gerard to force her still.

Once the rope was snug around her ankles, I tucked
quilts around her. "We're going to have a very quiet evening tonight, chosen one," I said, using spare laces to snug
the mask in her mouth. "I do not sit down with murderers.
I do not lie with them. Holy Mother Samele grant that you
never carry a child—mine or any other man's."

Malena's glare could have poisoned the world ocean
itself.

I detached a little bag from my waist, made sure the

three lonely seeds remained intact, and tucked the bag between her breasts. "I am returning the holy one's gift. Gildas gave them to me and told me that Sila wished me to be a slave as well as a whore. Tell her I prefer not." I trusted her to report my words exactly. I hoped Gildas would be in Sila's presence as she did so.

And then I peered around the end of the bed, met Jullian's very large eyes peeking out from his burrow, and grinned. "Time to go."

Regrettably we dared not take my pureblood cloak with its thick fur lining, so I pinned a plain gray blanket around Jullian's shoulders. The boy gaped at the writhing Malena as I handed him our remaining lengths of rope and grabbed the bag of knucklebones from the clothes chest. I dropped the dice and the armaments game pieces into the bag, as well, tied it at my waist, and pulled on my gloves to hide the last of my gards. Jullian, looking puzzled, pointed at my discarded boots. I shook my head, pressed a finger to my lips, and doused the lamp. At the last moment, I snatched one of the oaken legs of the chair the boy had broken over my head.

I held the door handle for a moment, listening. Only one person stood beyond the door. I hoped it was Jakome. A shudder of warmth raced up my spine, threatening my concentration, but I held tight to my focus. Making sure Jullian stood behind me, I pulled open the door.

"Malena?" growled the man on the dark landing.

Grinning in unseemly pleasure, I triggered the second piece of the lock spell. The lock burst in a shower of yellow sparks, illuminating Jakome's shocked face. Backhand, I slammed my arm into the join of his neck and shoulder. He slumped to his knees, retching, and I whacked the chair leg behind his ear to put him out of his misery for the moment.

Before very long, Jakome was bound as tight as I could draw rope, rolled up in a quilt, and deposited alongside Malena. I tied his orange scarf about my head and his dagger sheath about my thigh. His greasy brown cloak hung from my shoulders. As we pulled the iron door shut behind us, I triggered the last piece of the lock spell, unraveling the obstruction and fusing the broken pins in place.

Someone would have to ram the door from its hinges to release the two.

Jullian started down the steps, but I snagged the neck of his shirt and forced him to sit on the step beside me. "What?" he spluttered.

"We need to listen for a bit to learn the exact time." Given the early nightfall, and the span I'd used to eat and secure the two upstairs, the hour should be very close to sixth watch—poor Stearc's wretched hour. The fortress was filled with muted sounds—barked commands . . . roaring fires . . . the boots and grunts of departing patrols . . . grim laughter. I listened carefully for sounds from Sila's bedchamber. If the map was left unguarded . . .

The mystery of Sila's map grew on me like a boil. What use did Sila find in it? She already had my book and Gildas to take her to Danae sianous. Osriel must come first; to go after the map before securing the prince would be sheer lunacy. I wanted it, though. If I got the chance, I'd take it.

Of a sudden, fire ravished my limbs yet again, then abandoned me chilled and dizzy. The dark stair gaped and deepened in front of me like the maw of hell . . .

"Brother! Wake up!" Hands tapped my cheek and shook my shoulders in company with this anxious whisper.

I blinked. My heart sank. Jullian's scrawny limbs were knotted about my arms and shoulders, preventing me from sliding farther down the stair. My head was jammed uncomfortably against the curved wall and seemed to be several steps lower than my feet. "Ow!" I sat up, untwisting my neck and getting my legs below me.

"You fell . . . just rolled forward off the step."

"Dizzy," I said. "Part of that ugly business earlier. I'll try not to let it happen again. But if I should, just slap me. Kick me. Call me a gatzi spawn and get me moving."

There was no going back. I shook off the worry, took myself back into quiet, and focused on the plan. "I wasn't out for long, was I? They didn't call the watch?"

"Nay. Not yet."

"Sixth watch. All hail the mighty Gehoum!" When it came at last, the call rippled through the fortress, passed from one voice to another, advancing and receding around each level according to the caller's distance from our stair.

"I'm going to treat you like a prisoner," I said, prodding both of us to our feet. "When we reach the prison level, call for your mam to let me know."

When the watch cry circled the level just below us and came round again to the stair, I bellowed my own, "Sixth watch. All hail the mighty Gehoum!" I grabbed the neck of Jullian's borrowed shirt and whispered in his ear, "Fight me." Then I dragged him down the stair as fast as I could, right past the guardsmen changing their posts. "Filthy little beggar," I grumbled. "Ye'll sleep in yer cell again tonight, and every night, if I have my way of it. Don't think to get out of it by whimpering to no one."

I was afraid at first Jullian hadn't understood my instruction, but then he set to pummeling my ribs with such ferocity, I had to wrestle him under my arm, and still he would squirm loose. One of the guards we passed on the downward stair laughed and called after us, "Got a feisty one there!"

No one bothered us as we descended into the depths of the fortress, and Jullian had no need to call for his long-dead mother. The stair ended in a circular pit. Torches burned in sconces on the wall, but their light did not illuminate much past three dark openings in the wall. *Mighty gods . . .*

Two of the openings were blocked by collapsed walls or ceilings. The third opened into a passage, and from it issued a low keening I could scarce define as human, as if all the pain and despair this place had known had been drawn together into one terrible voice. Stearc's voice.

I set Jullian on his feet, but I did not release my hold on him. *To Gram,* I mouthed, and urged him forward, my hand on his shoulder, ready to sweep him out of the way if we encountered trouble.

The passage appeared to be deserted as the boy had said. And as his sketch had shown, his own cell was first inside the doorway. Its position near the exit and its door of open bars had left him better air, if the thick, unwholesome vapors of this place could be named *air*. Torchlight revealed straw and blankets and a rusty lamp mounted on the wall unlit. Perhaps it had been a guardroom at one time.

But the cells farther down the passage—all but two empty, according to Jullian—had no such amenities. I held my arm over my mouth and nose and worked as hard as I knew how to keep focused. My king lay dying in this fetid darkness.

We arrived at a thick iron door similar to the one on my tower room, only with a slot at the bottom for passing food and slops, and an eye-level grate for observing the inmate. A lung-stripping cough and fevered mumbling from inside the cell were sufficient to set me working on the lock.

Crude, warded by only the simplest magic, it succumbed more easily than the one on my tower door. I dragged the heavy door open, hoping the scrape of hinges would not bring guards running. The stench of sickness and rot escaped the cell in a flood, clogging my throat with bile. Torchlight from the passage revealed a dark form curled on the floor of dirt, rubble, and a scattering of moldy straw.

"Close the door all but a crack," I whispered to the boy. "Keep watch."

I ducked through the low door, stepped over a tin cup and an untouched bowl of something manifestly inedible, and dropped to my knees beside the prisoner. He clutched a threadbare blanket around his racked shoulders. The cramped cell felt cold as a tomb.

A cough broke into words. "Milkmaids merry 'neath a cherry blossom tree. Spring comes anon and they're beckonin' me." The chatter of teeth punctuated this rasping singsong.

"Quietly now," I said, and touched his shoulder. He jerked as if I'd stabbed him. The heat of his fever near blistered my hand, even through blanket and glove. "Can you sit up?"

From the far end of the passage, Stearc's formless wail sharpened into a bellow of agony. A shudder rippled Osriel's slender body. "Master's crying in the hall. Kenty's never got the ball. All fall. All fall. All fall . . ."

"He's been that way since they brought him," offered Jullian in a whisper. "Out of his head."

Great gods have mercy. Trying not to twist or strain his joints—Saverian had warned me to be careful—I rolled him onto his back. Osriel was almost unrecognizable in the poor light . . . more than being grimy and unshaven. His eyes were sunken, his neck swollen, his skin cracked and peeling. I fumbled at my waist for Saverian's amber vial and broke the wax seal.

Though the prince's eyes were closed, his unmusical croaking continued. "Grapes die in the fields. Warriors die on their shields. Angels dance in the trees. Gatzi dance—"

"Gram, listen to me." I lifted him up and cradled his lolling head, shook his chin, tugged at his hair. "I've brought you medicine from an old friend of yours. She says you must drink it all, even if it tastes like the dead man's boots."

His fevered mumbling ceased abruptly, and his eyes flicked open as if I'd dropped ice in his trews. He squinted in the feeble light, his gaze running from my fingers to my head. "Valen!"

I almost dropped him from the surprise.

His mind, it appeared, was not so sorely affected by his illness as his body. His hoarse expulsion of my name sent him into a fit of coughing, and his body tried to roll to the side and curl into a knot, as if to escape the force of the spasms. Every movement wrenched an agonized grunt from him. I would have sworn he was laughing, too, or sobbing. Or more likely both at once, as Stearc was screaming again.

Trying to cushion his pain, I held Osriel tight until his paroxysm ceased and his shallow, gasping breaths had slowed. "Let's get the good physician's potion down you." I emptied the vial down his throat, stuffed it back in my pocket, and used my teeth to yank the glove from my free hand. Whispering the words Saverian had said would speed the healing effects of the medicament, I touched his forehead and released magic in a tickling flood. Unfortunately we'd have to move him before the remedy could do its work.

"The boy," he croaked. "He's in this pit, too. And Stearc . . ."

"Jullian's here with us. We're going to take you out of here first. I'll come back for Stearc." Even if the thane had no torturers working on him at the present, I could not carry two injured men at once.

"He can't last much longer. You won't leave him here . . .

no matter what . . ." This was as close to a command as a man in Osriel's state could give.

"I'll do everything I can."

He squeezed his eyes shut and his mouth tight as I helped him to sitting. Shoulders, elbows . . . his every joint felt hot and swollen. "He has held all these wretched days . . . giving them some story. They haven't touched me."

Once he was sitting up on his own, I scraped together what straw and rubble lay within reach.

"Sorry, I need your blanket." I snatched it away, near ripping the worn fabric in half, and tucked it around the pile. With a poorly structured inflation spell, the mound somewhat resembled a body.

As I picked up the glove I'd pulled off to work the magic, Osriel grabbed my wrist and held my glowing hand where he could see. His face tilted up toward mine, unreadable in the blue glow. "Two wonders in a single day," he whispered. "A Harrower gives me a blanket out of mercy, and you appear at my side like Iero's angel. Did I die when I was not paying attention, or have you come to see to that?"

I bent down and spoke in his ear. "*My* grievances will be reckoned later, lord."

Jullian dragged the door open as I lifted Osriel to his feet and pulled his arm over my shoulder. After only a few agonizing steps, it became clear that this was much too slow. His joints could not bear weight.

"Wait," he said, "I can—"

But with one hand holding Osriel's arm, I bent down, caught him behind the knee, and drew his weight across my shoulders. He didn't scream, but the heat of his fever burnt through my clothes. "Is this our reckoning?" he gasped.

"No."

Jullian sped down the passage toward the stair. I hurried after him as quickly as I could, ducking to avoid the stone spans that supported the fortress floors above us. I tried not to jolt, as I could feel Osriel's muffled groans rumbling down my spine.

Stearc's cries had reverted from the rhythmic, escalating madness of a man under the lash to a constant drone. Even if his body survived until I could get back to him, what of his mind?

"Gildas and Grav Radulf are his questioners," said Osriel as we ascended the prison stair. "I hear them pass every day. They laugh." Hearing his bated fury, no promise of heaven would make me step between Osriel and Gildas, should such a meeting ever come to pass. Nor would I be so inclined did Iero himself command me.

I halted Jullian just below the main level, listening for movement both above and below, and trying to recall possible routes across the main hall to the outer wards. Sila's great hall surged with people and noise. We hadn't a chance of making it across to the exit doors. But according to Jullian's description, we had but to slip behind the guards on the landing and through an alley to the left to reach the inner court.

A heated shudder arrowed through my limbs, and the curved walls began to melt like frost wraiths at sunrise. I planted my hand on the grimed stone and forced the walls back into their proper shape. I would *not* falter.

"Two guards at the landing," I whispered to Jullian. "When I poke you, run for the inner court as quietly as you can. I'll follow."

"*I'll* distract the guards," said Osriel through clenched jaw. "Just signal me when."

I jerked my head. Remembering several instances of his unsettling magics, I didn't bother to ask him what he intended. So we crept upward to the juncture of the tower and the keep.

The smoky hall was a patchwork of cook fires and torchlight. The two orange-heads stood on either side of the arch that led into the noisy vastness. But no one guarded the path to the alley. Indeed, no intruder in his right mind would head into such a trap. But a torch blazed on the flanking piers, and the two men stood at such an angle they would surely spot any movement from our position on the stair. They carried bill hooks.

I tapped the prince on the hand and made sure he could see our problem, even from his awkward angle. He squeezed my hand in answer. He emitted a long sigh and the weight of him sagged even heavier on my back. I thought for a moment he'd passed out. Then I felt a low rumbling under my feet . . . or perhaps in my bones. Just enough to make me want to crawl into bed and pull the bedclothes over my head. The two guards, no disciplined warriors, shifted their stance uneasily, glancing over their shoulders. When a shadow darted past them into the hall, they pointed. A second one flew past, and they shouted, but no one paid any attention. The third set them charging into the crowd, yelling warnings, weapons leveled.

"Saints and angels," I hissed. "Could you not have done something a bit more subtle?" Every blighted Harrower in the place was on the alert.

Jullian and I sped through the junction and into the alley, which was not an alley at all, but a short passage that opened into the undercroft of the keep. The cavernous vaults were long emptied, and only broken chimneys and masonry foundations remained of the kitchens and barracks that had once adjoined the bays on the outside walls. Some halfway along, Jullian angled sharply toward the inside walls and up a few steps into the rubble-strewn interior yard—the heart of Fortress Torvo. The place was as dark as a well of pitch.

"Where—?"

I hushed Jullian. Anyone could be watching from the walls that rose starkly on all sides. We crept along the wall that stretched to our left, disturbing several scuttling creatures on our way toward the collapsed privies. I set Jullian feeling along the lower spans of the wall for a grating that might indicate the outlet of a drainage canal. We reached the corner without finding it. The mounds of rubble would disguise any remnant of the canal itself.

I squatted and set Osriel on his feet. Jullian lent his shoulder, while I touched earth and hunted the way with magic.

My bent did not serve well to examine layers of human-built works. Only the passages of people and their purposes made sense of structures. But after sorting through two centuries of death and ugliness in the courtyard, I found an old streambed that coursed this dry slope in the direction that I wanted, and I surmised that the original drainage canal had channeled the stream. We should be standing right on top of it.

Holding tight to my fading hope that I'd not stuck us

in a trap, I reached for Osriel. He stayed my hand when I moved to heft him across my back again, but accepted my arm under his shoulders. Jullian held close on the other side of him. The three of us proceeded slowly across the court to the far end wall, at the spot where the buried canal should pierce the foundation of the great hall. And indeed, set into the wall was a grate identical to those Max had shown me on the outer walls of the fortress—an iron-barred rectangle as high as my knees and twice that wide, and only halfway blocked by stones and dead thornbushes.

I lowered Osriel to the ground and pulled him and Jullian close, draping Jakome's cloak over us to muffle the sound. "I'm going back for Stearc. Max—Prince Bayard's pureblood—told me that this drainage canal tunnels under the fortress and exits outside the walls. But he's got the grates warded, and the moment we breach them, he'll know. I'd like to postpone that as long as possible, as I'd rather not end up in Bayard's hands after getting out of Sila's, so I'm going to leave you here. A certain touch on opposing corners will unlock the grates, if you need to get out before I return. Do you understand, Gram? Can you manage that much?"

The prince nodded. His magic would suffice.

"Good. Voushanti will be waiting for us outside the walls, off to the right. Give me an hour past seventh watch. No more. And mind your voices. These upper walls open into occupied chambers."

"Iero's grace," whispered Jullian. "I'll keep watch so Gram can rest."

I smiled and ruffled his hair. He hated that.

A hand squeezed my aching shoulder, then three fingers touched my cheek in the manner of a king to his knight. Osriel's hand seemed steadier and less fevered than earlier. My hopes crept higher. As I slunk away, I let magic flow into three whispered words, charging them with power to reach beyond the fortress. *Dead man. Parley.*

Moments later, I heard the response. *Bluejay. Parley.* Voushanti and his bought fighters would not attack the fortress, but would watch for us to emerge from the drainage canal.

The return across the courtyard seemed interminable.

I dared not hurry, lest some scuffing or stumble alert a watcher in one of the chambers that overlooked the yard. It was easier to walk quietly without boots, though the hose tied over my feet were getting a bit ragged. But eventually I reached the passage and the undercroft, and I raced back to the tower.

The hall remained in an uproar. A crowd of orange-heads, many with torches, centered on a few men arguing. Only one guard had returned to the tower stair. He shifted nervously, starting at every shout from the conflict in the hall, frequently spinning around to stare behind him, approximately in my direction. From the bag at my waist, I pulled one of the knucklebones and lofted it into the hall behind his back. He darted forward a few steps, and I slipped behind him and took the downward stairs three at a time.

I flattened my back to the wall beside the doorway to the prison passage. The torture session was ended, and the slow pacing of a single guard echoed in the passage. Praise be to Serena Fortuna, they seemed not to have discovered their missing prisoner.

The guard's footsteps paused. Soft fumbling noises came from just beyond the doorway, and then a trickle of water that grew into a stream. An opportunity not to be missed.

I took him from behind with angled blows to his neck. He dropped to his knees. Reaching around, I slammed a sidearm blow to his chest. My forearm glanced up to his throat, sending him to the floor clutching his throat and wheezing like a bellows. An elbow to the back of his neck stopped his clutching and wheezing.

Only after I had the scraggly fellow unconscious in his pool of piss did I remember Jakome's dagger strapped to my thigh. It had been a very long time since I'd possessed a weapon.

Had I been sure he'd caused Stearc's screams, I might have slit his throat and thought it justice. But it occurred to me that this might be the very guard who had shown a sick prisoner the mercy of a blanket. I was no judge. So I tied his hands with his orange scarf, emptied Saverian's vial of yellow broom into him, and tucked him under the blanket in Osriel's cell. Whenever he woke he would be so busy puking, he'd not be able to raise the alarm. I snatched up his ragged cloak and flop-brimmed hat, grabbed one of the torches, and ran for Stearc.

They hadn't bothered to lock the door at the end of the passage. The chamber was no cell, but a charnel house. Yet neither the implements on the walls nor the grotesque evidence of horrors held my gaze. In chains suspended from the roof beam hung the remnants of a man. The once powerful body of the Thane of Erasku had been purposefully destroyed by whips, murderously precise knife and ax work, and cautery irons. He had no feet. No nose. No ears. No fingers on his right hand, and only three remaining on his left. Had I not known who was held here, I could never have identified him as the proud warrior who believed in the honor of learning as much as he believed in the honor of his sword. The low despairing moan that seeped from his slack mouth might have been a threnody for the world's reason.

"Stearc, it's Valen come to help you," I said, throttling my rage. Using a length of timber, I scraped away the filth underneath him and spread out the guard's cloak.

"Valen?"

"I'm going to get you down."

"No . . . no . . . no . . . no," he rasped. "Must not falter. Will not." Blood bubbled from his lips.

"You've held long enough, Thane. They've not touched him." With my brutish lock spell, I burst his manacles and lowered him to the floor.

He cried out, little more than an animal's bleat. The bloody claw that was his left hand gripped my arm with desperate strength. "He is safe?"

"He will be with Voushanti and Saverian within the hour." Avoiding his dreadful wounds as best I could, I took Stearc's face in my hands, making sure his eyes met mine. "I'm going to take you to him, Stearc. You will not die in this vile place, but in the shelter of your lord."

Die he would. The instinct that had ever spoken to me of death and life told me clearly. But anyone with eyes must understand that will alone drove Stearc's heart and lungs.

"No!" His hand pawed at me, and he came near rising from the ground. "Don't let him— I honor him above all

men. My king. But I would not meet the Ferryman blind."
Terror radiated from him like fever. "I would not be
Voushanti."

How could I console such fear? I saw no means for Osriel to work his dreadful rites in Torvo's inner courtyard.
But that was poor assurance for a man who had spent his
last reserves of courage fifty times over. The prince might
have other means to capture souls.

"All right, then." Which set me a dilemma. I could not
leave Stearc living. "I would do you a last service, Thane.
Tell me what you want."

"A blade." He opened his bloody palm, rock steady. In
the command I heard a trace of his old accusations. He had
ever believed me a coward.

I gave him Jakome's dagger and wrapped his bloody
fingers around the hilt. Then I spoke clearly so he could
not mistake. "I will tell your king and your daughter only
of courage, lord, not of horror. The lighthouse will stand.
Teneamus."

He jerked his head. "For House Erasku," he whispered.
"For Evanore, for Navronne . . . *teneamus.*"

I took off my glove and laid my hand on his forehead,
determined Stearc would not die alone. His existence comprised naught but shadings of mortal agony . . . a map in
which every road led but to another shock or scouring,
and every border marked but new violation. My part in his
pain, shared through my bent and the gards on my hand,
ended mercifully fast.

Gripping the dagger with the remaining fingers of his
left hand, he used the palm of his mutilated right hand to
plunge the blade into his throat. Blood spurted from the
wound. His hands dropped away.

I stayed with him, and when the face of the world had
faded to naught but cold and gray, I whispered in his ear,
"Know this, too, warrior of Evanore; the blood of noble
Caedmon mingles even now with the blood of House
Erasku. Your beloved daughter carries Caedmon's heir.
And I vow upon the soul of our holy abbot that I will see
them both safe until the end of days."

The revelation did not violate my vow to Elene, for I
told her secret only to a dead man. But I believed Stearc

heard me, for his eyes grew fierce and bright just before the life went out of them.

I hung him from his chains again and removed all evidence of my coming. Let the butchers believe Iero's angels had released him from his pain.

Chapter 26

"**S**eventh watch! All honor to the Gehoum!"

As the call caromed through the fortress, I crouched on the prison stair at the verge of the main level. This was taking much too long. At any moment a replacement would be coming down to relieve the guard who lay vomiting in Osriel's cell. But a pair of cursed orange-heads stood just in front of me, one blocking the doorway to the great hall, one blocking the doorway of the alley to the inner court. Neither clattering knucklebones nor a shower of armament pebbles had distracted them. I had been hoping they would just go away. To get up to the gallery and Sila's chamber, I would have to run between them.

Forced to stillness, I had grown even more determined to take the map. I tottered on the verge of understanding. My glimpse of the Sentinel Oak had told me the map held two layers of information—perhaps that was what Gildas could not see. Sila was using the map in her campaign to squeeze the long-lived from their hiding places so that she could mingle Danae blood with Aurellian and Navron bloodlines. Something in the map would tell me her next move or which boundaries she thought to break. Though I regretted every moment's delay in getting Osriel free, I had to take the chance. The map could be the key to everything, and I had no intention of ever returning to this fortress of horrors.

The echoed call of the watch was slowing. Replacements

had arrived for the two guards. I had to move. I seated the guard's flop-brimmed hat on my head. Then I pelted up the stair as if newly come from the depths, sweeping Jakome's brown cloak about my shoulders and calling to the two guards, "Tell Nikred I couldn't wait for his lazy ass to show. I'm to relieve Jakome at the tower for the night."

The two grunted assent and turned back to their replacements, while I raced up the stair to the gallery. One torch burned outside Sila Diaglou's chamber, but no guard was posted. Soft light leaked around the door curtain. I held my breath and listened. One person inside, breathing softly.

I drew the knife, pulled back the edge of the curtain, and peered inside. Torches blazed on either side of the map. Ronila sat in front of it, her chin propped on her walking stick. Nothing for it but to slip inside, keeping my back against the wall.

"You might as well come in, abomination," she said, not even shifting her gaze from the map.

Of course, Ronila would have skills like mine. Once I had confirmed that no one else was in the room, I strolled over to the map, keeping the knife under my cloak. "Did you know my father, Ronila?"

"I suppose you deem yourself wise." Never had I heard amusement that tasted so much of gall and rancid life. She cocked her head at the map. "The answer is no. Cartamandua first came to Aeginea long after I had left. He is talented, I hear—talented at finding places he should not. As you are."

"He *was*," I said, staring at the map, trying to gauge its secret. Knotted cords looped from bolts in the wall through three bound eyelets sewn into the map's upper edge. Three strokes of the knife would take it down. "The Danae took his mind for a failed promise."

"Pah!" She blew a note of disgust. "The long-lived cannot admit they are as crippled as I am. Mixed blood will be *your* doom as it has been mine, abomination."

"You know not even the half of it, Lady Scourge." Though, in truth, I'd always thought the *blood* of my erstwhile mother's prophecy meant I'd die in battle or at least in a fight. I'd never considered it might signify heritage ... bloodlines ... family. Even queasier than usual at recalling the divination, I shoved the annoying hat backward and scratched my head. "Do *our* kind see the future? I've not been taught that skill."

"*I* see the future," she said. "In the hour he broke me, I told Stian what I planned. He didn't believe a crippled halfbreed girl could bring them down. But when he feels the world die, he will confess it at last. When he sees Tuari Archon himself lapping from my hand, he will admit my power, and I will see Stian Human-friend stand alone in the ruin of his making. Was it the proud son—the most arrogant of an arrogant race—who marked you or the old cat himself?"

"You made Sila a perfect tool for your vengeance," I said, unwilling to yield even so small an answer. "You hate the Danae because they did not allow you to be one of them; you especially hate the archon because Tuari killed your mother. You hate Stian because, out of fear for the Canon, he crippled you, and because he allowed Eodward and Picus to live in Aeginea, so that a human man became your temptation. You loathe humankind because it was humans who sullied your blood, and you hate both Eodward and the Karish god, because they stole Picus's affections that you believed should be yours alone. But I don't understand your particular antipathy for purebloods. That mystifies me."

She snickered at that. "My daughter, Sila's mother, was more Dané than human. Such grace ... such beauty ... When she danced in my kitchen, she made Stian's daughter, Clyste, look as a stick. The Aurellians ruled this benighted land ... and one of their knights rode through my village when Tresila was but thirteen. He dragged her to their pleasure house, forced her to service his common soldiers and Navron slaveys. Not the purebloods, though. She was not perfect enough to break their bloodlines. Thirty years they kept her a slave."

"But she birthed a child ..."

"You've yet much to learn of your Danae kin. Even halfbreed females can choose to conceive or not. One of Eodward's soldiers rescued Tresila from the Aurellian pleasure house. In gratitude ... in *gratitude* ... she gave him a child." Her tongue near curled with her bile. "The slut died bearing Sila. That's as well, as I would have killed her for it, as I did the cur who plowed her. You cannot measure my hatred for this world. Sila merely wishes no blot of green to remain on this map, but *my* vengeance will be sated only in the hour humankind reaps eternal desolation and no Danae gard lights the world's darkness."

No blot of green . . . I caught my breath and spun to look at the map again. This map was no ordinary fiché, where the significance lay in written symbols and proportionate distances, nor was it a grousherre, where disproportionately sized features demonstrated the mapmaker's judgment of relative importance. In this map the shifting colors told the story. My eyes raced across the expanse. The lands about Gillarine gleamed ocher. The meadow near Elanus yet green. The bogs—Moth's sianou—green. Kol's western sea and its bordering shores green. The tangled waste of Mellune Forest ocher. Sianous—living or dead.

When a sianou was lost, the Danae could no longer remember it. Sila wanted to force them out of their hiding places, out of their sianous and into human lands. She wanted them to forget Aeginea completely and merge with humankind. What if Janus had made this map to show the Danae the lands they had forgotten, so that Kol and the others could dance and reclaim those lands . . . repair the broken Canon . . . repair the broken world? Gods, I was looking at the answer!

Excitement surged through flesh and bone as I reached up and sliced through the first cord holding the map. "I'm sorry for all that happened to you, Ronila. Sorrier for what you did to your granddaughter, a child who did not deserve to be warped for your vengeance. But Sila's rapine cannot be allowed to succeed—nor can yours."

The second supporting rope at the opposite corner split like dry wood at the touch of the knife. Rolling up the bottom edge of the map with my left hand, I reached for the third cord.

Ronila lunged from her chair, grabbed one of the torches, and flung it at me. As the old woman toppled to the floor, bellowing with spiteful laughter, the ancient parchment exploded into fire like nitre powder.

"No!" I bellowed. I dropped the rolled map, and it crashed to the floor. Using hands . . . feet . . . cloak . . . I tried to smother the spreading fire. But sparks set my cloak ablaze, and searing heat drove me backward. The flames chased charring blackness across the lustrous colors with the speed of shooting stars.

The woven curtain behind me roared into flame. Shouts and footsteps rang from the gallery. Ronila lay in a rumpled heap. "You'd best go quickly, abomination," she said, waving me off with a hand streaked with azure. "My granddaughter will flay you."

Blazing ash floated in the air. Acrid smoke billowed from blackened, smoldering curls of vellum, my hope vaporizing with it. With every breath I wanted to crush the cackling crone, but I dared not compromise those awaiting me. I had no such strength as Stearc. I ran.

Whether it was only the smoke from the gallery or someone had discovered the missing prisoners or the fused lock on my tower cell, the stair was swarming with Harrowers. "The gallery chamber's afire!" I shouted when someone barred my way. And when a rough hand detained me and its owner snarled, "Who are you? I saw you go up . . ." I shoved him against the wall and said, "I'm Jakome's brother. Where is he?" Then I grabbed a woman warrior and another man and dispatched them to the "east tower," hoping such a thing existed, and the hunt for strangers quickly became the hunt for Jakome.

My hands were scorched and blistered, my gards peeking through the charred tatters of my gloves. I tucked my hands beneath my half-burnt cloak.

"Grandam!" Sila Diaglou raced past me, Gildas close on her heels. I pressed my back to the wall and ducked my head so that the flop-brimmed hat shadowed my face. Only the tether of Osriel's illness kept me from plunging my knife into one or the other of them; he might need me to get free. I galloped downward just as Sila screamed, "That was Magnus! The one in the hat! Take him!"

I dodged down the prison-level stair, just far enough to discard the hat. Then I raced upward again, tossing two knucklebones over my shoulder, and commanded two men to check on the clattering noise. The moment the two were out of sight, I bolted for the alley. The hose covering my feet, soggy with the guard's piss and Stearc's blood, disintegrated as I sped through the voluminous undercrofts. When I reached the arch into the inner courtyard, I paused long enough to rip them off before they tripped me. I draped the scorched remnants of the cloak over my head, so that at least my pale face would not be visible to those above. I had to hope it would suffice to block any view of my blue-streaked feet as well. Then I moved.

The temptation to dash through the yard straight to Jullian and Osriel nearly overwhelmed me. But the arrow loops on the second level were bright with firelight, and the fortress exploding with shouts. I crept softly, silently through the rubble.

I was halfway across the yard, angling toward the corner, when footsteps and voices echoed in the undercroft behind me. "I'm sure I saw a fellow run this way. Same one as came up the stair."

I dropped to the ground and held still under the ragged cloak, not even daring to look around to see if they followed me. Face buried in the dirt, I scrabbled for some spell that might give us time to get away, but I had naught in my bags of tricks that might deter a determined pursuit. *Stupid . . . cocky . . . arrogant . . .* Thinking I could get away with this. Allowing myself to be distracted and beaten by a bitter hag. Disappointment gnawed at my gut like rats.

"None would come in here. There's no way out but this." Though the sharp-voiced woman kept her excitement tight-reined, the close walls amplified her every word and footstep. I scarce breathed.

"Sila said to search everywhere."

"She'll tear every stone down before he gets away."

At least three of them . . . curse the luck. Light danced on the broken paving that pressed my cheek. I could smell the hot resin of the torches. One step in my direction and I would have to run.

"Over there, Braut! Summat's at the wall!" The three raced past me toward the north wall and the canal and my friends.

I leaped up, shouting, "Here, you damnable fools!"

They stopped, and turned my way, then looked back to the wall, where a shadow mimed a running man—though none of us were running.

"What is it?" They were pointing at me, and I realized the burnt cloak remained on the ground and the gards on my arms and feet glowed the hue of summer midnight. "Where's the other?"

As their resolution wavered, a great explosive crack shot dust and rubble from the wall, and in a roaring avalanche the remainder of the privies crashed down, pulling much of the standing north wall down with it. Osriel . . .

The three Harrowers retreated screaming—more in fear than pain. Had they paused two steps closer to the wall, the masonry would lie atop their heads. And I was no more than ten paces farther away. I leaped and dodged the debris, grateful my half-Danae eyes could penetrate the clouds of dust that fogged the yard.

"Glad I didn't choose to hug the wall," I said, as I skidded into the corner where Jullian and Osriel waited. "Now we move. Even *that* display won't hold Sila for long."

Jullian quaked like a spring leaf, his mouth opening and closing soundlessly as he gaped at the man he knew as quiet, studious Gram.

Osriel huddled in the blanket Jullian had given him, his head resting heavy against the grate, as if he had expended every remaining portion of his strength. But his dark eyes blinked open when I knelt beside him. "Stearc?" he said.

My elation at the moment's reprieve sank quickly under the burden of rage and disappointment. "I'm sorry, lord. He gave everything."

Jullian choked back a cry.

We had no time for grief. The two of them had wisely cleared the rocks and weeds away from the grate. I touched its opposing corners, as Max had instructed, and fed magic to the spell that vibrated in the iron bars. A pop and hiss and the grate flopped forward into a very dark hole.

"Jullian first, then me, so I can help you through," I said to Osriel, who had rolled forward onto all fours. He nodded without speaking, his head drooping between his quivering shoulders.

I reached out to the boy, but he scrambled backward. "*Aegis Ieri,*" he whispered, his head shifting frantically between Osriel and my glowing hand.

"You've no need of Iero's shield, Jullian," I said, as calmly as I could, considering my own heart clattered like hail-stones on a slate roof. "This was but magic—considerable magic, to be sure. Gram has hidden skills—inherited from his mother, as my talents and my strange appearance are inherited from my parents. Whatever else he may be, he is still the good man you know as Gram." It was the argument I used with myself every hour.

"I thought I knew *Gildas*," said the boy.

"Indeed Gildas fooled us all," I said. "But you know me, and I promised to protect you and get you out of here. We must go *now*."

Had any man or woman I knew committed such a feat of bravery as Jullian when he crawled into that blackness under Fortress Torvo with Osriel and me? I felt humbled. And very anxious. This was Max's route. Once I'd crawled into the hole myself and helped Osriel through, I set the grate back into the hole. It seated with a satisfying *snick*. I wondered if the unlocking spell worked from the back. In any case, I dared not leave it open.

After a brief attempt to confirm the route with my own skills—straight on, from what I could tell—I took the lead. Osriel tried to conjure us a light, but his hands were shaking with exhaustion. "Perhaps later," he whispered hoarsely.

Sighing with inevitability, I removed the rest of my clothes, allowing my gards to provide us soft illumination approximately the hue of cornflowers.

Osriel's eyes traveled my gards; then he turned away, unable to mask the beginnings of a smile.

Jullian needed a bit more reassurance after that. I pointed out Stian's mark on my arm and the sea creatures that seemed to have taken up residence on my chest, and asked if any demon he could imagine would have cats and fish among their markings.

He heaved a great breath and pronounced his rueful verdict. "I suppose no immortal demon would have bothered eating Harrower porridge either."

Even Osriel chuckled at that, though it set him coughing again.

We all needed something to take our mind off the place we traveled. The only thing worse than seeing the soured black slime we had to crawl through was smelling it. Osriel retched after every coughing fit. I tried not to inhale at all. Jullian vomited when he encountered a more solid lump that had at some time been a hound ... or perhaps a pig. None of us complained that it was winter. To make this passage in the heat would have been insupportable.

"My mother was not who I thought," I said to Jullian, hoping to mask the sounds of scuttering rats and the ominous creaks and groans from the masonry above us. Max must have enjoyed the thought of me enduring this place. "Nor was my father, as it happens, but it is my mother's race who display such marks as these. Her kind must go through four changes as they grow ..."

By the time I had told them a bit about my uncle and tide pools and distressed rocks, a whiff of fresher air floated amid the fetid murk. I quickly hushed Jullian's assault of questions and handed him my bundle of filthy clothes.

I crept forward the few quercae to the grate. Voices carried clearly through the frosty night, issuing crisp orders. Clanks and creaks were weapons being shifted in their owners' grasp. Sila kept more experienced men on the gates than on the interior watch. I hoped their eyes were focused outward.

As far as I could tell, the bailey itself was deserted. The drainage canal was blocked by rubble, which left us either the more exposed route straight across the bailey to the grate in the outer wall or a series of shorter jaunts between gallows and stocks and prison cages. For the time, Osriel's magic was spent. We could not depend on his power to hide us.

Still undecided, I touched the corners of the warded grate and quickened its unlocking spell. The grate fell smoothly into my hands. So far, Max's route had worked perfectly. But he would never trust me to show up with Gildas at our rendezvous three streets away. Warned by his wards that we were coming out, he would be waiting, and he would insist on knowing everything about my companions. Best go for speed.

"Only two bits still to go," I said when I returned to my companions. "Straight across the bailey and through another grate will take us under the outer wall. Do you need me to carry you, Gram? This is no time for pride. We must be quick."

"Saverian is very good at potion making," said the prince, already sounding stronger than he had earlier. "Just don't ask me to conjure a rat's squeak along the way. Hadn't you best take this and cover up? My attire is less . . . conspicuous . . . than yours."

I stayed his hand before he could shed the filthy blanket. "I—uh—hear better when I'm like this," I said. "The blanket's not big enough to hide all of me anyway. When you see I'm across with no disturbance, come after. Once we're outside the walls, the nearest cover will be to the right. Go as fast as you can and stay low. I'm hoping that only friends will be waiting, but . . ." I shrugged.

We moved to the hole. One careful listening revealed no change; a careful observation revealed no eyes turned inward from the walls. I crawled through and dashed across the bailey. My bare feet made no sound, and I caught the third grate as it toppled inward, lowering it carefully into the hollow under the wall. I scuttered through and across the blessedly short distance to the outermost grate, then quickened its spell. A glance beyond the wall showed me naught but night in Riie Doloure. I left the grate leaning against its hole and crawled back the way I'd come.

The two hunched forms moved steadily across the bailey in my direction, not invisible but dark and quiet. They had crossed three quarters of the distance when the doors of the great hall burst open, and torchlight flooded the steps. A patrol of ten Harrowers emerged and ran for the gates. More men took positions on the steps and spread slowly outward, approaching the gallows platform, searching on and underneath it.

Osriel and Jullian had flattened themselves to the ground at the first disturbance and blended well into the mottled landscape of rubble and refuse. But if they remained where they were, the searchers would surely find them. I considered ten different plans and discarded them as quickly. If I set one foot out of the hole to distract the hunters, every eye would be on me. Osriel and Jullian might reach the tunnel, but I never would.

Under, through, or over a wall, thieves and lovers learn

them all. The tavern reel's chorus defined my dilemma. There would be no way *through* a gate so well guarded, and no way to get back to the tunnel and *under* the wall faster than Harrowers could be outside it waiting for me. Which left *over* . . .

My stomach lurched. I closed my eyes and recalled the layout of the bailey as I'd seen it from the inside. The stair to the wall walk was some halfway between my position and the gates. No time to think. No time to doubt. *Holy Erdru, god of drunkards and madmen, preserve your faithful servant.*

I crawled out of the hole and darted up and over the wooden platform where Sila's judges had mandated death and mayhem, crouching low and putting as much distance as possible between me and the open grate in the corner. I was halfway to the gallows when they spotted me.

"Look!" Twenty voices at once screamed out. Everything seemed to stop for that moment, just as on the day Voushanti and I had stormed this same gallows under the shield of Osriel's enchantment to rescue Brother Victor. I spun in place. Searchers backed away. Some weapons clanked to the ground—not all, sadly.

Murmurings rose through the hush. *Sorcery! Ghost! Spirit!*

Stubbing my toes on broken planks and mounds of crusted snow, ignoring splinters that pierced my blistered hands, I climbed up onto the gallows. I quickened my simplest, crudest lock spell and touched the chains on the bloodstained drawing frame, where Luviar had been splayed and gutted like a boar. The iron shattered in a shower of red sparks. And then I did the same to the hinges on the gallows traps.

Angel! Guardian!

I dared not look to the corner. How long would it take for Osriel and Jullian to understand and move?

Somewhere behind the glaring torches, a snapped order imposed discipline. Boots crept toward me from the direction of the gates. I gripped a post, swung around it, and leaped off the platform, mustering what grace I could so as not to eternally sully all legends of the Danae. I landed on the balls of my feet with only moderate jarring of spine and limbs. Then I sprinted for the stair to the walls.

"Magnus!" Sila cried from the doors. "You will not escape! Your destiny lies with me!"

I had no breath to answer as I took the stairs three at a time. No wit to create some memorable farewell. I was too busy trying to remember what Kol had told me. *Drive thy spirit upward with the leap. Hold it firm and soaring. It is will that counters the forces that draw us to earth.*

For my king and my friend, I thought as I topped the stair and bounded across the wall walk with ten Harrowers charging from each flank. *Stearc died to keep Osriel safe.*

But it was not such noble thoughts that drove my spirit upward as I leaped from the wall of Fortress Torvo, or held it firm and soaring as I fell toward earth, but the remembrance of my uncle's healing grace as he danced, and a stubborn will that Ronila's malignancy would not destroy the beauty he had wrought.

Chapter 27

⤜——————⤛

I landed on one foot and one knee. Breathless. Not with fear, though I would have sworn I'd left my stomach on Torvo's wall. Not with pain, though grit and gravel and all manner of foulness had most uncomfortably embedded themselves in my knee. Exhilaration starved my lungs. I felt as if angels had borne me on their wings, as if I had lived my life in a cave and only now had glimpsed my first sunrise.

But four men with swords pelted toward me from the gates, Torvo's portcullis ground upward with a troop of Harrowers ready to burst from behind it, and five well-armed riders in Registry colors blockaded Riie Doloure. Their commander sat astride a very large bay, perhaps ten paces from me. Only my conviction that he would be waiting kept my eyes from sliding away from him. Max was a master at obscuré spells.

I could not but grin when I saw his face illumined by Torvo's torches. Not even when we were boys had I seen Max completely unmasked—which had naught to do with the pureblood silk that clung to half his face.

"Balls enough?" I called across the distance between us, opening my arms.

A slow grin broke through his awe. "Balls enough, little— Little bastard. Did you accomplish whatever you came here for?"

"Beware of Jakome," I said, grinning back at him. I would not take his bait. "He's false. But I've left you clean, do you but go now. If these Harrowers identify you . . . take my word, they *will* be out of humor."

Whether or not he believed me, he must have decided he could work no more advantage from the situation. Laughing robustly, he wheeled his mount and rejoined his men. With a snapped command of dismissal, they vanished into the city. I sprinted back toward the hole in Torvo's wall.

"Dead man!" I bellowed, quite unnecessarily, for Voushanti and a handful of leather-clad irregulars were already swarming out of the charred ruin of a tenement and inserting themselves between me and the oncoming Harrowers. Jullian was helping Osriel away from the wall. Between the two of us, we half carried, half dragged him toward the ruin where Voushanti had been waiting.

My back itched. I prayed that Sila had made it clear she wanted me alive. Bowmen on fortress walls in a night action could get twitchy fingers, and a glowing blue rock on a man's back would make a fine target.

Battle erupted behind us. Weapons clanged and shouts of bravado warped quickly into cries of anguish as we ducked under a fallen beam and into the blackened skeleton of a house.

Half of a blackened wall leaned crazily against a snow-clogged hearth. With my gards and the faint wash of torch-light from the fortress the only light, the mottled floor was tricky going. Pools of sooty slush made it difficult to distinguish pits where foundation stones had been carted away. Bundles of unburnt straw lay around the place, as if someone was trying to blot up the slush. The ruin reeked of lamp oil.

"This way!" A pale light bloomed at the back of the ruin, where a stone stair led downward. "Mother of Night, Riel! And Thane Stearc?" She must have read our faces. "Ah, a pestilence on these vermin."

Before we could blink, Saverian had Osriel seated on a bit of broken wall, draining vials of two different potions, Jullian wrapping the prince and himself in dry cloaks, and me dispatched to find us a way out. The physician's practical fury seemed to cleanse the air of Ronila's madness like a taste of fresh limes cleanses the palate. "Make it fast, Valen."

I hurried down the broken steps into the ancient lane

that had been uncovered two months ago by the raging fires of a Harrower mob. The noise of the fighting fell away quickly. The lane cut across a hillside, and its builders had installed high stone walls to hold back the dirt. But the stone houses that had lined the lane had vanished long before I was born, and the fires had burned off the vegetation that held the hill stable. Now mud had slumped down from the hillside, and I couldn't find the place I was looking for . . . a courtyard . . . a way out . . .

The intoxication of my leap from the walls deserted me, leaving a profound uneasiness in its wake. I felt cold, light-headed. The place, the night . . . everything felt wrong. I needed to get back. Voushanti and his men were sorely outnumbered.

In desperation, I knelt and touched the frozen mud, pushing magic through exhaustion and confusion. And there in front of me lay a silver path. A Dané had once walked here. More than one, perhaps, for just ahead lay a knot of silver—not an unruly tangle, but layer upon layer of loops and windings as Kol laid down when he danced. In the center of the knot grew a winter-bare apple tree, vibrant with life and health here in the midst of a city gone mad. I should have guessed this was a Dané sianou when I'd first found it, but I'd not known how to look.

Racing back toward the others, I gave the final signal. *Dead man. Harvest.* Voushanti would retreat to the ruined tenement to join us. *Bluejay. Harvest.*

The physician, the prince, and the boy crouched in the lane behind a fallen beam. Osriel held a decrepit sword, while Saverian hefted a rusty ax—perhaps better were hard to come by in the city. Jullian seemed to be their rear guard and sagged in relief at the sight of me, lowering a dagger half the length of his arm. The combat was deafening and very close.

Voushanti's bellow thundered through the din. "Fall back! To me! To me!"

"I've found the way out," I said, "or would you three prefer to stay here and fight?"

Osriel conceded me only a glance. "Saverian has propped me up to scare off Harrower crows," he said with a hint of laughter. "But altogether, I'd prefer a bed."

"As soon as Voushanti steps under the beam, we can go," said Saverian, dropping her ax. "Wait here and be ready." She ran up the steps into the ruined house.

"Hold on!" I bolted after her. "Are you mad?"

She ignored me as first one and then another of Voushanti's exhausted fighters yelled *haven* and stumbled through the crossed beams. Four ... five ... six of them ... and then Voushanti himself burst through. "Now, mage!" snapped the warrior.

As Voushanti twisted and skewered the Harrower who tried to follow him inside, Saverian touched the bundles of straw nearest the opening. Green flames exploded from the bundles, consuming another attacker, who stumbled screaming over his dead comrade. The physician ran from one bundle to the next until the entire front of the ruin was walled in flame taller than my head. Only one of Voushanti's goggle-eyed mercenaries stood his ground long enough to catch the bag Saverian tossed him. Payment in hand, he followed his comrades straight up the steep hillside behind the ruined house and into the night.

"Time to go," said Saverian, as Voushanti hacked at another man who braved the flames. "The fire won't hold them long."

Voushanti held the doorway until we were down the steps, lining the opening with dead and screaming wounded.

"Now, dead man!" I yelled over the roar of the flames. "Stay with me!"

As I led them down the ancient lane, I had a vague impression of Voushanti descending the steps in one jump and green flames exploding behind him. Shoving the roused fear and anxieties of battle aside, I sought clarity and memory enough to make the shift. A small courtyard ... healthy growth bared by winter ... high walls and the knee-high ring of stones in the center ... a pool of sustaining life—here an apple tree rooted deep in the hillside, there a well rooted deep in a mountain ... air touched with winter and smoke, here from straw burning to preserve valuable lives, there from hearth fires and kitchens ...

One by one, my charges hurried into the apple court, as I had named the strange little lane in Palinur—Jullian, fiercely determined; Osriel, flushed and wheezing; Saverian batting sparks from her jupon; and then Voushanti, blood-splattered and facing backward. From the smoke behind us burst another figure, a giant-sized warrior wearing a ragged cloak, dented helm, and orange badge.

When Voushanti took him down with an ax to his thigh, the Harrower bled his life onto the winter grass of the well yard at Renna, some two hundred quellae south of Fortress Torvo. It was snowing.

Jullian, who had spun around to watch Voushanti dispatch the Harrower, bumped into me when I halted at the stone circle of the well. I caught his arm before he stumbled over my feet and stuck me or himself with his dagger. "Easy, lad. I don't think any others can follow us here."

The mud-drowned lane, eerie flames, and rampaging Harrowers had vanished. Behind Voushanti stretched a colonnade fronting the cold inner wall of Renna's keep. The boy heaved a quivering sigh as he looked up at me. "Magic again?"

I squatted beside him and held out my arm in parallel with my glowing thighs. "Aye. It's one thing these are good for. You'll note that Gram is fairly well astonished, too."

Osriel spun so quickly with his neck craned up at Renna's heights that Saverian stood ready to catch him should he topple. "Well done," said the prince. "Oh, very well done, Valen."

Jullian leaned his head to my ear. "He's not just *Gram*, is he? All three of you call him lord. And he brought down that wall."

"He *is* Gram, but no, not *just* Gram. By now you've surely guessed his true name."

The boy acknowledged without words, his face a pale blur in the night.

"You've no need to be afraid, Jullian." I made no effort to keep my voice down. "Prince Osriel has found it necessary to keep people fearful of him . . . to protect himself and our cabal and his people here in Evanore. Abbot Luviar was once his tutor."

But, of course, there *was* ample reason to be afraid of Osriel, not for Jullian alone, but for all of us together. Grateful as I was to stand in Renna's shelter instead of Sila

Diaglou's tower, much as my legs felt like clay, my back wrenched, and my feet battered, my night's work could not be declared finished.

"And Voushanti"—Osriel gripped the mardane's shoulder and inspected him as if seeking the source of the blood that stained Voushanti's hauberk and leathers—"a magnificently executed retrieval. Your valor and your skill in arms are unmatched." His voice dropped a little. "You are well, Mardane? Saverian took care of you?"

"I am whole for now, my lord. The physician did as you commanded. I am bound to the sorcerer."

"To *Valen*?" On any other night, I might have missed the hint of dismay in Osriel's voice. He masked it quickly by a gallant bow in Saverian's direction. "And *your* skills, physician ... and friend ... remain unmatched and irreplaceable. What greater wonder can I demonstrate to these present than walking up yonder stair without reclining on Valen's shoulders or weighting my noble companion Jullian's arm?"

"Your physician prescribes food, wine, bath, and bed," said Saverian with no hint of sentiment, as she shoved her straggling hair away from her soot-smudged face.

"I must see Elene first," said Osriel, his momentary lightness shed like an unwanted cloak. "Perhaps you would accompany me, Valen, and tell us what you can of Stearc's end."

Ah, Mother Samele embrace Elene, who must soon be torn asunder by sorrow and relief ... and all the questions and fears this prince held for her. Her plight only hardened the resolution grown solid in my gut.

"I will, of course, lord," I said, standing up, while keeping a hand on Jullian's shoulder. "But I might suggest we not wake her to such ill news before I've had a chance to discuss the matter with you. Saverian, as the prince has downed multiple vials of your marvelous elixirs, would it compromise him too severely to speak with me for a little?"

She raised her eyebrows and twisted her mouth in her ironical fashion that illumined her awkward features with life and wit. "As Lord Osriel will tell you himself, I am *not* his keeper. He knows my recommendations and will likely do with them as he always has."

She rummaged in a pouch at her waist and tossed me another vial. Then she held out her hand to the boy at my side, let her magelight swell to a soft ivory where he could see it glowing from her fingers, and smiled in a way that instantly dispatched his awe. "Come, noble Jullian. You, at least, will enjoy what I have to offer in the way of food and bed. Prince Osriel has told me a great deal about you these past few years. He lives in awe of your scholarship . . ."

As the woman and boy headed for the stair at the corner of the colonnade, Osriel glanced my way and dipped his head, then addressed Voushanti. "Mardane, perhaps you would notify the watch that we have returned, and that Mistress Elene is not to be disturbed until I wait upon her."

Voushanti shifted his attention to me. Pinpoints of red centered his dark gaze. Only after I had given an uneasy nod did he bow to Osriel. "As you command, my lord prince." He pivoted and followed Saverian and Jullian out of the well yard, leaving Osriel and me alone.

"So we are to have our reckoning before even we get warm." Osriel spread his arms as if to welcome whatever I might bring, then seemed to think better of it. Shivering, he drew Saverian's heavy cloak tight. "It hardly seems fair to ask me to take you on when I've just seen you leap to earth from a height no man should survive, clad in naught but mythlight, and you've carried me out of hell to my own house in less time than it would take me to walk my own walls."

"Let us walk a bit, my lord. I'd not wish some lurking guard to hear what we might say." I pointed to the colonnade. Rather than taking the upper stair to the Great Hall and bedchambers or the lower stair to the passages where Saverian's workroom lay, we strolled along the covered walk so like those surrounding the cloister garth at Gillarine—the three-petaled lily of Navronne embedded in its stonework, the cherubic aingerou carved into the slender pillars, the square of grass alongside our path, centered by a spring-fed font. We rounded the corner in truth and memory . . .

. . . and we were there, staring up at the shattered tower of the abbey church, at the gutted remnants of the library and scriptorium, at the darkness of the deserted dorter. At the burnt and broken shell of a place once holy.

Osriel halted and stepped away from me, whipping his head from one side of the cloister to the other. "What have you done? Why have you brought me here?"

"I needed us to be in a neutral place," I said. "Away from devoted warriors, away from swords and dungeons and magic—or, at least, magic that is outside of ourselves. I thought at first to take you into the wild, to some place where you could not find your way back if this discussion goes for naught. But I've no wish to harm you, lord. This place ... I think we both care for it and will think twice before bringing any further evil to it. I thought perhaps to find my friend Gram waiting here."

In the azure light of my gards, his gaunt face appeared carved in ice. "I am your king and your bound master. I need discuss nothing with you."

He thrust this harsh rhetoric between us like the first feint in a dual. I didn't think I needed to remind him of his promise that once I took him into Aeginea I would be free to go my own way. Nor did I mention that to abandon him here in his present state without Saverian's medicine would likely mean his death. Instead I strolled down the west cloister walk away from the church. After a moment he joined me.

"I wish we were not so tired," I said, offering him my arm. He shook his head. "I wish you were not ill. I wish we had more time to debate and reason."

We rounded the south end of the cloister and walked past the refectory to the calefactory—an open room lined with stone benches and centered by a great hearth and a neat wood stack. "You need warmth, and I need open air. I doubt Nemesio would mind if we use his warming room. The brothers have taken refuge at Magora Syne."

In normal times the brothers kept the calefactory fire burning through the winter for the monks to stop in and warm their hands as they went about their work and prayer. Once I had laid the fire, Osriel summoned a spell to set it ablaze. He sat cross-legged beside it, hunched forward as if hoping to draw strength and nourishment from the flames as well as warmth. I sat on the stone bench where I could breathe cold air and see his face.

Even the bright flames could not push back the shadows of Gillarine. Too much death and sorrow lingered just beyond the light. Stearc's presence loomed very large. And I held the memory of the thane's last fear as a shield before my own.

"So speak," said the prince, once his shivering had eased. "You've not brought me here to play monk."

"I will ask you to hear me out before argument or comment," I said. "I've never laid all this out at once."

He did not respond, so I plunged ahead. "You are my rightful king, son of a man I honored and vowed to follow to the death. You are a man I have been astonished and pleased to name my friend, for one of the things I've learned since first I came to Gillarine is that I never before owned a true friend—one who would hold me fast as I fell into hell and strive to pull me out again, one who would trust me in matters of importance, one who would *know* me, for I believed I could not allow anyone to *know* me."

He propped his elbows on his knees and rested his chin on his clasped hands. Waiting for me to go on. Yielding nothing. A wall stood between us, and my purpose was to shatter it and expose what lay beyond—marvelous or terrible as it might be.

"I've not brought you here to explain why you betrayed me to those who would destroy me. I've convinced myself that you saw no other choices open to you." His unguarded smile when he first looked full on my gards had but confirmed my growing suspicion. "I believe you held a hope that my uncle would do exactly as he did. I believe you brought Saverian apurpose on that journey, knowing that her nature would prompt her to do exactly as she did, or if the worst came to pass, to amend matters as she could."

That surprised him. His head jerked up and his dark eyes met mine. Though he made no acknowledgment, I took his silence as confirmation.

I pushed on. "Rather I want to tell you what I've learned these past days, in hopes we can make some sense of it together before we fall off the edge of the world. Some you surely know, some you surely don't. I told you and Jullian some of what Kol taught me, but I didn't tell you about Picus."

"Picus?" Another surprise that shocked him rigid. "Where? How did—?"

"Please, lord, hear me out. Picus lives in Aeginea . . ."

I told him of the monk and his sin, of Ronila and her web of hate, of Gildas and Sila, of the lost map and my conviction that it had depicted the tale of the world's ruin. I laid out the evidence of Tuari's humiliation at the actions of his half-human brother, his retribution on Llio's wife, and his punishment by Stian. And I told how Saverian and I had both realized that Osriel's quest for power from the Danae could backlash and make matters worse.

". . . and so we are left with Sila Diaglou, entirely sane, entirely ruthless, and determined to purify Navronne and reshape it according to her peculiar vision, with Gildas, who schemes to become the lord of chaos, and with Ronila, who intends to destroy us all. They will cross Caedmon's Bridge in little more than a sevenday. I don't completely understand my skills, lord, but I have bound them to your father's service, to Abbot Luviar's vision, to Jullian's protection and the protection of two others whose names I cannot reveal. I would use them in the service of Navronne . . . in your service, too, if those two are the same. Tell me what is to happen at the mine called Dashon Ra on the winter solstice."

Osriel's eyes were closed, so that for a moment I thought he had fallen asleep. But he shifted and straightened and met my gaze unflinching, though his dark eyes held the bleakness of Navronne's winter. "I will position a small force at the Bridge, commanding them to lure the Harrowers into the hills behind Renna. Thanks to preparations I have made over the years, Sila will find the vale of Dashon Ra harder to escape than to enter—now I know she is half Dané, I'll have to consider more carefully how to deal with her own person, and her gammy's, I suppose. With enough magic entirely channeled into the gold veins at Dashon Ra, I can free the souls I have imprisoned. Bound by blood to my will, they must and shall do my bidding. I plan to give them the Harrower legions."

Cold horror struck me like a demon's hand. "Instill the dead souls in living hosts?"

He shot to his feet at my first word, gripping one column of the great hearth as if it were all that stood between him and dissolution. "Do *not* preach to me of the evil of this course until you have seen the future your sister, the diviner, has shown me. Were I to send a *living* army down upon Sila Diaglou's trapped legions to save this kingdom from such a future, no man or woman would fault me. Kings *must* command their people to die for them. Had I the slightest hope of an alternative, I would welcome it with all my heart. But I cannot condemn Navronne to centuries of starvation, disease, and enslavement for my lack of will to use what knowledge and skill I possess."

"But what becomes of such an army?" An army of revenants . . . living bodies possessed by the angry dead.

"Under my command, they will turn on my brother's troops. If my brother is wise, he will lay down his arms and come to terms with me. We must consummate the bargain quickly. Without an infusion of my blood, my warriors will have but seven days of life, perhaps twice that if the Danae keep their word. But those will be days they would not own had I left their corpses undisturbed on Perryn's and Bayard's battlegrounds. Perhaps they can make some peace with that."

I shook my head. "Not peace, my lord. And you well know it. Their souls' future will be forfeit. You will force them to trade seven days of breathing for the fullness of whatever life lies beyond this one. They'll not have even the time to seek out their families. And what of the Harrowers' souls displaced? Are they rightfully dead or are they lost to heaven as well? Or are they, in turn, prisoned in your veins of gold? Three days ago, I shared Voushanti's dying, lord, and such despair as I felt cannot heal what ails Navronne. If you win your throne by such means, how ever will you govern?"

"My warlords will protect me in the beginning. From there my own deeds must tell. I'll do what I can to hold back the night. And we must hope that the Danae, left alone and undisturbed, can heal the things I cannot." He braced his back against the graceful column, as unyielding as the stone. "I have pondered this course for three years, Valen. Could I see but a glimmer of hope in some other plan, I would leap at it. Luviar knew about Voushanti. He knew of my work with the dead, and why I donned terror

as a pureblood dons his mask. Indeed, he knew better than
I of all my strengths and weaknesses, and to the very end
he counseled me that his god would show me the path of
right. Yet even Luviar, in all his wisdom, could not tell me
another way."

I stepped out of the calefactory enclosure full into the
wind, for it felt as if the heat muddied my thoughts. "And
what if Tuari Archon betrays you?" For, of course, Osriel
intended the magic of the Canon to be channeled into the
veins of gold to empower his army of souls. "Ronila spoke
as if Tuari was already her tool."

The prince riffled his hair with his slender fingers, truly
puzzled. "Spite would be his only reason. I yielded every
point, gave him everything he asked for. To demonstrate
trust and buy the parley, I pledged him fair recompense for
my father's failure to return to Aeginea. To prove my faith,
I returned the treasure that was stolen—and it is his own
people who lost you again, after all. Our joined power on
the solstice will end the sianou poisonings. But in the event
you are right and Tuari upends the bargain, I do have an
alternative. Certain rites can release the power bound in
my blood as Caedmon's heir. It should be enough to do as I
want. Perhaps that is the only just solution after all."

And then I put together the clues and understood what
he had planned all along. No wonder Saverian would not
speak of it. Sila Diaglou had once demanded a scion of
Caedmon's house to bleed in her penitential rites, and Osriel had told me that blood consecrated to Navronne would
be supremely potent. He had told Elene that his plan would
end his last hope of heaven, but he had not meant that
merely as an acknowledgment of a monstrous crime.

"You think to have Saverian bleed you as Sila would,"
I said, appalled at what I envisioned. "You die in torment
to release this power in your veins, and she returns you to
life to use it. You would yield your own soul to win this
battle."

He let his head fall back against the pillar and closed his
eyes. "Actually I intend Voushanti to do the bleeding part.
I'll need him back from you before we begin."

To spend one's entire life dependent on the blood of
others—whom would he choose? Saverian herself . . . his

loyal childhood friend coerced into this macabre partnership? Not Elene. He had pushed her away, for love must surely wither in such a feeding. Voushanti ... their survival linked one to the other like conjoined twins?

"I'll not put Voushanti through another death to change guardianship, lord. Though I know he will obey you, even in this, it is cruel and inhuman and unworthy of you to ask it of him."

"We must all heed cruel necessity—whether prince, warrior, or halfblood Dané, whether man or woman."

And then did another consideration chill me. "Ah, lord, what did you promise Tuari to redeem your father's betrayal?"

"Only that which I shall make sure never to have—a firstborn child for them to nurture in my father's place."

"Spirits of night, but you—" I bit my tongue. I was sworn to secrecy on the matter. Of course the Danae would require balance in such a bargain, and if Osriel's firstborn was the price of the parley itself, this bargain would stand ... no matter what happened on the solstice. I was sworn to protect Elene and the child, whatever that might mean in the future. Osriel could not know. "Could you find naught else, lord?"

He dropped his head between his stiff shoulders and laughed—a sad, despairing humor. "How far you've come, friend Valen, from the rogue who tried to steal my nivat offering. You lack even a sprout of wings, yet I feel as if the judgment of heaven rests in your word. Can you not see? My father left his beloved kingdom—his people—in my protection. Do I wait another season, I'll have naught left to save. How can I ask of others what I would not give myself?"

I stared into the broken, snow-drenched cloisters of Gillarine and sought answers. Ruin lay in every direction that I could see. To stop Osriel left Navronne at the mercy of Sila Diaglou. But I had no confidence that even so determined a warrior as Sila could outfox the witch who had made her—and that made our end far worse. No wheat would grow from an earth of Ronila's harrowing. And Gildas, the monk who aspired to godhood, was the blind bargain in the game. At some point he would strike out on a separate course from his malignant partner. He intended me to be a part of it, and the hunger lurking even now in my blood gave me the unsettling feeling that my escape from Fortress Torvo had not concerned him as much as it should have. Though even a victory would tally an unsupportable cost, who else but Osriel had the remotest chance of stopping these three?

Not I. If I had a part in this conflict . . . in this world . . . it yet remained hidden from me. My mother's purposes were unfathomable. The impossible yearnings waked by my contact with my Danae kin seemed selfish and trivial beside the magnitude of the ruin we faced. And so I was left only with tangled vows and awe for those who would give so much for naught but sheerest love. I felt in sore need of counsel.

I wiped the sweat from my forehead and approached the drooping shape braced upright by the pillar. "Come, my lord, let me take you home to bed."

He cocked his head. "No argument? No fiery sword?"

I gave him Saverian's vial. When he had drained it and some of the rigidity had left his stance, I offered him my arm. He relinquished his pillar and allowed me to slip my arm under his shoulders. As we moved slowly through the cloisters, a flurry of bats flew out from the burnt undercrofts.

"Just . . . wait for me, lord," I said as I walked us back to Renna. "Don't tell anyone about your plan, and don't do anything irretrievable until I get back. I doubt I've the wit to find you another way, but perhaps my uncle does."

PART FOUR

Canon

Chapter 28

I crouched in the lee of a limestone scarp—the only shelter in the storm-blasted wilderness—and vomited up nothing for the fiftieth time in an hour. Had my throat not already taken on the character of raw meat, I would have screamed into the earth as my limbs seized with cramps, my gut twisted into knots, and my skin felt like the vellum of Sila's map as it charred into ash. Instead, I writhed and moaned and cursed, ready to devour the frozen mud or my own flesh did I have the least imagining it would taste of nivat.

The hunger had come upon me as I had traveled the first shift from Osriel's gates, as if my body knew that my responsibility for others' safety had ended for the present and it could now indulge itself. Determined to seek my uncle's counsel, I had ignored its warning and traveled the meadows beyond Caedmon's Bridge to the Sentinel Oak. Once in Aeginea, I shifted straightaway into the terraced land where, in the human plane, Ardra's prized vineyards lay dying. I had no notion of how to find Kol, even assuming the archon had not turned him into a beast or locked him out of his body. But if I could just find my way back to Picus, surely he could tell me how to locate my uncle or Stian.

Over the hours my craving had deepened, and the blizzard that had struck with the sunless dawn grew so violent I could not see. The onset of familiar cramps and tremors banished all my suppositions that relinquishing this renewed craving would somehow be easier than what I had undergone before. I could have torn through steel with my teeth to find the makings for a doulon. And this time I had no Osriel or Saverian to hold me together.

Miserably lost and dreadfully sick, I had wandered in circles for more than a day. And when my strength failed, I had crawled to this meager shelter to escape the storm. So much for great vows and resolutions.

A bout of coughing and sneezing felt like to push my eyes from my head. Somewhere in my mindless wandering, I had lost my bundle of clothes and provisions, which left me naught for wiping my streaming nose or eyes and naught to keep me warm now my gards could not. My shivering could have rattled even Renna's stout walls.

I tried to muster the sense for a seeking. Grateful that the sky did not shatter with my first movement, I rested my forehead on the snowy ground, pressed my palms to the earth on either side of my head, and forced magic through my fingertips. Instead of a nicely measured flow, power gushed through my wretched body in one enormous surge.

What felt like a hard-launched stone struck the center of my already tender forehead . . . which made no sense at all as my forehead yet rested on the snowy earth. But the image of the landscape struck me clearly: rolling meadows . . . not barrens, as they seemed in this grim weather. Dormant, yes, with the waning season, but in summer, thick with hazel and dogwood, grouse and falcons, roe deer, and myriad other creatures. The undersoil smelled rich with life and health. Well tended.

As I lifted my head a little and pressed the heel of my hand onto the unbroken flesh centering my forehead, a rush of warmth flowed up and around and over my back, flooding me with scents of clover and meadowsweet. Azure lightning threaded the snow all around.

"What thinkest thou to do here, *ongai*?" A woman's words peppered my skin like wind-driven needles. "To break my sleep without greeting . . . to broach so deeply. Such blatant rudeness requires explanation before I report thee for sanction." And then a bare foot struck me in the chin.

I fell back on my heels, clutching my rebellious stomach as a trickle of blood tickled my raw throat. *Sanction . . .*

captivity... breaking... Panic near shredded my wits. I scrambled backward ... and then I saw her.

Long arms wrapped about her knees, she sat in the snow—no, perched atop the snow like a bird, so weightless did she appear. Tousled curls the silvered rose of winter sunrise framed her round face. A butterfly, its lace wings tinted every hue of sunlit sky, hovered on her ivory cheek and trailed threads of dewy cobwebs down her shoulders and arms. What scraps of wit I had left escaped me.

"Thou'rt but initiate!" Her face blossomed in surprise as she looked on mine. She tilted her head, and her eyes traveled downward. "I could have thee sanctioned for—" Her examination halted in the region of my groin, wrinkling her glowing face into a knot. "No initiate, but a *stripling* male of full growth. You're failed, then. Hast thou no shame to come poking around my sianou like a mole in the heath? Unless thou'rt but some odd dream come to warm me this winter ..." Her pique trailed off in whimsy. "I've a fondness for dream lovers."

"You are ... so ... lovely." As I stammered this inanity, the surge of blood that spoke the goddess Arrosa's will seemed to flush the sickness from my veins. Though my state was no more sensible, at least I might not vomit on the small, pale feet that glimmered not a quercé from my knees. I inhaled deeply, dabbed the back of my hand against my bleeding lip, and tried to remember the polite address for an unrelated Dané female. "Shamed ... yes, *engai*. Forgive my rudeness. I've been wandering. Ate something I should not. I seek my vayar to discuss my future and, in my confused state, mistook the place."

"Ah, I once mistook mustard seeds for nivé, and they roused such a storm inside me, I could not dance the moonrise." Her smile set my gards afire. She touched my knee, releasing sparks of silver and blue. Did all Danae have moods that switched from storm to sun faster than flickers' pecks?

I leaned forward. Inhaled again. The afternoon smelled ripe as an autumn orchard. "Surely the moon wept on that sad night."

Pleasure rippled the brightness of her gards. "Sweetly spoken, stripling! Perhaps I should feed thee belly-soothing tansy before I sleep again. Thou'rt lovely, as well, and bring a powerful presence and a lusty vigor to my meadow." As she brushed her finger over my bruised lip, a veil of disturbance dimmed her starry brightness. "How is it possible thou art failed? More important, how is it possible a failed stripling can broach my sianou?"

"His blundering feet but sounded a dream, Thokki." Kol's voice cleaved the thickening air as the bells of Matins shatter a monk's wistful dreams. "*Envisia seru*, sweet guardian."

The female jumped gracefully to her feet, a move that did nothing to calm my urgent admiration. Woven spider-silk draped from one shoulder front and back. A girdle of strung pearls, wound thrice about her, caught it loosely at her hips, whence it fell to her knees. The veil hid naught of importance.

"Too long since the sight of thee hath delighted my eye, Kol Stian-son! Why are—?" A catch in her throat signaled alarm and wonder as her gaze switched back to me. She stepped away, arms crossed on her breast. "This is the Cartamandua halfbreed. The violator."

Kol spoke up before I could protest. "He is no violator, Thokki. Tuari's long-soured spirit speaks blight upon my *rejongai*. Blight upon my sister for her choice to bear him. Blight upon me for choosing to spare him the pain of breaking. Yet I have released his true being and found him reverent and gifted, though indeed clumsy as a bear in spring."

"Willing, then, I yield to thy judgment." Brow darkening, she touched Kol's arm. "Is it true they have passed over thee, Kol? That Nysse is the Chosen for the Winter Canon?"

He nodded stiffly. "But I am neither locked away nor beast-captive. I need not be at the Center to dance my part fully. And come spring"—he shrugged—"perhaps eyes will be clearer."

"Winter already bites deep, thus I have bedded early." She hunched her shoulders and wrapped her arms about herself, allowing her gaze to travel the gray dome of the sky and the wilderness of snow. "But I shall wake for the Canon and make my voice heard to argue this decision.

I'll not be alone in it. Thou shouldst challenge Nysse, Kol. The world is injured, and any who keep thee from dancing the Center tear at its wounds. Thou'lt have a care with this halfbreed?"

Kol stepped close, took Thokki's head gently between his hands, and kissed her hair. "I shall chastise my tendé for blundering so crudely into thy dreams, and then commend him for his choice of beauty to admire. Wilt thou partner me for a round this Canon, Thokki?"

She flushed cheek to toe—a fetching glory, to be sure. I near swallowed my tongue.

"I—" She tilted her head and looked askance at my uncle. "Thou needst not offer such a gift to keep me silent about this encounter."

Kol bristled. "I do not use a Canon partnering for bribe or payment."

"Of course," she said quickly. "I never meant insult. That thou wouldst mark my dancing in anywise near thy level humbles me. Honored and joyful would I be to partner thee."

"We shall be on our way. Come, *rejongai*." My uncle's curt command brought me to my feet and into a respectful bow, determined not to shame him further in front of Thokki. I sincerely hoped that he had not compromised his honor to prevent her telling tales of me. I wasn't sure he could forgive such a necessity.

I bowed to Thokki, as well, but deemed it best to keep my mouth shut. The language my body spoke was boorish enough.

"In the Canon, Thokki," said Kol.

"In the Canon, Kol," she called after us.

My uncle struck out across the fields without any word to me. Outside of Thokki's warm presence, his tension was as palpable as the bitter wind. He set a blistering pace. I struggled to keep up, doing my best to ignore the returning symptoms of my craving. We made two magical shifts, and though I felt the moves clearly, I could not have repeated them.

After the second shift, the snow yielded to a cold, pounding rain. The land stretched flat and gray as far as I could see. The air weighed heavy on my shoulders and smelled of river wrack. Sweat poured from my brow, and my knees quivered.

"Vayar," I called hoarsely as Kol began to move even faster. "We must talk. Matters of grave import. Please . . ."

My legs slowed on their own, threatening to give way completely as cramps and shakes racked my back and limbs. At first I thought he might abandon me in the rainy desolation, but as I willed myself a few more steps along his path, he spun and waited for me.

"What ails thee, Valen?" His speech pierced like shards of bronze. "I expected thee stronger, faster, and more attentive on thy return. I expected thee careful. Had I not kept my ears open in readiness, only cracked bones wouldst thou have to walk on this night. Thy coming rattled the Everlasting as crashing boulders, so that any who heed the movements of the air could feel it."

He rested his hands on his hips. "That thou dost dawdle and moon along the way is my responsibility; I should have taught thee better how to curb the rising heat of a stripling till thou shouldst encounter a proper companion. But it is naught but madness to risk thy safety by broaching the sianou of a sleeping guardian—a deed no stripling of any maturing shouldst be able to accomplish. Only by fair chance didst thou choose Thokki, a merry spirit who trusts her friends. Has sense left thee entire?"

I summoned control and stood straight, determined my ragged condition would not interfere with the world's fate. "Vayar, I bring news of the doom of the long-lived. These wild folk that poison the guardians are led by one who once lived in Aeginea. She means to destroy the Canon . . . destroy you all."

"We spoke of this before, and I told thee—"

"Her name is Ronila."

"Ronila!" His shocked echo split the air.

At the same time, pain lanced my middle, causing me to double over. He caught my arms just before my knees buckled. "Art thou injured? Broken? Come . . ." In a blur of pain and dark rain, he sat me on a muddy hummock, filled his hands, and poured rainwater down my throat. To my shame, it stayed down no better than any other contents of my stomach.

"I'm just sick," I said, wiping my mouth on my arm. Not even the fires of shame could quiet my shivering. "It's nivat—"

"Fool of a stripling! Thou art completely witless! Complain not to me of nivé, if thou wouldst ever have my ear." He grabbed my arm and, without another word, dragged me through a series of nauseating shifts. The world dissolved in churning gray and I completely lost track of body and mind . . .

"So, are you more sensible now?"

Sand in my mouth. In my eyes. Everywhere underneath me. Rain drummed on my back and cascaded over my head. I squinted into the murk. The pounding in my head was not just blood but waves, out there beyond the veils of rain that merged sea, air, cliffs, and sky into one mass of gray. Evaldamon. The salty residue in my mouth evidenced Kol had dunked me in the sea at the very least.

"Yes, *rejongai*. Better." I sat up, feeling scoured inside and reasonably clear-headed. Recollection of his warning postponed my questions about nivat and what he'd done to aid me.

"Tell me of Ronila," he said.

"The priestess who destroys your sianous is Ronila's granddaughter, raised to be Ronila's vengeance on humans and Danae alike. But it is Ronila and her toady that I fear most. They have some scheme . . ."

I told him all I knew of the old woman and Sila and Gildas. Though I did not describe Osriel's particular plan, I revealed how Tuari had pledged to spend the power of the Winter Canon into the golden veins of Dashon Ra and fuel the prince's dangerous enchantment.

". . . but once Picus told me of Tuari's hatred for humankind, I could not believe the archon would keep the bargain. I had to warn Osriel of the potential treachery. That's why I left Aeginea so abruptly."

Kol sat on his haunches, his mouth buried in his hands as he listened to my story. Through a sheen of raindrops, his dragon suffused his lean face with a sapphire glow. "Though my sire and I disagree with the archon on many matters, Tuari has always attended his responsibilities faithfully. He does not make bargains he has no intent to keep; nor would he ever compromise the Canon. When he failed to name me Chosen—the one of us who dances at the Center— none could understand it. My dancing is unmatched in this season." Honesty, not pride, birthed his claim.

"As Picus told thee, Tuari is least likely of all of us to join a human—especially Eodward's son—in any endeavor. Yet Dashon Ra *is* the Center of the Winter Canon, and he *has* named his consort Chosen. She could do this thing—divert the wholeness of the dance into the veins and not the land itself . . ." The words faded. His thoughts drifted deeper.

This was not what I wanted to hear. "Janus said the Chosen dances at the Center to 'bring all life to joining.' All life—human, Danae, birds, beasts . . . everything?"

"The dance of the Chosen joins *all* that is brought to the Canon by the long-lived—trees and rivers, mountains, stones, sea and shore, earth and all that grows, as well as all thou hast named."

"But only the lands you remember. You can't include the parts of the earth that are corrupt."

Kol straightened abruptly. "I have told thee, I will *not*—"

"I know that you and your kind forget places that have been poisoned, Kol. Janus once created a great map, hoping to show you the places you had lost. But he didn't understand that Danae could not make sense of such patterning. Somehow Sila Diaglou got hold of that map and was using it to judge her success in forcing your kind out of Aeginea." I could not let him avoid the subject any longer. "Vayar, you vowed to provide me truth and healthy guidance. As you see I need both of those now more than I have ever done, else we have no hope of untangling this mess. My mother intended me to help. You know that. I've just no idea how. Permit me to do so. Please, uncle, teach me."

Kol scooped a handful of sand, allowing the rain to wash it through his fingers. Only when his palm was clean did he respond. "Janus said he would help us reclaim the Plain. It is only a name in our tales of the Beginnings, yet we believe its importance equal to the Sea, the Mountain, and the Well. Thou hast judged rightly; we cannot bring it back into the Canon if we cannot find it. We cannot find it if we cannot remember. In the same way each of the sianous lost to the Scourge falls out of our memory and thus out of the Canon. Only the names linger to remind us of our loss."

Sorrow, grief, and shame clothed him as new gards. "Clyste traveled with Janus as he marked his papers," he continued, "returning joyful, for her eyes had seen these dead places. For one or two she was able to work a kiran to bring to the Spring Canon. With Janus's magics we would be able to find these places again and reclaim them all. But when at last the Cartamandua returned and unrolled his great skin, we could see naught but scrawling that twisted our eyes and turned our heads wrong way out."

"Ronila could read it," I said. "But in her spite, she told no one. She must have taken the map from Janus then, or perhaps Picus gave it to her when he came back to Navronne. The hag burnt your only hope to find the dead lands. Sila wants you to forget Aeginea and interbreed with humans. Ronila wants to ensure you never remember. Ronila wants you dead."

Kol scratched his head. "Neither of those could have taken it. Ronila was long away from Aeginea when Janus brought the great map. Picus too. I know that because the Cartamandua brought the skin map on his last visit, the same visit that Clyste lay with—"

He whirled about sharply, his golden eyes as bright as small moons in the gloom. Before I could ask what insight had struck him so forcefully, he yanked me to my feet. "Come, *rejongai*, we must resume your lessons. Take me to the Well."

"We've no time. And I cannot—"

"The long-lived do not grasp humans' constant invocation of time. *Before* and *after*, *soon* and *how long* seem to us but walls built to imprison you. But indeed, the change of season bites the air, and I see such danger and such possibility as tell me I have lived blind until inhaling this very breath that leaves my body." His hands near burnt their image into my shoulders. "If thou wouldst justify Clyste's fate, Valen Cartamandua-son, then do as I say, without thought, without distraction, without artifice, living only in the embrace of the Everlasting."

His urgency made my heart race. And as dearly as I

desired to determine my own course, the past months had taught me faith and trust. I trusted Kol in the same way I had trusted Luviar, when every mote of common wisdom said to distance myself from plots and conspiracies. In the same way as I trusted Osriel when the accumulated witness of my eyes and ears clamored for me to slay, not save him. But I hungered for answers as I hungered for spelled nivat. "I will obey, vayar, but I beg you answer one question: What have you guessed?"

"Many things, but only one sure. *Tuari* has given Ronila the map."

No matter how I pestered, Kol was adamant. He would explain no more until I led him to Clyste's Well. I had no capacity to judge what it might mean for the Canon if Tuari had been duped by his half-brother's daughter. *Duped*, to be sure, for if the archon was a person who attended his responsibilities faithfully, and who would never compromise the Canon, then he could not possibly have read Ronila's true intent. Yet no warning from Kol or from me could stop whatever scheme Tuari had devised. The archon had no use for either of us.

I had come to Kol for guidance. Thus, over the next hours, I indeed left everything behind and gave myself into the embrace of the Everlasting. We traveled the length of Navronne. Again and again I sank to my knees, placed head and palms on the mud, snow, or rocky ground, and released careful dollops of magic to seek a route to the Well. Though Kol's dunking had eased my immediate sickness, the yearning for nivat dogged my heels like an unwanted hound, as I sought out landmarks . . . rivers, seas, mountains . . . anything that might tell me where we stood and where we must go next. Subtle steps on this journey; I needed naught else to make me heave.

When storm and night and weariness left me too confused to continue, I attempted what I had never done before, seeking through the wind-whipped clouds above me to find the guide star. Fixed and firm, Escalor took its place in the landscape of my mind with the brilliance of my uncle's gards. Using its anchor, I knew which way to go next.

Thou shalt map the very bounds of heaven, Janus had told me, and wonder and gratitude swelled within me.

Happily, the harder I worked to juggle the fruits of senses and memory with the direction of magic and instinct, the less my nivat cravings troubled me. Not just in the way focused attention masks a nagging distraction, but in truth. My gards grew brighter as night closed in.

When my steps flagged, Kol taught me how to sniff out a Danae cache—a small stone vault filled with provisions and marked with an aromatic cluster of horsemint seed heads. I devoured every morsel of the dried apples and walnuts we found in the store. Kol watched me eat and eased my concern when my full stomach at last waked my conscience. "Replenish the cache next time thou dost walk these hills, and it will serve another who lacks time to hunt," he said. Beyond that he refused to speak, save for an occasional, "Attention, stripling. Thy mind doth wander."

My first shift after the cache took us from one ledge of rock to another and into calmer weather. The strip of blackness west of the ledge was the valley of the Kay. Only a few steps more and I led Kol down the slotlike passage through the cliff and into the high-walled corrie of my mother's sianou.

Saints and angels ... it felt as if we plumbed the very heart of winter. Ice as thick as my thigh sheathed the walls of the Well, glinting eerily with the reflected lightning of our gards. The pool had shrunk. Crumpled, broken ice hid its sunken surface. The wind moaned softly through the heights, swirling dry snow from the crevices.

"Inerrant thou hast come here, just as on the morn we met," said Kol, who remained in the dark mouth of the passage. "The Well has not faded from thy memory."

"No," I said, hoping he would now explain. "Its location is as clear to me as on the night I first walked here."

"Canst thou see ... ?" His voice trailed away as he walked toward the pool. After only a few steps, he sank to one knee and touched the ice-slicked rock. "Follow one of her paths. Prove it."

I knelt and yielded magic, and it was as if the hidden stars came streaking into the corrie, embroidering trails of silver light upon the dark stone. Everywhere, circles and twining loops, layer upon layer of threads, as deep as I dared plunge, all quivering with light, each one that I touched with my inner eye thrumming with stretched music.

The uppermost image was bolder than those that lay immediately below, the steps larger. This was Kol's own path, when he had danced his grief on the day we had retrieved Gerard's body from the pool. Carefully I studied the interlaced threads of his steps, comparing it to the images that his movements had etched on my memory. And then I peeled away that layer—as one could with the thin transparent layers of the stones that men called angels' glass—and examined the next.

My mother's feet had laid down a more intricate pattern than Kol's. I began to walk the silver thread. "She began here," I said, touching the place at the far side of the pool. "Here a small leap." A faint thread between a hard push and the landing. "Then a spin. A step and then another spin. The pattern repeated three more times . . ." As I walked I could almost feel her movements. "Here she paused, bending I think because the thread is uneven . . . another sequence of five steps and spins, and then here she made that twisting move as you do, on one foot, lowering her heel to mark each turn, again, and again . . . ten . . . twelve times . . ."

"Eppires," he said, suffused with awe. "Thou canst truly see her steps. I recognize this kiran."

"There are hundreds of paths here, layer upon layer. I could walk each one if you wished."

"Do this one again," he commanded, resolute. "And this time, shadow her moves."

"I cannot—"

"Do *not* say *I cannot*. I do not expect thee to dance, only to move in the manner of the kiran, to *feel* that I may also feel."

And so I began again. I pivoted and jumped in my own limited fashion. Wobbling. Awkward. I spun a quarter turn and tripped over my own foot, where Clyste had made three full rounds and landed on her toes. Filled with the remembrance of Kol's grace, I knew I must appear a lumbering pig with feet of lead.

I balanced on one foot for a moment at the first spot

where Clyste had paused ... and felt a feather's touch along my spine. At the next step I touched more softly on the ball of my bare foot and when I leaped to her next landing place, I recalled my leap from Torvo's wall and drove my spirit upward with the imagining of my mother's gift. I landed gently on my left foot, my knee and ankle bent. No wobble.

My skin flushed. Alive. Awake. As if the air spoke to me. As if a lover's hand touched my lips. The color of my gards deepened. Eyes fixed to the silver thread, I brushed my right foot forward and shifted weight, as the pattern told me ...

I finished the kiran on one knee, the alter leg stretched out behind me in line with my straight back, my fingertips touching my forehead. Only when I became aware of Kol's gaze did I break into a sweat of embarrassment. "I got caught up in it," I said, drawing into a huddle, wrapping my arms about my knee. I could not look at him. My crude miming must surely have appalled him.

"The ending position is called an *allavé*," he said dryly. "Wert thou to stretch the spine longer, round the arms as if embracing a tree, and lower the hips, while aligning the back foot and hip properly with the correctly curved shoulder, I might call thy position ... minimal. Now, touch the stone beneath thy feet."

The ice had melted along the silvered path. The stone, warm beneath my fingertips, swelled as if with living breath. "This is not usual," I said, half in terror, half in question, "for one of my poor skills."

"No. Not usual." Kol knelt beside me as my fingers traced the silver thread in awe and wonder. "In these few steps ... a youngling's raw beginning ... thou hast summoned life where none dwelt when we stepped through into this place. Think, Valen, is it possible thou couldst find other kiran shadows like these, without knowing their location beforehand or their makers? Without maps or books? Couldst thou walk the world, seeking with thy hands and thy Cartamandua magic these patterns scribed in seasons past?"

"Yes, I believe—" And then did my thick head begin to comprehend what he was asking me. Janus's map had failed to tell the Danae what they had forgotten, because they could not read the language of lines and symbols. But Clyste had seen my father's truer magic. He had taken her into places she could not find on her own . . . and she had been able to coax dead lands back to life with her dancing. Danae could see only living things, and so Clyste had chosen to create a living map—a child who could find what was forgotten and dance it back into the pattern of the world.

"Thou art the answer, Valen," said Kol softly. "Thou are the healing for the breaking of the world."

Chapter 29

A s a red tide departs a once-healthy shore, leaving behind a plague of tainted fish, so did my moment's exhilaration rush out to leave me aghast, aching, and empty. "How can this fall to me? I've so few skills ... scarcely begun ... God's bones, years ... lifetimes ... it would take me to seek out such places without the guidance of the map."

Not soon enough to tilt the world's balance on the solstice. Not soon enough to shield Osriel or Elene from dreadful choices, or save anyone, Danae or human, from coming treachery and chaos. And I was not fool enough to believe that this glimmer of life evoked by my awkward capering meant I could ever reclaim a sianou for the Canon.

"Best begin, then. Attend, stripling." Kol laid his hand on the crumpled surface of the pool. Around his spread fingers the blue-cast ice began to melt, until an oval hole penetrated the thick layer all the way to the dark water. He stood up, towering over me, his dragon etched sharp against the night. "Wash thy skin. Snow and ice would be excellent aids."

I glanced up sharply, fear and excitement prickling every hair I had left. "I'm to go on? The third passage?"

"No matter what else comes at the Winter Canon, thou must be a part of it. Only then wilt thou be long-lived and free to undertake this task of healing. Even a halfbreed is made new by the Canon, so that none can hinder thee without new cause. Once thou art past this change, we will speak of Tuari's blundering and thy prince's need, and how we might make answer to them. Those will be simple enough beside the matter of intruding thee into the Canon without dooming us both." He blinked and softened his stern aspect for a moment. "Thou art *willing*, *rejongai*? To take on the fullness of thy being? The responsibility it entails? To accept my teaching?"

My hands took a notion to rub my knees, even while my innermost heart told me that this was what I had come to Kol for. My answer had been given when I woke at Gillarine and saw a child had preserved my life, and in Gillarine's garden, when Luviar had deemed me worthy of trust, and again on Kol's own shore, when I understood that it was not disease or perversion or mindless rebellion that drove me. "I trust thee with my life, vayar. Yes."

A skim of ice had already formed inside the hole. I broke through the brittle layer, scooped out a handful of water, and splashed it on my face. The cold took my breath. Another handful on my head. *Gods in all reaches of heaven!* I scraped up shards of ice from the pond surface, and the coarse-grained snow caught in the crevices, and scoured the mud and sickness and dried sweat from my skin, rinsing with more of the damnably frigid water. Sea bathing. Wind scouring. What shape would this passage take?

I was soon ready to declare myself clean enough for any enchantments, but the direction of Kol's unsatisfied inspection reminded me of the exact nature of the third *remasti*—the passage of regeneration. *Sweet Arrosa, preserve and protect!*

Steeling myself, I doused my shrunken nether parts. I thought my skull might split from the shock of it. Surely I must be sprawled in some dark alley, my body gone doulon-mad, my mind locked into these perverse dreams.

"We shall attempt this passage here," he said, when satisfied with my ablutions. "In the usual course for a stripling, thou wouldst encounter groves or streams, fields or hillocks whose guardian is fading or ready to move on to a new place. Across the seasons thou wouldst learn and study these places, speaking with their guardians, weaving their patterns of life into your own. And on the day of thy third remasti, thou wouldst choose one of these places to partner in thy change. But at the tide pool on mine own shore didst thou show me another way of learning." He gestured toward the frozen pool. "So, learn of the Well."

Sitting on my heels, I laid one hand upon the stone bared by my crude echo of Clyste's dancing. The other hand I dangled in the dark water through the hole Kol had made. I closed my eyes and released magic, and the story of the Well unfolded.

Unlike the tide pool, or Picus's garden, or the meadows near Caedmon's Bridge, each of which teemed with layered life and growth, the grotto of the Well was a barren place. A few astelas roots lay shriveled in the cracked walls. Tucked into the rock near the top of the crags sat an abandoned aerie. But flowers and eagles had been intruders here. The Well was visited by rain, wind, and snow, but few creatures of any sort. A cold, lonely place, even in summer. The patterned music of the Danae, buried so deep in other places, lay very near the surface, as in a temple where gods and angels hover close to us. I breathed deep, exhaled slowly, and learned.

Stars lived here, even hidden above the clouds as they were. Cold and sharp as the rock and ice, their exposed light would arrow into the pool. I scooped water in my cupped hand, and it teased my tongue and palate with bubbles like sharp cider. But a sour second taste bloomed when my tongue touched a ragged black string that lay in my palm.

I shook the slimy thing off my hand, bent closer to the pool, and again plunged my arm into the cold water to the elbow. No fish, no creatures, no plants had ever lived here. But the stringy black growths slimed the smooth pale curves of the Well and even the disturbance of my touch broke off more feathery tendrils to taint the water. I reached deeper yet, toward the spring's source, through layer upon layer of porous stone. The deeper I probed, the warmer the water, as if the Well's source were the fires of the netherworld. I widened my exploration into the channeled rock, which spread the Well's bounty through a vast area of the surrounding lands.

Black slime clogged every watercourse. The channels lay barren and dry, and beyond them I found the withered roots of the forest across the vale, the starved confluence with the River Kay, sluggish and teeming with pestilence, Gillarine's soured barley fields, disease-ridden orchards, and cloister font—it, too, slimed with black.

Sick at heart I withdrew, sat up, and told Kol all I had found. Poison, death, blood-fed corruption throughout the lands where my mother's gift had once spread health and life.

"Thy learning surpasses my understanding, *rejongai*. Now I, too, know the Well." Though his finger touched my cheek gently, Kol's stern visage did not soften. "Breathe in the essence of all thou hast learned—good and ill, sweet and bitter—and weave it into thy spirit. Open thyself, as to a lover, yielding thy boundaries. Give and receive, reserving nothing."

Yielding thy boundaries ... My heart near stopped its rattling, and every terror of confinement and suffocation rose into my throat to strangle me. I knew what he meant for me to do. Now the moment had come, my instincts screamed of danger, of entrapment, of choking death and failure. But memories of Stearc's monumental sacrifice, of Jullian's courage, and of Elene holding life and love so dear, put me to shame. If I could not face my own small terrors, how could I take on Osriel and those he planned?

Near paralyzed with cold and fear, I crept gingerly onto the frozen pool. Facedown, limbs spread, I tried to imagine how to accomplish what Kol described. The bit of warmth I had engendered in the stone lay well out of reach, and the expanse of broken ice beneath me was hardly a lover's body. Saverian's bony substance might come close, but she was at least warm. The thought of the acerbic physician made me smile through my fear. *Naked again,* she would say to this. *Feeling grandiose, Magnus?*

Behind me the air shifted, and I heard a quick breath and the soft impact of a landing. Kol was dancing. Like Saverian's gifted fingers waking my skin, so did the wind of his spins brush my back and flanks, riffle my hair, and tickle my bare feet. His leaps and turns drew forth a stately drone of invisible pipes, and the countering rhythms of sawing strings filtered through ears, through skin, through the cold air I drew in with every tremulous breath. Music thrummed in my bones, and its harmonies played out in the air above me . . . in the ice beneath . . . in the tainted water below, and the earth that cupped this pool in its arms. My blood heated . . . and I became aware of every quat of skin where it touched ice . . . melting . . . dissolving one into the other . . .

To yield. To become nothing, trapped in stone. I wriggled a little, flexing fingers and toes to make sure I still had them. In the movement, a shard of ice gashed my belly. *Merciful gods . . . blood . . . water . . . ice.* A cold sweat drenched my body . . .

. . . and then I laughed. I rocked to and fro and rapped my head on the ice, chortling to think what Josefina and Claudio de Cartamandua-Celestine would say to this unlikely version of my doom. Never in Josefina's wildest divinations could she have seen me like this. *Facedown in a cesspool.* Great gods, I would *not* go back to that life. I would trade not one moment of this fear and doom and terrifying beauty for anything those two had offered me or any fate I had imagined for myself. Let it come!

Kol's music pulsed and drove, and a hunger deeper and more profound than nivat welled from my depths. Groaning . . . laughing . . . I let go of thought and reached out with my spread limbs to embrace the world of the Well . . . water and stone, forest and barley fields, streams and orchards, river and valley . . . reserving nothing . . .

. . . and I plunged through the ice and into the cold, wet blackness. Spears of ice pierced my skin. I dared not scream, because I could not breathe in the water. Yet the scream leaked out of my dissolving flesh, and the cold and the water passed through me as I fell . . . blind, for not even my gards lit this darkness.

Softly, rejongai, *settle. Do not fight. Do not fear. Feel. Touch this place and allow it to touch thee in return. Thy laughter is surely the heart of thy magic . . .*

Kol's breathless voice faded as hearing followed sight into the void. But I clung to his assurance that this was as it was meant to be. Thus I did not go mad when I fell through cold stone and gritty soil, and my thoughts disintegrated like a snowball striking a brick wall. All that remained was raging desire, as I plummeted deep into the molten fires of the earth and was reborn as the guardian of the Well.

*　　*　　*

I could not breathe. Could not move. Could not see. Sated, conjoined with flame and left hollow as a burnt-out stump, I could but exist for a while. Thus I did not panic when waking mind insisted I no longer had a body.

First, I knew the water. I flowed in stately rounds, cooling as I rose from steaming depths to surface ice, brushing against rocks and clumps like a purring cat's tail, and then sinking again to dissolve and dance in the fire. Starlight bubbled in my shallows—not so much as I would prefer—but tart and sweet, as intoxicating as the laughter of angels.

The black tendrils, on the other hand, tasted of decay, sapping my pleasure. My solid faces, cracks, and crevices— the curving walls that existed in and of myself—burned with the painful gnawing of the invasive slime. I grieved for the tormented dead whose blood had fed this poison, even as I swirled around it, prying it from my bones and dragging it down to the fire.

My veins were dry, clogged with the foulness, so that my fair limbs—my fields and groves and waterways that lived in the light—withered and languished. With rising anger I slammed against the barriers of corruption, shifting them enough that I could slip through—a few droplets, then a trickle to begin the healing. I had always been a quick healer.

Valen! Draw in thy sense and spirit. Reach for my hand. Already, I do feel thy life in the land . . . a glory, rejongai, *but we must go forward . . .*

The summoning waked tales and memories that had been scorched away in my passage: the tale of the world's end, the waiting legion of the dead, the friends depending on me. I could not rest here to scour and clean and repair my wounds. I could not sleep. Other duties called. Regretfully, I retreated from earth and bone. With what my mind insisted was a hand, I reached upward . . .

My uncle dragged me, coughing and gagging, from the frigid water. I collapsed on a skid of ice, kicking, writhing, and scraping at my skin. My groin was tangled in strings that stung like the tentacles of a bladderfish. "Get them off," I cried hoarsely. "Holy gods, get them off!"

"Easy, easy, *rejongai*." Kol held my arms as I writhed and flailed, coughing up water and trying to breathe. " 'Tis only thy new gards. Breathe. Be patient. The soreness will ease."

"Soreness?" I croaked, as I clutched my knees and curled into a quivering ball around my wounded parts. "It feels as if I've been whipped. And drowned before that. And before that . . ."

I could not fathom what had happened to me. Remembrances of overpowering need, of raging fire, of immeasurable release lurked somewhere below my present thoughts, too immense to bring into the light. And then I recalled my bizarre impersonation of water and stone, more vivid than doulon dreams.

"The Well has chosen thee, *rejongai*. Marked thee. I have danced here, and it lives in my memory as it has not since Clyste faded."

My uncle sat beside me, waves of heat radiating from his sweating body, as if he had danced the night through . . . perhaps several nights, judging by the starved hollow of my belly. For certain we had come here in the night. Now weak and cloud-riven sunlight glinted on the ice walls.

"If thou but knew all those of the long-lived who have attempted the Well only to emerge bruised and bleeding, weeping for their failure. Not only brash initiates, but mature dancers, worthy to take on great sianous. Valen"—I looked up at the severe pronouncement of my name to see my uncle's eyes bright as summer and his brows raised high—"this is not at all usual."

Weariness set me laughing this time. I tucked my head into my arms and longed for food and sleep and one of Saverian's balms to ease the vibrant sting in my flesh.

"And now we must speak of more lessons," I said, "and of the Canon and Tuari and those who wish to murder the long-lived, and I must learn what to do to save my king's soul and his"—no, even to Kol I could not mention the child—"and his subjects and my friends."

Kol sighed and offered me an insistent hand. "Lessons, yes, but I've brought thee sustenance, lest thy strength or attention should waver."

Ever a slave of my flesh, the prospect of food cheered

me greatly. As I accepted Kol's hand and proceeded gingerly to the almost sunny, almost dry spot where he had laid out his provisions, I kept glancing downward, afraid to look too closely.

"Feathers, I think," said Kol, inspecting me as I lowered myself carefully to the ground. "And braided ... something."

Unable to imagine what such decorations might mean, I shook off the oddity and devoured his small feast: two knotted carrots, four chewy figs, and three round, sticky cakes made of hazelnuts, dried blueberries, and honey. Every delicious bite warmed and strengthened me. I could have eaten ten times the amount.

As I ate, Kol taught. "When I danced in Picus's garden, my steps were not random. I designed a kiran, a pattern of movements to encompass a living landscape—the beasts, plants, trees, earth, stone, and water that comprise it, the air, the light, and the storms that shape it. I, and the others of our kind, dance many kirani throughout a season, not just at our own sianous, for many small places in Aeginea have no guardian of their own."

"So the silver threads I see are the evidence of a kiran—not just any dancing," I said, licking the honey from my fingers.

He acknowledged the point. "We bring these kirani to the Canon, dancing them in the various rounds throughout the day or night. The Chosen, the one named to dance at the Center, takes in all that is brought to the Canon in each dancer's kiran and joins them together as I told thee, building the power that thy prince desires to feed on. At the moment of season's change, the Chosen yields this power to the land through the Center, whence it spreads throughout Aeginea and into human realms through the connections that bind our two realms into one whole—"

"—the Well, the Mountain, the Sea, and the Plain, the sianous where the first of your kind were born of the Everlasting and took bodily form." My hands fell still.

He nodded. "It is also the duty of the Chosen to strip away those kirani that are incomplete or poorly effected, any that might violate the harmony of the dance and reduce its power. This stripping removes the kiran-hai—the affected land—from the Canon for the season. Though an embarrassment to the dancer who shaped the defective kiran, one season's removal does not poison the land or wreak irreversible harm. In the usual way, the kiran is repaired or improved and brought to the following season's Canon."

Kol braided his hair as he spoke, his wrenching twists and yanks speaking eloquently of his agitation. He tied off the thick braid with a solid knot, then pushed aside the strands of hair that had escaped his control.

"When I was but a nestling, the halfbreed Llio, Ronila's sire and guardian of the Plain, brought an unusual kiran into the Spring Canon. Tuari was Chosen—his first naming—and he removed Llio's kiran as flawed, tainted with too much of human influence. Llio argued that his steps were not flawed, but only new. When Tuari refused to reconsider, Llio—impetuous, foolish, driven to rage unnatural to the long-lived—tried to take Tuari's place at the Center by force, a forbidden act that threatened the entirety of the Canon. In the ensuing struggle, Llio fell and broke his skull. Before the dancing ended, he had returned to the Everlasting. It was as if Llio had been poisoned of our ancient Scourge while joined with his sianou, for we could not find the Plain again, and it quickly faded from our memories in all but name. So was the Canon sorely broken."

"The long-lived blamed it on the fact that he was a halfbreed," I said. *Llio's curse.*

"Aye. My sire and others have come to admit that the nature of the Plain as a channel to the human realm, and the nature of the Canon when we are wholly at one with our sianous, must have caused the breaking in some part, and not entirely Llio's human violence. Tuari does not agree. But those events and those that followed—the unstable storms, our own failure to regenerate, the weakening of the bond between our kirani and the land, the increasing incidents of the Scourge—have ever preyed on Tuari, plaguing him with doubts and leading him on a wavering course."

Kol's silence was the quiet between rainstorms as a line of squalls moves in from the sea. And so I waited.

Eventually he sighed and began again. "When Tuari summoned me from Picus's garden, he said he had been searching every channel of wisdom to learn how to restore the Plain and the Well, but all had failed. He had come to the conclusion that the human realm weighs too heavily upon the Canon, causing this imbalance in the world that we all see. He asked that my father and I consider abandoning our sianous for the Winter Canon to see if such removal might correct the imbalance. We refused, both Stian and I, for our kind emerged from the Everlasting in the beginnings apurpose to hold the four great sianous that join Aeginea and the human realm. Stian believes that to yield the remaining two would surely rend the world. Tuari appeared to yield to our misgivings. Now, hearing your tale, I surmise that he has reconciled with his kin-brother's child, Ronila, and given her Janus's map, hoping that Picus's teaching and her life in the human world would reveal to her its meaning, thinking she might show us a way to recover the Plain and the Well and these other lost sianous. If, instead, Ronila has spoken smooth lies and convinced Tuari that such recovery is forever impossible . . ."

". . . the archon might instruct his consort to repair this imbalance," I said. "And the Chosen can forcibly remove the kirani of the Mountain and the Sea from the Canon."

"I believe this is why he names Nysse Chosen. He hopes to repair the Canon by sheering it in twain." After speaking this grim verdict, Kol stretched his legs straight in front of him, linked his hands behind his back, and bent his forehead to his knees, raising his linked hands skyward.

I leaped to my feet, appalled, certain that Kol's theory was correct. Ronila had purposely destroyed the map in front of me, knowing that my news of it would be a torment to Kol and Stian. "Tuari may have yielded to your argument, uncle, but Ronila will find a way to kill you . . . you and Stian . . . and me, too, if she learns what's happened here. She wants to ensure the Mountain and the Sea are lost forever along with the Plain and the Well."

"I shall warn my sire," said my uncle, his voice muffled by his knees and the effort of his stretching. "We shall need his help to get thee into the Canon."

This made no sense at all. "I cannot pass for one of you, no matter my gards. I cannot dance. I've no idea what to do."

He released his arms, drew in his legs, and bounced to

his feet. "Return here at high sun on the solstice, and Stian will instruct thee. There will be sufficient distraction in the Canon for him to slip thee into his round."

"Distraction?"

Kol raised his arms and bent wholly to one side and then the other, holding each for longer than my sympathizing muscles could bear. Then he stood upright and bent forward from the waist. Supporting his weight on his arms, he slid his feet in opposite directions until it seemed he must rip himself in two. He settled his groin to the ice, then stretched his arms forward, flattening his chest to the ground as well. After a very long time, breathing slow and deep, he rose again.

"I shall issue challenge to the archon, asserting my right to dance the Center," he said. "If I prepare sufficiently, my kiran of challenge shall be of such a nature that none shall question my right, and for certain none shall pay any mind to a new-marked dancer in a minor circle of Stian's Round. *I* shall dance thy sianou, *rejongai*. Unusual—but then, all that touches thee is unusual. That the Well is reclaimed will ripple through the senses of the long-lived as a spring zephyr. And on solstice night when the season shifts, I shall infuse the gold veins of Dashon Ra with the power of the Canon and trust *thee* to put the world right again."

His confidence . . . his courage . . . left me breathless. "And if you fail, uncle? Or if Stian is caught bringing a half-breed into the Canon? Or if Ronila—?"

"Be off, Valen *rejongai*. I've work to do."

Chapter 30

❅━━━●━━━❅

The few-quellae walk took me from the Well into the ruin of Gillarine, and only twenty or thirty steps more transported me from the cloisters into Renna's well yard. The high walls left the yard in gray-blue shadows. A leaden afternoon—a proper reflection of my spirits. Flicks of sensation—a taste of moisture in the air, the feel of damp earth beneath my feet, the spongy moss between the stones—afflicted me with a yearning like that of a traveler on an evening road, hoping to see a warm and well-lit house over the next rise. And my gut felt uneasy.

I sighed and strolled toward the stair. I dared not hope that this third passage had somehow cured my doulon craving. I must speak with Saverian. I needed clothes. I needed sleep. I needed to know what day it was.

"Who's down there?" The gruff challenge came from high atop the wall that separated the well yard from the inner bailey. Someone had spotted me. "Gatzi's thumb! What's that?"

"There you are!" This shout, emitted in the squawking timbre of a young male, came from much closer. "Did you fall out of your head just because you spilt a bit of dye on you? You'll freeze out here, and His Grace won't like you tainting the well with dye!"

Confused, I glanced over my shoulder just in time to see a great bat flying across the yard, only I realized, as the dark mantle of wool fell over my head, that it was but a boy carrying a very large cloak. No sooner had I twisted the heavy folds so that my face poked out of the hood rather than into it, than Jullian shoved me into the deeper shadows of the colonnade.

"I've been waiting for you, Brother Valen," he whispered, as the guards on the wall speculated quietly on the likely parentage of a fool who'd walk naked in the freezing well yard after spilling dye on himself, and wasn't it an odd kind of dye to shine so brightly. "I didn't think you'd want to be seen . . . this way." He sounded disapproving, but then, he persisted in calling me *Brother*.

"I'm grateful," I said, fastening the clip at my neck. "It feels right to wear only the gards when I'm in the wild, just as wearing a cowl feels right in an abbey. But when I'm back amongst the rest of you, it's damned awkward. Tell me . . . how long was I gone?"

"A sevenday, it's been."

"Seven days!" Dismay erased what smattering of confidence I'd held on to. The solstice was but two days hence. Sila Diaglou would likely be crossing Caedmon's Bridge this very night.

"Everyone's worried, but no one will speak what's on his mind, especially to me. There's going to be a battle here, isn't there? A magical battle that will mean the dark age is come?"

"Yes." Jullian was no longer a child to be sheltered with sweet lies.

He straightened his back. "I knew it. They keep saying I need to be hidden in some fortress along with Mistress Elene and Brother Victor, but Mistress Elene vows she will ride out to war tomorrow. Mistress Saverian insists Brother Victor is too weak to travel anywhere, but he winks at me when she says it. We believe—Brother Victor and I— that there's only one place we ought to be when this battle comes. Prince Osriel told us how you took him there so quickly, and if you were to take us that same way, then Brother Victor wouldn't have to ride out in the cold. We've no other Scholar."

His boldness stilled my churning thoughts. "You want to go to the lighthouse."

He bobbed his head.

Simple logic and the boy's stalwart stance testified to

the rightness of such a course. Brave Jullian, the brightest student the abbey had ever nurtured, with the wise and capable Victor to mentor him, could become a Scholar well worthy of those who had died to give the world hope. To deny these two the chance to honor their vows to their god and their brotherhood would be to forswear my own.

I bowed to him with sincere solemnity. "In the name of the lighthouse cabal, I would be honored to transport the Scholar and his mentor to their duties. *Teneamus.*"

Jullian released a deep-held breath, no doubt erasing the pent arguments he'd held ready to hand, and squared his shoulders for the next challenge. "I suppose we'd best tell the others."

I grinned and started up the stair. "I'll tell them. But I'd give a good deal for a shirt and a mug of ale first."

"I've tunic, braies, hose, and all over here. The physician gave them to me to hold for you."

"Just tunic and leggings, I think. No braies today." The walk from the Well had kept my new gards stinging.

Osriel, Elene, Saverian, and Brother Victor were taking supper in a small dining chamber. The sight of my friends tucked away in the homely warmth of the firelit room struck me with a terrible sadness, poised as we were at the verge of the abyss.

Word of my arrival had preceded us. The prince had abandoned his meal and stood stiffly by the hearth. "Welcome, Valen," he said, gesturing to the table where two fresh bowls, spoons, and cups had been set. "Refresh yourself. You, too, young watchman. We've sent for more."

"Thank you, lord." I took a knee, hoping to reassure the prince that I wasn't planning to abduct him again. "It is fine to see you recovered from your ordeal." Though he was gray-skinned and gaunt as always, naught of weakness marred his posture, nor any outward sign of his saccheria.

As soon as he gestured me up, I turned to Elene. Her skin bloomed a much healthier hue than his. Even from across the room, I felt the robust life in her. Only her great eyes betrayed knowledge and grief beyond bearing. "Dearest mistress, forgive my not coming to you on our return from Palinur. Anything . . . anything . . . you need of me, please ask."

She lifted her chin. "Later this evening, after you have paid your service to His Grace, I would appreciate a private word. I wish to hear of my father's death."

"Of course, Thanea." I bowed deeply. Osriel would have a deal of trouble preventing his newest warlord from riding out to face her father's murderers.

Beside Elene sat Brother Victor, resting his diminutive chin on folded hands. I smiled and cupped my palms together. "Iero's grace, Brother."

He smiled and returned the gesture. "Good Valen. Well met."

I had saved Saverian for last. As I'd pulled on the clothes she'd left me, I had imagined her ironical smirk as she attempted to pry out what I'd been up to by inspection alone, and I had prepared a properly humorous and mystifying retort.

But her dark eyes smoldered, and she seemed on the verge of explosion. "Gratifying to see you've rejoined us, Magnus."

"Saverian," I said, swallowing my jests unspoken. How had I offended this time?

I took the vacant stool between her and Jullian. The boy was already laying a fine-smelling portion of meat over a thick slab of bread in his bowl. Timely and agreeable as Kol's provender had been, my stomach yearned for the hot and savory. I dug in and rejoiced when a serving woman brought in another tureen. Perhaps the uneasiness in my gut was just this and no warning of perversion.

The small room vibrated with unspoken questions. Yet, though they had already finished their meal, the company gave me time to eat by sharing news. Elene reported that Prior Nemesio and his monks were safely bedded at Osriel's remote hold at Magora Syne, that Thane Boedec and Thanea Zurina had arrived with their house warriors three nights previous, and that scouts had reported Harrower troops on the approaches to Caedmon's Bridge.

"I'm glad to hear the brothers are safe," I said as I refilled my bowl. "I presume Prince Bayard's legion accompanies the Harrowers."

"They follow," said Osriel, "but they appear to answer only to my brother, not the priestess."

"Thanea Zurina and her men rode out yesterday to meet the Harrowers at the Bridge," said Elene, a simmering anger scarce contained. "But Boedec's force is ordered to remain here along with Renna's garrison. His Grace seems to believe such a strategy does *not* condemn Zurina's house to annihilation. Though my liege forbids me, I've sworn to ride after her come the dawn and lend her my household's support."

I glanced up at Osriel, whose dark eyes had not left me, and at Saverian, who brooded and bristled, mouth tight as a pinchfist's heart. Then I blotted my mouth and decided I'd best forgo a third portion of the well-seasoned mutton, lest the tensions in the room crack Renna's thick walls.

"I've had a strange journey," I said. "I'd like to think I bring some small hope for this confrontation, but I'd best let His Grace judge. However"—I stood, raising my cup that brimmed with its third filling of Renna's best ale—"as this might be the last feasting night of the lighthouse cabal for a goodly while, I would like to wish godspeed and all good hopes to our new lighthouse Scholar and his mentor. Luviar himself could not have chosen better or braver."

No honorable Evanori may refuse to join a toast to a fellow warrior. Nor may he interject his own contravening opinions before the drinking's done. Monk, prince, physician, and thanea raised their cups and drank. As I was likely thirstier than any of them, I drained my cup first and got the upper hand in the ensuing remarks.

"Abbot Luviar would not have us forget our vows on this night," I said. "I understand the urgency of getting these two securely housed before the solstice. Thus I've offered my newfound talents to escort them to Gillarine. Yet, were I to attempt more Danae shifting before I've slept, I would likely deposit them in Aurellia or in the middle of the sea. Which means, Mistress Elene, that I must prevail upon you to delay riding out to war on the morrow, as you and Brother Victor will *both* be required to open the lighthouse. Am I correct in that?" I did my best to appear guileless.

It was Brother Victor who started laughing first. Jullian appeared to have acquired a healthy sunburn, but soon ducked his head and snorted into his sleeve. The prince blurted a modest chuckle that soon erupted into Gram's best humor, and even the two women, one beset by indignant grief and the other by gods knew what, soon joined in. Elene knew very well that her intent to ride off to the bridge was rash and futile.

Naught was fundamentally changed by our laughter. Grievance and worry held their grip on each of us. But no one argued with my pronouncement. Osriel returned to his chair, and we talked for a while of how the lighthouse had come to be. Brother Victor recounted the story of my novice punishment when he first showed me the astonishing library, and we spoke of what might be needed to keep the two scholars safe in a future that was naught but hope.

As Brother Victor and Jullian withdrew to their night prayers, Osriel saluted the monk with a hand on his heart, then turned to Jullian and bowed. "Brave Scholar, wisdom, courage, and honor must ever be our beacon through this storm. I can think of no one better suited to light our lighthouse."

Elene touched my hand as she made to follow them from the room. "I want to be angry with you, Valen, but you make it difficult."

"I must keep practicing, then. No one has ever noted such a difficulty."

"When you've done with Osriel . . ."

"I'll come."

Saverian had slipped out without a word to anyone. Her anger afflicted me like a saddle sore. Every passing moment seemed to aggravate it. Only duty kept me from running after her to settle matters. Osriel was waiting.

"As always, you tread the verge of treason, friend Valen." Cup refilled and in hand, he stretched his feet toward the fire. "But I do thank you for reminding us of our common purpose. And most especially— Elene will *not* hear logic from me."

Without waiting for an invitation I dragged my stool closer and perched. "And it is entirely *logic* that forces you to hold her back from danger?"

His color rose. "*Logic* is all I can afford. Believe it or not, Elene is her father's worthy heir, a dauntless and skilled warrior, and a leader warriors will respect. Anger makes her even more formidable. But for this mission, courage must take on a different face. Zurina knows exactly what I'm asking of her."

"To run. To let the Harrowers believe that her sex makes her weak and afraid, so they will think nothing of chasing her all the way to Renna and the world's end."

He drank and then swirled his cup idly. "So must I die on the solstice or not?"

"If Kol succeeds at what he plans, no ..."

I told him all. And as I feared, neither Kol's intentions nor the chance that I could heal the world's wounds changed his determination.

"If you bring me word that Kol has won his challenge, I will joyfully accept the personal reprieve," he said, after reviewing every nuance of my story. "And that you could be destined to heal these plagues and storms leaves me in awe and inspires hope for our future. My faith in you is immeasurable. But I must and will raise the revenant legion. Tales of hope and faith will not persuade Sila's fighters to lay down their arms, even if you were to stand before the hosts in all your glory to deliver them. Do I not fight the battle two days hence at Dashon Ra, then it must be fought another day in Ardra or Morian. Here I can set the terms. If you've brought me an alternative, Valen, then tell me."

And I could not. Though I believed Osriel's enslavement of dead souls would carry him down a path of wickedness no honorable intent could redeem, I had no argument to stay his hand. Sila Diaglou and her grandmother would leave Navronne in ashes and Aeginea desolate.

My conversation with Elene was little easier. We sat stiffly in her chilly retiring room. The hearth fire had already been banked. I spoke of her father's courage, but gave no details of his horrific end. And I confessed that I had not been able to redeem my promise to turn Osriel from his path. "I've brought him hope, though," I said, but did not reveal how slim. "How goes it with"—I waved vaguely at her belly—"you? You seem well."

"I could not hide it longer from Saverian. She says all seems to be as it should be. A hundred times I've thought to tell Osriel, but then I say: If he did not change his plans for me, why would he change them for a child he does not even know?" She did not weep or plead this time. Nor did she invite an embrace or comfort.

"Hold your secret close, mistress. Even so important a matter, from one who is dearer to him than all others . . . I doubt it could sway him just now. He is too locked into this course, and at the least, we need him clearheaded. But there will come a time when it's right." I hoped.

We agreed to leave for Gillarine at midmorning.

I returned to the tower room assigned to me, threw open the window, and sat on the bed to unlace my boots, imagining each of my friends doing the same. Each of us alone, anticipating the trial to come. Of a sudden I could not bear solitude. I relaced my boots and hurried down.

I gulped great breaths of air before descending the stair to Saverian's den. *You're being wholly irrational,* I told myself. *What difference does it make what she thinks of you?* No answer made itself known, and would have made no difference anyway. I needed to see her.

"Saverian?" I tapped on the open door.

"I'm here." The rattling and banging going on inside the low-ceilinged chamber where we had revived Voushanti served as evidence enough of that.

It was impossible to tell what she was doing, beyond removing every bottle, box, and packet from her well-ordered shelves and putting them back again. I stood awkwardly in the middle of the room, waiting for her to turn around to see who had come.

I cleared my throat. "I thought you might be interested . . . as my physician . . . as a matter of your studies . . ." Weak. Insipid. "As you weren't with me this time, and I found myself thinking about you right when something most astonishing happened. I fell out of my body—"

She spun about, a nasty-looking pair of sprung forceps in her hand. "You damnable, god-cursed, splotch-skinned toad. How can you let him do this? I'm to *bleed* him? Watch him suffer? Watch him die? And then perform this despicable enchantment to bring him back to lead an army of dead men?"

I felt unreasonably stung. "I tried to talk him out of it. I thought you knew what he planned."

"About the dead men's eyes, and giving the Harrowers to the dead, yes. That's vile enough. But not the other. Not murdering *him*. And of course Riel chooses to explain my part in his villainous little scheme after you *vanished* without saying anything to anyone. No one knew where you were going or when or if you might come back, and then the boy told us what Gildas did to you, and I can't conceive of how your mind or body can deal with the doulon again so soon. And every moment I thought we'd have to take Voushanti through another death ritual. He must either taste your blood soon or die again—it's surely some marvel of your damnable blood that he has survived this long. So comes tonight, and after worrying myself half sick, you stroll through the door all politeness and deference to Riel, and offering such kindness to poor, half-crazed Elene, and such honor to that brave child—able to work this magic of yours, twisting them all inside out for love of you. But I won't do any of it. Not for you, not for him, not for anyone. By this unmerciful, coldhearted, god-forsaken universe, I won't."

But, of course, she would, because she loved Osriel and believed in him, though it ripped her asunder. And somehow hearing that concern for me had some small part in her fury scratched the itch that had driven me down into her pit of a workplace to stand in the way of this outpouring.

"Please believe me, Kol is doing all he can to see that Danae magic will carry Osriel through what he needs to do. If all goes well, you'll not need to retrieve him from death. And I yet hope that somewhere in the great mystery that's to happen on that night, we'll find him an alternative to his legion of revenants. As for Voushanti . . . I've already told the prince that the mardane will *not* die again. I'll let the man suck my marrow if that prevents it." I stepped close enough I could feel the heated air quivering about her, and I could smell the salt in the tears she would never shed. "You know why Osriel's chosen you for these hard things—because he knows of no one more clever or sensible, no one more skilled. Because he knows you will do it only if you are convinced it's right, and we have no choices left. I'm sorry I didn't tell you where I was going. I was already half out of my head when I left. But I'd like to tell you what's happened, because you were with me through the other, and I need— I think you might understand the parts I've not told anyone ..."

I told her all of it—about my doulon sickness, about my guilt over Luviar and my shameful liaison with Malena, and my horror that she might carry a child of my loins. I told of exploring the Well, and how awkward and ungainly I had felt tripping over my feet in my mother's footsteps, and how quiet and lonely it had been to *be* the Well, and how terrified I was of losing myself, and how it was the memory of her touch and her good humor that had soothed my fear, so that I had been able to yield my boundaries when I had to ...

When I began to sweat and hold up her ceiling for fear of it crushing me, we moved outdoors—and still I babbled as I had never done in all my life. She asked sensible questions, and gifted me with thoroughly unsentimental encouragement when I confessed my doubts that Valen de Cartamandua could possibly be destined to heal plagues and pestilences, and she laughed when I told her of stinging tentacles and blue-scribed feathers in unlikely places.

When the stars had spun out their rounds, and she sat pinched and shivering in the well yard, no matter that I had given her the heavy cloak and wrapped her in my arms, I bent down and laid my forehead on her hair, inhaling its clean scent. "I thank you for this," I said. "I don't know what came over me. Next time, *you* must do the talking."

She pushed me away, quirked her mouth, and stuffed the cloak in my lap. "Perhaps I'll conjure myself into a tree, and you can dance around me—or I'll come to you when you are living as the Well and can't talk back."

I slept long and deep that night, and I dreamed of dancing around her and of hearing her speak in the rustling of leaves and bubbles of starlight and the silence of stones.

"I presume the lighthouse is still at the abbey," I said when Brother Victor joined Jullian, Elene, and me in Renna's well yard on the morning before the solstice. "Never thought to ask."

"It is," he said through the windings of scarves and cowl and the extra cloak Saverian had insisted he wear for our short journey. Jullian carried a leather case filled with medicines, each labeled with uses and doses. Saverian must have been awake preparing them all night after I'd left her in the well yard.

I glanced up and all three of them were staring at me expectantly. I tried to take on a properly sober expression. "Well, we should be off, then. I— You must excuse me, mistress . . . Brother."

Embarrassment quickly heated the still and bitter morning, as I wore naught but my gards beneath my cloak. I removed the cloak and draped it over Jullian's shoulders. Trying to concentrate, I motioned for them to follow me down the colonnade.

Once we walked Gillarine's cloisters, I held the others still for a moment, while I ensured no Harrowers lurked nearby. Jullian grinned as if he had invented me. I snatched my cloak from the boy, while Elene and Brother Victor gaped at the abbey ruins.

The little monk clenched his fist at his breast, his odd features lit from within. "Great Iero's wonders! Who could imagine that it might take us longer to reach the lighthouse from the west cloister, than to reach the west cloister from Renna?"

Victor led us around the north end of the cloister, past the church and the carrels where the monks had pursued their studies in the open air and around the corner by the half-ruined chapter house. He stopped short of the worst of the blackened rubble and turned down the alley that had once marked the ground-level separation of chapter house and scriptorium.

Just beyond a mountain of fallen masonry and charred timbers, a perfectly intact arch supported what remained of the upper-level passage that had connected the two buildings. Set into the wall beneath the arch was a niche where a soot-stained mosaic depicted a saint reading a book.

"Now, mistress," said Brother Victor, "I need you to lay your hands in the niche as we discussed." The monk placed his own small hands atop Elene's and closed his eyes.

A rainbow of light reived the day with magic, scalding my gards and near blinding me. The air crackled like burning sap and tasted of lightning. Neither Elene nor Jullian seemed to notice anything beyond the door that now stood open in the wall and the lamp that hung just inside, ready to show us the way downward.

"Brother, I am happier than ever that I never crossed you in my novice days," I said, shaking my head clear of sparks and glare.

He smiled and motioned us into the doorway. "You had naught to fear. Only in the service of the lighthouse am I exempted from Saint Ophir's proscription of sorcery."

While Jullian and the chancellor inventoried pallets and lamps, blankets and pots, to see what extra supplies they might need brought from Renna, Elene and I explored the two great domed rooms. Though her father had been one of the lighthouse founders, she had never been inside.

The walls of one room were devoted to thousands of books, while the storage cases that lined the narrow walkways held the collected tools of physicians, masons, tailors, and every other craftsman. The second room held the collections of seeds, as well as plows, looms, lathes, and every other kind of implement the human mind could invent.

"Ah, Mother of Light," whispered Elene as she gazed at the searing glory of Osriel's domed ceilings—the overlaid wedges of jeweled glass that shone as if the sun itself hid behind them. "These are the very image of his soul . . ."

She expressed a wish to be alone; thus I wandered back to the other room. The books were useless to me, but I found the tools fascinating. Beside a case that held a collection of pens and inks, measuring sticks, compasses, and the like, stood a tall shelf holding a collection of scrolls and flat maps. Many bore the Cartamandua gryphon. On the lowest shelf sat a number of books.

I squatted beside the shelf and ran my fingers idly over the spines. I pulled out one book, but it was all text, not maps. The age and the decoration of its thin leather cover named it Aurellian . . . which reminded me of a small puzzle.

"Jullian, back at Fortress Torvo you told me that Gildas used an Aurellian book to interpret my grandfather's maps. Why did he need such a thing? What did it tell him that the maps could not?"

The boy unrolled a palliasse, releasing a cloud of dust.

"He didn't use the Aurellian book so much to *interpret* the maps, as to tell him what to look for. It was a book of legends of the Danae. He said the stories told him where the holy places . . . the guardians . . . might be. And then he would know which maps to use to locate them."

The world held its breath. "Did he ever mention something called the Plain? Or the legend of Askeron?"

Jullian's brow wrinkled. "Not that I heard. But he'd not even worked a tenth of the way through the book. The Aurellian script was an ancient kind, written by some adventurer long before the invasion."

My brief hope sagged. Surely bringing some news of the Plain to the Canon might bolster Kol's challenge.

"Narvidius," said Brother Victor, poking his head from the storage room. "*Narvidius, Viator.* I know that book." He craned his neck to scan the vast shelves. "We have a copy here somewhere. That's how Gildas knew of it."

"Find it," I said, my excitement rising. "By Iero's hand, Brothers, find it before tomorrow."

Chapter 31

Vermilion streaks scored the ragged black scud whipped from the peaks of Evanore. The mountains themselves stood black, still, and immense, untouched as yet by the fire to come. Despite the livid ground fog that seeped through the iron gate of Dashon Ra to twine my feet, the air between the wakening mountains and this rocky perch snapped clear and brisk on this solstice morning.

My fists drummed softly on the rocks at my back. My stomach had surely shrunk to the size of a nivat seed. Every untimely bird squawk came near sending me crawling up the cliff. I tried to concentrate. I sensed the plodding hoofbeats and harsh breathing of thousands of men and horses advancing relentlessly from the north. Only light, dry snow had fallen in the past weeks—crystalline fluff that you could blow off surfaces as if it were dust. Sila's troops would experience no delays on the road to Renna.

I deemed myself fortunate to be in command of my senses and in control of this fiendish restlessness. Today was my birthday. The day I was to become one of the long-lived. The day the world could plummet into the abyss.

Firm, heavy footsteps approached from the direction of the stair behind Renna's Great Hall, and moments later, Voushanti strode past the outcrop where I stood waiting for him. Not an hour since, Osriel had passed through the gate and vanished into the fog-choked gully behind it. Before Voushanti could do the same, I stepped out of my hid-

ing place and called after him. "Mardane, do you endure
well?"

The warrior whirled around, sword in hand. "You're not
supposed to be here, sorcerer."

"I searched for you half the night, Mardane. More than
ten days have gone since our blood-bond was created."
Saverian suspected Voushanti did not want to be found.
"The prince told me that you are to lead his personal defense tonight, while he works his great magic."

"But this morning I am to bleed him. That *is* what you
command me, is it not—to aid him in this madness and then
save him from it?" If words could slash skin, so his would
have done. "I need naught else from you."

"I would not have you weaken, no matter what the day
demands. I may not be available to succor you later."

He turned as if to continue on his way, but his feet did
not move. Though his broad shoulders held rigid beneath
his mail shirt, his neck bent forward. "Indeed, I flag," he
said at last. "Do you know what to do?"

"Saverian gave me the words."

Voushanti pivoted smartly and waited for me, the unscarred half of his face gray and sagging in the half-light. His
knife's fiery kiss on my thumb burnt like the solstice sunrise.

"Live, mortal man," I whispered, frost pluming from
my mouth, "all desire and worth bound to my will until
heart stops, bone crumbles, and breath fails." A sour odor
crept through the air as I fed magic to Saverian's spell and
pressed my bleeding thumb to Voushanti's cold lips.

His eyes locked with mine, resentment and shame flaring scarlet in his depths. Though every instinct prompted
me, I did not turn away.

The moment passed. The enchantment resolved. I removed my hand.

Voushanti wiped the last traces of blood from his mouth
with his sleeve, averting his gaze. "May I go now? His Grace
awaits his torturer."

"Heed this command, Mardane: Obey Prince Osriel exactly in this dread matter. In all else protect him unto the
limits of your life . . . no matter his orders."

The warrior bowed curtly, stepped past, and vanished
into the gully.

I did not follow. Osriel did not wish any to witness what he was to endure at Voushanti's hands. No matter Kol's intent to yield the power Osriel needed, the prince could not be certain of it. Only a long, slow bleeding into the earth would generate magic enough to raise his revenants, and so he must initiate his grotesque alternative early on this still, cold morning, hoping that I would bring him news of Kol's aid before he was too weak to pull back.

Did Kol's challenge fail, Osriel would use the word trigger *bloodwitch* to summon Saverian to carry out her grim assignment. He had refused her plea to set up a second trigger in case he changed his mind. Furious, she had disobeyed his command to stay away, hiding herself and a supply of medicines, surgical instruments, and blankets in one of the stone sheds left by those who had mined Dashon Ra. From there she could observe Osriel throughout the day and ensure he did not fail too quickly.

Osriel's first scream rent the brightening morning. I shuddered. What faith he must have in the mardane. Voushanti had to take the prince to the precise juncture of torment without death, to induce him to forget hope, that Osriel's despair might create power for redemption. Faith and honor, love and duty ... I could not deny the virtues that drove the prince and his servants. But with every breath, in every bone, I knew this horror was wrong.

So I did not go to Saverian, though I hated the thought of her lonely vigil. And I did not drag Osriel away from his torment or Voushanti from his cruel task. The only way I could prevent the dread conclusion of this harsh beginning was to take up my own part in the day's events. By midday I must be back to the Well, where Stian would be waiting to take me into the Canon. The situation of Dashon Ra, the silhouette of its rocky parapet against the sky, the thinness of its air, and the gouged and damaged bowl carved from its heart already lived in my memory, ready to bring me back here again.

"Who's there?" Two warriors stood watch at the bottom of the rock-gate stair. They whirled and presented arms as I descended, clearly surprised to see anyone approaching from the direction of the heights. It was ginger-bearded

Philo who challenged me, along with Voushanti's other faithful lieutenant, the dark-haired Melkire.

I lowered my hood. "At ease, friends. It's just Valen."

The two men lowered their swords. "Should have known you would be a part of all this strangeness, pureblood," said Philo. "Perhaps you can tell us why we're posted here behind the hall and kitchens, instead of in the field."

"We've heard reports that the Ardran prince and Sila Diaglou herself are but half a day out in hard pursuit of Thanea Zurina," intruded Melkire.

"The *Ardran* prince ... *Perryn* rides with the priestess? Does Bayard, too?" It could be disastrous if Bayard brought a Moriangi legion here.

"The messenger said no Moriangi regulars rode with Sila yestereve," said Philo. "Only Prince Perryn and a handful of Ardrans. It was their route worried him the most. Zurina is leading them straight for the eastern approaches, showing them the secret ways not even the Aurellians could find. If they come upon Renna from the backside, they'll drop these rocks right on our heads."

This bursting unease from two well-disciplined warriors but reinforced my beliefs about this day's battle. Naught would be held back today—no secret, no life, no soul. Ronila and Gildas would unravel their plots, too, and like these two, I didn't know whence the attack would come.

"Zurina is no fool," I said. "She's surely got her reasons—and her orders. And certainly Thane Boedec and his warhost will be ready to meet whatever comes. Does Voushanti know that Perryn rides with Sila?"

"Aye," said Melkire. "He received the report."

"Good. Stand fast and have faith in your prince and your commander," I said. "Guard them well, warriors. And may your gods do the same for you."

"Godspeed, pureblood," said Philo. "It gives us heart to know you are with us."

I wished I had more reason to be optimistic. And this matter of Bayard ...

A few steps took me to a patch of bare ground behind the bakehouse. Though lacking a sample of Max's own blood, I squeezed a few drops from the fresh cut on my thumb and used it to touch earth with magic. Whether it was the half-

Cartamandua blood or merely the heightened alertness of this day that fed my skill, I located him quickly.

Spirits and demons ... Max had crossed Caedmon's Bridge into Evanore. Bayard's legions could not be allowed to join Sila's. So great a host could overwhelm Osriel's fragile trap, or break too quickly through the defense Voushanti would mount for Osriel. Osriel must not be forced to take action before Kol's release of power at the change of season.

I pelted through the halls and passages of Renna. In a great show of noise and sparks I burst a bar on the wicket gate, then promised the quaking gate guards dogs' faces if they failed to let me out. Bayard wouldn't listen to me. I needed to see Max.

Out on the open hillside, I stripped and bundled my clothes, tying them over one shoulder, and touched earth again. Carefully I recalled the landscape of the southern bridge approaches—a steep descent from the mountains over treeless slopes, leveling out only within the last quellé. As certain as I could be of Max's position along that road, I headed northward along Renna's rutted road to the point where it began its steep descent. Holding the two landscapes in my head for similarity, I worked the shift ...

Two riders pulled up sharply when I stumbled through a washed-out rut ten paces in front of them. Unfortunately, they were but the first of a sizable vanguard and neither of them was Max.

One sidewise glance and I dived off the road, tumbling farther than I liked down a precipitous slope of rocks and scrub into what appeared to be a snow-choked gully. I landed facedown and skidded farther yet, digging in my toes as my head and shoulders crashed through brittle branches and crusted snow. When I came to a stop, my head hung out over a precipice of at least a thousand quercae. My stomach plummeted the entire depth; thankfully, my body did not.

I held still, stifling my gasping breaths, while fifty other horsemen passed by and the two riders argued with each other about exactly what they had seen, and whether the slope was too dangerous to explore. As my legs began to cramp from my desperate hold, another man joined them.

"A naked *demon* glowing with light, you say?" said the newcomer, snorting in sarcasm after their lengthy description. "More likely a boulder tumbled off the cliff. Speak such foolishness again, and I'll conjure tails on your backsides."

"Aye, master." The clank of harness and whuffling of horses was followed by departing hoofbeats. But only two beasts had gone.

"Are you falling out of the sky now, Valen? Pardon if I don't come down to join you."

I crept backward crabwise. Once I found a firmly rooted branch to rest my foot on, I turned around and scrambled upward. "I need to talk to you, Max."

He dismounted and sat on the verge of the shelf road, waiting, examining me carefully as I crouched just below him so as to remain out of sight of the road.

"First you must tell me what you are," he said in as soft a voice as ever I'd heard from him. "And who you are."

I extended my arm so he could see. "I'm still kin—of Cartamandua blood. It just happens my father was not Claudio, and my mother was not human."

"Not human . . ." He stared at the sapphire sea grass and the snarling cat, but did not touch them.

"You're not half so surprised as I was. But much as I would love to share the tale—one could say I'm the younger brother of a map—we've far more important business. Bayard was supposed to wait at the bridge."

Max tore his gaze from my hand. All wariness now, he scanned the cliffs and the upward road, as if hordes of my kind might be lying in wait. "Bayard released Perryn to ride with him, believing him chastened by his tongue-tied captivity. Then the little fair-haired weasel rode ahead with the priestess. It makes Prince Bayard exceeding nervous—the idea of Sila, Perryn, and Osriel working some compromise without him."

"Listen to me, Max, and believe. There will be no compromises at Renna. The only way Bayard comes out of this with even a portion of what he wants is to honor his agreement with Osriel. You must persuade him. My master will not be denied this day."

Max leaned forward—all business—worried and angry. "You lied to me about Fortress Torvo. Used me. And yes, it seems you left me clean of blame. But it left my master chary of Osriel's schemes and *me* chary of persuading him to trust the Bastard. Why should I believe you now?"

"Have you touched earth since you crossed the bridge, Max? Have you allowed yourself to feel what haunts Evanore?" Even lacking Danae blood, Cartamandua talents should detect the sickness lurking in the veins of Dashon Ra.

"Osriel's wards." His voice dismissed the fears he named, but his pureblood mask could not hide those written on his face and in his eyes. He had felt the anger of the dead.

"Exactly so. Whatever you perceive, it is only the beginning for those who challenge Renna. Do your master and his men march on Osriel, they will curse the day they were born, and they will curse the day they died here. Do you understand me?"

"I'll think on it." He averted his eyes, shuttering fear behind perfect pureblood indifference.

Such feeble assurance did nothing for my confidence. Too many pieces of the day's puzzle remained tenuous. "I'll tell you a secret—*you*, Max, not your master. Perhaps if you understand why I could trust no one in Palinur, you'll give credence to my word today."

"Perhaps."

I prayed that I revealed only what no longer held importance. "Sila held three prisoners on the day I came to you. My master was one of them. Does that justify my deception?"

Dismissive laughter burbled from inside him and made it so far as his throat. But then his eyes met mine, and laughter died. "By the night lords . . . the sickly secretary."

His gaze traveled my length as I climbed back onto the road. "Believe, Max. You must find some way to persuade your master to hold back. If not, then in the name of heaven, look to your own soul and ride away."

I prayed my vanishing trick would leave him convinced.

The sun had traveled much too far from its fiery birth by the time I returned to Renna's well yard and shifted back to Gillarine. That such a journey should by rights have taken me three days did naught for my growing fever. I needed to

be at the Well. I would spare only a few moments to learn if
Victor and Jullian had discovered word of the Plain.

Once sure the abbey hosted no unexpected visitors, I
hurried to the lighthouse door and invoked the trigger
word *archangel*. The lighthouse door burst open. Jullian
must have been sitting on the other side.

"We've found it!" The boy bounded down the stair
ahead of me.

Brother Victor sat at a worktable half buried in books
and scrolls. "Iero's grace, Valen!" he said. "Read him the
passage, lad. I'm determined to find him a map."

Jullian proudly showed me the pristine copy of the book
Victor had named *Narvidius, Traveler*. My restless feet had
me circling the room as the boy read the Aurellian text.

> To discover the lost country, the seeker must di-
> vide the riverlands in twain, and the eastern half in
> twain again. In the innermost of these two last di-
> visions, known as the Barrowlands or the Haunted
> Plain by the local peoples, travel the winding thread
> of the River Massivius, called in ancient times Qazar
> or the "Twin," as it crosses a series of rocky berms
> and parts itself into two waterways. On a fertile isle
> between, enriched by the water's flow, once stood
> the garden city of Askeron. Here did great sorcer-
> ers raise the river water to their uppermost towers
> and channel it through the lanes and terraces, so that
> water flowed through every man's hold, the streets
> were ever clean of dung and waste, and the air was
> ever sweet with the roses and honeysuckle that grew
> in wild cascades from the walls.

The lost city of Askeron figured in numerous legends. Narvidius speculated that the sorcerers had grown
cocky and cultivated all of Askeron's terraces, forgetting
to leave a wild place for the guardian Dané to enter and
leave. Thus had the crops and gardens failed one dreadful summer. In that autumn, the river grew to a mighty
flood and washed away every trace of Askeron and left
the ground dead so that the eye of humankind could not
see its remains.

"There's no other reference to a *plain* in the book?" The link seemed tenuous.

"None. But we found no mention of the other particular names you said either—the Mountain, the Well, or the Sea," said the boy. "Though he writes of many mountains and seas. Surely holy Picus would not have told you of the story did he believe it false."

I wasn't at all sure of that. Holy Picus enjoyed his storytelling.

"We've few good maps of eastern Morian," said Brother Victor, beckoning me to his table. "No Cartamandua map. But I've found one that shows a divided river."

The monk showed me the sketchy rendering of a river that split into two only to rejoin itself on its way to the northern sea. A different, later map purported to show the River Massivius and its relation to several other rivers and the Trimori Road, the Aurellian trade route that led to the great port city, only this map showed no division in the river.

"Tell me the names of these towns and cities, and these other places," I said, tapping my finger on the words around the divided river. I had marched with Eodward to the defense of Trimori, along that very road, and it seemed as if we'd crossed a thousand rivers. "If I could but find some place I can remember well enough, I could transport myself there." I had no time for long expeditions.

Jullian began reading the names: Armentor, Vencicar, Pavillium . . . None was familiar. For each map, Victor and Jullian read me the marked distances and interpreted the key, but the Barrowlands were marshy and had a reputation for ill luck, thus Eodward's legions had avoided it.

Out in the cloister garth, I touched earth, bringing to mind all I had learned of the divided river, but a path failed to resolve. It would take me weeks of traveling to approach the Barrowlands and the River Massivius from anywhere I knew.

A crestfallen Jullian trotted alongside me. "Is there naught else we can do to help? Another map? Some question that needs answering? I want to fight in this battle beside you and Gram, but I know my best use is here and not behind a sword."

His earnest innocence, as always, made me regret the flaws and failures that left me unworthy of such admiration. "Here's a question: Find out what use Danae have for nivat. My uncle gets testy when I mention it. And I suppose I'm ashamed to press him. Perhaps if I knew what they do with it, I'd know how to prevent the vile things it does to me."

His face brightened. "I'll do it. I swear—"

"Be careful with oaths, lad," I said, smiling. "They'll take you where you never thought to go."

When I delivered Jullian back to him, I clasped hands with Brother Victor and thanked him for his help. "Lock your door, Brother. Stay safe. I'll come when I can to tell you what transpires."

"No one will find us." Brother Victor touched my bare shoulder. Somewhere in all the taking off and putting on, I had lost my bundle of clothes. I hadn't even noticed. "You shall be Iero's finger of grace this day, Valen. Do not doubt."

The silver-white disk of the sun had slipped past the zenith, and I was yet climbing the last steep hill toward the Well and my waiting grandsire. The day had grown oppressive—the air so cold and thick it was an effort to breathe. Not a whisper of wind stirred the dead grass that poked from the rocks in stiff clumps. The light was flat, a gray-white haze dulling the faint blue of the sky. I felt screams on the air. The taste of blood filled my mouth, no matter how often I spat or grabbed a handful of dry snow to wash it out. Was it that this land's king lay bleeding, or had Sila and her allies already reached Renna and bent their minds to slaughter and corruption?

I jogged lightly across the ledge and down the narrow passage through the cliff that led to the Well. A white-haired Dané squatted beside the dark, still surface of the pool.

"With all respect, grandsi—*argai*." He looked up sharply and I bowed. "Duties prevented—"

"Thy duty lies here and only here."

Stian's greeting halted my apology in the way of an avalanche—rock and ice and inarguable finality. Which, on this day when my turbulent insides already seemed to be digesting briars and knives, drove me to bursting. "My duty lies wherever I choose to pledge my service. Here at the Well. With my king. With my human friends. And with my Danae kin."

"This is impossible," he roared, shaking the ice-clad granite. "Kol is mistaken in thee." He jumped to his feet and strode across the corrie. In moments he would vanish.

"Wait, please, *argai*. Permit me . . ." Damnable touchy bastard. I dropped to my knees and laid hands on the stone, and felt a welcoming warmth flow up my arms. But it was a pattern I sought, the newest one—of course he would have danced here.

It began and ended at the spot where he had been kneeling. First a powerful spin. More turns than Kol's, but a heavier landing. I brushed one foot to the side. Shifted weight. Brushed the other. And then a leap—*drive your spirit upward, Valen*—scarcely landing before another, and then another, circling the pool. *Do not think of your loutish, graceless bumbling. Only of the steps . . . feel them . . . show him . . .*

Such twisted grief I felt as I moved through his steps, such wrenching guilt for blindness and stubborn pride, for anger and righteous belief. Stian's grief and guilt. Clyste, the brightest spirit ever gifted to the long-lived, had died here unforgiven. She had not dared tell her own sire of her hopes, and this shadow of his kiran told me she had been right to keep her secret. That was the worst. He would have woven her bonds of myrtle and hyssop himself. Pain drove Stian's dancing, relentless, unending self-condemnation for beliefs he could not recant.

I stumbled to the end of the silver thread. Trying to stretch my spine longer, lower my hips, and round my arms as to embrace a tree, I made my imitation of the *allavé*. I closed my eyes, determined to hold the position as long as possible, more afraid to hear Stian's scorn than to exhibit my incapacity. But, at the least, I understood him better.

To my astonishment, a hand grasped my back foot, shifted it slightly toward the center of my body, stretched it out farther, and left only my great toe touching the ground.

My forward thigh heated. My supporting ankle wobbled. But I squeezed my eyes shut and willed myself still.

The hands grasped my waist and pressed me down and forward, and then pushed my shoulders down to realign them with back, hip, and leg. I thought my burning thigh would rip. But I held.

"Remember," he said as he pulled my elbows wider and lower, twisted and kneaded my wrists until they felt like softened clay, and riffled my fingers until they rested light as ash on my forehead. Cradling my head in his palms, he drew his thumbs across my eyelids and forehead, smoothing away my frown of concentration. "Thou'rt a stick. Pounding will break thee . . . or leave thee pliable. Now stand up."

I drew in my back leg and pushed up, resisting the urge to groan or knead the muscles of my aching thigh.

"I could not believe what Kol spoke of thee," he said, his granite cheeks unsoftened. "Come. We must prepare. Nightfall opens the Canon."

Chapter 32

❖⟫━━━━━━━━━⟨❖

I held my tongue and followed Stian through the cliff passage. My actions seemed to please him better than my words.

We emerged from the passage into a wholly different landscape—a valley of tall pines decked with frost. Then Stian transported me through a series of breathtakingly fast shifts that demonstrated how rudimentary Kol had been with his teaching. No shift left me nauseated until the last, when we strolled onto a grassy hilltop, the high point of a ridge that protruded from the mountains. The oppression of the day, the anguish on the air, the blood and pain and unyielding winter came together here, leaving every movement an effort.

With only a gesture, Stian bade me stay where I was, while he wandered about the hillside. Every once in a while he would execute a breathtaking leap or a jump and spin that denied the god's firm hand that holds our bodies to the earth. At last he seemed to find what he wanted. He knelt and began to clear a spot of rocks and grass.

The view from the hilltop was magnificent. A little to the north, a small lake reflected the flat light, its outflow several small streams that shone like steel and gouged the hillsides. East of the ridge, the land dropped into a tangle of rock spires and knobbed hills that stretched to the horizon and the deepening blue of winter afternoon. The shortest day of the year. I was eight-and-twenty, and I was not mad. Not yet.

I turned to the west and caught my breath. A parapet of red-and-orange-streaked stone edged the ridge, dropping precipitously to a broad slope—the apron of the greater mountains to the south. The jagged rim reflected the very shape I had etched into my memory that morning.

"This is the Center," I murmured. "Dashon Ra." Only we stood in Aeginea, where no human had gouged and scraped and hollowed out this hilltop in search for gold. I knelt, and though I dared not touch the earth of such a place with magic, I believed I heard Osriel's harsh breathing and felt the seeping of his blood. "Be strong, my king," I whispered as if he might hear me across the distance. "Do not yield your soul too quickly. I *will* find you a way."

"Come here." Stian sat back on his heels and motioned me to do the same on the opposite side of the barren patch he had created. "Do not move. Do not interfere."

With the same powerful fingers he had used to correct my *allavé*, he scooped up the damp soil and spread it over every finger's breadth of my face and neck. "Do not touch it," he said as he closed my eyes and packed the soft soil over them as well. "Do not remove it until I tell thee."

My skin heated. Itched. Burned. Panic welled up from my depths. "Iero's grace! Please—"

He gripped my wrists firmly until my breathing settled. "When I lay a hand on thy breast, follow me. Move as I do, as best thou art able, and attend carefully the earth beneath thy feet. *Remember.*"

I could not imagine what he meant until he packed my ears with dirt, causing another bout of terror. He gripped my wrists until I understood he was not going to fill my nose or mouth.

A touch under my arms brought me to my feet. Thin cold air cleansed my lungs and whispered over my skin. Over my gards. I wriggled my feet and noted the surface of sere grass and thin soil, shards of rock and pricks of ice.

His hand touched my breast for one brief moment. Then the air moved. I panicked. This was impossible. But somewhere inside, the part of me that was coming to understand the language of the gards knew that he had spun in place and taken one step to the right. I did the same and managed not to fall. This time a shard of rock pricked my left great toe and a sprig of tansy tickled my heel.

The air moved again. Another spin. Another step right. Five more. A small leap from one foot to the other. Left, then right, then left again. Repeat. At the end of the sequence, I would have wagered my left arm that I stood exactly on the same spot where I had begun. Without sight or hearing, I had to focus on the gards, the shifting of the air, and the feel of the earth.

Hands touched my arms, extending them straight from my shoulders, kneaded my wrists, and riffled my fingers to ease their stiffness. Then he touched my chest, and we began again.

By the fifth time through, I heard the music, a stately rondeau. By the tenth, I knew every pebble and sprig of the ground, and I was able to concentrate on the spinning, sensing every twitch of Stian's muscles and striving to emulate him until I could sustain an entire revolution without wobbling.

When we completed yet another repetition—the fourteenth or fifteenth—Stian changed the pattern. He clapped his hands and stomped his foot at the same time, then clapped three more times rapidly. A step to his right. So odd not to hear the sound, but only to feel it. I mimed his moves. He repeated the pattern. Again and again, until my heart stuttered in the same rhythm. This one was much easier. Simple. Boring. One more and then he walked away. I waited for him to jump or spin, but he didn't. Fear nibbled at my mind, but I focused on his movements and did not rush. I executed the last repetition and walked after him. He would not lead me off a cliff.

The surface changed from grass and stony earth to sheer rock. Then to ice. He was shifting as he walked. When the rushing movement of a stream confused me, I hesitated briefly, then stepped forward. My foot found no purchase and I toppled . . .

Hands grabbed my arms and dragged me backward, holding me tight until I regained balance and firm footing, and longer yet until my senses calmed and I could feel subtleties again. I inhaled deeply. Just beyond my feet the rush of water drew its own wind and shed a fine spray. The hands released me and touched my chest lightly.

More careful this time, I swiveled right and followed him down a short, steep path and into fast-flowing water. Treacherous rocks underfoot, round and slick. Water so cold it stole my breath. But I did not fall or step into a waterfall.

When I stood ankle deep in the stream, Stian halted. A startling application of freezing water cleared my ears. "Holy Mother!"

"Discipline and obedience serve thee well. Wash now. Then we will speak."

I rinsed the dirt from my eyes. The stream that froze my feet was the outflow from the small waterfall and the deep pool at its foot. I dived into the pool and washed away the residue of the afternoon. When I climbed out again, shaking off the freezing water like a pup, my waiting grandsire inspected me, giving particular attention to my face.

"Did I get it all off?" I said, a bit impatient. My skin yet burned from the grit.

"The soil . . . yes." His middle finger traced an outline about my left eye, around my cheek and ear, and down my neck. "Fitting, I suppose, that it should be the Cartamandua beast."

"The Cartamandua—?" I slapped my hand to my cheek. "A gryphon? That means you— But I thought the remasti didn't happen until the Canon. I assumed you were testing me."

"The remasti must be *sealed* in the Canon. Wander away from Aeginea just now and this gard will fade, and thou shalt be no more than before. And indeed I used preparation for this night's deception to distract thee from thy fears. I would not have thee damage the dancing ground as thou didst gouge Stathero. Kol spoke to me of thy peculiar nature, and I did not dismiss *all* of it as foolery."

I could not help but grin. A gryphon. Great Mother . . . that would explain the feathers and braids down below— eagle's feathers and lion's hair. I stretched out my left arm and found that my gards had shifted. Talons wrapped my shoulder, draped by an eagle's wing. The breast and legs of the lion scribed the left side of my chest.

I bowed to Stian. "My thanks for your care, *argai*. I will strive to learn all you teach."

He seemed satisfied, if not pleased, as he beckoned me to follow. "As thou art prepared, we retrace our steps. Here is my plan for the Canon ..."

The daylight was failing.

"So if all goes well, if Kol takes the Center and holds the magic of the season's change, how long will I have to inform my prince?"

Even in its fifth variation, Stian could not seem to grasp my question. "The power of the joined kirani shall flow through his hands and feet. He does not hold it. *How long* has no meaning."

Stian and I crouched in the gully that penetrated the rocky rim of Dashon Ra. No iron gate barred the gully's western end. No fortress pressed its back to these vermillion cliffs. Not in *this* realm. Did the same steep-angled sunlight that bathed these cliffs shine on my dying king?

"How will Kol know the moment of the season's change? Will he do something so I'll know he's ready? Or just before?" I knew the dancing would not stop. He'd said they danced till dawn.

I felt confident that I could get to Osriel's side in the space of a few steps. After the afternoon's exercise, this hillside felt a part of me, and I would never shed the image of the ravaged mine ... and the souls that dwelt there. I just wasn't sure *when* I would need to go. At what point could I tell Osriel that Danae power was his for the taking?

"Thou shalt know the season's change as well as Kol. Dost thou not know when the wind shifts or the sun rises?"

"Yes, yes, of course I do." Faith came very hard on this evening, when every moment threatened disaster, when so much was new to me.

I peered out from our seclusion, and my breath caught as it had repeatedly over the last hour. How could I respond to the sights before me but with aching wonder? Danae, hundreds of them—male and female—roamed the hillside, greeting one another. Some practiced dance steps; some stretched out their limbs. Many wore veils of spidersilk that floated in the breeze, echoing or elaborating their movements. Others wore flowers in their hair—hair long and red like Kol's or white like Stian's, or palest gold, silver as moonbeams, or green as the sea. None black as mine. Stian had threaded my hair with vines to disguise it.

More Danae arrived, appearing in a wink of light here and there across the landscape. Age did not mar their ravishing beauty. Stian pointed out those who were eldest—recognizable by a luminous aura that left them almost transparent. And I noted Tuari, his rust-colored hair wreathed with autumn leaves, his haughty face marked with a roe deer, and his consort, Nysse the Chosen, with her cap of scarlet curls and a swan scribed on cheek and breast.

These two walked an arced path through the crowd, greeting the others, drawing them into ordered ranks behind them like a ship's wake. By the time Tuari and Nysse reached the apex of the hill, the other Danae encircled the hill in spiraled bands of light. Three initiates stood at the lower end of the spiral, their full complement of gards pulsing a dull gray like my own. A few immature initiates—young males and females lacking facial gards as yet—scrambled onto the rocks south of my position, where they could watch.

Here and there a latecomer winked into view and hurried up the hill. As Stian moved to join them, he glanced over his shoulder. "Our fate lies with thee, Clyste-son. Have care with it."

I bowed. "With all my heart and skill, Stian-*argai*."

He nodded and ran up the slope to join one of the ranks, greeting those on either side of him.

Great gods, please grant that I do not fail them. Breathing deep to calm my jittery gut, I hugged the rock and waited.

The last rays of the sun were swallowed by the horizon. From the hilltop, one of the eldest Danae began to sing a simple wordless melody, eerie, haunting, marvelous, wrenching, for it touched all the yearnings and confusions that had marked my life from my earliest days: the pain that had dragged me into perversion, the fury that had lashed out at confinement and tawdry concerns, the truth that had teased at me in temples and taverns, in drink and in lovemaking. The song called me to the dance.

Tuari spun on one foot, straight and powerful, then came to rest and touched Nysse's hand. She stretched one foot skyward, impossibly vertical. Tuari held her hand and walked a circle around her, turning her as she balanced on her toes. When he released her, she touched the next in line, a luminous elder who jumped and scissored his straight legs so fast they became invisible. He landed and touched the next . . .

And so the connection of movement and grace passed down the spiral around the hill until it reached the three initiates at the end. Their gards pulsed a faint azure. But not mine. My breath came short and painful, as I withheld my answer to the call. I had to wait. This was but the first round, the Round of Greeting, so Stian had schooled me.

A livelier song began the Round of Celebration. The ranks of dancers broke into smaller circles or duets or solo dancers, each following the music as they would. Soon other songs drowned out the voices—the songs of trees and wandering waterways, a pavane as stately as an oak, a gigue, light and joyous like the water. Or perhaps only I heard those particular harmonies, and others heard songs drawn from their own senses.

I climbed the gully wall and found a perch whence I could see farther down the hill to the lake, where the reflections of the dancers grew brighter as the afterglow faded from the west. Danae everywhere. An hour, they must have danced that second round.

The third round began with the Archon's Dance, a courtesy to his position. All others sat wherever they had finished the last round and watched attentively. Tuari was a powerful dancer. His jumps were almost as high as Kol's, his eppires charged with life, his positions held to the point of breaking. Though glorious in themselves, his movements spoke more of vigor than of grace. Yet at his *allavé*, the watchers all over the hillside offered their approval, slapping one hand against a thigh—the sound of hailstones rapping on a slate roof.

The next to dance was Nysse, for this third was the Round of the Chosen, where the archon charged the one judged finest among all Danae to demonstrate her skills and invited any who wished to challenge her naming to do so.

Indeed Nysse was lovely. She could weigh no more than cloud, for though her jumps were not so high as those of the males, she seemed to hang suspended in the air for an eternity and land without disturbing the grass beneath. Her willowy grace evoked the image of a pond where swans glided in the moonlight and once a year white lilies bloomed. Yet the dance affected me with a wrenching sadness, as it told how early snow had blighted the lilies and sent the swans southward over the mountains.

To feel Nysse's movements was to understand that every passing season weakened the bonds between the kirani and the land. When even so beloved a sianou as the Pond of the White Lilies suffered, the world must change or be lost. Her *allavé* drew a sigh of wonder and grief from the Danae host. Without a word, she had made a strong argument for the unlinking Kol feared.

As the slapping noise and cries of approval grew, Tuari spread his arms, inviting any to challenge his consort for the Center. I could not imagine who would attempt it. Even Kol must doubt. I crushed that thought before it could blossom. Three dancers tried, each one better than the last, though none were a match for Nysse. Few from the crowd voiced support for any of them.

An expectant murmur traversed the crowd as a fourth challenger strode up the hill and nodded to the archon— Kol, unmatched in his pride.

He began slowly, a simple series of steps and blindingly sharp triple spins, one and then another, scribing a circle on the hilltop, so that those on every side could see—every movement precise, composed, and very large. His body spoke that this was to be a monumental kiran, for he did not stop or slow or hesitate or miss the next ... or the next ... or the next ... And when he had drawn us tight enough, when I could not believe that he could possibly execute one more movement without flaw, he coiled and leaped into the air like the explosion of a geyser, soaring twice the height of a man, his legs split wide and straight. No sooner landed than he bent gracefully to earth as if to work a summoning, then rose and with his powerful leg drew himself into one eppire and then another, driving his body until my heart felt like to burst. The music he drew from earth and

sky began with the grieving strings of vielles and the cool
flowing sorrows of a dulcian—my lost mother—with hints
of mysteries and secrets, and moved with driving purpose
to trumps and songs of triumph.

I could not have said that those who watched held
breath as I did. They could not know how much depended
on this kiran. But when Kol had built the image of the Well,
so true that I could feel my own deep-buried fires, my veins
of stone, my bed of earth and wounded walls, wonder and
memory surged through the host. One and then another of
the Danae stood as if they could not believe what they perceived. Some spread their arms as if to bask in their awe.

By the time Kol stretched leg and back and bowed his
head in his *allavé*, every Dané in Dashon Ra was standing.
And when he rose to his feet, a great cry of joy and triumph
shattered the night.

"He said to prepare for a surprise, but who could have
guessed this marvel?"

I almost fell off my perch. Kol's friend Thokki stood
just below me, looking up with eyes the same color as her
gards—the hue of morning sky in spring.

"In the Canon, Thokki." I jumped down and kept my
distance, wary, ready to pounce if she cried out warning.

"Thou hast naught to fear from me, initiate," she said,
raising her hands as if to ward a blow. "Kol asked my help—
a matter of such astonishment that all else he babbled was
but chaff tickling my ear, save for his promise that his challenge kiran would vouch for his actions—as indeed it has.
He asked me in his sire's name to partner thee in Stian's
Round and disguise thy . . . limitations."

"I promise you that—"

"*Thy* promises carry no vigor with me, initiate. Kol's
and Stian's serve well enough." Her ready smile dismissed
whatever offense I might have taken. "Ah, see? Tuari has
no choice now."

I looked back to the hilltop where Nysse herself took
Kol's hand and presented him to the exultant Danae. Another cheer broke out as Tuari followed her lead. Then the
two of them backed away, leaving Kol alone at the Center.

Kol stomped one foot on the ground, then clapped his
hands together over his head. He set up a steady rhythm

that subsumed the random slaps and cheers and drew them into unison. Soon every Dané kept his pace, so that the earth thundered with it. They continued all together until Kol nodded, and a group broke off and set up a counterpoint of three quick claps in between Kol's steady marks. My blood pulsed in time with them. Simple. Powerful.

"Dost thou feel the call?" asked Thokki, tight with excitement. "This is Stian's Round."

My foot hammered the beat—the same rhythm Stian had driven into my head that afternoon. How had I ever judged it boring? All across Dashon Ra, the Danae formed circles large and small, wheels within wheels. Circles of light. "Aye," I said. "I feel it."

Thokki clasped my hand and grinned. "Then let us join in."

She paused, watching, as one great wheel expanded to catch up more dancers, burgeoning in our direction, and then shrank again, spinning off minor circles like sparks from a fire. "Now!"

We ran across the small dark gap and joined three others—two males, one female—in a minor circle. I stumbled at first, my heart in my throat.

"Welcome the initiate!" called Thokki as she stomped and clapped.

The others shouted, "In the Canon, initiate!"

"In the Canon," I croaked. Then I stomped and clapped, kept the rhythm and moved in the circle, and within three beats felt like crowing with the joy of it. I could have continued a lifetime with naught but this.

But the dance was not static, and Thokki leaned close. "Thy feet, initiate. Do not lose the pace. *Remember*."

She stepped back, and I felt sere grass and thin soil, shards of rock and pricks of ice underneath my feet. I spun in place and stepped to the right. Gods cherish all . . . a rock pricked my left great toe and a sprig of tansy tickled my heel. And so we moved into the patterns Stian had drilled into me. Simple steps and spins and short leaps about our small wheel. The music of pipes and tabors swelled from the earth and stars. My gards took fire with the deepest blues of lapis, sapphire, and summer midnight in the frostlands, and I thought I must be raised into heaven. And when Stian's

Round came to its end in a great crescendo, I thought the hands that reached under my arms as if to embrace me must surely be my grandsire come to welcome me. Kol had won, and I was Danae.

The arms squeezed upward, crushing my shoulders. "Take the halfbreed to the pond. And remove that one." Thokki stumbled forward and fell, her head slamming into the turf. "I'll have Tuari break her for this trespass."

No mistaking the crone's voice that gave the orders, or the stick that fell so brutally on Thokki's shoulder, or the shapeless form that moved into our circle from the night. Underneath her hood, golden eyes smoldered with hate, and her thin lips broke into a smile that none but I could see. Ronila.

Chapter 33

⟫————————⟪

"**N**o!" I yelled as a Dané with an unmarked face hefted a dazed Thokki to his shoulder and disappeared into the night beyond the circles. "Don't harm her. Please, you don't understand!"

The glare of sigils and starlight became a blur as I tried to wrestle free. But the owner of the well-muscled arms that gripped my shoulders locked his hands behind my neck. No matter my kicking and writhing, another Dané bound my ankles. If I could not walk, I could not escape.

The youth glanced up at me and wrenched his knots tighter. My heart sank as I recognized him as Kennet, the initiate whose legs were twined with oak leaves, Tuari's attendant who had bound me to a tree intending to break my knees. His tall, strong companion with the wheat-colored hair was likely the person crushing my neck.

The other three dancers of our circle gawked in disbelief as the two young Danae bound my wrists behind my back. "My kin-father, the archon, has charged me to root out the causes of our failing life," Ronila said to them. "What more cause could we discover than a halfbreed flaunting illicit gards in the Canon?"

"Don't let her do this," I said. "She wants to destroy us all!"

Ronila touched each of the three dancers on the shoulder. "Human interference has corrupted the long-lived, even he who is Chosen. *I* have paid the just price to preserve the Canon, and so must every violator. Go. Dance Freja's Round and restore innocence to the change of season."

The three glanced back uncertainly as they moved off to join Freja's Round or the Round of Learning, where one dancer would move about the inside of a wheel of light, striving to match every other dancer's most difficult steps.

"This is no violation!" I shouted after them. "Kol brought back the Well. It lives in your memory again."

Kennet's comrade hefted me onto his shoulders and carried me down the hill, past circles and spirals that twisted and turned like jewels of heaven strung on silken threads. Ronila hobbled alongside.

"I am made new by the Canon," I said, recalling Kol's teaching. "You cannot hinder me."

"The archon will render that judgment," said Kennet. "We but ensure thy attendance."

With only a few hundred steps we traveled far from the dancing ground and the Center. This pond lay in a nest of meadowlands in the lee of a gentle hilltop, very like the lake at Dashon Ra. But here spike-thin pines and dark spruce mantled the surrounding hillsides. Snow lay deep upon these meadows, frosting every twig and needle of the trees. And the new-risen moon set the crystals sparkling and laid a path of silver light across the rippling lake. The splendor of the scene pierced my heart.

Two Danae walked out of a rainbow flare and joined us at the lakeshore. "What urgency demands our absence from the Canon, Llio-daughter?" said Tuari. "The change approaches. The dance beckons."

My captors threw me to the ground at Tuari's and Nysse's feet. I rolled to the side, spitting out snow and dirt that filled my mouth. My cheekbone stung, sliced by a protruding rock.

"Behold, Tuari Archon," said Ronila, "all has come about as I warned thee. You asked me, as your kin, as one who has paid the just price of imperfection, to uncover evidence of the corruption that cracks the world. Here is the halfbreed Cartamandua found preening and prancing in Stian's Round. Canst thou mistake whose work this is?" Ronila's stick poked my back, where the second remasti had etched Stian's rock, and my arm, where the cat lurked amid Kol's sea grass.

"Thou dost accuse the Chosen and his sire of willful violation?" Sounding truly shocked, Tuari stooped to examine me closer. "How can this be the Cartamandua halfbreed? He wore no gards when I saw him."

"Clearly they have forced his body through some corrupt remasti," said Ronila. "Canst thou not feel the storm wind rising in the human realm? Look out upon the beauty of Aeginea, Tuari Archon, and tell me that human violence and filth do not threaten its annihilation."

"Good archon, gracious Nysse, I bring you hope of healing," I said, struggling to my knees. "Your kind were given guardianship of both Aeginea and the human realms. Surely no mere chance caused the first four Danae guardians to arise at the points of our joining. I beg you heed what you have felt this night. Kol has given you back the Well, where my mother was poisoned by this harpy and her minions."

"Who can say what deceptions Stian and his brood have wrought in our minds?" said Ronila, sneering. "The daughter who gave a child of our blood to a human. The son who steals the Center, as he stole this halfbreed from your just breaking. The father who once condemned you—Tuari Archon—to live as a crawling beast. They have brought a halfbreed to the dance, as your own proclamation of the Law forbids."

Tuari looked from Ronila to me, his rust-colored eyes flaring with anger and mistrust. "Did Kol and Stian bring thee to the Canon, halfbreed?" he asked.

"Ask him about Thokki, as well, *resagai*," said Ronila eagerly. "She who has lusted after Kol since he was nestling. Corrupted, as are all those touched by Stian's get."

"More pain and vengeance will not repair what's done," I said. "But I can help you heal the Canon without breaking it further. All I ask is your hear—"

"Thou art halfbreed, Cartamandua-son," said Tuari sternly, interrupting. "Thou hast reached maturing this night, thus the Law forbids me to break thee. However, those who brought thee illicitly to the Canon are forfeit. Answer truth, if thou wouldst have me hear another word from thy lips. I

will judge silence as agreement. Did Kol and Stian bring thee
to the Canon, using Thokki to shield thee?"

How could I weigh the consequences of my answer? I,
who was a master of lies, could likely devise a reasonable
story. But Ronila had built her life on lies, corrupted Sila
with lies. We stood at the brink of the abyss, and I needed
this man to believe what I told him. Surely it was the time
for truth. Kol and Stian . . . and Thokki, too . . . had known
the risks they took.

"Yes," I said, "because they believed—"

"There, you see?" crowed Ronila.

"Silence, Llio-daughter." Tuari held up a warning finger to the old woman. "I have sought thy forgiveness for
the wrongs I've done thee and thy dam, and thou hast offered me generous service in return. But I am archon and
would hear what healing this Cartamandua-son believes
he can bring to the Canon. Despite our hard experience
of him, Stian is no mindless actor."

Ronila pressed her hands together and bowed. "It is
but sincerest concern for the Canon that drives my crone's
tongue, *resagai*. Thou art most generous to allow thy flawed
kin to be of use."

"Speak, Cartamandua-son."

"I am born of a line of cartographers—human sorcerers
who can find their way through the world with magic . . ."
With cautious hope and urgency, I told the archon of my
bent. Of finding the Well before I knew of my parentage.
Of my ability to follow the paths of kirani laid down on this
day or those long past. Though I dared not mention that the
Well had chosen me as guardian—not with Ronila present,
not when I was captive—I told him how I had walked my
mother's kiran to build Kol's memory and understanding
of the Well, and what Kol believed about my talents.

"I know not what to believe," said Tuari, throwing up
his hands. "How can I accept that a human-tainted abomination, one ignorant of the Canon, can accomplish what
our finest dancers cannot? We feel the chaos of humankind; we suffer these poisonings and betrayals, and blind
though we are, we know our lands diminished. To hear
thy claim that *we* are responsible for this great imbalance
drives me to fury."

"Allow me to show you, good Tuari," I said. "I can help you restore what is lost."

"This halfbreed is poison, Archon," snapped Ronila, growling with hate. "Stian has set him to bring you down in—"

Tuari silenced her with a gesture, then turned to Nysse, who had been quietly attentive throughout all. "Kol's and Stian's violation—deliberate and well considered—risks the very survival of Aeginea . . . of our kind," he said in anguished indecision. "How can I allow it? And yet this halfbreed's sincerity rings true, and Kol's kiran hath bespoke a marvel this night. I must consider: What if his claims be true, and I refuse to heed?"

Before Ronila could burst or Tuari shatter with his vacillation, Nysse laid her hand on Tuari's shoulder. "The season's change is upon us, my love, yet clearly these matters cannot be settled in haste." Her clear voice rippled with light, just as the pond did. "Stian and Kol have certainly trespassed the Law. Thokki to a lesser guilt. Yet unless we can prove, without doubt, that their violations have done damage, Kol must dance the Center. To force him out on uncertain grounds could be judged an equal risk to the Canon. Nor will I have it said that private jealousy spurred me to take his place. His kiran was flawless, and none other can approach our level. Only in the dance and its consequences can we judge truth."

As a snarling Ronila clutched her walking stick and muttered indecipherable venom, Tuari kissed Nysse's forehead and gazed adoringly on his consort. "Nysse's wisdom frees my own thoughts, good Ronila," he said, his relief blinding him to the old woman's burgeoning malice.

But the archon immediately quenched my own surging hope. "By the halfbreed's own word are Kol and Stian guilty," he said. "We shall hold the Cartamandua-son as surety for their guilt until the dance is finished. If they value him sincerely, they will step forward to accept the consequences of their violations—myrtle and hyssop and forever unbinding. Then shall we give the halfbreed an opportunity to prove his promise of restoration. If they do not step forward, we shall judge their violations frivolous and force them to their punishment, proceeding with whatever is necessary to rend our unwholesome bond to the human realms."

"Whatever is *necessary*?" I cried. "You mean you would lock the guardians of the Mountain and the Sea in their sianous, and allow them to be slaughtered as was my mother. But, of course, Ronila will see them dead in any case. Tuari Archon, Ronila despises human and long-lived alike. In the human world, she names herself the Scourge. She has corrupted her granddaughter and taught her to poison sianous. She wants to destroy all possibility of recovery for the Canon, condemning the world to chaos."

But the weak-livered fool would hear none of it. "None shall be slaughtered," he said, insufferably condescending. "If you are what you say, we shall discover it. Ronila has long suffered the consequences of her mixed blood and aspires to naught beyond her place. I sought her aid to recognize human-tainted corruption, and by your own word, she has done so." He took Nysse's arm. "Kennet, Ulfin, secure the halfbreed until we are ready for him, and see that Thokki is returned to the Canon undamaged." The two regal Danae strolled toward the lake . . . fading . . .

"Archon," I called in desperation, "I can restore the Plain!"

Tuari paused and looked back, shaking his head in disbelief. "Bring us to the Plain in the hour of Kol's trial, halfbreed, and I shall deem all transgression worthy." He and his consort vanished in a streak of light.

Despite my futile struggles and impotent pleas, the two young Danae seated me on a jumble of rock so that I had a place to rest my back for the long night to come. Ulfin left to find out where their third companion had taken Thokki, while Kennet gathered a handful of reeds from the lakeshore and spread them on the rocks as if to sort them. Ronila crouched in the lee of a pine tree, watching us and jabbing her stick repeatedly into the crusted snow.

Urgency near drove me wild. Kol danced the Center and would do as he promised, but all would go for naught did I fail to let Osriel know. And even then, I must persuade the prince that allowing dead souls to devour the Harrowers must surely violate the Canon we were trying to heal. Then must I bend my thoughts to finding the Plain before

Kol could be imprisoned. I twisted my hands in their bindings of braided vines until warm blood welled from the raw scraping.

As I tore my wrists, Ronila drew a bundle from her voluminous robes. "Those of us half human can suffer from the cold," she said. "The gards are never quite enough. I would lend the Cartamandua-son my spare cloak. No ill in that, eh, lad?"

"Come ahead," said Kennet, who perched cross-legged beside me, head bent, braiding his reeds into a mat.

"I need naught from you, Scourge," I said, cursing the bindings that would not stretch.

"Oh, you need this." As the old woman approached our rocky perch, she juggled her bundle of brown wool and stumbled awkwardly over her walking stick.

Kennet reached out to catch her, and she fell forward into his lap, a shapeless heap. Startled, he looked down at her and grunted wordlessly. Ronila wrenched and twisted as if to free herself of his grasp, but his hands had fallen limp. She stepped back, and the young Dané shuddered and slumped sideways, his lifeblood gushing from the ragged hole just below his breastbone, his gards fading. His head rested on my thigh.

"Murdering witch!" I cried, horrified. Twisting my shoulders half out of their sockets, I slid my bound hands under me and around my legs to the front. Too late for Kennet. I pressed my shaking hands to his face and felt the surety of death.

Ronila backed away, laughing at my contortions. Dark stains covered her brown robes. "The long-lived take exception to those who slay their young. As you do. My faithful monk sends word that he plans to shred thy archangel before he bleeds him. He has only to choose which sianou to poison."

She turned her back and hobbled away.

I bellowed in wordless rage. The knife lay on the rock in a pool of Kennet's blood, and I fumbled it into my grasp. I sawed at the ropes on my ankles until they fell slack. Heedless of the blade's lethal edge, I cut my hands free. Some of the blood that slathered them was certainly my own. Weapon in hand, I sped after the retreating demoness . . .

... only to have the old witch shift and lead me past a different lake ...

... and again, so that I pursued her alongside a broad, sluggish loop of a river ...

... and again, to find my feet on a rutted cart road, skirting a river bend. Inside the river's loop, a jagged ruin loomed darkly through a driving snow, and in the moment I spun, blinking, to confirm that we had come to Gillarine, Ronila vanished in a burst of red light. Hand of Magrog!

Hate and fear driving me, I pelted toward the ruin, leaping the jagged foundation walls that were all that remained of the infirmary. I cut across the buried herb garden, and sped past the great chimney of the bakehouse and around the corner between the refectory building and the dorter. Then caution slowed my feet, and I crept through the ruined east cloister. I could not hide myself in the dark, but at the least I didn't have to announce my coming like a maddened bull. What better way for these demon gatzi to gain entry to the lighthouse than to prick Valen Blunderer into a mindless rage and send me charging forth to rescue Jullian?

Breathing deep, I called on my finest senses. The air tasted of fear and torment, and reeked of blood and nivat, so strong it came near choking me. No surprise that Gildas would wield my weakness as a weapon. Reawakened hunger ground my gut. But I would not run away.

I crept around the ruined scriptorium and down the alley toward the sounds of tight breathing and rapid heartbeats, grabbing up an iron torch bracket to supplement the bloody knife. The lighthouse door stood open, a soft light emanating from inside, illuminating a vision of horror in this once-holy precinct. Brother Victor's body dangled from the arch that bridged the alleyway. The pool of blood underneath him had long clotted and frozen.

Ah, merciful Iero, cherish your faithful servant. Yielding time only for this one prayer, I pressed my back to the broken stone, and crushed both deep-welling grief and an explosive lust for vengeance. Gildas and Ronila must have planned this damnable sight to send me further into frenzy. But my best honor to a man of reason would be to hold on to my own. My rage froze as cold as the night. I acknowledged no fear, as I considered spells ...

"Right on time, friend Valen!" Black cloak, hood, and boots made it difficult to identify the man who stood behind the shadowed arch. But Gildas's condescending humor was unmistakable. "We've not even gotten too cold awaiting you." He jerked one shoulder, and Jullian stumbled up the stair and into the light spilling from the lighthouse doorway. The boy's hands were bound behind his back, and a rope encircled his neck. "Did I not tell you that an archangel would be my shield when the last darkness fell?"

"The Tormentor readies a special pit for you, murderer," I said, tightening my limbs to pounce.

"Oh, I would not risk a move just yet," said Gildas. The monk waved a small knife, smeared with black, at Jullian's face. The boy tried to pull away, but the taut leash held him close. "Throw away your weapons, Valen, then proceed down the stairs and seat yourself on the stool beside the worktable. I expect to see your palms flat on the table when I bring our young friend down. One move of disobedience and I prick him with this blade. Doulon paste prepared from your blood would be a nasty balm for a wound, would it not?"

"Don't do it! He plans to—" A jerk of the rope silenced Jullian's anguished warning.

No curse seemed sufficient to the occasion. I tossed Ronila's knife and the iron bar into the rubble and did as he had instructed. The lower doors were thrown open, so that a table sat in plain view of the stair. In the center of it sat a bowl of nivat seeds. The scent near caved in my skull. Beside the bowl sat a leather pouch, a rushlight in a small iron holder, and a lidded calyx of silver, the size of my fist. No doubt the pouch contained linen threads and silver needles and enchanted mirror glass.

As I sat on the backless stool and laid my palms on the table, I summoned images of Victor and Kennet to divert my cravings into anger and purpose. I recalled the collections of tools and mapped out where knives, axes, or any other sharp implements could be found and estimated how long it would take me to reach them. Always too far and too long.

Though reason told me that one exposure to the doulon would not enslave the boy, even an hour of such craving for pain must scar a tender soul, no matter that soul's courage or resilience. I had been fourteen and far from innocent, and I would never be free of it.

Jullian descended the stair, Gildas behind him, clutching the short neck rope. Great gods, what I would have given for the ability to touch minds. If I could but induce the boy to dive or duck, yanking Gildas off balance, I could leap the table and take the villain before he could strike. But Jullian's face shone pale as quicklime, and Gildas maintained distance enough that I could not possibly reach him soon enough. The monk settled on a bench and forced Jullian to his knees in front of him, the knife poised at the boy's cheek.

"And so we have come to this day, Valen. The day the world ends." He tilted his head. "The gryphon gives you a rakish air."

I would not trade quips with him.

As ever, he grinned, reading me like one of his books. "So well disciplined. You've learned much since you first came here. You seethe and plot, seeing naught but obstacles as of yet, and so also you must know what I intend for you to do now."

One more doulon would not end me. I would control it. Wait for him to let his guard down. Kill him. I reached for the leather pouch.

"Not the pouch. Not just yet. Open the calyx."

I did and almost choked. The silver vessel held doulon paste—more than I had ever seen at once. It must have been made with two hundred seeds. "Just stick a knife in me," I said. "I'll do you better service as a corpse than what this will leave of me." I would be one twisted scab, a gibbering cripple.

"Made with your own blood. You've no need to use it all. Scoop out double your usual amount. Remember, I'll know."

I did as he said. Taking tight grip of my senses, I licked the tasteless mess from my fingers. "Iero have mercy," I whispered as the vile paste ignited the fire in my belly.

Every muscle spasmed at once, every quat of my skin screamed as if I had fallen into the everlasting fire. Yet even such pain as constricted my lungs and shredded my spine was not half enough to resolve the doulon spell.

In mounting frenzy, I slipped from the stool, ground my head into the floor, and clawed my skin, tearing at the cut in my cheek. All foolish notions of control, of retaining sense and purpose vanished. All I could think of was my need for pain.

"Go on now, boy, draw us a pitcher of mead, while I tend him. With a regular diet of nivat, Valen will become quite docile. Rely upon it, a slave who can shelter us in Aeginea shall make all the difference over the next few years as we await the deepening dark. Perhaps we'll teach him magic."

Gildas bent to whisper in my ear, his scorn mingling with the shrieking of my blood. "I'm going to let this build for a while, Valen. But don't lose hope. Just implant the lesson in your head. Relief comes only when I say."

The fire grew, and my mind broke. I writhed and moaned. I begged him to strike me. But only when my body seized into one unending cramp, and my heart balked and swelled into an agonized knot, did Gildas lay my left hand on the seat of the stool and slam a knife through it.

I screamed at the moment's blinding rapture, blessing Gildas for the divine release, though I had danced in heaven on this night and knew this was not at all the same. He yanked out the dagger, and I curled into a knot around my throbbing hand and my shame.

Time slumped into a formless mass, even as I struggled to retain some grip on it. *Stupid, vile, perverse fool, your king awaits you.* How many hours had passed since I had been carried from the Canon? My heart cracked to think that Danae were yet dancing without me.

From Stian's naming of the dance rounds, I had estimated the change of season would come some two hours past midnight. I would know, he'd said. But then, he had not thought I would be wallowing in a stupor, clutching a pierced hand and working not to empty my guts onto the lighthouse floor.

Gildas had returned to his bench. He cleaned his knife and coiled the rope he had used to hold Jullian. "Come, sit up, Valen," he said when he'd finished these tasks. "We'll share a pitcher of mead. Very good mead, I would imagine, as it was laid down in the early days of the lighthouse."

Behind him, Jullian was twisting his face like a mischie-

vous aingerou, and one of his hands kept making sharp
jerking movements. Something about the pitcher in his
hand. About Gildas. *Distract him* . . .

Gildas narrowed his eyes and glanced over his shoulder.
Jullian stepped around us, and I heard him set pitcher and
cups on the table behind me. I uncurled, pushed up with my
arms, and vomited into Gildas's lap. That he then kicked
me in the face with his slimed boot didn't matter. Nothing
could hurt me.

"Disgusting filth," snapped Gildas. "Find a rag and clean
this up, boy. My boots, too."

Jullian trotted off and soon returned with a ragged towel.
Once the mess was dealt with, Gildas ordered Jullian to
pour the mead. "Remember what I told you, boy. Whatever
I eat or drink, your protector eats or drinks, as well."

"Aye, I remember." So much for my muddled hope that
Jullian had poisoned the damnable monk.

Gildas watched as Jullian poured, then prodded me
with his boot. "Get up and get something in your stomach,
Valen, or I'll have to drag you to your cell. You remember Gillarine's little prison? You've chains and silkbindings
waiting."

Gildas and I drained our cups in perfect unison. And in
perfect unison, we gasped. The bone-cracking spasms came
hard and fast; the light splintered.

"J-Jullian," I croaked, aghast, "what have you done?"

Gildas paled and clutched his belly. Shudders racked his
limbs. "The wretched little beast . . . poisoned us both."

Not poison. The doulon. I wanted to weep and laugh all
together. So bright a mind, but the boy didn't understand.
This would hurt Gildas for a while. But me . . . two massive
doses in the space of an hour . . . The colored ceiling plummeted toward me, and I threw my arms over my head. My
skin felt as if it were peeling away from my bones. Gildas
screamed and collapsed on the floor.

"I'm sorry, Brother Valen. So sorry. I know it's awful."
Jullian kicked Gildas's knife away and shoved stools and
table out of the monk's reach. With the coiled rope that
had bound his own neck, he tied the weeping, writhing
Gildas's hands behind him. Then, grabbing me under my
arms, he dragged me, quat by quat, toward the stair. "I had

to pour from the same pitcher—give it to you both—else he'd never drink it."

Trumpets blared inside my skull and would not stop, no matter how I tried to crush them, and always the pain grew, squeezing harsh bleats from my ragged throat. In all my life I had never hurt so wickedly—and my body seized and begged for more. "Kill me. Please, god . . ."

Images flashed before my eyes and fractured before I could identify them. The world was crumbling, and even Gildas's groans could not put it to rights.

"Come on, Brother Valen. We've got to get you up the stair. I know what to do. I found out about nivat in a book. As you asked me to."

He forced me to crawl . . . nudging, shoving, yelling unintelligible words . . . into the night . . . into the cold that sent spears of ice into my lungs and my heart that hammered to bursting. Through the snow that seared my raw flesh. More steps. More stone. Endless misery. Endless agony . . .

At last he propped me against a ring of stone, grasped my head, and forced me to look at his face. He was so ragged . . . weeping . . . but he did not falter. "This is Saint Gillare's font, Brother. It's a part of the Well—your sianou. Nivat is like spirits for the Danae. When they have too much of it, they go into their sianous and it puts them right. You've got to go into the font. Back to the Well."

Snow drifted through the strips of stone above his head. I could not comprehend what he asked of me. "Sorry. Sorry. I can't . . ."

"You must let go of your body, Brother. Then it will be all right again."

He threw water in my face—bitterly cold and tasting of starlight—and my body understood. He shoved. I crawled. Once my aching belly rested on the font's marble rim, he tipped me forward, and I rolled into the burbling water. With a sigh, I yielded my boundaries and plummeted, and with water, stone, and the deep-buried fires of the Well, I purged spirit and flesh of my old sin.

"Just implant the lesson in your head, Gildas. Relief comes only when I say. Food and water come only when Jullian says."

Pain-ravaged, slimed with vomit and worse, the man who had once been my friend slumped against the stone wall of the abbey prison cell. The manacle that held his ankle to the wall gleamed bright in the light of Jullian's lamp. The mark on his cheek, where I had struck him to resolve his first doulon and teach him of perverse pleasure, was already swelling and would make a lovely bruise.

Jullian swore that no more than half an hour had passed from the moment I rolled into the font a madman until I climbed out again, refreshed and clearheaded. I would have believed it if he'd said days or weeks, for I'd had no sense of time at all. Yet I had carried with me the urgent understanding that I must return to physical form as soon as possible. Even so, we had gone to Gildas's relief only after we had buried Brother Victor in the herb garden.

Our prisoner croaked a laugh. "One doulon does not enslave me, Valen. I'll walk free and never look back." He spoke bravely now I had refused to soil my hands with his blood.

"Very true. So let me show you magic, friend Gildas. A talented physician taught me how to enhance the effect of medicines fivefold." I crouched beside him, placed my fingers on his brow, and triggered the spell. "The doulon is but a potion after all, which means—assuming a normal cycle of eight-and-twenty days, shortened by the extra-potent paste you prepared—you have perhaps two days until you feel the hunger ready to devour you. Perhaps only one. By that time, either the world will have fallen into the chaos you desire and no one will ever come to succor you, or Osriel of Evanore will be King of Navronne, and I will bring you to his justice for the murder of Brother Horach, Brother Victor, Thane Stearc of Erasku, Gerard of Elanus, and Clyste Stian-daughter. He will not be merciful."

Gildas lunged toward my ankles as I headed for the door. "Wait, Valen, I can tell you secrets—"

I slammed the prison cell door and locked it. "Never step within his arm's reach, Jullian," I said, as Gildas yelled after us. "Never open the door, but just shove a water flask through the slot. He will beg and wheedle and play on your conscience, but this is no sin to confine him."

"He didn't listen to Brother Victor," said the boy as we

climbed the three short flights of steps back to the alley and
the lighthouse door, trailed by Gildas's hoarse curses and a
last despairing wail. "I'll vow he didn't listen to Gerard or
Horach either. This is justice, not sin. Not at all what he did
to Thane Stearc."

"Exactly so. Now, I must go. You're all right with being
alone, lad?" I hated abandoning him. "You'll not go out
again?" Victor and Jullian had stepped out to retrieve what
was left of the abbey service books and stores when Gildas
took them.

The boy shook his head and hung the magical lamp on
its hook just inside the door. "Brother Victor showed me
how to lock and unlock the door wards without magic. I'll
be sorry he's not here to teach me more, but I'm not afraid
and not alone. Iero and his angels are with me. *Teneamus*,
Brother Valen."

"Indeed, I'm sure they are. *Teneamus*, brave Scholar."

I jumped lightly up and over the fallen masonry that
I had scarce been able to crawl over two hours previous
and sprinted for the cloister. As I worked the shift, the boy
closed the lighthouse door and the ivory light from across
the garth winked out, plunging the ruined abbey and the
world into a sea of night and winter.

Chapter 34

The battle had been joined at Dashon Ra. The earth itself had told me of the assault while I had purged myself of nivat in my sianou. And now my senses perceived the dread results. A cacophony of drums, trampling boots, and rage-filled cries blared about the ancient mine and its rugged approaches, and I smelled battle sweat and loosened bowels and warm blood dripping on consecrated ground.

The Harrowers threw themselves against Thane Boedec's warriors like the raging sea against the cliffs of Cymra, only these cliffs were not formed of granite, but of five hundred brave men who knew they were outnumbered ten to one. Strung out in a long crescent about the rim of the vast bowl, they had bent at the first wave. Torches and magelights flared bright in the driving snow, lighting the way for the frenzied mob that raced steadily upward from the east. Gods preserve my erstwhile brother, I saw no sign of Bayard's Moriangi. But the banner of Perryn of Ardra flew alongside the orange pennant of Sila Diaglou at the solid center of the assault. Their wedge had already driven Boedec over the rim and onto the downward slope to the mine's dark heart where Osriel lay bleeding—preparing to become a blood-addicted shell like Voushanti in order to preserve Navronne.

"We'll get you down there," said Philo. With his faithful comrade Melkire, the ginger-bearded warrior crouched beside me atop the west rim of the ridge, where Renna lay

below the rock-gate stair. "But we'd best be quick. Old Boedec is as strong as lords are made, but none were made to
withstand such odds as this."

Of course they weren't. Such was Osriel's plan. When
Boedec's line broke, the Harrower legions would rush
down into the bowl of the mine—and into Osriel's trap.
Only Voushanti and a handful of soldiers would stand
between the mob and our prince. At that point Osriel
would have to act—to summon power for enchantment—
whether the Canon had reached its climax or not. It would
be a race to determine which happened first. My blood
thrummed with the imminent change of season, and my
stomach throbbed with the pounding of Harrower drums.
And Osriel did not yet know that Kol could give him the
power he needed.

I snugged the dark cloak Voushanti had left for me and
raised the hood to hide my facial gards. Then the three of
us scrambled down from our perch and slipped and slid
downward between spoil heaps and broken slabs, through
snarls of iron and rope, and under rotted sluiceways. After
Melkire twisted his ankle in a trench, I led the way with
my better night vision, while the two warriors guarded my
flanks. Voushanti had pledged their lives to protect mine.

The oppressive horror of the souls' prison had not
waned. The music of this ravaged landscape was as frigid as
the frost wind that pierced flesh and bone, and as dissonant
as the clangor of weaponry from the approaching combat.
Yet something *had* changed here since the morning. On my
every visit, these prisoned souls' pervasive, virulent enmity
for all that lived had left me shaking and ill. But on this
night, I felt only confused anger and an overpowering grief.
What had happened to their hate?

The wind whined and swirled powdery snow into our
faces. Philo crept under a dry sluiceway, peering around
the rotting supports to ensure no Harrower flankers had
sneaked so far around the pitted vale. He waved us through.
After a long, shallow descent, we encountered Voushanti
and his sentries posted about the rim of the pit, a steep-
sided grotto the size of Renna's Great Hall, ripped out of
the core of the mine. The Center of Dashon Ra matched
the Center of the Danae dancing ground.

"Merciful Mother," I whispered when I gazed down into the pit, for surely this place was the inverted mockery of the Canon's heart. Where, in Aeginea, wheels of light turned to the earth's music, here a thousand calyxes sat upon the layered rocks and ledges that lined the walls of the grotto, each giving off a bilious glow. And with the stench of leprous decay speeded a thousandfold, a monstrous, corrupt magic shaped of human torment and royal blood poisoned the air and earth. Its source lay in the center of the pit, where a dark-haired man had been stretched and suspended facedown across the black, gaping mouth of some deep shaft or sinkhole. His wrists and ankles were bound to iron stakes driven into the rock. Wide bands of gold encircled his upper arms, smeared with the blood that ribboned his shredded back. Only slight jerking movements of his shoulders told me that he lived.

Recklessly, I galloped and slid down a crumbled, near-vertical stair, unwilling to take the long way around to the sloping cart track that led into the deeps at the north end of the pit. "My lord, I'm here," I yelled. "You need not suffer this. Voushanti, get him out! Saverian!"

The mardane followed on my heels. By the time we skidded to the bottom and dashed to the sinkhole, Saverian was pelting down the cart path, arms laden with blankets and medicine bags.

Strips of cloth bound Osriel's eyes. Tufts of wool stopped his ears.

I touched his hand. He jerked, the binding ropes squeezing blood from the raw wounds about his wrist. "Valen?" he whispered. "Tell me."

Stretching my arm across the empty blackness, I yanked the tuft of wool from his ear. "Kol dances the Center," I said softly. "The change of season is not yet."

A quiet noise that might have been a sob caught in his throat. I did not release his cold hand. "Hurry!" I called to the others. "Get him out of this."

Deep walls and howling wind muted the noise of the approaching battle. The mardane and his men slipped a wide plank under the prince's torso and another the length of his body, supporting him as they unbound his limbs. Carefully they lifted him away from the gaping shaft and onto

Saverian's blankets, where he lay quivering, gasping for breath. I could not imagine the agony of his fevered joints.

As I slipped off Osriel's blindfold, Saverian unstoppered a vial and pressed it to his lips. "Mother of life, Valen, I thought you'd never come," she said.

"Get me up," Osriel murmured into the blanket. "Help me into my armor."

"You're mad, Riel," said Saverian, near tears as she sponged some potion on his lacerated back and peeled away his shredded shirt. "You must stay down until I stop this bleeding."

"If I am not to share their fate, then I must *lead* them, at the least," he said, drawing his hands underneath his shoulders as if to rise.

Their fate ... He spoke of his prisoners. He had spent this day of torment listening to the dead.

Voushanti squatted beside us. "I'll send down your arms, Lord Prince. Then I'll deploy my line farther up the hill, as you commanded." Osriel jerked his head, but Voushanti looked to me for confirmation. I nodded, and the warriors left Saverian, the prince, and me alone.

"Valen, would you give him—?" Saverian's stopped breath made me look up. I had thrown back my hood, and she stared at me, blue sigils reflected in her dark eyes. I'd near forgotten my newest gards.

Smiling and rolling my eyes, I took the proffered flask. But she quickly averted her gaze, and even amid these matters of far more import, I selfishly wished she had not. I hated that she might think me some freakish creature.

While she prepared another potion, I helped Osriel sit up. I knew he needed to be on his feet to get his blood moving, to feel alive. Strength would come. He had reserves I could not imagine, and a physician unparalleled in any kingdom.

"Breathe a bit, get warm, and drink this nasty stuff," I said. "Then I'll help you stand. God's bones, you look a wreck." Gingerly I bundled blankets about his torn shoulders and helped him drink. His face was the color of ash, save for the bruises and blood.

He drained the flask and opened his eyes. A faint smile tweaked his bloodless face. "You're not so handsome as you might think, Dané. Looks as if Grossartius let fly his mighty hammer at your fine gryphon."

"And why is your hand bandaged?" said Saverian, the moment's crack in her brittle shell quite well sealed. "I'll vow you've not cleaned that wound any more than the one on your cheek."

"It's a reminder from Ronila and Gildas," I said, brushing dirt from Jullian's bloodstained linen wrapping my pierced hand. .

One of Voushanti's men arrived with Osriel's shirt, jupon, and hauberk, greaves, and gauntlets. Another dropped chausses, boots, and swordbelt at the prince's side. Osriel dispatched the two men with his demand for a scouting report. "Now I would have your report, Valen," he said, once they'd gone.

"Brother Victor is murdered," I said, grieving again that the chancellor's passing must be slighted amidst these dread events. "But Jullian is safely locked in the lighthouse, and Gildas is secured until his king can judge him. So we've only the priestess, her gammy, your brothers, and their soldiers to worry with. And Ronila is by far the most dangerous ..."

While Osriel downed two flasks of ale and another of Saverian's potions, I sketched out the day's events. "You can't imagine how fast Ronila can shift. Keep someone at your back at all times. And don't take one step toward her, or you'll find yourself somewhere else altogether."

"You've already taught me that lesson." Osriel reached for my hands for help to get up, and I hauled him to his feet. He grimaced and gripped his shoulders. "Would that I had a sianou where I could be taken apart and put back together again without this cursed sickness."

"Perhaps, as the land heals ..."

As I sensed the change that had come about in this haunted place, I recalled Luviar's words: *The lack of a righteous king speeds the ruin of the land.* The king and the land were so intimately bound, that his blood could charge it with power. They lived and died together. Osriel's great enchantment would be a terrible wrong, even if wrought with the Canon's magic and not his own soul's death. What could be less righteous than stripping the dead of eternity?

"Something happened with you as you suffered here today, didn't it, my lord? Something's changed here."

His gaunt face hardened. "Nothing's changed. Do you hear what's coming down on us from the east? Have you brought me an alternative?"

"Only this hope that we can restore the land. Lord, you must not sacrifice these souls." My conviction grew with every passing moment.

"Hope will not save us, Val—"

A thunderous blast shook the earth. As votive vessels rocked and toppled from their perches with a clatter, Saverian and I jammed Osriel between us and hunched to the ground.

A bloodstained young warrior, wearing the green of Evanore, raced down the cart path, Voushanti, Philo, and Melkire on his heels. "Boedec's broken!" cried the youth, chest heaving, looking wildly from one to the other of us. When Osriel stood up, half naked and scarred with blood, the boy went white.

"What is your name, warrior?" said the prince as calmly as if he wore ermine robes and crown.

"P-Prac of Noviart, Your Grace." The boy trembled so wildly his empty scabbard rattled.

"Report, Prac of Noviart. You've naught to fear from your duc, no matter how ill your news."

The young soldier straightened his back. "Prince Perryn's cadre split us in two, lord. Harrowers have engaged our reserves. Thanea Zurina has fallen. Her house—what's left of them—yet holds the left, but not for long." The left was the easiest approach to Dashon Ra. "The priestess d-demands parley."

"Philo, find this brave messenger a sword to fill his scabbard and a drink to ease his thirst, then bring him back here for my reply. Melkire, I want a report from Renna. We must have no interference from our backs."

As the three soldiers did his bidding, Osriel spun to me. "How long, Valen? I must be *here* when Kol grants us the power of the Canon."

My sense felt the night yet rising, a bowstring stretching its last quat. "Not yet, lord. Soon, but not yet."

"We'll not be able to hold the mob off you for three

heartbeats, Lord Prince," said Voushanti, his jaw pulsing—his only sign of agitation. "We should move you into the fortress."

Shaking his head, Osriel folded his arms and summoned Philo and the messenger. "Prac, tell the priestess I will meet her here or nowhere. I guarantee her personal safety, but offer no bond of truce with those who have tortured and murdered my warlords. Can you say that exactly?"

"Aye, Your Grace." The youth, become a man again with a weapon at his side and the trust of his lord, bowed. Philo escorted him back the way he'd come.

"She'll never come down here herself!" said Voushanti, near exploding. "She'll expect sorcery."

"She's attacked because we've told her my power is weak on this night. My warriors are in disarray. Will she not believe in a demonic prince brought low?" He spread his arms to display his wretched state. "All we need is to slow down the assault until Valen signals I've power to act. Return to your post, prepared to escort the priestess here when she arrives. And, Mardane"—Osriel glanced from Voushanti to me and back again—"I issue this command as your sovereign king. Valen has no say in it, no matter the bond between you. Is that understood?"

Voushanti bowed stiffly and hurried away.

"We need to put these aside for the moment," he said with a sigh, nudging his padded leathers and mail. "I'll keep the cloak, at least, lest I be too frozen to speak. And, Saverian, if you have more of the samarth, I would be grateful."

"Your purveyor of potions obeys, as always," said Saverian harshly, shoving a vial into his hand. "I don't know if I'll ever forgive you for this day."

Osriel drank and tossed her the empty vial. "I would regret that, whether or not you continue to keep me living. Now you'd best return to your hiding place. You, too, Valen. Sila mustn't know you've escaped her trap."

"Lord Prince, you must not—"

"Stay or go, Valen. I'll do what I must to preserve this kingdom."

I had no answer.

We upended a half-rotted cart to hide Osriel's armor.

The prince himself settled in the lee of the upturned cart. Bundled in blankets, he quickly lost himself in contemplation, the air about him fraught with spellwork.

Saverian gathered her flasks and jars and packed them away. I offered to carry her bags up to her hiding place.

"Stay with Riel," she said. "Another time, though, I want to hear about the Canon. You said so little, but your face—it's not only the gards that have left you . . . radiant."

"I'd like to tell you," I said, wishing I could erase the wistfulness that poked through her frayed emotions. My fingers twitched, as I fancied that I might touch the furrow between her brows and make it vanish. "As a part of your studies, of course."

"Of course." She started up the path, and I already missed her—so real, so human, our odd companionship grown as if by magic into a sweet tether, binding me to this human realm.

A hacking cough caused me to turn. Osriel's head rested on his arms. So alone in his harsh resolution . . .

Of a sudden I charged after Saverian, instinct pushing me where I'd no thought to go. "We need Elene here tonight," I said, breathless. "Something about his experience here today has made Osriel doubt his course. She, of anyone in the world, might be able to sway him when the time comes. I know it's a great deal to ask. And risky. Holy Mother, I've sworn to keep her and the child safe . . ."

Saverian agreed without hesitation. "Elene is a warrior of Evanore. She belongs where she can fight the battle given to her. I'll see to it." And then my friend, the physician, smiled in a most enigmatic fashion. "I think all your instincts are reliable."

I stared after as she hurried away. My blood warmed, bringing a smile to my own lips, while the wind erased her footsteps as if she had never been.

Melkire brought Osriel the news that Bayard's legion had camped on the slopes before Renna's gates. The Moriangi seemed in no hurry either to engage Osriel's garrison or to join forces with the Harrowers at Dashon Ra.

A clever solution, Max, I thought, as I perched on the rim of the grotto at the end opposite the cart track. *Be ready to make a quick assault in case Sila gains the upper hand, but don't jeopardize the alliance with Osriel by overt action.*

The rising blizzard hid the battle and muffled its clamor. Below me, Osriel had returned to his spellmaking. Fires popped up here and there about the pit—garish green and yellow flames that enhanced the vile colors of the luminous vessels and gave off a nasty odor. Shadows of unseen movement danced on the rocks, and the air filled with sighs and moans that were not the skirling wind. I didn't think such tricks would frighten Sila Diaglou or her vile grandam.

My fingers tracing spirals in the dry snow, I strained to hear the music from the other plane that existed here. A few steps and I could likely be on that hillside where the dance was reaching its climax. Sky Lord save me, how I wanted to be there. I rubbed out my idle markings and listened for Ronila. We could guess Sila's plans. The crone was the real danger.

Footsteps crunched beyond the veils of snow, and I heard Voushanti's gruff challenge.

"They're coming, lord," I called down softly. "I'll be close. The gods hold you."

Osriel threw off his blankets and glanced up. "Thank you for your care, Valen." He cocked his head with a quiet amusement that reminded me very much of Gram. "Tomorrow, remember, we renegotiate the terms of your submission."

I could not but laugh at such a bold pronouncement in the face of the world's end. "I doubt I'll ever be free of you, lord."

I ran lightly up a steep rib of rock that had once supported a wooden sluice. Lying flat on the ground beside the splintered trough, I could both get a superior view of the proceedings in the grotto and be in the midst of them with only two long strides and a stomach-lurching jump. Not that there was much I could do to help. Matters had moved beyond my talents.

Voushanti, Philo, and Melkire led the small party out of the storm and down the cart track. Sila's orange cloak floated in the wind, revealing the steel rings of a habergeon rusty with blood. Beside the priestess walked a tall, gray warrior, whose baldric of woad bore the steel house emblems of a Moriangi grav. This was Hurd, I guessed, the military mind behind Sila's legions. He might have walked straight from his arming room. Only his boots, caked in filth that blackened the snow, gave evidence of his day's activities. Behind Sila and Hurd stood her faithful henchmen, the scurrilous Falderrene and the needle-chinned Radulf, both carrying spears. No Perryn on this day. Most worrisome, no Ronila. Where was the poisonous spider who had woven this web? My back itched. Every nerve end quivered as I stretched my senses, but discovered no trace of her.

"Is my brother not bold enough to face me even under truce?" said Osriel, hunched and shivering. His wet hair straggled over his face, and his cloak flapped, revealing his battered state.

"Prince Perryn is destroying the remnants of your warriors, Bastard," said Sila, all serenity. The steel helm hung from her belt had molded her fair hair to her battle-flushed cheeks. "He saw no need to gloat. Though your tongue-block halts his speech, he channels his fury into his sword. Is it not time to call a halt to this slaughter?"

"Few dare challenge me on my own ground," said Osriel, waving a hand that trembled far too much. His scattered magefires snapped and billowed erratically.

Sila knelt and examined one of the votive vessels, passing her hand across its bilious gleam. A disturbance rippled through the earth under my knees. Her companions, even the formidable Hurd, squirmed uncomfortably and backed away. "I was warned that you dabbled in unwholesome arts," she said. "Tell me, has your halfbreed servant visited this place?"

"Pious Valen? Pssh." Osriel sneered. "True magic frightens him. He pretends he is an angel in a world that has no use for childish legends."

"He was to be mine tonight . . . so your brothers promised me. No matter what other terms we agree to, I will hold you to that. Are you not well, Prince?"

Osriel gathered his cloak tight, shaking violently. Three of his magefires flared and winked out. The dancing shadows slowed. "I've had my use of Valen and much good has it bought me," he croaked. "Have him if you will. I assumed you *already* had him. My spy reported his meeting with your monk yesterday."

Sila looked up sharply. "Valen is with Gildas?" *Nicely planted, lord. Make her doubt.*

Osriel shrugged. "These cabalist lunatics are inseparable. As to terms: I retain Renna. You cannot care; no gold remains here. And I'd keep Magora Syne; I've a fondness for the high mountains. I'll be neither *your* prisoner nor my brothers'. My warlords"—the prince began coughing, deep, racking coughs—"must be paroled—"

Sila watched dispassionately. "I think you are in no condition to make demands, Lord Prince."

Falderrene and Radulf stepped out from behind her. *Holy Mother . . .*

Osriel stayed Voushanti with a gesture and held his palm straight out. Green light flared for a moment from his fingers. But another coughing spasm soon had him clutching his chest, and the light winked out—as did the rest of his magefires. As Osriel's foolery collapsed, the livid gleams of the votive vessels paled as well, and one by one, faded into nothing. What did that mean?

I peered anxiously through the murk across the side hill, willing Saverian to stay hidden, worried about Ronila. When would the crone make her move? When I looked back to the pit, Falderrene had raised a yellow magelight to stave off the night.

"The remaining gold—we divide—" Osriel's breaths came harsh and strained between his bouts of coughing. He sagged against the cart that hid his armor.

"Soon, lord," I whispered. "Hold on. Stand up, or she'll pounce."

"I think we've heard enough," said Sila, turning her back on Osriel. Weapons bristled around her. "Falderrene, prepare your silkbindings. A sick man is no more trustworthy than a healthy one. Hurd, signal—"

Voushanti moved. He embedded his ax in Hurd's arm before the grav could bring his horn from his belt to his lips. Radulf reared back, aiming his spear for Osriel's breast, but Voushanti's sword sliced the devil's neck just below his needle chin. Philo bellowed, *"Avant! Avant!"* and placed his bulk between Osriel and Sila, while Melkire gave chase to Falderrene, cutting him down before he could reach the cart track.

Osriel, unruffled, retreated to the verge of the sinkhole.

Sila, protected by Osriel's bond, watched the brief skirmish calmly. "That was foolish, warrior," she said, picking up Grav Hurd's dropped instrument. "Do you think you can hold back what is to come?" The horn blast pierced the darkened pit.

Of Voushanti's sentries, only three answered Philo's summons, and ten yelling Harrowers raced hard on their heels. The pursuers cut down one of the three survivors before he reached the cart track.

In the distance, torches and magelights and screaming hordes broke through the last defenses of Dashon Ra and flooded the lower slopes. As earth and sky and past and future muddied one another like great rivers joining the sea, I burst from my hiding place, ready to snatch Osriel to safety . . .

The stretched string of the world snapped inside my chest. As Earth itself heaved a great sigh, I stumbled to my knees, shaken by the power of a blood surge more potent than heaven's own wine, more passionate than the drive to love's release. "Now, lord!" I cried, throwing off my cloak so he could see me on the verge above him. "The change!"

Osriel raised his fists. In the space of a thought, midnight boiled from the bowels of Dashon Ra—plumes of purple and green and black that hissed in the snow. Warriors the size of Renna's towers, steeds built to carry them, howling wolves with maws like caverns, and all with eyes of scarlet flame raced across the sky to surround the massed legions of Sila Diaglou and Perryn of Ardra, creating a barrier of terror that no man with half a mind would challenge. From the farthest reaches of Dashon Ra the shouts of battle lust and triumphant carnage transformed into wails of soul-deep terror. Yet these were but Osriel's long-set illusions, designed to trap the Harrowers in the bowl of the mine; the truer horror yet waited.

"Smoke and puffery," said Sila Diaglou, drawing her sword.

Standing at the verge of the black sinkhole, the prince touched the blood leaking from his torn wrists and drew circles around his eyes and sigils on his cheeks and brow. And then he touched his gold armrings and set his fingers glowing, and he knelt and touched the gold-veined earth, gleaming with the Canon's magic. My gards turned to ice. *Mother of night!*

Sila's new-arrived warriors gaped and moaned and let their arms fall slack.

"Grayfin, Harlod, Danc, Skay..." From the prince's lips fell a litany of names—Ardran, Evanori, Moriangi—summoning those he had bound to him until the world's end. With each name a splotch of gray slipped out of the pit intermingled with the purple and black clouds, and a shudder ran up my spine. The pall of illusion fell away from the votive vessels, unmasking their livid gleam.

The Harrower soldiers collapsed and buried their faces in their arms. While Voushanti's sword held Sila and a bleeding Hurd at bay, the mardane harangued his own four men to ignore the roiling heavens and to maintain their protective line in front of Osriel. Sila lifted her eyes to the vague gray faces that appeared among the towering phantoms, and for the first time, appeared uneasy. "What have you done here, Prince?"

"He is a bold sorcerer. I like that." A shapeless figure in brown hobbled away from a flash of scarlet light toward Osriel.

"Grandam!" Sila's shock raised the hairs on my neck. She did not expect Ronila here. Which meant the old woman was making her move ...

"No!" Cursing my distance, I leaped from my high perch, driving my body forward to clear the rock ledges below. I jolted to earth some fifty quercae from the prince and raced toward them across the grotto, yelling, "Take Ronila! Keep her away!"

"And our Bastard is a fine liar." Ronila waved her walking stick. "Even now the Cartamandua abomination comes to shepherd his prince onto your throne, granddaughter. I think it is time to be quit of this nuisance."

Osriel's men did not understand threats from old women. Ronila nudged an astonished Philo with her stick. Melkire merely shoved her back with the flat of his sword.

The old woman tottered and growled. But then she stepped deftly to one side, raised her walking stick again, and poked one of the surviving sentries so hard he staggered backward. I arrived in time to grab his arm before he toppled Osriel into the sinkhole.

"You will *not* touch my king," I yelled, spreading my arms wide to keep her away from the others, keeping a wary eye on her empty hand. "You will *not* do murder here."

Cackling, Ronila poked her stick at me—only this time, a blade protruded from the end of it, aimed straight at my gut. Voushanti launched himself into me, staggering me sidewise. Fire blossomed deep in my side. The witch growled and yanked the stick away. And then I was falling . . .

Crushed between Voushanti's prone bulk and iron-footed Melkire, I sagged only as far as my knees. Fear and instinct and every urgency of life demanded I stand up again. The old woman's leering face loomed in front of me as huge as the Reaper's Moon, her wild white hair a corona, her bloody blade aimed at my heart. A din of screams and wailing seemed to fill the universe.

Yet Ronila's blade did not strike. Her gleeful cackle twisted into such a wrenching intake of breath as comes only with pain. Shock dulled the feral hatred that glinted in her eyes. And even as I clutched my middle and stumbled to my feet, sure that my stomach and liver must fall out the hole in my side, the old woman wobbled and crumpled. Sila Diaglou stood calmly behind her, her pale hands drenched in blood.

"Child?" the old woman whimpered.

The priestess knelt and touched the blood bubbling from her grandmother's lips as if it were a great curiosity. "Could you not see, old woman?" she said. "I value the sorcerer far more than I value you. He is the new world. You are but the dregs of the old." Then she reached around Ronila's back and yanked out her dagger, wiped the blade on the stained brown robes, and stuck it in the empty sheath at her waist.

All the air in my lungs might have escaped through my punctured flesh.

The priestess proffered me a smile worthy of an angel. "There, my beautiful Dané sorcerer, the hag shall not threaten you again. It is not too late to join me. Malena awaits. Are you not curious—? Ah, the witch has wounded you!" Her smile quickly faded as Hurd, a belt wrapped around his bloody arm, gave her a hand up. "Do you need help?"

"Keep away from me, priestess," I croaked, stepping

back. I could not allow thoughts of Malena and what she might or might not carry to distract me. "Your kindness is as bloodstained as your hate."

"And I choose to keep my annoying servant." Osriel stepped from between two of his guards. "This war is ended, priestess. The lighthouse stands. The Canon shall be healed. Command this traitorous grav of Morian, my brother, and the rest to lay down their arms."

"Because you play with corpses?" Sila said scornfully, glancing up at the towering phantoms. "Once I speak to my troops, they will fight—no matter how frightened they are of your ghosts. You have no kingdom, Bastard of Evanore, and no subjects but the dead. My legions will follow me to the netherworld."

"They shall long for the netherworld, lady, when I am done," said Osriel, in such tone as would shudder the most jaded soul. "I give you fair warning. Lay down your arms, or curse the hour you first saw daylight."

"Your threats do not frighten me." And yet, they should. Was that the difference? Was it only those with souls who felt the fear of losing them?

"Then our parley is ended," said Osriel, and turned his back on her.

The prince hissed a command, and scarlet streams of light flowed from the sinkhole. From the gray faces in the clouds erupted a howl that only one who had experienced the doulon hunger would recognize. Or perhaps one who had tasted blood and despair. Of all in that grotto, only Voushanti and I did not stare upward. Terror was written on the faces around us . . . and pity, too.

Melkire pointed to the sky. "Skay," he said. "By the holy angels, it's Skay. And Bergrond. Merciful Iero, what's happening to them?"

"Hurd, form up these whiners," snapped Sila. "I will have Renna by dawn. We shall dismantle this prince limb from limb as we dismantle his house stone from stone."

The gray-faced commander bellowed orders to the ragged Harrowers, kicked and slapped them and got them moving up the cart track. Sila followed. A shoulder touch here, an encouraging word there, an admonishment not to heed the Bastard's illusions, and they moved faster.

Halfway up the sloping track, she looked back and smiled down at me. She waved her hand at Osriel, hunched over the gaping hole. "How can you bear this ghoulish prince, Valen? We need not be rivals. You are the essence of magic; I have rejected and forsworn all such power. You honor all gods; I acknowledge none. You care for humankind and the long-lived; I despise them all. You yearn for decadent pleasure; I need none of it. I am death, as is this prince of yours, while you, Valen, are life itself—more than any cold Danae. Come with me, and I will give you a world cleansed and purified. You can change its face forever, giving every man and woman the chance to wear silk or work spells or dance on the solstice." No matter her smile, her eyes chilled even so bitter a night.

"I do not argue with your vision, lady," I called up to her, "but that you slaughter children and destroy all that is holy and good to create it. There must be another way. I'll have no part of you."

"So be it." She shrugged and ran after her troops.

"Voushanti, you'll see to Valen?" said the prince. His voice sounded hollow, as if he walked yet another plane, or as if he had fallen into the sinkhole after his blood. He knelt beside the dark shaft, the scarlet streams of enchantment giving his pale skin a ruddy cast to match the blood marks he'd drawn. Yet Sila's words prodded me to move. Osriel was not at all like her.

"Lord Prince, don't do this," I said, limping across the drifted snow to his side. "Not before you tell me what you felt here this day. Not until you tell me why I sense no more hatred from these lost souls that only one day ago cried out for vengeance."

Despair and grief stared out at me from my king's bleak face. "Because I bled with them. Because I remembered them, as I promised when I took them captive. Because I knew their names." He dropped his eyes to the roiling pit. "And now I must command them to go forth and live and die an eternal death for me."

"Your very nature rebels at this crime," I said softly. "Let them go."

"I cannot."

I knelt beside the bottomless hole that stank of death

and corruption. "Think of the day we rode down from Renna, when you walked among your people who had been burnt out by the Harrowers. They had nothing before you arrived, and no more when you left save your care and your promise of hope. With but those few words from you, they stood straight and were able to do for themselves. You have given everything for love of these people and this land, and a lover does not torment his beloved. Use the power that has been given you. Let them go."

"You have brought me no other answer, Valen."

"Because it has lived inside you all this time, lord. Behind a mask. Hope is enough."

He raked his fingers through his dark hair. "I would condemn us all."

"Then we will die with love," said a soft voice behind us. "And honor. And faithfulness. But I don't believe we will die. I watched these Harrowers just now, and they are frightened, too, misled by a glamor—despair masquerading as hope. You are their king, Osriel of Evanore. Save them."

When Elene knelt beside him, it was almost as if I heard the earth heave another great sigh. Or perhaps that was only me, watching surprise and weariness unmask his love at last.

Chapter 35

Osriel stood beside the sinkhole and called on those he had named to attend him. And so did every one of the gray phantoms in the cloud turn their empty eyes toward him. How he bore the cold weight of their attention, I could not imagine, for when I, by chance, met the gaze of only one, it placed a burden of lead and earth upon my shoulders.

The prince removed his gold armrings and held them in the scarlet light, and the phantoms' eyes burned red and gold, so one could believe they listened. "Hear my commands and obey," he cried. "I charge you, by the bond I hold, find all who bear arms on this field of woe—your brothers in war, whole or wounded—and speak to each soul what you know of death and life. And at the ending, give this message: A new reign of law and justice shall come to Navronne with this new year. Do this, and I count your service to me ended. Duty done, make your way through the world as you will and find those whom you would comfort at your parting from earthly life, and when the sun touches the sky, be gone to your proper fate. *Perficiimus.*"

The gray phantoms vanished from behind the cloud warriors, and an unsettling energy infused the air and land, like the building tensions of a thunderstorm. All the anger and confusion I had felt here was turned to eagerness. To hunting. Never had I been so glad I did not bear a blade. I did not want to hear what they would speak. I'd seen and heard enough of death and life.

Voushanti knelt at Osriel's feet and spoke what none of us could hear. Osriel held out his hand. Voushanti kissed it, then handed over his sword and ax. And then the mardane turned to me, expressionless. I nodded, and he walked out of the pit and into the night. I did not think we would see him ever again.

Osriel knelt at the pit, his eyes closed as if he could hear his messengers. Elene kept vigil with him, her hand upon his shoulder. Philo formed up his three comrades at the foot of the cart track, weapons laid on the ground at their feet. The light of the votive vessels dimmed and faded. And so we awaited the end of the world.

Accounts differ about what happened on that winter solstice. Some say Iero's angels visited the homes of the dead all over the kingdom and brought them heaven's solace, while the Adversary himself visited wrath upon Sila Diaglou's legions, showing them the paths of hell and sending them home repentant.

Some say the Danae brought forth Eodward's Pretender, another young prince fostered in Danae realms. The guardians left him in the place of Osriel the Bastard, who had made one too many bargains with Magrog the Tormentor and was carried off to the netherworld. That this Pretender named himself *Osriel* was only to avoid the tricky business of Eodward's will. Two copies of that document came to light with the new year, both proclaiming Eodward's youngest son King of Navronne. All agreed that the first day of that winter dawned with a hope Navronne had not felt in living memory.

I know only what I saw.

When Osriel turned away from his enchantments, exhausted and at peace, Elene placed his hand upon her belly and whispered in his ear. It was the right time, when life displayed its truest mingling of joy and grief. For, of course, he had promised his firstborn to the Danae, and he could not break such fragile alliance as might come from this night's work. They clung to each other for a while; then he donned his armor and became Navronne's king, and Elene donned her fairest courage and became Navronne's queen.

*   *   *

I saw no more than that. Saverian found me slumped in the corner of the grotto, trying to find my way back to Aeginea, and offered to sew up the great hole in me instead. Once assured that the blood soaking her garments was soldiers' blood, not hers, I mumbled that my wound would surely heal of itself, and that her stitches would make my fine sea grass look like brambles, and that I had urgent matters to attend if I could just remember what they were. But indeed I came near collapsing on her boots from the great gouts of blood that would not stop oozing, though I felt shamed when I considered how Osriel had bled near a sun's turning and was yet spinning out enchantments and traipsing off to meet with his brother Bayard.

Evidently the prince persuaded Bayard to round up the hardened elements of the Harrower legions and Perryn's men, while Renna's household garrison and the survivors of Boedec's and Zurina's legions gathered the Evanori dead for proper rites on the next day. After what Bayard's men had seen happening in the sky over Dashon Ra that night, they were quite compliant. Many had been visited by the spirits of friends or brothers and had come to believe that Osriel had sent these spirits as a warning and a mercy to keep faith—as, indeed, he had. But I didn't see any of that. Saverian had taken me in hand.

"I must go back," I said thickly. It was very awkward after the physician had just spent most of an hour with her hands in my blood and flesh, and had given me some lovely potion to dull the wicked fire in my side.

"I suppose the ceilings are coming down on you again," she said, emptying yet another basin of bloody water down her drainpipe.

"Not too awful as yet. No, it's Kol." As sense returned, the remembrance of Tuari's impending judgment had me frantic.

She set her basin carefully on her table, as I slid my feet to the floor and put some weight on them to see if my legs would hold me up. "They're still dancing, aren't they?" she said.

"Until dawn. I doubt I'll be allowed anywhere close. Kol and Stian are already at risk of ruin for bringing me to the

Canon." There was also the matter of Kennet. For all the
Danae knew, I had killed him. I had to explain. Fear more
than blood loss threatened to buckle my knees.

"Go, then," she said. "I'll be here if ever you choose to
return to Renna."

As I touched her narrow face, drawing her worry into
a rueful smile, a cheerful determination captured my soul.
"None shall keep me away. There are things that even Renna's powerful house mage has yet to learn," I said, grinning
at the thought. "I do think the gods intend me to see to her
instruction."

I slogged back up the rock gate stair to Dashon Ra as fast
as I could, holding my bandaged side. Saverian had come
up with another cloak—I seemed to be shedding them
like snakeskins—and chausses, so I was able to walk un-
remarked through the grisly business of battle's aftermath.
The snow fell gently now, laying a soft blanket on the cold
faces of the dead. The waning night yet squirmed and wriggled uncomfortably, and I imagined souls passing on their
missions of warning and mercy.

Once out on the hillside, I thought to shift, but my steps
were halted by two weary veterans hauling a bloodstained
cart loaded with weapons and armor. "I've heard Boedec
had her, then lost her," said one. "She can slip through a
man's fingers."

My ears pricked, and I turned to listen.

"Harrowers turned on her," said the other man. "Ran
her off. I'd love to get my hands on her—slaughtered my
whole village, she did."

Gods, Sila was still loose! I pushed past them and ran
down the slope, touched earth, and poured in magic. Only
one other halfbreed Dané walked Dashon Ra.

She was hiding in the dry bed of the leat. I rested my
forearms on the rim of the great trough and peered over
the side. "Ah, priestess, what are we to do with you?"

"These whisperings are like to drive me mad," she said,
sitting up and shuddering as she glanced into the unsettled sky. "I'm glad for human company. Or at least mostly
human. You can kill me if you want. Better you than one
who holds grudges, which seems to be everyone. Perhaps

before you do it, you could explain to me what went wrong. I was ready to take him down. We would have taken Renna by midday. Then, all of a sudden, my warriors began weeping and mumbling. Even the commanders. No one would listen to me."

"Osriel held a more powerful weapon." I climbed up the great sluiceway and perched on the rim. "I don't want to kill you. I think I've given up killing altogether. Never was very good at it. Neither can I allow you to go free. I'd like you to understand what you've done . . . and what was done to you . . . and why Osriel is nothing like you . . . but I don't know enough words to explain it."

She sighed and brushed dirt from her face. "I'm too tired to listen. Besides, you'll not change my beliefs. This world is corrupt beyond saving. The universe cares naught for our human politics. It demands purity. Plague and pestilence will accomplish the cleansing I could not. Just more slowly and with more pain."

"You're wrong," I said. From our vantage I could see the fields of wounded and dead and those who tended them. "But clearly you must be judged by wiser heads than mine. Two realms have claim to your punishment, and I think . . . Will you come with me?" I jumped down from the trough and offered my hand.

She took it and jumped down beside me. "Nothing better to do at present."

I threw off my garments and gathered my thoughts and memories. We walked back toward the gully. I listened for music as we climbed the rocky parapet . . .

. . . and by the time we reached the top, the cries of wounded soldiers had become the music of a single vielle, its strings picking out a pavane. The dancers were paired, one lifting the other or lowering, closing or separating but always touching, entwining their bodies in a single expression of grace, never stopping, as the music never stopped in its round. As far as we could see across the grassy hillside, the lines of sapphire, azure, and lapis flowed and swirled and bent, but never broke. Kol and Thokki danced the Center, and if grace and strength could speak of heaven, then their partnering was divine.

Sila's face grew still. Stunned. "What is this?" she whispered.

The music swelled as it began another round, and slowly, one by one around the circles, the partners held their last position, then settled to the ground until only Kol and Thokki danced. He lifted her above his head, her arms and back and legs one smooth curve. Then Kol settled into an *allavé* with his own back straight and his leg a perfect line with it, and Thokki held above him. And then did the first light of dawn fall on them and the music fade.

"This is what you would destroy," I said, tears pricking my eyes.

She did not respond. Did not speak at all, as the Danae embraced and bowed and vanished, one by one, into the morning. "Come," I said. "We can go back now."

But a small knot of Danae gathered atop the hill, and as I suspected would happen, several more were waiting for us by the time we climbed down the rocks. Sila was strong but not strong enough to resist three determined Danae. I did not run. "It is time for judgment," I said.

Tuari and Nysse and ten more of the long-lived stood at the Center. Kol, Stian, and Thokki stood before them. They paused in their discussion, and all heads turned as we were brought up the hill.

"In the Canon, Tuari Archon," I said, bowing. "I have brought you the hand of the Scourge. She is of our kind, but was nurtured in Ronila's bitterness . . ."

The trial was long and required much discussion and argument. Such punishments as were to be meted out could not be Tuari's decision alone.

I was cleared of Kennet's murder. Ulfin knew that neither Kennet nor I had possessed a knife, and he had seen Ronila throw herself on Kennet as he himself brought Thokki to the pond.

For their part in bringing me to the Canon, Stian and Thokki were condemned to beast form for a gyre—a full term of the seasons. It was a bitter punishment and dangerous, lest some accident befall or some rash hunter fail to recognize them, but mild for the offense. The judges said they were brought into the conspiracy by their love for Kol and not of their own part, and indeed a marvel and no harm had come of my presence at the Canon.

But Kol was judged to have given long thought to his misdeed. He had begun my training and had failed to bring the issue of my talents to the archon. He had defied every precept of the Law and had taken fully on himself the risk of breaking the Canon. At noontide on the following day, he would be prisoned in his sianou, bound forever to slow fading with myrtle and hyssop. They accepted no plea from Stian to trade punishments with his son, no argument that Kol's dancing was unmatched in any season. And the marvel of the Well's recovery could not mitigate both Stian's punishment and Kol's.

Kol accepted the judgment without argument. "I did as was necessary," he said. "I saw no other way. I would do it again." Though many of the ten were uncomfortable with his sentencing, his own words condemned him.

"I can find your lost sianous, Tuari Archon," I pleaded. "I can find the Plain. I just need time." But they believed in swift judgment and would not yield. One look from Kol closed off further protests. He would not have me prisoned as well.

Sila Diaglou they condemned to beast form for as long as she might live. She said nothing. I did not know if she was yet mesmerized by the Canon or believed she was lost in dream. When they asked her what form she would prefer, she asked only that it not be vermin and that it be done right away.

Tuari took her. As she stood waiting to hear what they would do, he wrapped his arms about her from behind and whispered, "Do not be afraid." Before I could blink, both bodies had vanished, and a sparrow fluttered along the ground as if its wings were broken. Moments later and Tuari was back, kneeling beside the bird. He nudged it with his finger, and startled, it flew to a nearby rock. I wanted to watch her as she tried her wings, but a flurry of birds rose from the ground, wheeled, and vanished into the morning, leaving none behind.

The Danae dispersed, one and then the other. As a courtesy to Stian, they would not execute Stian and Thokki's punishments until Kol's was done. The three of them were taken away and I was left alone at the Center, weary and sick at heart.

At nightfall, I took Philo and a cadre of men to Gillarine to take custody of Gildas. Evidently the doulon hunger already burned his flesh. I did not stay to hear his pained sobbing and curses as they shackled him for the short journey to Renna's dungeon, but hurried to the lighthouse door. "Archangel!" I said, infusing the word with magic.

In three heartbeats, the door flew open. "Brother!" The boy peered outside as if to see if the moon had fallen or the earth cracked. The sheer joy that dawned on his young face warmed even such a cold night.

As I told him briefly of Osriel's great magic, and how we had hopes that my peculiar combination of talents might help set the weather back to rights, he served me a small cup of ale, taking as much pride in his hospitality as a new householder. He offered me cheese and dried figs, as well, which reminded me how dreadfully long it had been since I had eaten anything. My aching side and pierced hand had stolen my appetite.

"Do you think the brothers will come back to Gillarine now?" he asked, hesitant. "I can do very well here for as long as needed. But if they were to come . . . there would be singing . . . and they might raise the bells again. The quiet . . . I don't mind it, but . . ."

"I'm sure they'll come back. But you will always be the Scholar. The king will have it no other way." I stood to go. "Iero's grace, Scholar."

"Iero's grace . . . Valen. I don't suppose you'll be coming back here to take vows."

I laughed and looked askance at my gards. "I think I've vows enough for three lifetimes. But if you've matters to discuss with me, you can always go to the font, yes? See if I'm at home?"

He giggled like a boy again and thought that was very fine, and said he would read more in the book of Danae lore and discuss it with me to see if it was accurate. "If not, then I might write a new book that will tell the truth of Danae."

I left him then and jogged across the cloister garth to meet Philo and his prisoner.

"Brother Valen!" Jullian's call turned me around when I was scarcely past the font.

The breathless young scholar stood atop the alley rubble. "I forgot. Do you want to take the book?"

"It served me well, Jullian, and bless you forever for finding it, but you know it's of no use—"

"Not the book about the doulon, but your grandfather's book—the book of maps." He held out a square volume, bound in brown leather, the very book that had gained me admittance into the lighthouse cabal. "I thought you might have use for it."

"Saints and angels! Gildas brought it!" I had no way to carry it with me or keep it safe, but to use it . . . "Quickly, let's get back to the light."

Gildas sweated and his guards cooled their heels while I sat in the lighthouse doorway and paged through the book to find what I needed—a wholly unremarkable fiché, little more than a line drawing without colors or gold leaf or any other elaboration. One smiling aingerou lurked in a corner. Janus had scattered five rosettes across the rough outline of Navronne. Touch a finger to one of the rosettes and a symbol appeared beside it—one displayed the symbol for a mountain, one for a sea, one for a water feature such as a well, and one showed a spiral that Janus had called the Center, before I understood what that meant.

I touched the fifth rosette, the one drawn in the northern half of the map between the arms of a divided river, unmasking a symbol I had not recognized until now. Surely the tiny prongbuck marked the Plain.

Heart swelling with excitement, I touched the aingerou, drew my finger from the Well to the Plain, and poured magic into the enchanted page. In my mind appeared a certain route—a path of roads and fields, hills and valleys, images so vivid that I could use them to find a destination for a shift—a birthday gift from my Cartamandua father.

"The gods ease your pain, madman," I whispered as I closed the book and gave it to the boy for safekeeping. "I'll tell you all about it when this is over."

*   *   *

At noontide on the next day, when they brought Kol to Evaldamon for prisoning, I was waiting for them. Nysse, as always, stood at the archon's side, and ten other Danae had come to stand as witnesses. Kol, hands and feet bound with braided vines, gazed out onto the sea—deep green on this day beneath the winter sun. My uncle's proud face displayed no fear, though a Dané dropped a pile of fragrant green myrtle boughs and arm-length stems of dried hyssop only a few steps away. Stian and Thokki sat atop the cliffs under guard.

"Tuari Archon, I beg hearing," I called. "I have brought you that which must reverse this judgment."

When Kol glanced my way, I bowed. He nodded without expression and returned his eyes to the sea.

"What evidence can change what is confessed?" said Tuari.

"On the solstice, you said that if I could return the Plain to the Canon, you would judge these transgressions worthy, did you not, Archon? And worthy deeds merit no punishment."

Tuari's rust-colored hair was wreathed on this day with holly leaves. "I said this, but thou wert incapable."

"On this day, I am capable. Send whomever you will to judge me."

After some discussion, it was decided that Nysse and Ulfin would verify my claim, and that Kol's imprisonment would be delayed until our return. To the fascination of the Danae, I knelt and laid my palms on the earth. The route unrolled in my mind like a scroll of parchment, and I recalled the shore of the small lake until I could smell the marshland and hear the birds and the lap of the wavelets. "This way," I said, and we made the first shift into Morian, retracing the route I had worked out from Janus's map over a very long night.

In a matter of an hour, we stood in a thick winter fog on an island between the forks of a mighty river. I stepped along a long-faded silver trace and described the dancer's astonishing leaps and his intricate footwork. And soon Nysse herself danced a kiran, echoing Llio's last.

"It is the Plain, Tuari Archon," she said when we returned to Evaldamon. "I can return there at any time. With work, it shall live in our memory as clearly as the Well." Ulfin vouched for all she claimed.

And so were my uncle and grandsire and merry Thokki set free to dance again in Aeginea.

"So why art thou heartsore, *rejongai*?" said Kol, as the two of us strolled down the strand that evening at sunset. "Didst thou expect some other marvel than these thou hast described to me? The world is changing. And thou art fully of the long-lived and fully of the human kind. That is not at all usual. In the coming seasons thou shalt restore the Canon."

"I feel knob-swattled," I said, rubbing the wound in my side that ached more than it should. "Neither here nor there. The prince needs a pureblood adviser and has asked me to stay with him . . . and I desire greatly to do what I can to help him and teach him . . . but I want to be here and learn . . . and I need to travel and begin to reclaim what we've lost . . . and then, there is a woman . . . human . . . very human . . ."

Kol halted and put a hand on my shoulder. "Sleep, Valen. When thou art . . . knob-swattled . . . it is the call to sleep. Take thy season, and thou shalt wake clear and purposeful. It is our way. Necessary. No lesson is more worth the teaching. Renew thyself, that thy work shall be worthy."

"Thank you, vayar."

"Address me as Kol, *rejongai*. We get on well."

PART FIVE

God's Holy Book

Chapter 36

The drips and splats, dribbles and trickles have annoyed me for days. Pesky noises. I want to hear words, not plops and spatters. So easy to forget words when I nestle in the deeps close to the fire or flow through my clean and healing channels to mind the roots. Words land on my surface like pebbles and sink down to where I sleep, nudging me to wakefulness. I curl around them, cherish them, and comprehend matters that have naught to do with seeds or roots or beasts.

It is the woman comes most to bring me words. "The king has taken up residence in Palinur. Prince Bayard swore allegiance in the Temple District, and Osriel named him Defender of Navronne. He left immediately and is to live on his ships. Prince Perryn is branded a traitor on his forehead and is exiled in Bayard's service. The people do not know that Bayard is forbidden to set foot on Navron soil again. But his children shall be fostered in Evanore, while Perryn's are married off to foreign lords. Bayard is satisfied. Riel says he might find use for this onetime brother of yours—Max—who negotiated all these matters.

"The change in Riel is astounding. In these few short weeks, he has had no flare of the saccheria. No cough. No limp. No fever. Whether his pain is truly gone or just so much lessened that his dead nerves cannot feel it, I find myself weeping like a sentimental granny to see him ruddy-cheeked and able to ride and work and love his mooning wife. You will think me entirely changed.

"Those people not touched by the solstice magic are coming slowly to understand that he is not as they believed. It will take time and work, but Riel's peace—in the kingdom and within himself—are his best heralds."

I laughed to hear this and dived down to the earth fires and embraced them. My instincts had told me true: The land heals the righteous king.

Comes another day: "The queen blossoms, though not without sadness. The child will arrive with the summer. Two years Nysse Archon will give them together. But kings' children are often fostered, and unlike Caedmon, Riel and Elene will get to see their little one often as he grows. And yes, I know it is *he*, though I've not told them. And another secret, only for you, the child is also a she . . . for it seems our king got twins upon his beloved. Which will be firstborn and have to go, and which will dawdle and get to stay at home? Perhaps you can persuade Nysse to allow them to trade places from time to time! With Jullian as their tutor, they will learn. With you as their sworn guardian, they will laugh and thrive."

Joy and grief forever mingled. Ever will I give my friends what they need of me.

"Gildas was hanged yesterday . . ."

Justice. But I do not rejoice in ending life.

Did I make a child with Sila's handmaid? I will have to know before it breathes. No child of mine will suckle on hate.

"Bright news this day, dear Valen: The monks have come home to Gillarine. Brother Sebastian is named abbot. They send their prayers for you. They don't seem to realize what an unlikely messenger I am, who puts no faith in gods or prayers. I am helping Brother Anselm set up his new infirmary, and so they allow me to stay in the guesthouse despite my sex. They would like it better were I a married woman. And I would like—

"You must understand, Valen, I'm neither ashamed of my virgin state *nor* overprotective of it. Can you truly hear me? I must not believe it, for I would never say such a thing in front of you. In truth, I've never understood what men and women found together. My parents . . ." She spoke of a pureblood mother who came to regret the life she had given up for love, and a warlord father who resented that his wife held power he could not master. They grew apart and disliked the reminder of their connection in their daughter. A harsh and loveless lesson they taught. ". . . but at least I was clever enough to bury myself in books, not the doulon!

"Ah, friend, sometimes I think I hear you laughing as the ice melt dribbles into your pool—into you. Even if you are truly here, I suppose you sleep. Rest well, Valen. Riel needs you. The world needs you. And I . . . I will be pleased to see you and argue about gods and prayers, souls and immortal life."

She touched me that day—dipped her hand in the pool, and I burned with such fire at the remembrance of her hands that the trees on the ridge will be full green well before the spring change.

The dancer comes, too. He does not speak to me with words, but with leaps and spins and everlasting grace. He charges my dreams with glory, and my lands with the health and nurturing that I can only begin to provide. I feel the shifting of the air as he drives his spirit upward, and I yearn for my body that I can begin to learn how he does it.

The sun warms me on this day, and I feel lazy and still. And lonely. Yet, though the snows lie deep upon the mountains, the sap rises in the trees. I will sleep again another night or three or seven, but spring shall soon fill my loins and call me to the dance, and I shall have my way with living. *Teneo!*

Breath and Bone
began with...

Flesh and Spirit

by
Carol Berg

The rebellious son of a long line of pureblood
cartographers and diviners, Valen has spent
years trying to escape the life ordained for him.
His own mother predicted how he would meet
his doom—and her divination is nearly fulfilled
when he winds up half-dead, addicted to an
enchantment that converts pain to pleasure and
possessing only a stolen book of maps.

Offered sanctuary in a nearby monastery, Valen
discovers that his book—rumored to lead men
into the realm of angels—gains him entry into a
world of secret societies, doomsayers, monks,
princes, and madmen, all seeking the key to the
doom of the world. Now, to preserve the lands
of Navronne, Valen must face what he fled so
long ago. For he alone can unlock the mystery
that can save the world.

Enter the realm of

Carol Berg
SON OF AVONAR

BOOK ONE OF THE BRIDGE OF D'ARNATH

Magic is forbidden throughout the Four Realms.
For decades sorcerers and those associated with them
were hunted to near extinction.

But Seri, a Leiran noblewoman living in exile, is no
stranger to defying the unjust laws of her land. She is
sheltering a wanted fugitive who possesses unusual
abilities—a fugitive with the fate of
the realms in his hands.

Also available:
Book Two of the Bridge of D'Arnath:
Guardians of The Keep

Book Three of the Bridge of D'Arnath:
The Soul Weaver

Book Four of the Bridge of D'Arnath:
Daughter of Ancients

Available wherever books are sold or at
penguin.com

Read more in the Rai-Kirah saga from *CAROL BERG*

TRANSFORMATION

Enter an exotic world of demons, of a remarkable boy prince, of haunted memories, of the terrors of slavery, and of the triumphs of salvation.

REVELATION

Seyonne, the slave-turned-hero from Berg's highly acclaimed *Transformation*, returns to discover the nature of evil—in a "spellbinding" (*Romantic Times*) epic saga.

RESTORATION

A sorcerer who fears he will destroy the world. A prince who fears he has destroyed his people. Amid the chaos of a disintegrating empire, two men confront prophecy and destiny in the last battle of the demon war...

"Carol Berg lights up the sky."
—*Midwest Book Review*